The Entity of Souls

S. E. COWEN

The Element Trilogy:

The Keeper of the World
The Entity of Souls
The Treacherous Balance

Copyright © 2021 Sarah Cowen

All rights reserved.

Cover design: S. E. Cowen

ISBN: 9798597826233

For the two M's in my life - thanks and love

LOST

TWO WORLDS

Tungala 1405, The Seventh Month

The sound of new birdsong filled the air as the first creatures soared home to their nests, happy and comfortable in the branches of a revived tree. The once dry riverbed surged afresh with water, the sunlight casting rainbows of colour from every clean ripple as fish, *new fish*, that hadn't dared venture there for several centuries, flung themselves gleefully from the water, dancing in and out of each other, new plant life thrusting itself up from the once dead mud. But though the sight before him was beautiful, glorious in fact, a *miracle* long hoped and prayed for, there was one who couldn't enjoy it.

Bor, the chieftain of the Tribe of Water watched dolefully as the women of the tribe began on their still-daily collection of moss. Each woman, clad in the scales of their kin, chattered, smiled, laughed with her comrades as the children ran about them in their new paradise, screaming and giggling. Their world, their *true* world had returned to them. Gone, it seemed, was all care and worry, all memory of what had been only a short time ago. And in its place; bliss.

And yet despite it all, Bor couldn't let himself feel blissful. He couldn't let himself *forget*.

A week it had been now. A week since he had heard any news of the eight strangers and their mission, since he had watched them disappear beyond the trees; the human Explorer, the wizard, the warrior, the dwarf and four human women - a bizarre travel-worn group in search of a temple shrouded in mystery. But though he had been told little of what they were about, why they had been there, why they had entered his life, this he *did* know: they had succeeded. Tungala was safe. As was his tribe. And for that, proud as he was, proud as his *people* were, he knew he would not, he *could* not forget.

"Bor..."

A voice squawked in the chieftain's ear and he turned to find his second-in-command, Ckram, standing over his shoulder. The younger tribesman, just like the others, had a happy glow about him, a cheerful smile playing at the edge of his lips, a gladness to be alive during these times, but like his chieftain, he too looked concerned, weathered. Overseeing the rebuilding of their partly-destroyed village was hard work. The human's army had done their very worst.

"What news?" Bor asked quietly in the common tongue. This was how it was between them now, a sort of code to prevent accidental listeners and just to make sure, Ckram leaned in even closer.

"No word of the group as of yet... But another ship has been spotted on the horizon," he mumbled.

"Another?" Bor couldn't hide his surprise.

Ckram nodded.

"The five ships of the human have now been foundered. All lie at the bottom of the sea." No one could mistake the scowl on his face. "But this *new* ship is different. I believe it might be *her*."

And dejected as he felt, Bor couldn't help but perk up a little.

"Her?" he echoed, suddenly alert. "Are you certain?"

Ckram gave a sad smile.

"I am certain."

Thinking a moment, Bor then turned his eyes back to the moss fields and the river as it lay beyond. The sun was rising ever higher in the sky as he spoke. Soon it would be noon.

But what to do? Did he send a party out to her, or was he just to wait?

What could he possibly tell her?

And why, oh why, did he care?

The companions had no doubt succeeded in whatever their attempt to save their planet; the river, which had been barren for so many long centuries, springing so suddenly to life was a testament to that fact. Something had changed. The once silent land had been replenished with life. Where there had once been death and darkness and decay, animals, creatures of the forest had returned, loping and flying and swinging between the trees, and even as he sat there, surveying this wondrous new thing, insects buzzed lazily about his head, flitting up from the mossy-grass.

Yes, no doubt the group had succeeded in their quest. But at what cost?

And why should he be concerned?

This was a *human* affair now. Not a matter for him, for Ckram or *any* of his people. And yet...

Realising that Ckram was waiting for his instructions, Bor straightened up a little.

He owed them more than this. Everyone, every*thing* that drew breath did. And none would ever be able to say that he did not do his part and appreciate it.

"If the woman comes aground, bring her straight to me," he then ordered. "She must be made to know what has happened."

"Of course."

Giving yet another nod, Ckram then left to keep watch on the shoreline and discouraged once again by the company's failure to return, Bor turned away from the busy riverside and clambering to his feet, strolled back into the village to sit alone and ponder awhile.

—

Elanore of Lordan skilfully pulled the Karenza's helm to starboard as the ship's anchor caught beneath the smooth ocean surface. It had been over seven days since she'd seen or heard from any of the temporary members of her crew. Over seven days of fear, of silence and worry and yet despite it all, despite the odds, still the captain remained hopeful.

She had two choices, that much she knew.

She could choose to stay and wait, to stay and hope for life, or she could choose to leave, to go and never look back. And right then, she certainly knew which made the most sense...

"Eliom told me to go," she said to the air. "He said if there was no news within a week, and it's been longer than -" and realising no one could hear her, she soon forced a laugh, stroking the helm again as was so often her habit. Sense hadn't always been what drove her though. In fact, sense rarely made the sea captain do anything. It certainly hadn't been sense that had led her into this mess in the first place, that had made her walk into that inn back on the Western mainland and offer a complete stranger and his band of odd companions a ride...

Sense then, really meant nothing. Which in the end, left her with only one option after all...

"You be good," she murmured to the ship's wheel. "I won't be long."

Moving to the bulwark the captain then turned for the smallest moment to take one last look at her beloved ship before, throwing her arms up above her head, she dove straight into the sea. Just as she thought it might be, the water was pretty warm and after only a few strokes, the sea captain soon found the bottom and in what felt like no time at all, was wading into the shallows.

Scrambling onto the beach, it wasn't long before she spotted the rowing boat the company had taken many days before: the only small boat the Karenza owned. The wood was almost completely dried out, despite being such a short time since they had left, but otherwise, it remained intact and pulling wet hair from her eyes, Elanore soon made a mental note to reclaim it when she returned.

When *they* returned.

Brushing herself down, the sea captain then made her way across the strand.

The thick, ominous trees of the mainland loomed over her in a dense clump, but as she edged closer, she noticed something that gave her reason to pause. Much of the greenery just along the shoreline had been burnt. She had watched the flames from her ship some days before, and yet, up closer somehow the forest didn't look as frightening, as dark as it had from afar. Where there had once been thick impenetrable weeds of what looked like dead branches, amongst the burnt stumps, now there was growth; where there had once been eerie silence there was now life and movement. A sea bird cawed overhead, its mate landing on the upturned boat to rest and a small crustacean scuttled past as a light sea breeze fluttered the plush treetop leaves.

Strange how everything had changed, as if overnight. As if in one moment… And though it didn't take too many guesses to understand how, *why* was an entirely different matter.

Either way, feeling suddenly all the more urgent, Elanore hurried towards the first of the trees, desperate to push on.

She didn't get very far.

"Stop!"

The voice rang out loud and clear and alarmed, the sea captain instantly went for the long-dagger hidden beneath her cloak. But before she could even find it, four men had leapt from the underbrush, ambushing her in a moment.

At a cursory glance, all four of her assailants were dark-skinned and naked but for strange scale-like trousers that stretched from hip right down to feet. Each of them was armed with a loaded sling and one of them, obviously some sort of leader from the way he stood before the rest, made to move closer, signalling for the others to lower their weapons. Elanore didn't remove her hand from her cloak.

"Are you Elanore, Elanore of Lordan?" the frontman then asked. He had a strange, thick accent and Elanore could tell from his drawl that common tongue wasn't his native language. The sea captain eyed him suspiciously.

"I am," she replied. The truth then seemed to dawn on her in a moment and suddenly, she brightened up, dropping her hand away from her weapon as she realised what the man was saying.

The man knew her name. He knew who she was. And he and his companions were here, on this beach, at the exact same point she was, almost as if they had been expecting her… That could surely then, only mean one thing?

Her friends could be safe.

As if to confirm that fact, the captain of the troop then gave a little smile and nodded at another one of his men who darted off into the undergrowth. Within seconds he had disappeared, his dark skin and scales the perfect camouflage and the man turned back to Elanore.

"Come with me," he ordered, and before Elanore even really knew what was happening, she was being led into the trees.

—

Bor looked up as he heard his name clicked out and one of Ckram's troop appeared at the edge of the village.

"We have found the woman!" he jabbered in their native language. "She is ashore!"

The sudden commotion raised the heads of a few villagers as they paused in their daily work to listen, but seeing Bor's grim smile, all soon lost their curiosity.

Slowly, like one aged, not with time, but with some heavy burden, the chieftain rose to his feet and stepped from the hut.

"Good," he replied. "Where is she now?"

The tribesman glanced over his shoulder.

"She is with Ckram." And as if summoned that very second by the mention of his name, Ckram then emerged from the trees along with the rest of his small patrol group, amongst them a sturdy-looking young woman.

Bor took a moment to study their unusual guest, as did several of his tribe.

Clothed in a long leathery cloak, weathered and damp with thick boots and trousers, Elanore of Lordan was a human woman like no other. She was thick-set with brilliant auburn hair and an inquisitive face set with years of hard experience, and yet at the same time, she was attractive, and, Bor could somehow tell straight away, assertive. The perfect model of a ship's captain.

Pausing as they stepped into the village, Elanore couldn't hide her astonishment as she saw the tree-huts, the home of the Tribe of Water, even now being lovingly repaired after the battle just over a week before. But noticing Bor as he made his way towards her across the clearing, her expression soon shut down again.

"Welcome Elanore," the chieftain said.

The sea captain gave a wan smile.

"Thank you," she replied, showing that her voice was just as colourful as her coppery hair. Then, as if to prove Bor's immediate judgement of her; "but though this is all great, if you don't mind me asking; who are you people and how do you know who I am?"

As one so easily suspicious himself, Bor couldn't help but acknowledge her own mistrust with a nod. Too well he remembered the tribe's reaction to the travellers only a matter of days before. Elanore was watching him though, waiting for answers and gesturing to the central hut of the village, the greatest and oldest of trees, he gave a small smile again of his own.

"Come. Let us sit and I will explain everything." And not really seeing any other choice, Elanore obliged, turning away from the staring eyes of many tribesmen, once again paused to watch.

As the unlikely paired entered the great hut, the sea captain halted for a moment on the threshold.

"That's beautiful," she murmured, pointing to a large tapestry decorating the entire inner wall of the hut. Bor just nodded, trying to put aside all thoughts of the last human to stop and notice the same, before he motioned for Elanore to take a seat.

The only furniture in the entire room was a great long table, standing barely a foot from the ground and the sea captain planted herself at the base of the wood amongst cushions and downy blankets peppering the floor. They were surprisingly snug, and, she couldn't help but notice, made almost entirely of some kind of plant, but though they felt soft and almost warm to the touch, she knew that she could never be truly comfortable. Not here anyway. Not until she knew. For sure.

"So…" she started almost as soon as she was down. "Please. Tell me what you know."

Bor took a seat at the very head of the table, as was obviously his want and leaning his arms on the smooth wood, he levelled the human with a dark gaze

"Where to begin," he mused. And then; "Perhaps, from the beginning. I am Bor, chieftain of the Tribe of Water and over a week ago, I met with eight travellers just south of our village."

There was a flash of something like joy on the sea captain's face.

"So, they passed this way? Edmund of Tonasse and the others?"

Bor nodded again.

"Yes. They did. We offered them shelter for several days and learnt a little something of their mission here, of their journey to the Temple of Ratacopeck. But, on the third afternoon we were ambushed by a great army…"

"Renard." Elanore scowled the name under her breath like a curse. "I spotted his ships on the horizon but by then I was well hidden. I took the wind due south for a few days."

Surprisingly, this information didn't seem to be news to Bor.

"When Edmund told us of the Karenza, I suspected such a thing. My scouts caught sight of your vessel this morning."

Elanore couldn't help but be impressed.

"But what about the attack?" and suddenly keen, she too leaned on the table, the great wood hard beneath her elbows. "Were they hurt? Did they escape?"

"We spied Renard's fleet before he had the chance to land ashore," Bor replied. Elanore was sure that there was something of a smugness to the leader's voice, but she chose to ignore it. "The company managed to flee just as the battle started."

The Karenza's captain couldn't help but give a small groan of relief. This was what she had been hoping for. Eight against hundreds had never been a good statistic…

"We managed to slay Renard's fighters," Bor continued, "but Renard himself managed to escape. He went after the group… but I do not know what became of him." And he gave something of a shrug. "We hope that he got lost in the trees. The forest is almost impossible for those who do not know the path."

Impossible unless you have a map and a wizard on your side, Elanore thought gratefully before biting her lip. Something told her that she knew the answer to her next question already, but at the same time… she also knew that she needed to ask it.

"And where are they now? Edmund and the others. Have they returned?"

But any tiny hopes Elanore might have had on that front were instantly dashed as Bor slowly sat up, removing his arms from the table with a sigh. His face was bleak.

"It has been over a week now since they left," he said, "and over a week since we last saw any sign of them." His eyes shifted to the floor for a second. "To be very truthful, I begin to fear the worst…"

Elanore had known that the 'worst' was probably true. No one could have failed to notice the brilliant light shooting across the sky, feel the impact of that giant force that six days ago had blasted out across the realm, but though she had seen it, felt it, experienced it for herself, a small part of her had been holding out that somehow the companions might have escaped, might have been clear of the explosion, might be safe.

Bor studied the sea captain's expression carefully and then, as if reading her mind:

"You saw, as we did, the great light?"

"Yes," Elanore's expression was dazed. "I did." But not knowing how much Bor was aware of what the group had been there to do, what they had achieved, she offered nothing else.

Not that it mattered anymore. It was over now, Tungala was safe…

"Whatever happened," the chieftain added. "Whatever it was that they did, it has given my people joy after so many centuries of struggle and sorrow and for that, we owe them everything."

This took Elanore by surprise, and for a moment, she looked blank.

"What do you mean, given you joy?"

Bor glanced pointedly at the entrance to the hut and in the dim light of the empty tree, Elanore couldn't help but notice how much he seemed to blend into the shadows. Dark skin, dark lips, dark hair, dark eyes…

"For hundreds of years we have lived, somehow survived without the River Gragnoth," the chieftain then explained. "We have struggled along, working with what we had left in a dead land. But six days ago, the waters came. The river began to flow once again and life returned."

"The river started flowing again?" Elanore was amazed. "How can you be sure that… that Edmund and the others had something to do with it? How can you-?" Before she could finish though, she was cut off by the arrival of a young tribeswoman. Unlike the men of the tribe, the woman had scales reaching from her toes all the way up to her neck, covering every inch of her body bar her head and as she hurried into the space, she bowed bashfully to Elanore before turning to Bor. Slightly irritated by the disruption but intrigued, the captain inclined her head back, as the shy woman and Bor proceeded to have what Elanore could only assume was a conversation. Every word or phrase was a meaningless flurry of throaty clicks and squawks, but clearly delivering her message after only a few moments the woman then just as quickly turned and left, looking anxious and Bor cleared his throat, rubbing his eyes wearily.

"Anyway…" he carried on, seemingly unruffled by the interruption. "Six days ago, there was a great light. The ground shook. An immense power swept the land. Many of my people fell where they stood. In my lifetime, I have never witnessed such a great force! It caused even the great trees to bend! But when the power had receded, the river, where it had once been dry, was living again, and the forest… it was no longer barren and dark but full of life." He paused for a moment, looking at Elanore as if determined to make her see sense. "Can it truly be believed that it was all a coincidence?"

The sea captain shrugged. It did make sense… but how and why that was, she couldn't fathom.

"Whatever it was Edmund of Tonasse achieved, it appeased the gods," the chieftain insisted and although Elanore wasn't quite sure what she thought about that, she didn't argue. Instead, she moved back to her main concern…

"Have you sent scout parties to find them?"

For a moment, Bor's eyes flashed with slight indignation.

"Of course," he challenged. "But they found nothing. We have been much preoccupied with our own matters. Of repairing our homes, burying our dead…"

All of which was our fault… Elanore thought before lowering her gaze.

"Of course," she echoed. "I'm sorry."

Bor's nostrils flared, but he seemed pacified. For now. Drawing himself back to the table, he then met Elanore's eye.

"I must be honest with you," he said, and his voice fell a little. "I fear that the company have not survived. They would have returned to us before now, I am sure of it. If they were close to the blast, then they are almost certainly dead."

Dead.

The word pounded the air like a hefty weight and Elanore, crushed under its blow, blinked heavily. Of course, a part of her had been expecting this, she knew that, but saying it aloud? The word somehow made it all seem so final.

They were dead. Her comrades were dead. Logic told her that Bor was right, there was no way they could have survived such an explosion.

They would have come back. They would have come back to find her.

Wouldn't they?

As Elanore already felt herself begin to flounder, to let the helplessness, the injustice of it all sink in, the chieftain suddenly got to his feet. He'd obviously said all that needed to be said on the subject for now, and for him, the human's grief was too much to bear.

"You are welcome to stay for as long as you see fit. But do not hope for their return..." he said to Elanore. "I am past hoping myself."

The sea captain didn't look up. Instead, she leaned forward until her forehead was almost resting on the table, her bright hair swooping down to cover her face.

"Thank you," was all she said. "I may have to take you up on that."

And with a nod, Bor then headed back out into the sunshine, leaving her to sit alone in the dim light of the hall as she contemplated the fate of eight companions she had once considered friends...

A frantic clicking awoke her and Elanore's eyes slowly opened to dim blackness. Through the window of the hut, one twin moon cast a glow at her feet but though she was conscious, still the sound didn't cease.

"Huh-?" she mumbled drowsily. "What-?" but before she could finish, or really even start, hot breath was then in her face, hot breath and a dark shadow looming over her. And something was shaking her by the shoulder. Hard.

What was going on?!

Elanore's brain roaring into action, the sea captain then sat up, grabbing instantly for her knife.

In the very faint light, she could just make out a figure. It was tall, slim, a woman, and she was backing away from her now, clearly frightened.

"What is it?" Elanore found her voice. The knife was tight in her hand. "Who are you? What's going on?" But instead of replying, the dark figure only stared.

Difficult as it was to see her in the white moonlight, Elanore could tell that the intruder was a tribeswoman. She was darkest black, almost nothing more than a silhouette, yet in the glow of the night something glimmered on her skin…

"What is it?" she tried again a bit more gently. "What do you want?"

The woman just stared at her, at her and her knife, her expression hidden, only the whites of her eyes visible. But then…

"Coo-me."

It was more a noise than a word and for a moment, Elanore couldn't understand.

"Coo-me," the woman repeated. And then, suddenly desperate, she began to make little muffled gagging and clicking sounds, as if trying to speak, to find something to say, only to realise that she simply couldn't. Whoever the woman was, she was uneducated, and, just as Elanore suspected, not human.

"Come," the tribeswoman then eventually managed. "Come." And she began to gesture eagerly, obviously wanting Elanore to follow her.

Lowering her blade, the sea captain got to her feet.

"You want me to come with you?" she hissed. For some reason, she was afraid to raise her voice.

The woman nodded quickly.

"Come!" she cried, her new favourite word. "Come!"

Turning on her heel the woman then hurried from the hut and Elanore, pausing only seconds to pull on her cloak, soon followed suit.

As she stepped out into the warm, clear night, the light of the moons shone into the captain's upturned face, causing her tired legs to stumble as she shielded her eyes. The tribeswoman was just ahead, turning back every now and again to check that the human was still there. To Elanore's surprise however, instead of being led back towards the main meeting hut, where the sea captain was half-expecting to go, the scaled woman began to head towards the trees at the edge of the village clearing and before long both found themselves pushing their way through the now plush undergrowth.

"Where are we going?" she demanded as the woman scurried on just ahead. But before there was even a chance to reply, before there was even a chance for Elanore to start wondering if the whole episode was some kind of trick, they came across a group of dark figures.

There were seven of them in all; six of them, facing into the night, crouched at the ready, loaded slings at their sides as if expecting attack. They were almost invisible in the night, in fact the sea captain almost missed them entirely but for the seventh who, upon hearing the two women approaching, soon straightened up and turned as if to greet them.

THE ENTITY OF SOULS

Even in the darkness, Elanore recognised him.

Bor gave a small nod of greeting, which the tribeswoman with Elanore returned.

"My scouts have spotted someone approaching," he then whispered, glancing at Elanore. His voice was so surprisingly soft that to an outsider it would have sounded like a breath of wind on a still lake.

Immediately fully awake, the sea captain fumbled for her knife again.

"Who is it?" she muttered, her thoughts turning straight to Renard.

Bor's gaze flitted back to the way ahead.

"They are not certain. My men only detected movement not too far away." And alarmed, Elanore squinted into the dark underbrush beyond Bor's men as if hoping to spot the intruder herself.

"Could it be Edmund's brother?" she breathed, turning back to Bor. *He would pay for the pain and death he has caused…*

But Bor too was on the alert now as he gazed off into the dark trees and even as she spoke, Elanore suddenly became aware of the swishing of leaves and branches, the plod of feet...

She froze along with the rest of them, for some reason her heart in her throat.

A branch snapped loudly.

The steps weren't quiet. Whoever it was wasn't trying to hide. And…

Was that more than one pair…?

The captain straightened up, every sense pricked and aware.

Another branch snapped, and then another.

It definitely sounded like more than one person, perhaps even more than that… a group even…

Elanore drew a long steady breath. She could feel her palms sweating.

Could it be?

But then, just like that, the sound of footsteps halted, as did the swishing and all of a sudden, the air was utterly silent.

Bor's men remained perfectly still. Each and every one like a shadow in the dark, a motionless invisible patch of black. Everything was hushed, frozen, waiting and without knowing she did it, Elanore flinched as a night bird cawed somewhere close by, flying off into the night.

And then, it was over and everything seemed to be happening all at once.

There was the quiet shuffle of something moving again and a figure appeared from the foliage. As it did so, the first of Bor's men reacted and raising his weapon, shot a stone at the figure's head. But just as the pebble snapped into the air, there was a deafening shout from beyond the branches and all of a sudden, the trees around them were bursting with a white light, bright and fierce as day.

With surprised yells, the group fell back, all except Elanore, who, shielding her eyes, immediately smiled. No, not smiled, positively grinned.

She had recognised that shout, recognised that voice; she would have known it anywhere.

And, just like that, as if to confirm her desperate hope, another equally well-known voice then rang out.

"Bor! Tell your men to lower their weapons!"

It was hoarse and exhausted but still him and as Elanore watched as the chieftain immediately did as the man instructed, she saw the same smile light his own face. He knew the speakers too.

As the group waited gladly, four figures then stepped out of the shadows: two men - one a warrior, muscular and tall, with a sword in his grasp and spiky unkempt hair, the other, the second speaker, a man, with a square jaw and long traveling cloak; a dwarf with a bushy beard, wielding a big double-edged axe; and a wizard, clothed all in white and gripping a great staff the end of which was glowing...

"Edmund!" The cry escaped from her lips in a wonder-filled yell as Elanore of Lordan, throwing her knife aside, rushed forward. "Eliom! You're alive! Thank Tungala! I thought - well we *all* thought-" But overjoyed, awestruck as she was, the second she had reached the Explorer, her eyes scanning his face, she broke off.

There was something not quite right. Yes, the human looked fatigued and drawn from the long trek through the forest and his chin was growing stubble - she'd been expecting that - but at the same time there was something else. Something deep within his eyes. A deep sort of numbness...

She looked to the others, each in turn. But no matter where she went, all of them had it, the pained, almost forced nothingness as they met her gaze. And as if awaking from a strange dream, it was then that she realised.

"Where are the others?" Her eyes turned to the trees beyond the small group, expecting to see the four women of the company staring back at her. "Where are the elements?" But there was no one else... There was nothing but trees and empty blackness beyond the light and knowing what this meant, her stomach did a funny flip.

No... Surely not. It wasn't possible.

"The elements have fallen."

The warrior, Fred, was the one to say it and for a moment, Elanore just stared at him, her own face completely blank.

They had fallen?

The elements were gone?

The elements were *dead*?

But before she could open her mouth to say another word, even if she had been able to, Bor then stepped forward.

"Come," he said briskly to the five dazed companions as if he were ordering his own men, "We will discuss all manner of things in the morning. But for now, you must rest."

It was Eliom, the wizard, who spoke out for them all then. He seemed a lot less affected than the other three, but though he appeared cold, maybe even heartless, Elanore knew that this was his way.

"Thank you, Bor," his voice, despite its calmness, also somehow tired.

Filled now with a confusion of emotions, shock, grief, happiness and impatience at not knowing what had happened, Elanore followed Bor silently as he then led the four shattered travellers into the village and a well-needed rest.

—

Flames engulfed him everywhere, burning and scalding and roaring. The heat was intense and the pain…

Somewhere, he could hear someone screaming, again and again. And again. And he knew somehow that it was his own voice and that he was shouting, crying, calling her name just as he had before, just as he would again.

And then as it always was, he saw her face. The same face that had haunted his dreams for the past four nights. The same face that plagued his every waking moment.

Large round eyes, lush red lips and dark hair shimmering in the light. Perfect and wonderful.

And gone.

She was speaking to him, smiling, just as she had every night.

It was always the same and though he knew it, part of him still yearned for it, yearned for the sound of those precious words.

"I don't have a choice."

They were spoken quietly and regretfully, but beautifully, like a flowing waterfall on a spring day, so alive and yet destined to fall.

And then he could hear his own voice, again, calling her name, pleading with her uselessly.

"Bethan!"

She was still smiling.

"Bethan!"

But though he called her name again and again, she said nothing.

Bethan!!

And as he watched, her face was erupting into flames, burning hot reds and whites biting at her flesh…

Eating at her eyes…

Drowning her cries…

Edmund of Tonasse awoke with a yell and flung himself to a sit, panting. His bed was drenched with sweat, his blankets tangled about him, trapping him in his dreams and for a moment he just remained there, breathing, trying to clear his head, blinking in the soft morning sunlight as it filtered its way into the hut. His whole body couldn't seem to stop shaking and with a moan he rubbed his eyes. Somehow they were wet with tears even though he couldn't remember crying…

For a moment, he struggled to recall, as he had every morning over the past few days, where he was and how he had come to be there. But then, it hit him, and unravelling himself from the moss coverings, he soon pulled himself to a sit and swinging his legs to the side of the bed, clambered to his feet.

As his weight shifted to his feet, his whole body ached, and yet, for a long moment, he ignored the pain. This was the discomfort of a few days spent on the ground, amongst other things. It was nothing compared to what it *could* have been and as he turned automatically to search for his tunic, it was then that he noticed the figure standing in the doorway.

Edmund didn't even flinch.

"What time is it?" he asked instead, reaching for his sword and cloak as he recognised Eliom – The Wise.

The wizard was leaning on his staff but upon being addressed, he soon straightened up.

"It is nearly noon," he said calmly. "Bor is waiting for you in the main hall."

Pulling on his tunic, Edmund strapped his sword scabbard around his waist and then straightened up himself with a little sigh. Though he knew he was probably safe there, amongst the trees, he felt naked without the weapon now.

"Come on then," he replied briskly and without another word, he slid his way past Eliom into the sunshine. He didn't dare look his friend in the eye, but just as the Explorer expected, Eliom soon followed, matching his stride to his companion's as he marched with strange determination towards the centre of the village.

As was custom in recent days, the pair walked in silence for a while.

"I can do something for the nightmares," the wizard then eventually murmured. As usual he sounded cool, removed. "If you would only *allow* me."

But instead of gratitude, Edmund's head snapped round and he glared at his friend, his expression angry.

"Have you been-?" and he tapped his forehead fiercely.

"I do not need magic to know of them," Eliom said, still calm. "I heard you crying out from across the village. It was disturbing the others."

Thrown a little, Edmund opened his mouth to respond, but just then, Thom came trudging up to interrupt. The dwarf seemed a little surprised to see the Explorer.

"Oh," he commented gruffly, soon falling into step beside them. "I was not expecting you to be ready. Fred said you were still asleep…"

He was looking at Edmund carefully, but when the man didn't respond, Eliom gave a warning nod and the three quickly fell back into a heavy silence.

As they reached the centre of the huts, they were then met by Bor who, holding out a hand to them all, beckoned them into the main hut.

Already inside were the serious-looking warrior, Fred; the ship's captain, Elanore of Lordan and also another tribesman that Edmund didn't think he'd seen before. He had the same dark skin and scales covering his legs as Bor and a few markings on his chest, setting him apart as someone of rank, perhaps a captain.

Now that the last three had arrived, everyone took a seat amongst the mossy cushions and rugs and as they settled, all eyes seemed drawn to Edmund as if expecting his guidance. But though the Explorer had come as requested, he seemed as if he wasn't really there at all, for avoiding all eye contact with his companions, his hands in his lap, he did nothing but stare at the table top before him.

Bor then, was the first one to speak into the oppressive stillness.

"This is my second-in-command, Ckram," he pointed out, gesturing to the new man with the chest markings. Ckram, who was sitting at the right side of his chief, inclined his head and Eliom, Fred and Thom responded in kind.

As he often seemed to do, Bor then sat up in his seat and leaning his elbows on the table before him, he levelled his gaze at the four new outsiders.

"It has been ten days since you parted from us," he began slowly. "Ten days with no sign of your return. Tell us, what has happened since we saw you last?"

The way he spoke, in his controlled, composed manner made him sound, not concerned, not worried or distressed but only as if he was mildly curious, and for some reason this made the listening Edmund's fists clench.

What has happened?? How could the chieftain act as if it had been nothing, as if he was asking where they'd been like they'd simply stepped out on a merry jaunt? The Explorer couldn't help but scowl to himself.

How could *any* of them sit there and discuss it all like they didn't care, like they didn't know….? *How?*

Because, and the little voice of reason buried deep inside of him seemed to speak up for the first time. *Because they didn't.* They *didn't* know. Bor, Elanore, Ckram and his people had no idea. Not really. They couldn't possibly *know* the full extent of what had happened at the Temple of Ratacopeck.

The truth was; *none* of them really did.

Edmund closed his eyes with a deep breath and the calmest, as always, Eliom was then the first to try and explain.

"Since leaving your village, we travelled for three days and nights," he said. "On the second evening, we reached the Temple and made camp there until the following morning."

Bor nodded but made no comment.

"On the third morning since we left you, we then made for the entrances."

"Entrance*s?*" the chieftain questioned. He really didn't know anything about it, as was to be expected and Eliom glanced for the slightest second at Edmund. But though the wizard was clearly prepared to divulge exactly what had gone on, the Explorer had opened his eyes again and they were rooted to the table. He was giving them nothing.

"Indeed," the wizard then continued. "Each woman, each *element*," the word seemed to send a deep chill thrilling through the air, "was to enter by a separate path. Water to the north…"

"I went with Bex," Thom piped up, before immediately falling silent again as all eyes turned on him. Eliom gave the smallest smile.

"Yes, Bex and Thom headed north; Fred and Meggie to the south…" The warrior raised his head at this point as if to corroborate Eliom's story. "Earth was to stay eastward. And…" Eliom paused. "I travelled with Saz to the far western door." For a moment, for anyone watching closely, the wizard's mouth seemed to contract a little. But then it was as smooth as stone once again and taking a moment, perhaps to regain his thoughts as the others all continued to stare at him numbly, the wizard paused before continuing.

"Within a day we had reached the entrances and again, we took camp for the night."

Bor stirred, his brow furrowed.

"You took camp again? Why did you not enter straight away? Why did you wait?"

Instead of Eliom however, this time it was Fred who answered him.

"We thought it wise not to enter until daylight," he said. "None of us were certain of what we would meet once inside." And from the way he spoke, no one listening could doubt that it had been his idea to remain cautious. The Temple then, was still to be a mystery.

"And we were right to do so," Eliom added. "For once entering, each of us were… tested."

"Tested?" Elanore looked shocked. So far the sea captain had sat silently, abnormally so, her face pale, just absorbing it all but now she was suddenly alive. "What do you mean *tested?*"

Eliom didn't need to look at Edmund this time.

"Tested," he repeated, leaving it at that. Now wasn't the time to relive such things. None of the four companions wished to elaborate on what they'd been through, the tight bonds, the hideous creatures, handing over the necklaces… for distant as it felt, the pain was still there, still fresh; the sheer helplessness, the humiliation…

"Once inside the inner temple itself, we were then faced with four elements of the past," Eliom carried on steadily. "They were what some might call 'spirits'; beings from a long-distant time when the orb's power was released before."

Those who had not been there perked up at this point, wanting to catch every last word that came from the wizard's mouth. Although Bor and his tribesman had known next to nothing of this 'orb' or the element's task, except to save Tungala, both were eager to listen.

This 'orb' then, the potential destroyer, had been used to save their planet *before*?

Elanore, knowing a little more than some of the others, shifted uncomfortably.

"When you say distant time…" she murmured.

"I am not sure exactly," Eliom replied in all honesty. "But the beings claimed to be at least two hundred years old."

The whole hut seemed to stir again, all except for Fred and the wizard himself. Two hundred years was the blink of an eye to both their peoples.

"But how had they returned to you and why?" Bor interjected. His dark face betrayed only the smallest fear and Fred looked directly at him.

"We have no idea how they came to be there," the warrior admitted. "But as to *why*… They were acting as some kind of gatekeepers, to offer the new elements the ultimate choice. They told us what was to pass…" And at that moment, he fell quiet again, plunging the hut into complete silence as those who knew, reminisced and those who didn't, guessed.

Death. The unspeakable word swamped the room and unable to hide it anymore, Elanore let loose a single sob, her hand flying to her mouth as Bor's black face whitened a little. Edmund meanwhile, just closed his eyes again.

It haunted him; the temple, the fire, burning and blinding and the white stone pillars, the space. *Her*. Bethan. Her face, her eyes as she'd stared up at him, full of sorrow, of determination. The feel of her lips beneath his as he'd kissed her, pressed her close for the first and final time. The horror as he'd watched her disappear into those flames.

And then the orb. He could see everything all over again, witness as it roared towards the sky, the force blasting out across the stone, recalling the very second he'd watched that great power, magnificent, terrifying, unstoppable flooding towards him and realised that he and his friends were going to die too. The tiniest moment when he'd also realised that he wasn't sure he *cared*…

It was Bor who finally broke the tense hush. Much as he might be able to sense the hurt around him, painful as it was, there were still matters to discuss and leaning even further on the table, he once again looked to each member of the group in turn.

"And what of Renard?" he said. "To our misfortune, we did not slay him during the battle. Did you see him? Did he find you?"

Eliom, Fred and Thom all glanced at Edmund again then, who sat as motionless as a statue. But still he didn't move, still he remained silent, only the smallest twitch of his jaw showing any emotion.

"Yes we *saw* him," Thom growled before anyone else could say another word and Eliom threw him such a steely glare that the dwarf immediately shrank back as if he'd been hit.

Turning back to Bor, it was then the wizard who spoke again.

"He also fell."

Bor frowned, his dark eyes glistening, but he said nothing more. It was no secret that the chieftain, the whole Tribe of Water in fact had wanted Edmund's brother dead after the devastation his army had caused to their village, the innocent deaths that had come about by his hand, but much as he wanted to, sharing his joy at the news in front of Edmund felt wrong right then. Fred too, looked a little pleased, but made no comment. It was no secret either that the warrior had longed for the young man's death for his own reasons.

Elanore straightened up. Her eyes were damp with unshod tears, none of them for Renard.

"But that was all *days* ago!" she challenged. "Why didn't you return sooner?" And for the first time, she sounded almost angry. Good as the captain was at hiding most of her emotions, she couldn't hide her concern.

"All of us were knocked cold by the blast of the orb," Fred said. "We thought ourselves dead but then we awoke a day later to find ourselves back outside the Temple."

"And it was *exactly* as we had left it," Thom chipped in. "Not a crack anywhere, not a stone out of place despite the whole place collapsing round our ears!"

"It appeared precisely as we had first seen it."

At this, Bor looked incredulous, as did his second-in-command.

"That is not possible!" he said. "How could the building have survived that blast? How even could *you*? The trees, the whole forest was bent to the ground and the light-!"

Eliom shook his head slowly.

"It is magic beyond even *I* have witnessed," he muttered, as if to himself and for anyone studying his face right at that moment, they would have seen something like concern etched on his brow. Before anyone *could* study his face however, a sudden a voice then spoke out, causing everyone to turn in alarm.

"We should have known all along," it stated simply and all attention turned once more on Edmund. His own eyes were open now and he was no longer staring at the table. Instead, eyeing the room in general, his gaze had settled on Eliom, with an expression entirely dark. None could mistake the grief and with it the anger quavering beneath that weary voice but as the others looked from human to wizard and back, none either could mistake the look of knowing that passed between them.

"How *could* we have known?" Unusually, it was Thom who was the one to ask, voicing everyone else's concern. But it was no matter who had spoken it, for like one hit, Edmund instantly snapped his head around to glare at the dwarf.

"Ask *him!*" he demanded and to everyone's shock, he pointed right at Eliom. "Ask the *wizard* here what he saw. Ask *him* about the vision he received *the night before*. He *knew* that this would happen but he did *nothing!*" and as his accusing finger shook, his eyes were back on the wizard's face as if challenging him, waiting for him to deny it.

This none of them had been expecting and suddenly realising what he was saying both Thom and Fred straightened up.

"Is this *true*?" the warrior asked in disbelief. "Did you *know* what would happen in the temple?" But Eliom, who was still looking calmly at Edmund, did nothing for a moment.

"I did see a vision," was his serene reply, his answer aimed at Fred but his eyes never leaving Edmund's. "But it is not as Edmund suggests. And it is not strictly accurate that I kept it to myself. I did not know what it meant so I sought Edmund's counsel..."

Edmund's face reddened a little, but he seemed no less angry.

"But you could have guessed!" he challenged and then suddenly, he was up on his feet, his fists clenched again as if ready to hit out. "And what you told me... it made no sense! How could I have helped you understand it? *You* were the one who Saw it!" And before he knew what was happening, the hurt and rage were running away with him. "How do I know that what you told me was the truth? That it was even what you *Saw*? How do *we* know," he gestured almost drunkenly at the others, including them in his pain "that you didn't *want* the elements to die?! You *knew* about the existence of the Dark Mist and yet you chose to keep it from us!" Fred and Thom looked even more alarmed – they had known nothing of this. "You chose to make me –" and he blinked, unable to say the words, before stumbling on. "How-how do we know you're not lying about this?"

But Edmund had gone too far. Calm, serene, detached as the wizard was, the Explorer had passed all point of reason and all of a sudden, the whole hut seemed to darken as the wizard too was somehow back on his feet. Filled with an unknown fear, the others then shrank back in their seats as Eliom – The Wise raised his staff, the ancient wood emitting a deep red light, causing the wizard's suddenly enraged face to elongate, the shadow twisting up towards the ceiling.

Edmund, seeing this change in his friend, also widened his eyes in fear, but stood firm.

"Do *not dare* accuse me of being a liar Edmund of Tonasse!" Eliom then roared, in a voice unlike his own. It was loud, deafening almost and boomed through the hut like thunder. "In all the years we have known each other, have you *ever* had reason to doubt me?!"

Edmund's face reddened all the more. Everyone in the room realised that they were holding their breath. But before any more angry words could be said, the light from Eliom's staff had dimmed and he was back, back to the peaceable wizard they had known.

"You are not yourself, friend," he said simply and as if these words held some great magical weight, Edmund's rage suddenly left him. Just like that, it was gone and as if stunned by the reality of his own harsh words, he opened his mouth to apologise. But though Eliom brushed any regret aside with a nod, and the whole hut seemed to breathe easy again, Thom was still indignant.

"What was this vision, Eliom?" he demanded loudly. "You told us of no such thing before!"

Some of the others flinched to hear him ask it, afraid all over again but Eliom simply turned his attention to the dwarf, his expression unchanging.

"I did not have the time," he replied. "As Edmund rightly said, I received a vision the night before we entered the Temple and only managed to speak to him of it briefly."

Bor and Elanore, who had kept well back during the short argument, soon shifted in their seats, attentive once more. Meanwhile, Eliom glanced at Edmund again, whose gaze had turned back to the table top and the Explorer gave the smallest nod, his hands clasped together in his lap as if to prevent them from causing any harm.

"It was vivid and yet indecipherable… at the time," Eliom then started, facing the rest of the group. "At first I Saw a great light, so bright that I felt as if I were staring directly at the Sun itself. I know now, after witnessing the orb, that my beliefs of it being the Keeper of the World were true. I then…" but he quietened at this point as if wondering whether to go on. Whatever he might feel or not feel himself, the grief of what had befallen the elements was obviously still very near for them all.

"Go on," Thom encouraged, but his voice wasn't quite as gruff as usual. Even he could detect that whatever Eliom had seen, wasn't going to be good. They all could…

"I Saw flames and heard cries of pain…" Eliom continued and though he seemed to pause again as if unsure whether to continue, the other three members of the group couldn't help but shudder as they remembered those very cries, the bloodcurdling screams none were likely ever to forget as Edmund's brother had stumbled and fallen back into the blaze of the orb. All could recall perfectly the horror as his body had burned before their very eyes; his very being turning to ash in less than a few drawn-out seconds...

Edmund gave a small throaty sigh and shut his eyes again, as if the wizard had spoken the name aloud.

"That wasn't really him," he muttered, more to himself than anyone else.

But when he realised that everyone was looking at him again, his head rose a little and he added a bit more firmly; "Renard wasn't himself. I don't know what happened to him but he wasn't always like that. Once he was my *brother*..." but then his voice seemed to catch in his throat and he said no more.

Hearing Edmund speak so openly, there was a long, full silence before anyone dared say another word. Outside, the sound of the tribe at work, of the children playing seemed like a mockery.

"All that I Saw begins to make sense..." Eliom was almost thoughtful. His hand lay calmly at the staff by his side, but though he seemed at peace, his voice was still hushed. "Next, I Saw burning and creatures turned to ash. I Saw stars and their destruction – a warning, a warning of what might have occurred... if the orb had not been released."

Suddenly, Elanore let out a moan.

"They really had no choice," she whispered before; "I mean, I knew they had to go but I didn't think..." and she wiped her forehead, her eyes glassy, "I didn't think it would be like *that*."

Eliom was grave.

"Beyond this I Saw what was to be, I Saw a valley, beautiful and alive, yet at the same time I could hear wailing, the sounds of deep sorrow. I know now that it foretold of how Tungala would exist... afterwards. Restored but..." and again, no one needed to hear his final words to understand what he meant, for they all knew.

Tungala was restored but at a cost.

Having spoken his part, Eliom then lowered his gaze, as if in thought and the hut fell once again into a deep quietness. No one wanted to say anything. No one *could* say anything, the horrible weight of all they had just heard and for many, just relived, lying heavy on every heart and to everyone's surprise, it was Edmund who was the first to respond.

"Excuse me," was all he said and suddenly, as if he couldn't bear to hear any more, were it to come, he was back on his feet again and stumbling to the door, disappearing out into the sunshine to leave the others staring after him wordlessly.

As if the odd spell that had kept them all in place was now broken, Bor then stood up. His movements were those of a much older and frailer man.

"I think that we should postpone this discussion until another day," he announced. "I fear that I was too abrupt in asking you to meet so soon. I can see that, as of yet, the... memory... of what happened at the Temple of Ratacopeck is still too strong."

Eliom bowed to him. Somehow the wizard was on his feet too, though yet again, no one had seen him rise.

"Perhaps it is so," he replied reasonably. He too then left, hurrying after Edmund with long calm strides and the rest of the group began to disperse, moving their separate ways, none of them sure of what could happen next or where their lives would lead after such devastation.

—

The woman awoke suddenly, as if from a dream. No, not a dream. A terrible, burning nightmare of fire and pain and tears and letting out a low, guttural cry she flung herself to a sit and retched with all her might, throwing up onto the dry, sandy ground.

Her eyes and throat were sore, her skin tingling with a strange warmth, her limbs oddly stiff and as she wiped her bitter-tasting mouth with a pale, trembling hand, she forced herself to take several deep, shaky breaths.

Where was she? What was going on?

And neither answer coming to her at all, for a while she just sat there, numb, confused, dazed, just trying her best not to throw up again. Her head was throbbing, worse than throbbing, pounding like the beat of a heavy drum thudding into her skull and with a whine, she soon lowered herself back to the ground, curling up into a ball as she stared out at the land ahead.

She was sitting on what looked like a sun-baked prairie. The sparse landscape was vast – it stretched for miles in every direction – and it was empty, dead but for the odd clump of dried-out scrub and rough hot rock. The whole place was a wasteland and almost instinctively, the young woman's eyes turned to the sky through fluttering mud-cake lashes. It was bright blue above her and hot, like a summer's day and yet... *not*. There was something not quite right about it, something out of place and unable to comprehend anything, or so it seemed, the woman swallowed, her parched throat raw.

There's no sun, her brain managed. That was what was strange. There was no real light, not really. It was almost as if the whole place hung with some kind of luminescence, casting the air above her in a strange reddish-blue glow. In fact *everything*, the woman then realised, as she dared to move her head and stare out into the distance, seemed to be red. Red, red, glowing red.

She pulled her hands from her face. They seemed to radiate with it too.

And the silence. That was the worst part of it. There was no hint of noise anywhere. Not even a gentle wisp of a wind.

Somehow she had expected sound and for an odd moment she wondered if she'd gone deaf and reaching up again, she stroked the sides of her face tenderly.

No. She had heard her own cry. She could hear her own breath, shallow and ragged. Her tongue tasted like acid.

Where then, was everything?

"Greetings."

The word was so sudden, so out of the blue that the woman almost cried out again. But as she snapped around, squirming in the dust it was then that she saw him; a man, a human man. He was standing over her and as she raised her dry eyes to his face, she saw two attentive green ones staring right back at her.

She hadn't heard anyone approaching... Had he been there the whole time?

Hello, she opened her mouth to reply, but finding that she didn't really know what else to say, she soon closed it again. It was rude not to reply, somehow she knew that, but the man didn't seem to mind. He was just staring at her, long and hard as if waiting to understand something not of her control. And then, as if making some kind of decision, he took a step closer and holding out a brawny hand to her, gave a smile.

"Here," he said and without thinking, the woman, uncurling herself slowly, took it, climbing to her wobbling feet like a deer on its first legs. Her naked toes scraped the dirt, grazing her skin and it was only as she glanced down that she then noticed another strange little detail.

She had no shadow, and neither, she saw, looking at the man's equally-uncovered feet, did he.

It was a tiny almost irrelevant realisation that was instantly forgotten until much later, but then so was the niggling feeling at the back of her head. The feeling that grew stronger as, turning back to the man, who now stood face-to-face with her, she saw his smile widen.

She knew him. She *knew* this man, just as he clearly knew her. But *how*...? The woman blinked painfully. *How*, she had no idea.

Who was he?

The information was *there* - she knew it - in her head, but for some strange reason, she couldn't seem to access it, almost as if it had been put away just out of her reach.

Or as if it were something utterly unimportant not worth remembering...

It was only as the woman stood there, trying her hardest to recall who this apparent stranger was, that it then dawned on her and with a panic-stricken gasp that split the silent air, she almost fell.

Her memories.

They were gone. And not just who the man was; that wasn't the worst of it.

She couldn't remember anything. *Anything*. Not even her own name, where she was from or how she had come to be in this dry, dreary place.

Faces and pictures swam in her mind's eye. Little tiny scraps of things she had known, seen and experienced but she couldn't seem to work out what they were or how they all pieced together.

Somewhere in there was a river, clear and vast. And *cool*. She had swum in it, washing the mud from her hair, from her tired body. And she had fallen, only for another man, another stranger to help her up, to keep her from drowning. She could feel his warmth now, see those deep ocean-like eyes full of concern, full of...

And then there was a group of girls, all of them identical. But though they looked as children they weren't. They had been armed and fierce, with fangs like creatures of the night and they had chased her, chased her with endless energy and fury before...

A necklace, bright and shining, a dazzling gemstone, lying in her palm. She could remember it, feel the weight of it, feel the smoothness on her skin. Feel that somehow it had mattered to her...

And the man with the blue eyes. The way he had pulled her to him, the way her chest had almost burst as he'd pressed his lips to hers, warm, soft and urgent as if...

The woman let out a heart-wrenching sob. It broke away from her suddenly, echoing off across the eerie plain and hearing it, the man with the green eyes grabbed her fully by the arm, as if detecting her weakness. Again, the woman tried to speak, but her mouth and lips were dry, so dry, that all she could manage was another hiccoughing cry.

The man then spoke again. Now that she could concentrate on it, his voice seemed distant and muffled and yet close, all at the same time.

"Do not be afraid," he said, a note of grimness in his voice. "Some of your memories will return in time."

In time?

The woman gave a cough and rubbed her throat. She felt ready to retch all over again. Instead of pounding now, her head felt light, dizzy...

"What- what," she finally managed to croak. "What is this place?... Am I... am I... dead? I remember flames and burning and ..."

But the man held up a hand.

"No, no," he interrupted solemnly. "You are not dead." But then giving a small sigh, as if afraid someone might overhear, he continued in an undertone; "But you may as well be. Perhaps death is kinder... *some* people seem to think so... Although I cannot say I am one of them."

He gave an odd little smile, and shocked by his words, the woman seemed to study the man's face properly at last, her eyes ever widening.

"Who *are* you?" her voice managed to squeak, wavering with something like fear. Those green beady eyes and that thick head of hair. She knew them and yet...

The man let go of her arm, letting his own flop down to his sides as he turned to stare up at the distant sky, deep in thought.

"I know you..." the woman continued, more to herself than to this half-stranger, "I just... I can't..."

But the man soon cut her off again.

"My name," he said, "I have long forgotten, but I now call myself Barabus."

Barabus. Instantly, the woman recognised the word and something clicked in her mind, a new memory. She could recall a room - no not just a room, a gigantic hall, made all from stone, white and bright and fiercely hot - and standing before her had been him, Barabus, along with three others. All men and yet all…

"Ghosts," the word slipped out before she even knew what it meant. But then it dawned on her and giving a start, the woman stared at Barabus like he was going to hurt her. He was just as she remembered him, just as he had been in that fearful place, young - no more than twenty at least - and grim, only now, somehow, he seemed so much more *solid*. He had touched her, he had held her, she had felt his flesh, strong and very much alive…

"You were…. You were a-" she started but the man known as Barabus, gave a shrug.

"I am old," he replied, as if being a spirit one minute and apparently alive the next, was the most natural thing in the world. "Ancient beyond your comprehension. My people walked your world many hundreds of years ago and for that, I cannot return to it as you are. To *that* world, I was dead and buried long ago…"

Much as it made her head spin, now that he had spoken it aloud, the woman somehow knew he was telling the truth. Yes this man was young, young as she suspected she might be, and yet without really knowing how, he was *older*. The way he spoke, the way he moved, the knowledge in those eyes, all seemed *different* somehow, as if he had stepped from another time, long forgotten. And though he spat the words with disdain, though she had a feeling he would deny it, the woman also knew that wherever, *when*ever it was, Barabus still wished to be back in '*that*' world, alive and *un*buried.

That world…

The cold realisation hit her in the face like a slap.

"*That* world?!" she then echoed incredulously, all thoughts of Barabus pushed aside. "Hold on! What are you saying? Are you saying we're not on Tungala anymore?" *Tungala* – that much she could suddenly remember.

Another world? Was it even possible?

But though she looked at Barabus, hoping that he would laugh or maybe just smile again, mocking her for her foolishness, the man only continued to look thoughtful.

"Many would say we are, yes, but others perhaps, no," he answered mysteriously. "I like to think we are."

Yes? She was in another *world?!*

The woman could feel all blood draining from her face as she tried to understand, to comprehend what Barabus was telling her.

No, a voice cried inside her head. *It's impossible. Other worlds don't exist…*

And yet…

Where was the sun? Where were the twin moons? *Where even, were the shadows?*

And if she was *here*, where was *Tungala?*

So many questions and all of them she wanted, *needed* answering. So many holes filled her memory, so much nothingness and yet despite it all, there was one demand that seemed to burn deeper than any of the others.

"Who is he?" she blurted out. "The man with the blue eyes?"

The man with the blue eyes. The man who had pulled her close, pushed his lips to hers, warm, safe, sad…

"I know him. He's there, in my mind," she tapped her forehead. "But I can't… I can't remember…"

She looked at Barabus urgently but though she expected an answer, the man instead did something very strange. He opened his mouth as if to speak, to tell her what she needed so desperately to know, but before any words could come out, he suddenly gave a shudder and snapped his lips shut.

Without any warning he then turned on his heel and before the woman could react, had started off across the prairie.

"Hey!" the woman cried in alarm and with no time to lose, she made to run after him. The ground was rough beneath her naked heels and stony too, but though her clumsy feet almost brought her down, she flung herself on, quickening her pace until she was almost beside him. The man walked quickly, his stride long and determined and though she couldn't begin to understand why, the woman knew it was because of her.

"All right," she tried anxiously, out of breath. "If you won't tell me anything else, please just tell me this…" and going on a whim, she grabbed Barabus's arm, forcing him to stop and turn to look at her. "Who am I? What's my name? Please just tell me that at least…"

"Your name?"

To her surprise, Barabus looked confused for a second and he glanced at her, then once more at the sky as if trying to decide what he should say. Finally though, he seemed to give in to whatever troubled him.

"Your name?" he repeated. "I suppose it cannot harm. No one ever told me mine, but it was different then…" and he paused again, contemplating before; "Your name, I believe, is Bethan."

Bethan.

The woman's breath caught in her throat as she froze.

Bethan. That is me.

"I'm *Bethan*," she whispered to herself aloud, just running the word over her tongue. "Bethan." The name felt alien and yet…

She frowned.

"You *believe?*" she asked suddenly. "You mean you don't *know?*"

Barabus's face seemed to flush for a moment.

"I know what I have heard, what it was someone called you," was all he said on the matter before, growing suddenly annoyed he gave a hurried sigh; "but who you *are*, I cannot tell you. You must discover *that* for yourself." And with that, he marched off again at an even quicker pace.

For a moment, the woman now known as Bethan just stayed where she was, rooted to the spot, her mind whirring.

Bethan.

Though the word felt odd to her, it also felt *right* and along with it came more memories, more gaps to fill.

She could recall a woman calling to her from across a country garden, as she'd sat under a great tree, the happiness of childhood wafting about her like dust mites.

Her mother. How beautiful she had been, how bright. And yet gone now, she knew. Long gone…

She could remember a room filled to bursting with parchments and scripts. Tables and cases filled with them. Dim yet warm; familiar, like the feeling of a well-loved rug. Someone was speaking to her, asking her to help them find a particular volume, her favourite book as it happened…

And then, just like that, there he was again. The man with the blue eyes. Only this time he wasn't holding her. This time he was calling to her, crying her name, screaming it in anguish…

With a gasp of air, Bethan blinked and tried to focus on the here and now. Barabus, with his tall stride, had gained a fair distance and suddenly realising that if she didn't follow him, she would be utterly alone, Bethan almost sprinted to catch him up.

"Wait for me!" she panted. Her voice barely echoed across the strange space. "Where are you going?"

Barabus, hearing her approach, hesitated, but only a little and turning to glance at her, he nodded off towards the horizon where, Bethan noticed for the first time, there stood a block of what looked like squat dark boxes miles away.

"I am heading for civilization," the man replied briskly, "as should you. You never know who could be lurking out here."

Bethan couldn't help but be struck by the way he'd said 'who' instead of 'what', but thinking herself to have little other choice, she took one peek back the way they'd come before following on, jogging to keep up with her odd companion's long gait.

Looking back, she could faintly make out the damp patch on the dry weathered ground where she'd thrown up and remembering how ill she still felt, she rubbed her throat. It was still so sore and parched. She needed water. She needed food and, she looked to Barabus' stern-set face, she also still needed *answers*…

MEMORIES

*T**he flames engulfed him once more as the sound of screaming filled his ears.*
And then, right on time, he saw her.
Her beautiful face was full of sadness, of fear, and yet she was struggling to be brave, to smile. For the others. For Tungala. For him…
And she was speaking to him, those same words. Nothing else.
"I don't have a choice."
She didn't and he could hear his own voice again, calling her name. He shouted along with it, his throat hoarse.
"Bethan!"
Her face faded as fire took over.
"Bethan!"

"No!" Edmund screamed and woke, sweat pouring down his face to mingle with the tears he hadn't known were there.

It was pitch black, the middle of the night, or at least very late, and taking a moment to calm his thudding heart and wipe a hand across his brow, the Explorer detangled himself from his drenched blanket and sat up, swinging his legs to the side of the bed with another groan.

The night was cool and clear and every now and again, as he sat there for some minutes, just breathing, his eyes closed against the world, a fresh breeze would waft through the door of the hut, gently cooling his burning temples. But even though he was awake, even though the world of dreams had been set aside, still the images he had seen, the images of suffering, haunted him. Even thoughts that had once been a pleasure to him, felt like swallowing ash.

He could remember the Dark Mist and the beach, the soft warmth of Bethan's smile, and yet at the same time, he could feel the icy cold water, see her unconscious face beneath the waves, just as he could feel her smooth lips beneath his own, the warmth of her hair running under his fingertips…

Edmund gave another moan and gripped the side of the bed with white fists, shaking his head as if the movement could somehow empty his thoughts.

He *had* to stop this, he told himself firmly as he had so many times before. He *had* to forget…

He had to.

And yet just as he had every time, he knew that he *wouldn't*.

All of a sudden, there was a slight noise from the doorway and though he had half expected it, the Explorer immediately tensed up, on the alert, automatically reaching for his sword.

"It is late," a voice commented.

And squinting out into the night, Edmund could, sure enough, just make out the very dark shadow of Eliom standing at the entrance to the hut.

Dropping his hand, the Explorer soon turned away.

"Indeed," he grunted in reply.

Eliom then whispered a few words and Edmund saw a small circle of faint yellow light appear in the darkness, the shining end of the wizard's staff. The light gradually grew until the whole room had a dim glow, allowing Edmund and Eliom to see each other and shielding his eyes as they stung in the gentle brightness, the Explorer got to his feet, and barely glancing at Eliom, made his way over to the window on the other side of the room as if to stare out at the night.

"You should rest," Eliom carried on after a few moments of - on the human's part at least - awkward silence.

Edmund continued to stare out of the window.

"I'm always *resting*," he replied lamely. He could tell that Eliom was referring to his nightmares again. He hadn't slept properly for almost a week now and he was aware of just how much the wizard knew it. But knowing just as much that his nightmares were the *last* thing *he* wanted to talk about right then, he soon swivelled back to confront his friend.

"Why aren't you resting yourself?" he demanded, even though he already knew the answer. Eliom didn't *need* sleep. He rarely did and seeing how much the dim glare irritated Edmund's tired eyes, the wizard soon covered the light from his staff with a hand.

"I heard you shouting," he answered simply. "I came to ensure that you are well."

Edmund turned away again and reaching for his tunic, began to pull it on.

"I'm fine," he replied automatically.

But instead of arguing back, half as Edmund expected, Eliom said nothing in reply.

He didn't need to.

"They're dreams, that's all," the Explorer then continued with what was supposed to be an offhand shrug. But his words weren't going to fool anybody. His whole body was shaking from exhaustion and much as it irked him, he knew that everyone, whether wizard or not, could see it.

"My offer is still open to you," Eliom said quietly as Edmund finished buttoning his tunic and started to pull on his sword belt. "But where are you going at this hour?"

"For a walk." Edmund's reply was gruff as he scanned the room for his boots and cloak. "I'm awake now so I might as well stay awake."

Instead of getting rid of the wizard however, Eliom soon turned in the doorway, gesturing at the blackness beyond.

"May I join you?" he asked calmly and Edmund paused to glare at him. He didn't really want the wizard's company. He wanted to be left alone, to ponder on things. Plus, he knew that if Eliom accompanied him he would keep pestering him about the nightmares. Yet at the same time, the Explorer *also* knew that if his friend was determined to walk with him, to stay by his side, he would do so whether he gave his permission or not.

"If you like," Edmund replied instead, trying to sound nonchalant but failing to do so again.

He then picked up his sword and made for the doorway, trying to avoid the wizard's enquiring gaze only to find, to his surprise, that Eliom had stepped back into his path and much as he then tried to sidestep around him, the wizard wouldn't let him go.

"Why will you not let me help you?" Eliom was insistent this time, more than he had ever been before. There was concern there and perhaps a hint of impatience in those usually cool tones, but though he knew deep down that his friend meant no harm, before he realised it, before he could control it, Edmund felt the now-familiar stab of boiling rage, of grief, well up to meet it.

"I don't need any help! *Especially* from you!" he exclaimed, trying to push past the wizard once more.

Short of physically shoving him though, still Eliom wouldn't relent.

"You must let what occurred at the temple, remain there," the wizard asserted. "We *all* must. It is in the past now. We must look to the future." And Edmund stepped back to glare daggers at him.

"I know!" he growled, for the absurdist second, wanting to reach for his sword again.

"There is nothing you can do now. There is nothing you could have done *then*."

And hearing his companion so matter-of-fact, Edmund's teeth ground together horribly. His heart was pounding like some ferocious beast trying to escape.

"I know!" he repeated. But still the wizard wouldn't stop.

"They are gone. The elements are gone. There is nothing more you can do..." he said.

"*I know. I KNOW!*"

And suddenly losing all power over himself, Edmund's shout stopped both in their tracks.

Somewhere, an animal, disturbed by the sound, scuttled off into the trees, screeching loudly and woken by the noise, a few fires began to flicker in neighbouring huts. But though there would be a few irate villagers in the morning, at least it was over. For as soon as Edmund had exploded, had let his emotions out, all of his anger, all of his strength suddenly seemed to drain away and he was left weak. Weak, useless and foolish.

"I know..." he echoed again, his voice feeble and releasing the sword hilt he hadn't even realised was now in his hand, he soon lowered his gaze from Eliom's.

The wizard's stare was strangely fierce, as if something had been awoken deep within him too, but seeing his friend back down, a change seemed to happen in the wizard too and with a blink, he then moved away from the door, unblocking Edmund's path.

"I am sorry," Eliom apologised, for a moment, his words sounding deeply heartfelt. "I was rash with my words. Perhaps you are not ready to hear them just yet..."

But Edmund shook his head.

"*I'm* the one who should be sorry," he answered sadly. "I know you're only trying to help me. And I know I'm being..." he sighed.

Despite his apologies though, Eliom clearly wasn't finished just yet.

"If you will not let me prevent the nightmares then at *least* let me give you something to help you sleep more easily," he said quietly.

The wizard wouldn't stop, Edmund knew, until the Explorer was safe. But though he also knew that this made his argument pointless, still he could do nothing but shake his head again.

"I'll be fine," he whispered and before his oldest friend could say another word, he took his chance and pushing his way past Eliom, disappeared into the black night.

—

"Has anyone seen Edmund this morning?" Elanore commented, causing some of the others to glance up from their food.

Thom shrugged and Fred shook his head.

Eliom did nothing.

"Thank you," Fred said as he accepted an extra plate of breakfast fish from a little tribegirl. The girl merely smiled shyly and ran off to play with her friends.

Thom took a great bite from a hunk of moss bread before speaking up.

"So, we seem to have been delaying this for as long as possible," he grumbled, picking the crumbs from his beard. "But surely now is the time..."

Elanore glanced up herself.

"Time? Time for what?"

Fred, meanwhile, carefully dismembering his fish with a knife, looked less confused.

"To decide," the warrior mused. "What happens next."

And Thom nodded, reaching for yet another fish.

"Exactly. What *does* happen next? Where do we go from here? We cannot live in this place forever."

But though everyone had been thinking it, for a moment, no one seemed to know how to respond. Much as he might have started the conversation, even the dwarf seemed reluctant to offer any ideas, yet gradually, as if pulled by some natural instinct, all eyes soon fell on Eliom. Somehow all felt the wizard to be the authority on the matter at present, but even Eliom, who wasn't eating anything, as usual, looked uncertain and his own eyes turned towards the sky as if for guidance.

"I would suggest that every being does as he or she is want," the wizard then mused. "Whether that be to set sail and head back for the West and home or to continue here." Nevertheless, there was something oddly doubtful in his voice and after another short contemplative pause, he soon turned back to the breakfasting group. "But…" he added. "We must, of course, wait and see what Edmund decides."

Edmund.

This made the other three look at each other uncertainly and it was Fred who then voiced what they were all clearly thinking.

"I am not certain that Edmund is… well," he chose his words carefully, "in the right frame of mind, Eliom. I know I speak for us all when I say that he has been the most affected by what happened… And I fear it may cloud his judgement."

But surprisingly, instead of defending his friend as he so often did, Eliom's mouth turned down at the corners, the tiniest hint of a frown clouding his usually clear features.

"You may be right," he muttered after a time. "He *has* been affected badly. He has lost a brother as well as…" He trailed off into insignificance.

Thom sat up, gulping down the last bite of his meal with a belch.

"Well maybe we should elect someone else to lead us," he suggested, feeling braver now that it looked like Eliom was on the majority's side. "We have done what we set out to do. Our debt is paid."

"Debt?!"

But this was a step too far and all of a sudden, the wizard changed. Just like that, his gaze, cool and serene was fierce, aflame with unforeseen anger and Thom gave a start, finding himself just as suddenly afraid…

"Is that why you are here, Thom? To repay your *debt*?! A life for a life?" Eliom demanded. His staff glowed a little.

Thom's face reddened as the other two turned to look at him in surprise.

"No! Of course not! That is to say I-" the dwarf spluttered, but the wizard wasn't finished.

"He *may* have been affected," Eliom continued firmly "but I am certain that he will not let his own feelings surpass his judgement. What is this talk of electing, Thom?" His voice was quieter now, yet still it seemed to carry on the wind like a sharp hiss. "We did not *elect* Edmund to lead us. We all chose to follow him. He has led us this far and now you who consider yourselves his *friends*," he was addressing all of them now, "wish to abandon him? Can you think of any *other* to lead us? I see no one here who would be up to the task. So I suggest that these thoughts go no further."

Stunned, the other three lapsed into a guilty silence. Of course the wizard was right. Edmund was and would always be the natural leader of their group. Human and, in the eyes of many, weak as he was because of it, it was just always, somehow, going to be the same. Each of them trusted him, each of them were willing to follow him and yes, each of them knew deep inside, they were willing, if it came to it, to die for him.

The first to realise, Fred looked sombre.

"Of course, you are right, Eliom," he apologised, his voice quiet and regretful. "It was wrong of us to doubt."

"To doubt what?"

And giving a collective flinch, straight away warrior, dwarf, sea captain and wizard swivelled to find Edmund himself standing at the edge of the group.

The Explorer's eyes were red and bloodshot and stubble was starting to push its way onto his chin again, despite shaving the day before. It was obvious that he'd had yet another restless night. But despite this, and what had happened in the hut the day before, his face was utterly expressionless.

No one answered his question. Instead, Eliom bowed his head, as if in welcome and giving a wan smile in return, Edmund moved into the centre of the group and seated himself on the grass in a space next to Elanore. Everyone was secretly relieved as he then took some bread and began to eat, slowly and silently.

Still none of them spoke, but before anyone could have much of a chance, it was then that Bor appeared from the entrance to the main meeting hut only a few metres away.

"Good morning," he addressed the whole group pleasantly. "I trust you all slept well."

Everyone nodded, including Edmund, before, slurping a canteen of fresh water down in one, Thom then wiped his mouth with his hand and without warning, as if the last few minutes had never happened, pounced straight back on to the issue at hand.

"So, what is our plan now, Edmund? Where do we go from here?"

The tension in the air suddenly created by the dwarf's words could have been split with an arrow. But to everyone's surprise, calmly, gradually, Edmund swallowed down his first mouthful of fish and turning to the dwarf, levelled him with a look that could only be described as completely uncaring.

"I don't know," he half-shrugged, rolling the next mouthful in his teeth. He glanced at the rest of them briefly. "Does anyone have any suggestions?"

But though asked the very question they had been trying to answer themselves only moments before, everyone merely stared at him. Somehow they'd been expecting their leader to insist upon going back to the temple, to demand that they stay there for the sake of the elements, to suddenly rage with fury, to cry out, to do *something*... Not *this*. This new approach, this *new*, calm Edmund was something different entirely.

As if detecting the effect his friend's new mood had caused, it was then Eliom who spoke up.

"Perhaps we should return to the West," he suggested. "It is time for us to return home." And he glanced at Thom. "Or at least, to the homes we have made for ourselves."

Edmund nodded, taking another bite of his breakfast.

"Of course," was all he said.

But Thom obviously wasn't finished and looking first at Edmund, whose tired eyes were now on his food, he instead, turned to Eliom.

"When?" he asked. "When shall we leave?"

And Eliom seemed to pause for a moment, almost as if he were waiting for Edmund to answer, before, seeing that he wasn't going to, he looked to Elanore.

"Elanore," he then said. "When can the Karenza be ready to leave?"

As usual these days, the sea captain had just been sitting, listening attentively but silently to the scene unfolding before her, but noticing Eliom's attention, she soon gave a start.

"She can ready at any time," she shrugged. "She'll need stocking with food supplies for the journey, but other than that, I'd say that... at the latest... she could be ready by tomorrow?"

And just like that, it was then that Edmund choked on his food.

"Tomorrow?!" he exclaimed, all indifference gone in a split second.

Elanore nodded cautiously. This was it. This was the sort of reaction they'd been expecting all along. Dreading even...

"I cannot see why we should not leave tomorrow," Thom said. "There is no purpose to staying here any longer..." but determined as he seemed to be to go, even *he* couldn't hide the pain of his odd grief as his mind fell on what they would all be leaving behind.

Edmund though, still looked stunned at the idea of leaving the next day.

THE ENTITY OF SOULS

"I didn't realise you meant so soon!" he cried and then, turning back to his food with suddenly shaking hands; "Well, if you really want my opinion. Then perhaps we should stay for another week or so…"

The suggestion rippled across the group with varying emotion.

"A *week*?!" Thom challenged "Why?" and Edmund turned on him.

"You n-never know…" he stuttered, clearly struggling to speak his feelings aloud. "We might need to stay…"

"For what?" and Fred too piped up with a hint of impatience despite the fact that he knew what their leader was trying to say. They *all* knew what Edmund was trying to say, why he didn't want to leave, but none of them seemed willing to prevent it. Only Eliom, aloof as he was, could really see where the conversation was leading and knew it wasn't good.

"Stop," he warned quietly, but just as if he had shouted it, everyone instantly obeyed.

To the surprise of the rest, it was then that Bor, who they'd all forgotten had only been standing a little way off all this time, made his presence known.

"If you *are* to leave tomorrow," he said smoothly, "then where will you go? If, as you say, you intend to return to the Western Realms, where will you make berth? From what you have told me, Stanzleton has been destroyed. Surely you should head somewhere else?"

Eliom looked thoughtful again.

"Very true," he mused.

But Fred seemed ready with an answer.

"Well, wherever we go, it should be West. Although reluctant, I for one intend to return to my people. It has been many years since I stepped foot in Mawreath. Now may be the time for me to do so once again… And I am sure everyone else would like to return homewards too."

Thom and Elanore bobbed their heads in agreement.

Finishing his meal however, Edmund cleared his throat.

"Then if that's your decision. I can't stop you," he said solemnly. "If the rest of you wish to leave then I'll remain here, by myself," he glanced at Bor. "If that's alright with Bor of course…"

The chieftain, looking not at all surprised, gave a gracious nod as the others turned to stare at Edmund in alarm.

Eliom's eyebrows rose but his face remained calm.

"We cannot force you to return with us, Edmund," he replied gently, "but I am not certain that remaining here will-"

Edmund positively glared at him.

"I have no home in the West," he snapped. "I've no reason to go back there. So for now, at least, I'm going to stay here."

"But what of your parents?" The wizard didn't seem to want to give in. "Edmund, surely they must be told. Renard-." But the mention of the flesh and blood he had lost, only made Edmund's face crumple with fresh anguish.

"I just - I can't!" he exclaimed weakly. "Not yet! I-" But even thinking about it, the Explorer could see their faces, see in his mind's eye as they heard of the death of their son and he knew that he simply couldn't bear to watch his mother break down, watch as his father, determined to remain strong, tried to comfort her uselessly. The son they loved. The son they had thought was a genius, a marvel. Their youngest. Dead.

No. They had never known of his plans, of where it had taken Renard, of how it had ended him and as far as Edmund was concerned, for the moment at least, they never would.

He could feel his eyes starting to prick with tired tears and climbing to his feet, he wiped them quickly.

"Excuse me," he choked out and then, before anyone could object, he was striding off towards the trees.

No one said a word to stop him. All of them knowing it would be useless to try.

"He needs time," Elanore mumbled into the quiet. Her own face told the story of a similar pain, a similar loss. "That's all."

"That is all very well, but how much?"

And Thom, giving a small sigh, turned to the others pleadingly.

"I am not desperate to leave this moment but we cannot stay here forever. We do not belong here."

Fred frowned in thought before, suddenly he was then clambering to his feet as if he had half a mind to leave himself, right then and there.

"And it is clear that the longer we *do* stay..." he added. "The more it takes its toll."

No one needed to ask what he meant and it was then that Eliom, who was still watching after Edmund, turned back to Elanore.

"Elanore," he said softly, barely taking his eyes from the spot where the Explorer had disappeared into the foliage. "Please make all the necessary arrangements to leave tomorrow. We will begin heading West in the morning."

Though all three looked amazed, none of them argued and nodding her assent, Elanore too got to her feet, looking to Bor without a word, who soon gestured for her to follow him back to the main hut where they could start organising the supplies.

Fred meanwhile turned to Eliom.

"What about Edmund?" he asked bluntly. "He is very determined."

But Eliom just nodded, his gaze still riveted on the clearing's edge.

"I will speak with him," was all he said. And with that, the wizard headed off into the trees after their leader.

—

Bethan's throat was painfully dry now.

For days on end, it felt as if she had just been walking, walking, walking in the dirt; the dry warm dirt of a world she didn't know.

For all she knew it *could* have been days. She was so thirsty, so hungry, so tired, every second felt like an hour, every hour, a lifetime and so much so, she had no *idea* how long she'd really been like this.

All she did know was that nothing seemed to be changing. The buildings on the horizon, the tiny blobs of civilisation Barabus had promised her didn't seem to be getting any closer.

Bethan had tried to speak to him, to ask her constant companion how much more she would have to endure, but every time she opened her mouth, all she could do was croak. Her whole body was crying out for water and feeling as if she was going to throw up again, she halted, resting her hands on her knees to take deep, wobbly breaths.

Barabus, noticing her slow down, also paused.

"I was ill constantly for the first few weeks I was here," he mused, the first words he'd said in a long time. "Some believe it is the shock…"

Puffing her cheeks out as she desperately gulped in some warm air, Bethan nodded absently. He really wasn't helping.

"Need… water…" she just about managed to rasp and realising her frustrations, Barabus threw a glance back to the buildings ahead.

"Not too long now," he said. "Only a couple of hours I would say."

Hours?!

The word sent a fresh stab of pain through Bethan's gut and she groaned, as acid rose to the back of her mouth. She knew there was no way she would be able to last that long, not without anything to drink, anything to sustain her. Even the reddish hue glowing all around her seemed too bright, too painful for her eyes.

And the sickness…

Paling, Bethan then finally succumbed and leaning forwards, retched, throwing up what was left of her empty stomach. The taste was foul, the mark on the caked ground barely a splatter. Her head was spinning, and overcome with weakness, she collapsed to her knees.

Barabus, all the while, watched with mild disgust, before, seeing her fall, he soon reacted.

"Come now," he said and moving fast, he suddenly grabbed her by the armpits and before she could register what was happening, was dragging Bethan unwillingly back to her feet. She let out a feeble whimper of annoyance, the only sound she could muster, but her companion wasn't having any of it.

"Once you fall down, you will struggle to get back up again," Barabus pointed out, holding Bethan at a stand until she was strong enough to do so for herself. "And if *that* happens, we will never reach the city."

Bethan just coughed, her head lolling to her chest.

Suddenly she felt overwhelmed by a strong, and, she was pretty certain *alien*, urge to die. She just wanted to lie down, right there in the middle of nowhere, and sleep. Forever. Never to wake again. Never to exist.

Awful didn't begin to describe how she felt. And not just physically.

She had no memories. She had no past life. She didn't even know who she was, where she had come from, *anything*. All she really had was a name. That was it. A name and a few scraps of pictures in her mind's eye.

What kind of a life was that?

Not one she felt that she wanted. Whoever she was…

"Come on."

She could feel Barabus releasing her, giving her the space to stand and then walk unaided. But she wasn't ready.

Bethan took a few reluctant steps forwards… and vomited again.

Barabus gave an audible sigh.

"This will not do," he said in that strange archaic way of his and then, once again he was reaching out to hold Bethan up as she bent almost double. "How about this?" and leaning down, he tried to meet her eye. "I will carry you as far as the city. Just until we get you something to drink." And not waiting for an answer, Barabus then crouched and taking the almost comatose Bethan by the waist, draped her like a sack across his shoulders.

The woman barely weighs a thing, he found himself realising. The transition had obviously been harder than he'd thought. He seemed to remember being stronger. But then it had been so long ago, he didn't know if that was really the truth…

Once certain his burden was secure, Barabus then made off towards the city again without another word as Bethan gradually fell into a restless sleep, all the while remembering, dreaming of another time she had been carried like this, sometime in her past life… By the man with the blue eyes.

—

"Edmund!" Eliom shouted to his friend's back as he stormed on ahead. "Edmund! Stop!"

The Explorer seemed to carry on striding for a minute or so, but a part of him then realising that it was useless to keep going, reluctant as he was, he turned back to find the wizard pacing towards him through the trees.

Instantly, the familiar anger that had been his almost constant companion of the past days, snapped at him as he saw his companion's calm yet concerned face.

He just wanted to be left *alone*. Why couldn't the wizard seem to *understand that*? Why couldn't he just stop being so-?

Taking his last few gaping steps, Eliom then stopped, moving into Edmund's path to study him for a moment. The Explorer's own expression was a mask of grief, of fury and bitter guilt; those same emotions Eliom had seen increasing day by day. But just as he could recognise them in an instant, so he could recognise that before long they would be all that was left of his friend.

Before too long, the Edmund of Tonasse he had known would be gone, which meant that he had to act, and fast.

"Why do you feel the need to stay here?" he asked outright as Edmund tried yet again to avoid eye contact. "Speak to me."

But though the question was direct, Edmund's gaze was firmly set on the trees behind the wizard's shoulder.

"Surely you should know the answer by now, Eliom," came the cold reply. "Why do you *keep* asking me questions you already know the answer to?"

So, it had back come to this. It had come back to empty blame all over again.

Eliom remained calm.

"I do not wish to delve into your mind. You know that. I never truly See unless given permission."

But though he had given his reasons, or reason enough, Edmund just sneered, delivering the wizard a sudden shock as he saw for a few seconds, not the face of the friend whose life he had followed with such interest, but the face of the Explorer's dead brother...

"Why don't you want to read my mind?" Edmund demanded. "Why don't you *really*?" and as if to challenge him, it was then that he glared straight into Eliom's face.

The effect was instant and the wizard recoiled as he saw into the Explorer's eyes, saw the vision deep beyond and pictures, unwanted, unheeded, flashed through his mind's eye like the flicker of flames. Visions of the elements, of Renard's body burning and bubbling, of the orb's blinding light, of Bethan's face, so full of sorrow, so full of pain, flooded his senses...

Quickly, the wizard forced himself to look away, without knowing it, his own face mirroring the horror of what he had seen and watching his companion's reaction, Edmund, his anger momentarily forgotten, paled, looking suddenly frightened.

"What is it?" he demanded. "What happened? What did you See?" But Eliom shook his head and moved away as if to clear his thoughts. He hadn't meant to search into Edmund's mind and yet somehow it had happened. Somehow the magic had worked beyond his control like never before and though Edmund then frantically tried to gain eye contact with his friend again, Eliom shifted away from him. He didn't want to see anymore. He couldn't.

"Eliom!" Edmund cried out. "Tell me! What did you see? Why won't you look at me?"

But again, the wizard shook his head.

"You have suffered much, my friend," he muttered. "We have *all* suffered much."

Suffered. Was that the word for it?

And suddenly it was then Edmund's turn to move away.

For a moment he looked about ready to march off again but before he had a chance to, Eliom was there, back by his side.

"I *know* why it is you would stay," the wizard said and Edmund swivelled back to face him, their eyes meeting all over again.

This time, to Eliom's small relief, nothing happened. All he could see now was the man's overwhelming grief. But then, Eliom didn't have to be a wizard to see that. It was there for everyone.

"She is not coming back."

Finally someone had said it and Edmund shook his own head, a small, bitter smile crossing his face.

"I wouldn't expect you to understand, old friend," he replied. "You don't know what it is to love…" And Eliom just blinked at him. In the dim light of the thick trees, his white cloak and tunic seemed to glow, making him seem even more inhuman.

"True," the wizard reasoned. "I know that I cannot feel as you do, that my… kind do not require, are not *permitted* to feel as you do. Nonetheless, do you truly believe me to have a heart of stone?"

Edmund said nothing. But as he watched his friend speak, he couldn't help but notice how *different* he looked suddenly, how unlike himself, almost as if he too, despite all he knew about the wizard, was suffering in some way…

"I cared for the elements," Eliom spoke the words as if they lay heavily on his tongue. "I grieve for them, in my own way. And I grieve for the loss of your brother." He gave something of a sigh. "I grieve for you. And that is why I ask you these questions. I have watched you every day and I have heard you every night. You do not sleep. You barely speak. You try to hide it, but you pick arguments with your friends when all they are attempting to do is help you… *All* have suffered whether much or little. So do not be mistaken in the fact that you are the only one who is hurting."

His admittance was a shock and speechless, Edmund just stared at his friend as he waited for the wizard's surprising and yes, he knew it deep down, *wise* words to filter slowly into his brain.

He was right, of course. Eliom, as he always seemed to be, was right. Everyone *had* suffered, not just him. Just as the wizard had implied, it wasn't fair for him to be so angry with everyone, with the people who cared about him most in the world, the people who shared his pain. He was no worse off than any of them.

Or was he?

"But it's all my fault, Eliom," he muttered after a time. "I feel so *responsible*. If it weren't for me, none of this would have happened. No one would have been hurt. Bethan and Renard wouldn't have died... Saz-"

Eliom held up a hand firmly.

"You cannot believe that this was in any way down to you," he stated simply, as if through saying this, all of Edmund's guilt and regret would somehow melt away. "It was ordained long before you were even born that this would occur-"

"But you always told me that we are in control of our destinies!" Edmund interjected sceptically. "You told me long ago that I had the choice. '*Every action that you take, affects what your life holds*', you said! I had the choice to carry out this quest or not... I had the choice as to whether I would fall in love-" he broke off and Eliom gave something of a sour smile.

"You made the right choice Edmund. That is all I can say," he replied. "*Think*. If you had never ventured on this journey then Tungala would have been doomed. In less than a few months we would all be destroyed. If you had not taken this path you may never have met Bethan...."

"I wish I'd never met her!" Edmund cried furiously and a single tear of hurt escaped from his left eye, rolling down his cheek and falling to the ground. "I wish I'd never set eyes on her!"

Eliom watched him evenly.

"You do not mean that," he said calmly and straight away Edmund shook his head, immediately regretting his words. Of course he didn't. He'd loved every minute he'd shared with Bethan over the past month, through the good and even the bad. And deep down he knew that if he were to turn back time, if he were to go back those few weeks, knowing what he knew now, he would *still* have gone to meet her, to journey with her to the temple no matter what the consequences, no matter how selfish...

"Can you not see why we *must* leave tomorrow?" Eliom looked, as he always did, serene and thoughtful. "Staying here will only bring you more grief. You cannot allow yourself to be swallowed up in misery, Edmund. It accomplishes nothing. We must leave and move on."

Move on? Already Edmund could feel his anger beginning to grow all over again. What did the wizard know about *moving on?*

"But what if I don't *want* to?" he spat, his voice rising once more. "What if I *want* to stay here?"

"It is not a case of *want*," Eliom insisted, his own voice suddenly also rising into what could only be resentment, if he had been able to feel it. "It is a case of *must*."

Edmund could see the difference in his friend again, like something had changed, something deep within but he was too full of his own hurt to try and understand it.

"*Why* must I?!" and suddenly he was yelling.

Eliom's fist clenched tighter about his staff. He seemed to be struggling somehow to hold himself together.

"Because one cannot live in the past," he said.

"I'm *not* living in the past!" Edmund retorted.

"Edmund!" And right then, just as he had in the meeting hut the day before when Edmund had called him a liar, the wizard's whole face changed to one of rage, the tip of his staff glowing a deep dangerous red. The whole forest seemed to burst with it. "She is dead Edmund! Bethan is *dead* and there is *nothing* you can do about it!"

His voice reverberated around them, shaking off through the trees towards their friends and Edmund froze, his mouth dropping open.

"What-?" he started, stunned by his friend's uncharacteristic outburst but then the realisation finally hit him full in the face.

Bethan was dead. The woman he had known for such a brief time and yet loved like none other, was gone. She was dead.

He'd known the truth, of course he had, but he'd also never *really* accepted it. Never truly accepted that she was gone forever, that he would never see her beautiful face or hear her beautiful voice ever again. He hadn't accepted that it was over.

Bethan was gone.

Detecting the hurt that he had caused and clearly confused by his own reaction, Eliom, much back to his old self, soon opened his mouth to apologise before shutting it again. The words had been necessary. They both knew it, however angrily he had spoken them. And after a little while, Edmund, coming back to his senses like a new man, gave a long sigh.

"Very well," he then murmured in a voice not quite his own, the voice of defeat, of numb acceptance. "We'll have it your way. We'll leave tomorrow."

—

Bethan tried feebly to open her eyes, startled to find that she was numb. Completely numb.

And she wasn't entirely alone.

Voices were coming from somewhere, voices she didn't recognise; but wherever they were, they were faint, almost inaudible and her body didn't seem to want to respond to them. It wanted to lie there, with just her and her scraps of memory. Perhaps forever.

Forever felt safe.

Safe and warm.

"This one may take a while to recover," she deciphered one deep voice say. It was close, just above her. "Look after her. She is still in shock."

Another voice, this time female, then replied; "Of course. But who is she?"

"She is Bethan."

Bethan then felt a tugging at her shoulder, or rather more a kind of weak, irritating pull. Her body was so deadened, so exhausted that she was barely able to register it, but register it she did and giving a moan, she tried to open her mouth to demand whoever it was to leave her alone.

Go away, she wanted to scream. *Just go away.*

"Bethan," The woman's voice spoke again and just like that, the movement stopped. "You *must* sit up and drink. You're very dehydrated." and remembering just how incredibly thirsty she was, Bethan's eyelids slowly fluttered open.

Blinking a few times to focus, she was then only half-surprised to find herself lying on her back, looking up at a low stone ceiling. A faint reddish light was floating in from somewhere to her right and moving her head just a fraction of an inch, a young woman soon came into view.

She looked about Bethan's own age, - however old *that* was, she realised with a stab of horror - and was quite short with unkempt black hair cut raggedly to her chin.

Seeing Bethan stir into consciousness, she gave a little smile of what was probably relief.

In her hand she held a canteen of liquid and Bethan stared at it greedily, wanting to reach out and grab the nourishment from her fingers. But her hand muscles didn't seem to want to move either. They too seemed to want to stay put, lolling uselessly at her side, just like everything else. Dead and gone. She felt like screaming all over again, but the woman seemed to know this and leaning forwards to prop Bethan's head up with one surprisingly strong arm, she gently tipped the canteen to Bethan's mouth, giving a small laugh as her patient drank hungrily; the liquid, whatever it was, dribbling down her chin and onto the blanket-less bed beneath her.

"There," the woman cooed. Once the liquid had gone, she then moved the canteen away and taking Bethan by the shoulders, helped her to a proper sit. Already, Bethan could feel her energy somehow beginning to return and glancing about her she found herself truly *seeing* for the first time.

She was in what appeared to be a bedroom. It was simplistic, with a cupboard and a bucket in one corner and a few shelves with various glass sculptures and some age-eaten books in the other.

The only other piece of furniture in the room was the bed. It was quite hard and plain and it had no blankets or sheets, merely a downy sort of mattress with some feeble cushions for pillows. It smelt like dust, yet fresh. Like something clinical and rarely used.

Bethan then turned to the black-haired woman. There were a few moments of staring silence before eventually, she managed to regain the use of her voice.

"What is this place?" she then tried. "How long...?"

But the woman stopped her straight away.

"You've been asleep for several hours. But don't worry, rest is the best remedy for you." She then swept her arm wide, as if introducing her to the room at large. "You've reached the City of the Diggers. Or Elements, if you prefer..."

"Elements?" Bethan echoed doubtfully. Something in her mind flickered at the word, but she couldn't focus on it enough to think why.

The woman pointed to herself as if she were conversing with a small child.

"I'm Belanna. If you need anything, just shout out." And with nothing more than that, she then turned and quietly swept to the door at the other end of the room.

Alarmed, Bethan waved a feeble hand only just in time.

"Hey!" she cried. "Hold on! Wait!"

The woman, Belanna, turned back with a look of blank patience.

"I can't remember things," the patient blurted. "All kinds of things. Like who I am- how I got here and...why-?" She tried to make a move as if to stand. "Can I leave this place? What even is-?" But it was as if Belanna and her previous companion were in some kind of conspiracy together.

"Rest," she answered sweetly. "All will be answered soon enough." And then she finally disappeared from the room.

Bethan just sat there for a few moments, watching the empty space the woman had left, unsure what to do.

Should she really rest some more, as her nurse had instructed? Now that she was awake, she found herself suddenly filled with fresh energy and questions, so many questions, pushing their way round her brain, vying for her attention all at once...

Slowly and carefully, so as to give her body a chance, Bethan then slid to the side of the bed. Surely having a bit of a look around wouldn't hurt? Perhaps it could even *help* and swaying slightly as she got to her feet, she took a few tentative steps towards the door.

Something brushed against her knees, making her stop and looking down, she was mildly surprised to find herself wearing a long dress of pale beige. The fabric was thin but not very giving and as she took another step, she noticed that it rustled when she walked. It had long sleeves and a plain neckline and hitching it up to her calves to stifle the sound, she edged towards the exit, trying not to wonder about why she had never noticed it before, or how long she'd been wearing it.

The door was simply an archway, as plain and pale as the rest of the white room and as Bethan carefully peered out, she saw that it led out onto a long corridor. Everything was white stone here too, but still the red glow she had noticed out on the scrubland seemed to be casting a hue over everything meaning that even white wasn't quite *white*.

The corridor was completely empty and after several moments of watching and waiting and realising that she was quite alone, Bethan took a few brave steps out. On either side of her doorway were two others of a similar shape and size - all as basic as each other. Looking towards the end of the hall, there was also some sort of outlet at the very end of it, to her right, and glancing about her again, Bethan shuffled quietly towards it, discarding the grip on her dress hem. The noisy cloth fell back to her feet but she barely noticed. Her gaze was somehow drawn to what lay ahead, the little opening, a hole in the wall and as she finally neared it, she couldn't help but smile to herself. It was a small ornate window, one half opaque lacquer, the other totally open. Functional yet pretty.

But as she moved even closer to peer out into the gap beyond, Bethan felt her heart do a funny flip as she then saw the view laid out before her.

Far off into the distance, as far as the eye could see, were rows upon rows of two-storey buildings, and squat huts carved from stone, all white, blending into each other and the dry surroundings. It was a world of white-red stone and glass.

But what had made Bethan start was the sight *beyond,* for towering past the huts, towering above everything else, casting a deep shadowless presence across the whole city – for a city it was - stood a gigantic structure. It too was carved from white stone and glass; a platform, with four great stone trellises wrapping their way from the very base all the way to the top and at the very top itself, four colossal glass orbs placed in a diamond atop the great podium.

Seeing the construction, Bethan felt suddenly sick all over again as something like a memory slammed its way into her head.

Suddenly she could remember a giant white stone hall.

It had been hot, *burning* hot and there were flames… and a platform - just like the one she saw before her, but greater and somehow different. For the four webs of stone had been four ladders, ladders thin enough to climb…

And as for the glass orbs-

"Should you not be resting?"

The sudden voice interrupted her thoughts and swivelling to find Barabus striding up the corridor towards her, Bethan blushed as she realised that she'd been caught.

"I've rested already," she pointed out, turning back to the window. "And I'll rest some more later."

"Fair enough," and to her surprise, instead of chastising her some more, Barabus joined her in looking out at the view.

"I can see you are feeling better," he said with a faint smile.

Bethan nodded, never tearing her gaze from the city scape beneath her.

"It's beautiful," she answered and then, nodding towards the great platform; "What is it? Why is it there?"

But yet again, Barabus seemed determined to give nothing away and moving back from the window, he gave a chuckle.

"Surely you should know that answer," was his reply and Bethan glanced at him, feeling suddenly irritated. Why was he *laughing* at her? Why, instead, wasn't he being more supportive in helping her to retrieve her memories?

And *why oh why* did he seem incapable of giving any straight answers?

"Why can't you tell me anything?" she then retorted aloud, her voice perhaps sharper than she'd intended it to be, but despite this, still Barabus shook his head.

"It is not right to tell others about themselves. It is for *them* to discover." And then, seeing the look on Bethan's face, he sighed. "Bethan, I *would* help you, but in all honestly, I know nothing about you. And the truth of it is; it is prohibited."

"Prohibited?" Bethan looked suddenly startled. "What's prohibited?"

"Many things." Barabus's response was equally unhelpful and Bethan just stared at him.

Was he being serious? He looked as if he was and that would probably explain a few things. But…

"Prohibited?" She pushed again. What kind of a place, a *world* was this?! "Prohibited by what?"

"Not so much a *what* as a who," Barabus retorted, looking completely unmoved as Bethan actually took a few steps towards him and then; "you will find out soon enough but he is known as the Builder."

"The Builder?"

The name meant nothing to her. No flash of memory, no sudden sickness, nothing. But as if suddenly afraid the very man, or being would appear upon mention, she turned back to the corridor as if to check. "Who's this Builder?"

As she glanced back down the hallway however, all thoughts of the Builder were gone in an instant as she realised for the first time that they weren't on their own. There was someone else moving slowly along the passage towards them. Another rustle of a long dress.

It was another woman, pale and tall with a head of short blonde hair and as she looked up from where she had been watching her feet shuffle along the white-stone floor, Bethan saw that she wore a pair of spindly spectacles…

It was as the women's gazes inevitably met that Bethan then let out a cry as memories, thick and fast exploded into her head, fresh images, flashes of this woman. A quiet smile, a short man with a beard, a gemstone…

No. It couldn't be.

And shocked to her core, Bethan gave another moan.

She *knew* her. She *knew* this woman! She *remembered* her and feeling the nausea overwhelm her once again, Bethan stumbled, dizzily grabbing for Barabus's arm in some desperate attempt not to fall.

"Bex?!" she just managed to whisper. "Bex is that *you-*?" but then, her eyes rolled back in her head, and just like that, Bethan fell to the floor in a dead faint.

HOMEWARDS

Edmund was woken by an almighty yell.

It screamed out across the hut, rattling through the sunny space and he sat up sharply, grabbing for his sword before realising the all too painful truth; that he was alone and the sound had been his own, the sound of the recurring nightmare, of his sorrow.

Not again. Would it never end?

And wasting no time, the Explorer got straight up and on to his feet, busying himself with bathing his hot, sweat-stained face in a basin of river water and pulling on his shirt, all the while trying to push the haunting image of the burning woman he loved from his head, trying as he always did, to forget what had happened....

As there always seemed to be, he then heard the movement in the doorway.

Don't get angry, he told himself. *He's only trying to help.*

But looking up he was surprised to find, not Eliom, as he'd come to expect, but Fred.

Despite the fact that the whole village had no doubt heard the Explorer's outcry, the warrior made no comment about it. Instead, he was donned in his travelling cloak, his sword sheathed ready at his side and with a pang of mixed emotions, Edmund suddenly realised why it was he had come.

"We are ready to leave whenever you are," Fred then confirmed and not knowing how else to respond, Edmund nodded.

"I'm coming," was all he offered before, watching the warrior leave he then hitched his own cloak on, tied his scabbard around his waist and left the hut without a second glance.

The others were all at the meeting hut in the centre of the village, each of them clothed for travel and ready with large packs fully loaded with food and supplies for their journey ahead. Amongst them were also Bor, his second-in-command, Ckram, and a small group of villagers wanting to say their goodbyes.

THE ENTITY OF SOULS

Seeing Edmund striding towards them, the other four companions hoisted their packs onto their backs and as the Explorer reached the group, he too shouldered his own prepared pack without a word, before, finally, once everyone was ready to go, he then turned to Bor.

Bor's face was all serene politeness. Whether he felt any emotion at their parting, was difficult to tell.

"Goodbye Edmund of Tonasse," he then said, offering his hand, as was human custom. "May our paths cross again someday, on better terms." And taking the chieftain's palm gladly, Edmund shook it.

"Thank you, Bor," he replied, meaning it, as he stepped back to allow the others a chance to do the same. "Really. Thank you for everything you've done. I fear we've brought nothing but suffering to you and your people. And I don't know how we can ever repay you for what -" but Bor, who was now clasping arms with Fred, raised a hand.

"No," he insisted. "Without you, none of this," and he beckoned at the new paradise that was the forest around them, "would have been possible. You have brought us life where once was death. There is no debt to pay."

After all partings had been exchanged Bor then beckoned to several of his followers, all sturdy-looking tribesmen.

"My men shall guide you back to the shore," he said before turning to Ckram and clicking out several orders. Ckram, listening, gave a nod and repeated the orders to those men behind him who all immediately stepped forwards.

The companions looked at each other. Taking one last glance at Bor and the Tribe of Water, they then followed the tribesmen as they wasted no more time making their way towards the farthest end of the village and back into the tangle of trees.

Bethan found herself back in bed, staring up once again at that same plain ceiling. The room was quiet, empty, just as it had been before, and yet, she wasn't on her own; for sitting at the end of her bed was a figure. *The* figure and throwing herself to a sit, Bethan soon found herself staring straight into the just-as-surprised face of the woman called Bex.

"You *are* real," she muttered, more to assure herself than anything and Bex gave a thin smile.

"So are you," she replied, tucking a stray strand of hair behind an ear.

As she moved, Bethan couldn't help but notice how incredibly pale her fellow companion looked, pale and exhausted, her eyes an almost blank film of confusion.

What had happened to them both? Did Bex know? Could she remember? But as if to confirm her thoughts and in a way, fears, Bex only leaned in closer.

"Do you know why we're here?" she asked quietly. "Do you remember anything?"

Bethan's heart fell.

"No, I-" and she paused, remembering what Barabus had spoken of right before she'd fainted. Something about how information was prohibited… about the Builder. "A bit," she then continued, her own voice low. "I have little fragments of images in my head that don't quite add up. Snippets of people and places but seeing *you*," she studied her confidant up and down as if for the first time, "has brought back *so* many memories. I remember now, there was four of us. You, me and two others. We were on a *journey*. We were going somewhere and I remember that I had a green necklace and that you," she pointed shakily to Bex's neck, "you had a blue one."

Bex looked suddenly excited.

"Yes!" she hissed. "I remember that too!"

"What else?" and Bethan couldn't seem to hide her own excitement, as her heart now began to race with hope. Perhaps with Bex's own recollections, she could begin to piece together more of her life, more of herself. Perhaps she could remember how she had come to be there, who it was, the man, she had left behind… "What is this place? What do you know? Do you know who I *am*?"

But instead of answering, her pale companion just looked bewildered and realising that it was too much, too fast, Bethan forced herself to calm down, sinking back against the wall behind her bed.

"I'm sorry," she said solemnly. "I'm just so desperate to know… *everything*. I feel so lost…"

Bex smiled again.

"It's all right," she said. "I was like that a few days ago." And then, when Bethan said nothing; "We're in the City of the Diggers. That's all I really know."

"Yes, I know that much too…" Bethan mused, recalling the woman, Belanna's words. "But how did we *get* here, to this whole *place*?" for some reason she didn't want to use the word 'world', it felt too strange. "And why *are* we here?" When Bex glanced behind her towards the door, Bethan then realised that she too knew about the Builder…

"I've been told some things," she then whispered, moving even closer along the bed so Bethan could hear her clearly, "but not a lot. Some *other* things I've picked up myself." And Bethan couldn't help but lean forward hungrily, ready to devour every word.

"A few days ago - I think. Although I forget. Every day seems to last a lifetime here- Anyway. A few days ago, I awoke to find myself here, in a room, just down the corridor from this one," Bex then began to explain. "I couldn't remember *anything*. Anything at all and I was terrified, but I met a man called Gergo. He told me my name…"

Gergo. The name meant something to Bethan and it took only a moment for her to recall that he had been one of the men in the room where she'd first met Barabus. That he had been a ghost too.

"He *also* told me other things, *secret* things that he said he wasn't supposed to tell. Things about this city." She paused hesitantly, and Bethan leaned even closer.

"Go on," she encouraged.

Bex pushed her spectacles further up her nose. The frame, Bethan noticed, was a little wonky.

"Well, this city was created by the 'Builder', as Gergo called him." Bex sounded cautious.

"The Builder?" Bethan echoed. She was right. There was that name again. "Yes, Barabus mentioned him." She then looked at Bex long and hard as if ready to judge her reaction before; "He also told me that we're in another world. Different to the world we're from…"

But to her surprise, Bex didn't seem at all put out by this news.

"Yes, we are. The Builder supposedly 'built' this place. And Gergo told me that we're not here by chance. That we were *summoned* here."

"Summoned?"

Bethan's eyebrows rose. She didn't remember being *summoned* by anyone…

"Yes," Bex said, the look on her face saying it all – she thought it was farfetched too, "*summoned* somehow. Gergo didn't really manage to say anything else. I've a feeling he wasn't even supposed to tell me as much as he did. I think he was afraid…"

Bethan nodded. But she was unable to hide her disappointed. She was craving for information. They both were. Any information to help in the search for what was lost, in the search for their missing lives. And knowing she simply couldn't leave it there, Bethan lowered her voice all the more.

"What about… before?" she asked.

"Before?"

"Yes. Before we were here. What exactly do you remember?"

Bex said nothing for a moment, frowning as she concentrated on her memories, but despite her longing, Bethan didn't push her.

"I can recall things from my childhood," she then replied and her face, still so white, reddened a little as her mind's eye returned to fondness she had forgotten. "I remember my parents. I remember their accident years ago and I remember… I remember seeing them again. Only I was dreaming, but *not* dreaming…" she looked suddenly very confused. "It was a sort of nightmare as well. I was attacked by someone. A man. We were stuck in a mist. A dark mist... and I dreamt of them all but it felt really real... Does that make sense?"

A man. In a dream.

A dark mist...

Bethan's face lit up. *This* was the sort of thing she'd hoped for.

A mist.

"The Dark Mist!" she exclaimed as recollections of those fateful three days came cascading back, hand-in-hand with others. She remembered a ship now. She'd been on a ship and a mist had taken them and then she'd found herself on a beach... with a man.

Bethan's heart sank again as she saw him.

It was the man with the deep blue eyes. The figure who haunted so many of her other thoughts. The nameless man...

She recalled being in the sea. Swimming. With him. It had been beautiful and warm and they had been smiling, laughing together. But then it had turned cold. Cold as death. And the rain had begun, the driving freezing rain and storms and-

Bex, seeing that Bethan's mind was now a hive of activity, sat silently, allowing her companion to relive her memories uninterrupted. But noticing the sudden distress on her weak friend's face, she took her by the hand.

"Bethan," she soothed. "Bethan, what is it? What do you remember?"

Bethan blinked a few times as something like tears sprang to her eyes. But then she was back in the room and her gaze was on Bex's face, pleading.

"Please," she then demanded, "who is the man in my mind? The man I keep seeing. He always seems to be there but-"

Bex's forehead crumpled.

"Which man?"

"The man with the blue eyes," Bethan snapped, but noticing Bex's blank reaction, Bethan could see that she knew nothing of him either.

"I'm sorry," Bex apologised meekly. "I can recall others, others who were with us. But not him. I don't remember a man with blue eyes..."

Bethan pulled her hand gently away from her friend's grasp.

"It's all right," she shrugged her off in frustration. There was no use getting angry about it, she knew that. Hard as it was; for now she would have to wait, whether she was impatient or not.

"Tell me more," and suddenly desperate for her companion to carry on, Bethan tried to smile. It was as if every new revelation opened a new door in her mind, releasing a part of herself back into existence. She was hungry for more. Hungry for anything.

"Well," Bex said thoughtfully, "like you said, we were on a journey together..."

"Yes, I remember that," Bethan mumbled absently.

"And there was eight of us."

"Eight?!" Bethan thought she could only really call to mind six. Herself, two other women, the small man with Bex and of course, the man with the blue eyes... but even as she thought this through, two others started to emerge. One had been a swordsman, a warrior, who at first had frightened her and another a being of magic, a wizard with a staff...

"I remember some of our companions.," Bex continued unheeded. "I remember you and two other women, just like you have. One short with long hair and another about our height with blonde hair and..."

"Saz..." the name escaped Bethan's lips before she even had a chance to think about it and as if the word had acted as some kind of catalyst, both women seemed to brighten.

"Yes!" Bex cried, sounding thrilled all over again. "She was Saz! I remember now! And two men... and... and a dwarf. The dwarf was Thom. I remember he was with me. Alone. We were travelling to meet you and..."

Bethan's mind whirred with eager anticipation.

"And Eliom!" Bex burst out. "The wizard!"

"Eliom! Of course! I remember him!" Bethan replied. The pair's voices were starting to grow loud now as their eagerness took over.

"And there was a building, a giant building we were all heading towards. Can you remember *why?*" Bex asked. "I don't remember much about it, do you?"

But before Bethan could even contemplate answering, they suddenly became aware of another sound, the sound of footsteps and the swish of someone in the doorway...

"Bethan!" Belanna exclaimed sharply and then, noticing Bex as she swivelled to look, she glared at them both. "You should *both* be resting!"

Bustling into the room, the woman then took hold of Bex's arm and pulling her firmly but gently to her feet, began to steer her back into the corridor.

Unable to fight, Bex just stared back at Bethan helplessly as she found herself herded through the door. But as she reached the doorframe, she turned, just managing to make eye contact with her friend and mouth the word 'tonight' before disappearing from view.

Bethan gave a sigh and slumped back in her bed, her mind a flurry of thoughts. She felt beyond annoyed that their talk had been interrupted. She hadn't had the chance to tell Bex about the building, the temple, which was now, at that very moment, fresh in her mind's eye.

She could recall everything about it now, from what she had remembered about it before and the platform to the ornate white stone pillars and the intense fire that she and the others had stepped into, little knowing the consequences...

—

Edmund watched soundlessly as Ckram and his men heaved the small rowing boat to the water's edge.

The other four stood beside him looking awkward. They'd offered to help make the boat ready but Ckram had had none of it. He'd *insisted* that his men would do *everything* for them, as a last thank you and none of them had been able to persuade him otherwise.

"I still cannot understand what they have to be so thankful *for*," Thom muttered gruffly and though the Explorer glanced at him, it was Eliom who spoke.

"We may have brought them bloodshed, Thom," he said, never moving his eyes from the working tribesmen, "but we have also provided the gift of water. To them the river is everything and to them, *we* are the ones who have replenished it."

"It wasn't us," Edmund interjected darkly and the conversation collapsed back into watchful silence.

Once the rowing boat was in the water Ckram then finally turned to the group, beckoning for them to clamber in. None of them needed telling twice and wading into the shallows, Elanore was the first, followed closely by Fred; Thom, who struggled perhaps more than the others due to his short legs; Eliom and then lastly, Edmund.

Once again, the Explorer found himself thanking the tribesmen for everything they'd done, although, from the blank beams on each of their faces, he knew he wouldn't ever be entirely sure if they'd understood his gratitude. Either way, all knew it was time to leave and with a few more squawks from Ckram, the tribesmen released the boat and grabbing hold of the oars, Fred and Elanore soon set them on course for the awaiting Karenza as those who weren't rowing turned to look back on the quickly shrinking beach.

For a long while, Ckram's men stood in the shallows, watching their visitors venture off towards the horizon, but once the tribesmen were nothing but insect-like blemishes against the trees, the group then turned their full attention on the ship ahead. Only Edmund hung back a little, his gaze still rooted on the land, on the forest, as if secretly, intently searching for something, or someone... Perhaps for a glimpse of the temple. Perhaps for a glimpse of *her* – he didn't know, but even as he thought about it, he already felt the boat slow and then a dark shadow was casting itself over them all.

"Homeward bound!" Elanore cried cheerily, unable to hide her joy as the Karenza towered over them and after securing the boat with the deftness of a professional, she was the first to leap nimbly onto the ladder leading up to the deck and was gone in less than a heartbeat. Her companions, meanwhile, all took a moment to pause.

It had been a few weeks since the four friends had stepped foot on board the Karenza and though for all it was somehow good to see her friendly sails waving in the breeze once more, at the same time, the ship also brought with it a sense of sorrow, fresh memories of what they had known and lost…

"Come on," Fred said to no one in particular. The words almost fell dead in his throat, but obeying, Thom grabbed hold of the rope and began to climb without a word, followed by the warrior, Eliom and finally Edmund.

As all four companions reached the deck there was a strange stillness in the air, as each took a moment to reaffirm their surroundings. Right ahead was the gigantic main mast and the crow's nest high above their heads, with the winch and chain of the anchor beyond. To their right, beyond the smaller foremast was the forecastle deck with the ship's wheel and beyond even that the long bowsprit reaching out to the sea with the wooden horse head still sporting its fiery mane defiantly at the ocean. It was just as they all remembered it. In fact, *exactly* and almost eerily so, from the black scorch marks and, in some places, ruined boards - a reminder of the fires only matter of weeks before - all the way to the stern on their left and the trapdoor leading down a sharp ladder to the two cabins below. One living space for them and one for the women…

Already Elanore was hurrying here and there, untying this rope and loosening that. None of them were sure whether she just hadn't noticed the oppressive gloom that had suddenly settled over her crew, or whether she was simply choosing to ignore it, but either way, taking charge once again, she threw them all a glare.

"Come on you lot!" she chided gently. "We need to get moving! Eliom and Fred," the pair looked up, "anchor – you know what to do. Thom – crow's nest and Edmund," the Explorer seemed to look at her as if he couldn't quite believe she was there, "I'll need help making the boat fast. Then we need to set a course due West." And sniffing the sea air like it held some kind of magical property, she then folded her arms. "We should be out of here in no time!"

ELEMENTS

For both of the tired travellers, the outer city was a thankful sight, or so Meggie had herself believe. Then again though, in the few days that she'd known him, she'd never really been able to work out *what* her companion was truly feeling. He had one of those faces; not unfriendly, but at the same time, *closed*, unreadable. Almost like a certain wizard she could remember all too well…

"I have to admit," the man known as Nickolas remarked. "I *am* surprised at how long you have lasted."

"Oh?" and Meggie glanced at him as they walked. "What do you mean?" She tried not to sound insulted, but unlike him, she knew that hiding her irritation wasn't always her forte and detecting he'd obviously touched some kind of nerve, Nickolas gave a small smile.

"I did not mean it as a slur," he replied in that strange ancient way he spoke. "Just that, when it happened to me, I was not…. *right* for a long time. I lost my memory for nearly a month," he paused. "And even now I cannot recall things that I once knew."

"Oh," Meggie repeated. For some reason, she couldn't seem to hide her sudden misplaced guilt either.

Since her arrival in this desolate place days before, she'd met Nickolas, who, to his complete astonishment, she'd immediately recognised as the spirit, or *man*, she'd witnessed appear a few minutes before in the Temple of Ratacopeck.

If it *had* been a few minutes… for Meggie wasn't really sure of the time anymore.

What Meggie *was* sure of however, was that when she'd walked into the temple flames with the other three women, she'd found herself there, in another *world* - as Nickolas had put it - lying at his feet in the middle of nowhere, a vast desert of nothing, her head swimming and her stomach churning. And unreadable as he had come to be in the days afterwards, Nickolas appeared to be completely astounded by her, for not only could

Meggie remember the temple perfectly, but also everything *else*, from the beginning of her journey to save Tungala - her *own* world - and beyond, far into her life before that. She appeared to be completely.... well, *fine* and as a matter of fact, though he would never show it, Nickolas found himself secretly afraid of the small woman with the long hair and catlike eyes.

He'd never known anyone to be so... *normal* after what had happened. It just simply *didn't* happen and it was this more than anything that actually worried him.

No doubt this wasn't going to last. No one *ever* came through the transition from one world to another lightly and that included his charge.

Which could only mean that it was simply a matter of time.

Most likely Meggie's body was just slow to react to the shock and that at any moment everything would change. But whether it was going to be soon, or days, weeks, *months* down the line, Nickolas had known after only minutes in her company, that he would have to be there, to watch her carefully, to be ready and all the while, where possible, show her *nothing* of his concern. After all, the last thing he needed – they *both* needed - was for her to somehow panic and break down before she was truly ready.

No. For now, he would just have to wait it out and help where and *when* he could...

"*I'm* not sorry I still have my mind and body intact," Meggie was muttering to herself and Nickolas gave another little smile. There was something about this gutsy woman that amused and yet saddened him. *How the truth would truly crush her...*

The pair then plodded on as they had for days, in silence, and taking yet another chance to glance about her at the dry sandy ground littered with nothing but rocks and shrivelled shrubbery, Meggie rubbed her dry eyes. She wasn't sure why she hadn't noticed it before, but the whole place seemed to be seeping with some kind of light and it was really starting to make her head ache.

"Why is everything.... *red?*" she asked after a time. Her voice seemed muffled somehow in the great space.

She looked up at her tall companion but though, yet again, his square stern-set face gave her nothing, for some reason, this didn't seem to stop her from staring longer than she should have.

It was as if she couldn't quite seem to tear her eyes away from him. There was something there, something small, like a memory or a sense of familiarity, a sense of *recognition* being with him; although much as she thought about it, Meggie couldn't seem to quite work out *why*. She didn't *know* the man, that was for sure. In any real sense of the word, Nickolas was a complete stranger to her. And yet...

Nickolas's own gaze was still on the collection of squat buildings ahead. Civilization.

"There are some things that I cannot tell you," he replied, glancing down at her as he felt Meggie's stare. "You know that." But though the small woman blushed a little, she didn't give up.

"Yes 'I know that' but I still don't know *why*?" she demanded boldly. "Who's to stop you?"

But Nickolas's expression didn't change.

"I just... I cannot."

And he turned back to the way ahead but though his *face* gave nothing away, Nickolas's *voice* certainly did. It was tense, with a hint of warning and Meggie could see then that, much as she had tried in the past few days, she wasn't going to get anything out of him just yet.

Much as she wanted to know, to *understand* just what on Tungala had happened to her, she also didn't want to annoy him. Nickolas was the only person she'd met in this strange new world. And, for all she knew, he might *remain* so.

"It is only a short time before we reach the outer city," her companion continued, his voice back to its normal deep self. "But I must warn you... it is not the nicest of places. We will only be there a night before we move onto the City."

"All right," Meggie nodded with a sigh.

None of it made any sense to her. She had no idea *where* she was, or *where* she was going. But to be honest to herself, at that moment, she didn't really care. All that mattered somehow was that she was still alive. She still had all her limbs and, despite what Nickolas seemed to be worried about, she still had all her memories. She was still *Meggie*. For the time being...

"Will I find the others, in this 'City' place?" she asked Nickolas and this time, he nodded.

"I should think so. Everyone goes there. No one stays out *here* for too long."

"I wonder why," Meggie couldn't help but snort and to her surprise, her sarcasm made Nickolas suddenly laugh. The sound was pleasant and Meggie couldn't help but join in. It was somehow nice to joke after what had seemed to her, so long a time of sorrow and danger, and encouraged by her companion's change in mood, she began again.

"I've got a question for you that maybe you *can* answer," she smiled. "You know, a few days ago, when I asked you how it was that you were a *ghost* at the temple, in the other world- my world- and yet now you're fully alive-?"

But though she had meant well, Nickolas suddenly seemed to clam up all over again, as his lips pursed, his whole stride stiffening and Meggie faltered.

So much for trying not to annoy him. She'd already failed.

Although, she reasoned perhaps too late, starting back with the question of why he was no longer *alive* in Tungala, probably wasn't the best idea she'd ever had. It was obviously a sore point for him, she could see it in his eyes...

THE ENTITY OF SOULS

Maybe those kinds of questions should be left for another time.

"I'm sorry," she interjected, turning her gaze quickly to the ground as she felt her face reddening again. "I don't mean to keep harassing you."

Despite the impression he'd given however, Nickolas surprised her again by giving a shrug.

"I too had many questions when I came through the flames," he said and somehow Meggie could tell that he wasn't just trying to be kind to her.

And then, even more unexpectedly, Nickolas gave yet another small smile.

"Ask away."

Meggie's eyebrows rose cautiously.

"Really?"

"Really."

"All right." And taking a moment to really think, to really consider what she could say without hurting her companion again, Meggie frowned.

She had so many questions, most of which she'd already tried and got no response. What then, could she ask? Except…

She cleared her throat.

"Well, what do *you* remember… of when *you* were…" she almost said *'alive'* but stopped in her tracks. Somehow, she knew that Nickolas wasn't dead. He was walking there, right next to her and she had felt his flesh, the firm grip of his hand as he had helped her to her feet at the first. And yet he wasn't, at the same time, *alive* as she knew it, or rather *had* known it. He had been a ghost in her world. He was so old, he'd told her a few days before – one of the few things he *had* told her- that to Tungala, he *was* dead.

Although just *how* old he was, he hadn't said…

Nickolas, sensing her struggle, gave another weak smile.

"When I was living in your world?"

Meggie nodded eagerly, pleased not to have to say it.

Nickolas turned his eyes back to the way ahead.

"Not much," he said meditatively. "I cannot recall anything of importance. Or at least, nothing that really matters to anyone but myself." Something in his eyes glistened as he spoke though and feeling positive, Meggie tried to press him a little more.

"Tell me," she pleaded. She could see that he obviously wanted to talk about it but wasn't quite sure how or whether he should. Whatever it was that was preventing him from speaking to her the truth about what had happened, about where they were, was clearly holding him back now.

"Well, I remember the little things," he began. "Things that I once took for granted. Like the feeling of grass beneath my bare feet or the feeling of a clean summer's air filling my lungs. The smell of a morning in springtime and the taste of fresh water and bread in my mouth…" he halted a moment and to her surprise, Meggie's chest felt suddenly heavy.

He was right. They *were* little things. Things up until that very moment she had nearly always taken for granted and yet hearing him speak, seeing the uncontrolled longing on his face, she felt all of a sudden very afraid.

"Don't you eat or drink?" she found herself demanding as she realised that her throat was parched and she was desperately hungry. It wasn't the worst of her fears, but somehow it helped to mask them, to push them aside a little.

Luckily for her however, Nickolas laughed again.

"Oh yes! There is food and water here. And as you can tell, there is still air to breathe... but," and again he was back to the past, "it is not the same. It is *never* the same..."

If he'd meant this to help though, it hadn't, for instead of relief, Meggie only felt worse.

She was suddenly very frightened of this place.

She was frightened of staying here forever, old and forgotten with no enjoyment for food or the necessities of life anymore.

She was frightened of ending up like Nickolas.

And with these fears came a strong, overpowering longing to be back in her world, back in Tungala.

At first, she'd seen no appeal in her return. She had no family left; they were all dead. She'd been alone for years. And she had only ever had a handful of friends, friends who she'd happened upon by pure chance - or perhaps by fate, she couldn't be sure - as they'd battled to reach the temple together.

Strangely, she'd felt no remorse at being flung into this strange existence but now, suddenly, as she realised what it really *meant* she was beginning to have her regrets... and without realising it, she stopped walking.

Panic, thick and fast was starting to well up inside of her. Panic unknown, wild and so strong that for a moment, she was only vaguely aware that Nickolas was still talking to her, was still reminiscing. She only caught his last few words.

"...when I was younger. I remember her smiles but then..."

But Nickolas trailed off the moment he realised something was wrong. Meggie's face had paled to almost a white and her breathing was coming rapidly.

He halted.

"Meggie?" he asked. This time there was no mistaking the worry either in his voice or on his face.

Meggie felt suddenly dizzy.

She couldn't breathe. She felt sick all over again. But only this time it was worse. Her fingers were starting to tingle. She was going to throw up and leaning over, Meggie retched, horror pouring into her every thought as she realised what was happening.

The shock. The illness Nickolas had warned her about. She hadn't got away that easily and unable to control her limbs any longer, Meggie's crashed to her knees in the hard dirt as her legs gave out from under her.

"Meggie!"

She could hear Nickolas shouting her name, feel his solid body against hers as he threw himself at her, only just managing to catch her before her whole body hit the floor.

She tried to call out, to reply, to tell him what was happening, but all that came out of her mouth was a moan.

She was terrified. Her whole body was shaking.

She didn't want to go! She didn't want to lose her memories! She wasn't ready! What would happen to her?

She could already feel herself slipping into unconsciousness and was fighting with all of her will to stay awake.

Nickolas's words kept swimming round and round in her head.

I was not.... right for a long time. I lost my memory for nearly a month. And even now I cannot recall things that I once knew.

Even now I cannot recall things that I once knew...

"No..." she muttered.

No...

She could still feel Nickolas's firm hands holding her up and his voice, muffled as it was, calling for her to stay with him.

"Meggie!" he was crying urgently. "Stay awake! Meggie! We are nearly there! You can do it! I know you can..."

But his words were wasted. It was too late and finally giving up, Meggie fell limp in his arms, her eyes rolling senselessly to the back of her head.

—

Dromeda propped his feet up on the chair opposite with a small sigh and rubbing the back of his shaggy head, leaned back to stare up at the ceiling.

White. Always white. And he shuddered, not for the first time, as he remembered when he'd last been in this place, lying in a room just like one of those beside him. Dead to the world. Quite literally...

Although not *quite* like these rooms. *These* rooms were smaller, grubbier, simpler – if that were possible. But then again, it was only to be expected here, in the poorer parts of the outer city.

He was counting the seconds until he could get out of there.

As he hummed a little tune to himself, a fragment of song he had once known, a woman then exited from the room to his left and seeing him, she paused to stare. Dromeda realised, with a small scowl to himself, that she probably hadn't seen two humans together in a long time. In fact, the chances were, she'd probably never seen *one* in her life before now.

"You can go home now, you know," the woman said offhandedly. If that *was* the reason she was staring at him now, she was hiding it well.

Dromeda barely even blinked.

"I know," he answered with a bit of a scowl. "As long as you do not require me anymore."

Not even slightly put off by his apparent bad mood, the woman shook her slender head.

"She'll be fine without you."

Dromeda didn't need telling again and with these words, he leapt nimbly to his feet, preparing to leave. He was sick of this place already anyway. Sick of these people. But as he made to move off down the long corridor to the double doors and beyond, he halted a moment before doubling back.

"You are *certain* she will be all right if I leave her?"

The woman nodded her head. It was her turn to look annoyed. But some kind of sick respect, or perhaps even *fear* held her back from saying anything else.

"I may be the only one she remembers," Dromeda pointed out and the woman glanced back to the room she had just left as if expecting someone to be standing there.

"I'll find you if she wakes," she insisted and then, seeing that the woman wanted rid of him, Dromeda gave another sigh and started back towards the exit.

He didn't need telling again and it was only then, as he passed the third doorway from the end, that someone else spoke.

"Dromeda!" and knowing the voice, he swivelled around to see a tall muscular figure emerging from the room he'd just passed. It didn't take him a second to recognise it.

"Nickolas!" he exclaimed and he hurried forward to meet his friend.

"Well met!"

Embracing him, Nickolas then held Dromeda out at arm's length for a moment or two, as if to study him and taking this chance to do just the same in reverse, Dromeda couldn't help but note the dark bags under Nickolas's eyes and taut lines of stress just at the corners of his mouth. His friend hadn't slept properly in a while.

"How long have you been here?" he then asked his companion, unable to hide his surprise.

"Only a few hours," Nickolas replied and Dromeda's eyebrows rose.

"I did not see you arrive," he pointed out unnecessarily. "Took you a while to get here."

"We were very far out," Nickolas justified.

"Ah."

There was then a pause and Nickolas glanced down the corridor.

"What are you doing here?" he asked and Dromeda nodded at the room Nickolas had just exited from.

"Same as you."

"Ah."

His companion gave a distracted grimace and Dromeda felt suddenly aware how bad his exit looked.

"It is strange that we are both here," Nickolas then remarked instead, as if desperate to make conversation. "In the past all were moved straight to the City."

Dromeda shrugged.

"Perhaps times are finally changing," he mused. "I can tell you though…" and he took a second to look about him then as if to check no one was listening before leaning in closer, "the sooner we reach the City the better. This place is… I just *cannot* like it."

Just as he half-expected, this made Nickolas give a wary sigh and realising that even now his friend would never agree with him, Dromeda rolled his eyes.

"I know what it is you would say," he then interjected before his companion could scold him. "I know that *you* believe the Diggers are no different from us, but you are *wrong*. You are fooling yourself if you think they are not. Besides…" he shrugged again noncommittally, "this place is so *rundown* compared to the City."

Just as he'd suspected, Nickolas could only look disapproving.

"I agree with you on that point. You know that. But you also know *why* it is rundown, Dromeda." On the word *why,* Nickolas's voice almost became a warning. "Just because these people *are* different from us does not make them worthy of rebuke," he continued and Dromeda rolled his eyes again mock-impatiently.

"I know."

He didn't want to argue with his friend over the matter right then. In his mind it was already settled. And much as they had spoken about it in the past, he knew his opinion was never going to change, no matter how hard his friend tried to make it otherwise.

"How is your element?" he asked, changing the subject swiftly.

At this, Nickolas's brow knotted in concern.

"She was fine until about an hour or two ago…" he said and Dromeda's eyebrows rose higher.

"Fine?" he echoed in disbelief. "What, *completely* fine?"

"Fine," Nickolas repeated, rubbing his forehead in confusion. "She seemed… well, normal. No memory loss. Nothing. And then a little while ago, she just… collapsed." Dromeda's eyebrows continued to rise until they were almost impossible to see under the line of his long shaggy hair.

"What about yours? How is she?" Nickolas spoke in what would have been a conversational tone had it not been for the tense look on his face and Dromeda shrugged yet again.

"She was unconscious from the beginning and has not yet woken up. I had to *carry* her here, Nickolas. A hard slog, I can tell you. The Diggerwoman said I could go home... well, not back to the City, but where I have been calling *home* the last few nights..."

"You mean to say, you have not been staying *here*?" Nickolas challenged, clearly surprised and Dromeda couldn't help but look even incredulous.

"Here? No!" he retorted. "I have bad enough memories from the *first* time I stayed in one of these places. And in fact, now that you are here, I have a right mind to return to the City and leave you to it."

"You would leave her here?!" Nickolas's voice was almost a shout.

And yet, Dromeda's face was blank.

"Well. There is no real reason for me to stay. You know how much I *hate* the outer city. *You* are here, you can wake her..."

But Nickolas was incredulous himself now.

"I am here for *Meggie*," he pointed out sharply. "You should look after *your* element. You cannot leave her here alone!"

"I am-"

And for a second, Dromeda couldn't have looked more shocked than if Nickolas had reached out and hit him across the face. Utterly confused, he spread his hands wide in supplication.

"Nickolas, why are you being like this?" he then demanded suspiciously. "We knew the job we had to do. The job we were assigned to do. I cannot understand why you care about the welfare of your element so much. She will be fine.... Eventually. They always are..." he snorted. "No doubt you will meet again in the City. And anyway..." but then suddenly, as if a flame had sparked to life in his head, he stopped and slowly, a smile of realisation began to spread across his face. "Oh!" he cried. "I understand now! You like her!"

At this, Nickolas turned away from his friend with a bitter laugh and a shake of his head, but when he said nothing in his own defence, Dromeda was even more stunned. *Was it really true? Had his friend really become attached?*

"You do?" he cried teasingly but, though he was laughing, his companion wasn't in the mood for games.

"You sound like a *child* Dromeda!" Nickolas retorted and then, his voice a menacing hiss, he rounded on his friend; "Do you not remember? Do you not remember what it was like when *we* walked through those flames? Do you not remember the pain, the illness, the anguish? *Do you not remember what it was like?*" And suddenly Dromeda was no longer smiling.

"Of course I do," he growled. "I remember it every day!"

"Well then, how can you *possibly* just leave her here?" Nickolas demanded. "She *needs* you. Just like *you* needed somebody once…"

Just like you needed somebody once.

Once.

The word sent a surprising stab of long-buried pain through Dromeda, making him fall silent, and obviously realising enough was enough, Nickolas seemed to soften. Breaking away from his friend, he then moved to a chair just beside the doorway and giving a small moan, slumped into it in exhaustion.

"You are right," he then carried on, as if the past few moments hadn't happened, "of course I *like* her. *But,*" and noticing the mischievous grin flicker its way back across Dromeda's face, he held up a hand, "not in the way that you *imply*." He gave a shrug. "She has spirit. And most importantly, does not deserve to just be *abandoned* here. No one does. And I, for my part, will wait until she is ready to leave. *Even,*" and he looked up at his friend pointedly then before burying his tired head in his hands, "even if it means staying here."

Long after his companion had finished speaking, Dromeda just watched him, but when his face didn't surface again, he moved towards the corridor wall and leaning the weight of his body against it, took a moment just to think.

Though he would never admit it, his emotions were all over the place.

He hated this place. *Hated* it. The whole building was grubby, silent and forlorn and every second he was there he was reminded of all those hundreds of years ago when he too, had been ill and unable to wake. But at the same time, though everything in him wanted to leave, to *run* even and never look back, the voice of conscience, the voice awoken by his friend's anger told him that he should stay, that he *had* to stay. For her sake. For, as Nickolas had so rightly pointed out, his element would need him.

For all he knew, he could be the only one she recognised when she woke up, the only one she could talk to. The only one who could save her. And the elements were all there to help each other. To keep each other sane, for if they didn't, what was the point?

How could life be even slightly bearable anymore?

It seemed a long time before either element roused, but as if he had finally, unwillingly made his decision, it was Dromeda who moved first and pushing himself from the wall, he shuffled across the hall and heaving himself into a spare chair next to Nickolas, gave a sigh.

"I will stay then," was all he said. "For you and for Saz."

Nickolas never even looked up. But though his head was still in his hands, Dromeda was sure he saw the twitch of a nod.

—

Bethan flinched as a hand touched her shoulder. It was the middle of the night and having crept from her room to meet with Bex, she was feeling undeniably jumpy. At the first touch she turned, ready to run, but before she could so much as move, Bex's friendly face appeared in the gloom.

Without a word, the other woman then pressed a finger to her lips and taking Bethan by the arm, began to lead her towards the end of the corridor.

Bethan followed without comment, clutching the hem of her dress as it began to rustle. Bex did the same and together they moved almost silently.

Reaching the swinging double doors at the end of the hall, Bex then released her and leaning forward, pushed one cautiously. To their relief, it swung open without a noise and the women slipped through it, Bethan gripping the edge of the door as they fled to stop it from slamming back into place and alerting anyone else of their presence.

The women then found themselves, to Bethan's surprise, outside.

Bethan had half been expecting more corridors and rooms lined together in one great white maze but instead they were standing in what appeared to be a small square surrounded by other squat-like buildings. In the middle of the square was a fountain, which would have looked impressive if there had been more than a tiny trickle of water gurgling from it. Everything was white stone, only just visible in the blackness.

Down one side of the square was a little alleyway, darker than the rest and like one who knew her way, Bex didn't hesitate in pulling Bethan towards it.

The alley led out onto what appeared to be a wider street with more white stone buildings, all silent and dark. There were no moons or stars to be seen in the sky. Only the reddish hue that seemed to cover everything, provided any kind of light.

Bex guided Bethan further down the alley until they came out onto the street and though Bethan felt like stopping to ask if her companion knew where she was going before they got well and truly lost, she decided against it. From the way Bex was directing her, so quickly and decisively, it was clear that she had been here before and sure enough, even as Bethan was thinking it, her companion soon dragged her across the street, ignoring the natural pull of the road which stretched on for a good half a mile or so to their right. Turning instead left, back into another, thinner alleyway, they were then in yet another square surrounded by buildings, only not with a fountain or statue at the centre, but, to Bethan's surprise, a tree.

This was the first full-grown greenery that Bethan had seen in this strange place although, despite this, she couldn't help but notice that the shrub in fact barely looked green at all. Its leaves, instead, were a sort of dull grey and droopy, the branches sagging as if under a great weight.

Even in the darkness she could see that the whole plant looked about ready to die but despite this, Bex began to hurry Bethan towards it, as if by rushing to it they could somehow save it. It was only as they got to within a few feet that Bethan then saw why it was Bex had dragged her all this way.

In the centre of the square, in the shadow of the tree - or what Bethan supposed *would* have been a shadow, as curiously, the tree didn't have one despite the odd light - was a long flight of stairs, leading down to another street many steps below.

Still without a word, an explanation, Bex pulled Bethan towards the stairs and they began to descend them quickly.

By this point, both women were starting to get out of breath and with every step Bethan could feel her uneasiness growing as she tried not to slip or fall.

Where was Bex taking her?

What if they went too far and couldn't find their way back?

She was already beginning to forget how they'd come to be there in the first place… Had it been right and then left or left and then right?

But just as Bethan was about ready to give up and stop, on the forty-fifth, or so, stair, she felt a great tug on her arm as Bex suddenly hauled her to the right where at first there had appeared to be nothing but solid wall, but in fact was a small recess. The gap was hidden from the stairwell by an overhanging piece of dying shrubbery and conveniently, just large enough to fit two people very snuggly inside.

Bethan and Bex huddled into the space and the moment she was comfortable, Bethan then finally turned to face her friend, impressed.

"Gergo told me about this place," Bex explained modestly, her voice a low whisper.

"It's a good place to hide…" Bethan commented.

"And talk. I don't know why, but I have a feeling that people around here," and Bex nodded back to the stairway "don't like us *discussing* things. Did you see the way that that woman, Belanna, separated us when we were talking before? That's what happened with Gergo. He was interrupted and whisked out just like that…" Bex lowered her voice even further so that Bethan almost had to strain to hear it. "There's something not quite right about this place. But if only I could remember how we *got* here to begin with…"

Bethan perked up then. Finally it was time to share some of her new memories with her friend.

"I remember!" she hissed and Bex's face positively lit up. Though the tiny space was dark, Bethan could still just make out her companion's expression through the gloom.

"When you asked me about the building earlier, the one we were all heading towards? Things began to slot back into place." Bethan talked quickly. "I remember *exactly* what happened in that building. It was a temple of some kind, a gigantic hall made of white stone. Just like this place. It was full of great pillars, and I remember everything from the tiny little ornate details, the pictures and words carved on the stone to the platform and the fire and..."

"Platform? Fire?" Bex echoed, desperately trying to keep up.

"Yes!" and then, "have you seen the great statue? The one here. I saw it from the window back at... well... wherever we were."

Bex's face contorted in blank confusion for only a moment.

"Yes! I have! I remember now! The statue? The weird stone platform with the four glass orbs on top of it?" and Bethan nodded eagerly.

"It was there. In the temple. We were there, us two," she gestured at both of them in turn, "and then there were the other two women, Saz and-"

"Meggie!" Bex suddenly burst out. She looked surprised as if she hadn't even meant to open her mouth let alone speak any words, as if the name had somehow spurted out, but too excited to care, she gave a laugh before, remembering where they were, covering her mouth with a hand.

"Meggie," Bethan repeated, speaking the name she had once forgotten. "Yes and Meggie. And then the others were there. Eliom and Thom and a warrior and... another man. The one with the blue eyes..." Bethan felt her heart pang then as she thought about the tall man who seemed to disturb her thoughts constantly. Oh, if she could only remember!

"Yes..." Bex mused. She was beginning to recall things herself now, memories tripping over themselves to be set free, to be spoken aloud. "That was where we met the four ghosts, or spirits or- well they're not ghosts *or* spirits..."

"And we climbed the platform."

"And then..." but Bex trailed off and the two women stared at each other fearfully.

Neither of them needed to say it. For they both knew. They both remembered.

Then they had walked through the flames.

And awoken here.

In another world.

"I think that-" Bethan began again but before she could finish, before either could start to contemplate what any of this *meant* both heard the sudden noise from outside and froze.

Footsteps. There was someone coming down the stairs. And whoever it was, wasn't alone, for accompanying them was another pair and with them, two voices, both of them male. Without realising they did it, both women then held their breath and leaning closer to the edge of the alcove, strained to listen as the conversation grew louder.

"The Diggers are causing trouble again," one exasperated man said. He obviously had *no* qualms about keeping his voice down in the dark night for his words carried easily. "So the rumours say."

"I heard only yesterday that they were witnessed trying to reach the City," the other man then replied. He too wasn't speaking softly, but even so, there was more caution to his tone. "If it were a matter for me, I should say they ought to remain where they are. It is the best place for them."

"Most of them do," the first man sounded reasonable. "But there are more and more of them working here and not enough of *us*. At least thirty to one they say."

"Yes," the second mused. "There *are* too few, Arcameaus, but one day that will no longer be the case. You have walked this world longer than I, you who were one of the first."

The footsteps then paused only a step or two up from the women's hiding place and alarmed at the possibility of being discovered, Bethan and Bex's hands found each other, as they gripped one another tightly in the dark.

"Indeed," the first man then spoke again. His voice sounded weary.

The second man though, didn't seem to detect it.

"Yet you have never aged a day. Even after all this time, I still find it amazing."

But though his companion clearly meant to compliment, the man known as Arcameaus didn't seem to think so.

"You *know* very well why *that* is," he replied smartly, his voice suddenly a warning.

"And yet, I have never understood, even now, how it is that the Diggers are so different," the second man said as if nothing had happened. "They are not like us. They age, they breed, they die much like-"

"They are part of this place. They were created on this world. *We* were not. They are its true inhabitants. Not us." Arcameaus sounded almost impatient.

"But we are the *chosen*!"

"Yes, we are and yet... the Diggers are truly the Builder's. They have been drinking his water, watching his red sky and breathing his air their entire lives. We are only... *guests* here."

There was a snort.

"Guest is not the term many would choose."

"No, perhaps not." Arcameaus' voice was flat. "But we are here now. And will forever be until such a time as the Builder reveals his plans."

And whatever that statement really meant, there seemed to be something of a shocked silence then before someone gave a wry laugh and the second man, clearly the sceptic, began again;

"You are not one of those to believe-?"

"And can you say you are truly not?" Arcameaus challenged. "It is clear the Builder has brought us here, preserved us just as we were the day we entered those flames *for a reason*..."

"But why? I know the risks. But one has to wonder…" The second man's voice suddenly dropped to a whisper. It was clear from the way he spoke that he wasn't as knowledgeable as the first. And despite the fact both men sounded no more than youths, he somehow seemed younger.

"You know that the *reasons* are not to be spoken of, not to be speculated," the older man cautioned.

"I do not see why. If the Builder has gone through so much difficulty to hold us here, to keep us as we were – *are* - then surely he would not *destroy* us for simply *speculating*. We have a *right* to know. What can he possibly do?" and he seemed to lower his voice even further. "We cannot *die*."

The first man sounded a little put out, as if what his companion suggested was somehow treasonous.

"The Builder is god here. If he wants to smite you, he will do so."

"But as to *that*," the second man insisted. "If he has, as you and others suggest, *collected* us for some reason or purpose, what *is* that purpose? Who even-" and suddenly it was as if he was beside himself with years of unanswered questions, "who even knows who the Builder is? Has anyone ever seen him or *her*? No one in living memory has ever-"

"Because it would bring them death," the first man interjected solemnly, cutting the conversation straight away. "No one has ever met him. Just as, as you say, no one has ever aged. Just as no one has ever died. Just as no one has ever escaped this place. And no one ever will. Not until the right time."

And the second man paused as if considering his next move before;

"I have heard tales…"

But before he could get any further, the older man seemed only to grow more impatient again.

"They are mindless rumours. No one has ever escaped," he repeated. "No one ever will."

"One of the others knew of him. We spoke of it only last week. He was brought here not too long ago. The last element; element of earth I believe. Although I forget his name… Eastern-sounding…"

His words trailed off into an awkward silence followed by the shuffling of feet as one of the men shifted his weight.

"The new batch should have arrived by now," the older man then pointed out, obviously trying to change the subject. And to the listening women's surprise, the younger man took the bait.

"Yes. I have heard that two of them are here. No doubt at the *building* recovering. And as for the other two…. Someone spotted them on the outskirts, in the outer city with the Diggers. Women this time. As was to be expected…"

Arcameaus gave a sigh.

"Your mind works too much, Narabu. It is not good to ponder too deeply here. It will only lead to trouble. I thought you would have learnt your lesson by now...."

"Perhaps."

The word sounded uncertain but final and clearly taking it as such, Arcameaus then took the lead.

"Come now, it is late," he said and then, just like that, without a warning, the footsteps began again and startled by the sound of movement, Bex and Bethan both flinched, holding their collective breath all the more. To their immense relief though, instead of stopping again, the men soon passed by their cramped hiding place, heading on down the steps as their conversation continued.

"Over a thousand years..." the younger man, Narabu mused, his voice echoing off into the night as the men moved further away. "I sometimes wish I had never walked through those flames..."

"I wish it every day," the older man replied and then they were gone, leaving the two hidden friends to just sit there, still clinging to each other in the darkness as they both tried to make sense of everything they had just heard.

DREAMS

Edmund dragged himself wearily from the sweat-drenched bunk with a sigh.

Images of the nightmare still fresh in his memory, filled his thoughts.

There it had been again. The dream of Bethan.

The same words.

The same face, just looking at him.

The same flames eating her alive.

The same scream. And the same feeling he'd experienced every night as he'd woken, knowing there was nothing he could do. Waking with nothing but his guilt and his sorrow for company.

When would it end? And, as he asked himself every day, so he bargained every time, did he even *want* it to?

"Well," he whispered to the air generally. "That's over with."

He was awake now and buckling up his sword scabbard and pulling his cloak across one shoulder, Edmund then wasted no time in hurrying for the ladder leading to the deck, feeling suddenly desperate for some fresh air. As he carefully pushed his way past the other occupied bunks, Thom let out a particularly loud snore.

His cries then, hadn't disturbed anyone else.

That made a change.

And taking two rungs at a time, Edmund climbed to the cabin door and creaking it open carefully, stepped out onto the deck.

A fresh blast of sea wind met him full in the face along with the first rays of a new sunlit day. But though he felt unable to enjoy either right then, the Explorer took a moment just to breathe, stretch and calm himself.

What day was it? He had no idea. What even was the season? He seemed to have lost all sense of time. Just as he seemed to have lost all sense of anything lately.

That would have to change, the inner voice of reason chastised. He would have to move on.

I know.
He owed it to his friends. To his parents.
I know.
To himself.
"I know."
But just not yet. Not yet.
And so it was Edmund of Tonasse, without another moment's thought about anything, shuffled towards the crow's nest with a leaden heart.

—

"Anything?"
And Fred, glancing up, shook his head as the Explorer joined him on the crate, the wind pulling across his face to sting away any last signs of tiredness.
"The night was quiet," he pointed out.
"Good."
"And there is a good north-westerly wind. We should reach land quicker than expected. In less than a week I would say."
"Excellent."
Looking at Edmund for a moment longer, Fred's gaze then turned back out to sea. The warrior's face gave nothing of his thoughts away but barely a moment passed before he then began again; "What will you do?"
And Edmund, surprised, just stared in dull confusion.
"What will I *do?*" he echoed. "When?"
"When we reach the western shores again," Fred said, never taking his eyes from the waves below. There was no judgement there, no pressure for him to admit anything and understanding dawning, Edmund soon followed his friend's stare. For the first time in a long time, he didn't feel angry that someone was suggesting the very thing he feared, the very thing he fought against. The future.
Maybe then, he was making progress at last.
"To be honest with you... I'm not sure," he admitted truthfully. "I haven't thought about it. Not *really.*" And not necessarily for the first time either, it suddenly dawned on him that once they reached their destination and he left the ship, he had no idea what was going to happen next.
Years he had spent researching, dragging together piece by piece the puzzle Ophelius had left behind, ready to save Tungala from an unimaginable fate. And yet now it was over. All of it, over and gone, and all of a sudden, as he sat there, just watching the waves smooth back and forth beneath them, he just couldn't seem to see the way forward.
What could he possibly do now? Go back to exploring? Go back to the life he had known before with no brother with no... *her?*

The little voice inside his head, the *other* voice that had seemed to keep him the most company over the last week or so didn't seem to think so.

What's the point? it said. What did he even care anymore? He had lost his only brother. He had lost the woman he loved, what did anything else matter?

Even as he thought this though, Eliom's words seemed to rise up from nowhere to meet him, giving him pause to think.

You cannot allow yourself to be swallowed up in misery, Edmund. It accomplishes nothing, he had said, confirming his own decision from only minutes before.

His life wasn't over. The wizard knew it and deep down, he did too.

No. Whatever he did, wherever he went from here, he had to get control of himself, he had to deal with whatever was holding him back, to deal with the despair, the pain of what had happened and somehow make a world for himself all over again.

Somehow. And remembering yet more of the wizard's suggestions then, Edmund gave a weary smile.

"I know I really ought to visit my parents… They deserve to hear things from me," he added doubtfully. But even as he said the words aloud, just as he had fought against Eliom when the wizard had proposed just that back in the village, he knew that right then, he simply *couldn't*. Not yet.

He was afraid to. He knew it. More than anything he was *frightened* of admitting what had happened out loud, of telling, reliving the story all over again, because of what it would mean. If he spoke of it, if he drew someone else in to their tale, he knew that he would then, finally, have to accept it. He would have to deal with Renard's and Bethan's death and *accept* that they were well and truly gone.

And what if they blamed him?

Despite Eliom's assertions, despite even his own, Edmund knew that he still held himself responsible for what had happened.

What if his parents did too? Could he really bear it? Could he really bear to see, to relive his own anger, his own grief afresh?

Rubbing his tired eyes, Edmund's gaze then turned to the sunrise ahead as it cast striking reds and ambers across the dry sky. A small part of him found it beautiful.

"What about you?"

He turned the question back on Fred but instead of questioning it, to his relief, the warrior's brow just furrowed pleasantly.

"Me?" he replied without any sign of emotion. "I too *ought* to return to Mawreath. It has been a long while since I set eyes on Soph and I must inform Kell of Crag's death."

Crag.

Edmund lowered his head as he remembered what Fred too had lost. With so much that had happened over the past few weeks, Fred's warrior-brother's death had been pushed aside, but never forgotten, either by the warrior or, he knew, himself. After all, it was due to Edmund's brother that Fred was now without his other half, the other part of his soul.

There would be few to mourn Renard's death.

"I'm truly sorry, my friend," the Explorer confessed, the apology more deeply heartfelt than the warrior could possibly know. "What will Kell do?"

Fred shrugged, his face, a controlled mask of sorrow.

"They will undoubtedly give her a new life-partner – there are often partners to be had - although I know he will be sorely missed. I believe she was with child when last he saw her. Granted, by now, the young one would have already started its training."

Edmund nodded glumly, not knowing how to reply but immediately feeling for Kell and the unknown child. Even though Fred's kin didn't 'marry' for love but were paired up at birth to become life-partners, often the pairing led to a fond attachment, perhaps even what could be described as love.

As he thought about it, for some reason he couldn't explain, the question then just slipped out.

"Fred," he started. "How do you feel about Soph? Do you *love* her?"

The words seemed to come from nowhere and from the way he gave a start, the warrior was surprised too, but instead of replying, Fred just continued on his vigilant watch for a while, his expression turning thoughtful.

"My people differ from yours in that regard, as well you know," he then said. His voice gave nothing away of his surprise at Edmund's sudden curiosity. "So, my idea of love is perhaps… not the same." His mouth crinkled at the edges. "That is the problem with humanity, as I see it. You *choose* to love one another and suffer the consequences of it. To my mind, it is so much simpler to be paired at birth, such as we are. It is… *logical.*" And moved by something unseen, he stared at Edmund afresh then, curiosity in his own eyes. "Humans have the choice to stay detached if you wish to. To not feel love. So why do you still choose it?" he asked. "*We* are taught to 'love', as it were. We are bonded together as if one. But it is not the same…"

The way Fred spoke, so matter-of-factly about it, about emotions, about how he felt, filled Edmund with instant doubt. For a moment, something deep inside him made him question himself, his own humanity, for he felt in a way that the warrior was right, that love, in a way, *was* a choice.

Wasn't it?

"You choose whether you care or not too!" he retorted out loud, confused by his own thoughts. "You can choose to love those you're paired with. You loved Crag! You-" But he faltered then as he tried to control the eruption of words that had somehow collected in the back of his throat from bursting out. He didn't want to seem stupid in front of the great warrior.

Fred looked troubled.

"Yes, this is true," he admitted. "I loved Crag. But it was the same love I feel for my own flesh. He was a part of me. It was a bond unbreakable. Not an attachment chosen and created. We warriors are never alone, until death…"

"But what is a world without love?" Edmund challenged almost angrily. "I *know* it sounds foolish and sentimental and to you, to Eliom and Thom, yes, humans seem *weak* because we are ruled by it but I *choose* to love because without it…" He gave a sigh. "You loved Crag, that much is obvious. You care for your friends, for Tungala, so we're not so very different you and I…"

It was as if he'd simply run out of words to say then as Edmund fell silent and the salty air rushed in to gush between them.

For a few minutes the Explorer just searched himself, amazed at what had come out of his own mouth. He felt as if someone else, someone wiser, more worldly, had been speaking from within, a stranger speaking truths he had never really considered before.

Even Fred seemed to have detected something new, or unfound in him for he looked at his friend then as if he'd never quite seen anyone like him before.

"You speak wisdom, my friend," the warrior then said seriously. "You are, without doubt, one of the wisest humans I have ever met."

And Edmund couldn't help but give a scornful smile.

Of course, the compliment meant a lot, especially coming from Fred, but at the same time he knew how the warriors of Mawreath and many other higher races for that matter, viewed humans. To them, humanity was seen as one of the most careless and ignorant races on Tungala and both of them knew it.

"That's not saying much," the Explorer found himself joking in return and for a moment it was like the old carefree Edmund was back again as the pair exchanged a smile.

As seemed to be usual though, any instant of normalcy was soon ruined, for as Fred then turned back to the sea, in the blink of an eye everything had changed, as the warrior leapt to his feet, sword drawn and rushed to the portside of the lookout, his cloak cracking behind him wildly.

He had spotted something and startled, Edmund jumped up too to follow, staring down on the waves far below.

At first, all he could see was foggy blackness where the growing sun hadn't quite touched the ocean depths. But then, just like that, a roll of thin morning mist shifted to reveal something in the water.

It was a small black rowing boat and inside it sat a solitary figure.

The person was difficult to make out from this distance but as if he could recognise them clear as day, Fred didn't lower his sword. Instead, his expression darkened.

"Witch," was all he said and straight away, Edmund's stomach lurched.

A Witch? Here? Now?

But even before he could try to contemplate, the Explorer found himself moving straight away towards the ladder.

"Stay here and watch!" he commanded to Fred's back. "Shout if she- *they* make any movement. I'll go and wake Eliom!" and without another moment's hesitation he disappeared onto the deck below.

Edmund, Eliom, Elanore and Thom, closely followed by Fred, all stood on the deck. Fred and Thom had their weapons drawn, ready to spring as Eliom and Edmund, along with Elanore close behind, all stood at the bulwark, peering down on the boat as it drew up alongside them.

Just as the warrior and Explorer had seen from the crow's nest, the boat wasn't empty. Inside sat a lone figure, but the person, whoever they may be, was shrouded entirely by a long black hooded cloak that, even as their vessel bumped the side of the Karenza and the stranger shifted to look up at the awaiting party, completely shadowed their face.

Edmund felt every hair on the back of his neck stand erect.

Like one possessed, he then leaned forward over the bulwark, his own hand white on the hilt of his sword.

"Who are you and what do you want?!" he shouted. His voice was louder, braver than he felt and for good reason. If Fred's prediction from the lookout was right, if this eerie stranger *was* a witch or another wizard, then they could all be in a lot of trouble…

And not for the first time, the Explorer couldn't help but be thankful they had Eliom with them.

The dark figure in the boat stood up but didn't raise its head again. It still seemed determined for no one to see its face. But then, it spoke, and like a breath of cold winter wind, the whole deck seemed to shudder.

"I am come to seek you, Edmund of Tonasse. For I Saw what must occur at this place," it said in the smooth high voice of a woman and instantly knowing what this meant, the group stirred anxiously.

"It *is* a witch," Thom growled under his breath. "Fred was right."

Witch. The word sent a sliver of dread through them all and unable to hide his fear, Edmund glanced at Eliom. The wizard's face, as always, was completely indifferent. However, though he had expected it, somehow, seeing his friend completely unmoved seemed to give the Explorer some kind of new strength and encouraged, Edmund found himself turning back to the stranger below with a wary eye.

"Who *are* you?" he repeated. "And how do you know my name?"

But the witch-figure remained motionless.

"I am a friend. Let me up and I shall speak with you," it replied evenly and not knowing what else to do, Edmund looked to the others. He could see distrust on all of their faces. All apart from one. For suddenly, Eliom's expression had changed. In the moment since Edmund had looked away, since the woman-thing had spoken again, his face was now almost *thoughtful*, as if he were trying to recall to mind something from a distant past, something he hadn't contemplated for a long while, something that disturbed him…

Before Edmund could say anything more though, the wizard seemed to collect himself and meeting the Explorer's eye, gave a small nod.

"Allow her aboard. She is harmless," he said.

"Harmless?!" Thom scoffed, but suspicious as he was of the stranger, Edmund also trusted the wizard's judgement and ignoring the dwarf, he soon nodded to Elanore.

"Let her up," was all he said and obeying, Elanore headed reluctantly for the ship's ladder, ready to help where she could with securing the boat.

Meanwhile, the others stepped away from the Karenza's edge. In spite of Eliom's assurance, Fred and Thom didn't lower their weapons and for a moment, Edmund also felt his own fingers unable to let go of the sword at his belt.

He felt Eliom's presence by his side before he heard him.

"She is harmless," the wizard repeated quietly and if scorn had been in his nature, Edmund could have sworn his look was scathing.

But though the Explorer then loosened his grip; he didn't move his hand away,

"I hope you're right, old friend," he muttered instead. "Or we're all in danger."

—

The tension on the Karenza was almost touchable as the stranger stepped up onto the deck some time later, its face still shrouded in darkness. Seeing the figure up close, Fred and Thom instantly stiffened and Elanore took a step back from the ship's edge, as if expecting their visitor to attack, but though no one made a friendly move, the black newcomer didn't so much as flinch.

Instead, they simply stood there, leaving the company to eye each other for what felt a good long while, nothing but the wind and the lapping of the waves making a sound until eventually, what had always been bound to happen, inevitably did.

Without a word, the figure suddenly made as if to move towards them and instantly, the crew reacted. Fred and Thom both rose their weapons, ready to defend themselves as Elanore, unarmed and defenceless, took another leap back. At the same time, seeing what was about to happen, Edmund, grabbing for his sword again, flung himself forward with a cry, trying to get between the stranger and his friends. As he did so however,

Eliom too answered and with a shout unlike any they had heard, the wizard stepped forward and throwing his whole body behind it, slammed the bass of his wooden staff onto the deck.

The whole Karenza seemed to shudder as the force of Eliom's power boomed through the air, throwing Fred, Thom, Elanore and Edmund to the ground. Only the stranger remained standing, but before anyone could so much as move, could so much as turn on their friend in angry confusion, a deep cackle suddenly rippled through the air.

It came from beneath the black hood.

"You are friendly, I can see," the figure then spat. It made no more attempts to move further from the edge of the deck, but suddenly, as if noticing him for the very first time, its head snapped around to look straight at Edmund before; *"You really are too pathetic for words. You always pretended like you were the hero when all you are and ever have been is weak."*

And all defence forgotten, Edmund's hand fell limply to his side and he gawped open-mouthed as the words of his brother, spoken in anger at the temple, were shot back at him. And not just the words. The voice... Renard's voice. Exactly as he remembered.

Exactly.

But how could this be? How was it *possible*?

Unless...

Seeing the Explorer's distress, Fred and Thom moved as if to attack again but Eliom soon stopped them.

"Do not touch her!" he cried, his voice surprisingly loud.

But though the pair turned to glare at the wizard in disbelief, Edmund, pale-faced, only had eyes for the cloaked intruder.

"*Wh-what* did you say?" he stuttered. "How do you-? Who-?"

But the figure simply let out another throaty cackle and finally having enough of the whole thing, Fred, ignoring Eliom's command, took yet another step forward, his sword tight in his hands.

"Show yourself!" he demanded angrily as he tipped his blade toward where the stranger's throat would be beneath that dark shroud.

"Who *are* you, *witch*?!" Thom added with a snarl.

And as if the very word spat with such hatred were the trigger, the figure then finally complied and reaching up a small white hand, pulled its hood back to reveal its face.

Just as they suspected, it was a woman, but though woman-shaped she was, she was unlike any the group had ever seen. Her face spoke of someone who was young, young and pretty with curved cheeks, a sharp jaw and plump lips and yet there was something about her. Though she looked no older than Edmund in human years, just like Eliom she *felt* older, more ancient; ageless even, as time itself.

She had jet-black hair, long, beyond her shoulders and her skin was a deathly grey, verging on white. It was her eyes though, those shrewd eyes so dark, so black, so cold that even the light of the morning sun couldn't seem to make them shine, that somehow seemed to draw each and every one of them in. For as all looked upon her, all somehow knew that here was someone alive and yet somehow not, feeling and yet frozen, in the present and yet also inexplicably, the past and the future; a figure so striking that for a moment, all anyone could do was stare at her, frozen by the sense of power that seemed to somehow ooze from her every pore.

Only Eliom seemed untroubled by the woman's appearance and as she glanced coldly at each of the group in turn, it wasn't long before her gaze landed on him. Her black eyes seemed to study his face for some time, as if drinking in every last morsel of detail before her sharp face then softened a little.

"Eliom," she then breathed. "It has been too long a while since last I set eyes on you."

Eliom gave a deep nod, not meeting her stare.

"Eldora," he muttered in greeting. "Welcome."

Eldora?

This caught the others' attention and as one, all then swivelled their amazed gaze from the woman to the wizard in shock.

"You *know* her?" Thom cried incredulously.

To their surprise, Eliom nodded again.

"Yes," was all he offered and the woman, whose name was Eldora, turned her cold gaze upon the dwarf, also making no move to explain her connection with their friend.

Feeling instantly uncomfortable under that dark penetrating look, Thom couldn't help but be reminded of all those weeks ago when he had stood before Emmine, the elven queen. Just like the beautiful elf, this strange woman seemed to omit some kind of power he did not fully understand, to read things with her eyes that no one else could see. It made him feel vulnerable, naked, and not knowing what else to do, the dwarf averted his own stare.

Eldora's expression was cold, yet curious but even as she eyed the dwarf, reading his expression, her face fell suddenly blank, as if drained of all thought, all emotion and as she opened her mouth to speak, a voice poured forth not quite her own.

"*They took Trolenda! They took her!*"

The company looked at each other with frightened suspicion as the dwarf's words came to light and Thom's mouth, reacting much in the same way as Edmund's had, flew open as he lowered his axe.

But Eldora didn't wait for anyone to act, to say a word. Her voice carried on and suddenly it was changing again, her words a flurry of different tones and confusing words.

"*No one has ever met him… no one has ever aged. Just as no one has ever died. Just as no one has ever escaped this place. And no one ever will. Not until the right time… I'm sorry. I-I didn't realise… If I'd known – I would have given the necklace up sooner… the elements must make a decision and that one way or another, this decision will have dire consequences. But the real question is; which consequences outweigh the others?… I love you.*"

Edmund's eyes grew wider and wider as the woman let flow more and more. Parts of the speech, parts of the voices he recognised, he had heard before, but how did this *woman* know? How was it possible?

I love you…

As his own words were quoted back at him in just the way he had spoken them, desperately, earnestly in the temple, the sorrow that he had shoved decisively to the side, came flooding right back as hot tears of anger pushed themselves to the corners of his eyes. But still Eldora continued;

"*With this test, I have determined your self-sacrifice… We need your help. We all need your help!… She is dead Edmund! Bethan is dead and there is nothing you can do about it!!*"

And suddenly, just like that, Edmund couldn't take it anymore and ignoring his friend's warnings he leapt forwards and grabbing the woman roughly by the arm, he shook her, *hard*.

"Stop it!" he cried. "Stop it! *Now!*"

Fred, Thom and Elanore did nothing to prevent him. Hurt was also etched across their faces as they too listened to the woman's babble. Only Eliom moved, wielding his staff and before Edmund could so much as reach for his sword, he found himself on the floor all over again, thrown back by another violent blast as the wizard shouted an incantation.

Pain seared through the Explorer's body as he fell and knocked almost breathless, he simply lay on the ship's deck for a moment or two, completely stunned.

The others were all stunned too. None of them had ever seen Eliom use magic in such a way against one of his friends before. And yet even as Edmund then tried to get up, suddenly drained as all anger seeped away to leave the familiar dull numbness, the wizard made no move to help him.

"Do not hurt her," was all he said as if in way of explanation. He seemed almost *angry* and straight away the rest of the group felt an odd fear clutch at their hearts. Everyone knew how powerful the wizard was…

Finally managing to haul himself to a sit, Edmund looked up at Eliom, but instead of addressing him, of demanding to know what had just happened, he instead, turned to the woman, his mind still on one thing.

"Why do you talk like that?" he said, rubbing his elbow. It was tender, bruised from the fall. He was lucky it wasn't broken. "How do you *know* these things? Who *are* you?"

The woman's face, which had remained frozen in its glazed state, even during Edmund's attack, then suddenly loosened and she blinked as if waking from a trance. As if no one else were watching, Eliom then strode across the deck and making to take the woman's arm himself as if she might fall, inclined his head towards her.

"Are you well?" he asked softly and she nodded before straightening up to glare at the Explorer, her expression cold.

"You ask who I am," she replied, her voice returning to itself. "I shall tell you. My name is Eldora." Everyone stared at her. "And I am a Lectur."

There was a small gasp, possibly from Fred, but the rest of the group, bar Eliom, simply looked blank. Edmund's expression meanwhile, slackened in surprise as he finally got to his feet.

"A Lectur?" Fred echoed in amazement before anyone else could speak, his voice barely above an awe-filled whisper. "I had heard that they were no more!"

The woman didn't look at him. Instead, she seemed to want to keep her eyes on Edmund.

"We are few, it is true," she replied a little sadly. "But I assure you. We *do* exist."

She shifted on her feet, as if tired and Edmund, looking at this woman in a new light, then noticed for the first time as her cloak parted a little, that Eldora was armed with a curved dagger: a typical Lectur weapon.

He'd read about Lecturs before, *long* before, heard murmurs of them on his travels but had never dreamed that he would one day meet one. As Fred had rightly said, the whole race was believed to have been wiped out long ago with other creatures of old, long extinct. And for good reason...

So why then was Eldora here? And more importantly, why *now*? What did she want?

Edmund's stomach roiled a little, his chest feeling suddenly heavy.

The Lectur couldn't seem to take her sharp eyes off him and *that* to him, could only mean one thing.

She had *Seen* something. Something he had to do or was about to by chance and she had come either to encourage or, to prevent him...

"I don't mean to be rude," and for the first time, it was then that Elanore spoke up. Seeing that the strange woman obviously wasn't much of a threat but judging that something was amiss from the others' reactions, her arms were now folded, her brightly-coloured head cocked to one side matter-of-factly. "But to be honest, even in my travels, I've never heard of, let alone come across a Lectur before. What *is* a Lectur?"

Instead of being offended however, Eldora gave a small smile, her eyes finally breaking away, thankfully, from Edmund's anxious face.

"A witch," Thom growled again. "Like I said."

Eldora glanced at him as if he were an irritating patch of moss, nothing more.

"I am no *witch*," she snorted before; "I See the future, the past and even occasionally, on a day such as today, the present. But apart from that…" she smiled again, "my powers are but poor… compared to Eliom's." And her beady eyes then turned to Eliom with what could only be described as adoration. The wizard met her gaze briefly but there was nothing there in return, nothing but controlled coolness.

"What are you doing here, Eldora?" he asked instead softly and the Lectur's death-pale face was proud.

"I Saw that I was meant to be here. A few weeks back…And I Saw you," she nodded towards Edmund, "and I Saw the rowing boat and this…" she gestured sarcastically around her with a limp arm, "*grand* ship. And I knew that I must come… although that is all that I know. It is *you* who must tell me why."

This last point was directed straight at Edmund, as she once again glared at him, but the Explorer could only return her look in amazement. He hadn't been expecting *this*.

"Me?!" he stuttered, pained by the Lectur's fierce expression. "*I*-I don't know why you're here…" and Eldora gave a sniff of obvious disdain. Whoever this strange being was, she clearly thought the same thing all other beings of power seemed to; that humans were beneath her.

"You humans are weak," she muttered in confirmation and then, turning to Eliom, she gave another strange little smile. Obviously the wizard had some sort of hold over her, but Edmund couldn't quite interpret yet what exactly this hold *was*.

It was clear that the Lectur had indeed met Eliom before, but it was difficult to tell under what circumstances, for every time she laid eyes on him her face either flashed with rage, or softened with a kind of hidden affection. This time, her expression became soft, and there was something dejected lingering at the corners of her mouth.

"I am tired," she then stated quietly. "I have rowed all night. Eliom, please show me where I might rest."

Rest? The Lectur was *staying?*

Half to everyone else's surprise though, Eliom gave a polite nod and obeying, he led the way to the cabins with a sweep of his hand, leaving the other four staring after them in complete bafflement.

"Well," Thom said the second the pair were out of earshot, "what was *that* about?"

"What?" Fred asked blankly, his thoughts obviously elsewhere. He looked troubled.

Thom shrugged.

"I do not trust her if you ask me," he mused mysteriously, heading back towards the cabins himself. "Yes... I do not trust her."

Elanore meanwhile looked at Fred and Edmund.

"Very weird," was all she said and then following suit, she headed back towards the stern of the ship, leaving the warrior and the Explorer alone.

The moment everyone else had gone Edmund then turned on his friend.

"What are you thinking?" he asked directly, his voice shaking a little, disturbed as he was from his encounter with Eldora and her hollow eyes. *He hadn't missed the warrior's concerned expression* and blinking as if waking from a daze, Fred gave a frown.

"I am not certain," he replied slowly. "But no doubt we will find out her purpose here when the moment is right." Looking at Edmund solemnly he then finally sheathed his sword. "Know this, my friend. She will be important to our fate. Somehow... I have heard that Lectur's do not See needlessly."

And with that, he then made his way across the deck and as if forced back into normalcy, Edmund found himself wandering back towards the crow's nest to keep a watch on the dawning horizon.

—

Eldora sank with a groan into the spare hammock as Eliom stood at the cabin door watching her.

For some reason he was yet to understand, he did not want to enter, for as he looked around, scanning the empty space, he became aware of some kind of alien pang in his chest, a twitch of something as he recalled the last time he had stepped foot inside this room, the room where the four elements had slept...

Even Elanore never came in here now but took rest in the ship's hold beyond. And yet right then, Eldora was sitting, lying in what used to be, he believed, Saz's bunk...

The sensation grew stronger, burned brighter for the smallest second before he buried it.

The Lectur meanwhile, completely oblivious to the unseen struggle beneath the serenity of her companion, got herself comfortable before taking a moment to gaze up at him.

"Give this to Edmund," she then said knowledgably, and from under her cloak she pulled out what appeared to be a small grey sack tied at the top by a tattered length of string. "It will help him to sleep."

Eliom didn't even question how she knew of Edmund's sleepless, nightmare-filled nights. Instead, reaching into the cabin, he took the bag without question and tucked it away in his own pocket, being careful not to touch the white woman's fingers, even for a moment.

Barely seeming to notice his reluctance, Eldora all the while glanced around her curiously, her black eyes absorbing every hammock, every wooden slat on the wall, every neatly-folded blanket until, several minutes later;

"The woman who was last in this bed," she started slowly. She ran her hands lightly over the blanket by her side on the hammock. "I detect that there was a woman here. Who was she?"

Again, Eliom seemed not even in the least bit surprised by this question.

"Her name was Saz," he replied shortly, but something in the way he spoke had obviously stirred something else in the Lectur for suddenly, she was glaring at him, her head cocked to one side.

"I see your pain," she said almost curiously, despite the fact that to anyone else watching, Eliom would have seemed calmest calm. She then gave a tart sniff. "Did you love her?"

Eliom's face tried to remain indifferent, but he could see where the conversation was leading and despite himself, his brow furrowed a little.

"You know that I cannot love," he answered stiffly. "We have spoken of this before."

But just as she had all that time ago, Eldora snorted.

"That is a *lie*," she argued. "You know it and I know it."

Eliom shook his head but still he was calm, almost frostily so.

"I am incapable of love. You above all others should know that."

But despite his assertion, Eldora replied with a stubborn shake of her own head. She looked suddenly alive, livid with the emotion she had suppressed for so long. Her eyes were blacker somehow, dark as nothing.

"You love your friends. You would die for them so why not her? Why not *me*?" she demanded.

When Eliom didn't answer though, the Lectur stared into her lap, gazing distractedly at her hands, long and thin and white, for a short while, as if trying to calm herself. Her long hair almost shadowed her face.

"If I had known you were here…" she began again quietly.

"…you would still have come."

Eliom's voice was soft, almost *caring* but not the caring that the Lectur wanted it to be, *longed* it to be. It was a sort of caring through some kind of pity and she didn't want his pity. She *scorned* his pity…

Before she could speak however, before she could defend her own pride, Eldora felt the familiar pull at her mind and her eyes glistened as they glazed over, rolling to the back of her head. Her voice changed and words erupted from her mouth, her body no longer under her control.

"*It is broken… Why did you not tell me of this before?*"

Her voice then shifted again, almost as if she were holding an imaginary conversation with herself and Eliom recognised the words straight away as those he had shared with Saz on the Karenza's deck only a few weeks before.

"I suppose, I just didn't want to be a burden. With everything going on I just-... You are never a burden, Saz. You are vital. To us and to Tungala's future..."

Saz.

He could see her face now, clear as day as she had spoken to him, as she had tried to hide her pain...

And suddenly, unexpectedly, the wizard found that he simply had to turn away, to leave, to not hear any more, the strange hurt in his chest growing stronger with every moment. Swivelling to go, clutching at the doorframe in his odd desperation to get out, he heard Eldora calling after him, suddenly back to her usual self.

"Eliom! No! Wait! I am sorry!"

But it was too late. The wizard was gone.

—

Edmund sat, simply staring, mesmerised by the calming monotony of the ocean rolling and drifting below. He could feel its gentle sway, even from the top of the crow's nest, something soothing, gentle, secure as he gazed into the nothingness, his mind slipping into the old thoughts and dreams he'd had a thousand times or more since Ratacopeck.

Bethan. Her face, her words, her eyes, her lips. Every moment they'd spent together seemed to play over and over again in his mind's eye.

He ached to see her again with every part of himself but a dull shield seemed to cover his heart.

He was never *going* to see her again. He knew that. He truly truly knew that but this was how it was every day now; the hopeful fantasy and then the crushing reality. Each time the fiction was somehow different. One time she would turn around and agree to come home with him instead of climbing that fateful ladder, another she would just somehow magically reappear by his side as if nothing had happened. But always, always he would see it again; the flames, the power engulfing her as she'd walked to her fiery death and again, he would know the reality of it all, the reality that she had gone.

"Edmund."

Edmund felt a friendly hand on his shoulder but he didn't bother to turn around. Instead, he simply shook himself free of his memories to continue his blank stare into the oblivion beyond.

"So, who is she?" he asked as Eliom, removing his hand, took a seat beside his friend on the upturned crate and without so much as a hesitation, Eliom gave something of a sigh.

"An old acquaintance," the wizard muttered. If he knew anything of what Edmund had *really* been thinking right before he arrived, he showed no sign of it. "She asked me to give you this." And he reached into his cloak, pulled out the small grey sack and dropped it into the Explorer's lap.

Edmund looked at him then. The wizard seemed almost troubled, exhausted, the smallest of bags collecting under his weary eyes and it couldn't help but make his friend concerned. Whoever this Eldora was, despite what Eliom said, she was clearly *more* than he was letting on, and more than anything in that moment, Edmund was determined to find out *why*.

"An old acquaintance?" the Explorer retorted aloud. "She must be more than that! You used magic against me so that I wouldn't harm her! And what is *this* for?" he gestured to the little grey bag.

Eliom noticed the bitter tone in Edmund's voice and straightened up stiffly.

"It is to help you sleep," he replied with caution, remembering his friend's reaction the previous times he had offered to help him. "And as for Eldora - it was vital that I stopped you. You were upset. You could have injured her and I apologise if I truly hurt you…"

The wizard's apology however was soon lost on Edmund as the Explorer recognised the familiar wave of anger that had raged up inside him so much over the last days threatening to flare again.

"She gives me something to help me sleep as if she knows me!" he snapped. "She talked of the elements as if she knew *them*! She said things that only *we* had spoken, had heard-! She said them out of spite!"

But straight away, Eliom shook his head.

"No. She cannot control her Seeings. No Lectur can."

His voice was soothing. He could clearly detect Edmund's rising tide of fury and for some reason he almost *feared* it. But when his friend said nothing in reply, Eliom knew that now was the time to tell the truth.

"I met her many human years ago, when your parents', grandparents would only have been small children," he started with another small sigh. "At that time, Lecturs were not quite as sparse as they are now. They were still rare but-"

"Why did so many of them die out?" Edmund interrupted. Just as the wizard had hoped, his anger was quickly subsiding to be replaced by curiosity – the mark of an Explorer.

"As I explained before, Lecturs cannot control what they See. Hundreds never experienced the present. They lived *only* in the past and future, flitting between the two and naturally it drove them mad. Lecturs, like wizards, are blessed with long lives, but many of them never see, or rather *saw* adulthood."

Edmund could only meet this comment with a shocked silence before Eliom continued;

"You may wonder why *any* survived; but Eldora is not a full Lectur. Her mother was a Lectur and her father a human. She manages to live in the present for most of the time but there are some periods where she receives visions…"

"But where did Lecturs come from?" Edmund asked. "I've read about them. Is it true that they're descended from the Elves…?" but straight away Eliom shook his head heavily.

"No. Thom, in his way, was correct. They *were* originally witches. But something happened. A half-breed was created; half-elf and half-witch. This was where it started. Before long there were many descendants and Lecturs were born in their hundreds. It was only after many generations that the Seeing became a problem, controlling their every thought and breath. Hundreds died and now there are only a handful left on this world. Many are only half-breeds like Eldora; otherwise they would not have survived as long."

Again, all Edmund could do was gawp. He'd had no idea. No idea of the pain, the suffering of an entire race just for being born… and for a moment he almost felt *sorry* for the cold Eldora. And yet…

"But how did you meet her?" he then asked critically. "Why have I never heard you mention her before?" and realising that there was no holding back now, Eliom looked almost uncomfortable.

"In truth, I lament our meeting… but I doubt there would have been an alternative," he replied so *uncertainly*, that Edmund couldn't help but stare at him in new surprise.

The Explorer had rarely seen Eliom like this, almost unsure, almost… *human* and it made him feel uneasy. Uneasy yet thirsty. He felt thirsty to know more and luckily for him, Eliom didn't disappoint.

"I met her in the farthest Eastern Realms," the wizard admitted. "I was travelling alone, as was my want in those days. She came to me and told me that she had Seen me a while before and had come from a great distance to find me; or so she claimed. She had travelled from her homeland in the north to seek…" and the wizard paused a moment as if trying to find the right words, "someone whom she might love."

Love?

Eliom?

Edmund's eyebrows rose almost to his hairline. But though Eliom continued to look uncertain, even, in some way, ashamed, he didn't blush or appear embarrassed.

"Of course, I rejected her," he added. "I regret hurting her but I had no other choice. I *cannot* love in the way that she demanded… And besides, even if I *could*, it is forbidden. I would have been demoted as a wizard."

Edmund wasn't sure if he could look more shocked if he'd tried. Of course, he knew of Eliom's inability to express emotion – it was the doctrine of all wizards to suppress their feelings at all times, an obvious secret -and he had grown used to his friend's cool calm ways, the ways he had known almost his entire life and yet at the same time, he had never felt less like he knew the wizard, *truly* knew him, until now.

"The order can *demote* you?!" he interjected, astonished. "They can stop you being a *wizard?*"

How had he not known this?

But Eliom shook his head again sharply.

"No! I was born a wizard and I shall *die* a wizard. But I *can* be cast out and not recognised in the eyes of the Council," he warned. "I can be stripped of my powers and left to die like a human…"

Edmund just stared at him. When Eliom talked about his own death like that, his own mortality, it somehow felt strange. For some reason, he'd never considered his friend actually *dying*. He simply couldn't imagine it and foolish as he suddenly knew it was, he realised he'd somehow always imagined Eliom to be indestructible, untouchable, a force against time and nature. Against mortality.

And yet, at the end of it all, Eliom *was* mortal…

"Wait," he said in confusion, suddenly thinking of something else that needed considering. "If Lecturs can see into the future and Eldora Saw herself with you, then surely it should have happened? Surely you *should* have loved her."

Eliom's brow shifted.

"Ah. But remember many years ago, when I told you that you can control your own destiny?" The wizard's voice would have sounded patronising, but Edmund knew him better than that. Even though both of them were fully aware they were in no way equals, Eliom had always treated his human companion with the utmost respect. "Lecturs can only See *one* outlook of the future not *the* future itself. They cannot always shape it."

Edmund remembered very well Eliom's words. He had been only young then, desperate to prove himself and ignorant of the future. Eliom had warned him of Renard's betrayal, of the love he would one day feel for Bethan, all information he had seen in a vision and yet Edmund had ignored it, hoping, just as Eliom had instructed him, to control his own fate. And yet…

"But I couldn't," the Explorer whispered. "I *couldn't* control my destiny." *Or Renard's. Or Bethan's.*

He had spoken the words out loud, not for sympathy, not for guidance, and yet Edmund was surprised to find that instead of the comfort, the words of wisdom he had come to expect anyway when speaking with his friend, there was a flutter of light fabric as Eliom suddenly got to his feet.

"I must talk with Elanore," the wizard murmured softly instead. "The winds are rising in the north. We may want to steer clear of them if a storm is afoot." And with that he strode towards the ladder.

A little troubled, Edmund gave a glum nod, but didn't try to hold his friend back. As long as he had known the wizard, still he was an enigma to him and as if detecting the human's pain, as Eliom reached the side of the lookout, he turned back briefly.

"Will you use it?" he asked and Edmund, confused for a moment, looked up to see his companion staring at the grey sack which still lay, untouched, in the Explorer's lap.

"Oh." Edmund glanced at it. "Thanks. But I don't need help sleeping,"

The reply was short, automatic and Eliom made no move to argue. Instead, he simply stared at his friend for some time, saying nothing. But then again, he didn't need to, for even without speaking them, Edmund knew exactly what his words would be, and, as he took the sack in his hands, weighing it deftly between his fingers, he began to accept then that they would probably have been wise ones.

———

"Bethan!" he yelled, *his voice almost hoarse as he shouted over the crackling inferno.* *"Bethan!"*

"I don't have a choice."

Her own words split the gloom, quietly, as though she were whispering in his ear and yet deafening over the flames. But she was so far away. Her face fading and burning.

The same face he saw every night.

The same face he wished he could see every day.

But just as Edmund realised that he was going to wake up soon and pleaded with himself not to, for fear of losing her, the woman who lived only in his memories now, another figure came into view.

All he could make out was a white silhouette, but for some reason he couldn't see even that properly. The flames licked and ate at his eyes, making them smart.

He then heard another soft voice. It seemed to be coming from him, from inside his own mind, speaking with his own tongue. No, not his…

"Edmund, wake up!"

But though he recognised the voice, somehow he couldn't seem to remember who it was. The flames were so hot! His flesh burning, his sorrow screaming…

"Edmund."

And with a gasp, Edmund opened his eyes and sat bolt upright in bed only to give a start as he saw, in the near-pitch-blackness of the cabin, Eliom standing directly above him, his hand on the Explorer's shoulder.

Wiping his brow, Edmund tried desperately to control his breathing, his body sweaty and exhausted, but though he knew it had only been a dream, that he was back in reality, still his head spun and catching a breath felt worse than hard.

"Eliom," he gasped feebly. "What…?"

But Eliom put a finger to his lips. His staff was emitting a glow, high enough for Edmund to see him by but low enough not to disturb the others as they slept peacefully. Somewhere nearby he could hear Thom snoring, as usual.

"You were screaming," the wizard admitted and Edmund gave a small sigh of relief. For a brief moment he'd thought that something had happened, that the ship was once again in danger, that Eliom had needed him for some urgent matter. But no, he had woken him because of the dream.

The dream that the wizard had *invaded*…

And just like that, the flicker of groggy confusion, of relief was suddenly replaced by a stab of resentment. He could feel it growing within him like a coiled snake ready to spring.

"What right do you have to enter my head?" he demanded hotly, his voice not very low.

Eliom released his hold on Edmund's shoulder, glancing at the other two bunks as he did so. Luckily the others were still sleeping.

"Follow me," he then commanded and strangely, despite his irritation, Edmund felt the immediate urge to obey. In fact, he was sure that the wizard had to have used some kind of magic to make him do so, as following him felt like the *last* thing the Explorer wanted to do right then.

His anger boiled all the more.

Eliom then made his way towards the trapdoor leading to the deck, and stopping only briefly to grab his cloak, Edmund followed. As the door swung open, a strong nightly breeze rushed in, turning the Explorer's sweat to an immediate clammy chill.

Once on the deck, Eliom then led Edmund to the far portside of the ship before pausing to turn to him. The spell he'd obviously put on his friend to make him obey, also, somehow kept him silent, for however much he wanted to, Edmund found that all of a sudden, he couldn't speak. His mouth simply wouldn't open, his voice simply wouldn't work and stunned that his friend could do something like this, he tried desperately to express his anger, his complete indignation through his eyes. But though his pupils burned like fire, it was if Eliom couldn't see it.

The wizard looked urgent, as if he didn't have a lot of time and it didn't take long for Edmund to work out why. Any minute now the spell, which had only been brief and weakly made, would break and both of them knew that Edmund's rage, that uncontrollable grief he had yet to quench, would take hold of him, making him shout and curse at his friend, maybe even strike out...

"Edmund, I apologise for entering your dream. I know that the dreamsphere is a private place and that *no one* should have to see what you have seen, but you must *understand* that I am trying to *help* you," the wizard entreated. And then suddenly it was like he was angry too, frustrated and his staff gave an extra burst of light. "You humans are so *stubborn*! This much I have seen... but will you not let me *help* you? You *cannot* carry on like this forever!"

It was only at this point, as Eliom last few hurried words spilled out, that the spell holding Edmund then broke. To the Explorer, it felt as if a great weight had suddenly been lifted from his body. Air rushed into his mouth, and he opened his lips preparing to shout and scream and rant... but again, nothing came out. The way Eliom had spoken with such pained frustration had stopped all that.

Was the wizard right? Was he just being stubborn by not letting Eliom in? Was his friend simply just trying to help?

"Dreams are *natural*," he retorted, finally finding his voice and with it, his fury all over again. "*You* dream!" he pointed straight into Eliom's face. "Don't you?! I don't prevent *your* dreams! So what right have you to prevent mine?! I'm fine! Stop worrying about me!"

But Eliom's eyes flashed.

"You have been through much over the past weeks Edmund. These dreams are *not* natural and if you let them, they *will* control you!!" he re-joined, his voice uncharacteristically hard. "Just let me help you! How many times must I ask?"

Edmund cursed aloud but said nothing else as Eliom took a deep long breath, as if to calm himself.

"I have seen greater men fall in situations like this, Edmund. I have seen them reduced to dribbling infants at the first sign of death. You may believe yourself brave, but...!"

"Brave?!" and Edmund actually *growled*. "Is that what you think of me? You think this is to do with some idea of *bravery*?!"

"No!" Eliom's voice came out at a bellow, making Edmund flinch but then, more quietly, as he studied his companion's livid face; "I think that *this* is all to do with your guilt. This is not a matter of pride, of bravery. It is a matter of pain and fear."

Edmund had been about to snap back but once again Eliom had left him speechless with his obvious wisdom. It *was* guilt, he knew; he had been through this before. Again and again. Guilt and fear of what had happened, of what *would* happen once the dreaming stopped...

There was then a long, edgy silence as the wizard and Explorer simply stared at each other. Around them the wind was starting to pick up, whipping into their faces in a cold blast of wet, the waves continuing to roll on their rough way, carrying the Karenza ever homewards.

Eliom was right again and enraged as he was, Edmund knew it. And finally, he could feel the snake of anger, of rage at the world he had been carrying with him all this time beginning to really subside.

"I..." he began after a time, before stopping again. He still just didn't know what to say.

Thankfully however, Eliom soon stepped in.

"You did not use the sleeping potion Eldora gave you," he stated. His voice was very much back to itself now, calm and soft and soothing and shrugging, Edmund gave an awkward frown.

"I just don't trust her, Eliom," he said almost apologetically. "I know you say she's harmless... but I still don't trust her."

Eliom nodded fairly.

"That is understandable," he replied. "You do not know her. But I hope that you know and trust *me*."

This made Edmund give a start and turning his full attention on his friend, the Explorer looked aghast.

"You *know* I trust you Eliom! I would trust you with my life!" he cried pitifully.

But Eliom merely stared back at Edmund, his usual indifferent mask hiding his true thoughts and it was then that the Explorer realised not for the first time in his life that if he had trusted his friend, *truly* trusted him, then he would have done what the wizard had suggested all along. He would have allowed Eliom to help him sleep, to take the nightmares away, to ease the pain. The wizard was powerful and wise. How could a mere *human* have thought he knew better?

And yet something was still holding him back. The same something that had held him back all this time, that had prevented Eliom, or anyone else for that matter, from getting too close; the one reason why he hadn't accepted his friend's offer of ridding him of his nightmares before.

"I'm worried," he then finally admitted aloud. "I'm worried Eliom, about... forgetting her." And as if even saying it was too much, he turned to look out over the crashing water. "I mean, I *want* to forget the dreams, the horror... but her?!" He felt suddenly numb. "I'm worried that... well... if the dreams stop... with time I won't be able to remember her. Even now I find some memories of her fading...I just...." And he looked back at his friend then, pleadingly, as if yearning for him to understand.

As usual, the wizard's expression gave nothing away.

"I see..." he mused, although there was something in his voice that told Edmund that perhaps he'd known about the Explorer's concerns all along but that he'd just been waiting for his friend to understand them himself.

"So you see why I *can't* stop the nightmares…" the human assumed. "I have to keep the pain in order to… keep her."

Instead of agreeing as Edmund had secretly hoped however, Eliom looked slightly thoughtful.

"No…" he mused slowly. "I still see good reason to cease the nightmares."

Edmund gave a sigh, his fists clenching as his anger flared again for a second, but before he could say a word, Eliom took over.

"You cannot sleep," the wizard explained patiently. "You are exhausted every day and you wake others during the night with your screaming. We *need* you Edmund. You are our leader. How can you lead us when you are only half-awake? How can you lead us when you spend all your time wrapped in guilt and self-pity? No one is asking you to forget everything that has happened. No one is asking you to forget Bethan. As your friend, I am simply asking you to look to the present and then on to the future. There *is* no future with Bethan or even Renard. Although it grieves us all, they are both gone."

The wizard then turned to the waves himself, his expression once again oddly troubled.

"It was inevitable that this *event* was to occur… I believed that perhaps it could be changed but…" And as he faltered, sounding uncertain again, Edmund tried not to let it show in his face how much this display of *doubt* in his friend concerned him.

"You will not forget her, Edmund. Is it not a saying amongst humans that a loved one remains always in your heart?"

Edmund nodded half-heartedly.

"Yes," he said. "It is."

"Then there she shall remain. There and in your thoughts. I can guarantee that." And he reached out and touched his friend on the shoulder then as if casting some kind of spell that could promise just that. "I see your guilt. You blame yourself every day for this tragedy. For Bethan's death, for Renard's, for Saz's, Bex's and for Meggie's. But I will continue to tell you, until you truly believe; it was *not* your fault. It was beyond your control. It was the elements' decision to walk into those flames and theirs alone. There was nothing you could have done about it. Without their sacrifice, we would *all* have risked the fate of Tungala and it is over now. Let us not dwell on the past. We need you to lead us into the future."

Eliom's last words were met with utter silence as Edmund just stood, expressionless as a confusion of thoughts and emotions whirled around his head. But though everything felt like one big mess, one thing seemed now to stick out above all the others. Finally, it was if the wizard had lifted the lid on his bitter, angry selfishness and he knew now what he had to do.

What Eliom had said was true. He couldn't live in the past. He had to carry on. He had to think of the others now.

Much as he often didn't understand *why*, they needed him.
They were his crew, his friends, his journeymen and he was theirs.
And he owed it to them to carry on.
He owed his life to the living and so it was with that in mind that Edmund of Tonasse finally gave in.

It was late, very late. The darkness had reached a new intensity and Edmund sat on his bunk, motionless. He'd been in the same position for the last half an hour, never moving, barely even blinking, in one hand Eldora's little grey sack and in the other, a goblet of warm clear liquid which Eliom had given to him only an hour or so before.

All around him he could hear the sounds of heavy breathing, snorts and snoring, the sounds of deep sleep, his own breath laboured with exhaustion as slowly, arduously he moved his head to glance, not for the first time, down on the objects in his fingers, all the while a mental argument raging in his head.

He knew that he should take the potions. He knew that it was for the best that his nightmares stop and that he should sleep for a full night, and yet that same unconscious voice was still trying to stop him. Still clinging on and fighting. He didn't want to forget Bethan... It was his fault that all of this happened... he *deserved* those nightmares... he *deserved* to be reminded every night of what he had done...

Eliom, himself, had gone to bed, but Edmund had an eerie feeling that the wizard wasn't asleep. Eliom rarely truly rested and for all the Explorer knew, he could be watching him right at that very moment, just waiting for him to do the right thing and take the plunge. To trust him.

Trust him. He trusted Eliom. He knew he did. But then, knowing it wasn't quite enough. He also knew that he had to show it.

And so finally, giving a tiny sigh, Edmund drew the cup to his lips, letting it lie there for a while, warm and smooth. The liquid within smelt of hot metal, making him gag a little. But he *would* drink it and his heart quickened as he realised the full extent of what he was about to do.

In one quick movement, the Explorer then threw his head back and gulped the liquid down in one, closing his eyes with a cough as the fluid slid down his throat towards his stomach.

There. He'd done it. He'd really done it.

The nightmares had gone. And for a moment he just sat there, his eyes resting shut, breathing deeply, before, moving to the sack, he then untied it and being careful not to spill any of the contents, tipped it up, pouring a soft pink powder into his hands. Eliom had told him that he only needed a small handful. Anymore and he would sleep for weeks, perhaps even longer, so he would have to be extra careful.

Not that it was easy to tell in the dark...

Edmund knew for certain now that Eliom really was watching him. He could feel the hairs on the back of his neck rising up and tucking his blanket more tightly about him in a show to get more comfortable, he slowly brought the powder in his hand towards his nose until they were almost touching. Then, as instructed, he muttered under his breath a few words in the ancient language just as Eliom had taught him.

The sounds he made felt strange, like a curious kind of burning and yet somehow, they also felt *right* all at the same time. With a shudder, the Explorer then took a quick, short breath and snorted the powder right up into his nostrils.

For a good minute, all Edmund could do was choke and sneeze, doubling up over his bunk, his hands pressed to his face in a desperate attempt to keep quiet. But then things started to change. He could feel it already; the overwhelming drowsiness, the heaviness on his eyelids and before he knew what was happening, the sack had fallen from his bunk, tipping the pink powder all over the floor as he slumped back against his pillows.

A warm sensation was spreading its way across his chest, reminding him briefly of returning from the Dark Mist... His whole body was heavy and yet weightless and he felt for the first time in as long as he could remember, *peaceful*.

Slowly but surely, his eyes then began to roll to the back of his head and finally letting go, Edmund found himself slipping into a deep and comfortable sleep...

―

Blackness surrounded him in its warm, relaxing embrace. Only it wasn't really blackness, more like blankness. A nothingness.

A peace.

This was what it felt like. He had almost forgotten...

He could hear himself sigh, breathing deeply, in and out, in and out, a gentle hypnotic rhythm and it was soothing; soft and perfect like a drawn-out moment of happiness long forgotten.

But then, there was light. Bright light white, erupting everywhere and though he stood —yes, somehow, he had legs- his hands over his eyes, his eyes shut, still it was there, a part of him somehow. Without and yet within.

And then all peace was erased as he saw the fire. It was a great orb of flames and molten metal, so hot, so pure and white that it burnt into the very back of his mind. A great white circle, ebbing and flowing and boiling.

And before he knew what was happening it had started to dim and very slowly, he realised that he was no longer standing alone.

There was a figure in front of him, before the scorching ball of white; an old man, an ancient man. He was small, about a foot shorter than himself and he wore a long, simple cloak of grey yarn. His face was wrinkled, showing barely blue eyes encased between folds of skin above a long wispy grey beard that reached almost to his knees.

In the man's hand was a roll of parchment and as soon as he'd caught his attention, he began to wave it like one would a flag.

His voice was quiet with the weakness of the elderly and yet it emitted a surprising strength.

"You give up too easily," he rumbled in a faintly Eastern accent. "If only I had known this could happen, I would have tried to inform you more directly...." And he shook his head. "No, but I could not do that. Even now I cannot tell you the truth... Even now I can be cursed... I would not have cared before, but now, now I know his powers. He can doom me for eternity if he chooses. He knows how to bargain with death... But that is not important."

The man seemed intent on getting everything he wanted to say out as quickly as possible.

"What is important is that the map was not what it appeared," he said with barely a pause for breath. "You must go back... But first you must come to me... I knew about you... Of course I knew there would be others... There always are. I had thought that my message would get through... I had thought that you would understand... Although it may have been best this way... But there is *a way of getting them back and only I know it*... Go, quickly! Only those who are destined will find a way!"

And then suddenly, he was gone and, in his place, just like that, was a woman.

She was tall and striking, beautiful, *with long dark hair that seemed to emit a light all of its own*. She looked afraid, but made no sign either to move away or towards him; she simply stared at him with large round eyes.

Yet, even as she did so, the surroundings then began to change and shift around her to reveal a dry prairie. Suddenly the light was gone, but in its place a red eerie glow and far off into the distance he could see a great platform, a monument, hundreds of metres high, stretching like a giant knife into the sunless sky.

On the platform stood four great globes of glass, one green, one orange, one blue and one as clear as water.

The woman then opened her mouth but it wasn't her voice that spouted from her lips; it was that of another, someone entirely different altogether.

"You cannot defeat it... The entity...The balance is too delicate! But you may be able to save them!... There may be a small window... No more can I say, for the Builder has many ears..."

She seemed desperate for him to understand, to make sense of her ramblings, but before he could even open his mouth to reply, to ask, he saw it. The great flame, wiping across the prairie. The platform crumbled under the force of it and then it was rolling towards them, ready to annihilate them both.

The woman just smiled at him, sadly, lovingly.

But then she was gone, buried, crushed beneath the heat.

And finally letting out a yell of terror, Edmund awoke.
.

REVELATIONS

Feeling a tug at his arm, Nickolas rolled over, opening his eyes blearily. It was dark; meaning that he'd been sleeping for either less or *more* time than he'd thought and suddenly worried, he sat up, alert.

The touch had been a Digger-girl. She was smiling at him apologetically, but with excitement in her eyes and even in his exhausted, pent-up state, Nickolas realised that the child had probably never touched a human before. As he always did, he found himself wondering briefly whether, beyond the intrigue and novelty, she resented him for that, for being there. For being alive.

But he knew better than to ask aloud. She was only young. So very young…

"What is it?" he almost snapped and then, remembering his manners, he tried to slow himself down. "Is it Meggie? Is she all right?"

The girl nodded silently.

"She's awake, *sir*." The word, as it often did, grated on him a little, but he left it alone. Some Diggers used it, some didn't. Who was he to change that?

Dromeda, who had also been sleeping nearby, then awoke with a yawn.

"What is it?" he too asked the girl. Unlike his friend though, Dromeda didn't seem to care *how* sharp he was and though it made Nickolas scowl slightly, he left *that* alone too. For now.

"Meggie is awake," was all he said and satisfied there was no emergency, Dromeda nodded and closing his eyes again, fell back into a doze.

Nickolas meanwhile turned back to the Digger-girl.

She was quite pretty, he noticed. She could have quite easily passed as a human.

"Take me to her," he then entreated kindly and the girl gave another nod before hurrying out of the room, closely followed by a now wide-awake Nickolas.

—

"Logon?" Meggie called out in sleepy confusion as she saw the blurry figure standing over her. "Logon, is that you?"

"No," said a voice, and realising her mistake straight away, the element blinked, trying desperately to focus her fuzzy mind.

"Sorry, Nickolas," she mumbled, trying to sit up, but failing. She felt weak, her limbs like rock. "I thought you were someone else, I-"

Nickolas however, looked utterly delighted.

"You can remember me?" he cried and confused for a moment, Meggie just looked at him.

"Of course I do!" she said. Her voice came out in a sort of quiet slur. "We were heading to the outer city and then… Then…" her brow furrowed, "then I don't really know what happened."

And despite his sudden excitement, Nickolas couldn't help but clench his fists. This was the moment of truth. The moment when everything could change all over again.

He would have to tread carefully.

"But before?" he started, speaking slowly. "Do you remember… *before?*"

"Before?" And managing to finally prop herself up on her elbows, Meggie levelled him a quizzical, wide-eyed stare. "Before what?"

"Before…"and Nickolas paused, searching desperately for the right words. For some reason, his heart was pounding. "Before you arrived here…? In this world."

For some time, Meggie just continued to stare at him and as she did so, Nickolas couldn't help but dread that the very worst had indeed happened; that just like so many others before her, Meggie had somehow lost herself…

But then, slowly but surely…

"Yes," she said, sounding uncertain, before realising what that truly meant, she suddenly brightened. "Yes! I can!" and her mouth spread into a wide, relieved grin. "Nickolas, I'm still *me*! I can remember everything! I can remember Tungala! I can remember the grass and bread and water and-"

Nickolas just shook his head in wonderment.

"You *are* a mysterious one, Meggie," he muttered, not able to quite believe it. "For as long as I have been here, no one has ever made the transition without severely suffering for it. Although," and he rubbed the back of his neck, "you *did* have me worried for a while…"

Just like the Digger-girl, Meggie gave a little smile of apology. Only this time it felt somehow sweeter.

"Sorry," she laughed and Nickolas couldn't help but give his own smile in return.

She was fine. His charge, Meggie, was fine. And though he would never understand *how*, he felt somehow grateful…

Perching on the edge of her bed, he then studied her again.

"And who is Logon?" he asked, trying to tease her, even though, for some reason, he felt more curious than he was letting on. Right then any details from Tungala, anything he could find out about what had once also been his, felt like a dream come true. And if he could maybe learn a little about Meggie in the process…

But though she had been all laughs and smiles seconds before, almost the moment the words had fallen from his lips, Meggie's grin had gone.

"Oh," and instantly sobering as he realised he'd gone too far without knowing it, Nickolas straightened up, feeling suddenly awkward. "I am sorry."

Meggie gave a little shake of her head.

"Don't be," she replied. Her voice was frostier than before; although whether that was due to *his* inquisitiveness or *her* memories, Nickolas wasn't quite sure. "He was my brother. But it's a long story…"

And as she stopped talking, there was then a short, and in Nickolas's opinion, weighted silence as the companions sat together, both at a loss, so it seemed, for something to say.

Nickolas wondered if he should leave, to let her rest, and having that thought, he soon got back to his feet. As he did so though, something suddenly came over him and as if desperate to keep the conversation going, he instead, moved away from the bed and cleared his throat, his face, until then, sparkling a little with mirth, locked down once again.

"So, how do you feel?" he asked pointlessly.

Trying to give another smile, Meggie shrugged.

"Tired I suppose," she replied. "But other than that…"

She was looking up at him with those big green eyes almost as if she expected something; what that something was though, Nickolas had no idea and finally deciding it really was best to go, he turned for the door.

"I will leave you to rest then," he muttered and before she could so much as react, he was walking towards the corridor. For some reason, Meggie didn't understand, he seemed suddenly colder, more awkward than before. But just as anxious as he suddenly was to escape, Meggie realised she was for him to stay.

"No, wait!" she cried out. "Don't leave me here! Where are you going?"

Nickolas only paused in the doorway.

"You need to sleep, Meggie," he replied matter-of-factly. "I will just be outside."

Meggie though was having none of it.

"I've slept already! I feel like I've been sleeping for weeks!" she almost pleaded. "In fact," and she hesitated, "how long *have* I been here?"

And hearing the hint of fear in her voice, Nickolas turned fully back to her then.

"Not very long," he replied, feeling suddenly exhausted himself, now that the relief had worn off. "No more than a day or two. Although I have to be honest - I am not *entirely* certain. I begin to lose track…"

"A day or two?" Meggie echoed, then with a hint of sarcasm; "Is that *all*?"

She gave a laugh and Nickolas couldn't help but smile all over again.

There was something about the little woman that he found refreshing, *appealing* it could even be said and knowing that this time at least, she had won the argument, he stepped back into the room.

"When you are ready, and fully rested, we will head for The City," he said. "But until then-"

"The City, is that where the others are?"

And crossing his arms and leaning against the wall – he really *was* tired - Nickolas shrugged.

"I do not know where your other two companions are. But," and straight away, he looked serious again. "The element of fire; she is here…"

Meggie's whole face then changed in an instant.

"Saz!" she exclaimed. "She's *here*?!"

"Yes," he began. "She came with-" but then, watching as Meggie positively sprung out of bed, he leapt forward as if to grab her. "Wait, I do not think-!"

"Where is she? I need to see her!"

Meggie had jumped to her wobbly feet in a moment. As she did so though, she heard an odd rustling and glancing down was vaguely surprised to find herself clothed in a long beige dress.

Distracted, the element paused to finger the thin fabric for a moment. Had she been wearing the dress before? Back when she had first arrived there? She couldn't seem to remember…

Glancing at Nickolas, Meggie was then just as surprised to see that his outfit too, a simple tunic and trousers, was also beige and that somehow this didn't seem right to her.

Hadn't it been white? Hadn't he been wearing white before?

No.

In the temple… It was white in Ratacopeck, not here…

Nickolas, meanwhile, following her eyes, looked bewildered.

"Are you… are you all right-?"

But with a shake of her confused head, Meggie's moment was over and she looked up at him pleadingly.

"Where is she?" she repeated. "Where's Saz? Please take me to her!"

There was something in the tone of her voice, something urgent that unnerved the already increasingly concerned Nickolas.

"You can see her but she is unable to talk," he replied cautiously. "She has not yet gained consciousness. My friend, Dromeda, is taking care of her. He carried her here almost a week ago."

And hearing his explanation, Meggie's pale face fell.

"She's *still* unconscious?" she muttered and Nickolas, suddenly worried, despite himself, that the shock would make her collapse all over again, took an extra step towards her, readying to grab her arms in case she should fall. The little element's legs were shaking violently, but seeing that he meant only to help, Meggie just continued to stare at him.

For a second, as she saw Nickolas move towards her, her natural response of stubbornly refusing any aid, was about the kick in, but for once, she managed to stop herself. She knew it had been a mistake to get up, she could feel it – her whole body was quivering, ready to drop at a moment's notice. But whilst she knew she was weak from the shock, weak with exhaustion, she also knew that she wasn't ready to do any more resting; not when Saz, when someone she knew from *before,* from her own real and true world, not this strange fantasy place of beige clothes and odd light, was so close.

Asking for help this time won't hurt, she reasoned to herself. It was either let him help or admit defeat and go back to bed.

And so it was that reaching out a trembling hand, she then laid it on her companion's arm.

"Please," was all she said and understanding immediately, Nickolas tucked the tiny fingers into the crook of his elbow and bending so as not to cause her strain, gently led his charge back towards the archway that served as a door and out into the corridor beyond.

As they walked slowly along, so it was Meggie finally took the time to properly study her surroundings. Beyond her room, a small space with nothing but a simple bed, was a long squat building carved all in white. Along one side seemed to be a long corridor with three or four archways leading off to her left into other unfamiliar rooms. Further along was a pair of high-backed chairs propped against the wall and a swinging double-door leading to the dusty street beyond.

As the pair made their way down the corridor, passing the other archways, Meggie tried to see into each room beyond, but it was too dark. The morning light was only just beginning to shine through and there appeared to be no one else around.

Eventually Nickolas then stopped outside the final doorway.

"This is it," he whispered.

For some reason, he didn't seem to want to raise his voice and Meggie glanced up at him uncertainly.

"Aren't you coming in?" she murmured.

But Nickolas shook his head.

"It is not my place," he said, and removing her hand from his arm, he took a step away from her.

For a second, Meggie felt a stab of something like hurt pang through her chest. She knew that feeling well, the feeling of betrayal, of sadness – she had experienced it more than her fair share in life - but why she felt it then, she couldn't understand. After all, how had her companion possibly let her down? Why had she even assumed he would come with her? What interest, after all, was *her* friend to *him*?

What interest even, was *any* of this to him? Why was he even still *there* in the first place?

Focusing on not falling, Meggie then took hold of the doorway and with sudden fear in her heart as to what she might find beyond, she stepped through it.

The room was much like the one she had left. It was white, as usual, and with only the minimal amount of furniture. To her left was another high-backed chair, empty but for a spare cloth someone had left and directly before her was a low bed with a simple mattress. Atop the mattress lay a thin, pale body.

Only a few steps in, Meggie was half relieved to hear the deep rhythmical wheeze of someone sleeping and feeling a little braver, she soon moved towards it.

Up close, Saz's blonde head was unkempt and clammy. Her face and lips were pale, almost lifeless, but for a film of sweat lining the underside of her nose that rose and fell with every breath.

There was no blanket covering her, but Meggie soon understood why. The element too was garbed in a long beige dress but whilst Meggie's was light, Saz's was darker, almost brown where it clung to her legs and torso, sticking to the sweat coating her fevered body and stifling the air with the strong smell of sleep and musty wetness.

For a while, Meggie just stared, drinking in every detail she recognised of her friend and every detail she didn't over and over again. It felt like years since she'd last seen her, since she'd last seen *anyone* she knew from the old world and though it felt somehow wonderful, it also felt oddly alien.

"Oh Saz," she murmured sadly. "What's happened to you?" And realising even as she said the words aloud, just what they could mean, she slumped onto the edge of the mattress heavily, her eyes suddenly pricking with hot tears.

What if Saz couldn't remember anything? What if she awoke and didn't recognise her?

Her heart quickened.

What, even, if *none* of them did?

What if Saz, Bex and Bethan were all lost and it was just her?

Alone.

Again…

Meggie's body gave an extra shudder.

She really *was* tired. And not just physically either. Mentally. *Emotionally*, though she would never willingly admit it.

Sitting on the edge of the bed, she thought then about calling for Nickolas, about asking him to lead, maybe even *carry* her back to her own room, but though she knew she needed it, she also knew she wasn't going to.

No, exhausted, upset as she was, there wasn't anywhere else she wanted to, she *could* be right then but right there, by her friend's side. And so it was that Meggie let her weak body slide to the cool bare floor and resting her aching head against Saz's mattress, the little element closed her eyes and drifted into a peaceful doze.

Edmund paced the deck like a man crazed. He hadn't stopped moving from the moment he'd woken - he simply *couldn't* and though Eliom had tried his best to calm him, Fred to make him see reason, Thom, even, to *growl* it out of him, he just wouldn't cease. He was just too exhilarated, too heightened with emotion to do anything else; anything but march and keep marching as if the movement itself could bring him closer to the truth.

"It doesn't make any sense!" he cried wildly, not for the first time. "You said I wouldn't dream, Eliom! You *said*... And yet I took the potion and I dreamt again!"

The whole crew, with the exception of their new visitor, stood huddled in the morning breeze, wide-awake and yet desperate to go back to their warm beds.

"Perhaps the potion simply failed," Thom was the one to argue but though the others nodded their agreement, Edmund just bit his lip frantically, before turning to Eliom with a pleading look in his eyes.

"You *have* to believe me! It was different," he begged. "I've never had a dream like this before. Couldn't it *mean* something?"

The wizard, as ever, stood calmly at the edge of things, his staff slack in his hand. Despite the early hour and lack of sleep for all, he alone remained patient, willing to hear his friend out.

"It *is* possible," he reasoned, "but I cannot understand why-"

"It is not often that a human is subject to visions, Edmund," Fred interjected cautiously and Edmund rubbed his forehead in frustration.

"I know, but it can't have been a coincidence," he repeated for the third time that morning. "It just *can't*."

Elanore meanwhile frowned, pulling her cloak more tightly about her exposed neck.

"Maybe it's not," she offered, glancing at the rest of the group. "I mean, I don't usually take heed of this kind of thing but if Edmund thinks-"

Eliom's staff clacked gently on the deck, somehow drawing all attention back.

"Tell us again what you saw," he mused. "Perhaps we may be able to arrive at a conclusion." Though his voice was quiet, as always, it carried over even the strongest whisp of sea air and whilst the rest of the group shifted uncomfortably, Edmund seemed to brighten. Reaching up to massage his temples, as if the movement would somehow help sharpen the memory, he then began;

"Everything was black," he said. "Not really black, just nothing. And then, suddenly, it was white. Bright white, like a great light shining. Like the orb perhaps; a big burning circle of fire. And it was so *bright*, I - my hands," he glanced down at them as if half-expecting them to be different. They were trembling a little. "My fingers were almost transparent. The light was outside of me and yet it felt like it was *part* of me at the same time. Like I was *making* it. And then that's when I saw him," his eyes moved back to Eliom, then on to Fred and Thom as if gauging their reactions. "A man – and he was old, *really* old. He was small, wrinkled, with a long beard, simple robes and some parchment," he gave a frown. "I don't know what it was, but he was waving it at me. It could have been a chart, or a map or…"

"A map?" Eliom echoed pointedly.

"*The* map?" Elanore realised and Edmund's expression lit up all over again.

"The map! Of course! It *had* to be! And-and the man, he spoke to me… he said something about being cursed, he said I had given up. He said…" the Explorer puzzled for a moment, clearly trying to remember the exact words. "He said something about a 'he' and how 'he' could doom him 'even in death'. Then he spoke about the map – yes that makes sense now! - he said that the map isn't what it appears. He told me to 'go back' but first to come to him. Then he talked of getting 'them' back and something like 'only those who are destined'-?"

"-will find a way?" Fred interjected. He and Eliom exchanged a meaningful look then before their attention immediately snapped back to Edmund as he suddenly gave cry of delight.

"Of course!" he cried. "From Ratacopeck! Eliom, you told me about it. That phrase was written over the temple entrances in the ancient tongue of the wizards. But what does it-?"

"Did you *see* anything else?" Eliom interrupted firmly.

"Yes," the Explorer seemed barely put out, as this time, his face fell. "I saw *her*. I saw Bethan. She spoke to me, but not in her own voice. It was a woman still, but not one I recognised. She spoke of a Builder and a being of some sort - an '*entity*' she called it. She said about how the balance of something was too delicate but that we might still be able to save them. It didn't really make a lot of sense. And then, after that?" his brow furrowed. "I don't really know. There was a platform, like the one at Ratacopeck – and it burnt. There were flames… and then, then I woke up."

The rest of the group all looked at each other. In every face could be read mixtures of curiosity, of confusion, doubt and differing levels of sleepless impatience. Half of them were convinced, the other half not, but no matter what they were feeling, all of them knew what had to happen next and almost as one, the companions then turned to Eliom, the voice of wisdom and reason, ready to listen.

"Can you interpret it?" Edmund asked the wizard hopefully. He was almost out of breath with anticipation. Something in his heart, in the back of his mind told him that his dream had *meant* something and that, despite the rest of the crew's unimpressed attitudes, he had to find out *what*.

Eliom's expression never changed, but realising that all attention was now on him, he met the Explorer's gaze with something like concern.

"I can of course *speculate*..." he then spoke carefully. "You know that I have in the past. *But*," and to everyone's surprise, he then *frowned*. "But I have not always estimated correctly or even, occasionally, been well-timed..." And even as the wizard spoke, Edmund found himself remembering Eliom's vision from the night before they'd entered the Temple of Ratacopeck. If the wizard had more accurately understood what he'd seen - the glowing orb, the cries of sorrow - perhaps none of this would have happened. If he'd known what would be waiting for them, Edmund wouldn't have allowed the group to enter the temple. He wouldn't have allowed the elements to walk through those flames and no one would have died...

But they'd already been through all this. Every day since it had happened Edmund had fought with himself, with others, considering all of the options they could have had and knowing that now was *not* the time to bring it all back up again, to question an event that he was starting to move towards accepting hadn't been in *anyone's* control, Edmund instantly pushed the thoughts aside.

"You're the only one who can even come *close* to the truth, Eliom," he pleaded instead. "You *have* to try. What if it's important? What if it's about the elements?"

The elements. He had said it out loud and it was then that Fred, who had been keeping a close eye on Eliom's face this entire time, as if trying to see something the others couldn't, stepped in.

"Could they still be alive?" he asked. He spoke carefully, slowly, but straight away, Thom was the first to give a snort of derision, crossing his thick arms.

"*Not possible*. We saw them burning with our very eyes. No one could have survived that inferno," the dwarf snapped. "*No* one. We saw how Renard-" But Edmund, who had secretly been hoping the same thing himself, turned on the dwarf angrily.

"They could have survived, Thom! There might have been a way!"

"I cannot see *how*..."

"Why not? *We* did! *We* survived!"

Thom visibly bristled.

"That is not the same!"

But before any more could be said, Eliom then raised a hand and, just like that, the two fell silent.

"Stop," he said. "Arguing will not help in this matter."

And turning once again to Edmund, the wizard then delivered his final verdict, shocking them all.

"I am sorry," he said. "But much as I may wish to. I cannot help you."

No one could have mistaken the instant the Explorer understood what his life-long friend was telling him. No one could have mistaken the stunned disappointment. But though no one could quite believe that Eliom, the great and wise wizard of old, *couldn't* provide an answer, before anyone else could have time to register their shock, they realised that their friend wasn't quite finished.

"*I* cannot help you," the wizard repeated and then; "But I know someone who *can*…"

And at the exact same second that Eliom spoke, all suddenly became aware of the sound of approaching footsteps echoing across the wooden deck as Eldora strode purposefully towards them, her black cloak billowing in the dawn breeze.

—

"Good morning." The Lectur spoke to the group assembled on the deck as if she'd simply come across them all on a morning stroll.

Despite her easy manner though, no one said a word in response. No one, even, so much as reacted.

No one except Eliom.

"Just in time. As always," he commented serenely. But though he sounded much as he always did, there was something about the way he spoke that, to the trained ear of certain among his friends, sounded almost cold.

And Eldora too, as she turned her steely gaze on her companion of old, seemed suddenly icier.

"I Saw that I must be here," she replied, her voice stiff. "And so, I came," and she cast her eyes fleetingly over the rest of the group. "Even if it is a rather *peculiar* time of the morning…"

Positively itching to speak however, Edmund didn't have the patience right then for the Lectur's odd kind of small talk.

"Eldora," he demanded. "Can you interpret my dream? The powder that you gave me, something happened and I saw-"

But to his surprise, instead of the cold retort, instead of the hard look he had half been expecting, Eldora held up a white hand.

"Hush. I know what you saw," she said. "And yes. I may be able to help."

"*May?*" Despite the unwanted hurry to leave his bunk, Thom had still found time to grab his axe on the way and he leant on it now, levelling the Lectur with a firm glare of his own. "You *may* be able to help?" he scoffed. "You say that you Saw yourself here, on this ship, but that you did not yet understand why. *This* might be the reason you are here, witch…"

No one could mistake the dwarf's logic, but at the same time, no one could mistake his obvious dislike either and clearly detecting yet another argument on the horizon, Eliom shifted a little, taking the smallest warning step into the centre of the group.

Eldora meanwhile, who had merely bristled at being called a witch, coolly turned back to Edmund.

"Give me your hand," she commanded, holding out one of her own before giving an irritated sigh as the Explorer didn't take it. "I cannot harm you. Perhaps I will be able to See more clearly what your dream foretold if you let me touch you."

The word 'foretold' somehow seemed to pacify Edmund – proof that the Lectur might believe him where the others hadn't, seemed to fill him with an odd sense of hope – so this time he obeyed and reaching out, took the white fingers in his own.

For a moment he was shocked. Where he had expected Eldora's skin to be cold, icy and smooth like white granite, he was surprised to find warm flesh and beneath that, the rough layer of what felt like calluses…

At the same time, the second her skin touched the human's, Eldora's eyes seemed to flicker and then roll like orbs of ghastly white to the back of her head as her eyelids closed. Her fingers twitched in Edmund's firm grip but she made no sound.

The rest of the group meanwhile, watched in silent amazement, none of them quite knowing what to expect or what to think as the pair, the white cold Lectur and their exhausted leader then just stood there, hands clasped, neither moving, neither even seeming to breathe as, for a good long while, nothing happened.

The sun told them it was well into morning now as the light grew stronger, casting a bright orange glow across the pale tired faces of the Karenza's crew.

Minutes began to pass. Minutes as the never-ending waves rolled softly beneath their feet, and as patience finally began to wear thin and stomachs to rumble, the group soon began to move about, to shift themselves, Elanore heading back towards the cabins and beyond, to the hold, to gather food for breakfast whilst the weary Fred and Thom, realising they weren't going to be returning to their bunks any time soon, began to stroll the length of the deck one at a time, pacing through their tiredness.

Only Eliom remained where he was, his eyes never leaving Eldora's face, his expression giving nothing away. At one point, he even opened his mouth as if to speak, but as if thinking better of it, he then closed it again.

Edmund all the while was struggling.

At the first sign of some kind of answer to his urgent pleas he'd felt relief and *more*; elation, excitement at the prospect that what he thought could be true… But now that feeling was starting to wear off and not for the first time, he was starting to realise just how exhausted he really was. His whole body was shuddering with it, crying out with lack of sleep, though he desperately tried to hide it, to keep still for fear of somehow disturbing whatever it was Eldora was doing. His legs were throbbing, longing for rest, even just to *move* instead of standing there, frozen, waiting. And all the while he could feel his grip loosening. Feel his head beginning to spin…

"No!"

Suddenly Eldora's eyes snapped open with a shriek and Edmund almost wrenched his hand away completely as he saw her face; for though her eyelids were open, in place of the Lectur's pupils was a film, deadly white and bulging, her eyes left like fleshy white orbs. The rest of her expression meanwhile seemed to *fall*, her eyebrows drooping, her lips slackening as if she had somehow fallen asleep – or *worse*- standing there all that time, her long bone-like fingers still firmly encased in the Explorer's hand.

Halting on his latest stride, Thom stared wide-eyed at the Lectur.

"What is wrong with her?" he murmured as Fred too started at the sudden change. But though he looked for a second as if he were about to reply, the warrior soon hushed the dwarf with a quick glance as the Lectur then cut in.

Her voice was normal and yet somehow louder, *thicker* as if she was speaking, not through the air, not with sound but somehow *through* them as the whole group froze to listen as one.

"The man. He is calling to you," she began. "His name… His name is Ophelius and he talks of a journey and a map." Ophelius. The effect of that name rippled out across the deck like a rush of wind. "He cannot tell you what it is that you should seek, for fear of the Builder. The Builder, who can curse him even in death." She barely seemed able to pause for breath. "He knows you, Edmund. He knew that you would come searching for the map. He thought that you would understand what he had hidden… But he cannot tell you more but this; Those you have lost may be returned. But first you must find him. You must go to his body, his tomb and he will show you the answers that you seek."

The whole deck stood, hanging on her every word in stunned silence as the Lectur paused. Edmund's heart was already in his mouth, pounding in his ears as her words, like some slow-moving liquid, began to seep themselves together, to make some kind of sense in his head, as he searched desperately for meaning. But then;

"A woman. One who will not reveal her identity," she suddenly started again. "She says in a voice not her own that there will be a window of opportunity." The Lectur's eyebrows twitched ever so slightly. "She speaks of an entity. But she too, is afraid. She too tells us that those you have lost can be reclaimed."

The last three words were gone in a split second, sucked into the still silent air, but to the listening companions, each one felt like a jolt to the heart.

Can be reclaimed.

Those you have lost can be reclaimed.

And as suddenly as she'd opened her eyes, Eldora blinked, her pupils returning to normal and just like that, she snatched her hand away from Edmund's as if his very touch burned her flesh.

She was done. The vision was over and like a flame bursting into life, the reaction amongst the group was instantaneous.

There was a loud clatter as Elanore, who had just reappeared on the deck with their morning meal dropped the platter she was carrying, her hands flying to her mouth with a stifled cry. Thom immediately wobbled, leaning on his axe suddenly as if the revelation of those last few moments had been too much for his short legs to handle and Fred just continued to stare at Eldora in complete wonderment, as if unable to quite understand…

Eliom meanwhile, lowered his gaze from the Lectur. His eyes closed for a second and if anyone had been watching him closely, they would have seen his fingers tighten for the briefest moment on his staff. No one, however *was* watching him, for all eyes, as one, then seemed to fall on Edmund.

Exactly as he had been throughout it all, the Explorer simply stood there, his hand, though now free, still outstretched towards the Lectur as if half-expecting for her to take it again and tell him that what she had just told him, told them *all* was completely wrong, completely impossible.

And yet she didn't.

She didn't take it.

Instead, she too was just staring at him, just watching as his whole face seemed to drain of colour, his eyes widening but blank, not quite ready for the truth of what any of this meant.

No one knew if Eldora had quite understood what she had just said, whether she, through all her Seeings, knew of what it was they had lost up until that moment, but whether she did or no, the Lectur saw what was about to happen before any of the rest of them did and all of a sudden, she lunged forward.

For a moment it looked as if she was trying to hurt him, to wrestle him to the ground but all soon became clear as the Explorer then fell, his legs finally giving way under the exhaustion, under the strain, under the guilt and the pain suddenly, *finally* lifting in one unlooked-for moment. The Lectur caught him just in time and he stumbled into her arms, before toppling sideways to his knees on the deck. Something like a gasp erupted from his chest.

"They're alive?" he breathed shakily. He couldn't even say *She*. He couldn't even dare think it.

But something in the eyes of Eldora shone and a small smile spread across her face, the first sign of real feeling, of warmth she'd shown that morning.

"Yes," she then murmured in reply. "The elements are alive."

WHERE TO GO

"**B**ethan," came Belanna's cheery voice, making Bethan wake with a start.

"Wha…?" she mumbled blearily. "What time is it…? What's going on…?"

For a moment, Belanna didn't answer as she fussed about with a jug of water, pouring Bethan a canteen and placing it on the floor at her feet. But then;

"You're moving today," she replied absently. "Best to be up and about while it's early."

"Moving?!" and all of a sudden, Bethan felt very much wide-awake as a little flip of something like excitement shifted in her belly. "Moving where?" Though she knew it didn't make a lot of sense, for the tiniest of seconds she wondered if she was going home. Back to her own world, which, she realised gloomily, she hardly remembered anything about.

What if she was moving to be with the others she remembered?

Or what if she was moving to be with the mysterious man with the blue eyes?

Belanna's answer, however, wasn't what she had hoped for.

"You're moving to another house. Similar to this one, but your own," she replied, cleaning her hands on an apron at her waist. All the women in this place wore aprons, like some kind of odd uniform.

Bethan's unconscious smile faded.

"But what about Bex?" she asked slowly. Suddenly she was very much aware that she didn't want to lose contact with the only person she *knew*, her only connection, the only trapdoor to her memories, to herself… And ultimately the only one she felt she could trust right then. Belanna seemed friendly and Barabus, of course was helpful enough, but there was something about him, something odd that she didn't quite understand. Something that made her feel a little uneasy around him…

Belanna smiled, obviously amused by her continual questions.

"Bex will be moving too."

And Bethan let out an audible sigh of relief.

Well, *that* was something.

As if that made her decision, she then got to her feet.

"I'm going to see her then," she stated, trying not to trip as her dress tangled about her legs.

She made to stride for the door, but the second she moved, Belanna's whole demeanour changed and suddenly, she had grabbed Bethan by the arm.

"I'm sorry, Bethan..." she started. "But there-"

"You cannot see her."

And recognising the voice as it cut across Belanna's, Bethan soon turned to find Barabus standing in the doorway. His arms were crossed, his expression serious and for a moment, Bethan found herself wondering just how long he'd been there...

What was going on?

"Why not?" She looked first at him before turning back to Belanna.

"Because..." but even Barabus's uncertainty was obvious. "You have to go now."

Bethan cocked her head to one side, careful to hide her thoughts, to hide the mild panic now thudding through her chest. Why the sudden change? Why the sudden demand?

"I won't be a moment," she reasoned carefully. "I just want to say goodbye."

But Barabus remained where he was, cleverly blocking the exit.

"You cannot," he repeated. "New regulations. I am sorry."

New regulations?

Bethan just continued to stare at him, her heart positively racing now, just like her thoughts. Someone had to know about their meeting in secret, about what she and Bex had heard in the darkness of the steps. That was the only explanation...

The question though was, *how?*

"Regulations? What *regulations?* Made by who?!" she tried.

But to no one's surprise, Barabus just glanced, with an awkward clearing of his throat, at Belanna. The woman's face looked somehow *guilty* now but neither of them said anything. It was obvious neither of them were *allowed* to, for some reason. No doubt the same reason no one seemed to want to tell her *anything* around here...

Clearly neither of them knew what she had done after all then...

Perhaps now was the time to reveal just how much she understood.

"Is it the Builder again?" she said more calmly than she felt. "Isn't that who makes the rules around here?"

The reaction was just as she'd been expecting. Barabus's eyebrows flickered as he sucked in his next breath just that little bit *too* sharply. Belanna meanwhile, looked suddenly anxious to leave, and without so much as another word to either party, she soon did so, Barabus stepping aside briefly to let her pass.

The second the woman was gone, Barabus then rounded on her.

"Do not speak so freely of the Builder," he hissed and he sounded suddenly so *angry* that Bethan felt herself physically shrinking away from him.

Perhaps it wasn't such a good idea to reveal too much after all…

"You're the one who told me about him!" she replied, trying to sound innocent. "You told me he created-!" But her play-acting wasn't going to fool him. He could tell that she knew more than she was letting on; that she had heard something more than what he had told her. She could read it in his face.

"Who have you been talking to?"

Though his voice was all forced calmness, Bethan detected a threat beneath his tone.

What was *wrong* with him? Why was he being so aggressive suddenly?

"No one," Bethan muttered. "Only Bex. No one else…" but instead of pacifying him, this only seemed to make Barabus rear up all the more.

"Who?!" he demanded. "Who have you been speaking to?!" His arms were uncrossed now and for a moment, Bethan thought he was going to move towards her. She shuddered.

"No one!" she insisted. "I don't know what you want me to say!"

"Was it a Digger? Was it a human?" Barabus seemed desperate to know.

"Who? I haven't been speaking to anyone!" and though Barabus continued to glare at her, Bethan, with some relief, could see the doubt in his eyes that she knew anything important after all.

Again, he opened his mouth to speak, but then, as if deciding that shouting was going to get him nowhere, instead of speaking, he gave a sigh and surprising Bethan, he then stepped away from the door and just like that, the matter was dropped.

"Come on," he grunted and without another word on the subject, turned to leave. "Follow me."

Bethan hesitated, feeling stunned.

What about Bex…? But already her companion had stopped to wait for her.

"Come on," he forced. There was still something dangerous in the way he spoke and realising that she didn't have much of a choice, Bethan found herself following him reluctantly into the corridor she had ventured down with Bex only the night before. In the light of the morning, it was pale and plain.

Everything was white, the walls, the floor, the swinging doors – the whole place felt like some great big stone box and feeling suddenly suffocated, Bethan felt her palms begin to sweat. Even in those few seconds, Barabus had already stridden ahead of her and running to catch up, she swallowed her fears, knowing she had to say, to *do* something.

"I'll tell you who I've been talking to if you answer *me* a question," she blurted. Her voice was barely audible but Barabus still glanced at her as they reached the double doors at the end of the hallway.

"I have already told you too much," he said. His voice wasn't apologetic, it was *troubled* and frustrated, Bethan paused. She tried not to let her gaze wander down the corridor to the other end and Bex's room beyond, but she couldn't seem to help herself.

Bex was right there, right within reach and for a second she had the smallest impulse to run.

"You've hardly told me anything!" she cried instead, making Barabus stop too as he reached out a hand to push the closest door.

He turned to study her then and as he did so, Bethan, considerably a few inches shorter, couldn't help but feel like she was looking up at some great immoveable statue, his lips cast into a frown, his eyes hard.

"I have told you about the worlds. About the past," he muttered, resolute. "I was *supposed* to tell you *nothing*." But still just as determined, Bethan leaned in closer. The pair were almost touching.

"Well then, just answer me this," she intoned. "Why has the Builder suddenly decided to change things? I've seen-" but she stopped herself before she could reveal any more about the conversation she and Bex had overhead the previous night. "Why are Bex and I being separated? *Really?*"

For a moment, Bethan thought that he was going to refuse her again; his stone-like face told her so, as he stood just eyeing her in that suddenly very cramped space. She could feel his breath on her face, practically feel the warmth from his skin through the thinness of his tunic almost touching hers. It reminded her of another time, of another's touch. Only *that* time it had sent a thrill through her, a shiver of pleasure; *that* time had felt *right* compared to *this*…

Bethan wanted to do nothing more than move away, to distance herself from her companion and her strange memories, but before she could do anything, Barabus suddenly seemed to soften.

"I do not pretend to know why things have been changed," he murmured. If he had any idea of what Bethan had been thinking, he didn't show it. "I can only guess that the Builder does not want any more… *mishaps*."

Mishaps? What mishaps?

Was he talking about their secret meeting on the steps after all?

And surprised, Bethan finally recoiled giving Barabus the chance to shrink away from her stiffly and wrenching open the double doors, step out into the morning air.

"Move," he commanded, the word putting a stop to any more conversation.

Bethan knew she wouldn't be able to argue this time. But even as she began to process what Barabus had just told her, as she followed him out into the city, she couldn't help but feel a sense of relief.

Yes, Barabus may try to stop her and Bex from seeing each other again but judging by his reaction, she was pretty confident that he didn't know what had happened. Now that she thought about it, the way he had said it, so casually, the 'mishaps' he spoke of were clearly nothing to do with her. Which could only mean one thing; no one knew what happened the night before or more importantly, about *where* it had happened, about the hole in the wall on the forty-fifth stair, under the overhanging shrubbery...

"It's settled, surely?" Edmund insisted. "It's *obvious* what we have to do! We have to do what he said! We go East! We travel to Ophelius's tomb! He has the answer to finding the elements!" and he stared around at the others as they all looked at each other, challenging them. His gaze was fierce, his head clearly focused for the first time in days, and yet, to his amazement, some faces were definitely doubtful.

"Thom?" the Explorer pleaded, appealing to each of them in turn, and the dwarf twitched uncomfortably.

"Of course. I am with you," he replied, his voice oddly quiet. "I *did* wish to return home. But," he clutched the handle of his axe more firmly, "I must be here for Bex as she would have been for me..."

Edmund was surprised by this, as, evidently, were the others. None of them were sure they had ever heard the dwarf say anything quite so heartfelt before and moving on with hope, Edmund turned to the wizard.

"Eliom?" he continued. If *anyone* was going to agree with him then surely it would be him. And to his relief, the wizard didn't disappoint.

"I believe it is best I stay with you, Edmund," he replied diplomatically. "As always, I remain at your side for as long as I am needed. I will not abandon Saz and the others now..."

And encouraged, Edmund nodded gladly before turning to Elanore.

"Elanore," he asked. "Can we use your ship?"

The sea captain looked surprised but she barely even hesitated.

"Yes! Of course!" she cried. "The Karenza's yours for as long as you need her!" and she gave a grin. "With me too of course!"

Edmund couldn't help but grin back. He wasn't sure whether he'd ever be able to stop smiling. Not right now. The impossible dream was coming true. Right before his very eyes…

Though no one had asked her, it was then that Eldora spoke up.

"I feel that my task here is not yet accomplished," she said sedately. "So I too, will remain with you…"

And hearing her speak so softly, his beam faded for a second as Edmund looked at her. Before, the dark Lectur had seemed cold and intimidating. Even in the light of what had happened, she still *did*, but much as a part of him for some reason he couldn't fathom, didn't want her there any longer than necessary, he also knew that he owed it to her to obey her wishes and more…

Finally, the Explorer then turned to Fred.

"Fred? Are you with me?"

The warrior stood up slowly from the crate he had been sitting on for the last ten minutes of their discussion. But unlike the others, as Edmund met his friend's eye, he could see the uncertainty even before he spoke. And as Fred sheathed his sword, the blade that he'd been sharpening meticulously throughout, the fateful words then came.

"I *must* continue as planned. I must return to the West," he said, before seeing Edmund's face fall; "I am sorry. I have fought with you and I would yet die for you, but it has been long in the coming. I have thought the matter through much over the past days and it is time that I sought Soph and although I will perhaps not yet return to Mawreath, I must tell Kell news of Crag…"

"But what about the elements? Surely you owe your allegiance to them?!" It was Thom who had spoken, had snapped where no one else dared say a word, but before it could escalate, Edmund himself soon stepped in.

"Thom," he warned the dwarf. "It's fine. Everyone has the choice to make their own destiny." He glanced at Eliom, the wizard's words of wisdom echoing in his head. "If Fred's choice is to head west then who are we to stop him?"

The dwarf scoffed.

"I *choose* to help the elements," he retorted. "My *own* fate can wait. We owe them that much at least."

Edmund shifted uncomfortably. He knew that Thom was only trying to help but much as he wanted the warrior with them, he knew that they couldn't push the issue…

"Thom we can't-" but before he had a chance to finish, Fred had cut in.

"No Edmund," he said. "It needs to be said." And suddenly, just like that, his whole demeanour changed from doubt to complete surety. Thom's words had obviously struck deep. "Thom is right. I have a duty here. I was bound to the elements and to this task I am still bound." And as if to make it clear he then looked at each of the group in turn. "I will seek Soph and Kell once the elements are safe again."

Surprised but secretly glad, Edmund didn't argue as his friend met his eye. Instead, he sighed as if with that one breath all cares, all worries and sorrows of the past had fled.

"So it's settled then?"

This time it was his turn to look around and to his delight, in every face he saw nothing but determination.

No one needed to say it. He knew it now.

They were in this together, just as they had been from day one and just as they would be until the end. And feeling suddenly elated, he found himself smiling all over again.

SECRETS

The darkness tormented her but no matter how much she cried out, how much she screamed, howled to be free, it held her trapped.

Let me wake! She would shout, again and again, without a sound. But no one, nothing ever seemed to respond. No one could see the tears that were not there, hear the wails that never sounded in the blackness, feel the crush of her hand beneath fingers that never moved.

Was she alive? She didn't know. Death seemed to consume her every thought.

Am I alive? Can I live? Will I live again?

And yet she was there. She could think, she could feel. She was aware of the heaviness of her body – her fingers, hands, arms, legs, the still beating of her heart. It was just no matter how much she begged, pleaded, her body just wouldn't obey. It just lay there – yes, she knew she was lying at least, and on a bed too – deathly still, deathly silent with nothing but the darkness…

How long she had lain there, she had no idea. It could have been minutes yet it could also have been days or maybe even months – time was like one long abysmal stretch to her now. One long *nothing*.

Let me wake! Why won't you let me wake?

Am I alive?

She tried shouting all over again.

Let me wake!

She was a prisoner in her mind, entombed in the small black box of her thoughts.

And yet today… or perhaps yesterday, maybe even tomorrow - whatever time she was in – she knew was different. For today she was no longer alone.

The voice was faint, very faint, but it was still there.

"*I must've fallen asleep. When will she wake up?*" it said, clearly speaking to another, not to her, and sure enough, another then replied.

"*I do not know. But you should rest. You are exhausted.*"

"*No.*" The first voice sounded determined. "*I'm staying. Saz needs me.*"

Saz.

That's me, she thought to herself slowly. *That's my name – I am Saz. The voice is talking about me.*

But though she tried to open her mouth, to declare this fact out loud, nothing happened.

Let me wake!

Why won't you let me wake?

Everything in her ached to move, to open her eyes and *be* and yet there was something holding her back. The blackness...

Am I alive?

The voices were still speaking.

"Another hour or so of sleep will not make a difference. How about I promise to wake you if she stirs?"

There was a doubtful pause.

"But what about you?"

"Me? I have rested enough. And besides, I *am not the one who needs it!*"

"...*All right,*" the first voice seemed to give in very reluctantly. *"But the second that she moves, mind you, you come and get me!"*

"Yes, of course. I will stay here."

And then, suddenly, Saz found herself beginning to grow aware of *other* noises, sounds she hadn't noticed before; like footsteps and the gentle swish of material as someone moved away; and breathing, the slow quiet sound of life.

It was her own and with it, she suddenly became very aware of other things. Like how her fingertips tingled, the backs of her calves ached and her eyes... she could feel her eyelids.

Let me wake!

They quivered. Slowly she was gaining control.

Let me wake!

Her lips twitched. They were dry. So very dry.

She felt hot, damp, stiff...

Let me wake!

And finally, her eyelashes began to part.

Light, bright and beautiful cracked through the blackness. It was dazzling white, pure white and it *hurt.* But then, as her eyes began to adjust, she saw something else. A crack. The white was cracked and - she squinted a little - *dirty.*

I am in a room, her brain told her. *And the ceiling is white.*

And blinking - for she could do that now, open and shut, open and shut- everything then came to sharp focus and thrilled at her sudden control as she felt the creeping sensation of muscles in her neck, Saz hurried to move. Flinching as her stiff body throbbed – just how long *had* she been lying there? - she peered down at herself from the corners of her eyes.

Just as she'd thought, she was lying on a bed. It was plain, barely more than a mattress… and beyond… beyond was a room, white and just as plain with no other furniture save a high-backed chair propped in the corner. The chair, she saw, was empty but for a cloth folded on the seat.

There was nothing else that she could see, and no other sound but that of her breathing.

Whoever the voices belonged to then, had clearly gone.

Or so she thought…

"Meggie!" a man suddenly cried. He was the second of the voices she had heard in her stupor, only this time he spoke so much *louder* and jerking her head to the side, Saz then realised that she wasn't alone. The stranger had been standing above her the whole time, just out of eyeshot and as he saw her move, he soon stepped into view.

He was tall, very tall, with a strong frame and a stern face, but before she could process any more, there was a rush of frantic footsteps, a swish of material and a woman appeared.

The woman's face was tired, anxious, but it was smiling, and grabbing Saz's hand – Saz gave a start as she felt it – she let out a sharp breath as if she'd been holding it in for a long time.

"Saz!" she said, in a voice Saz instantly recognised. "Saz, are you all right?"

She was studying Saz's face, as if waiting for something, searching for some kind of reaction, her weary green eyes large with worry and having a feeling she knew what it was the woman wanted and eager not to disappoint, Saz's dry lips then pulled themselves into a weak smile.

"Meggie," she managed to whisper. "Meggie. What happened?"

Hearing and clearly understanding her words, for a moment it looked as if the woman now known as Meggie was going to cry, but instead she simply gave a sniff and glanced at the man behind her, before turning back to Saz with a look of complete relief.

"You remember me?" she murmured, her voice choked.

Saz closed her eyes again, baffled by this whole new thing called life.

"Of course I do. Why wouldn't I?" she mumbled and Meggie gave a laugh.

"Well *exactly*," was all she said as if the whole episode were one big joke. "Why *wouldn't* you?"

Saz was aware of everything now, from the tip of her nose all the way down to her toes.

She was thirsty, she realised and, she twitched a hand, trying but failing to reach for the uncomfortable clumpy mass on top of her head, she was *filthy*, clammy as if her whole body was encased in some kind of warm wet film.

But though her mind instantly began to search, to piece herself back together, she realised that she had no idea where she was or how she had come to be there in the first place.

Not *really*.

She remembered another white room, that much she was sure. But it had been different to this one; cleaner, brighter and larger, *so* much larger - *ginormous* even.

And it had been hot, burning hot with fire. With the flames, the giant orb of flames beneath a platform...

Even now she could feel the heat of that inferno, the slippery dampness of her hands on the ladder as she had climbed towards-

And then, suddenly, Saz's whole body seemed to freeze in shock.

"The orb!" she cried breathlessly. "Meggie! The flames!" And her eyes grew almost to the size of plates as fresh sweat broke out on her forehead. "We – we!" she couldn't even say it. "Are we dead?! What happened!?"

Meggie remained calm but her grip on Saz's hand grew suddenly firmer and as she spoke, her other hand moved to Saz's shoulder, as if to keep her pinned to the bed.

"Don't try and move," she commanded quietly. "It's all right. Just stay there."

"But-" Saz tried to speak again but as she did so, she became aware of movement and turning to her side she noticed the re-arrival of the tall man she never noticed had left, through a doorway to her right. He was followed by another, who, the moment he looked at Saz, then turned his shaggy dark head back to the first.

"You are right. She is awake," was all he said and confused, Saz opened her mouth, ready to demand to know just who these strangers were. Seeing the way Meggie turned to look up at the first man though, her whole manner one of complete trust, she soon closed it.

Whether she knew the men or not didn't really matter right then. What mattered was that she was back. The darkness was gone and she was ready to move.

She was alive. Or at least she *felt* alive and suddenly desperate to be free, to use her limbs again, she began to push herself up against the mattress, struggling to a sit.

Meggie tried to protest, but Saz wasn't having it. Gently she pushed her companion's hand aside.

Once she was up and her head had stopped spinning Saz then levelled all three of them with a sharp gaze.

"So," she commanded. "Is someone going to tell me what's going on?"

Saz chewed slowly on the hunk of bread, her eyes glazed as she tried to digest everything she had just heard.

"I know." Meggie all the while looked *guilty*, as if the whole sorry affair was somehow her fault. "It's all a bit... hard to take in."

Hard to take it?
No kidding.

And Saz took another numb bite of her food. She was starving. Even if she *was* in another, alien world – or so Meggie had told her - and she didn't know why, she still needed to eat.

Blinking away her thoughts for now though, she tried to look unconcerned.

"When are we heading for this 'City' then?" she replied eventually and her companion gave yet another small shrug.

The women were still in Saz's room where they had been for some time now, Nickolas and Dromeda leaving a while before to let the pair talk alone. There was no doubt that Saz was stronger and much her old self now that she'd had the opportunity to eat and drink something; nevertheless, however much she tried to enjoy it, the bread and water Meggie had given her were somehow not quite *right*; not quite the way she remembered them to be. There was something remarkably tasteless about them, and the *air*… in fact, the whole place, the whole '*world*', as Meggie had called it – Saz still couldn't quite get her head around that – seemed somehow tasteless and… *wrong*.

"Tell me then," Saz screwed up her eyes. "Is it me or is everything kind of… *red?*"

Meggie glanced around her, mimicking Saz's face as she too tried to concentrate on the reddish glow enveloping them both.

"No, it's not just you," she replied. "But I have no idea *why* it's like this and Nickolas won't tell me. In fact," she frowned a little, "Nickolas won't tell me much of *anything* at all. I get the feeling he's not *allowed* to."

Saz gulped down her last mouthful a little too quickly.

"Not allowed to? Why? Who does he have to *ask?*" she coughed.

Meggie, also finishing her meal, wiped the back of a hand across her mouth.

"No idea. But," and her voice dropped almost to a whisper, "there's definitely something wrong with this place. It's all very strange!"

Saz knew she couldn't agree more. But then, the more she thought about it, about what had happened, about being there, however unfamiliar, *alive*, the more an idea began to form, the nudge of something that brought with it the tiniest thread of hope…

"Hold on," she began slowly, waiting for her thoughts to take shape, "so if you say we're not *dead,* simply in a different world," she scoffed at herself "– if I can say *simply* - then surely Eliom and Edmund might be able find us…"

Meggie's eyebrows rose and Saz found herself a little surprised that her fellow element hadn't considered this possibility before. The answer seemed obvious to her.

"Perhaps," Meggie mused. "Though how on Tungala they'll be able to, when up until a few days ago I don't think any of us thought other worlds were possible…"

Saz's face was resolute.

"If anyone can find us, Eliom can. I trust him," she said automatically. But whilst for her it was enough, this only seemed to make Meggie annoyed.

"Yes, but, it's not just a matter of *trust*, Saz," the little woman almost snapped. "Eliom might be a wizard but however powerful he is," she spread her hands wide, "we're in *another world*! I mean, we don't even know where we are! Eliom probably thinks we're dead. And why not?" She gave a sigh. "I would too if I was him."

The idea sent a dribble of something like fear shuddering through Saz but before she could even think of a response, there was then a small cough at the door. It was tiny, more like an "ahem", but instantly on the alert, the women both swivelled to find, to their surprise, two strangers standing in the doorway; a slender lady with a timid face and with her, a beefy no-nonsense-looking man, his arms crossed.

Clearly the one who had coughed, the woman, wasting no time at all, then took a step over the threshold looking straight at Meggie. She seemed a little nervous, almost like being there was the last thing she wanted, although neither companion knew why until;

"Meggie," she then said. Her voice trembled slightly. "It's time to leave."

Leave?

The word made both women sit up and pay attention as Meggie glanced at Saz before turning back to the two figures. The man was eyeing her oddly and for some strange reason, she didn't yet understand, something deep inside told her that these two people weren't in fact *human*.

She cleared her own throat.

"Leave?" she challenged. "Why? I'm fine here."

Whether it was what she had said or the tone she had used to say it, the man, who Meggie realised, was obviously there for such a moment as this, then took his own thundering step forward, his expression quickly changing to a scowl. He didn't uncross his arms.

"You *will* come with us," he said. "Now."

And Meggie, small as she was in comparison, squared her shoulders a little.

What was this? Who were these people?

"I will *not*," she argued, her little fists clenching. "I don't even know you!"

What she had hoped to gain by refusing though, she wasn't sure, for the man only scowled all the more.

"It is *forbidden* for you and the other to remain together," he snapped.

There was that word again. *Forbidden. Not allowed,* and both Meggie and Saz gaped, the smaller of the two's face reddening with anger.

"Forbidden?" she dared fiercely. "Why? I told you! I'm fine here! I don't want to go!" And then, suddenly realising; "Where's Nickolas?"

But at her companion's name, the man only shuffled closer. The whole place seemed to shake with his every step.

"You have no choice. You can either come with us willingly or by *force*," he replied and his voice was so aggressive that Saz instinctively reached out to grab Meggie by the arm, not as if afraid for herself, but for what her friend might do next.

"It's all right." And sure enough, giving Saz a look braver than she felt, Meggie soon laid Saz's hand aside and getting to her feet, she stood before the man, her own arms now clenched across her chest. The intruder was at least twice her size with biceps as thick as her neck. A nasty vein was pulsing on the side of his red forehead.

This was going to be harder than she thought...

"Well my *choice* is to stay here!" the little woman then exclaimed boldly. "I don't care if it's *forbidden* or not!"

Even thinking about it later, Meggie still had no idea what she'd expected to accomplish by standing up to the man; whether she'd ever really thought that by defying him, he would change his mind and let her stay. What she *did* know, however, was that she *should* have expected what then happened next; both women should and somehow had and yet still it came as a shock, as suddenly, without so much as another word of warning, the man then lunged forward and before she could even flinch, his crushing fingers were seizing Meggie's wrist, almost wrenching her from the ground.

Instantly, Saz gave a cry and scrambled forward, trying to regain any part of Meggie that she could, trying to pull her back, but it was too late. The man had her and tears sprung to Meggie's eyes as a howl of pain erupted from her chest.

"Help!" she cried out desperately. "Saz! Nickolas! Nickolas!"

Where was he anyway? Why wasn't he there to help her?

She could feel Saz by her side, readying herself to fight. But her friend had been weakened by what had happened to her and whatever use she might have been at full strength, she was none now, as the man simply pushed her aside and she fell to the floor, gasping for air from a shove to the gullet.

"Get off me!" Meggie screamed, writhing in the great man's grasp. She could feel the bones grinding in her wrist, her whole arm on fire with the pain...

And then, just like that, she felt a shudder and the pressure was suddenly released and Meggie, free, fell to the ground.

Above her head there was a commotion and thudding onto her side with a gasp, her arm throbbing, the little woman only just looked up in time to watch as a cluster of figures then appeared, writhing in a mass of bodies. One was the beefy man's, the other two... to her relief and equal dread, Meggie recognised as Dromeda and Nickolas.

All three were tangled in a brutal fight. Dromeda had a hold on the man's neck and was squeezing it, his large knuckles white with anger whilst Nickolas, trying to dodge the man's flailing limbs, was hitting out at him every chance he could. The man's companion, the slender woman, had already fled in fright.

Saz and Meggie, both still on the ground, watched in horror as Nickolas finally managed to gain a hold and without warning, smashed his fist into the man's chest.

An audible crack split the room. For a horrific second, Meggie wasn't sure whether it was Nickolas's fist or the man's rib cage that had made the sound, but then her doubts were answered as the beefy-man let out a yell and also fell, Dromeda on top of him, his grip still tight.

Nickolas, meanwhile, straightening up, wiped at a small wound at the side of his mouth, before glancing once at Meggie as if to make sure she was all right, he then turned back to his still-fighting companion.

"Dromeda!" he warned, his eyes flashing, his breath short. "Leave him! Leave him now!"

But Dromeda's own face was wild with nameless rage as he continued to squeeze the man's neck, the man, whose face was red and quivering, his mouth and eyes gaping open, desperate to draw breath...

"One... less... Digger!" Dromeda panted. His whole body was shaking now, shuddering under the force of pinning his victim down.

"*Leave him!*" Nickolas bellowed. He sounded angry and yet he made no move to stop his friend.

No one could mistake the conflict in his face, but appalled by the sight before them, both Meggie and Saz let out a cry. Despite what he'd tried to do, neither of them were ready to see the man *die*...

"Stop him!" Meggie half screamed, appealing to Nickolas. "Please!" and as if he'd been waiting for her word all along, Nickolas then finally seemed to react. Quick as a flash he leapt at Dromeda, and pulling his friend's arms apart with vicious force, he bowled him to the floor, pinning him down with both hands.

"I *said*, that's enough!" he exclaimed.

His voice, although still loud, had lost its edge but luckily, the moment Dromeda's fingers lost contact on the beefy man's neck, his whole body then seemed to relax.

In that tiny second, whatever had caused his blood-lust was gone and waiting a moment to catch his breath, he soon nodded to be released and just like that, it was over as Nickolas immediately clambered off him, turning to offer his friend a hand as he got to his feet.

Once both men were up, sweating and gasping, they then turned to the women.

"Are you all right?" Nickolas asked Meggie straight away, indicating her wrist and for a second Meggie just blinked at him, the rush of the fight and the sight of Dromeda's rage having erased all memory of what had happened only seconds before. Looking down she then saw the red handprint already turning to yellow on her skin. She could feel the dull ache there, like a painful memory.

The wrist was only bruised. She'd live…

Dromeda meanwhile, looked to the now-unconscious body lying at their feet with a scowl.

"Nickolas, we must leave for the City. Now!" he demanded. "We are not safe here."

Nickolas turned to him, his expression concerned.

Before he could make a decision though, another figure then appeared in the doorway.

It was the slender woman back again, and she had brought someone else with her, another woman. Surveying the room with a quick glance, both gave an audible gasp when they saw the body of their comrade on the floor. One even gave a little shriek. But then horror was replaced by anger.

"The Builder will know of this- this *treachery*, human!" the first woman spluttered. "You will be *punished!*"

Though neither of them knew what she was talking about, the way the woman spoke made Meggie and Saz both give a start of fear. To their surprise though, rounding on the strangers both, Dromeda's scowl became a sneer.

"He cannot *touch* us Digger-rat! He *needs* us! There is *nothing* you can do!"

The two women visibly bristled and Nickolas shot Dromeda a warning glance. But his friend either didn't notice, or chose to ignore it.

"He may not *kill* you, human!" the other woman then spat in defiance. Her face was red with pent-up rage. "But he *can* make your lives a misery! He is God!"

Dromeda clenched his fists. But enough was enough and detecting another fight, Nickolas grabbed his arm.

"No," he muttered. He sounded surprisingly calm. "Dromeda."

"We must leave," Dromeda repeated at a hiss and then, inclining his head towards Nickolas, away from the women's probing eyes; "We cannot head for the City now. That much is clear. But wherever we go, we must do it *at once!*"

"Why can't we head to the City?"

Meggie, who had stood mute throughout the exchange, leaned in too then, her voice a tiny whisper. She never took her eyes off the two women who seemed too, to be huddled towards each other, speaking in hushed tones, clearly trying to decide what to do. There was no way they could hope to fight two men and two women on their own, that much was obvious. But how they intended to go from there, to inform the Builder – whoever that was, or if that was indeed their plan – no one knew.

Nickolas and Dromeda flinched as if they'd momentarily forgotten about the presence of the other two.

"Too dangerous," Dromeda replied shortly. "We will only be under further scrutiny there. And if *they*," he flicked his head in the women's direction, "intend to inform of our *troubles*..."

"To this... Builder person?" Meggie intoned.

Dromeda nodded.

Nickolas all the while seemed deep in thought, his mouth set in one stern line.

"We have nowhere else to go, Dromeda. We *must* head to the inner City. Despite the Builder, we will be more protected within its walls. There are fewer Diggers there, so perhaps word will not spread; we will be able to blend in-"

"What are you planning?!"

It was one of the women. The pair had obviously made their decision – whatever that may be – and the four companions turned to them again. Even though these women were spitting and snarling at them, still red-faced in anger, all four humans could tell that they were actually afraid of them, of what they could do. Their worried glances at the unconscious man on the floor gave them away.

Fighting then, was not an option. If the group tried to leave, the two women wouldn't be able to stop them and with this in mind, Meggie soon touched Nickolas on the hand.

"Can we go?" she asked pleadingly. "I don't care where."

Nickolas gave her a fleeting look as if to somehow read her thoughts but then, he gave a nod.

"Let us stay on course," he muttered. "The City it is."

The decision felt final and leaping into action, Meggie then grabbed an anxious Saz by the arm, dragging her forwards as they headed for the door the two men following, knocking the two angry women aside on the way. Neither gave any resistance.

"You will pay for this!" one of the women shouted instead, as she stumbled. But it was too late; the small group of companions had already disappeared up the white stone corridor and out into the morning light.

—

The wind at her back, the Karenza was charging south eastward, as aboard her deck, Edmund of Tonasse sat on a crate, watching the beckoning horizon draw ever closer.

Already he thought he could make out land ahead, but he knew that it wasn't the land they had left behind. It was flatter than the Gulf of Gorgan, but not only that, it *felt* different somehow too. More *hopeful*.

Then again, maybe it was just the mood he was in.

Edmund smiled to himself. He hadn't felt so cheerful in weeks. And honestly, he just didn't know how to deal with it. The knowledge that the elements were alive, that *Bethan* was alive, had rejuvenated him. He felt like a new man; like a carefree man, the man of his youth before he had known what it was to worry, to feel such sorrow, to know such pain...

The Explorer blinked.

Renard...

There was still and would always be-

"So where are we off to then?"

And Edmund turned to find Elanore standing beside him, her bright hair whipping in the wind as she too pondered the horizon. In her hand she held a roll of parchment, wrinkled and sea-worn; the Karenza's map.

Edmund glanced back to the wisp of land ahead.

"We're headed to the Far Eastern Realms again, but this time, just beyond the border, further south and inland."

"Ah yes."

The sea captain took a seat beside the Explorer and throwing the map to the ground, began to roll it out, securing one end with a candlestick, the other with her boot. The map was old and fading but still legible, showing a spread of land from as far as the western territories and the Cliffs of Namer, all the way to the Far Eastern borders and the seas beyond.

Edmund merely watched as Elanore then perused over the chart for a few moments, making her silent calculations and decisions based on experience and not for the first time, the Explorer thanked the gods above that they had happened upon such a woman.

"Well," she then said after a time, "the best way, I would say, is up the Great Madid River, but *only* if the wind keeps in our favour – otherwise there's not enough of us to row." She frowned in thought. "Other than that, we *could* go around and approach the land from further east, by the seaward route..." and she drew a path on the map with her finger.

"How long would that take?" Edmund asked.

"From the sea?" The sea captain pursed her lips together with a *tsk*. "We're probably looking at a week? Maybe two?"

Edmund was stunned.

"Two weeks?!" he exclaimed. Despite himself, he couldn't help but sound disappointed. Now that he knew there was a chance, however big or small to reclaim what was lost, he was desperate to take it...

"Yes," Elanore pointed out. "*But*, if we take the river, and if the wind turns *north* when we do so, then it would take us maybe... five days?"

Five days?
Edmund frowned.
Still a longer time than he would have liked but…
"It would be shorter…" he mused fairly.

Elanore gestured to the river on her map and traced it up towards the town of Ophelius. Named after its famous prophet, this was where the tomb lay.

"If we head up here, we'll pass several towns and villages along the way. I'm not sure how many are human and many might not be friendly… but most of them are close together, so we might not need to make port… I'm not sure, as I haven't travelled that way before. My experiences are all further south."

She glanced at Edmund then. "*You've* been there before. You're the one who excavated Ophelius's tomb in the first place. How did *you* get there?"

But straight away, Edmund pointed towards the mass of land further east.

"I came by land. I sailed beyond and then trekked across the mountains," he said shortly before tracing the shape of the river with his own hand. As he went, he read the names of the other towns and villages along the blue line of the parchment; Merchant's Wreath, Yawton Corner, Basherby… Some he recognised, whilst others…

"We'll take the river," he then said decisively.

"All right," Elanore nodded and, the conversation now over, the sea captain got back to her feet, gathering the old map up in her arms as she did so.

"Let's hope this wind keeps to our advantage then," she said. "Or it'll be an uphill struggle."

But Edmund smiled loosely.

"I shouldn't worry about that with Eliom around," he said. "He'll know what to do."

"He usually does."

The cold voice rang out across the still deck, startling them and both then turned to find Eldora striding towards them. Her long dark cloak was wrapped all the way to her eyes, almost as if the sun above chilled her and seeing her approach, Elanore couldn't hide her scowl.

It was no secret that the sea captain, in fact, that the rest of the crew entirely, were still unnerved by the Lectur's presence. Much as she had been willing to assist Edmund, and aware as they all were that without her, none of them would have known of the elements' true fate, there was still something *odd* about their guest, something cold and *otherworldly* that each of them knew in their heart of hearts, they would *never* be comfortable with.

So it was that before Eldora was so much as a few feet away, Elanore had then turned to Edmund.

"I'll leave you to it," she whispered and with a stiff nod to the approaching figure, she hurried her way towards the cabins leaving Edmund and the strange Lectur quite alone.

The Explorer, meanwhile, watched Eldora's approach, his expression unmoved.

After Eliom's revelation of Eldora's sad ancestry and the strange passion she held for him, Edmund knew he couldn't *completely* dislike their new guest. By pretending that only the Lectur could interpret his dream, Edmund was beginning to suspect that Eliom's plan – yes, *plan*, for when else had the powerful wizard not at least *tried* to understand a vision? - to somehow make the Explorer trust perhaps even *like* Eldora, had in a small way worked. And yet though he no longer truly feared her, at the same time, in its place wasn't *friendship* but a strange sort of wary pity. The Lectur's beady eyes were deep and mysterious and her voice always chilly. And though she marched towards him with such purpose as if, again, she had Seen herself to be there, alone at his side; for a moment all Edmund wanted to do was turn around and walk away.

It was too late though, for without waiting to be invited, Eldora was there, sliding down next to him on the crate, her white face close to his.

"We are to take the river?"

Only the slight rise in the Lectur's voice indicated that it was a question. She didn't even bother to hide that she'd obviously been eavesdropping.

Either that or she has Seen the road ahead…

Edmund, resigning himself there and then to the fact that he couldn't escape, nodded.

"Good," Eldora mused and then, coming straight out with it; "I feel that perhaps my time shall arrive during that voyage."

"Time?" Edmund couldn't help but look surprised. "Do you mean this… *task* you feel you've yet to accomplish?"

His voice gave away perhaps more than he'd wanted to and Eldora turned her black eyes on him scathingly.

"I can see that you doubt me," she muttered. "This does not shock me. You *are* human after all."

Ignoring the jibe though, Edmund lowered his gaze, turning his focus suddenly to his hands.

"I don't doubt you," he said pointedly. "I think I'm probably past that now…" and as he looked at her again, he saw something of a painful glimmer in her dark eyes, which only confirmed what he was thinking.

Eliom.

So it was true then. The wizard *had* lied to him. He'd been able to interpret Edmund's dream after all. But he'd wanted Eldora to do it, to take the lead and Edmund, for one, whilst he had his suspicions, really had no idea *why*.

The thought unsettled him.

"I just…" he turned to his fingers again, "I doubt the *reason* for why you're here. Why you're doing this 'task' you're supposedly here to do. We should all have the freedom to lead our own lives. You shouldn't do something simply because you Saw it happen and believe it to be set out for you…"

Suddenly Eldora gave such a careless laugh, that Edmund gave a start.

"You do not believe that yourself for a single moment!" she taunted. "You *hope* it to be true! You believe in destiny just as much as I, although you try to deny it. You sound just like Eliom, trying to convince yourself that you can *change* things."

Edmund reddened a little.

"No, I've just learnt from the mistake of following what you believe is *meant to be*. Or trying to fight *against* it…" he said, forcing himself to sound calm.

Eldora stared at him, a knowing look in those cold eyes.

"You speak of the quest to release the orb," she said wisely. "It was foreseen by Eliom that you would venture on such a journey. But even if he had not Seen that you must go, you probably would have undertaken it anyway…"

Something in the way she spoke, in the way she *knew* things that she shouldn't, angered Edmund Somehow this woman, this *being*, seemed to tangle him up inside.

"I wouldn't!" he retorted. "If I'd known that all of this… this *suffering* was going to occur because of it! I would never-"

But Eldora only laughed more, an icy, callous laugh. And then, holding up a white cool hand; "Be calm, Edmund. It is too late now. What is done is done. And anyway," she lowered her gaze as if to entice him closer, "are you not *defying* destiny by going to bring the elements back?"

Edmund didn't reply. But already the moment was gone and as if she'd suddenly grown bored of his company, the Lectur then turned entirely away from him, her piercing gaze scrutinising the rest of the deck.

"Although, one has to wonder how you know that what you are doing *now* was not predestined also…" she mused, clearly not finished with the subject just yet. "That is the strange thing about fate. How do you know that you are not still trapped in your own destiny? Just as you were at Ratacopeck?"

Edmund didn't need to ask how she *knew* any of this but straight away he realised that the Lectur's words were getting to him, making him feel uncomfortable all over again.

What if she was right? Could all that had taken place up to this point, this rescue, all be fate? Could he really be in control or was this all some sort of cruel trick?

What if he was never *meant* to get the elements back?…

If she knew anything of her companion's conflicting emotions Eldora didn't show it. Instead, she was then turning back to him, a new gleam in her eyes, as if ready for the next challenge.

"Even so. Whatever the outcome is… we will never know. We can only ever speculate," she concluded.

"Whatever the outcome?" Edmund shifted about to face the Lectur properly. "We *will* succeed." The statement was a lot like a question, as if a part of him hoped that Eldora with her power to See would confirm it, reaffirm the hope he had learnt to cherish since the night before.

But Eldora only laughed again.

"I am sure you will," she replied vaguely. "I am sure you will."

There was something in her expression that even in that tiny moment changed then, a new pain in her hidden face. Something was troubling her, Edmund could tell. She seemed too apathetic to argue with him now, and again he found himself wanting nothing more than to leave, to make his excuses and get as far away as the ship would bodily allow him to. But though he knew that was what he wanted, he also knew that he *wouldn't*.

He had a feeling, however small, that the Lectur had deliberately sought him out, had perhaps Seen herself there with him, that she had some kind of purpose in mind and uncomfortable as he was, he knew he wouldn't be able to leave until he had discovered just what that might be…

"You are lucky," she then said out of the blue and there was such sadness, such angst in those three words that Edmund couldn't help but be surprised, reminded as he was that Eldora had feelings. Despite her cold, callous appearance, the Lectur wasn't emotionless…

The Explorer didn't answer. Something told him he didn't have to.

"You love the woman. I have Seen it. I have Seen *her*. You care for her and she in return cares for you; something I once wished and find myself, despite my disgust, *wishing*, I had."

This admittance of her knowledge, of her deep feelings was so unexpected that for a second, all Edmund could do was stare at her. Having gone from knowing nothing of Eliom's past with this woman a few days ago to learning of her love for him, all the way to the Lectur's sudden admittance, he was finding it all rather difficult to take in.

"Eliom *can't* love," he replied carefully after a time. "Not like that."

But Eldora sighed, her breath slow and tired.

"But that is a lie. I *know* he can love. I have seen it. *Not* as a Lectur," she added bitterly, watching Edmund's astonished face, "but as a human – that frailer part of myself," her eyes glazed for a moment. "I *know* he can love. He just *chooses* not to… A weakness on my part, for if *I* were given the choice-"

"Eliom can't love you the way you want him to," Edmund repeated firmly, before Eldora could go any further.

The Lectur's eyes flashed like hot coals. Suddenly she then glared at him, really glared, the power of those black black eyes like a shove to his chest and unable to bear the force of it, Edmund found himself moving away from her on the crate, tearing his own gaze to the deck.

"He can care for *you*! He can care for this woman, *Saz*! And yet he cannot care for me? Someone who once offered him love freely?" Eldora bellowed, her voice carrying out across the water. Somehow her cloak had fallen from her face now to reveal her cold raging lips.

Saz? The explorer's brow crumpled in confusion. What did *Saz* have to do with it? The Lectur was paranoid...

"He cares for you!" he instead retorted aloud. "Why else would he have used his powers against *me*, someone who you claim he loves, to protect you? He hurt me!"

It was a slight overstatement, the wizard had hurt the Explorer's *pride* more than anything but this suddenly seemed to silence her and her lips pursed, Eldora then drew back, her cold glare fading.

Edmund realised that he was holding his breath and releasing it slowly, he ventured to turn back to her, to watch as her expression changed from complete rage to sorrow in one slow instant.

To his utter surprise, the Lectur then let out a low sob and closing her eyes in sorrow, her head fell to her chest as tears began to well at her eyelashes.

She really was pitiful, a being in torment, in pain, and not knowing what else to do, Edmund found himself drawn towards her on the crate. Reaching a hand out, he almost touched her, but something stopped him and instead he balled his fingers to a fist, letting his palm fall back to his knees.

"Listen," he murmured. "There may yet be someone else. You might find someone who can love you the way you want..."

But though he had only been trying to help, almost the second the words left his mouth, he knew they had been stupid ones. Eldora's love, her *infatuation* for Eliom had burned for years, he could fully see that now. In secret she had yearned for him, for however many long decades, perhaps even *centuries* – Edmund's head span.

Who was he, a mere tiny human to tell her to move on and find another?

And just as he'd suspected, Eldora gave a derisive snort and opened her eyes.

"I thought that *you*, of all people would understand," she said. Her voice was beyond chilly now, her tears gone. "You claim to be in love yourself. But perhaps you are not. You cannot know what love truly is if you expect me just to give up." She gave a derisive sniff. "I was told that you are wise for a human but clearly they were mistaken..."

Taken aback, Edmund bristled.

"What other choice do you have but to give up?" he demanded in his own defence. "Eliom isn't like others. He won't somehow *come around*. You've waited this long, you continue to wait, for what?"

Eldora's lips trembled with indignation.

"Did *you* give up?" she retorted. "Even when you believed your lover to be *dead*, did you give up on her?"

Edmund said nothing. Clearly the Lectur's own feelings repulsed her. He could see it in the way she spoke, the way her face moved; it seemed to leak from every pore. She hated Eliom deeply for his rejection and yet she couldn't help but continue to long for him. She was stuck in a state of self-loathing, a kind of mourning not much different than he had been in only a day or so before, trying to convince himself that he needed to move on, that Bethan was dead...

The Explorer took another deep breath to calm himself. Was this why Eldora had come to him? Had she just needed someone to set her straight? Someone to tell her to hold on or to give up? A *friend*?

Is that why Eliom wants me to trust and like her?

Because he could offer what the wizard couldn't? He could *feel*?

Suddenly overwhelmed by another great urge to leave, Edmund then found himself on his feet.

"Excuse me," he mumbled and made to move away. But it was too late.

All of a sudden, he felt the vice-like grip on his arm and before he could react, he was being jerked back towards the crate and Eldora, her cold fingers digging into his flesh.

She was strong, crazily, *amazingly* strong for as he struggled to right himself, to get away, she was then leaning towards him, her body pressing him close. And then, before he knew it, her lips were on his and she was kissing him urgently, passionately, painfully...

Stunned for a moment, Edmund just let it all happen. He let her arms entwine in his, let her soft – yes *soft* – warm skin brush against his own, her mouth surprisingly sweet and inviting... But then everything came flooding back and like her very touch was hot iron, he suddenly wrenched himself away, springing back to his feet, his face flushed with embarrassment, anger, *guilt*...

"Wh–what are you *doing*?" he spluttered breathlessly and in a moment of confusion, he drew his sword, pointing it straight at the Lectur's throat. "What were you-?" and he wiped his mouth with the back of a hand, his eyes suddenly wide with understanding. "Did you *plan* this? Did you *See* this? Is *this* why you came?"

But much as he'd half-expected Eldora to laugh again, to mock him with her cruel smile, she merely stared at him for a moment, sorrow all too evident on her face.

THE ENTITY OF SOULS

"I only wished to know what it is to be loved..." she muttered mournfully. "That is all."

Edmund was shaking now, quivering with a flurry of angry, baffled emotions. The hand that held his sword trembled as his breath still came in gasps.

"Well!" he snapped, taken off-guard by her reply and, not knowing what else to do, he sheathed his sword again. "You can't ask it of me!" And with that, not waiting for another word, the Explorer then turned and at long last fled across the deck as fast as his legs could carry him.

—

"Eliom, Edmund said I should speak to you about the wind? We'll be heading further north-east very soon," Elanore told the wizard with a sheepish smile, as the pair sat inside the male cabin, Eliom on his own bunk and her in the bunk opposite.

Eliom nodded politely.

"Of course, if I can assist in any way..."

And Elanore's smile widened. She'd had no doubt that the wizard would say yes, but she knew she'd had to ask.

"I will begin immediately. But," and for a moment, Elanore swore that the wizard looked *concerned*, "where is Edmund? Where are the others?" he said, getting to his feet and grasping his staff. It had been lying at his side the last few minutes as he'd sat in a strange meditative state, exploring the magic in the air as Elanore waited patiently for him to wake.

Eliom didn't often meditate. On the road to Ratacopeck he'd not had the time or the inclination, but now that their journey had reached a lull, the wizard had decided to try his relaxing and searching technique once more, building up his mental strength for the times ahead. Unbeknownst to the others, something had disturbed him and he was determined not to let that continue...

"Fred and Thom are in the crow's nest and Edmund's with Eldora, on deck," Elanore replied. None could mistake the bitter turn in her voice at the mention of the Lectur.

"Really?"

Eliom's brow crinkled and he looked concerned all over again. Before the sea captain could say another word, he was then suddenly on his feet and striding towards the cabin door, his white cloak billowing in the small space.

Confused, Elanore watched him leave, on her lips a word of question but before the wizard could even reach for the steps, Edmund had appeared at the trapdoor and without so much as a word, he charged down the ladder into their midst.

The Explorer looked flustered and out of breath, his face red and his hands shaking and alarmed, Elanore too got to her feet.

"Edmund?" Eliom asked. His voice was as calm as it always was but even Elanore could tell he was worried. Seeing Edmund's expression, she found that she was too, but one glance at her and the empty cabin and the Explorer was shaking his head. Whatever the problem was, the sea captain noted, it was clearly something only to be shared between him and his oldest friend.

"We need your help with…" he then started, turning back to Eliom as if remembering himself.

"… the winds, yes," the wizard interjected. "Elanore was just telling me." He was still looking at Edmund uneasily.

"Right, yes." Still Edmund seemed out-of-sorts, but soon realising he was in the way as Eliom glanced towards the deck above, he stepped away from the stairs.

Eliom hesitated and for a moment, Elanore wondered if the reason he'd moved so suddenly to leave her was now standing right there, out of breath. Whether that was the truth of it or not though, seeming to have a change of heart, he then nodded to his friend and grabbing hold of the ladder, ascended in barely a few strides.

Elanore cleared her throat. She wanted to say something, to ask what was wrong, but already Edmund had turned away from her, moving towards his own bunk and not knowing what else she could do, so it was the sea captain then moved towards the ladder herself to follow her companion up onto the deck and set the Karenza's new course.

—

Eliom leaned far over the bow of the ship, his cloak swelling and curling in the growing wind. His eyes were closed, his staff held high, his mouth working furiously as he murmured his chant, the ancient words that would chart the Karenza's course.

Elanore, Fred, Thom, Eldora and now Edmund all stood in a quiet huddle just watching, feeling as the once gentle breeze lifted, sending a rippling current of air blasting across the deck. The sails billowed, straining against their ropes with a loud crack as they caught.

Change.

The word was almost palpable in the air as if the magic itself could speak. But the wind was fighting it.

Change, the wizard demanded. *No*, the wind seemed to reply and for a good few minutes they continued to struggle. All the time the breeze grew to a steady howl and then a roar as nature fought back.

"Hold onto something!" Edmund shouted at one point as the roar turned into a gale and the group were almost thrown from their feet.

But Eliom's will and power were resolute and like the sudden blaze of a candle, he won and the wind changed. Suddenly the windstorm had dropped and then it was howling again, pushing the sails back inside themselves, flapping dangerously. At the same time, everyone stumbled, thrown off-balance as the Karenza shuddered, starting to pick up speed.

Within moments Eliom then lowered his staff and opening his eyes he stepped away from the ship's edge leaving the airstream to ebb to a manageable blast.

"We are on course," was all he said and the others just smiled amongst themselves as the Karenza shot like an arrow towards her goal.

Edmund threw back his head to gulp at the flagon of water as he leaned over Ophelius's map in the flickering light. Many minutes he had been searching, thinking, his whole focus on the way ahead. Or at least *trying* to be...

"It is still bright outside."

And as Eliom stepped out of the shadows Edmund glanced only briefly at his friend before returning to his work. For some reason he couldn't seem to meet the wizard's eye.

"The wind's strong," he replied feebly, taking another mouthful of his drink. "I thought I'd be able to concentrate better down here." Though this was only really part of the truth. In reality, he didn't want to see Eldora again. In a group it was fine, but *alone* after what had just happened...

The Explorer inwardly shuddered. But half to his surprise the wizard seemed satisfied with his weak excuse for the time being, for he didn't argue.

"Searching for something?" he asked instead, gesturing at the parchment in Edmund's hands.

Edmund sighed and turning the map over, stared more closely at the scrawled writing and detailed lines plotting the course to the Temple of Ratacopeck.

"I'm searching for anything that will give us a clue as to what we're supposed to do once we reach Ophelius's tomb," he explained, rubbing the paper gently beneath his fingertips. "Perhaps if this were the original and not just a *copy*..." he trailed off, his thoughts briefly drifting back to Renard.

If his brother hadn't stolen the map and turned against him in the first place...

"I am certain you would not have missed anything, if it were there," Eliom pointed out, taking a seat opposite Edmund and blowing on the lamp softly. The lighted splint inside it, instead of going out, glowed even brighter.

"You'd think so," Edmund mused. "I've scoured every inch of this map, but I can't seem to find anything that even so much as mentions what happens *after* the elements walk into the flames." He gave another sigh. "All we have to go on is what I Saw, what Eldora-" but he paused abruptly, trying to hide his emotions and Eliom held out a hand.

"Perhaps if I were to take a look…" he said.

Edmund tried to shrug.

"Be my guest."

The wizard took the frail-looking parchment in his large hands and stared at it, just as Edmund had, his eyes studying every bit of surface, trying to scour every tiny bit of translated text. After a while he then began to mutter words of the ancient language under his breath, turning the map over in his hands as he did so. But after only a minute, and no change in either Eliom or the parchment, the wizard gave a small sigh and turning once more to Edmund, he handed the map back.

"I detect a certain aura about it… which is unusual considering this is only a *copy*," he said, detecting Edmund's questioning glance. "The original must indeed be powerful for me to sense such a thing here. Ophelius was obviously wise in his knowledge of incantations."

Amazed, the Explorer couldn't help but gawp.

"Are you saying it's magical?!" he asked. "Why would it have some kind of *power*?!"

But Eliom frowned a little.

"I am not certain," he admitted. "My only certainty is that it does."

And not sure how else to take that information, Edmund looked down at the map in his hands as if expecting it to either spontaneously crumble or cast some kind of spell. His fingers shook a little.

He'd had no idea…

"What do you suggest I do?" he asked then. Should he try to find out just what this power was? If he even *could*… What if it was the answer they were looking for? But Eliom only tilted his head to the side as if thinking deeply.

"I am sure it will reveal its secret in time," he replied, ever mysterious, before, looking at his friend directly, his frown then deepened. "Just as you will…"

Edmund lowered his gaze.

So Eliom *knew* that he was keeping something from him. He knew that something was bothering him and had been since he'd first appeared at the cabin entrance after his talk with Eldora.

The Explorer opened his mouth to respond, for a moment wondering if he could really lie and deny that he had any secrets, deny that anything had happened. But he knew there was no point. If Eliom *really* wanted to find out what was disturbing him, he could just read his thoughts. Edmund knew that when the wizard asked questions, tried to show concern, he was only being respectful. One look into another's eye and he could get all the information he ever wanted. One quick delve into his mind…

THE ENTITY OF SOULS

Edmund coughed uncomfortably, suddenly finding the map very interesting indeed.

"I will not *demand* that you tell me what it is that haunts you, Edmund," Eliom then said, his voice soft. "But as always, I may be able to help." And he too seemed to look uncomfortable, if ever he could, as, for a second he looked away. "Was it something you discussed with Eldora? You seemed... *upset* upon your return and you seem pained now when I mention her."

Edmund could see for definite that lying really wasn't an option now. Just as he always seemed to, not as a wizard, but as his oldest friend, Eliom understood him, could read him, with or without magic. The Explorer shifted in his seat.

"Eldora. She-" he started and then paused, thinking rapidly.

What if, despite his assertions, Eliom really *did* feel something for the Lectur? At the time, when even presented with the idea, it had seemed utterly absurd. But then again... just as Edmund had told Eldora herself - the wizard *had* used magic against him, had tried to *hurt* him, however little, just to protect her. He had used magic against his *friend*.

What then, if the wizard truly loved her in return but just hadn't realised it? And if he did, what if hearing about the kiss sent him into some kind of jealous rage? Or worse, cost Edmund their friendship?

But almost as soon as he'd thought about it, reality returned, the firm beliefs and truths he had always known and the Explorer almost laughed.

He *knew* that Eliom didn't love her. He *couldn't* love. It was impossible. Friendship was all the wizard could ever offer, and even that, the human knew, was at a stretch.

Wizards were required to feel nothing, to care for no one. They travelled alone, unaided and unloved. Eliom had made a conscious choice to associate himself with humans, or more specifically, with Edmund – even though until that very day and perhaps for the rest of days, the Explorer had never understood *why*.

But that didn't mean he *was* human.

And anyway, Edmund found himself reasoning. *He would have told me. Wouldn't he?*

Much as he knew that he would never fully understand all there was to know about the wizard - he had come to accept this over the years – and though so much was still hidden beneath that calm exterior, he was almost certain that Eliom would have shared his feelings with him.

If he'd had any.

Not that, really, any of that was relevant right now.

Because she kissed me. His logic kicked in. *She kissed me. She forced me. It wasn't my fault.*

Or was it?

And a cold shiver of something unpleasant wound its way down Edmund's spine.

It couldn't have been him, could it? He couldn't have led her on? He couldn't have made her feel as if he cared for her?

Could he?

And suddenly, the Explorer found himself desperately trying to recall every word he had spoken to her, every moment they had shared in the short time they'd met, looking for any sign…

Could he have said something to make her feel like that? He didn't think so. And she had known he loved another. *She* was the one who had brought up the matter of Bethan…

Bethan. The name somehow made him feel guilty right then…

"Eldora," he then ventured aloud again after what felt like an age. "We were talking and then she-" he hesitated again, watching for Eliom's reaction, "she kissed me."

Having said it out loud finally, it was like a strange weight had been lifted from his shoulders and for a moment, the Explorer felt almost *light* with relief. But as soon as he looked up into his friend's face, as if waiting for the wizard's approval, waiting for the acknowledgement that he had been a victim of an unforeseen accident, everything changed, for instead of calm understanding, Eliom's own expression was one of sudden, uncharacteristic horror.

"I tried to stop her!" Edmund insisted, feeling suddenly afraid that his fears were actually about to come true and that Eliom really had held a flame for the Lectur after all. "But she wouldn't let me pull away! She *knows* I don't love her! She started talking about Bethan and her frustrations about-"

But instead of flying into a rage, Eliom suddenly lowered his head and turning away, he almost slumped against the cabin wall.

"I am sorry," was all he said and taken aback in mid-flow, Edmund just looked utterly blank.

Sorry? What did the wizard have to be sorry for?

"It wasn't *your* doing… it was *hers*!" *I think,* the Explorer's bewildered brain added. "Not that I can really blame her… or even you-!"

"If I had not rejected her, none of this would have happened," Eliom pointed out and he looked so remarkably upset that for a second, the stunned Edmund honestly didn't know what to say. All he could do was let out a bitter laugh.

"You said so yourself, you *can't* love," he tried. "It's no one's fault. Not even hers. She just longs to be cared for. All I can do is pity her. And now I…"

He trailed off then but Eliom only looked at him quizzically.

"You, what?" the wizard asked slowly. "I detect something more you are not telling me…"

THE ENTITY OF SOULS

And Edmund wiped his brow, feeling suddenly very tired. He hadn't been prepared for any of this; *none* of it. He'd only just managed to put a lid on his own emotions but *this*, this had just made everything all confusion all over again. *Nothing* got past Eliom.

"I feel sort of..." he then replied equally slowly, "*guilty*."

"Guilty?" Already Eliom looked almost himself again, his expression back to nonchalant curiosity. "But you have no reason to-"

Edmund gave another mirthless laugh.

"What if I led her to believe that I care for her? What if it's *my* fault? I might have said something or..."

Why didn't I stop her sooner?

The realisation hit him like a slap in the face, but Eliom shook his head, something fierce in his eyes.

"Eldora knows you do not care for her. She knows that you already care for another..."

Bethan. And Edmund closed his eyes.

"And what of her?" he then said aloud, trying to push aside the overwhelming feeling that he had somehow let her down, that he had betrayed her. Yes, he'd pulled away from Eldora. But not as fast as he ought to have done. A small, very small part of him might even have *enjoyed* it... "What of Bethan and the others?" and he opened his eyes again, meeting his friend's pleadingly. He hadn't meant to take it this far, but suddenly all of his doubts were just pouring out. "What if we don't succeed in finding what we need to get them back? What if my dream was just a hoax? I'm worried for them, Eliom. We can't let them down now."

Just as he had hoped though, the wizard gave a small, comforting smile.

"We *will* succeed, Edmund. I know it," he replied with such certainty that for a moment the Explorer wondered why he had ever thought otherwise. "You were hopeful before. Why has your attitude changed so suddenly?"

It was a fair point and Edmund thought back to his conversation with the Lectur, before the kiss...

"It was something that Eldora said."

Eliom waited.

"She said, how do I know that what we're doing now wasn't predestined as well?" and Edmund turned to his friend, his councillor, uncertainly. "Eliom, what if we're *meant* to fail? What if everything about destiny is true and it's already *preordained* that we're to fail, not succeed? I tried to fight destiny for so long. I tried to fight what I knew about Renard, what I knew I would feel for Bethan. I tried to do what you said and control my own fate but it seemed to be controlling me all along. What if it's the same now? What if I can't control- *none* of us can control- whether this mission is going to succeed or to *fail?*"

But again, just as he had before, Eliom shook his head, his expression all calmness.

"We will not fail," he intoned forcibly. "You will not let us fail."

And though Edmund knew that the wizard was right, he hoped that it was enough.

"Edmund."

At that moment, another figure then appeared at the cabin ladder and Edmund, not wanting anyone to know of their conversation, leapt to his feet quickly. As he did so, the map fell from his hands, curling to the floor, but before he could bend to pick it up, disaster happened. In his hurry to scurry from his bunk, the Explorer had jarred the half-drunk flagon of water he had set down by his feet and wobbling, the carton fell to its side, spilling water in a great slosh across the wooden floor… and straight onto the parchment.

Forgetting everything that had just happened, Edmund dove to pick up the map with a loud curse. But it was already too late, the paper was soaked through in seconds.

"Edmund. I am sorry!" the new figure exclaimed, stepping into the light to see the damage that had been done. It was Fred. But Edmund just held the sopping wet map in his hands, watching helplessly as the ink started to run, the paper itself to dissolve as lines and words disappeared before his very eyes.

He cursed again.

"Eliom?! Can't you do something?!" he exclaimed. They *needed* this map. The *elements* needed this map. Without it… He couldn't even *begin* to think what it would mean.

Straight away, Eliom was there, his hand on the parchment, muttering words under his breath, breathing magic. But though the map suddenly began to dry, to harden, crisp and stiff once more, it was ruined. The ink was gone. More than gone – Edmund, Fred and Eliom all leaned in to look on it in astonishment – it had *vanished*. The parchment was entirely, utterly blank.

"It's useless now!" Edmund growled in frustration. "What have we *done*?!" and angry, he made as if to screw the paper in his fist. But Fred soon stopped him.

"Wait!" the warrior cried, grabbing Edmund by the wrist and jabbing at the corner of the parchment with a finger. "Look!"

And sure enough, just as he spoke, clear as day, something began to appear. Black marks began to curl themselves up from the thin fabric, arising into symbols, into *words*, words that none of them had seen before, words rising to the surface of the blankness as if they'd been there all along.

Edmund's hands shook as he held the map eagerly in his hands, as slowly but surely, the whole parchment began to fill up with a black scrawled writing. It was scruffy but legible; but most oddly of all, it was written, not in the language of old, as had been the original, but in the common tongue, free for all to read and understand.

"What does it say?" Eliom asked calmly, not being quite close enough to see and Edmund's voice trembled in astonishment as he began aloud:

"*I bid you welcome in the hopes that you may have discovered this note before you endeavour to reach the Keeper of the World. I am sorry I have not spoken out before but I feared to inform you in any way but this. The Builder's spies are everywhere. He is powerful beyond even my understanding–*" Edmund paused for a second, his eyes widening in excitement as the realisation then hit him. "Eliom!" he cried, turning to his friend. "Do you know what this *means*?"

"It means that this map is not a copy, as we first believed," Eliom answered. He looked almost triumphant. "It is the *original.*"

Fred looked amazed.

"You mean to say we had the *original* all along and Renard stole the wrong map all those years ago?"

"Exactly!" Edmund exclaimed, not quite able to believe it.

Did you know that you took only a copy, brother? He thought to himself. Was it an accident or did you never intend to betray me after all…?

Turning back to the parchment, he then read on.

"*However, I urgently entreat this of you now, through this small magic, that you, my friend, have cunningly seen through; you must not,*" the word 'not' was underlined twice, "*under any circumstances lead the elements to the orb. The Keeper of the World is a trickery that has fooled many for tens of generations. I, myself, the biggest fool of all.*

Granted, if you read this now with a heavy heart for they are lost and you believe it is too late, I also tell you not to fear. They are not gone forever. The elements are not dead. I cannot tell you exactly where they are, for I am pressed for space and even now, it is not safe to speak of it. In the wrong hands, the information could be catastrophic.

All that I can say is that they are in another place, a place very much parallel to this one, fashioned by the Builder and they can, they <u>must</u> *escape and you who read this, must help them.*

I cannot say more now, but you must go to my resting place. Inside my crypt there is a secret compartment, guarded by all the magic I know and have ever known. You must find it with care, for I warn you that it will only open for the worthy. If it rejects you, do not try to break the spell, for it cannot be undone.

Inside this compartment is the answer you seek.

One day I hope to meet you in death, in the knowledge that you have succeeded. It is of great importance that you undertake my instructions, not only for the elements' sake but also for yours, Tungala's and those chosen as the elements of the future.

Yes, there shall be more to come unless this ceases now…

Nevertheless, until the day that I meet with you face-to-face, good luck and may the gods, whoever they may be, shine down upon you.

Ophelius."

As Edmund's last words faded, the cabin fell into a stunned silence, the warrior, wizard and Explorer all taking a moment just to understand and think.

It was a lot to take in, a lot to try and realise and Fred was the first to react.

"Should we trust him?" he asked matter-of-factly. "How do we know this is not some kind of-?" but he paused, not knowing how to finish.

Straight away though, Edmund nodded, his face serious.

"If he can bring the elements back, yes," he replied. "This is the proof we've been looking for. This is exactly what my dream said we should do."

"Very well."

And before anyone could begin to discuss what else Ophelius had written, about the Keeper of the World, about the elements being in another 'place', about this mysterious 'Builder', right at that moment there was a shout from above and the trio turned to the cabin door.

It was Elanore. She was standing at the entrance to the ladder looking pleased.

"Just thought you'd like to know that we've reached the river mouth!" she cried and instantly discarding Ophelius's instructions to be pondered over later, the man, warrior and wizard then glanced at each other before making their way up onto the deck as quickly as they could.

AN UNEXPECTED HELPER

The evening was beginning to rear its dark head and feeling a sudden chill, Bethan shivered. Even though it was supposed to be summer in her old world, the nights in the world of white stone and mystery, were cold and still and no matter what she did, she just couldn't seem to get warm...

Barabus, meanwhile, was marching on ahead.

He hadn't said a single word for at least half an hour now and his stony silence left Bethan feeling utterly miserable. White stone building after white stone building had passed by, every one the same, or similar, but on the same variation and the further they walked, the more she secretly worried.

How was she *ever* going to find her way back to the hole in the stairs, the hideaway she and Bex had found together? All day, as they'd moved through the City, she'd felt a growing sense of dread. Every alley, every turning looked as identical as the last and with no sun, or even a moon to give her a sense of direction she was starting to feel more and more hopeless of ever finding her way back to her friend.

Barabus was angry with her. That much was obvious after their argument that morning. But now it appeared, she was stuck with him. Stuck and-

"Here."

Suddenly, Barabus then slowed and before Bethan knew it, he was stopping outside a small hut-like building.

It was squat with only one floor - just like all of the others around them; and just like the others it was crafted from white stone, made dirty by dust. *Unlike* the other buildings though, this one had two men standing at the door, two men who looked remarkably like guards and Bethan inwardly groaned as she saw both of them straighten up to reveal glistening swords slung at their sides the moment they saw Barabus approaching.

They're here for me, she realised. *They're here to stop me going back.*

But determined not to look too dismayed, she gave both a little nod as Barabus, completely unfazed, ducked past them to open the door of the house for her.

Not knowing what else she could do but follow, Bethan then stepped into a small room with a table, a washbasin, a large oil lamp and a bed. It was plain and even colder than it had seemed outside and without knowing it, looking around her, she couldn't help but feel an overwhelming sense of homesickness... wherever *home* had been before.

Not for the first time that day, the man with the blue eyes sprang into her thoughts. Somehow she ached for him. Ached for his arms and more importantly, for the comfort that he brought.

Whoever he was, she knew that she had felt safe with him. Safe and *warm*.

But where was he now?

And wherever he was, was he thinking of her too?

"Welcome to your new home," Barabus said, spreading his arms out mock-majestically. "If you need anything, just ask one of the Diggers outside..."

Diggers. She had heard the word used several times now.

The City of the Diggers. And the overheard conversation on the stairs...

They are not like us. They age, they breed, they die... the Diggers are truly the Builder's.

The Diggers. Were they the native people of this world? And was that truly their name?

She supposed it must be and even as she thought about it, much as the handful of people she had met since arriving in this place had seemed human, seemed like her, she had somehow known that they were different. A feeling in her gut had made them alien to her.

Digger. It seemed such a strange term...

Although no stranger, she supposed, than the Builder.

Bethan gave the little room another cursory glance.

"Why are the Diggers even *there*?" she snapped, knowing very well the answer. *How was she supposed to sneak out and meet Bex in secret if she had a pair of guards watching her every move?*

"Because you are not allowed to leave here." Barabus sounded smug. If he'd been surprised by her sudden outburst, he didn't show it.

Bethan meanwhile, felt a strange sickness swelling in her stomach.

"Why would I try to leave?" she whispered dryly as Barabus turned to do just that.

But obviously annoyed on some level by her lack of gratitude for being moved to what he clearly considered to be a nicer place, her companion soon scowled.

"You could at least thank me," he retorted.

Thank him?

Bethan just stared at him.

"For *what?*" she cried. "For separating me from the only friend I have?"

But Barabus only ground his teeth together before turning back towards the only exit.

"No one comes in, or out," he then commanded to the guards loudly before he finally left, slamming the wooden door behind him.

"No, wait!"

But it was too late, he was gone and feeling suddenly crushed with the weight of her own helplessness, the second she was alone, Bethan then gave in to her feelings at last and fell to her knees on the hard ground, her eyes swimming with tears of frustration. Before she could stop herself, she was crying, and curling herself into a little ball, a small huddle of flesh and bone doubled-up on the floor, longing for a world she'd almost forgotten, the young woman fell asleep.

—

With a listless sigh, Bethan rolled over, trying as she had for the past hour to find a comfortable position on the lumpy mattress. The bed was better than the floor had been at least, but still she couldn't seem to sleep.

Inside the hut, all was deathly quiet; outside, the occasional shuffle and little snippets of conversation as the guards amused themselves on their long watch, ever reminding her of her situation.

As a prisoner.

Despite her many hours of tears, somehow they were welling up again but determined to stay in control this time, Bethan blinked them away furiously.

It was very dark now. All she could see was the faint red glow of the sky through the single window. The expanse was starless, something she found instantly odd, but thinking about why that might be, long-forgotten memories soon began to well to the surface of her exhausted mind.

She remembered her home now. Her *true* home. The little red-bricked cottage with the old tree in the garden... the tree, she remembered, that had been destroyed. Uprooted. Stolen from her.

She could recall herself as a little girl, sitting out in the garden under that tree on a soft spring night, staring up at the stars far above her, her mother telling her that the bright specks were other worlds, other galaxies and gods far far away...

Bethan could sense herself beginning to feel drowsy again, the memories themselves bringing a sort of comforting warmth with them.

How safe she had felt then. How safe and how loved...

And now?

Now she didn't know *what* to feel...

"Wait a moment! Where are you going?"

She heard the change before she even knew what it was.

Something was happening outside. She could hear voices again, only this time, there was a *woman* amongst them…

And brushing her tiredness and thoughts away in an instant, Bethan sat up, listening hard.

"Barabus sent me to check on her, Haydn." The woman's voice spoke hurriedly. "So let me through."

"You know we're not supposed to let anyone in," came a guard's reply – Bethan had no idea which one. She hadn't bothered to ask their names.

"Come on… If Barabus said so," the other guard sighed.

"How do you know she's telling the truth?" but though the first sounded annoyed, he also didn't sound too convinced.

"Just give me five minutes." The woman was insistent.

"If you're lying…"

"Why would I *lie?*"

Before long, Bethan then heard the sound of someone scraping at the door and then a loud creak as it swung open.

Panicking, Bethan instantly fell back against her pillow, closing her eyes half shut as if to sleep as, through the darkness, she just made out a figure, a slim shadow sneaking into the room.

She could feel her heart beginning to pound in sudden fear.

Who was this stranger? Was she safe? she wondered, as slowly, the person began to move closer, shuffling towards the bed, then bending *over* the bed, examining her…

And then, suddenly, the whole room seemed to flood with light and giving herself away, Bethan gave a cry, flinging her hands up over her half-closed eyes in the brightness.

"What are you doing just lying here in the dark?" a woman's voice spoke out, the same voice from outside and Bethan opened her eyes to find Belanna, the Diggerwoman – as she now knew her to be - standing by the now-burning, oil lamp in the corner of the room.

"Belanna!" she replied, squinting at her visitor again as her eyes grew accustomed to the light. "What are you doing here?"

Belanna, however, didn't seem her usual cheerful self. She seemed on edge about something, for every now and again her eyes would flit to the closed door and when she spoke, her voice shook, unnerving Bethan even more.

"I've asked myself the same question," she said, wringing her hands together uneasily and Bethan sat up, preparing herself.

"Did Barabus send you?" she asked her cautiously.

Belanna glanced back at the door and Bethan guessed that she didn't want the guards to overhear them, but shaking her head, she then moved closer to the bed, lowering her voice.

"I am here to help you," she whispered so quietly that for a moment, the other thought she'd misheard her.

"You're here to help me?" she echoed. A part of her leapt with fresh hope, with excitement at the idea of escaping from Barabus's prison... and yet at the same time she couldn't help but feel suspicious.

Belanna was a Digger. She had been created and had lived here, lived this way, for all of her life. Why then would she risk herself to help a human, a *foreigner*, someone she'd only known a matter of days at the risk of supposedly upsetting the Builder?

But as if detecting her doubt, Belanna shook her head again.

"You shouldn't be kept here," was her explanation, perhaps the only one, Bethan realised, she was ever going to get. "I'll speak with the guards and then we'll leave and I'll take you to meet your friend, Bex," she hissed.

"All right," Bethan said, unable to find any good reason to argue – not that she wanted to - and getting to her feet in a hurry, she pulled the blanket from the bed and wrapped it around her shoulders, ready for the cold night air. Watching her, Belanna then wasted no time, and beckoning for the human to follow, she extinguished the lamp and headed back towards the door. Bethan obliged and fumbled her way through the darkness, her whole body quivering with nerves.

"Excuse me," Belanna called and then, opening the door, she was once again confronted by the two guards. In the darkness, both of them somehow looked taller, more threatening than Bethan thought they had before. They also looked incredibly fed up.

Stepping aside to let Belanna through, one of them then threw out an arm as he saw Bethan.

"You know the rules, Belanna," he said warningly. "You're lucky we let you in in the first place."

But bold as brass, the Diggerwoman looked up into the guard's face, ready with her plan.

"She's unwell. She needs to go for some fresh air," she lied. "I'll bring her straight back."

It was a pretty rubbish excuse but whether or not she had fooled the first guard, the second guard wasn't having it. He shook his head firmly.

"No. Absolutely not."

"I'll be with her," Belanna pleaded. "She won't escape. She's weak. She hasn't eaten a proper meal in days. And can you really blame her?"

Amazingly the second guard then turned to the first and Bethan held her breath, wishing with every fibre of her being for them to let her go.

"Perhaps this time-" the first said to the second doubtfully.

"But what if Barabus finds out? And the Builder... the Builder sees all-"

"The Builder won't mind," Belanna chipped in. It was plain to see that they were starting to crack. "As I said, she's not well. A walk outside is the best remedy for her."

Whether the reasons were foolish or not, Belanna had made her argument well and after a few moments of quarrelling in hushed voices, the guards then nodded and to Bethan's immense relief – and surprise - finally stepped aside.

The Diggerwoman didn't hesitate for a moment.

"Come on," she said and taking Bethan by the crook of her arm, she then led her away into the night.

Only after they were a considerable distance away did Bethan dare to breathe freely again.

"Thank you," was all she said, and quickly the pair made their way further into the City to meet Bex.

—

Halting, Nickolas flung his arm out, stopping Meggie in her tracks and causing Saz, who had been right behind, to walk straight into the back of the pair, closely followed by Dromeda.

"Why have we stopped?" the latter demanded in a harsh whisper and Nickolas pointed to the way ahead where a group of figures were huddled at the end of the next alleyway.

"Diggers," he muttered. "A whole group of them. They might know…"

And understanding, now that the elder elements had explained, Saz and Meggie both glanced at each other. Dromeda meanwhile pounded a fist into the palm of his hand and made as if to move off.

"We can take them…" he started. But straight away Nickolas gave him a warning glare.

"Now is *not* the time for another fight, Dromeda. There has been enough violence already. They are innocent people…"

"*Innocent people*," Dromeda scoffed, but he said no more on the subject.

Scanning the white stone passage ahead, Meggie then leaned in closer to Nickolas, keeping her voice low.

"Where are we?" she whispered.

Nickolas glanced at her and then out towards the group only a few metres in front of them. He still had his arm out across her like a barrier.

"The outskirts of the outer city," he replied shortly.

"If we go now, we can make it," Dromeda pointed out. He sounded edgy. "It is dark."

It *was* dark, the night was a black one and the Digger streets this far out of the city were badly lit, the odd lamp casting only a faint glow across the buildings around them.

If they were quiet and fast enough, they could probably slip by the group ahead completely unnoticed and realising that his comrade had made a good point, Nickolas gave a nod, letting his arm fall.

"Let's go then!" he hissed and without warning he then hurried forward at a half-crouch.

The others sprinted after him into the blackness and within moments they were at the cluster of Diggers and then past them without so much as a stir.

Down one alleyway, turning right into another, then right and left again the quartet then slowed as the buildings suddenly ended to reveal a vast dry flat of land right ahead.

Across the plain, in the distance was a knot of great lights and more buildings but it was the sight even further afield that drew the eye of both Meggie and Saz, for nestled amongst the throng of white huts towered an enormous stone sculpture, sparkling like a torch in the reflective flames of a thousand lamps.

A gigantic platform…

"The City of the Diggers," Nickolas hurried, as he noticed the two women stop to stare at the impressive stretch before them. "That is where we are headed."

But though he had meant it to rush them on, Meggie's eyes were like round saucers.

"That statue," she began. "It looks like-" Before she could finish though, an angry cry suddenly split the night air. The group of Diggers had spotted them after all. Word had clearly already spread of Dromeda's fight with one of their own and the elements' escape, and all were now rushing to reach their weapons, their feet already slapping on the hard dirt road as they rounded the corner towards them.

"Run!" Dromeda shouted, pushing Saz before him.

"Go!" Nickolas added and without thinking, he grabbed Meggie by the hand, almost wrenching her off her feet as he tore out onto the plain.

Without questioning it for a second, Meggie let herself be led, her already tired legs pumping as fast as they could as she tried to focus on her breathing and not the familiar aching cramp that was creeping across her thighs. The group had spent most of that day in bouts of walking and then running, hiding from anyone they saw, dodging detection, desperate to escape towards the City and the effort was really starting to take its toll.

Only once they were well and truly racing across the hard dust-laden space, did the smallest element then dare to steal a quick glance back. The group of Diggers, all male, were shouting and calling, but they weren't as keen as the group had feared. Already most of them had given up the chase, satisfied just to spit and curse in the dirt. For some reason, they seemed reluctant to venture beyond the last buildings of the outer city and even those who had, soon ground to a halt, turning back from the lowlands.

"Well, that was pointless," Dromeda panted sarcastically as he too looked back. "Fools. The lot of them."

Nickolas opened his mouth as he clearly so often did, to defend the Diggers but feeling Meggie drag like a dead weight on his arm, he seemed suddenly to remember that he was still holding her.

Slowing a bit instead, he turned to study the little element.

"Are you all right?" he asked.

Meggie nodded, but she was plainly exhausted and realising that for every stride he took she suffered three, Nickolas slowed right down.

"I think we can walk now," he said and giving a little smile, he then released her hand.

Meggie just looked up at him, still too breathless to speak but whilst she would never admit it aloud, she couldn't help but notice how oddly bereft she felt. Her companion's hand was large – it had encased hers easily – and warm, but most importantly it had been *solid*, solid and somehow comforting. In those few minutes she felt like she'd run further, moved faster than she ever would have managed alone but now, without it, without *him* and his support the element really wasn't convinced she'd even be able to *walk* let alone run anymore. Every part of her seemed to beg for a bed...

"Nickolas!" Dromeda's shout startled them both. "Help!"

And Nickolas and Meggie turned to find the elder element kneeling in the dust, Saz out-cold in his arms. She had fainted.

"Saz!" yelped Meggie, instantly hurrying to her friend's side. "I *thought* she looked pale..."

"She has not had *nearly* enough time to recover," Nickolas reasoned and ever practical, he reached down to feel the element's forehead. It was cool and clammy, just as he had thought it would be. The fear of being chased had clearly been the final straw.

"Will she be all right?" Meggie demanded as her companion straightened back up.

But Nickolas's expression gave nothing away.

"It will just be the shock," he reassured. "It affects everyone differently..."

Dromeda all the while was watching Saz, his face blank.

"She will slow us down, Nickolas," he then pointed out, not even turning to look at his friend. "It could be dangerous..."

This statement, sudden as it was surprised the listeners both, but none more than Meggie, who gawping, suddenly turned on him, her green eyes flashing.

"You're *surely* not suggesting that we *leave* her here are you?!" she challenged. "Because if you are-"

Dromeda scowled.

"No, of *course* not!" he shot back, sounding as if he'd meant to do exactly that. But before Meggie could argue back and the matter got out of hand, Nickolas had stepped between them.

"*I* will carry her," he said pointedly. Though he sounded just as angry, just as outraged as Meggie, still his face remained calm. "She will not be a burden to me." And gesturing for Dromeda to hand her over, he then took Saz's limp body without a fuss and draping her carefully over his shoulder, straightened up and started back off towards the City.

For a moment, Dromeda and Meggie both just watched him, neither of them sure what to make of what had just happened but with one more glare at each other, still bristling from their small but vital argument, the pair soon followed him on into the night.

—

"This way," Belanna said, her voice still quiet, still afraid of being detected and Bethan followed her, being careful where she trod. It was extremely dark now, even the odd red glow in the sky seemed to provide only the very smallest amount of light, with the occasional oil lamp on the street to aid their way. The further they went though, the more Bethan could feel her nerves and excitement growing. Despite the monotonous similarity of every white stone street, every white stone house, she was convinced that she was starting to get her bearings. There was that crack in the wall she had noticed on the way out of the City, there was this rock on the corner. There was that lamp hanging at a slightly different angle and then, there was that tree... The one withered tree...

Bethan felt her pulse quicken as she saw the steps and then even more so as Belanna then led her towards them, heading for the street below.

Fifteen, sixteen, seventeen... Bethan found herself silently counting as they descended. *Twenty-four, twenty-five, twenty-six, twenty-seven...*

As they reached the thirty-second stair, only then did she begin to worry.

What if they were in the wrong place after all? What if she never found the hole in the wall again? Or, more disturbingly – what if Bex hadn't been able to make it? What if she too was trapped somewhere with no one to help her...?

Forty-two, forty-three, forty-four...

"Is this it?" Belanna asked and trying to focus, Bethan stared at the overhanging shrubbery on the forty-fifth step like it was something out of a dream. Relief hit her in a wave.

This was the place all right. This was it.

But how had Belanna *known?*

"How did you-?" she started, suddenly feeling even more afraid. But Belanna soon gave a reassuring smile.

"I overheard Gergo telling Bex about it in the first place. Don't worry."
And Bethan took a deep breath.
"Right, of course," she said, trying to hold her nerve.

She had no idea *why* she felt like this, so afraid all of a sudden, so uncertain. Was this really who she was? Who she had been back in her own world? So easily scared?

Wasting no more time, Bethan then reached for the curtain of shrivelled plant hiding the entrance to Bex's cubbyhole and pulled it aside in one sweep.

The tiny space beyond was completely black, and, Bethan thought, completely empty, but then:

"I thought you were *never* going to come!" and sure enough, there was the sound of movement, of something or someone shifting, the flash of a candle being lit and Bethan almost let out a cry of delight as Bex then appeared, stepping out of the gap to join them on the stair.

In the flicker of the tiny candle flame, Bex's face was pale, strained with worry but clearly just as relieved as Bethan was, she soon sprang forward, pulling her friend into a tight hug.

"I thought you weren't coming!" she repeated, her voice just above a whisper. Even here they would have to keep as quiet as possible. "My new *house* - if you can call it that - isn't too far from here thankfully. So when I-I…"

But to Bethan's surprise, she suddenly seemed to notice Belanna and stuttering, she froze, her whole body rigid with shock as she pulled away from Bethan, her eyes wide in fear.

"What is *she* doing here?" she challenged at a hiss. "Why did you bring her?" And confused, Bethan looked from one woman to another. For some reason she'd assumed that Bex had known Belanna was helping her, helping *them*, maybe even that Bex had sent her in the first place. But judging by her friend's reaction…

"It's all right. Belanna brought *me*," she explained uncertainly. "She says she wants to help."

Belanna didn't say anything to either confirm or deny this, but obviously trusting Bethan's judgement, this seemed to pacify the other for now.

"All right then," she said stiffly and then, finally gesturing to the empty hole in the wall, "Let's talk in here." Before, casting another glance at Belanna as Bethan reached for the plant again, she frowned a little. "Though it might be a bit of a squeeze with three of us mind you."

"We'll be fine," Bethan defended the Digger and not losing another moment, she clambered in, closely followed by Bex and a still-silent Belanna.

As soon as they were settled, Bex then went straight to the point of asking Bethan about what had happened since they had been separated, what Barabus had told her, details of her new prison, where it was, what it was like. Some of these questions, Bethan couldn't answer and Belanna had to fill in as Bex cut in with her own details. However, after what felt many minutes of catching up, it was finally then that the trio dared to breech the subject of their future.

"What I can't understand, no matter how much I think about it, is why are we even *here*?" Bex pointed out. *And what did they do now they were?*

"I know, it doesn't make any sense," Bethan answered truthfully. "Nor does this sudden ban on seeing each other. This Builder person - whoever *they* are - is obviously afraid we're going to do something."

Bex spread her hands wide. The candle now in her lap flickered crazily, making shadows dance across the three faces.

"Like what?" she cried and then, surprising the others both she turned suddenly to Belanna. "Do you know anything about what's going on? Have you been told anything?"

Of course. Belanna was a Digger – she was a part of this place, a part of whatever it was, of what it might become – surely she had to know *something*?

But though both human women suddenly had high hopes of finally getting some answers, Belanna shook her head almost straight away.

"Sorry," she replied sombrely. "All I know is; that for as long as I can remember, there have always been humans. And you have always just suddenly *appeared.* Turning up in the prairies, in the City. Just as there have always been Diggers," she gestured with one hand "there have always been humans," she gestured with the other. "But they have never been the same. You are not *born* here, not made, so to my people, to *us,* that makes you special. Some call you the 'chosen', others 'the special ones'; a people to be revered. To us you are likes gods – because you don't age. You don't grow old like us and you don't die. You are always the same, *immortal.*" She frowned. "The Builder brings you here for a reason, but what that reason is…"

The Builder. There was that name yet again, spoken in devout fear.

"And who *is* this Builder?" Bex asked, leaning in eagerly. "Is he a man? A Digger?"

It was a simple enough question but for a moment, Belanna just looked at her like she was crazy.

"The Builder is… the Builder," the Digger replied. "There are rumours, speculations that he was a man once, another immortal by a different name. But none have ever seen him face-to-face, save one."

For some reason this sent an odd shudder down the spines of both listening women.

The Builder is god here. If he wants to smite you, he will do so.

The words heard in secret at their last meeting there sprung to mind.

God. Another immortal. Neither of them really knew what they thought about that, but knowing that they weren't ready to stop yet…

"You say only one has seen him face-to-face," Bex was the one to carry on. "Who? Who was it? Was it a human or a Digger?"

Belanna looked at the pair in turn. Both of them could tell that she was nervous. Knowledge was obviously not a thing shared here, that much they had already learnt just from Barabus and Gergo, but this was something else. This wasn't like the others, the humans who knew next to nothing of the Builder, but had still been forbidden to speak anything of him.

No, Belanna knew more, understood the nature of this thing but she held back, not because she had been told to, but because she was frightened, truly deeply frightened. She had been raised in a culture of fear, of mystery surrounding her supposed creator, the ruler of her world. Breaking through that was like denying who she was.

"He was a human. A man," her voice shook a little. "He came with the last group of humans before you. About two hundred years ago," her eyes glazed for a moment. "Humans always seem to arrive in groups. I never really thought about *why* before…"

"And this man?" Bethan coaxed.

"Yes," Belanna suddenly hurried. "Yes, he met with the Builder… and then he *left*."

"Left?!" Bex and Bethan both echoed at the same time.

No one has ever escaped this place. And no one ever will… They both well remembered the words the two men had spoken on those steps not so long ago.

I have heard tales…

"Yes," Belanna insisted. They could tell that she was starting to feel very uncomfortable now. "He left, he escaped from this world, back into your own. Although I don't know how and don't ask me to find out. He just kind of *vanished* one day," she bit her lip. "But this was before I was even *born* so I can't tell you any more…"

Bex and Bethan looked at each other, wide-eyed.

It was true then. The rumour the man had spoken of was true. A human had left, had *returned* to Tungala… And almost instantly the realisation, the spark of hope was there, the desperate question and the *need* for its answer reflected in both of their gazes.

"Do you think *we* could leave?" Bethan was the one to say it. "Could *we* find a way back?"

Was it really possible? Could they too return to the world, the lives they had lost?

But the moment she had spoken, Belanna's eyes widened too and for the first time, the Digger looked truly panicked.

"Oh no!" she cried. "You can't – you mustn't - even *try!* You'll be caught and-" she turned from one to the other over and over again, pleadingly. "The

THE ENTITY OF SOULS

trouble it would cause-! The Builder-" And she gave a shuddering sigh as Bethan rested a hand gently on her arm.

"It's all right," Bethan soothed, trying to hide her obvious disappointment. "We're only talking about it. We wouldn't do anything to make trouble for you willingly... And anyway," she gave a sad smile, "I doubt it's that easy."

After all, where did they even *start* trying to escape from a *world*? Especially when they had no idea where this world even *was* in relation to their own.

Belanna seemed to calm a little.

"What I don't understand is; why do you *want* to leave?" she then asked. "Is your world so very different from ours? Is it so much better?"

And again, Bethan and Bex glanced at each other.

In one instant both humans knew that the answer was *yes*. It was like asking if they could breathe, if they could move; it was a part of them. But *why* that was, neither of them really seemed to know. Yes, the food and drink were better there, and the trees, the grass, the people, those little comforts they had known and understood all stood out, but *really*, deep down?...

"I have someone," Bethan then realised aloud. "Someone I need to go back *for*. Someone I-"

She broke off, not really understanding, but Belanna, looking suddenly interested, soon picked it up again.

"Who?" the Digger asked. "Who is it? Who do you want to go back for?"

Bethan hung her head.

"Well, I don't know his name..." she answered, feeling very sheepish. "I can't seem to remember it... But he had –*has*- blue eyes. And..."

Those eyes...

Belanna all the while smiled knowingly.

"Ah, a lover," she laughed. "I can see it in your face!" and embarrassed even more, Bethan felt herself blushing. She hadn't really thought about it, she realised. Hadn't really considered what this man was to her. But then the way she had felt with him, the way she felt *now* just thinking of him, the way she remembered him kissing her, desperately, hurriedly – those weren't the kind of feelings, the kind of moments you shared with just a friend...

"Belanna."

Straight away, as if she'd been waiting all along for the Digger to relax a little, Bex then brought the subject smacking straight back to the matter at hand.

"I'm sorry, but I need – *we* need –" she added, including Bethan in her sudden quest for knowledge, "to know more. If you can't tell us, do you know *where* we could find out how the last man escaped?"

Just as both thought it would, Belanna's smile instantly disappeared.

"I *told* you not to ask," she replied, the fear in her eyes back again. "I'm sorry. I wish I could help you but..."

"You *can* help us," Bethan tried gently. "Please Belanna. You must know of *someone* we can talk to. How did *you* find out?"

And the Digger looked away from them both, fiddling with her hands. Until that moment, none of them had really noticed how incredibly cramped and uncomfortable they felt in that tiny space, huddled together in the cool darkness. In the dying light of the candle, the air felt suddenly thicker, stuffier.

"I can't tell you who told me," Belanna then began slowly. "I daren't. But..." and though she squirmed in her makeshift seat, she gave a small smile, "I *do* know of something that might be useful to you. It's a bit... *farfetched* and I'll need to find out more details, ask the right people, but I know there *is* a connection somewhere..."

"Connection?" Bex looked confused. "A connection to what? To our world?"

Belanna was thoughtful.

"Possibly- I would think so- yes," she stuttered, talking more to herself than anything. "But that's not what I was thinking. I'm thinking..." She rubbed her mouth, her eyes glazed for a second. "I'm thinking of the connection between *this* world and the next." And then, when the other two looked utterly baffled; "you know, the *next*. The world of the dead."

Bethan and Bex weren't sure if they could possibly have looked more horrified than they did right at that moment.

The world of the dead?

Was Belanna serious? Was *that* her suggestion?

Everything in her face said she was and yet...

Both women had only just come to understand that by walking through the flames of their own world, they had stepped right into another. The fact that they had done just that, that another world had existed in the first place, had taken everything they had thought they'd known and turned it on its head. But *this*? The idea that there were *more* worlds, and not just that, but a world where the *dead* went, the *next place* that all living beings feared *existed* and the suggestion that they might be able to just 'find a connection' somewhere, perhaps even walk straight through? *That* felt utterly utterly... *wrong*.

Bex's voice came out in a croak.

"What are you-" She cleared her throat. "What are you *saying*?"

And Belanna continued as if she couldn't see the sheer astonishment on her companions' faces, "I'm saying that if you were to find it, maybe you could go there and *maybe* you could speak with the human that escaped." She looked curious for a moment. "That's assuming humans on your world die, right?"

Bethan just about managed a nod.

"Yes," she said. Her mouth felt oddly dry. "Yes, humans die. We-" She turned to Bex. "He *would* be dead on our world."

If he had lived again to begin with, she added as a silent afterthought. For she remembered the temple, she remembered Barabus and the others, how they had seemed like ghosts; *were* ghosts.

It had been too late for them, she reasoned. They had left the human world too long ago to come back; to live. But then again...

How did they even know whether this world, the world of the Builder, was the same as theirs? What if *time* was different here? What if, to those they had left behind, she and the others had been gone not days but *years*?

Bethan felt her heart almost stop at the sobering thought.

They had to hope it wasn't the case. *They had to.* And if that was so, they had to hope that the man who had escaped had returned to their world in time to live out his normal mortal life. In time to *die.*

It was all a big *if.*

"I think that-"

But all of a sudden, the women then heard a noise outside.

A shout had erupted from somewhere and as if the sound were the herald of doom, all three companions gave a start, shaking themselves as if from a deep sleep.

"It's late," Belanna then hissed, alarmed by the noise. No doubt it was a Digger wandering home through the blackness, calling to a friend, but even so, she looked urgently at Bethan. "We should be heading back."

"Heading back?"

Surprised and forgetting for the smallest second where they were, Bethan almost shouted herself. For some reason she'd had it in her head that by breaking her out of the little prison Barabus had made for her, Belanna had been breaking her free, *for good.*

The Digger looked just as surprised.

"Of course," she said. "I thought you knew that! If you went missing, those guards would tell Barabus and Barabus holds a lot of power in the City. He'd turn my people and yours against you. So until we know what your next move is, until I've found out what you need to know about the connection, you should lie low."

Bethan hesitated, but knowing that Belanna was ultimately right, she gave a sigh.

"All right," she gave in and shifting her body in the cramped space, she made an effort to stand, followed by Belanna.

Only Bex remained where she was a moment, the candle almost out, her expression thoughtful until;

"Wait!" and as if suddenly remembering something she threw a hand out to stop the Digger in her tracks. Her face was suddenly eager. "The human? The man who escaped. What was his name?"

"The man?"

Unperturbed by the sudden request, Belanna paused to think.

"His name was long..." she muttered. "Old. I don't know if I can remember it...I..."

"Please. Try." Bex sounded urgent. There was a glisten of something in her eye.

She knew something, or was starting to, that much was obvious but *what*, neither Bethan nor Belanna could yet understand.

"It was something like Auph..." Belanna tried. "Orp.... No. Off..."

The women waited in tense silence as the Digger rolled the various sounds over her tongue, searching for the right fit.

"Offee... Opho... Oh yes!" and then, just like that Belanna's face lit up. "I remember now! Ophelius. Yes! That was his name... Ophelius!"

MEETING

"Tie that sail, Thom!" Elanore ordered, her voice battling with the wind as the dwarf nodded, pulling ever tighter on the ropes.
"Edmund! The wheel! Level us up!"
Edmund shouted in the affirmative and pulled at the ship's wheel, using what felt like all of this strength to keep it steady as the Karenza bounded over the gushing torrent of the river. Pockets of fast-flowing water hit the keel relentlessly, socking the ship upwards, but thanks to Eliom's spell, the wind remained strongly in their favour, dragging the vessel north despite the force rising to crash against them.

"Rocks ahead!!" came Fred's deep bellow from the crow's nest and Elanore glanced up at him, whipping her flailing hair from her face.

"Hard to starboard!!" she then yelled at the helm before running towards the bow of the ship to look out on the terrain ahead.

Sure enough, jagged rocks, the remnants of broken cliffs either side were poking their way above the surface like gnarled teeth. Though the banks of the river mouth were far enough apart to house at least four Karenzas side-by-side, they were going to have to be careful.

"Right! Sharp right!" Elanore shrieked in panic as the ship lurched towards a particularly dangerous-looking rock and Edmund immediately threw all of his weight onto the ship's wheel, forcing it down. The Karenza jerked but steadily began to turn.

"Straighten up!" Elanore shouted, trying desperately to guide the Explorer through the menacing, needle-like formation. But it was useless, the obstacles were scattered everywhere, and for the briefest of moments, the sea captain found herself wondering why she had ever agreed to any of this…

Noticing a rock too late, she then clung to the bulwark with all of her might.

"Hold on to something!!" she screamed and without the slightest hesitation, everyone instantly obeyed.

There was a deep throaty crack and then a groan as the whole Karenza shuddered. And then she was buffeted into the air, pivoted by the blow, and before anyone could stop themselves, the whole crew were tumbling to the deck.

"Eliom!" Edmund cried out wildly, the first to regain his balance. "Eliom! Can you do something?!"

But the wizard was way ahead of him. Stepping past Elanore, he strode to the very prow of the ship, his staff raised, a deep ruddy purple already glowing from its end. As he stood there, his gaze on the river ahead, a sudden beam of light shot from the wood straight into the water, and as the others watched, spread its way across the wide river-mouth in one giant beam.

There was another loud groan, like the moan of a deep-sea creature, then, before the crew's very eyes, like the jaws of a folding trap, the rocks ahead began to *shudder* and retract, disappearing beneath the surface as if they had never been.

Just like that, they were gone and with the last of them fading from view, the water took on an almost *glassy* calmness, glistening innocently in the sun.

After a time, Eliom lowered his staff and glanced at the others as they approached him, as if noticing them for the first time. He said nothing though. He didn't need to and the first to greet him, Thom's face cracked with a smile.

"Eliom, my friend," he said, "you never cease to amaze me…"

Edmund and Fred also smiled. Elanore meanwhile, sighing in relief that that one small battle had been won and her ship was still in one piece, then looked suddenly solemn as she turned around, searching the deck with her eyes.

"Where's Eldora?" she said. Her voice was a little frosty and remembering the Lectur, Edmund's smile immediately faded as did Fred's.

Eliom however, as calm as ever, gestured towards the cabins.

"Not to fear," he replied. "I believe she is still below deck. I seem to recall she has little fondness for water."

Little fondness for water?

Thom snorted.

"One has to wonder *why* she's here then…" he muttered.

And though no one could escape his logic, neither did anyone seem to want to comment. Instead, all eyes were drawn to their new surroundings.

Since entering the Great Madid, the ship was now flanked on both sides by high cliff-land swamped with trees and bushes. Everything was green, green and thick, the canopy above them leaving barely room for the sky - yet despite all the signs of life, the whole place, just as it had in the lands of Bor, felt utterly *dead*. The air was close and musty, pressing in on them like a heavy weight and there was no sound of life, no movement, but for the wind slapping against the sails.

It all felt very... *odd*.

"It is quiet..." Fred remarked. His hand was already lying on the tip of the sword hilt at his side, his fingers flexing as his eyes scanned the treetops overhead.

To say the least... Edmund thought. But instead of speaking it aloud, turning to look at the others, his face was sombre.

"I suggest we stay on our guard," he said. "We don't want to disturb anything...!"

And turning away from the land ahead, the Explorer then headed back to the helm.

—

The first thing Meggie noticed when she woke, was the pain.

Her neck was aching, as was her back, the hard dusty ground where she'd slept having offered her no comfort whatsoever, but the worst of all was her wrist. Where the large Digger man had grabbed her and squeezed, where she had thought herself only bruised the day before, was skin now almost purple and swollen to twice its normal size.

No doubt it was at least strained, she thought to herself as she tried to flex the useless hand, only to flinch as more pain shot down her arm.

Her mouth felt dry, her eyes scratchy and sore from the dust of the plain. She had no idea how early it was or how long she had been asleep. But she did know that it was day and sitting up, she finally took a moment to get a proper look at her surroundings.

It looked far less impressive by daylight, the City ahead; more squat and grubby somehow, but still that bright patch on the muddy horizon *felt* more welcoming than the outer city they had left behind.

Even so, Meggie still watched the way ahead with dread.

Nowhere seemed safe right then. The group of Diggers in the outer city had told her that much. They had been complete strangers to her, she'd never set eyes on any of them before and yet they had wanted to do her harm. She assumed it was because they somehow already *knew* about what had happened, about the fight, about Dromeda and Nickolas beating one of their own, about her refusal to be separated from Saz. It was the only thing that made sense to her. And if they had known, had been informed so quickly then how long would it be before *everyone* knew, how long would it be before word reached the City ahead, before they were chased there too, frightened for their lives?

Would they ever really be safe *anywhere* from now on?

"Good morning."

Meggie physically jumped as Nickolas's voice pierced her thoughts.

He sounded husky, his own throat dry and turning to look at him she saw that he too seemed to be suffering from a night spent rough. As he sat up, kneading his shoulders, rolling his head to relax his neck, he let out a long yawn. Somehow the movement, the mannerism reminded her of an animal, a cat she used to feed in the back alley of a house she'd lived in once and recognising the similarities, she couldn't help but smile.

Nickolas looked bemused.

"What are you grinning at?" he teased, pausing mid-stretch.

"Nothing," Meggie said, but even looking away, for some reason her smile only seemed to widen.

Blinking back the rest of his sleepiness, Nickolas then wasted no time in getting to his feet and reaching for a pocket in his trousers, Meggie had never noticed before, he surprised her by pulling out a hide flask.

"Here," he said. "It is a little stale but will help."

And Meggie took the flask without a word, trying not to wonder where the animal hide had come from to craft it in the first place... There certainly weren't any animals *here* that she had seen.

Gulping down some of the water she then made a face. He was right. It *was* stale. Stale water, a few days old and not quite... *right*, not the way she remembered it. From before.

Not that she could afford to be picky.

Many things weren't how she remembered them now...

"Oh," Nickolas suddenly exhaled sharply and looking up as she handed the flask back to him, Meggie was startled to see sudden horror in his eyes.

For a second she thought he was looking beyond her, back to the outer city, back to the danger they had left behind. Perhaps the mob of Diggers had followed them after all...

But then.

"Your wrist!" he exclaimed and suddenly remembering her injury, Meggie felt her face physically redden. Carefully she placed the swollen hand behind her back.

"It's nothing," she muttered. "Really."

But Nickolas didn't seem convinced and holding out his hand like a parent to a disobedient child, waiting for a stolen object to be returned, Meggie found that she couldn't help but bring her wrist forward for his inspection. There was something authoritative about the elder element, something she found strangely difficult to resist or refuse and right then, she realised that she wasn't really willing to fight it. After all, for all she knew, he might know a way to stop it throbbing...

"Looks broken," Nickolas said seriously and he took the wrist gently in his large hands, running his fingers over the swollen skin like a true physician. His touch was soft and her eyes wandering for a second, Meggie couldn't help but notice as she looked up, that the cut at his lip, the wound from his fight with the Digger man, seemed to be gone.

I've had worse injuries than this, she felt like commenting drily, but something stopped her. And not just the fact that there was now movement beside them, that someone else was waking up.

Dromeda stirred loudly, sitting up like one primed for action in a moment.

"Morning," he said, giving a brief stretch as he turned to his two companions. Something flickered across his face as he saw them, the woman and the man, holding hands, something Meggie didn't quite catch. Whatever it was though, clearly had an impact on Nickolas, for instantly he released her wrist.

"Good morning," he replied. But though Nickolas's tone was friendly, as the other element climbed to his feet, Dromeda's expression turned sour as his eyes flicked from Meggie to Nickolas and then down to the still-sleeping Saz.

Moving closer to his old friend, his back to Meggie, he then spoke, his voice lowered.

"Nickolas. There is something I must discuss with you," he intoned. "Urgently."

Hearing the strange insistence in his tone, Nickolas's brow furrowed. For a moment though, he just looked at him.

"Anything you have to say can be said in front of Meggie, I am sure," he replied evenly, glancing at Meggie as he spoke only for the little element to meet his gaze in surprise.

Why was he bringing *her* into it? Was she supposed to feel flattered he wanted her included? Pleased? Or was this about something else entirely? Either way, she could tell by the way that Dromeda was eying her and more importantly, eying the swelling on her wrist that whatever he had to say really wasn't going to be something she *wanted* to hear. He was looking at her almost disapprovingly. No, not with disapproval, almost as if he *envied* her. But *why* she couldn't begin to guess…

"It's all right," she said eventually and turning away from both men like it mattered nothing to her, she gave a shrug. "I'll check on Saz."

"Meggie," Nickolas started, but without so much as a backwards glance, the element was already striding to where her companion lay only a few feet away.

When it came down to it, whether she cared what Dromeda had to say or not was irrelevant, for as she busied herself with kneeling by Saz's side and straightening out the blanket – the only one they had- covering her still-unconscious friend, her ears couldn't help but pick up every word of the following conversation.

"Nickolas," Dromeda said the second he'd turned his back fully on the women, before, taking Nickolas's arm, he soon pulled him a little further away. "What do we do now?"

Nickolas inclined his head a little, looking confused.

"Do?" he echoed. "You know what we *do*. We continue for the City and once we are there, lie low for as long as possible. After that, I do not know…"

Dromeda's face, however, easily betrayed his concern.

"Nickolas," he reasoned. "They are slow." He didn't need to look at Meggie and Saz for anyone to know just who 'they' were. "Saz has still not awoken, and Meggie," he cast a backwards glance at the little element, "she is injured now. We need not-"

"*Enough*!" Nickolas's hiss was surprisingly fierce. And then suddenly, as if he'd been waiting a long time just for this moment, he seemed to flare up, his eyes aglow with anger as he stepped away from his friend looking utterly disgusted. "I *really* hope for your sake you are not trying to say what you did last night!" he spat, his voice almost loud.

Dromeda though, seemed ready for him.

"Do we not want to *live?*" he argued hotly. "Word will have spread even to the City by now – you know what the Diggers are like! If we are seen with them, it will only mean trouble for us. We should save ourselves and *leave them.*"

His final two words echoed across the plain like the sentence of death and hearing them, Meggie felt herself freeze.

"Can you not *hear yourself?*" Nickolas's mouth was a thin, dangerous line now. "You know just as much as I, that regardless of what happens now, we will do nothing *but* live. We cannot *do* anything else! The Builder will not *allow* us to die!" He gave a dry, inhuman laugh. "We have *lived* here for hundreds of years and yet you speak to me of dying?! And *you*," he jabbed his finger at Dromeda's broad chest, "you are just as, if not *more* responsible for this mess than they are," he turned his finger on the now fully-listening Meggie. "*You* were the one who would not release the Digger guard! Yes, Meggie and Saz are disobeying the Builder – with *our help*, might I add. But *you* have committed far worse. You tried to murder one of his own!"

As if he couldn't control his anger, he turned away then as if to leave but as if desperate for his friend to see reason, Dromeda suddenly grabbed Nickolas's arm, gripping it hard.

"The Builder may not kill us," he spoke through his teeth. "But he *could* make our lives not worth living!"

Nickolas though, had clearly heard enough already and pulling furiously away, he rounded back on his friend, his whole face a mask of hardness.

"If he *could*, do you not think he would have done so already?! We have been in this place," he threw his arms to the sky; "we have been at his '*mercy*' for long enough!!"

THE ENTITY OF SOULS

Dromeda shook his shaggy head.

"But we have never willingly disobeyed him before! And now... because of *them*!-" and this time it was his turn to jab a finger in the direction of the women.

"And when have *you* ever cared about obeying the Builder?" Nickolas demanded. "They need our help! Do you not understand?! I thought you of all people would be leaping at the chance! You, the one who-"

"We were only told to *watch over them*, Nickolas. But not like this! *Not like this*," Dromeda seemed to be pleading now and there was something in the way he spoke, something that Meggie, listening closely, couldn't help but notice. The elder element had obviously never seen his friend quite like this, had obviously never pushed Nickolas this far. And it *frightened* him. "You are right. I hate the Builder just as much as you do, if not *more* but-!"

"Then, let him do what he likes," Nickolas snapped. "We are helping them. And the matter is not up for debate." And as if all anger, in one moment had drained from him, he then looked his friend fully in the eye, his voice, for the smallest moment, softening. "We were like them once, Dromeda. Do you not remember?"

"Of course I do." Dromeda looked stunned. "How can you ask that? I remember it every day-"

"Then stop this idiocy!" His friend's mouth was a firm line again and obviously intending these words to be the last he spoke on the matter, Nickolas then turned full on his heel and began to stride out across the prairie, away from his oldest companion, away from Meggie and the still-unconscious Saz, away from the rage none of them had quite expected.

Dromeda, oddly breathless, watched him go with a scowl.

"The Builder sees all here, Nickolas!" the bellow slipped from his mouth before he could stop it. "Your care of them will cost you!"

Nickolas paused but didn't turn.

"At least I know what it means to care," he replied, his voice cold and shocked into silence, Dromeda, merely stood, staring after his friend as he left.

Meggie looked up to see Nickolas approaching. His expression had fallen back into a sort of unreadable sternness in the few minutes since the argument but though he obviously wanted to pretend like nothing had just happened, Meggie couldn't meet his eye.

Did he know she had heard everything? That she had heard Dromeda's true opinion, and in return, - Meggie felt an odd feeling of warmth in her gut – heard how much Nickolas was willing to risk to help her, to help them all?

And not knowing what else to do, she turned her attention back to Saz, feeling her forehead – it was cool - tucking the blanket more snuggly round her – how many times had she done *that* in the past few minutes alone, just to be seen to be doing *something*? *Anything* but listening…

She felt Nickolas stop just above her. His leg was close to her cheek, but though they never touched, Meggie felt as if a great heat was radiating between them, like the ashes of an angry fire still sizzled there even after the flames were gone.

He surely had to know, it had been impossible *not* to hear those words spoken in bitterness, in resentment and fear.

I can't stay silent, and feeling suddenly nervous, Meggie then cleared her throat.

"Look," she tried. "I-We really appreciate what you've done for us. But I-we-" she licked her lips, "I understand if you can't help us anymore…"

She trailed off, not really knowing what else to say, but noticing that Nickolas didn't seem to be in any hurry to jump in and argue with her, she chanced a look up.

The elder element was studying her, his expression wan. His mouth twitched, but seeing her upturned gaze, he soon gave a sigh.

"You heard," he stated. He sounded guilty and realising then that she had probably made things worse, Meggie quickly buried her feelings, flashing a quick smile.

"It was kind of hard not to," she joked. Was it really eavesdropping when they had practically been shouting at each other? Technically no, so why then, did she feel so bad?

Seeing her own sheepish smile, Nickolas gave a small one of his own. Before Meggie could say another word though, he was crouching by her side and for a rare moment, the pair were eye-to-eye.

"Meggie," he then said. His voice was firm, but suddenly very soft and looking into his eyes, Meggie found herself feeling just as suddenly very uncomfortable. They were very close now, his knees almost touching hers, his hand placed barely a fingers-breadth from her own and still his whole body seemed to be giving off some kind of heat. The whole air was thick with it. "Dromeda and I both made a choice to help you," he continued. "Even if he does not see it that way now. He will. We will remain with you for…" and he hesitated for a second as if not quite sure where to finish. "For as long as… as you need."

As long as they needed? How *long* would that be?

And suddenly hit by the realisation of what he was saying, what his small flounder could mean, Meggie looked away, feeling the hairs on the back of her neck stir.

THE ENTITY OF SOULS

You know just as much as I, that regardless of what happens now, we will do nothing but live. We cannot do anything else! Nickolas's angry words buzzed in her ears like insects.

Nothing but live...

She'd made the connection before, touched upon it tentatively right before she'd collapsed all those days ago, finally succumbing to the shock of being in another world, but she'd never really, *truly* put two and two together.

She knew Nickolas was old, *very* old, that much she had gathered from his ghostly presence back on Tungala, but how, *why* he was still alive here, but not only that, still *young*, no older than herself, she'd never really properly considered.

Was this what happened here? Did people truly never age? Did people truly never die? Did they just stay, just live in this world of sand and stone, *forever*?

And was that her fate now too?

Feeling suddenly a little queasy, Meggie pushed her thoughts aside. She was aware that Nickolas was still looking at her - she could feel his eyes on her face - making her wonder if he knew what she had just been through, no doubt the same, terrifying, confusing conclusion he had come to when he too had walked through those flames...

"You and Dromeda have known each other for a long time..." she said quickly.

"Yes. You could say that," Nickolas's smile was wry. If he somehow knew what she had just been thinking about, he didn't show it. "Do not worry for us though. Arguments have always been a part of our friendship."

With a sigh, he then rubbed the back of his neck, almost as if he held a great burden there, he was aching to get rid of and his eyes fell to the still-sleeping Saz.

"Listen," he then continued. "Do not judge Dromeda too harshly. He has known much sorrow before now. He can find it a... *challenge* to trust others."

Meggie wasn't sure she could look any more surprised, but sensing that that was all Nickolas was going to say on the subject, she didn't argue.

"Thanks," she murmured instead and then, when her companion looked at her again, his own expression puzzled; "For helping us, I mean. For keeping us together. We – I – never wanted you to be in harm's way..."

Nickolas gave a shrug. Whether he was good at lying or whether he really didn't care though, Meggie couldn't quite tell.

"Dromeda is worrying about nothing. I doubt we will have an issue," he said. "The Builder will not harm us. He needs us. Although, before you ask," he held up a hand as if expecting Meggie to leap on the point; "I do not know what he needs us *for*. Just that he does."

Meggie tried not to look too interested but it was difficult not to - her companion had never willingly given her this much information before. Nickolas though, carried on as if he'd said nothing.

"As for if the Diggers try and harm us... well..." he grimaced but went no further.

Meggie glanced down at her wrist. Even in the short time since she'd woken, she could swear that the swelling had lessened a little.

Was it even possible...?

"We should make a move soon."

Before she knew it, Nickolas was then back on his feet and the moment between them was gone.

"Time is getting on."

As she too stood up though, Meggie knew that she wasn't finished yet. Despite his plea for her not to delve any further, there was something in what Nickolas had said that she knew she couldn't let lie. She didn't know if his own free mention of the Builder had made her feel braver, more certain of getting the answers she craved or what; but whatever it was, she felt suddenly willing to try.

"Wait," she said and then, barring him with one hand as if afraid that once her companion turned to leave, she'd never get him back, she hit him with it; "I know you told me not to ask. And I know you said you don't know anything, but what *does* the Builder want with us? Why are we here? Why didn't we die when we came through those flames...?" and then, as if suddenly realising the truth for the first time, her eyes flashed. "And why did you *lie* to me – to us?"

Nickolas looked like she'd slapped him in the face.

"Lie to you?" he echoed. "When did I-?"

"In the Temple!" Meggie's expression was suddenly fierce. "In the Temple, you lied to us! You told us we would die, that by giving ourselves up to the Keeper of the World we would be acting as a sacrifice! Yes," she was rambling now, "it wasn't *you* that lied – it was the other guy. Barabus or whatever his name was – but you were still *there* and you didn't *say anything*!"

Nickolas's expression was mournful.

"I wish I could tell you what you want to know, Meggie. On my very existence I would. But I cannot. The first three questions alone, I cannot answer simply because I do not *have* the answers – I did not lie when I said that even after all these years I do not know why we are all here, what the Builder's purpose is in bringing us to this place, why we did not die, why we *still* do not die." His eyes lowered. "And as for the last..." and shamefaced, he trailed off.

"Let me guess. You weren't *allowed* to tell me," Meggie challenged hotly. "You make out like you don't care whether the Builder can harm you or not *now* and yet it obviously frightened you enough to lie to us *then* when you *knew*," she jabbed a finger at his chest, "you *knew* what it meant! You *knew* we would end up here! Stuck here, just like you!"

She had every right to be angry, incensed by the trap she and the others had unknowingly walked into, but even so, meeting her eye then, Nickolas visibly bristled.

"Admit it," he said. "You believe me a coward!"

And the statement was so sudden, so matter-of-fact that completely thrown for a moment, Meggie just gawped.

"A coward? N-no!" she spluttered, completely taken off-guard. "No. I don't think that, I just-"

"No!" Nickolas argued. His whole body was suddenly very tense. Patient as he seemed to be, something in what she had said had clearly rattled him. "You are right! I should have spoken out. I should not have cared then about what the Builder would do if I disobeyed. If he wished to harm me, to *punish* me, he would have done so already. I have already disobeyed him by being here, by trying to help you. What do I have to lose by disobeying more?"

Disobeying more?

Realising what she had done, but that instead of feeling relief, joy that he was finally going to let her in, she felt nothing but fear, Meggie eye's widened. It was all very well her mocking the Builder and his commands but what did *she* know? How did she know that the Builder, wasn't going to harm Nickolas after all? What if he really did have the power to extinguish Nickolas's life, just like that?

She had no idea who this Builder was, *what* he – or she- was, what he was capable of... What if he was watching them now, just waiting to crush them? And the very hairs on the back of her neck fully rising now, Meggie couldn't help but steal a glance over Nickolas's shoulder as if half-expecting some other-worldly figure to appear.

"Don't tell me anything else!" she then cried. "Just don't!"

Nickolas however, just looked more annoyed.

"Why? What have I to fear now? The Builder will not harm me!"

Meggie glanced at him again, her expression firm.

"I know you seem very sure about that but-"

"*But* I want to tell you," Nickolas gave another dry little smile. "I *want* to tell you why we lied." And unable to help herself, unable, she realised, to stop him now even if she had wanted to, Meggie fell silent.

"I want to tell you, because I want you to know it was not because of cowardice. Yes, we were afraid, we were very afraid – we had been threatened. But not in the way you might imagine. Before we were sent back to our old – to your world, we were under strict instructions from the Builder's fighters not to breathe a word about this place, or our lives, when we returned, would, as Dromeda said, not be worth living. But that is not all-"

"But why did we need to think we'd *die?*" Meggie interjected. Still none of it seemed to make any sense to her. Surely the choice whether to save Tungala or not would have been easier if they had known, if they had been told that instead of dying, they could live on…?

That was still assuming that what they had done had prevented anything at all…

Meggie's face suddenly paled.

What if it had all been a trick just to lure them there? What if there had never been any danger of Tungala being destroyed in the first place? What if it had *all* been a lie? Or, more frighteningly, if it was the truth, what if what they had done *hadn't worked?*

"Tungala-" she muttered. "What-?" but seeing where she was going, Nickolas soon stepped in.

"But that is it exactly," he said. His hand, she noticed, was on her arm, although how long it had been there, she had no idea. "The fear for our own lives was not the only thing holding us back. The Builder's fighters told us too that if you did not walk through the flames, if you did not sacrifice yourselves for the greater cause, the salvation of your world, Tungala would fall. Whatever it was holding the Keeper of the World at bay, whatever it was preventing the utter destruction expected, was still placated by you passing through the fire."

Meggie hesitated. For some reason, she was holding her breath.

"So you're saying that what we did, even though we didn't die, still worked? We still stopped Tungala from being destroyed?"

"Precisely," Nickolas confirmed. "Or at least, this is what the Builder's fighters said…"

The Builder's fighters?

Meggie's blank confusion said it all.

"And who are these people who fight for the Builder? Are they Diggers?"

"No, they are not Diggers. They are the Builder's… *creatures*, for want of a better description. Giant beasts like none you have ever seen before." Upon recollection Nickolas's own face seemed to pale of all colour. "You may remember them. One has great colossal talons," he curled his fingers into claws, "with the head of a bird and long leathery wings. Its eyes are the clearest thing imaginable-"

Meggie gasped.

She did remember. All too well.

"The keepers of the necklaces!" she cried. It was impossible *not* to remember the beast that had tortured Fred, tortured *her* into giving up the gemstone necklace she had carried as the mark of an element. The key to Ratacopeck. The key to the Keeper of the World and the gateway to…

Gateway.

Meggie paused again. *There* was a word she hadn't thought about. Something she hadn't really considered, and as if everything was suddenly slotting into place, she gave a start.

"Hold on!" she almost shouted. "You said just before, a minute ago, that you were sent back to my world. To Tungala. I mean," and she gestured vaguely at her companion, "you were there. We all saw you..."

"I was there, yes," Nickolas replied slowly. If he had any clue as to where this was going, he didn't let on.

"So if you were *there*," Meggie mused and then, at the moment of triumph as all made sense, she lifted her eyes to him gleefully. "It has to mean that there's some way of me, of *us* getting out of here!"

Of course! How could she not have considered it before? How could she not have realised that Nickolas, Dromeda and the other two elder elements had been *back* to Tungala? How could she not have made the connection that if *they* could do it, she could too?

For a moment, she felt utterly stupid.

If that was the case, then why couldn't she and Saz, and, when she found them - *if* she found them - Bethan and Bex go back to Tungala? Why couldn't they return to the lives they had known before?

Blinking, Meggie realised that she had been staring at Nickolas the entire time without even seeing him.

"I-" she started again. But suddenly distracted by the realisation that her arm felt much cooler than it had before, she glanced down to notice that her companion had removed his hand.

Something in her chest ached. Although *why*, she had no idea.

Perhaps...

"Do you think it's possible or-?" but then, chancing another look up into Nickolas's eyes, Meggie instantly found herself frozen in place by what she saw there. For instead of the elation, the excitement, the joy for her, she had been expecting, Nickolas looked, *annoyed*.

"What?" she demanded and shocked, Meggie suddenly felt her own anger beginning to rise. "What is it? What's wrong?"

This time, Nickolas didn't flare up though. Instead, his voice still quiet, quieter perhaps than it ever had been before, he stood his ground.

"You wish to leave," was all he said.

It was a statement, not a question but realising instantly what he must be feeling, Meggie bit her lip.

He missed Tungala still; that much was obvious. All these years he had longed for a way to escape, to return to the life *he* had known all that time ago. Over time he had buried it, realised that it was nothing but a dream, nothing but a fantasy and then she had come along, reminding him of what it was to live, what it was to question, to make half-thought-out plans that she had no right to.

That was why he looked so upset. Because he knew that he could never have what was in her grasp.

Right?

Meggie could feel her face reddening.

"I don't know if I do," she admitted. And the truth was, she *didn't*. She had considered it before, right at the beginning, but whilst she too longed for things missed, just as he did, something, without even really knowing it, was holding her back. And that something was growing stronger every day…

"All of my family are, well, gone," she explained aloud. "There isn't anyone there to miss me… as such. Though to be home, to see Tungala again, it would be-"

But seeing Nickolas's expression fall, Meggie realised all too quickly that his attitude wasn't because of his own disappointment. No, she had been stupid not to see it, not to recognise it even in someone she had only known for such a short time. The sadness, wasn't meant for him.

It was meant for her.

He pitied her. Because if there was indeed such a simple way back, a simple path to take, Nickolas would have taken it; they *all* would have. All of the humans. All those who longed for the comforts, the pleasures of their own homes, their own world. They would *all* have escaped by now and the world they stood in would truly be a world of Diggers, a world of the Builder's own making.

He knew what she was saying was utterly impossible but hadn't had the heart to tell her the truth.

"Oh."

And the word fell from Meggie, just like any hopes she might have had. "I see."

Nickolas looked pained but not completely helpless.

"Returning to Tungala cannot be *entirely* incredible," he tried, with something like hope. "There was one man, some time ago. He is, *was*, much younger than myself. Or rather, he was from a *time* much younger than my own, since he was technically no different in age…"

"And why *is* that?" Meggie blurted, feeling frustrated all over again. "Nothing makes any sense here! You've been in this place for… well…" she hesitated, not really wanting to consider it too closely, "a long time but you don't look-" but as she gestured at her companion, she faltered completely as it suddenly, inexplicably hit her just how very tall he was. Nickolas towered above her by a good few feet, his broad shoulders twice the width of her own, his head inclined towards her, intent on her every word, his hair hanging in little curls to just above his eyelashes… "old," she finished weakly.

Seemingly unaware of Meggie's scrutiny, Nickolas straightened up.

"I have considered the matter many times," he said. "And all I can guess is that the Builder is gathering us for something. Something for which our youth plays great importance."

Our youth.

Meggie visibly gulped. Somehow she didn't like to think of what the Builder could possibly want with them all, what this great *gathering* might be for...

"Tell me though," she said instead. "You were an element as well. So you were given a gemstone necklace, right? A necklace that represented one of the elements? Earth, fire, air, water..."

Nickolas, looking a little surprised, nodded.

"Yes. Of course," he said. "I believe it is the same for all of us. I was, *am* an element of air."

Element of air? Could it really be? And forgetting whatever it was she'd been about to ask, Meggie's face lit up.

"You're an element of air?" she exclaimed, not quite believing it. "I'm the element of air too! Or *was...*" she frowned. "Weird..."

Nickolas though, only surprised her again by letting out a chuckle.

"I hate to ruin this moment," he said. "But I knew that you carried the air."

"You knew?" Meggie looked even more amazed. "How could you have *known?*"

Nickolas shrugged.

"Because we are all paired with our compatible elements. Every time a new element, a new human, enters this world it is expected for a previous element of the same to assist them. I knew that you were the element of air the first time I ever saw you."

"The first time *ever?*" Meggie lifted an incredulous eyebrow. "Now that *can't* be true! How could you possibly have known then? I wasn't wearing the necklace – I didn't even say a word to you!" There was something in his use of the word 'compatible' that for some reason unsettled her.

Compatibility implied fate, implied that there was something within each of them, air, earth, water or fire that made each the same as their predecessor, making the idea of the Builder's 'gathering' all the more real and frightening...

Nickolas however, never got a chance to reply, for right at that moment, they both saw movement and turning as one they came face-to-face with Dromeda.

Since his argument with Nickolas, the elder element had spent much of the last minutes standing aloof from them all, perhaps afraid to approach them after his harsh words, perhaps just taking a moment to think, to calm himself. Whatever his reasons had been to stay away though, he had returned and seeing him approach, Meggie's whole body tensed.

For a second she glanced at Nickolas as if half-expecting for him to react and begin shouting again, but the men eyed each other and then with a small, almost imperceptible nod from both, all anger between them, all argument was gone and forgotten.

Just like that.

"We should move on," Dromeda pointed out as if nothing had ever happened and regardless of his interruption, he glanced at Saz. "Shall I carry her or should we try to wake her?"

Meggie glared at him. Though she knew it was a small victory on Nickolas's part that Dromeda seemed to have come to his senses and was agreeing to carry on with them – at least for now -, she also knew that she couldn't leave things the way they were. Nickolas may be happy to carry on as if Dromeda had never spoken his thoughts but Meggie wasn't. No matter *what* Nickolas had said about how she should go easy on him, she was still *angry*.

"So," she said instead, looking Dromeda straight in the eye. "You're coming with us, are you?"

Dromeda, for a moment, seemed confused and then surprised before, realising what the little element had overheard, his own expression then hardened.

"Ah," was all he said.

"Yes. I heard you," Meggie retorted, her voice cold. "I think everyone in the *City* probably could."

She wasn't sure, but for a second, Dromeda almost looked sorry - *almost*, but before she could open her mouth again Meggie was then surprised to feel the touch of Nickolas's hand on her arm all over again and looking up at him, she saw that his face was stern.

"It is over, Meggie," he said. "Dromeda is truly sorry. He spoke in error and we should leave it at that." And he too looked at Dromeda then, his fierce eyes almost a warning. "He will not make the same mistake again."

Dromeda said nothing but with the tension over, Nickolas then turned back to Saz.

"I think maybe we should let Saz rest. She is still in shock. I fear if-"

"If what?"

The words were no more than a mumble, but all three of the listening elements heard it and giving a collective start, turned to watch as Saz stirred. Her eyes were flickering as she began to wake and forgetting all else, Meggie was back on her knees at her friend's side in a moment.

"Saz!" she half-sighed. "You're awake!"

Saz mumbled something again in her half-conscious state, but too groggy to do much more than that, she just gave a little smile.

"Here," and being careful not to jar her still-throbbing wrist, Meggie reached out to aid her dazed friend to a sit, Nickolas and Dromeda closing in overhead, ready to help. "How are you feeling?"

"Mmm," Saz managed and then, as her eyes finally opened and she took a proper good look at her companions, her smile widened. "Though next time you feel like arguing… can you do it a bit more *quietly*? You woke me up."

All three of her watching companions couldn't help but grin in return then, all of them clearly relieved in their own way to see the fourth of their group finally with them.

"Can you stand?" Dromeda asked. He sounded concerned, making Meggie steal a look at him. But whilst her eyebrows rose again, she said nothing.

"I think so," and seizing the elder element's arm gladly as he offered it, Saz clambered to her feet, taking a moment to look at their sparse surroundings before getting straight to the point.

"How long until we reach the City?" she asked. "I swear it's no closer!"

Nickolas looked out towards the City almost as if he'd forgotten it was still there.

"If we move quickly, by the end of the day – I should think," he replied with a thoughtful frown.

"Well," and Saz gave a small sigh as if the weight of their very destiny lay on her strengthening shoulders. "We'd better get a move on then," she said briskly.

Bethan lay on the bed staring up at the ceiling, her face utterly blank.

Hours that morning she had spent like this, just staring; staring at the walls, at the blank blank ceiling with nothing else to do but watch and wait. But over time, watching had turned to nothing- there were no shadows to chase here, no sense of time passing, just empty oblivion- and as for *waiting* – she had no idea what she was waiting *for*. For Belanna to return and free her? She wasn't expecting the Digger to come back any time soon. For Bex to come and find her? Bex was probably just as trapped as she was.

No, she had nothing to do now. Nothing but to just lie there. Lie and ponder. And remember.

With nothing else to occupy her, one by one she found herself dragging each memory of her old life to the forefront of her mind, inspecting it, reliving each tiny detail before placing it beside others just like it in an attempt to piece together the lost puzzle that was herself. For now, she was simply trying to recall all the details she could of the journey that had brought her to this place, and nothing more.

Just as she had discussed with Bex, she could recollect nearly every member of the travelling band now. There had been the other three women; Bex obviously; a short woman called Meggie and another called Saz. And then a dwarf, Thom; a wizard, Eliom; a man - no - a warrior, Fred; a woman, the captain of a ship the name of which she couldn't recall just yet - Elanore; and a man... the man with the blue eyes.

The man with the blue eyes.

She had spent over an hour alone on him, just rolling every name she could think of over her tongue, sometimes aloud, sometimes in the recesses of her quiet mind, as if trying each one for size as she desperately tried to remember who he was; the man from her memories, the man in her dreams, the man, who, every time she thought about, every time she imagined his face, made her breath catch in her throat and her mouth curl into a little unknowing smile.

But every time she thought she had it, every time she thought that things were ready to slot right back into place it would all slip away. The more she tried, the more desperate she was, the more determined her memories seemed to keep themselves under lock and key until, after a time, she took to trying to trick herself, to trick her brain into submission. Quickly she would focus her thoughts on memories of her earlier life, those fragments from her childhood, her mother, a withered tree in the garden, a green gemstone necklace – and then just like that she would switch back to the man, calling out a name she hadn't yet tried in the hopes of it making sense, of it being the one. Still though, nothing seemed to work...

Still he was an enigma.

Who are you? She felt like screaming. *Why can't I remember?*

"Good morning, or should I say, afternoon?"

Bethan gave a start and sat bolt upright on the bed, her face blushing as the blood rushed to her face. For a silly moment she had half-imagined that it would be him, the man. But to her disappointment it wasn't even close and seeing the intruder, her expression fell straight away into a frown.

"Barabus," she said shortly. Her head span from the rush of her sudden movement and she swayed a little as her fists clenched handfuls of the sparse bedspread.

From the doorway, Barabus looked at her as if she were some wild animal and he was judging whether it was safe to approach or not, but seeing her giddy he soon moved towards the bed and taking a seat as far away from her as he possibly could on the mattress, he began to rummage in a cloth bag at his side, pulling out a loaf of flatbread and a flagon of water.

"Here," he said dumping his load on the centre of the bed. Bethan eyed it vacantly. "I have brought you some nourishment."

"Thanks." But though she could already feel the well of saliva building in her mouth as she stared at the bread, Bethan felt just as suddenly very determined to refuse it. "You're very kind. But I don't want it."

Barabus looked at her, his own expression cold.

"You must eat," he commented. "Starving yourself will not help anyone."

"Really," and Bethan physically turned herself away from the food, away from *him* knowing that she was acting a lot braver than she felt. "I'm fine."

She was acting like a child, a part of her knew that and for a moment, Barabus shifted his weight on the bed as if he meant to get up and walk away. As if quickly changing his mind though, he moved closer instead.

"I *am* sorry about this," he then said and then, when Bethan wouldn't turn back; "I know you think me heartless for keeping you here against your will but really it is for your own protection. In fact, I-"

Her protection?

This had got Bethan's attention and unable to help herself, she swivelled to face him, her glare incredulous.

"Protection?! Against what?!" she demanded. "What could I possibly need *protection* from?"

But instead of arguing back, Barabus moved even closer to her, his voice low, conspiratorial and for a moment, Bethan thought she saw what looked like *sadness* in his eyes.

"Protection from *yourself*," he then said quietly. "I brought you here to protect you from making any rash decisions. To prevent you from injury."

There was a silence as, bewildered, Bethan just shook her head for a moment. For some reason she hadn't really been expecting an explanation like *this* and she would have been the first to admit she wasn't quite sure what to make of it.

"Well I don't *need* protecting," she retorted aloud. "I wasn't doing anything wrong! Bex is the only person, the only other living being I know from my own world and you're trying to keep us apart!" She pointed a threatening finger straight at Barabus's chest. "Bex is the one remnant I have of the life I knew before I was dragged here *against my will*. So why won't you let us stay together?"

"You have never been 'dragged' *anywhere* against your will!" Barabus growled, his own anger rising, "If I remember correctly, you chose to walk through the flames! You chose to come here! You and you alone decided your fate!"

His last word seemed to echo hollowly in the tiny room as he halted, his eyes wide, his fists clenched. Finally getting to his feet he then took a deep breath as if determined to calm himself.

Bethan meanwhile, all fight gone as she realised the truth, simply stared into her lap. She felt suddenly heavy, as if her head were too much for her neck, her neck too much for her shoulders; heavy with the helplessness, the sorrow that had claimed her only hours before. The realisation that she was stranded, stuck, alone, and there was nothing she could do about it.

Right now…

"If I'd known I'd be coming here…" she muttered.

"You would have acted in exactly the same way," Barabus sounded firm. "We all would. We all *do*." And though again, Bethan snapped her head round to look up at him, her face aghast, ready to be offended that he could presume to know her, somehow she just couldn't bring herself to say anything. Somehow she knew he was right.

Barabus began to pace the little room.

"I know it may not seem a consolation now, but this world is better than the death you would have experienced," he continued.

The death you lied about, Bethan wanted to add.

"Here we cannot die."

Bethan got to her feet as well. The dizziness was well and truly gone now.

"Yes," she agreed. "And what kind of life is that? What kind of life am I going to lead stuck in this room?" her face was grim. "I think I'd prefer death over imprisonment!"

At this though, Barabus gave an ugly scowl. His gaze seemed intent on the floor.

"You know nothing of what you speak! You know nothing of death! You are young!"

Bethan's hands balled into fists.

"So are you!" she cried and then suddenly, as if the words had taken everything from her, she slumped back on the bed, dejected.

Was this what life was going to be like for her now? Anger, sorrow, loneliness? Barabus wasn't going to let her go willingly – that much she could already tell. But what if she had to stay there? And not just there, in that room – what if she had to stay in that new world? What if what Barabus and others had said was true? What if humans really didn't *die* here? What if she just carried on living and living and living there with no chance of return, of escape?

Escape.

Bethan's mind went back to the hole in the stairs.

Belanna had said that she could possibly find a way of them talking to the dead man, the only one who had ever managed to escape from this place…

Ophelius.

The name meant something to Bethan but like so many things, she couldn't recall where she'd heard or seen it before.

But still…

Even *that* wasn't a certainty. Nothing was. It was only a small hope, a small chance. One that she had grasped with all her might only a matter of hours before but even now she was beginning to feel slip through her fingers.

More than anything Bethan just wished that she was back in her own world, the world she little remembered and yet knew she loved, she cherished. Just like the man.

The man from her memories.

Every time was the same: how she longed even to see him again, just once, to feel his arms warm and strong around her, to feel his eyes boring into hers, his lips lingering on her own...

And overwhelmed suddenly, Bethan felt tears begin to spring unwillingly to her eyes, to escape where she couldn't and alarmed at the sudden unexplained change in her, Barabus looked almost frightened.

"There, there," he tried softly, in a voice quite unlike his own and slowly he moved back across the room to sit near her again. Though he reached a hand out, he didn't touch her. "I did not mean to upset you. Only to make you *see*. This world is not so bad," and he gestured to the doorway where the guards outside still stood, no doubt listening to them talk. "The people here are friendly enough. You will learn to endure, perhaps even to enjoy life again."

But Bethan was almost sobbing now. She couldn't help it and much as it disgusted her to cry in front of him, to show so much raw emotion, she also realised right then that it might be the only weapon she had at her disposal. Barabus obviously didn't understand *why* she was so upset. He had clearly long forgotten the yearning for home, for the world he had left and that, in its own way put her at some small advantage. She was weak before him and weakness was one thing Barabus couldn't seem to deal with...

Leaning in closer Barabus cleared his throat.

"Bethan, if you desire, I will remove the guards. As long as you promise not to leave," he pleaded slowly, clearly trying to find some sort of comfort that would stop her tears.

Bethan ceased crying almost immediately.

Perhaps there was hope after all. Perhaps she could find a way out of this...

She wiped her eyes with the back of a hand.

"Would you really do that?" she sniffled and Barabus gave a smile. It was weak and lop-sided but a smile nonetheless.

"Yes," he replied. "Of course. But like I said; *only* if you give your word that you will not try to leave."

Bethan stared at him. Already he looked relieved that she'd finally managed to gain what looked like some semblance of control over herself, but despite this, she still didn't know what to make of him.

For all his faults, despite his misguided imprisonment and fierce manner, Barabus *had* looked after her. He hadn't left her alone to suffer, mindless and exhausted when she'd first arrived. He had been the one to give her her name, to return her back to herself in some small way, to bring her to civilisation and now he was offering to remove the guards from the door when there was a high chance she would try and escape. Could she really make a promise to him not to try when she knew she had every intention of breaking it?

Unaware of her thoughts though, Barabus looked away, his mind already moving on to other matters.

"I am not so very different from you, you know," he mused. "Despite what you may think."

And not knowing what else to do, Bethan continued to watch him, her red-rimmed eyes wide.

"I don't see *how*," she mumbled. But the fight had entirely left her now. Arguing seemed pointless, venting her frustration obviously fell on deaf ears. "I'm nothing like you."

Barabus sighed, his expression unusually affected.

"I think perhaps in the same circumstances you would be," he replied. But it wasn't an argument. He too seemed to have given up for the moment and Bethan couldn't help but realise with a guilty thrill that it was probably down to fear. He didn't want to see her to cry again. That much was clear.

Bethan's voice was icy. There was arguing and then there was standing up for herself.

"I would *not*," she said a little more forcefully. "I would never imprison someone against their will."

They were back to that, back to the glaring issue again but to Bethan's amazement, Barabus didn't rise to it. Instead, he only smiled, the grin of an experienced man amused by naivety, a worrying expression to the younger woman who couldn't seem to understand what was funny but then; "you and I are the same," Barabus insisted. "We must be or we would never have been paired."

Bethan just blinked.

"Paired?" she echoed. What was he talking about, paired? She'd never met the man until a handful of days ago. Although young in face and body he was far older than her, so how could they even remotely be 'paired'?

"Yes, paired..." Barabus said almost as if he couldn't quite believe she hadn't noticed it before. "Do you think I helped you completely out of choice?"

And stung a little, Bethan paled, for of course he was right, she *hadn't* noticed; not until now at least, now that it had been pointed out to her and almost thrown in her face.

She had never thought about why it was that the four men from her own world, the four ghostly men who had stood before her and the other three women, leading them to the flames, were the same men they knew here. Why it was Barabus had been the first man she had met in this new world, why or how he had come to be by her side, and stuck by her, just as Gergo had initially taken care of Bex. It had all made an odd sort of sense – it had all felt somehow *right* – if anything in that place *could* be- but how and why she had no idea...

"I don't understand," she tried. "How could we be *paired*? We are *nothing* alike!"

"Oh, but we are," Barabus replied. He looked almost smug. "We are both, or should I say, *were*, carriers of the element of earth. And though it may seem an accident, it was not by chance that you and I were chosen by the Builder for that part."

Element of earth.

It was the first time she had heard him use that term, but it wasn't the first time she had ever heard it. The men on the stairs, the conversation she and Bex had overheard...

He was brought here not too long ago. The last element; element of earth I believe.

At the time the word 'element' had meant something to her but she had pushed it aside. Just as she had pushed it aside when Belanna had named the City the City of the Diggers or the City of the *Elements*.

But now?

Now, as the word settled in her mind, swirling about in her consciousness, Bethan could feel her head starting to swim all over again as memories took hold.

"But why do you need me? What do I have to do with this?"

"We need you because you are the key. Well, one of the keys."

The man with the blue eyes and Fred, the warrior. They were all sitting together in a room that she recognised now as her own dear home.

"What do you mean one of the keys?"

"Well." The man with the blue eyes was looking at her so patiently, so kindly. *"There are four of you; fire, water, air and earth - that's you."*

"The four fundamental elements? The four elements of life?" Bethan could feel her own past amazement bubbling up inside her.

"Yes. Exactly. Each of you represents one of these elements." And then, suddenly, the man was sitting up in his chair. *"Tell me, do you have a necklace?"*

"Yes... I'm wearing it."

The necklace she could remember, the family heirloom, green and beautiful. It had all been part of a greater plan, of a bigger picture. And suddenly, Bethan felt like a large part of her past life had finally revealed itself to her.

The elements. Bex, Saz and Meggie. She knew now why they had walked through those flames. She could remember now why they had journeyed so far, why they had sacrificed themselves, thinking that they were saving Tungala, their own world, thinking that they were saving the people they loved...

It was not by chance that you and I were chosen by the Builder for that part...

And then, as she managed to get a hold on her thoughts, Bethan found that she was shocked, shocked by what Barabus was essentially telling her and shocked by his sudden honesty. She'd tried in vain to get any information about this world, about what had happened, about the Builder from him, from Belanna, only to be given the smallest scraps in return. But this? This was something else. The idea that the Builder had chosen her, had known about her, not only now but from childhood, from the time she received the necklace from her mother, was mindboggling.

Somehow it made everything seem much much bigger and, in its way, much much worse…

As if detecting he had said too much, Barabus was then on his feet again before Bethan had so much as a chance to gasp.

"I will leave the food with you," he said quickly, nodding towards the long-forgotten bread he had brought, still sitting untouched on the bed. "It is getting on to noon. I have things to attend to."

"Wait!" and realising that he really was going to leave after that, Bethan leapt up to follow him. "What are you trying to say? That we are related or something? I don't understand! I-"

But Barabus didn't look back as he stepped towards the door

"I shall dismiss the guards," was all he said. And that was it. In a moment the door was pulled open, the elder element had stepped through and then he was gone, the wood swinging back in Bethan's face with a slam.

"Anyone heard from Darius recently?" the Digger called, lazily scratching his head with one hand as he used his knife to pick at a loose thread on his shirt with another.

The other six Diggermen mumbled and groaned in the negative.

"Think he was on some assignment in the outer city. Something to do with the new humans," one of them shrugged. His mouth rose in a sneer and several of the others shook their heads scornfully, one even spitting on the dry ground.

"No matter how much the Builder might wish it," the spitter added. "I wouldn't do *that* job for the world." And the others just jeered in response, several raising weapons as all the while, the group of humans looked on in worried silence.

"I can only assume they are not our admirers," Dromeda scowled under his breath, in earshot of Nickolas, Meggie and Saz. The four were huddled so close to each other that even breathing seemed loud.

"Well then, let's not give them a chance to find us," Nickolas added and the other three nodded. It seemed the best solution, but even so…

"What are we going to do though?" Saz asked, her voice shaking nervously. Her eyes never left the way ahead. "They're blocking the way into

THE ENTITY OF SOULS

the City." And straightening up a little, Nickolas took a quick moment to get his bearings. Sure enough the four companions were crouched at the very edge of the inner City. Each building here was exactly like the last, short and squat and white but everywhere he looked something seemed to be obstructing their path. To their right was an alleyway leading towards the City centre, but though it would have been their best route, it was blocked by a cart laden with heavy barrels, any attempt to move of which was bound to draw attention to themselves. On their left were more buildings but each were pressed tightly together with barely room for even Meggie to squeeze between them. Finally, behind was the prairie, the dead landscape separating the outer city from the inner and directly ahead, down the longest path were the Diggers, sitting in the middle of a small square.

The elder element squinted as if trying to study the six figures more closely. Each of them, he was secretly afraid to see, were armed.

Did they know? Was that why they were here? To stop them?

The thought wasn't entirely impossible…

"We will just have to make our move when they are not looking," he then muttered after a time. What other choice did they have? They couldn't go back. It was too late for that now. "Dromeda," and looking at his friend pointedly, Nickolas watched as his companion gave a little nod. Without so much as another word, Dromeda then broke away from the group and ducking into the main alleyway ahead, he slid along the side of the wall, heading straight for the little gang of Diggermen, his steps almost silent.

"Where's he going?" Meggie hissed, remembering to keep her voice low.

But Nickolas only glanced at her.

"Be ready to run," was his only reply.

Meggie turned to Saz and Saz smiled weakly back as they both hugged the back wall of the alley, waiting for the sign, whatever it may be, to spring up and run.

Meanwhile, reaching the end of the alleyway, Dromeda seemed to freeze for a second but then, suddenly, he stepped out of the darkness and without warning, began racing straight towards the six lazy men.

For a moment all three watching companions held their breath, trying not to cry out as their fourth got closer and closer to the little rabble until…

"Hey!" one Digger cried out and suddenly, Dromeda was rolling to the ground and then in one movement was up again and running, sprinting across the little square away from them all. "Hey! That human's got my sword! Hey! Stop him!"

For a heartbeat nothing happened, the other six Diggers slow to react, some sitting up, looking stupidly about them as others got to their feet. But then there was another cry.

"There he is!" and all of a sudden, all six of the group were up and ready, bloodlust in their eyes, in the taut fingers tightening around weapons and all were moving towards the top left corner of the square where another alleyway led off into the edges of the City, and where Dromeda now stood bold as brass, his arms waving, sure enough, clutching in one hand the sword he had stolen.

Meggie straightened up in alarm as if she was going to make for him herself, to somehow help, whatever her opinion still was of the elder element. But before she could have the chance, Nickolas had slipped his large hand over hers.

"Now!" he ordered and only just having time to grab Saz by the wrist, Meggie felt herself being jerked up and then along into a scattered sprint as Nickolas ran the full length of the remaining alley and burst into the now-deserted square, pulling both women along behind him.

Instead of turning left after their companion, all three hurried to the right, charging down the next space between the buildings in their bid to reach the centre of the City.

Behind, they could hear shouting and the rush of feet as Dromeda led the six Diggers on a merry chase. They sounded close, very close and almost stumbling, Meggie took a moment to pause and turn, craning her neck to see where the commotion was coming from.

For a second, she couldn't see anything, the way behind them was empty, with nothing to show for their escape but some half-smudged footprints in the dirt, but then she almost let out a cry. Dromeda's face was flushed from running. In his hand was still gripped the sword but most importantly, as he rounded the corner after them, all seven of the Diggers followed, their own weapons raised and ready, curses and shouts of fury spilling from their lips

Meggie felt Nickolas give an extra hard tug on her arm.

"Keep running!" he bellowed. "Do not stop!"

Dromeda too was shouting, gesturing for them to keep going, pushing them all along. But Saz, at the rear of the trio, was slowing down too, trying to look back as Dromeda and their assailants got closer and closer...

Staring about him frantically, Nickolas yanked the women to the right, taking another unplanned street. They weren't going to be fast enough – that much was quickly dawning on them all. They weren't going to be able to shake this angry mob off. Not unless...

"Quick!" he cried and suddenly he was veering off to the left this time, dragging the group down an even smaller and dimmer alley and then, before either women could respond, could even take in what was happening, he had wrenched open the front door of one of the buildings and they all burst into a darkened room, the door slamming shut behind them with a grinding bang.

For a good few minutes all three of the elements just stood, panting in the pitch-blackness, trying to gain control of their breathing and still their frightened hearts, straining to hear what was happening outside. But everything was silent now. The shouting and the cursing and the running seemed to have ceased, or rather passed on along a different path.

Surprisingly, Nickolas's hasty plan seemed to have worked. Dromeda and the trail of Diggers were gone. For now...

The first to recover, Meggie stared about her, squinting into the blackness around them. She could still feel the warmth of Nickolas's hand clutching hers. He was standing very close to her, enough to make his breathing, deep and fast, the loudest of all. She could feel the heat of it brushing across the top of her head in quick blasts.

She could *also* feel the grip she still had on Saz. Her fingers had tightened with fear, enough to make her bruised wrist throb, and realising that she must be causing the other element pain, she quickly released her hold. Nickolas released his too, but Meggie could still feel his fingers brush against hers, never too far away.

"What about Dromeda?" Saz was the one to ask. Whether it was the sudden darkness or the fact that they probably weren't completely safe yet, she still kept her voice hushed.

Nickolas shifted in the blackness.

"Stay here," he whispered. "I will go for him."

"No!"

Too late did Meggie realise and with a cry, she was groping in the blackness for that hand again, for an arm, for any part of him she could grasp just to make him stay. "You can't! What if you get caught?!"

But it was too late. The fingers were gone as was the brush of breath across her head. He had moved away and before either could say another word, both women heard the sound of the door opening, saw the brief splash of dim early-evening light and in a moment, Nickolas was gone.

For a good long while Meggie and Saz just stood there, in the blackness as if frozen in place, still breathless and uncertain until;

"Do you think we should try and find a lamp?" Saz suggested. She still spoke in a whisper, even though the street outside was eerily quiet and distracted by listening for any approaching movements – hopefully Nickolas and Dromeda's - Meggie just nodded before remembering where they were.

"Yes," she muttered absently. "But not too bright. We don't want anyone to know we're here." By 'anyone' of course, she meant the seven angry Diggers and remembering their plight, remembering just how fiercely they had taken after Dromeda, Saz bit her lip.

"Do you think they *know?*" she hissed. "Who we are, I mean. About what happened in the outer city?"

Meggie took a few small steps further into the building, her arms outstretched to protect herself from falling. Her eyes never left the space where she knew the door was.

"I hope not," she replied, trying not to sound anxious. Because if they did, if news had already spread to the City that they were not only disobeying the Builder's instructions but that they had defied and attacked one of the Diggers...

Pfft!

Suddenly there was a loud click in the blackness, a yellow flicker and then the room was flooded with light.

Straight away the elements flinched, Saz even letting out a yelp as they instantly turned to each other, both expecting her companion to be the source. But both were empty-handed and both looked just as shocked as they then realised that they weren't, as they had thought, alone...

Squinting in the light, Meggie scanned the space with new eyes.

They were standing in a room, much like those they had known in the outer city; plain, with a simple bed, a simple table and a simple basin. It also had an oil lamp in the corner, the source of the sudden light and crouched in a worried ball beside it, was a figure, a woman, who even now, as she lifted fingers from her own stunned eyes, was climbing to her feet, her legs unsteady as she gave an audible gasp.

Right at that second, as she stepped up and out of the direct glare, Saz and Meggie then saw her, *really* saw her and both responded in kind, both hearts suddenly jumping afresh.

"Bethan!"

The word came out as a sort of collective sigh, a cry of utter surprise, and for a moment, the figure just stared at the two of them as if her own amazement was the greatest of them all. But then;

"M-Meggie? Saz?" and the moment shattered, Meggie and Saz, forgetting their fears, both broke into grins and ran forward to embrace their lost friend.

AN INTRUSION AND A REVEALING

Elanore rubbed her cold hands together, blowing on her fingers and watching as her breath sent wisps of warm mist swirling into the night air. Summer it might be, but all could feel it; the chilly air drawing in beneath the shadows of the empty trees flanking the banks of the river.

It was the cold of darkness, of night and shadow, but also – the sea captain couldn't fail not to notice it – the coldness of foreboding, and resting one hand on the Karenza's wheel, stroking it like a loved pet to steady her nerves, her eyes cast themselves on the way ahead. All the while the silent blackness tugged beneath her as the ship continued to push herself further upriver, the mysterious wind conjured by Eliom buffering the sails at her back.

The world was strangely silent here, like a world at peace, but despite it all, Elanore didn't feel like resting.

Not quite yet. Not, at least, until she was sure…

"You seem anxious."

The cold voice rang out so suddenly that Elanore jumped before, spinning around, she soon stiffened, her teeth setting on edge as she recognised the speaker.

Eldora the Lectur was wrapped in her usual dark shroud, revealing only a very small part of her pale face. In the darkness she looked taller somehow, elongated, but in her frail-looking hands, disturbingly white against the night, she carried a candle.

The single light cast a feeble glow across the deck and turning back to the helm, Elanore could just make out the very tip of the ship's prow, a glimpse of the horse's fluttering mane and beyond into the abyss of night, before the flame guttered and everything fell back to dimness. Again she touched the Karenza's helm, smoothing the soft wood beneath her fingertips as she thought of how to respond to the statement she knew was really a question.

Should she speak the truth aloud? The truth about her fears, her thoughts, her doubts? Her concerns about their absolute and utter aloneness; for after all, where were the other ships? For almost a day they had been travelling upriver and yet they had seen nothing, no vessels, no people, no other signs of life...

Wasn't that enough to make one anxious? And yet...

Elanore glanced at the Lectur, but avoided her pit-like eyes, almost invisible in the blackness. Just like the others, it was no secret that from the first moment they had met, the sea captain hadn't liked Eldora. There was something about her, something dark and strange and unnerving and, due to her frightening ability to See, *unpredictable*. And Elanore didn't like that. She didn't like unpredictability – not in *that* way – in a *bad* way. Unpredictability was dangerous. And more danger was the last thing any of her crew needed right now. Especially on a night like this...

Without knowing it, the captain's grip tightened on the wheel and for a moment, she thought about just leaving. She knew she wanted to. She was exhausted, in desperate need of rest after a long night by the helm, ever ready to take control of the ship just in case...

Yes, Fred was in the crow's nest, taking his watch, but something had kept her out there, above deck, alert and ready for trouble. And yet as Eldora made her final approach, stopping only just short of the sea captain's shoulder, Elanore knew that however much she might not want to, she was going to be remaining there a while longer. Etiquette, if nothing else, dictated it. That and...

"You fear me."

The Lectur's voice was like a long throaty hiss on the air and Elanore felt her whole body shudder with it as her face reddened at the unexpected remark.

"No – I-" she flustered. "I'm not *afraid* of you."

"It is all right. I am quite accustomed to fear. I *understand* fear," Eldora replied. She sounded as if she were smiling a little, though it was impossible to tell through her coverings. But as if coming straight to her true business, she then turned fully on Elanore, the candle swishing dangerously close to the sea captain's ear as her cloak billowed. "Tell me," she said. "How did you come by such a vessel as this?"

"The Karenza?"

And stunned into uncertain silence, Elanore hugged the Karenza's wheel even closer. Eldora was standing very close now and yet despite this, the captain could feel no warmth radiating from her, no *presence*, almost as if she were a ghost, an other-worldly apparition, untouchable and cold.

The sea captain took the smallest step away.

"I bought her myself, if you're trying to *imply* something," she answered a little hotly before, after another uncomfortable pause, she gave a sigh. "My brother and I bought her together."

She didn't know why she'd said it. She'd had no need to mention him, to tell the truth to this almost complete stranger and yet somehow it had slipped out and straight away, Eldora's gaze turned to the river ahead as if searching its depths for answers, for knowledge, for a name Elanore knew so well, loved so well and yet had dared not speak aloud for so long...

"Elender."

The Lectur spat the word so forcefully, as if it had fallen unbidden from her reluctant lips, that Elanore instantly swivelled to glare at her.

"How *dare* you!" she growled, feeling suddenly furious. "How *dare* you speak his name like that! He was a good man!"

But Eldora didn't meet the captain's eye. Instead, again, her eyes appeared to be smiling, yet not, this time, in some smug defeat. It was almost as if she understood the pain, the sadness...

"That I am sure," she replied. And then; "I have Seen him."

"Seen?" and as if the very wind had been knocked from her, Elanore paused. *This* she had not been expecting. "What - what have you Seen?"

"Only a little." But the Lectur seemed suddenly very reluctant to say any more. "I Saw how it was you purchased the Karenza together. I Saw your hopes, his dreams. I-" she faltered as if realising for the first time the effect her words could be having on her companion.

Elanore's face was a mask of well-practiced nonchalance but there was something dark in the depths of her eyes, years of grief that would never pass.

"Why did you ask me then, if you already knew?" she snapped, blinking back tears that weren't there. Why had the conversation taken this turn? Was the Lectur just trying to taunt her? To make her speak of her brother aloud, to relive the pain of his death? Did the creature have no feelings?

"Elanore."

Elanore turned with something like relief as another figure then appeared at the helm.

Edmund, wrapped up tightly in a cloak, also carried a candle, the likes of which out-shone Eldora's and as he crossed the deck in the dim light, he looked first to the Lectur, his face hidden in shadow before turning to Elanore with an expression the sea captain could only describe as apologetic.

"Is everything all right?" he asked. The request sounded overly casual, like a need for an update on the passing night, but Elanore could tell that it was really meant for her.

She relaxed a little.

"Fine, yes," she said a little frostily as she too glanced at Eldora, keeping the pretence alive. The Lectur barely seemed to have noticed that the pair had become a trio; her gaze was cast once more on the blackness ahead. "All seems very quiet." *Too quiet.*

Edmund nodded absently.

"Good. Good. I couldn't sleep, so... I thought I'd give you a chance to rest. I can take over for a while here. If you want."

Elanore looked at the wheel beneath her fingers reluctantly, but nothing in Tungala, not even the thought of leaving the Karenza in the hands of someone else, even someone she knew and trusted, was going to stop her right then from getting away from the Lectur. She wasn't going to need telling twice and giving a nod and a smile she gestured to the helm.

"All yours," she commented. "Give me a shout if anything happens."

"Of course," and with that the sea captain was gone and Edmund took up his new place, one hand on the wheel, one hand still clutching the candle.

He was nervous and he knew exactly why. He too could feel the stillness in the air, the nothingness, he too was unnerved by the Karenza's solitude but that wasn't the worst of it.

He was nervous because this was the first time he'd been left alone with Eldora since the kiss.

The kiss.

Edmund inwardly shuddered to think that it had even become a *thing* in his mind, a named incident, something he knew he wasn't going to be able to brush off so readily. A part of him feared the memory, whilst another feared that she would try to do it again, or worse, hit out at him, blame him for not being able to return her feelings, that long-lost but never forgotten burning within.

Maybe he should say something. What, he had no idea. But *something*. Something to warn her off? Something to comfort her? Something maybe to satisfy his own strange guilt? *Something.*

But even as he turned then to Eldora, to speak, maybe even to apologise, he saw that *none* of those were going to be appropriate, for the Lectur was frozen like a statue of ice, her eyes on the horizon still; only not, for they had rolled back to white, her expression entirely blank and realising exactly what it was he was seeing, Edmund recoiled in horror before the words, in a voice not her own, then fell from her lips.

"*You cannot defeat it... the entity... the balance is too delicate!*" she cried loudly and Edmund stood agape as he recognised the voice speaking, the voice from his dream so many nights ago, the voice Eldora had interpreted.

"*There may be a small window...No more can I say, for the Builder has many ears....*"

And then the Lectur's speech changed pitch and quality as it rose to a frenzy of high-pitched squeaking.

"*Bring me to your leader... You have trespassed through our domain, Edmund!*" and startled at the mention of his name spat with such malice, Edmund searched Eldora's blank face in growing trepidation.

Who was this? He didn't recognise the voice, or the words. He couldn't place them anywhere, which to him, had to mean only one thing; the Lectur was Seeing the future, *his* future. She was Seeing someone, something yet to come and before he knew what he was doing, Edmund found himself grabbing Eldora by the arm, his grasp desperate as a cold shiver of foreboding shuddered down his spine.

"Who are you? What domain?" he demanded as if believing for a moment that the voice being transmitted would reply. But despite his sudden force, Eldora carried on, her words becoming all the more fervent;

"*We are going to take you to our Chief now... She wishes to speak with you... Stop this at once! Or we will kill you all!*"

Kill you all. The words rang in Edmund's ears like icy stabs.

This wasn't good. This really wasn't good...

"Stop *what* at once?" he cried, positively shaking Eldora under his grip. "Who *are* you?!"

But before any more words could be said, several things then happened all at once.

Instantly, Eldora ceased talking, her eyes refocused and she let out a sigh as she came to, confused and unaware. At the same time, Edmund caught a flutter of movement in the corner of his eye and releasing his hold on the Lectur, he turned, reaching for his sword only to feel a sharp pressure at his neck and the side of his temple.

"Don't move," a little voice hissed in his ear, "or I will slay you where you stand."

And shocked, Edmund took a sharp intake of breath as he felt a twinge of pain at his throat. He quickly froze.

"Now," the owner of the little voice and Eldora's Seeing then continued matter-of-factly, "without any more fuss, bring me to your leader..."

—

Eliom sat up in bed fully awake and fully ready.

Something was wrong. He had known it the second he'd awoken from his trance, he had known it even the moment trouble had dared to breathe upon the air and in less than a second, the wizard was on his feet, staff in hand and striding for the cabin door.

The magic of old burned at the base of his tongue and he let it flow free, quietly, peacefully, aware of Thom sleeping nearby, the only one to rest that night. His staff began to emit a glow and he followed it gladly through the blackness, up the steep steps and out onto the deck.

Instantly the cold night hit him full in the face. But this was not all.

Before he even had a chance to draw breath it was on him, pounding him in the jaw, the shoulder, the abdomen. Flying creatures, bombarding him one by one in the darkness, taking their shot then swerving away into obscurity, a great flurry of them...

Eliom shielded his face with a hand.

"*LIGHT!*" he then bellowed, pounding the end of his staff to the ground and straight away the entire deck flooded with white, illuminating everything in one glorious spark.

For a second, everything seemed to freeze as if in one brilliant snapshot of time, but then the creatures rallied and with barely a moment to take in his surroundings, the wizard was hit again, this time in the arm, followed by a burst to the chest. Quickly, Eliom threw himself to the ground, rolling onto his back.

Above his head he could see them now. The night sky was blacker than black with them all, roiling and flapping and screeching. Creatures of the darkness with long leathery wings and sharp black snouts. Hundreds, no, thousands of them and all with-

Eliom aimed his staff high into the midst of the swarm as yet another beast made its charge, aiming straight for his eyes with sharp sharp talons. The wood emitted a new, wailing scream and letting out a cry of its own, the creature soon dived away again, snorting and howling in unseen pain. But though that single unit was finished, plenty more circled to take its place and the wizard barely had time to move before he was firing shot upon shot of sound. The things were everywhere, like hordes of black thick insects flooding the air, unrelenting and fierce.

"Eliom!"

Through the throng of cries he heard Edmund's shout loud and clear.

"Eliom!"

And knowing that he could not hope to hold the beasts off one by one forever, the wizard urgently searched his mind for the spell, the words that had served them all well once before, that had saved the element Meggie's life.

There was no light, no noise, no big show, but straight away the magic worked, as the creatures, as if angered by this new enchantment, shot towards him with fresh rage only to find themselves smashing into the invisible wall that had suddenly appeared in the air, rebounding off across the sky. Eliom watched as one creature flew full pelt towards him, only to crash into the field and only just manage to veer up from a stunned nose-dive before it was too late.

Undeterred now, the wizard then got back to his feet, finally taking a moment to examine his foe more closely.

The flying creatures were in fact some kind of rodent. They were dark, with beady little eyes, large ears and fast gristly wings the span of a handbreadth. But it was not the appearance of these flying missiles that struck him the most.

Each little scruff of dark sinew and bone carried a rider, a tiny, human-shaped rider as tall as an index finger and about as thin too, with tiny robes of black and amber, minute hands, fingers and perfect sandaled feet. Their faces, all female to the wizard's eyes, were beautiful, stunning even, and yet terrifyingly fierce for in each minutely-crafted hand they wielded a pair of long spears with what looked like a bloody thorn carved at each end, making each staff almost twice their height.

Nimphs.

The word came to his mind as if it had always been there and straight away the wizard, in a rare moment of almost-fear, paused as he realised what it meant. What it truly meant. What these creatures truly were. And most importantly, how much danger he and his friends were now in.

Forcing himself to react as he strained to hold the air shield, the only thing still keeping him alive against his tiny foes, Eliom then dashed across the deck, the bats swerving violently from his path.

He could see Edmund through the mass of black now. He was at the helm, another figure, Eldora, with him. Both of them were surrounded in a swirl of moving, flying bodies and, as he moved closer, he even saw, to his horror, that several of the tiny people had dismounted and were now clambering along both of their shoulders, one dangerously close to Edmund's neck.

Slowly he lowered his staff, ready to cast another spell, but right at that second Edmund suddenly seemed to notice his friend and with a grunt he gave the tiniest shake of his head.

No, he mouthed and stepping even nearer, Eliom then saw that the person on Edmund's shoulder, the one closest to his companion's throat was speaking to him, her face leaning in towards his ear and, most importantly, her two thorny weapons pressed like fangs against his exposed skin.

The little woman had a high-pitched lulling voice that despite her size, seemed to carry through the din of flapping wings.

"Bring me to your leader *at once*, human!" the wizard heard her spit shrilly and Edmund flinched as the thorns touching his neck moved. One more push and the sharp barbs were bound to penetrate, but this didn't seem to bother the tiny woman in the slightest. In fact, she almost looked to be enjoying herself, her bright little face almost shining in satisfaction as she clambered closer to Edmund's neck, her revealing cloak – a different colour from the others, blue and black – shifting like flowing silk across her tiny shoulders. "I warn you…"

"I *am* the leader here," Edmund shot back, his voice choked in a desperate effort not to move more than he had to. "You're talking to him."

"*You?*"

Despite her obvious contempt though, for a moment the tiny woman seemed to consider it, her miniature eyes half-closed in thought, before, noticing Eliom for the first time, she levelled the wizard a menacing glare and turned back to the Explorer with a look of complete scorn.

"Do you expect me to believe that?" she challenged. "A human?" And she gave a laugh - the sound glorious yet deadly – before, all at once, she was serious again. "If you are the leader here then call your wizard off."

For someone so small, she seemed awfully sure of herself and though Eliom studied the tiny being with his usual calm collectedness he said nothing.

"He's not my wizard," the Explorer replied, putting great emphasis on the 'my'. "We're a free group here. We're not-" But the woman-creature obviously wasn't patient enough for specifics.

"Call him off!" she snapped, throwing Eliom another glare, "Or I'll kill you *both*."

The threat, coming from such a tiny little mouth, to anyone else, in any other situation, might have seemed ridiculous, laughable even, but as Edmund then met Eliom's eye and all manner of secret meaning passed between them, Eliom suddenly gave a sigh and holding up his other hand as if in defeat, lowered his staff.

Instantly, released from the wizard's spell, the flying black beasts swarmed about his head, diving closer and closer, snapping at his face, his head and arms, for a moment, blocking all view he may have had of the frozen Edmund and Eldora. But though the faces of each tiny rider were screwed in fearsome rage as they aimed their barbs and fang-filled rides at the wizard, Eliom noted with interest that none of them touched him. Though all teeth and thorns and threat, none of them seemed to want to draw close enough to cause any *harm* and though he knew that it wasn't much – he also knew that it was still *something*.

Through the loud flutter of hundreds of leathery wings, the wizard could still hear Edmund's voice.

"Who are you? What do you want with us?" the Explorer demanded.

The little woman laughed again, the strange bewitching sound filling the deck like something enchanting yet toxic.

"Who am I?" she taunted. "I am Hoclee and you have trespassed through our domain, Edmund, for which you must pay the price!"

Edmund.

The word shot through the black throng like a curse and recognising his own name spoken, the Explorer couldn't hide his astonishment.

"How-?" he cried. "How do you know me?! I have no-"

But Hoclee just gave a carefree sneer. Though it was an ugly look, her small, perfectly-formed face was still somehow radiant.

"You're not very observant, are you?" she pointed out. "We've been trailing you ever since you entered the river mouth. And. You're. Not. Welcome. Here!" With every word, she drove her thorny spears further into Edmund's skin, making him flinch. She hadn't yet broken through, but it wouldn't be long and both of them knew it.

Suddenly, the little thing known as Hoclee then loosened her weapons and striding further along her captive's shoulder, she made an effort to stare him full in the face.

"Now tell me," she demanded, "why are you here? Why do you trespass?"

And Edmund, finally freed from immediate danger, took his chance to release a long-held breath, quickly scanning his surroundings as if weighing up his chances of escape before he gave his answer.

"We're simply passing through," he said slowly. "We mean you and your...*people*, no harm. All we ask for is peace."

"Passing through, you say?"

The little woman again seemed to consider a moment, her tiny head tilting first to one side, then the other as if ready to accept this perfectly reasonable explanation. Perhaps it *was* all a misunderstanding after all; perhaps they could go their separate ways, as the man had said, at peace.

And yet - Hoclee's tiny eyes shifted back to Eliom suspiciously. And yet they had a wizard and – her eyes moved to Eldora, who had neither moved nor spoken a word since the ambush –a witch of some kind, a Seer. And not only that, she had been informed by one of her rank, that in the nest above was another strange being, a warrior...

She looked again at Edmund. *And yet all lead by the weakest of all... a human. Curious.*

It was a strange group and no mistake, but though the tiny woman seemed ready to give in, to give the nod, the order to leave them be, something seemed to catch her gaze.

There was a movement, a slight twitch in the watching Eldora's face, a gleam of knowledge in her black soulless pupils and as she caught it with the corner of one miniature eye, it was like something then clicked in Hoclee's mind. Something in that small second seemed to come to her and just like that, without a word, without so much as a warning, the little woman then spurted forwards, back the way she had come along Edmund's shoulder and with a cry, aimed and lunged, stabbing the tips of the thorns in both hands straight into the Explorer's neck.

For a second there seemed to be an odd sort of stunned silence as Hoclee froze, her spears held in place, as she and the watching Eldora and Eliom saw the blood of her victim begin to well to the surface. But then, with a cry of pain like none of them had heard before, Edmund gave a great yell and with a thud, crashed straight to his knees.

No!

Immediately, Eliom made to start forward, a rare expression of horror flashing across his face as he began to prepare the spell in his mind, the spell to heal and then to slay...

But there was nothing he could do for his friend now.

It was too late and he knew it.

Edmund of Tonasse had been poisoned.

Pulling her weapons mercilessly from Edmund's skin, their ends snagging as she did so, Hoclee grabbed the Explorer roughly by the ear, and propelling herself up onto his cheek, using his nose for support, she then stared straight into his eyes.

"Now tell me!" she repeated, her voice now a vicious hiss. "Where are you going? Why do you trespass? Tell me or I will end your crew!!"

Already Edmund's breathing was starting to grow sharp and shallow, his eyes watering in unknown pain as the tiny wound on his neck began to bleed openly.

"I don't-" he started.

"*I will give the order!*" Hoclee raged.

"I-I can't…"

"*Enough!*"

And the wizard's voice split the deck like a thunder clap as again, he made to move towards his friend. But no matter where he turned, Eliom found himself surrounded by a cloud of rodents, each tiny rider's face as menacing as the last, informing him that he no longer had any hope of using magic now.

Not *obviously* anyway. Not without further risk to his friend's life.

Hoclee hadn't delivered Edmund a fatal dose; the wizard, with something like great relief, had been able to tell that the second she had stabbed him. She had only nicked the very surface of his skin, enough to draw blood but not enough to kill.

He wouldn't then, die.

At least, not instantly.

But the pain…

"What do you want with us, nimph?"

His voice was uncharacteristically harsh and Eliom stepped towards Hoclee, his staff raised a little in warning to any more of the horde who dared to come too close. Still none seemed to want to touch him, to land on him as they had the others.

Hoclee's attention flicked back to him instantly as she eyed his staff with her beady eyes. For a moment she looked afraid – this wizard was strong, she would have been a fool not to notice – but then, fear was replaced quickly by cold anger.

"You have trespassed through our domain," she repeated matter-of-factly. "And for that the penalty is death."

Edmund let out a tiny groan. The unknown poison was fast taking effect. His whole face had broken out in a sweat, his hands quivering.

"This is not *your* domain," Eliom replied, his voice even again. "This river belongs to no one. It flows freely."

"This is *our* land!" Hoclee visibly bristled. "We have claimed it for our own. By that right it is ours and we do *not* suffer trespassers."

The wizard's expression didn't change. Though Edmund let out another sound, he didn't break eye contact with their foe.

"But surely we cannot be the first you have encountered," he reasoned. "There are colonies, towns further north as well as-" but before he could finish, a sudden commotion from across the deck distracted them both, and turning, the wizard felt his placid face fall as he saw the three figures marching through the flurry of blackness towards them.

It was the rest of the crew; Elanore, Fred and Thom - only they weren't *marching* as the wizard had thought but *being* marched, for each of them were covered in dark beasts, some perched on their shoulders, some on their heads and some on the front of their clothing, scrabbling and pulling and clinging to keep hold as the three walked. Elanore was shouting to be released, cursing aloud, as was Thom, but only Fred seemed to be putting up a good fight. The warrior, obviously taken unawares enough not to draw his sword, was now using every other weapon he had at his disposal, as he bit, kicked and scratched at the things all around him, tearing them from his shirt, clawing them from his chest and face under a mass of noise and fluster and blood...

Obviously amused at the sight of such torment, Hoclee's little face up lit as the trio approached, her smile broadening as the three eyed both Eliom, Eldora and then Edmund in alarm.

"Stop!" she then bellowed, her entire demeanour changing as she saw Fred mercilessly tear one of the black rodents from his arm, throwing its tiny rider from her reigns. With a scream the tiny woman fell to the deck and, most likely, her death. "Stop this at once! Or we will kill you *all!*"

But though he clearly heard her threat – the warrior looked up from his business for but a second – Fred carried on regardless, desperate in his bid for freedom. Several riders flew at him with their thorns raised, ready to poison, even to slay, their faces contorted with indignation, but still the warrior continued to bat them away, punching the air, slaying where he stood, stronger perhaps than any of them had bargained for....

For a second Hoclee looked desperate but then, turning to Eliom;

"Stop him! Now!" she ordered, and quickly, she was scrambling back to Edmund's neck, her deadly spears poised at the bleeding wound which even now was starting to ooze some kind of yellow pus. "Stop him or Edmund *will* die!"

Eliom's face betrayed nothing but for just a moment he seemed to pause as if considering their options before turning to the warrior, his face unreadable.

"Fred," was all he said and hearing something perhaps the others didn't, Fred, breathless and angry, instantly ceased his fight, straight away allowing himself to be flooded with rodents and their riders, his whole body heavy with the weight of them. He looked utterly murderous but he too could see now how dangerously close their leader was to death.

"Now, lower your weapons," Eliom then reasoned with Hoclee and half to everyone's surprise, the miniature woman complied, stepping away from the seeping neck.

Edmund's entire body was soaked with sweat now, his face ashen white and quivering. Intense pain seemed to well up from the very tips of his fingers, feeding itself through his blood to every part of his body, stabbing, gnawing, twisting. He gave a gasp as the agony reached his chest, burning and roiling, the wound, the very start of it all, twinging.

Everything was just one big blur now, a hot fuzzy blur, his brain turning to fug and though he was mildly aware of the presence of the others, all he could hear, all he could feel was the touch of his tormenter, the tiny hands and feet, the tiny voice of the little woman...

Biting his lip hard, he tried to speak out, his breathing nothing more than short rasps.

"What... do... you... want with... us?" he asked her. "What... *are*... you?"

Hoclee's face, though small, seemed to fill his entire vision, and, despite his pain, despite his addled, spinning consciousness, he couldn't help but notice how *attractive* it was. She was *stunning*, truly beautiful and for some reason, even now as he suffered - perhaps even *more* so now – he seemed to find it compelling, a force that somehow drew him in...

"You don't know?" Hoclee sounded surprised more than anything as she leant on one of her staffs almost companionably. Now that she seemed to have everyone under her command, she was suddenly more relaxed. "We are nimphs, nimphs of the air and water." Her beautiful lips twisted in a cruel smile. "But don't be misled by the tales of our beauty, of our *weakness*. We don't forgive easily..."

Nimphs. Of course. Edmund had heard the *tales* she spoke of, the myths lost in time of the water women, the women of the wind and the air, of the earth and their ferocious beauty. Their *fatal* beauty, luring in the unfortunate souls of men to do their bidding unto death...

Slowly he tried to close his eyes as more pain shot along his limbs, but despite knowing what she was, what she was capable of, he couldn't seem to tear them away from Hoclee.

Thom meanwhile, seemingly unaffected by the nimph's odd power, gave a snort.

"Forgiveness?" he spat. "You have nothing *to* forgive! We have done nothing wrong!"

"Oh?"

Hoclee didn't even deem to look at him. Instead, she gave the smallest nod and the nimphs on Thom's shoulders moved a threatening step or two towards the dwarf's neck.

Thom, watching the figures through the corners of his eyes, growled but fell silent.

"Tell me," Eliom was then the one to speak again. His voice was slow, thoughtful and, as usual, completely calm. "Are *all* the old tales of nimphs and their kind untrue?"

Hoclee frowned a little but still she did not take her eyes from Edmund as if luring him in, bit by bit, casting her spell...

"It depends on what you have heard, conjurer," she replied fiercely.

Eliom seemed to consider for a moment.

"I have heard that nimphs are a people of honour, a people true to their word who do not enter into a promise lightly."

And despite herself, the little nimph couldn't help but look a little proud.

"This is true," she said shortly. "We are."

"Well then," the wizard continued, "I entreat you to make a pact with us. Let us keep our lives and you, your land. Let no more blood be shed."

And this time Hoclee turned, her eyes seeming to flicker for the tiniest instant.

"A pact, you say?" she asked with interest as Edmund let out another groan. Suddenly the Explorer sagged forward, almost toppling to the deck, but without so much as a stumble, the nimph soon rebalanced herself on his shoulder with ease. "What are you proposing?"

But before either could say another word, one of the flying rodents broke away from the mass of flapping and with a sharp dive, landed atop of Edmund's head, its rider pulling expertly at the tiny reigns connecting her to her steed.

"Hoclee!" the nimph cried, sounding urgent. She looked angry. "The Chief wishes to speak with the human."

At this news, Hoclee's expression changed in one moment from surprise to something like disappointment. But quickly recovering, the nimph then lunged forward again and, grabbing hold of Edmund's earlobe, clambered swiftly up the side of the Explorer's face, using his hair as leverage.

Within seconds she and the other nimph were then conversing in minute, inaudible voices before, giving another nod, she turned her back on her comrade, leapt swiftly back onto Edmund's shoulder and was once again looking him in the face.

The Explorer could barely keep his eyes open now, his chest rasping in its fight to breathe. He could only just manage to see her.

"We are going to take you to our Chief now. She wishes to speak with you," Hoclee spoke quietly and then, pulling on his ear; "Do you understand me?"

Edmund could only nod, his head numb and yet as heavy as lead.

Yes, he tried to mouth. *I do.*

Unable to help himself, Thom shifted again.

"Now?!" he retorted. "It is the middle of the night!"

"Quiet!" Hoclee snapped and the dwarf gave a surprised yelp as one of the nimphs on his shoulder suddenly pricked him with one of her spears. The barb hit him squarely in the jaw, not enough to poison but enough to hurt and as if he had been waiting for this opportunity all along, it was Fred who then reacted. Suddenly, in one swift move, the warrior was springing forward. Like a spry animal that had been waiting to pounce, he finally whipped out his sword, at the same time, dislodging the nimphs clinging to his chest, arms and shoulders with a single swipe.

The move caused utter chaos as the black beasts flapped up into a storm, thrashing and swirling, confused, angry, readying themselves to attack. But before they could do anything, sensing their only chance, Eliom had stepped into their midst, instantly shouting aloud the spell he had been holding, preparing at the back of his mind for the last few minutes.

Suddenly thick, violent flames exploded from both ends of the wizard's staff and he spun it around, wielding the weapon like a whirling, fiery sword, striking the vermin aside, burning them to the ground as nimphs fell left and right to the deck, writhing and screaming in surprised agony.

This was it and seeing that the fight was on, Thom, with no axe, then also leapt into action, smacking here and there with his thick bare fists, throwing punches at anything small and black whilst Elanore, also struggling to free herself from the animals, took to tearing at her clothes and hair, taking great clumps of rodent and throwing them as far from her as she could.

The creatures and their riders were everywhere, one great swarming mass of black chaos, some flying to attack, others away in fear whilst even more tried to defend their comrades as best they could, for even in such a short time, it seemed as if the four companions were starting to make headway, to fight their way through the thick bodily darkness as more and more beasts fell…

"STOP!"

The scream rendered the air so loudly that for a second it felt like everyone and everything halted to listen.

"STOP IT NOW!!"

And as one, the wizard, warrior, dwarf and sea captain all then paused to turn in disbelief as they realised who had spoken.

It was Eldora the Lectur.

Her head was uncovered now, her black hair flowing in the wind whipped up by the wings of their captors, but other than this she hadn't moved. She had made no effort to free herself, spoken not a word the entire time, not made even so much as a sound.

She had been completely silent, and yes, almost completely forgotten. Until now.

Now her eyes were unusually wide, her pale face frantic and she was eying, not the flying creatures, but each of the remaining crew as if in *fear*.

"Stop," she then repeated more quietly. "Do not harm them. Do not harm the nimphs."

The nimphs?

And stunned, all four of her companions froze just that little bit longer to stare at her, aghast. But though the pause was nothing but a moment, it was still enough, for in the breath, the nimphs took their chance, and within seconds, had landed in groups on each of the crew's shoulders, heads and torsos, each rider ready with her spears pressed against bare and clothed skin whilst the rest scrabbled back into their surrounding positions.

Everyone's eyes, including Hoclee's, were on the Lectur who was now, oddly, watching Eliom.

"I have Seen that we must not harm these creatures," she then explained as if speaking to him alone, waiting for his approval. "We must let them take him."

And with that she then turned to Edmund, who had remained hunched and shaking on the deck throughout the brawl, his eyes closed, suffering etched into every part of his being. It wouldn't be long now until his body shut down altogether…

With barely a hesitation, Hoclee, until then, still standing on the Explorer's shoulder, gave a sharp whistle and from out of nowhere it seemed, a rider-less beast, larger and more magnificent than all the others, broke away from the horde. Landing daintily beside the nimph, the thing inclined its head and without ceremony she leapt onto its back, grabbing for the tiny reigns thrown about its neck with the movement of an experienced rider.

"The dwarf is right," she then spoke aloud, surprising them all. "It *is* late," before, looking at Edmund alone, all smiles, all fierceness gone; "my Chief will speak with you in the morning."

And with that the nimph then gave another whistle and taking its cue, her ride launched itself into the air, swirling up to join its smaller companions as the tiny army prepared to head off.

"But what about Edmund?" Eliom was the one to shout. "The poison-!"

"You're a wizard." Hoclee leaned forward against the tiny saddle to peer into Eliom's eyes. "You'll think of something to keep him comfortable for the rest of the night!" and with yet another whistle and a pull at the reigns, the nimph's rodent was swallowed up into the night, followed on by the throng of others behind in one long swirl of shrieking black. In less than a minute, there was nothing left but the bare Karenza and her crew of six, surrounded by the corpses of the dead they had managed to slay.

For a moment the small group just stood there, shocked and uncertain, each of them filled with questions about what had just happened. But now was not the time for answers, now was the time for action as Edmund then let out a feeble cry and finally, keeled over completely, his head hitting the hard deck with a crack as he rolled onto his back. Suddenly his body was convulsing as foam spewed violently from his mouth and alarmed, the others ran to him.

"Edmund!" Elanore cried, the first to speak as she rushed to his side, only to stop and draw back as she saw the pus at the side of his neck.

"What is wrong with him?" Fred meanwhile demanded, instantly falling to his knees and reaching for his friend's shoulders in an attempt to stop him from harming himself. "What happened, Eliom?"

"He was pierced before you arrived," Eliom replied, his voice ever calm. "He has been poisoned. Quickly, Elanore! Bring some water!" And the sea captain nodded and scrambled off across the deck towards the cabins, almost tripping on the bodies of the dead rodents as she did so.

Tearing off a piece of his own tunic, Fred tried to mop at the foam churning from the Explorer's lips, but there was so much of it, he could do nothing but smear it away. All the while, Thom stood over them both, looking anxious.

"Can you cure him?" the dwarf asked of the wizard but even before he had finished, Eliom was shaking his head.

"Unfortunately, this time I cannot. Only the antidote can. The poison used by the nimphs is… *complicated*."

"Complicated?" Thom retorted. "What do you mean by *complicated*?"

But seeing the shock his admission had brought, Eliom instead glanced at Eldora. The Lectur was standing, exactly where she'd been left, her face more ashen-pale than he had ever seen it, but with no hint of any expression now, any sorrow or sign she could even see what was going on.

"I cannot cure him," the wizard repeated firmly, leaving her and his thoughts quickly then to focus on the issue at hand. "But I will not let him die. He did not receive enough poison to kill him outright but he *will* be - he *is* - in a lot of pain and it will take much strength on his part to pull through entirely."

"Entirely?" Fred echoed and he looked up at the wizard as if his own life depended on it. "Eliom, what are you saying? How long do you think he will remain like this? Are we talking hours, days? Or…?"

But all Eliom could do was shake his head all over again. Despite his wisdom, he had very few answers. On the surface, he knew not much more than the rest of them.

"Let us hope he will be well enough to speak with the nimph Chief in the morning," was all he said, "or we may *all* be in grave peril."

Bethan became aware of the breeze first, like a soft breath across her face.

It was the woman she knew, Saz, fanning her softly with her hands, her face, concerned whilst the other, Meggie stood by her side, a flagon of water at the ready.

She didn't remember fainting. She was starting to recall a few things but collapsing wasn't one of them. Yet though she didn't remember feeling even so much as dizzy, she also knew that she couldn't have been unconscious for long. Though the lamp still burned, the corners of the room were dark, the ever-red glow of the Digger world seeping in through the black window. It was still night time and yet somehow, as she lay there, just taking everything in, it felt as if she'd awoken from a long long dream, a nightmare with a faceless figure in a black cloak, taunting her…

"Bethan," Saz soothed, noticing her comrade awake and hearing the sound, Meggie snapped to attention and leaning forward, offered the element the flagon fearfully. The little woman seemed distracted and every now and again she glanced at the door.

Sitting up drowsily, Bethan took the water with thanks, giving herself a moment to recover. She had no idea what had really just happened, how she'd ended up back on the bed again, why Saz and Meggie were here, how –

The two women were staring at her now with mixed expressions.

"What are you doing here?" Saz was the first to ask as she watched Bethan down the flagon, wiping her mouth with trembling fingers. She didn't seem to want to address Bethan's sudden collapse. "I mean," she looked utterly shocked. "I knew you were *here*, that you must be, but not," and she gestured at the tiny room, "*here!*"

"I could ask *you* the same question!" Bethan replied. "I had no idea you were even…"

She glanced at Meggie who was positively staring at the door now as if her gaze could burn through it, her face taut with concern.

"Where are they?" the little element muttered under her breath, almost as if she'd forgotten the others were there. "They *must* be in trouble… they should've been here by now."

Following Bethan's gaze, Saz just laid her hand on Meggie's shoulder as if reassuring her that all would be well and unsure what was going on, Bethan's brow crinkled.

"Where are *who*?" she questioned. "Do you have someone else with you?"

She had been sleeping when the pair had arrived and thought she'd heard a man's voice, but then…

"Yes, we do," Meggie replied shortly. "Nickolas and Dromeda."

"They're some of the-" Saz started before something making her pause, she soon gave an odd smile, "some of the *people* here. They've been helping us."

Bethan nodded, understanding dawning.

"The past elements," she said and then, as Saz looked surprised; "yes, I know all about that."

"*All?*" Meggie cut in and she tore her eyes from the door for a moment, searching Bethan's face.

Already it had come to this. Both Saz and Meggie looked a little nervous.

"How much do you know?"

Bethan though, frowned.

"Not much, sadly," she admitted. "No one's really told me much. Sorry."

She didn't really know why she was apologising, but something in Meggie's face had made her feel like she had to. The element looked *angry* about something.

"Although, if you remember us," Saz mused, either completely unaware of her friend's mood, or ignoring it. "Does that mean you-?"

But Bethan cut her off straight away.

"No," she said. "I can barely remember anything of my life from *before*. Everything's a bit of a blur to be honest… Some things more than others…"

Meggie and Saz glanced at each other again.

"Well, there's plenty of time for that," Meggie insisted. But though she sounded unworried, her focus was still clearly on the arrival of the elder elements, for all of a sudden, she strode for the door, reaching out for the handle.

"Don't!" Saz reacted, leaping back to her feet. "What are you doing?!"

Meggie didn't turn back.

"I'm just going to have a look," she hissed. She sounded angry still, frustrated, but before she could touch the wood, Saz had hurried after her.

"Don't Meggie! The Diggers might still be out there! They'll see the light! Nickolas told us to stay here!"

"I *am* staying here!" Meggie argued, but obviously pacified, she stopped.

Bethan looked from one to the other in the dim light. Part of her still couldn't quite believe that they were here, her fellow elements, in the flesh, the reality of her past life…

"So how are you even *here* in the first place? Why haven't I seen you before now?" she asked Saz, hurrying to break the tension.

Saz rubbed her neck and Bethan couldn't help but note how pale and weary she looked.

"We were in the outer city - another place on the outskirts of this one," she then explained. "Meggie and I, we found each other, well, by accident I suppose. And then the Diggers, they tried to split us up… some sort of command from-"

"The Builder?" Bethan offered and Saz nodded, looking surprised all over again.

"You *know* about that?"

"That's pretty much *all* I know," the other replied. "But then that's what happened to me too! I was separated from Bex by some new rule. Suddenly it became *forbidden* for us to be together…"

"Bex?!" Meggie interjected. "You've seen her?"

Bethan couldn't help but smile, unable to hide the delight at being back on familiar ground with friendly faces, faces of her past, of the world she had known.

"Yes! I don't know where she is *now*, but Belanna - she's a Digger- she's been helping us," the element hurried as Meggie and Saz looked shocked. "She's been helping us meet and-" all of a sudden though, Bethan let out a gasp and her hand flew to her mouth.

"Barabus!" she then cried. "He might come and check on me! If he finds you here-!"

It was Saz's turn to frown.

"Barabus? The past element from the temple?"

"Yes," Bethan said. "He's the past element that's been with me all along… *but* he's not like the others," she added hastily as she saw Saz visibly relax, "he won't be happy to see you. *He's* the one who brought me here. I had guards only a little while ago!"

"You mean he's not trying to keep you and Bex together?" Meggie sounded surprised.

Bethan looked sombre.

"He refused to," she spat. "I don't know why. He's just-"

But just then, there was a commotion at the door and the three elements froze. All of them could hear what sounded like hushed, fierce voices then a shout, followed by a scuffle and then suddenly a loud bang as the door was then thrown open slamming into the wall and four figures burst into the room.

The first two figures were men that Bethan didn't know. One had a dark shaggy head, muscular arms and in his hand, a sword soaked in blood. The other, on the other hand, was slimmer, with a stern face and though he too held a weapon, it was clean. Both were panting, out of breath.

The two other figures meanwhile, Bethan recognised straight away.

"Belanna! Bex!" she cried in complete amazement. "What are you doing here?"

But instead of answering, Belanna, who was looking extremely frightened, immediately rushed forwards, shoving Bethan's bed between herself and the two men in the suddenly-crowded room. All the while, Bex just halted in shock, her mouth hanging open as she saw Saz and Meggie.

All three elements took a second just to stare at each other before they then broke into grins and hurrying together, embraced with cries of recognition, a moment of joy soon interrupted as the man with the shaggy hair and bloody sword then gave a growl and without a moment's hesitation went straight for the bed and the cowering Digger behind it.

"Dromeda! No!" Saz cried, seeing the look in his eyes. "She's helping Bethan and Bex! Don't hurt her!"

The man with the shaggy hair paused, as all the while, the other man just stood, looking about him dazedly, barely seeming to notice the actions of his companion before his gaze finally fixed on Meggie.

"What is happening?" he asked as he looked from her to Saz then on to Bethan and Bex.

Meggie's smile returned.

"This is Bethan and Bex," she said, gesturing, to them accordingly. "The other two elements."

"Pleasure," and the man, Nickolas, gave both new women a short nod, his expression giving no sense of any surprise, his face, instead, dark. "We cannot stay here," he then added, addressing both Meggie and Saz. "The Diggers were not far behind us. They *will* find us here and-"

"Not if we kill them," the man known as Dromeda snarled. *His* eyes were still fixed on Belanna and the Diggerwoman visibly paled.

This time though, Nickolas gave his friend a warning glare.

"No more deaths tonight, Dromeda!" he hissed, his voice suddenly angry and realising what this meant, Saz and Meggie looked at each other, alarmed.

"No *more*?!" Saz cried. "You mean...?" but she didn't need to finish. Watching as Dromeda, without comment, started to wipe the bloody sword in his hand clean on the fabric at his thigh, no one was in any doubt as to what had happened.

"We cannot stay here, it is not safe for any of us," Nickolas repeated softly, addressing Meggie once more as if the decision somehow rested with her.

The little element bit her lip but didn't say anything.

"We will not be *safe* anywhere," Dromeda pointed out and sighing, Nickolas finally lowered the blade he had been clenching in his fist the whole time. Since he hadn't been carrying a sword before, Meggie and Saz could only assume that, like Dromeda, he'd stolen it. The long blade however, slotted nicely into the simple belt of his tunic as if it had always been there.

"You may be right," he commented and then, as if having another thought, he glanced at Bethan. "Is this your house?"

Bethan returned his look doubtfully.

"Well, I suppose," she admitted. "Though I would hardly call it *my* house..." Even so, Nickolas gave her a small smile, putting her at her ease.

"I only ask because we need somewhere to stay," he explained. "It is late. We are tired. Can we be permitted to sleep here?"

"Of course!" and this time it was Bethan's turn to smile. She couldn't help it. After the depression of the last few days, of the heavy sense of helplessness she had battled to keep at bay she could hardly *not* smile. After so many hours of nothing, everything seemed to be happening all at once. "Yes, please stay!"

"Hopefully Barabus won't be back until morning," Bex chipped in. "I'm sure he would have come if he was going to by now. It's very late-"

But at the mention of the elder element's name, both Dromeda and Nickolas seemed to stiffen.

"Barabus?" Dromeda interjected sharply, looking up from his cleaning. "Do you mean, the Barabus *we* know?"

"Who else?" Nickolas said, watching his friend carefully as the other's expression clearly fell. "He will have been paired with an element just as we were." And speaking of Barabus, he then gave an uncharacteristic scowl, turning away from Dromeda, as if fearing that his own obvious dislike would only cause more problems…

The ensuing silence was then interrupted by a little cough from the other side of the room and all attention fell on Belanna.

All this time the Diggerwoman had remained behind the bed, away from the humans, her hands out in front of her as if ready to defend herself at any moment, but now she dared to take a step forward, a step towards the door.

"I've done what Bex asked and brought her here but now… I'll be going," she muttered. She was clearly still terrified of the two men, especially Dromeda, who every now and again continued to glance at her like she was some kind of threat he was ready to address.

"No, Belanna! You don't have to leave!" Bex insisted. "They won't hurt you. I promise."

But Belanna's mind was not to be changed and she shook her head, positively running for the door.

"No, I really must go…" she replied. "My family will wonder…" and then, seeing the disappointed look on both Bethan and Bex's faces, she gave a little smile. "I promise I'll be back in the morning. I've got some information for you." And with that, she then made her way outside, closing the door silently behind her.

The lamp gave a little flicker, casting the rest of the group into temporary shadow, but despite this, Meggie didn't miss the excited look exchanged between Bethan and Bex at the Digger's final words.

"What information?" she began but before either could say a word, Nickolas had stepped in.

"It is late," he repeated. "We should rest. We may have to leave early tomorrow." Again, he seemed to be speaking only to Meggie. "The Diggers will no doubt know by now, if they did not already, *why* we are here… We will need to move as soon as we can." And the room fell into an anxious silence.

Whether each element knew the full extent of what their companion was saying or not, everyone agreed that rest was all they could do now and so it was, each picking their spot, two women on the bed, two on the floor, Nickolas by the door and Dromeda by the window, all soon settled down to rest and, as best as they could, sleep.

—

"How long have you been awake?" a voice whispered into the darkness and Bethan gave a start.

It was one of the men, Nickolas, but unable to see in the midnight gloom, she didn't bother to glance about her. She could tell he was near, his voice wasn't too far and over the sound of deep breathing all around she was just able to hear the shuffle of movement as he made his way towards her.

"All night, I think…" she replied quietly. Beneath her, she felt the bed wobble and then buckle slightly. This was followed by a *pfut* as a small flicker of light kindled next to her.

Sure enough, Nickolas was perched on the edge of the bed now, the lamp burning low in his hand. Beside him, and her, on the bed itself was the sleeping Meggie with Saz on the floor to the left and Bex on the floor to the right. Dromeda lay under the window curled in a tight ball, his new and now clean sword lying in wait at his feet. Nickolas's own commandeered sword lay propped against the door.

"You should be sleeping," Bethan pointed out, shying away from the light after so long of unfathomable blackness. Nickolas shrugged.

"Someone needs to keep watch," he replied and Bethan gave a wan smile. Something about the man reminded her of someone she trusted, someone she felt safe with…

"I can keep watch," she mumbled dimly.

"Perhaps," and for a moment Nickolas's gaze seemed to fall on Meggie, before he was back to looking at her again, his eyes questioning. "Is something troubling you? To keep you awake? If you are concerned about the Diggers finding us…"

"Oh, no!" Bethan turned away. "I'm not worried about *that*. At least not *really*." Her brow furrowed. "I-"

Nickolas shifted a little on the bed.

"Apologies," he hurried. "I did not mean to pry. I thought – Oh! Are you all right?" and surprised at his sudden urgent question, Bethan turned back to him, only to discover much to her alarm that she was crying. Silent tears, unbidden and unlooked for were dribbling in tiny streams down her cheek and wiping them away quickly she tried to smile again.

"Yes," she insisted faintly. "I'm fine."

But she wasn't. Because in her mind's eye, a new memory was coming to light.

She was in a shadowy forest, a dark wood. She could hear the sounds of the night birds, the swish of the wind through the leaves, the call of the midnight insects. She could smell wood – almost taste it on her tongue- tangy and sweet. And there was something else; sweat and... blood. She had a wound on her head. She could feel how it stung. But someone was dabbing at it, nursing it...

The man with the blue eyes. The man without a name. He was holding a ragged cloth and sitting so close to her she could so easily have reached out and touched him.

She *could* have. Only she hadn't. She had hung back and now he was speaking to her.

"*Bethan.*" Somehow her name felt so right on his lips. His voice was soft, caring, *loving*, she realised now.

And she was replying, flustered, uncertain.

"*Sorry. I'm fine. Honestly. I'm just a bit shaken I suppose, by everything. By everything we have to do, what it all means... Sometimes it all still seems so much to take in. Sometimes – Sometimes I feel like I was crazy to just drop everything and follow you.*"

Then, he'd taken her hand in his, so softly, so gently. She could remember her surprise at his rough and callused skin, the way his fingers curled around hers and the feeling of warmth, of strange happiness that had risen with it. She had felt so safe in that moment...

"*Bethan,*" he had said. "*You know I wouldn't ever let anything happen to you, right? You are never alone in this. Never,*" and right then she had only been able to nod, too overwhelmed as she had been by it all. Just as she was overwhelmed by her own sorrow now; her own sorrow at being just what he had promised she wouldn't be - without him.

Realising that Nickolas was still looking at her, Bethan blinked, rubbing her eyes furiously with her fists for a moment as if to clear her head.

"I'm fine," she then repeated more strongly. "I was just remembering something... someone...But I can't..."

"But you cannot recall who?" Nickolas offered and Bethan nodded glumly. The elder element's expression was difficult to read, but there was understanding there, kindness and she welcomed it.

"I wish I could know who he was... I wish I could see him again... There are so many things I didn't say to him. So many things we never..." she trailed off, not knowing how to end.

Nickolas fiddled a little with the lamp between his fingers.

"It is always hard to leave loved ones behind," he reasoned. "Always painful. It took me many a year here before I could even recall any of my family..."

And he spoke so lightly, with so little emphasis or care of the words for himself that Bethan couldn't help but pause and wonder for a moment.

He was the same, she realised, *truly* realised; the same as her, as Meggie, as Saz and Bex. He too had taken that decision to walk through the flames, to sacrifice himself, to sacrifice the life he had known for *this*... this emptiness, an emptiness and pain that had faded with time – how *much* time, she didn't know – but enough to make him a shadow of himself, enough for him to forget how it was to feel that pain, that love, along with everything else he'd felt before; enough time for those emotions to mean nothing to him. He had once loved, whether it had been a lover, family or friends, but that was gone now. That love had become *nothing* and that, to her, was truly horrifying because one day she knew that she *too* would be just the same. One day she *too* would forget what sorrow, what longing was, because that would become the *norm*.

One day, she would have lived here for so long, she too would just, *forget*.

And struck dumb by her realisation, Bethan barely noticed that Nickolas was still speaking.

"I never found love. Not in the way others did," he was saying. "Others *do*. Not whilst I was alive. But I hope that one day you will find him again."

Bethan tried to give a little smile, but her heart wasn't in it. She knew that the element was just trying to be kind, to make her feel better. But something told her, deep down, that that was all. There was nothing else he could do. Nothing *she* could do. She would probably never see the man with the blue eyes again. And one day, like everything else, he would fade to nothing, his memory long forgotten...

Just then a voice cut in, causing both to turn in surprise.

"You'll find him again if you follow Belanna's plan and escape."

It was Meggie. Her eyes were open but she was still lying there as if she had been lying there the whole night, just listening to them talk.

Forgetting her troubled thoughts for a moment, Bethan gawped at her.

"How did you know?" she demanded, her mind turning back to Belanna and her secret meeting with Bex and the Digger.

Meggie almost laughed.

"It didn't take much to guess," she whispered. "When Belanna said she had some information, I don't think I've ever seen you or Bex look so happy!"

Bethan smiled and faced suddenly with two women, Nickolas looked from one to the other in confusion.

"Escape?" he asked, his voice rising. "What are you *talking* about?"

But both elements ignored his question. The less said about it right then, the better. They didn't want any of the others disturbed and instead, turning back to her thoughts again, Bethan leaned in close as Meggie finally pulled herself to a sit.

"Meggie," she then started after a time. "Do you remember... Can you remember what happened before we were here?"

At this, Meggie glanced at Nickolas and as the two made eye contact, Bethan was surprised to see some sort of understanding pass between them. The little element seemed to be assessing the situation and he was giving her all the answers she needed in that one look.

Odd for a pair who had only known each other for such a short amount of time...

"Yes," Meggie then answered. "I remember..."

Bethan leaned in even closer.

"Everything? Your family? Your friends?" she said and Meggie looked uncomfortable for a moment.

"I remember my family, yes," she intoned. "I have memories of before they died. But apart from that... I don't really have anyone else *to* remember."

Died.

And realising what she had done, Bethan opened her mouth in dismay, only for Meggie to hold up a dismissive hand.

"It's fine," she insisted kindly. "You can't remember parts of your own life. You can't be expected to recall any of mine." To which she gave a sheepish smile. "And besides... it sounds a bit... well... the only real *friends* I suppose I have, are you, Saz and Bex. And of course, Fred, Thom, Eliom, and Edmund, if they're still alive. Though," and suddenly, she paused clumsily as if remembering who it was she was talking to. "I'm not saying they're *not* alive. We don't know what happened. I mean," she flushed, "there's no reason to think that-"

Bethan thought, didn't seem to be listening. Instead, the element had completely frozen, her mouth hanging open in a little 'o' as her expression fell into blank shock.

"Wh-what did you say?!" she then spluttered from nowhere and Meggie, confused, halted in her tracks.

"Which bit?" she replied. "The bit where I said about you being my friend as well as the others or-?"

"Who?!" Bethan was urgent now. "Who are the others? You said their names! Tell me their names! Again!" and suddenly, without warning she was grabbing Meggie by the hand, squeezing it tightly until her knuckles were almost white.

Trying not to cry out – the hand was attached to her still-injured wrist – Meggie searched her friend's excited face with concerned eyes.

"Um," she began slowly, "their names...? Yes. I said Fred and Thom and Eliom, the wizard, and then Edmund..."

Edmund.

That was it.

The name.

And suddenly it was as if Bethan's whole body, which had been holding on to something, struggling, straining from the moment she had arrived there in that world, suddenly let go and she gave an almighty sigh, her hand releasing Meggie's in a moment.

"Edmund," she murmured, trying the sounds on her own lips. It was as if the name had been the key to a locked door, the key that had turned in the latch and now the door was flung wide and suddenly memories, information, faces, names, words, voices, smells and sounds were flooding into her mind's eye in a crashing wave.

Edmund of Tonasse.

The man with the blue eyes.

The man who had spoken to her in so many fragments of memory, so kindly.

The man who had mopped her head when she was injured.

The man who had been with her through the worst and yet best of times.

The man who had kissed her in the shadow of the great flames...

His name flooded about her now as if it had always been there, as if she had known it all along but it had simply hung there in the air, waiting for her to remember... Waiting to take action, to bring everything once more back together.

Edmund.

And in the confusion, the strange jumble of emotions, sights and sounds brought to her afresh as she relived every moment with him like a new chapter in her head, she could hear someone speaking.

Someone was calling *her* name now. Almost shouting.

It sounded like Meggie. Or maybe it was Saz. Maybe even Nickolas.

But she didn't know for sure. And, for the moment she found she didn't care.

Suddenly she was lost and it was all too much. She could feel her stomach churning, the very edges of her vision darkening.

She was losing herself in it, in everything, too soon. And then she could feel her head drooping, her limbs like dead weights, tumbling onto the bedspread. And finally overcome by it all, so it was that Bethan then keeled over and with one last gasp, fell to the bed, her eyes rolling lifelessly to the back of her head.

FOUND

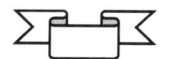

SACRIFICE

The morning was a sunny one. Even beneath the thick dark trees flanking the Great Madid river, where nothing else stirred, there were mottled shadows just beginning in the early hour mist, casting themselves hopefully across the Karenza deck where one lone figure stood.

All in black she felt nothing of the growing warmth. She felt nothing, in fact but coldness. The coldness of her cool white skin, the coldness of regret, of long-lived emotions spent, but also the coldness of clarity. Of inescapable fate, for Eldora, the Lectur was deep in thought fraught with Seeings of her purpose, the purpose that had brought her here, to this ship, to these people; the purpose that she was beginning to realise only now. The purpose that, yes, loathe as she was to admit it, terrified her more than she would ever show.

Through what had remained of that long night, she had battled with her thoughts alone, on the deck, not daring to venture below where the others had been awake, fighting to keep their leader alive.

Seizure after seizure had crippled Edmund of Tonasse for hours; eyes rolling, foam spitting, coughing up blood. A part of her detested it all. The weakness in it, the *degradation* and she had held no desire to witness the spectacle of a man reduced to a spewing, convulsing wreck. And yet...

Another part of her, a much smaller and well-hidden part, had wanted to stay, had wanted to help him. To *feel* something just that once. Something more than the constant bitterness at the very core of herself.

Eliom.

The Lectur brushed a stray tear from her eye as her thoughts turned back to the vision she had Seen that night. The vision of her own future.

She would do this for *him*; she had already decided that. She would do it for his care for Edmund. And much as she hated it, she knew there was no getting out of it.

She would do it to save the wizard she loved, the wizard who had rejected her.

She would do it for *him* because she had no other choice.

And as she turned her gaze to the sky, the warm morning stillness was then broken by the sound of fluttering and flapping, of screeches and organised chaos. And then, they were on her, the swarm of rodents, swirling, cascading like a wave of dark towards the deck, their tiny riders almost invisible in the daylight, swamping the bulwark, the sails, the ropes and pulleys and crates, in a mass of churning black.

With a quickening heart, the Lectur then glanced wordlessly towards the cabins.

The nimphs had returned.

Let them come.

—

"He *must* drink it! Keep his head still, Fred!" Eliom commanded as Fred struggled against Edmund's shuddering body, exhausted but determined to cling on.

Elanore, who had moved to hold Edmund's legs, all the while glanced at the wizard in tired concern.

"We've tried this before, Eliom, and it didn't work!"

But despite her protest, the wizard's face was solemn.

"It is all we have," he replied softly. "We must continue…"

"He is weakening." Fred sounded more tired than anything. "The poison is destroying his body!"

"*Argh!*"

The shout was loud and everyone turned to watch as Thom, who was desperately trying to hold a cup of boiling liquid to Edmund's quavering mouth, was soon nudged by the Explorer's thrashing head and dropped the cup, spilling its contents all over the floor. The splashing fluid steamed against the wood, trickling into the crevices and almost receiving a face-full of it, Elanore gave a yelp, stepping away as fast as she could before any could touch her.

Thom gave an exasperated growl.

"What is the point?!" he cried fiercely. "Elanore is right. Nothing is working!"

The sea captain reddened a little but helpless as he might feel, Fred immediately rounded on the dwarf, his own expression livid.

"What are you suggesting, Thom? That we *give in?*" he hissed. "Give him the medicine! Or if you cannot…"

Thom stiffened.

"Of course I can! I suggested nothing of the sort I-"

"Enough!" And detecting the tension a sleepless night had caused, Eliom soon raised a hand. "I will make more of the liquid and we will try again. It is daybreak. It cannot be long now."

As if his very words heralded what they had all been waiting for, there was then a movement at the door and everyone swivelled to see that Eldora had arrived.

The Lectur, casting her eyes about the scene quickly, looked a little flustered, but quickly regaining herself, she soon turned to Eliom.

"The nimphs are here," she said coolly. "And they have brought their chief. She wishes to speak with Edmund…"

Regardless of her news, Thom, Fred and Elanore all looked at the Lectur with complete disdain. She may have been unpopular before but she was doubly so now.

Where had she been all night? Why hadn't she been down in the cabins with them, trying to keep Edmund alive? And, none could quite forget her actions from the day before either; how she had virtually helped the nimphs to overpower them right at their potential moment of triumph…

"Tell this *chief* that if it were not for her, Edmund would quite *easily* be able to speak with her!" Thom grumbled and this time no one argued with him.

Without the actions of Hoclee, none of them would be suffering right then…

"What should we do?" Elanore interjected quietly. She too was addressing Eliom. "Edmund hasn't been conscious in hours. How is he supposed to *speak* to anybody?"

It was a good point and for a moment it looked as if the wizard was careful in planning his response. Slowly his gaze turned to Edmund, his eyes running from the tip of his friend's head all the way to his toes as if assessing every part of him for some kind of hope.

The Explorer had mostly stopped fitting, for the moment, but his face was remarkably pale, except for the stain of yellowed blood about his lips. His eyes were closed and moving hurriedly in their sockets, his fists clenched in pain and his forehead, his neck, his whole body in fact, soaked with sweat.

There was no way that he was ready to be moved, let alone talk.

Which really meant that they had little option…

"*I* will speak with the Chief," he finally said, before looking back to Eldora; "You may stay here I will-" But the Lectur soon shook her head.

"She said that she will speak with Edmund and *only* Edmund," she said. Her voice sounded cold but not entirely unfeeling as she then cast her eye back to the suffering Explorer. "Is there really no way of waking him?"

"No," Thom shot, glaring daggers. "If we knew how to wake him, we would have tried it already! Although some of *your* expertise might have come in use…"

Eldora though, shot a glare back as fierce as the dwarf's.

"I am sure I could not be of any use to *you,*" she remarked.

Thom looked annoyed but instead of stepping in at this point to prevent conflict as he usually did, Eliom remained where he was, calm, collected and so deep in thought that as if sensing that something important was about to be said, the whole cabin fell silent.

Sure enough, after only a minute, the wizard gave a small sigh.

"There may yet be a way I had not considered," he said slowly.

There was no hint of real hesitation, of doubt, of any fear in his words but in the absence of Edmund's input, Fred was the first to notice it.

"Yes, but what is it?" he demanded. "What is the risk?"

"Risk?" Elanore just looked blank, having detected nothing in the wizard's speech.

Eldora, meanwhile, looked utterly horrified.

"If you are suggesting something that would risk your *own life* for this – this-" she began before Thom cut her off with another growl.

"I am merely suggesting that I attempt a similar spell to that I used in the Dark Mist," Eliom replied sedately. "I can try to enter Edmund's mind and from there draw him out of himself, back to consciousness."

Fred paled slightly but said nothing. Elanore though, looked appalled herself.

"Hold on," she started. "Do you mean the spell that nearly…" but somehow she couldn't finish and before she could even try, Eliom had given a little smile.

"I survived," he said smoothly.

"Yes, but we all saw the effect it had on you!" and hearing the fear in her tone, Eldora glanced at the sea captain, genuine concern on her face.

"What effect?" she demanded sharply. "What happened?"

"It is irrelevant," Eliom replied. "Once again the need outweighs the odds. If Edmund is, as I suspect, in a feverish dream, I may be able to retrieve him. If I cannot… then I may as well have tried."

There was a silence as everyone took the fact of the matter in, the fact that they really didn't have much of a choice. The wizard had clearly decided the best course of action and there would be no stopping him.

And so it was that taking up his staff more firmly, Eliom moved towards Edmund's head, Fred numbly sidestepping out of the way to let the wizard closer. Taking a seat by his friend's side, Eliom then took the Explorer's temples in both hands, drawing in a deep breath as he did so. But even as he started to close his eyes, preparing himself to link with Edmund's mind, it was then that he felt the cold clutch at his arm.

It was Eldora and looking up, he was met with her black beady eyes, dark, hollow and yet so deep he found himself almost lost in them. A flash of something crossed her face and for the first time, he saw how truly frightened she was, frightened and not just because of her worry for him...

Something was wrong. He knew it. He had known it the moment she had walked into the room. There was something none of them knew, something she was hiding. But what that was...

"Be careful," the Lectur then whispered in a voice so trembling and unlike her own, that the others, overhearing, for a brief moment, thought that she was Seeing another vision.

Eliom bowed his head.

"Of course," he replied before turning back to the immobile human at his side.

And as the others watched, the great wizard's eyes then closed and slowly but surely, he began to seep into Edmund's toiling mind...

Colours.
Hundreds of confusing colours.
Blue, red, yellow, orange, beige, pink.
They flashed through his mind's eye so quickly that for a moment, he felt faint, stunned.
And the noise. The noise was almost worse. Snippets of sound, loud voices echoing in a cavernous space. Parts of conversations, parts of words...
Fred and Thom in the waking world. He would recognise those voices anywhere. But their sentences were so disjointed they were more like sounds, sometimes deep and long, sometimes quick, hurried, nervous.
One thing Eliom did know for certain however, was that he was entirely on his own.
Edmund wasn't here. His mind, his thoughts, weren't here. There was nothing of his friend. No heartbeat, no breathing, no voice...
Which meant he would have to go deeper. He would have to probe, stretch himself further into Edmund's mind, into his very core, a dangerous risk he knew he was going to take no matter what the consequences...
And so it was, taking a breath of his own, he forced himself onwards, delving deeper, pushing into the very fabric of Edmund, the colours spinning faster and faster, Fred and Thom's words disappearing into oblivion along with, for a moment, thought and feeling and all else that made him, him.
But it was too late now. He couldn't go back. Not yet anyway...
Not until...
And then he found it. Suddenly, pain, searing, agonising and real ripped through his body and he was wailing in torment. He was there. Edmund was there and he could feel what the Explorer felt. They were one, mind and body. They were one and the same.
He could feel the muscles cramping in his neck all the way through to the base of his spine; the bones in his arms and legs shaking uncontrollably as every nerve burned like an invisible flame.

Desperately he tried not to cry out again, but it was difficult not to. Difficult to see, to breathe, to think.

Quickly he clamped his eyes shut, screening everything in painful blackness. But now, through the screams of pain that despite his best efforts seemed to be erupting from his own mouth, he heard a voice; a voice he recognised and yet was so removed, so very different from Edmund's actual voice that for a moment, Eliom didn't know what to make of it.

"Who are you?" it demanded, loud and angry.

Eliom gritted his teeth, trying to block out the rushing agony.

"You know who I am," he replied. "I am your friend."

Friend. The word seemed to fall like some kind of curse as the voice took a second to think.

"We are one now, Eliom," it said after a time. "Which means you know who I am."

Eliom managed to open his eyes, but it was as if they were still closed. He was surrounded in darkness now. Darkness and intense, burning, scolding heat.

"You are Edmund," he managed. "Edmund of Tonasse."

"Yes, and no," the voice corrected. "I am, as you say, Edmund. But I am not as you know him to be. I am more and I know why you are here."

Eliom took another deep breath. He could feel somehow, in the very back of his consciousness that Edmund's worldly body also did the same.

"So you know then what it is you must do," he replied slowly. "What you must allow."

But the voice seemed reluctant.

"The poison is strong. It's not time for waking yet," it said. "We should stay here."

Eliom tried to reach for his now sweating brow but the more he did so, the more he found that he couldn't move his hands. His whole body was limp. Every feeling bar the pain seemed to be gone.

"If you do not wake, you could die," he answered the voice severely. He knew that no matter how powerful he may or may not be, he wasn't going to be able to last much longer there. It was becoming more and more difficult to concentrate, to speak, to remain separate, himself...

"The pain is too strong," Edmund's inner voice argued weakly, "but then, you already know that."

Eliom tried to nod. The effort was almost impossible.

"If you refuse to wake up, I will have to force you," he warned. He sounded calmer than perhaps he felt, the panic of human suffering already eating at the edges of his serene mind, and the inner voice gave a laugh.

"You wouldn't dare go further. If you did, you'd definitely die. It would take magic too strong even for you, old friend."

The use of 'old friend' threw Eliom a bit. He felt as if he were talking to a stranger, not the Edmund he knew. Somehow the poison had taken hold of his friend's deeper self. Somehow it was affecting his thoughts, making him reluctant to wake up, to live.

"You will awake!" he commanded loudly.

The inner voice didn't answer.

"*AWAKEN!!!*" Eliom shouted, every fibre of his free concentration forced towards the inner voice, Edmund's mind, honing in on it, cornering it.

"*There's nothing you can do!*" the voice shouted back, but it quavered, obviously frightened, and Eliom, too felt the unquenchable fear rise within him. The magic of controlling another being, of pushing himself so deeply into Edmund that he became Edmund, was highly perilous. Few wizards ever attempted it. But he knew that if Edmund's mind didn't comply, he would be forced to take action.

"*You know what I will do...*" he cautioned. "*I need not speak of it.*"

Still the inner voice said nothing.

"*AWAKEN!!!*" Eliom ordered again, more forcefully.

"*No...*" But Edmund was weakening. He could sense it. The Explorer was weakening, just as he was weakening. It wouldn't be long now... Just a little longer...

"*By the power of the Great Order! I command you to awaken!!*" Eliom then bellowed, his voice deafening in the crevices of Edmund's mind.

The voice said nothing as if pausing to draw breath, to argue back.

But through the silence the wizard knew already that he had won. He could feel the life draining from him, from Edmund, the rugged purpose to refuse falling away and suddenly, the darkness that had surrounded him was starting to fade, to lighten to a pale grey and through the odd mist he could see an image.

Was it a face?

Was it someone he knew? Thom? Fred? Elanore?

But though he knew that Edmund was awaking it was as if the poison was desperate to make one last attack. There was a cry, his own and Edmund's combined as the pain seared through every vein, every muscle. He could feel tears, alien and wrong springing to his eyes, feel foam bubbling at his mouth, his chest constricted.

Desperately the wizard began the process of pulling himself away, of detangling himself from the web of his friend's mind, to become Eliom once more. And yet still the agony lingered, even as, slowly but surely, Eliom silently slipped from Edmund back into himself, his own consciousness, once again his own entirely, falling into blank screaming nothingness....

Eliom gave a great gasp and sat up, blinking furiously, every part of him relishing in the rush of being back in his own body, his own space.

Already the pain in his limbs was starting to ebb away as his mind recalled his own nerves and muscles, his own veins that weren't filled with poison. And yet the process was slower than he had expected.

He felt... *tired.* Drained.

Strange.

And closing his eyes again, the wizard took a moment just to breathe in and out, waiting for complete feeling in all of his limbs, checking himself over in his mind.

Physically he was fine, or at least, he would be. But as for mentally…
"Eliom!"

It was Fred. The warrior was at his shoulder; Eliom could feel his presence like a familiar warmth and somehow it helped to soothe him a little. "Eliom, what happened?"

The wizard then opened his eyes to find Fred, Thom, Elanore and Eldora all staring at him.

All of them looked worried.

"You collapsed and were shaking all over!" Elanore continued on. "And then you just sort of, *stopped*. We thought – well- we thought -" she paused.

Stranger still.

He didn't remember falling or being unconscious at all. Except…

Feeling suddenly, uncharacteristically weak, Eliom just shook his head and glanced briefly at his hands, only to notice that they were extremely pale. No doubt his face was too.

He had known this would happen; it had happened before when he'd performed a similar magic to save his comrades from the grip of the Dark Mist, the fog that had taken their minds out on the ocean. And yet somehow this time it had been different.

This time he hadn't been able to pull himself away so easily. And this time he *felt* different afterwards. This time it was almost as if a part of Edmund's inner self had latched onto him, refusing to let go, remaining with him as he'd torn himself away to shift one back into two and because of it, he felt - the wizard struggled to settle on his senses, on the word itself - he felt *changed*.

Eliom the wizard, ancient, wise, great as he was, had, somehow, changed.

Slowly aware of the fact that the others still had their eyes on him, perhaps waiting for some sort of explanation, some sort of command, Eliom then made a move to stand. But before he could even attempt to speak, there was another movement, the sort of movement they'd all been desperately hoping for and all attention snapped to Edmund's body on the floor as the Explorer then stirred, his eyes flickering as he began to wake.

Straight away, Fred knelt by Edmund's side, aiding his friend to sit up and Elanore quickly reached for some water, handing it to Thom to give to their leader. Eliom too looked on with something like relief as he witnessed the success of his spell. But though all eyes were on the recovering Explorer, one pair still remained on the wizard.

"I would ask after your welfare, but I know how you would respond."

Eliom felt before he heard Eldora's presence as the Lectur moved to his side. Unlike Fred, however, the woman's aura was cold and hard, like a stone wall of gloom - of *guilt* - and the wizard did not raise his gaze. Instead, he took hold of his staff, feeling the soft familiar wood like new strength in his hands, and standing it upright, finally clambered to his feet.

Eldora didn't give up.

"You should rest," she pointed out in a voice only loud enough for him to hear, the way she spoke, the quavering beneath her words, speaking volumes. Half of her, the half that still, despite all, loved him was relieved, happy that he was alive and concerned for his safety whilst the other half, the part that despised him, hated him for his continual rejection of her, wished that he had... gone.

Something stirred inside him. Something like sadness.

"Eliom."

Edmund whispered his friend's name and Eliom turned back to him, the Lectur, as she always was and would always, despite his best efforts be, pushed aside once again. The Explorer's face was white, his eyes bloodshot, his lips almost invisibly pale and every now and again he would wince, his entire body tensing as his limbs continued to cramp in and out of their painful poison-induced spasms; but he was awake. He would never be cured, not without the antidote to the nimphs' poison, but he was awake, he was alive, and that was all anyone could care about right then.

"Here," Thom murmured, handing Edmund the flagon of water. The Explorer gave a weak smile and took it gladly, but his nerves were still quivering, his muscles too weak to hold on and he let out a groan of frustration between clenched teeth as the canteen soon slipped from between his fingers, the fast Fred only just in time to catch it before it hit the deck.

"This is ridiculous! He is in too much pain to move, let alone speak!" the dwarf growled. "He will not be able to do as the nimphs ask. We must demand more time."

"We do not *have* more time," Fred responded in kind, leaning down to feed the Explorer from the flagon himself. Edmund for a moment turned away, embarrassed at his own inability, but the warrior soon encouraged him with a nod. "He is far from cured. And who knows how long his body can last?"

"They must have an antidote for their own poison," Elanore suggested helplessly. "Maybe we could make some kind of deal... after all, they seem adamant they'll only speak with him. And if he's the one they want maybe we can-"

"*I* will go and reason with them!" Thom cried bravely, his fists clenching to give some idea just what *his* reasoning would mean. "Demand that they give us the cure..."

But Fred straightened up from Edmund's side.

"You will *not*," he snapped. "Even *I* can see that we should not fight them. It is not a battle, currently, that we can win. We are far outnumbered. And now that we know what those weapons of theirs are really capable of..."

"No."

As the two friends glared at each other, ready to argue their case, for a moment, the word was almost missed. But it was definitely there, and the first to notice it, Elanore turned to look at the Lectur who had spoken it, in something like shock.

"I will speak with them again," Eldora then said. "Let me go."

"*You?*"

This got everyone's attention and warrior and dwarf swivelled in surprise.

"They will probably hurt you," Fred pointed out matter-of-factly. He sounded more shocked than anything, but no one could mistake the coldness there either.

Eldora shook her head.

"They will not harm me," she replied. Her voice was equally as cold, complacent and for a moment, the trio watching her all felt like none of them *wanted* to argue, to try and stop her – to try and potentially save her life.

"How can you be so sure?" Thom replied with a scoff. "Have you Seen that they will let you live?"

Eldora's eyes were like fiery coals.

"Do not mock me dwarf," she spat. "I am going. And you will not stop me!" But though she sounded strong, her white face a sneer not to be reckoned with, there was that quiver again, something hidden behind her words and the only one to notice, Eliom, who all this time had been listening but offering nothing, felt again, just as he had when she had first entered the cabin minutes before; that something was wrong, that beneath her cool exterior, the Lectur was hiding something.

Perhaps he could find out what. Perhaps just this once he could dare to delve somewhere private, uninvited, undetected. Perhaps just this once he could break his own personal code - but as if sensing his thoughts, his capabilities, and where they were leading, Eldora turned straight back to him, her expression one of warning.

No, she thought. Her voice came like one loud and crisp on the air, but only he, the wizard, the mind reader, could hear it. *Leave me. Do not probe further. All will work out for the best. Trust me.*

And before Eliom could even pull away, the Lectur had then swept back towards the cabin ladder and in seconds, the door to the deck was open and she was gone.

—

Eldora stood back on the deck surrounded by the black swarm of creatures. Even now, somehow, there seemed to be more of them, more even than there was sky, each one carrying a tiny fatally beautiful female rider with her fatally painful spears tipped to kill. All except one.

Before the Lectur, perched on the highest candle bracket now sat the largest of the animals. It was even larger than Hoclee's ride, about as large as two handspans, its eyes bulbous and white, blindly ugly, its ears round, its teeth hideous, but it made no threat. Instead, it simply sat there, still, silent, like a mother watching its young fluttering about her head.

The beast was riderless, but it was not alone, for alongside it, taller than all the other nimphs, with robes, not of black and amber but red and gold and blue, stood a tiny woman.

The woman was beautiful, strikingly so, more even than the stunning Hoclee, with long flaming red hair, a curved waist and perfect bosom. Her eyes were sharp, intelligent and fierce, so spectacular, that even the cold Lectur felt herself almost intoxicated by them, mesmerised to do nothing but stare and, for the moment, gawp. But then;

"Who are you?" the chief of the nimphs spoke. Her voice was surprisingly deep for someone so small, but sensuous, and unaffected as she believed herself to be, Eldora felt a shudder of something achingly pleasant sliver down her spine.

Closing her eyes a moment, she gave a sigh.

"You know who I am," she then replied, her own sharp voice a harsh contrast to such loveliness. "Just as I know who you are."

Her words sent something like a bolt of tension sparking into the air as the nimphs flying all around the Lectur's head began to whisper amongst themselves, the beasts at their beck and call, fluttering and jerking nervously. A few spears came dangerously close to Eldora's skin, but she didn't even flinch.

She did not fear them anymore. Not now anyway.

The chief of the nimphs meanwhile raised her hand, demanding and receiving instant order.

"Where is your leader?" she said. "I asked to speak to your leader. Not you."

"He is unwell," Eldora replied and noticing the figure of Hoclee sitting on her steed nearby, watching the situation unfold, she turned her black eyes on the tiny figure pointedly. "One of your people poisoned him."

The chief, noticing Eldora's glare, turned for the briefest of seconds to Hoclee and then back to Eldora. If she was surprised to hear this news, she didn't let on.

"We only do what is necessary to survive," was her snooty response. "We cannot be blamed for that."

"Just as these people cannot be blamed for trespassing where they were unaware," Eldora pointed out. Already it had come to this. "What do you want from them?"

"Them?" The tiny woman gave the smallest of sneers, lighting her glorious face for a second and making even the chilly Eldora catch her breath. "You speak as if you are not a part of this vessel and its crew?"

Eldora just blinked, her expression stony.

"As for what I want," the chief continued, little put out by the Lectur's attitude. "That is something I will freely discuss with *their* leader." She held her regal head high. "Now, bring him to me!"

She had known this would happen, she had Seen it, just as she had Seen that morning what would follow, but still she could not keep the anger, the fear from welling up within her and for a moment, Eldora glared true daggers.

"If he were to receive the antidote for your toxin, the human would be well enough, I am sure, to speak with you," she replied fiercely.

But clearly unaffected by the Lectur's hard stare, the chief only scoffed all the more.

"Why do you assume we have any?" she retorted. Seeing that Eldora wasn't going to back down any time soon though, her smile faded a little; "I see that there is no fooling you, Lectur. Although it strikes me as odd that you would refer to your leader as 'human'. Do you have no respect?"

Eldora said nothing, but her silence revealing everything, the tiny woman smiled all over again.

"Interesting… very interesting…" she murmured and then louder; "Very well! We'll have it your way. Hoclee!" and rising to attention instantly, Hoclee drew her ride closer.

"Yes, my Lady?" she said.

"Fetch some solution, quickly," was her answer and turning back to the cold Eldora, the chief then looked stern. "He *will* speak with me within the hour. Any longer and I'll give the word to dispose of you all."

Eldora nodded curtly and without further ado, released from the strange hold this tiny being had over one and all, she hurried back below decks to relay the chief's message to the others.

—

"What if he *cannot* speak within the hour?" Thom demanded gruffly once told the news.

Eldora just glared at him.

Elanore meanwhile glanced urgently at Eliom as she mopped Edmund's sweaty brow. Studying him, the wizard already looked to have regained much of his strength following his delve into the Explorer's consciousness but though he stood tall, moving about the cabin with quiet ease, still he looked very drained; not quite yet himself.

The sea captain bit her lip.

Anything now would clearly be a risk, a great risk, but what other choice did they really have?

"Eliom!" and giving a cry to attract the wizard's attention, Elanore tried to keep the obvious despair from her voice. "Eliom, his eyes are closing again!"

It was true; Edmund's eyes, after staring dazedly up at Elanore, were beginning to roll back, the whites of his eyeballs quivering as his body gave a heavy shudder.

"No!" Eliom cried.

The word was like a command, weighted with untold magic, but the poison had taken hold like never before and in one swift movement that surprised them all, the wizard then seemed to come alive. In less than an instant he was at Edmund's side, staring down into his face, taking the Explorer by the head. But then, instead of closing his own eyes, readying himself to perform the dangerous spell all over again, his hands moved to his friend's shoulders and suddenly, without any warning, he began to shake him roughly, like one would shake another from a deep sleep.

Aghast at the wizard's sudden, uncharacteristic violence, Elanore quickly stumbled out of the way.

"Is that really going to - ?" she started in concern, but then Edmund gave a groan and to everyone's shock, his eyes slid open again.

Staring up at Eliom, the Explorer looked confused, unfocused, his mouth opening and closing as he tried to form his friend's name on his lips. All the while the wizard moved in closer.

"Do not let it take you," he hissed in his companion's face, desperately fighting for eye contact as he gripped the Explorer tightly. "You must control it."

Edmund made some incoherent noise at the back of his throat in reply, the only thing he could manage as his breath fell back to short rasps, his mouth hanging open helplessly. His eyes began to close again and again, but every time they did, Eliom was ready with a fierce shake and a commanding word as the others just looked on in stunned silence.

Just then, there was a flutter at the door above and all turned to watch as a large black beast swept into the cabin.

Circling the room once, the thing gave a sharp screech before landing atop a candle bracket on the wall above Edmund and Eliom's heads. As it settled, a tiny figure then leapt from its back, carrying with it a glass vial almost twice its size. It was Hoclee and staggering to the very end of the bracket, she barely hesitated for a moment before, taking one step back, she then launched herself straight into the air.

Everyone watched in pure horror as the nimph's tiny, fragile-looking body plummeted towards the ground, a distance to her, comparable to jumping from a high cliff. But within seconds and with nothing more than a grunt, she had landed on her feet on Edmund's chest, the vial still held fast in her arms, none the worse for her fall.

"Make him drink this," she said, her voice calm and smooth as she held the glass out to Eliom.

And without question, the wizard nodded and taking the vital antidote, brought it up to his eye level, staring through the misty glass to study the pearly white liquid within.

"This contains rootweed," he muttered knowledgably as the nimph watched him.

"Yes." Hoclee sounded suddenly haughty. "There are many things we can acquire through fair trade with travellers."

Both Fred and Thom rose an eyebrow at the mention of 'fair' trade, but neither said a word. Now was clearly not the time to anger the dangerous little creature and they both knew it.

With a few quick flicks of his wrist, Eliom stirred the remedy before, unpopping the little cork, he brought the vial to Edmund's mouth.

Almost instantly a look of sheer revulsion passed across the Explorer's face as the cool liquid trickled between his lips. Weakly, he squirmed and tried to move away, but Eliom soon held him down.

"He must drink it *all*," Hoclee stressed as a shadow of worry flickered on the wizard's brow. "It won't work otherwise."

Eliom looked at the others as they all still stood, just helplessly staring.

"Fred," he instructed. "Hold him." And stepping forward to help, the warrior took hold of the Explorer's head, grasping him firmly. Edmund visibly struggled against his grip, but he was so weak now that Fred barely seemed to twitch.

Elanore all the while continued to look horrified.

"You're hurting him!" she suddenly cried out. "He doesn't want it! You're just making it worse!"

"It is for the best," Eliom justified. But no one could mistake the odd uncertainty in his voice as he then leant forward, bringing the vial once again to his friend's sickened mouth.

Edmund's eyes opened wide as, coughing and spluttering, he struggled to pull away from the foul liquid.

But it was no use.

"I am sorry friend," Eliom muttered and without further ado, he forced the Explorer's mouth open and tipped the entire contents of the glass vial down Edmund's throat.

—

"How much longer, my Lady?" Sashlee, the nimph lieutenant intoned. But instead of getting a response, another nimph nearby took up the reply.

"He will be ready!" she hissed. "Stop your complaining!"

Sashlee bristled, pulling at the reins of her ride as it twitched beneath her.

And the chief of the nimphs all the while said nothing, *did* nothing but seemingly stare out across the riverbed as if surveying her very own territory.

THE ENTITY OF SOULS

Sashlee's beast gave a squawk as she kicked it.

"They *hope* he'll be ready," she then sneered and the other nimph who had spoken, shot her something of a dirty look.

"Anyone would think you would hope otherwise?" she commented.

Sashlee gave a beautiful shrug.

"What does it matter if he doesn't?" she snorted. But though she seemed all confidence, her bright eyes fierce, she still spoke in a whisper as if worried the chief might overhear.

The other nimph sniffed sharply.

"If Hoclee heard you saying that..." she warned, equally as low.

And hearing the other's name, Sashlee's face flashed with something like anger.

"She doesn't worry me," was her best retort. "She couldn't even finish that human off!"

"She was under orders!" The other nimph was clearly seething. "And anyway, since when was it honourable to kill first then-?"

"Honourable?" Sashlee shot back. Her ride flinched as her voice rose a little and the chief's own beast seemed to detect something too as his ears twitched and he shifted, glancing briefly at Sashlee as if he could see her with his big sightless eyes.

The nimph paused before continuing.

"Honourable?" she then repeated at a low murmur. "It was *her* who poisoned the man in the first place!"

"And why do you think that was?" the other nimph said pointedly. "She was doing her best to protect us! You only wish you'd acted first!"

Sashlee opened her mouth to spew even more anger, but just then there was the sound of more fluttering wings and a rush of wind as Hoclee appeared from the throng of still-circling nimphs and pulling her creature into the small space beside the chief, leapt effortlessly from her saddle.

"He is ready, my Lady," was all she said to the chief before shooting Sashlee a sideways glance. Her expression was icy, as if she could somehow detect what had been said in her absence.

The chief of the nimphs finally seeming to take notice, gave a serious smile.

"Good," she replied and then, levelling Hoclee with an intense stare; "You did the right thing. Although I know some would disagree." And Sashlee, who was listening intently, felt her delicate cheeks burn as the chief glanced at her before continuing. "I sense that we may gain something far greater than we may have hoped from these people."

The chief then gave a sigh, her tiny eyes brushing once more across the river before turning back to her second-in-command.

"Hoclee," she ordered. "Remove the others. I wish to speak with the human alone." And without question or comment, Hoclee gave a quick bow and sprung back onto her ride, flicking the miniature reins as the creature launched itself back into the crowd of black.

Sashlee meanwhile, seeing her chance, sat up briskly.

"My Lady!" she cried. "Is that really wise? What if the human is dangerous? Or the wizard-?"

The chief shot her another weary glance.

"Do you doubt me, Sashlee?" she asked, her voice as fragrant and enticing as a flower yet dangerous as a thorn.

Sashlee looked aghast.

"Of course not, my Lady!" And she bowed hurriedly in the saddle, making her mount shift uncomfortably. "I only meant–"

"He knows what we are capable of. He knows the danger should he try to cross me," the chief continued, gesturing at her own weapons – two long spears housed in special slots at the side of her saddle. "And besides, he is human." She looked almost amused by the word. "What could he possibly do?"

"But, my Lady," Sashlee pleaded. "If you would only-" but the chief's patience obviously wearing thin, she held up a hand.

"Enough," she said, her voice still pleasant yet menacing. "Violence is not always the answer, Sashlee and the day that you learn that will be the day that you too will become a Lady. Until that time though, you must follow Hoclee's lead. Now, leave me." And unable to argue anymore, Sashlee gave another quick bow and tugging at her own reins, swooped away into the crowd as they began to disperse, fluttering, squawking and wheeling off into the thick trees to leave the Lady of the nimphs quite alone.

Before long there was then the sound of footsteps, slow and laborious and as she watched, three figures stepped out onto the deck.

One was a tall, muscular man, or what *appeared* to be a man, for the nimph chief knew differently. Here was a warrior of the far west, a fighter of Mawreath, a being to be feared and alongside him, a wizard in long white robes carrying with him a withered staff. To her and to any other, *he* looked as young as a human, as handsome too – if that was such a thing - and yet she knew him to be older than the hills, older than the trees, even perhaps the river she and her clan had claimed for their own. And the one in between, propped up by the other two as if somehow, he was the rarest, the most precious of all? A pale yet resolute human.

His face showed everything of his agony and yet his jaw was set against it and weak as she knew him to be compared to his companions, the nimph chief couldn't help but admire his dumb courage. She too had experienced the suffering of that deadly poison – every nimph had known the bite of it at least once in their lives – and she knew what pain it was to bear. Still, looking at both the warrior and the wizard in turn, the Lady then stood to her full height.

"I wish to speak with your leader *alone*," she pointed out, her luxurious voice ringing across the now achingly-silent deck. "As you can see, I am very much without friends," and she gestured at the empty space around her with something of a smile.

All three of the companions could feel it, the strange pull, the odd spell of that grin, the draw of that beautiful face, but still Fred glanced at Eliom, unsure.

Before he could retort though, he was then stopped short by Edmund.

"Leave me," he said. He seemed barely able to speak above a hoarse whisper. "I'll be fine."

It was the first time the Explorer had managed to say more than a word and Fred, still looking uncertain, leant in close to his friend's ear.

"But you can hardly stand!" he hissed. "Perhaps if we ask for more time…"

"No," Edmund's reply was soft yet surprisingly firm. "Trust me. I'll be fine. Really," and weakly, he waved the warrior away.

Again, Fred looked to Eliom, but as if the wizard could see some new strength in their companion that he couldn't, the wizard only nodded. Reluctantly the pair then released their hold on Edmund and with one backwards glance at the tiny vision of radiance that was the Lady of the nimphs, exited the deck, leaving the Explorer to his fate.

—

"What happened?" Bex demanded in a frantic whisper as she looked over her friend, watching for any sure sign of life.

But Meggie could only give a concerned shrug.

"I don't know!" she admitted. "She asked me about life, about things, you know… *before* so I was telling her and then suddenly she just seemed desperate to know about…" And then it came to her. "I think it was something to do with Edmund. She said his name and then just sort of-"

At the mention of the Explorer though, Bex had suddenly brightened.

"Edmund!" she breathed. "*That* was his name. I couldn't remember him until now…"

Couldn't remember him? Meggie glanced at her companion quizzically, only to be interrupted by a movement from across the room.

"Perhaps that could have been it," Nickolas said from his position by the window where he'd been keeping watch for the past few hours. Meggie, Bex and Saz, all awake now, were sitting on the bed where the still body of the unconscious Bethan lay, wrapped under the blanket. She hadn't woken yet after her discussion with Meggie the night before and all of them were admittedly worried about it.

Meggie looked up.

"What do you mean?" she asked the elder element as his gaze turned back to the growing morning light. "Perhaps *what* could have been it?"

"Well, perhaps by telling her of this man, this Edmund person, you unlocked more memories to her past she had forgotten and wasn't yet ready to remember." Nickolas sounded unmoved. "Her body must have just shut down."

Saz looked horrified.

"Is she going to be all right?" she said, but looking not in the slightest bit concerned, it was Nickolas's turn to shrug.

"Yes. I am almost certain of it," he replied. "As you yourself know, Saz, we all react to the shock in different ways." And glancing at Meggie he gave something of a smile and unable to help herself, the little element returned it gratefully.

Saz all the while frowned.

"I'm surprised," she commented after a time. "I thought of *all* people Bethan would've remembered him." And thinking back to what had happened at the Temple of Ratacopeck and the embrace they had all witnessed before the base of those horrible flames, Bex nodded in agreement.

Meggie meanwhile, still seemed to be watching Nickolas, as if lost in her own thoughts and memories.

Getting to her feet suddenly, the little element then headed for the single washbasin in the corner of the room and like one possessed she splashed some lukewarm water onto her face and rubbed it through her dusty hair, before straightening up and without so much as a word, walking straight for the door.

"Hold on!" Nickolas demanded as he saw the movement from the corner of his eye and instantly leapt up to bar her path. "Where are you going?"

"I can't just sit here." Meggie met his severe gaze with her own. "I'm going to get us some food."

"And where are you hoping to do *that*?" Nickolas retorted, making a good point. The moment they left the little hut, there was bound to be trouble. Who knew how quickly word had spread about the rogue humans and what they had done?

Just then, Bex gave a gasp.

"Barabus!" she cried. "He could be here any minute! What if he finds us all-?"

Barabus. They'd almost completely forgotten about him, about why Bethan was in that hut in the first place…

"Surely he won't *really* be a problem?" Saz reasoned. "If we explain, he'll understand, won't he? After all, he's one of us."

But at the use of his fellow element's name, Nickolas's whole expression seemed to darken.

"I do not think we can rely on Barabus to aid us," he said, a definite bitter emphasis on the word 'us'.

"What are we going to do then?" Meggie insisted, shifting anxiously on the balls of her feet. "We clearly can't stay here much longer. If we don't-" but as her eyes scanned the room, she gave a sudden start as she realised that something, some*one* was missing.

"Where's Dromeda?!" she cried and sure enough, at the mention of the other element, Saz and Bex both turned to the patch of floor under the window where they'd last seen him and now expected him to be, only to find to their surprise that it was empty. Nickolas though, not even mildly alarmed, just nodded towards the door.

"He has gone to return the swords," was all he said.

Return the swords?

Shocked, Meggie gave a burst of disbelieving laughter, for a moment too surprised to argue her case for being released too.

"He's done *what*?"

Nickolas gave a slight smile.

"It took a bit of *persuasion*," he added, before, more seriously; "We should not steal. Not even from the Diggers. Especially not from the Diggers. Not without just cause. Plus, we already have-" At that moment though, he was interrupted by a knock on the door.

The sound was loud, invading and instantly everyone froze, all four of the conscious elements seeming to catch their breath as all attention flew to the flimsy wood and their only escape.

The first to react, Nickolas then reached for his tunic and slowly began to draw out a knife, until then hidden at his waist. No one knew where it had come from or how long it had been there, but gesturing with his free hand for Meggie to join the other elements on the bed, he then edged towards the door silently, his weapon at the ready.

There was a long, heavy pause as all waited, afraid and unsure. Then came another knock, slightly quieter and suddenly the door was creaking open and the group let out a collective sigh as a nervous-looking Belanna stepped into view.

Closing his eyes briefly in something like relief, Nickolas quickly covered the knife before hurrying to close the door behind the Digger as she entered and, seeing all the strained expressions, looked suddenly sheepish.

"Sorry," she said. "I didn't mean to frighten you."

"It's all right," Bex replied, the first to react. But then, getting to her feet; "Have you seen Barabus?" It was the name that had instantly sprung to everyone's mind at the Digger's entrance but Belanna only shook her head.

"I haven't seen anyone," she remarked. "The streets are very quiet this morning. Almost *too* quiet."

Noticing Bethan lying on the bed, the Digger's eyes then widened and she immediately glanced at Nickolas as if somehow suspecting that *he* had had something to do with it.

"What happened to her?" she cried, making as if to rush to the bedside.

"It's all right," Saz explained hurriedly, echoing Bex as she saw how distressed the Digger was. "She's just sleeping. She should be awake soon."

It wasn't strictly the truth but it was enough to go on, for suddenly Bex was looking agitated.

"You said last night that you have some information for us, Belanna," she burst out. "Have you found out any more about the escape?"

"Escape?!" The word seemed to send a thrill through the quiet room as Saz sat up, looking then from one woman to another in surprise and Nickolas, his attention once again caught, moved back to the window, turning silently to listen. "What escape? What are you talking about?" she demanded.

All desire to leave having fled, Meggie all the while moved back to the bed to take her place again at Bethan's side.

"Apparently there may be a way of getting out of here," she remarked, sounding so unsurprised that Saz, glancing in stunned shock first at Bex and Belanna, soon turned her attention on the little element.

"You knew? You all knew and you didn't tell me?!" she demanded hotly. But Meggie, hearing the anger behind the question, shook her head.

"Bethan only mentioned it last night. And she only said there *might* be a way."

"And we don't know how… yet," Bex added quickly. "So really, we know no more than you."

Saz still looked perturbed, but obviously pacified for now, she then turned back to Belanna, ready to listen as the Digger opened her mouth, positively quivering with nervous excitement.

"I may have the answer you need," she then confirmed. "I may have found something that can help you."

The words sent another shockwave of expectation buzzing through the room. But before anyone could so much as comment, the bed unexpectedly shifted and out came a groggy voice.

"What have you found?" it said and hearing the words, the other three elements gave gasps of delight as they realised that Bethan was finally awake.

—

"I am here," Edmund said to the nimph chief through half-clenched teeth.

Despite the assurances he had made to his friends, the pain of just standing there was almost unbearable. The muscles in his legs were crying out to give in and collapse, his mind foggy with the strain of just staying conscious. But though every moment seemed to feel like his last, though it hurt even to draw each painful breath, he could feel himself somehow reviving. The spasms that had crippled his body before seemed to have stopped for now, the froth at his mouth had all but gone and though it still hurt, he could now breathe without rasping. Slowly but surely the antidote was starting to work.

With a few smooth steps, the Lady of the nimphs mounted her ride and with a gigantic screech from the beast between her thighs, lifted off, swooping into the air with ease before dropping towards the deck. As she did so, it was as if something had snapped within him and suddenly Edmund's knees gave way and he crashed to the deck with a disgruntled groan as the creature with its precious cargo landed barely a few feet in front of him.

For several moments, it seemed, neither Explorer nor nimph moved, Edmund just remaining where he was, flat on his stomach, trying desperately to regain his strength before, with one huge effort, he then pulled himself to a kneel, dragging his fatigued head up to look upon the tiny woman.

Seeing the chief of the nimphs as she was, so tiny, so fragile on the ground, made her seem far less threatening somehow and yet…

She was stunning. Painfully, achingly so and just as he had with Hoclee, Edmund suddenly found that he couldn't seem to do anything else but stare; stare and stare at her until his eyes began to water…

The chief too, held him with her own gaze before she gave something of a smug chuckle.

"So it would seem that you are, Edmund," she said, putting that extra emphasis on his name.

Edmund. There it was again – that hold the nimphs seemed to have, and the Explorer blinked, trying badly to focus.

"You seem to know my name," he retorted. "But I'm sorry – I don't know *yours.*"

He didn't really know what had come over him, whether it was the pain, which even now as he stared at the little thing before him, seemed to be ebbing; the exhaustion; or that strange power the nimph seemed to have over him – but he didn't feel quite himself.

If the nimph could detect any of this though, she certainly made no sign. Instead, she gave something of a smile, a brush of sunshine, almost as if she was impressed by his sudden odd courage.

"You are quite right," she replied. "But that can soon be amended." And she fluttered her eyelashes, long and luxurious making Edmund feel himself almost physically lean towards her.

"My name is Charlee, or at least it *was*, for I am now known as the Lady of the Water, the chief of the nimphs."

Surprising Edmund to no end, the chief then began to untangle herself from the saddle of her beast and leaping nimbly to the deck without so much as her deadly spears, proceeded to walk, all several inches of her, towards the Explorer.

"I will not harm you," she continued, as if it were *he* at the severe size disadvantage, not her. "No one will. But only if you comply with my request."

Her request. So, already it had come to this and for a moment, Edmund could only gape. The way the Lady moved, the way she spoke... it was all mesmerising. And all - he knew deep down - pure enchantment.

These people were not to be taken lightly, the last of the poison still fighting in his veins told him that much. One more dose and he would almost certainly be dead.

"And what exactly *is* your request?" he tried weakly. His knees were starting to seriously ache now and for some reason, his fingers were tingling. What more did his body have in store?

The Lady of the Water seemed to ignore him though. Instead, she turned her eyes to the morning sky as if the blue clearness held the answers.

"I know where it is you are heading, Edmund," she then replied and then, when the Explorer almost choked on his own gasp, she gave another chuckle.

"Oh yes, I *know*. I know many things that you, human do not, *cannot*. I know, for instance," and this time she turned back to him, watching his face as if waiting for his reaction, curious to see his response, "where the elements are. I know *why* they are there and most importantly of all, *what* you must do to reclaim them."

Just as she had no-doubt expected, *this* took Edmund by surprise and in a heartbeat, he had straightened up, all attention.

All of a sudden, as he looked into those tiny vivid eyes, he felt an overwhelming urge, an alien urge, just to grab the nimph and crush her in his hands until everything he now wanted, *needed* to know just sort of spilled out of her. But caution was the only way forward. He was counting on it. They all were. So it was the Explorer forced himself to remain calm.

"Well, any information you can give would be greatly appreciated," he replied instead, trying to sound as humble as possible as his voice shook.

The chief was looking at Edmund carefully now, studying him and as he watched her, the Explorer had a feeling that just *asking* her for the answers wasn't going to get him very far.

She was fishing, he realised with a churn of fear. She was dangling the bait before him, showing him what was on offer if he complied with her demands; which could only mean that whatever this 'request' of hers was, it was unlikely to be something that he or the others would be willing to give...

"Unfortunately, I cannot offer you all of the answers you seek," the Lady of the nimphs then replied, finding the sky somehow fascinating again. "But I am prepared to give you some information as a gesture of my good will.

And," she paused with a sniff, "perhaps to offer you a small apology for your injuries..." She glanced only briefly back at him as if not too willing to dwell on *that* point.

Edmund meanwhile couldn't have been listening more eagerly if he'd tried.

Perhaps he could learn something in spite of everything... *if*, he reasoned, the nimph *knew* anything. After all, the nimphs had learnt his name through eavesdropping. What was to say they hadn't learnt of the elements and their purpose the same way too? Maybe he was being played right then for a fool...

But whatever he had expected, however much he thought he had been shocked before, it was *nothing* compared to what happened next. For as the chief then told him what she knew, Edmund recognised instantly the words he had heard before, *exactly* before – the words from his dream so many nights ago.

The very dream that had allowed him to hope all over again...

"The elements, they are not dead," Lady Charlee began. "They are simply in another place, another *world*, some might call it. An entity."

"An entity?" Edmund echoed the phrase dumbly, forgetting altogether his doubts of the nimph's knowledge as he tried to make quick sense of what she was telling him. "An entity of *what*?"

The chief of the nimphs spread her tiny arms wide.

"*The* entity," she said. "Or, if you do not know of it - the Entity of Souls, as I once heard it called." And she gave a frown, the movement seeming to soften her whole brutally beautiful face. "I cannot tell you what it's for, or even the *true* identity of the one who created it. But know this," and she levelled Edmund with a meaningful glare, "the elements are *needed*. It is not by accident that they were taken there, selected for the Builder's purposes. And he will not give them up easily."

Purposes? The word sent an odd shiver through the Explorer's poison-torn body.

Only those who are destined will find a way. The words Eliom had seen at the Temple, the words from his dream seemed to flash to his mind's eye. Only those who are *destined*...

"This entity though," he asked fearfully, "is it something harmful, dangerous? If it is a *world* can we get there? Or can it be destroyed?"

The chief however, as he had half-expected her to, shook her head, ready with the words ingrained in his memory from that tortuous night.

"You cannot defeat it... The entity and this world, the balance between them... the balance is too delicate. *But*," and here she seemed to pause almost for effect as Edmund listened impatiently, willing her to go on. "But you may be able to save them, the elements. There may be a small window of opportunity..."

This is what he had remembered. This is what he had been secretly waiting for, but when it seemed as if the nimph wasn't going to go on, the Explorer grew even more restless.

"Where? When is this window?" he demanded aloud. "What can I do?" This was more, he knew, than he had ever hoped for and the excitement, the thrill of the potential knowledge was all he could think about now. But though he was eager to know more, to glean everything the chief of the nimphs had, the Lady Charlee only frowned again.

"I am sorry," she replied, for the first time sounding like she meant it. "But no more can I say, for the Builder has many ears. He is very powerful and I dare not tell you more, not for my sake, but for the sake of my people." She gave a sigh, the sound like a puff of breeze. "I cannot sacrifice them for you."

It was understandable, what she had said, much as he might hate it; and for a moment, Edmund found himself reminded of the hidden words of Ophelius;

The Builder's spies are everywhere. He is powerful beyond even my understanding.

Who *was* this Builder and what were his intentions? Edmund found his mind buzzing with more unanswered questions, but before he could say anything, excitement quickly changed to worry as the nimph chief then continued.

"This brings us back to our agreement," she stated, interrupting the Explorer's thoughts and reluctant as he was to go back to the matter at hand, Edmund felt himself starting to weaken all over again. It felt as if whatever had kept him going throughout the conversation had suddenly fled and pain, thick and fast, hit him like a wave. Unable to hold himself up any longer, he slowly lowered his hands to the deck, holding himself up on all fours.

"And what *is* our agreement?" he asked, unable to hide the concern from his voice just as he was unable to shake the horrible feeling that whatever they were about to discuss wasn't going to be good.

Lady Charlee looked serious.

"You have trespassed on my land," she said. "And for that you must pay the price. All travellers must pay."

Edmund shifted uncomfortably.

"We have little to offer as payment," he argued. "We have barely any money, or goods of any value and as for food-" But at the mention of food, the chief let out a laugh, high, strong and glorious.

"We have no need of your money or your goods! You're right, your ship has barely anything to offer on *that* front," and hearing where this was likely to lead, Edmund felt an icy thump of fear hit his heart.

"No," the nimph chief said, suddenly sobering. "Your payment for passing and now for the knowledge I have just shared with you, is much greater than that!"

Edmund briefly closed his eyes. So, the information she had told him *had* been a kind of bait after all and he had willingly, stupidly, fallen into the trap.

"But," he started urgently. "We have nothing else to give! I don't know what we can-"

"Oh, but you do," and the Lady looked him full in the eye like one tradesman to another, waiting for the private understanding, for the message to draw home. "You have exactly what we need. You have life. You have a crew…"

A crew? Life?

And unable to believe what the nimph was implying, what she was *saying* and yet somehow knowing that it had always been coming to this, Edmund could only gawp.

"All we ask of you is this; you must surrender one of your crew members to us," the chief then confirmed, plain and simply as if there had been any doubt as to what she meant. "We do not mind which one, the choice is yours. But one of your group *must* give themselves, willingly, to me and my people before the sun sets this very day and in return, I will grant the rest of you safe passage up the river."

The request was laid out, the choice opened and utterly stunned, Edmund found himself without words.

He hadn't bargained for this. None of them had. And yet…

And yet - the stone cold realisation of it hit the Explorer like a slap in the face - perhaps they *should* have.

The nimphs had supposedly been following them since the Karenza had entered the river. They'd been watching them, listening to them and grasping not only their names but who each of them *were*. And for the first time, Edmund understood, *really* understood what that meant.

The Karenza's crew were valuable – more valuable perhaps than any gold, any jewels, riches or materials they could possibly have offered instead. They had a wizard, one of the very few magical beings left in Tungala; a warrior, a *Mawreathan* warrior, a being with strength, with ferocity like no other; and a dwarf – one of the very few to venture above ground, hardy and tough and skilled with an axe. Even Elanore had her value – a weathered ship's captain with a vast knowledge of the oceans and her own vessel. And as for the Lectur, though only a guest, she was born of a powerful race of Seers almost lost in myth, perhaps even one of the last of her kind.

Where else could anyone have seen such a crew, such a pick of irreplaceable individuals? And where would they again?

The nimphs were powerful in their own right. They had their poisons, their numbers and their magic. But ultimately, they were small; tiny beings in a much larger world. They needed more, they needed protection and that was why they needed their beauty. Humans would do where others weren't available. Humans were weak, easily drawn in by their charms, to serve in whatever way the beings needed. But a warrior? A dwarf? A *wizard? That* was something else.

They would give the nimphs so much more, if the opportunity arose. For, more immune to the nimphs' magical wiles, they would need more convincing. They would need to offer themselves, give themselves freely to service, which meant that opportunities didn't, indeed, arise like this very often...

Edmund felt suddenly numb.

What had they done?

"And what if we refuse?" he eventually managed at a whisper. Suddenly he was finding it hard to speak as a new ache made its way through his body, a new suffering, a new horror at what now lay ahead. The life of one of his crew, the life of one of his friends for the chance at saving the elements'.

How could he make that choice? How could *any* of them?

There had to be another way, another bargain he could make, but turning back to the chief of the nimphs, there was no hint of a smile on her face now.

"If you refuse," she said as if the matter were an easy one. "Then we will have no other option but to kill you all."

—

Bethan lay sprawled on the sunny grass, flicking lazily through the ancient wrinkled pages of Mythes, Legends and Folklore, *a book so well used that the print was almost unreadable. Quickly finding her favourite passage, she paused to read;*

> The Warr of the thyrd sentury was consydered a great and marvellous vyctorie for humanekind. Once a mynoritie, these fearsome warriors drove the defeated races of Nymphes, Gremlines, Dwarfes and Lecturs farr and wyde, reducing them to nothing but the stuffe of legend. Loste in the mistes of tyme, these peoples, driven into hyding by man's magnificent army, alle now lye virtually forgotten. Somme historians even doubt whether such creachures ever actually existed.
>
> Nevertheless, whether facte or fiction, mythe or folklore, the disappearance of the Elven Princes remains a most questionable tragedie. Many have queried why it was that upon the days of enlistment, the disreputable leader of humanity itself sanctioned the Elves, cousins of the trees, to join theire forces. Formidable fyters indeed they were, but where arr they nowe? Despite such vyctorie, the Elves, much lyke their foes, disappeared into obscurity... into obscurity... obscurity...

Blinking stupidly, Bethan gave a sigh and treated the hefty book to a good slam. Even trying to lose herself in her favourite stories didn't feel like enough today...

"You'll break it," a voice, warm and deep spoke, and squinting up into the light, Bethan gave a smile to see him there, standing in the mud, in the gap where her tree had once stood. Her beloved tree.

Odd how she hadn't noticed him there before. Though what was even more odd was how out of place he seemed, standing there in his travelling cloak and dirt-encrusted boots in the middle of her back garden.

But she didn't get up.

Instead, he moved towards her, his cloak fanning out behind him, a great shadow against the yellow light.

Edmund of Tonasse.

Just the very thought of him seemed to make her stomach flip, like an excited little girl. She felt breathless with it, almost overcome and as he neared her, she could almost feel his presence on the air.

Slowly he knelt by her side and looking down on her, he took her upturned face in his callused hands.

"That's not the way for a Bookkeeper to behave," he teased.

Odd again that he was armed – she could see the hilt of the sword at his belt, even though there was no danger here.

Her grin widened.

"I'm not a Bookkeeper," she replied. "I'm an Explorer now. Like you."

"Oh, are you?"

Edmund laughed.

The sound was wonderful to her, soothing as the summer air. His eyes, she could see, were half-closed in the glowing light, his face shy, uncertain. He was new to all of this – she was too, but suddenly overwhelmed, Bethan found herself reaching up and with one tug, she pulled him down to the grass beside her.

His arms were around her now, encasing her in safety. She could feel his breath on her face, hear the thrum of his heartbeat, smell his scent, musky, warm, grassy and-

Was that blood?

Suddenly, Bethan pulled away, feeling uncertain herself. He was staring at her with those deep blue eyes, drinking her in, his chest rising and falling calmly beside her own. But though he looked perfect, though it all felt perfect, Bethan knew in her gut that something wasn't right.

They weren't alone. Not as she had first thought and glancing back up into the garden again, it was then that she saw him.

It was the man. The man clothed all in black, his face turned away from them. The man who had haunted her dreams before. The nameless, faceless man who never revealed himself...

He was standing where Edmund had been. In the mud. Soundless and motionless.

"Edmund..." Bethan started.

She felt suddenly, unexplainably afraid but though she turned back to the space where the Explorer had been less than a second before, he was gone. He had vanished, leaving her behind and she was alone again. Alone with the man in the black, who even now was

turning, turning towards her, the great hood of his cloak a shadow across that unknown face…

"Apparently there may be a way of getting out of here."

There were voices. Voices she knew, at first all seeming to talk at once and then, one at a time, holding a conversation above the idyllic grass.

"You knew? You all knew and you didn't tell me?!" *one voice sounded angry.*

"Bethan only mentioned it last night. And she only said there might be a way," *another replied.*

Bethan sat up.

Bethan.

That was her name. They were talking about her. They knew her too.

"And we don't know how… yet. So really, we know no more than you," *another voice altogether finished.*

And then it was that Belanna spoke.

"I may have the answer you need," *she said*. "I may have found something that can help you."

And with that, the man in the black disappeared and Bethan opened her eyes.

—

Meggie handed the almost-empty flagon to Bethan and watched as she glugged the water readily.

"That better?" she asked and the other element nodded with a smile.

"Much."

Bethan still felt groggy, confused by what had happened, by what she had seen in the garden… But questions and wondering about all that felt suddenly irrelevant.

What the Diggerwoman, Belanna, had to say, had to answer to her half-awake question was, right then, the most important thing for her. It was the most important thing for any of them, for even Nickolas, who had been keeping out of the way in his watch by the window, couldn't hide his interest as Bex then took the plunge and sitting forwards on the bed eagerly, brought the point back to what they were all waiting to hear.

"Tell us," she said to the Digger as all eyes then fell on her. "Tell us what you know."

And for the longest time, Belanna seemed to pause.

In the aftermath of Bethan waking and the bustle it had caused, being given a moment just to herself, to breathe and think, the Digger had clearly lost her nerve even more. Anxious as she had seemed before, it was nothing compared to how she seemed now and for the first time, those of the five elements who hadn't before, finally realised what it was they were asking of her.

Whatever she might tell them now, whatever she might give was some step, however small or insignificant, to helping the elements escape – but so it was a step, a much greater step than perhaps she had taken so far towards disobeying the Builder.

The Builder was, as far as anyone knew or believed, her creator, her god, and whether she herself believed that or not, the consequences of going against them were bound not to be good… Already all of them had witnessed the rage, the *violence* others – Diggers and humans alike – had enacted in the name of this being, let alone the supposed power of the Builder themselves, so all of them knew that whatever she said, whatever she did, carried a big risk for her.

Belanna however, though quiet, though pale and worried-looking, was made of sterner stuff than perhaps any of them, including herself, had bargained for. And so it was, glancing around, as if to make sure no one else could possibly overhear, the Digger leaned in closer to the four waiting elements on the bed.

"Just as I thought I might, I've found a way of travelling in to death freely, without actually dying," she started as the whole room seemed to hold their breath.

"Death?" The word just kind of slipped from Saz's mouth – and she wasn't the only one to be confused either, as both Meggie and the listening Nickolas rose an eyebrow. "What do you mean? What has *that* got to do with anything?"

Of course, none of them had been a party to Belanna's previous revelation and the Digger looked at her.

"By crossing the connection into the world of the dead, you may be able to talk to the last man to escape this world – the *only* man – and find out how he did it," she explained hurriedly. Now that she had decided to help, she obviously wanted it over and done with as quickly as possible and seeing her fear, neither Meggie nor Saz asked who this 'only man' was.

The others meanwhile remained silent, just giving their companion a chance to speak.

"I visited a Digger I know, a relative of mine. He told me that apparently there *were* documents, records dating as far back as my father's forefather, telling of Ophelius," – both Saz and Meggie looked surprised to hear the name they knew so well – "My great forefather made a detailed recording of how the human returned to his original world. It is even rumoured in my family that my great forefather may have helped him! But whether he did or not…" she gave a frown, "all of his writings somehow disappeared years ago. Though it was never revealed why…"

Meggie snorted quietly.

"It's probably not hard to guess," she muttered before gesturing for Belanna to go on.

The Digger wrung her hands together.

"Because of this, I couldn't find out exactly how Ophelius escaped. *But* I did find the information I was initially looking for…"

She paused again for a long breath, the elements watching her silently, not daring to make a sound for fear of missing something. Nickolas meanwhile turned his concentration back to the window, but though his expression was unreadable, he was obviously still listening.

"When I spoke to you last," Belanna then continued, looking at Bethan and Bex, "I remembered something, nothing more than a rumour really, about a connection into death, some kind of door or barrier out in the desert somewhere that someone could simply step through and find themselves in… that place," she looked uncomfortable. "This relative of mine, he has only once left the City; only once ventured beyond, into the forbidden lands where the Builder lives. But he has seen it. He has seen the barrier with his own eyes, a place, he says, where the connection between this world and the next is so thin that a person really could just walk through. He has seen it – he knows it to be true," she repeated. "And this, I believe, is your best chance."

The sheer magnitude of what the Digger was telling them was almost too much to take in and for a moment, the four women just looked at each other blankly.

"You speak of a barrier, Belanna," Saz then began. "Of a connection, but death is… well… *death*!" And she looked at her fellow elements as if to confirm what she was thinking. "How can it be another place? How can we just *step* into it?"

Belanna looked slightly surprised.

"Because death *is* another place. It is another world," she breathed. "We Diggers have long believed it. Just as you came to us from another world, so must we move on to the next once our time here is finished."

"And we clearly stepped through some kind of connection – barrier - whatever you will, to get here in the first place," Bex reasoned aloud. "So I suppose it's not completely crazy to believe that death could be another world too, just like this one, with another barrier, another door we could walk through?"

"Exactly," Belanna agreed, giving something of a smile to hear some acceptance.

The other three women just continued to look at each other though, a mixture of fear, of untold excitement and disbelief glowing in each face.

"You say this relative of yours has seen this place, this barrier in the 'forbidden lands'," Bex then continued, trying not to show her obvious concern about the word 'forbidden'. "But where exactly is that?"

"It's a few days north of the City," Belanna said. "Beyond the gates."

"And how will we know when we've found it?" Bethan was searching for details. "What does it look like?"

Belanna's face twisted in thought.

"*That*, I don't know. But," she was quick to add as she saw disappointment dawning on the faces all turned to hers, "my relative told me that you can tell where it is by looking for a great boulder shaped like a tree." The others took this information eagerly before Belanna then spread her hands. "He said he knew it was the barrier to death and no other because he felt something of a pull. He could feel his life almost *wanting* to leave him, he said, when he saw it. Like he *had* to enter through…"

The description sent a chill through the air, but even before they could think about it, Belanna had finished.

"But that was all he told me. That was all the information I could get, willingly…"

It wasn't much to go on, the word of a Digger, a rough description, an odd sign, but it was *something*, and baffled, dazed as they were all now feeling, the four women couldn't help but smile.

"Belanna, I can't begin to thank you," Bethan said earnestly as she saw that the Digger really had given them everything she knew. "You truly are the greatest of Diggers!"

Belanna blushed but then quickly glanced at the door as if worried that at any moment the Builder him or herself would march in.

"I'm truly glad I could help you – even if it's only in a small way," she admitted. "But I have to go. I can't stay here for long. I'm…" and she looked then at Nickolas, who still seemed to be staring out the window, his jaw set.

"It's fine, Belanna," Bex said. "You've done more than we could ever have hoped. You've already risked a lot for us. You don't need to risk any more."

Belanna nodded, but despite her sudden urgency to leave, she seemed to linger for a moment.

"I wish you all the best," she murmured. "I really do. And if I don't see you again-" and she hesitated again as if struggling to find the words to warn against the unspoken danger that was no doubt ahead. "Please be careful!"

"We will," and leaping up to thank her each in turn, personally, the four women watched Belanna the Digger, perhaps for the last time, as, just like that, she left, the door pulling softly shut behind her.

The first few minutes following their companion's exit, no one said a word, each simply watching the space where the Digger had been, as if waiting for more. But then, the spell of silence seemed to break and Saz turned to the others with the inevitable question on everyone's lips.

"So, when do we leave?" she demanded bravely. "The sooner we get out of here, the sooner we can be home!"

The element's enthusiasm sent a ripple of more growing smiles amongst the other three. Whether believable or not, finally they had some answers, something firm. Finally, they could make some kind of plan.

But though everyone felt the thrill of potential freedom like a physical shudder, Nickolas, no longer aloof from them all, soon turned to the quartet, his face grave.

"I must warn you – it will not be as simple as that," he pointed out, an oddly harsh ring to his voice. "The journey will be a dangerous one," and then, when no one tried to stop him; "The forbidden lands are not called 'forbidden' for nothing! To the north of the City are the main gates, but after that – there is *nothing*. Nothing but desert for miles and miles. We will have no protection, nowhere to hide, to run to – we will be exposed to any threats. And as for the gate itself-" he rubbed his forehead wearily as if the idea alone made him feel exhausted, *"that* will be guarded. Heavily guarded. Do you think none have ever tried to leave this place by those means before?" And then, he let out a sigh. "I do not know how Belanna's relative ventured beyond the boundary, but he will not have done so easily!

The words hit the room with a cold thud as one by one, the smiles of elation, began to waver on the face of each element.

He was right, of course. The gate was bound to be guarded and the way ahead and beyond, bound to be tough, otherwise the almost-plan they were now forming would have been tried countless times before. They all knew that, understood it *really*. But the thought of it – the pull of the world, *their* world and the home they had known with all of its beautiful yet brutal intricacies was too much.

If there was just a chance, however small, of returning to what they had loved and lost, surely they had to take it? Surely they had to *try*? Fear for what lay ahead surely couldn't be enough to stop them? And as Meggie, the longest to linger, watched Nickolas's face, she could see the sudden change there as he too seemed to realise it, to recognise the same wild hope that he had felt so long ago – the hope of escape that he had never seen through, and the reckless courage it brought with it. To him *that* world was dead now, a passing dream; but to them it was a reality, a reality they had to and would grasp for, whatever the cost.

They would go, the elder element realised in that moment, whether he warned them or not. Just as he would have done in a heartbeat all those years ago, when he too had entered the unknown. So the choice then, was no so much what *they* did now, but whether *he* would do it too. And right then, he knew he didn't even need to think about it.

"Of course," Nickolas added quietly, breaking his own silence. "Whatever you decide to do – I will stay with you for as long as I am needed."

Chancing a glance up, he then met Meggie's gaze, expecting to see her smile at his offer. But whether he was expecting gratefulness there or not, she was staring at him, he saw, with something like concern on her face, not for what he had just said but for something he very much hadn't…

Quickly though, the moment was gone, whatever its meaning as the element soon turned away.

"Thank you," was all she said, as if speaking for them all and giving a nod, Nickolas too turned and went back to his window, all words lost.

"All right," Saz meanwhile started again. She looked shaken up by Nickolas's hard truth, but the thrill of potential action couldn't be held back for long. "We're going to have to think about this more carefully. We don't want-"

But just then the door flew open, banging wildly on its hinges and the moment for planning was gone as everyone looked up to see Dromeda rush in, panting for breath.

The elder element's face was wild and like one possessed, he scanned the room hurriedly with his eyes as the room gave a start of alarm.

"Dromeda-!" Nickolas began, leaping to his feet as he too saw his friend's obvious distress, but before he could say another word, the other element threw up a hand.

"We must leave at once!" he cried breathlessly, without so much as a greeting. "*At once!*" and then, the words all five of them had been dreading to hear came without any more delay; "Barabus! He is coming!"

Down in the cabins, the crew all stood, stunned into silence as Edmund relayed all that the Lady Charlee had said.

Even after his telling had ended, no one seemed able to so much as move, shocked as they were by what had happened and ultimately the impossible decision ahead.

Only the Explorer, who had had more time to process what had happened, to think, was ready with a solution.

"Of course, I can't ask this of any of you," he said. "As a human, I am the least valuable of us all, so I will have to surrender myself."

But instead of making the situation better, this only seemed to send the rest of the cabin into an uproar.

"Don't be stupid! *You* can't go, Edmund!" Elanore objected.

At the same time, Fred shook his head firmly; "No! Absolutely not! *I* will go!" whilst Thom leaned on his axe, grumbling; "No one will go but I. I am of the least use here!"

There was clearly going to be no agreeing as of yet and Elanore gave a groan of annoyance before then turning to Eliom almost pleadingly.

"How do we even know she's telling the truth?" she cried. "How do we know she won't just kill us all anyway and have done with it? And *how* even," she added in frustration, turning also to Edmund, "*how* does she know about the elements and this so-called 'entity' place?"

Eliom, who until then had remained apart from the others, stepped forward.

"I believe that if we come to an arrangement with the nimphs, they *will* uphold it," he said calmly before looking at Elanore. "Despite their size, they are not to be underestimated. The chief may have spoken with a Seer, or perhaps even experienced a Seeing for herself… It may also be that we will never understand where she acquired this knowledge."

Turning to Edmund, who was beginning to pace, all remaining pain from the poison forgotten in the light of the situation, the wizard then rested both hands on the top of his staff.

"I think, perhaps, that we should decide what happens next wisely," he then offered. "There may yet be another option."

And Edmund glanced up at his friend, but instead of joy, his expression was incredulous.

"Eliom, if you know something, then tell us, because to me it looks like there *isn't* another option," he was almost shouting in his exasperation. "They don't want anything else! And there's no way we can fight our way out of this." He gestured to his neck where the mark of Hoclee's poison was still visible. "We're ridiculously outnumbered and I was just *scratched*. Think what would happen if the nimphs decided to truly fight back? No!" and he spread his arms wide. "There is no other choice but for me to go. How can I ask one of you to sacrifice yourselves for this task when I was the one who brought you all here in the first place? You didn't need to follow me."

The argument was a fair one and for a moment, no one said anything as if, to the shock of all, they were all in sudden agreement. Eliom seemed to just cock his head thoughtfully for a moment, ever tranquil. But then; "That is why it is wisest for you to remain on this ship and continue," the wizard reasoned slowly. "If indeed, there is no other option but for us to comply, someone else must go."

Edmund rubbed his head in defeat.

"The nimph can't ask us to make this decision," was all he could return. "I for one can't. I *won't.*"

"What do the nimphs *want* with one of us anyway?" Thom question aloud bitterly. "Are they just going to use us however they see fit and then kill us?"

But either no one really knew the answer, or was willing to give it and once again the floor quickly fell to Eliom.

"The logical way to handle this situation is to let someone volunteer themselves," he said, looking at each member of the group in expressionless turn. "The nimph asked someone to give themselves willingly. Let someone make the choice."

This however, only seemed to cause yet more argument.

"I have already chosen! I said that I will go!" Fred spoke up, touching the sword at his side as if daring anyone to deny it. "And I intend to!"

"Myself also!" Thom added loudly. "I offered myself and I will not go back on my word."

"Maybe I should be the one," Elanore butted in. "If we're talking about value, I'm not as important as the rest of you. You all started on this journey together – you should finish it together."

But though all three had said their piece, no one made to move for the door, no one seemed to make that definitive step and Eliom continued to watch them all patiently.

"It is a brave offer, a noble offer, you each make," he said. "But none of you are willing to go. Not really. Not in your heart of hearts." He seemed to be getting at something, making some kind of point, as if he could see the solution and was waiting for it to come about, but sighing, Edmund turned to the ship's captain.

"Elanore," he said, running with what small hope he may have. "I know we've been through this before, but is there no other way to reach the tomb? Some other route, some road we could have missed?"

But though he hoped for answers, for a sudden moment of thrilling realisation, Elanore only shook her head.

"I have checked and re-checked the map. The only other options we have are to head back down river and out to sea, approaching the land from the east. Or, come at it from the west, above the gulf and trek across land like you once did…"

"And how long would either take from here?" Edmund asked, even though he knew the answer and sure enough, Elanore winced.

"From here? Probably a couple of weeks. Or if we're *really* unlucky, possibly even three or four," she reasoned.

"A *month*?!"

A month felt too long. Far too long. They knew nothing about this new world the elements were in, this *entity*, as the Lady Charlee had put it. How were they to know that they weren't in danger? That they weren't fighting for their lives and here the Karenza was, just *sitting* there, wasting precious days, *minutes* deciding their own fate?

Edmund's frantic pacing got worse. The antidote seemed to have finally worked its magic. He felt almost entirely better now. The pain was gone but though his mind was free of the strain of trying to hold on to some form of consciousness, it still felt fuggy as he searched desperately for an answer, something they could have overlooked that wouldn't cost lives in this world or the other, the impossible choice…

As he did so, a figure then stepped forwards, who so far had remained silent and yes, forgotten.

It was Eldora, her face even whiter than usual, her black coal eyes darting nervously from one face to another. But though she seemed, for the first time any of them had seen her, afraid, her expression was fixed and almost before she opened her mouth, Edmund somehow knew what she was going to say.

"I will go," she mumbled without ceremony. "The nimphs can take me."

At first it seemed as if no one had heard her. The room remained silent, Edmund even continued to pace - but then like one being, everyone turned to stare, as if noticing her for the first time and nearly all looked stunned.

Edmund was the first to react.

"I can't ask it of you, Eldora," he dismissed her, not daring to make eye contact with the Lectur. "So don't even think about it."

But though Eldora's bottom lip quivered, she was determined, all of them could see it.

"It is me they want," she insisted. "I should be the one to go. I willingly offer myself."

Again, no one seemed willing to say a word, no one but the Explorer, who suddenly froze as if realising that the Lectur was deadly serious.

"They don't seem to care who they have!" he retorted, his words a spit of anger, of exasperation that no one seemed to be listening to him, before, quietening a little; "You can't go either, Eldora. You're not part of this… this… *mission*. You haven't been with us for long and-"

"That is why it would be wise for me to offer myself," she interrupted, and no one could mistake the hard edge to her cold voice. "You do not need me. I am not a vital member of this crew. And you need not lie and pretend that any of you ever cared for me."

Cared for me.

The words felt like an icy slap across every face. Much as they may have tried to hide it in front of her, perhaps even to themselves, they all knew the truth of the matter. The Lectur had never been welcomed among them, not properly. Her cold, fearsome ways had and never would make her friends and for that, love was rare.

Of them all, the Lectur would be the least grieved for, each member of the crew knew it, but to be told so boldly, so brutally…

"That's not true," Edmund tried, but the words sounded unconvincing even to himself. "And as for needing you… You said so yourself, when you came here, that you have a purpose to fulfil," and as if the matter were over, he started pacing all over again. "No!" he repeated. "Enough of this! No one needs to sacrifice themselves. I was wrong. There must be another way. We will find another way…"

But still Eldora wasn't giving up. The moment had come and though she looked at none but Edmund now, she knew that she wasn't alone in believing it.

"This *is* my purpose!" she said frostily. "I know that now. And you cannot stop me." And she drew to her full height, her eyes fiery before it then came out; "I have Seen it."

The admittance sent the room into an even deeper silence as Edmund froze again and the others just stared. Only Eliom seemed unmoved as he observed without comment.

In the hush that followed though, attention was then drawn to the deck above as everyone clearly heard the muffled flutter of hundreds of flurrying wings.

The nimphs had returned to their leader's side and once again, the crew of the Karenza were trapped.

Seeing the effect her words had had on the rest of the crew, Eldora then lowered her gaze, her cold façade dropping for the rarest moment as the full realisation of what she was saying, what she had known but kept secret, swamped over her.

"I Saw last night, when they arrived. I Saw them take me away..." She gave a small sigh. "I understand now why I was drawn here. I was brought here so that none of you would have to be sacrificed. So that you may carry on your journey... and succeed." She levelled Edmund with a stare, woman to man. "*That* is my purpose. *That* is why I came."

"But-" Edmund opened his mouth to begin, but though he tried, suddenly he found he simply had nothing to say. What *could* he say? What could anyone say? How could anyone react to that? How could anyone now deal with the strange pang of guilt they now all felt?

All along they had treated the Lectur with cold distance, with, in some way, contempt and yet all along she had been there, not to cause problems for them, to frighten and mystify them, but to *save* them, to save the elements, four women she had never even met and probably now never would...

It was too much. Far too much and feeling suddenly far more determined than he had before to stop this, to fight, Edmund then turned to Eliom, Eldora's last desperate hope.

"Surely there must be something else we can do? Lectur visions don't set the future! They can't always be accurate, can they?" he demanded, remembering his previous conversation with the wizard.

But Eliom was grave.

"You know the answer to that question as well as any of us," he replied quietly. "You said yourself that there is no other way out of this. We must give the nimphs what they want." And from the way he spoke, it was clear that *this* was the conclusion he had expected, *this* was what he had been waiting for and Eldora sniffed quietly, wiping at something near her eyes.

"I go gladly," she said with determination and then, glancing at each of the others in turn as they all watched her, not knowing what to say, what to do, she gave a cool little smile. "Do not fear for me. Fear only for yourselves. You have a long road ahead. A long road with much to gain and yet much sorrow," her brow crinkled. "The care you take for each other... is crucial. The consideration you share for one another, the friendship I have witnessed in even such a short time amongst you, will be the envy of all. It was something I once wished for myself," and none could mistake the fleeting look she passed at Eliom, "but have now understood will never be. I, however, remain happy in the knowledge that you will all endure, for now, to continue on your most noble cause. I would not call it friendship, or even care, but it is what it is. And there is nothing you can say to stop me. I will go."

And just like that, the fate of Eldora the Lectur, of the Karenza and her future seemed decided. And no one argued.

After what felt like many minutes of awkward silence, it was then that Edmund approached the Lectur across the cabin.

"Do you know what will happen to you?" he asked carefully. "Have you Seen that far?"

Eldora's smile was wry.

"Do you mean, will ·they kill me?" she replied and then, watching Edmund's colour drain a little; "It is probably best for you not to know."

Just then, the sound of beating wings grew louder as the cabin door flew open and in swept Hoclee on her flying steed. As seemed to be her routine now, she circled the room before landing, once again, on the candle bracket and pulling on her reins to calm her ride, she sat up to her full height in the saddle.

"It is time, Edmund," she said commandingly, her eyes on the Explorer. "Make your choice and be done with it." She made no indication as to whether she had heard what had just gone on or not, but either way, Edmund wasn't the only one to look horrified.

"But your chief said we had until sunset!" he exclaimed. "It's still morning!"

Hoclee however, despite her proud air, looked remarkably apologetic.

"I'm sorry, but we are running out of time. We've received word from our scouts elsewhere that there is evil afoot on land. We must attend to it straight away," she explained. "So, have you made your choice?"

Before Edmund had a chance to reply though, Eldora had stepped forward.

"Yes," she said. "I am to go."

"*You?*"

And Hoclee took a long look at the Lectur as if analysing her for whatever task it was that lay ahead, whether death, torture or something else entirely...

"Very well," she then said, flicking her wrists to cast her ride back into the air. "Follow me. Alone." And with that, she disappeared back outside in a fluster of wings and downy fur.

No one moved for a few moments, unsure of what to do, how to react.

With a final sigh, Eldora then headed for the steps leading up to the deck.

"Wait!"

The word seemed to fall from Elanore unbidden, surprising everyone, including herself. But running with it, she moved towards the Lectur. "You can't just *go*. Not without so much as a goodbye!"

And the others, suddenly encouraged into action, all nodded their agreement and for a second, Eldora turned back to look at the captain, her black eyes sparkling with perhaps a hint of gratefulness at the human's obvious attempt to make her feel wanted, to feel missed. But the Lectur knew her place, she knew how they felt about her. And turning back to the stairs, her voice was cold.

"I must go," she muttered. "The nimphs are waiting."

No one would try and stop her now. The decision really had been made and the silence was the only goodbye she could expect or need. Except...

Suddenly, shocking them all, Eliom then hurried forward and taking the Lectur firmly by the arm, he spun her back around to face him.

"Eldora," was all he said, the word spoken softly in a voice unlike his own, as the pair exchanged one long, meaningful stare.

No one would ever know, could ever guess what passed in those last moments between the wizard and the Lectur who loved him, but after they were over, Eldora gave a miserable smile, tears evident on her stone cheeks and lowering her watery gaze, she turned and left.

For an agonising minute, the slow, sad creak of her footsteps heading up towards the deck and her fate, echoed in the quietness. And then there was nothing. Nothing but a strange bereftness as the others just waited with baited breath, none of them knowing what to do; Eliom standing at the door; Edmund leaning against the candle bracket, his head in one hand; Fred and Thom merely staring after the Lectur; Elanore sitting on a bunk, listening numbly for the sound they were all secretly expecting.

And then, it came.

The great fluster of wings fluttering and gliding and flapping filled the air for a second or two, becoming, it seemed, the very air itself and then, slowly, began to fade to nothing, the deck and the cabin below falling slowly into silence, leaving the group safe to breathe at last as those that remained, glanced at each other.

Edmund was then the first to move. In a moment of seeming decision, he ran for the door, shoving past Eliom and charging up the steps to the deck above, flinging open the cabin door with a crash as he stepped onto the deck.

Everyone heard the moan and knew what it meant.

There was no one there. The deck was completely empty.

The nimphs and Eldora the Lectur had gone.

The Karenza had paid its price for freedom.

—

The reaction was almost instant as those who weren't already standing, leapt straight to their feet, Bethan clambering out of the bed in such a hurry that she almost fell.

Nickolas meanwhile, pushing past Dromeda, rushed straight to the door to peer out into the alley beyond.

Straight away he was back inside, pulling the door to, quickly.

"Too late," he hissed to Dromeda. "Barabus is already here. He's coming down the street!"

The elder element cursed under his breath.

Glancing at Nickolas he then reached under his tunic and just as his companion had before, pulled out a small knife, until-then concealed at his waist.

"It may not come to that," Nickolas muttered, throwing up a wary hand as he saw what his friend intended. Dromeda however, only scoffed.

"You know better than to say that to *me*," he said and Nickolas looked pained.

"Don't," he warned again. "Weapons are pointless here and you know it!"

But though Dromeda opened his mouth to reply, he never got the chance.

Just as it had earlier, the knock on the door stopped everything and straight away, the room fell silent, each member of the group once again frozen in fear, every heart beating that little bit faster as, for a long moment nothing happened, nothing stirred, until;

"Bethan?" a voice called out. "Bethan, are you awake?"

Muffled as it was by the wood, many of them recognised the sound of Barabus and the first to react to it, Dromeda visibly gripped his knife even tighter, making Nickolas look even more worried. Meanwhile, all eyes fell on Bethan as the element paled.

"Should I answer?" she mouthed at Nickolas, the somehow-leader of the party.

The elder element, concentrating still on Dromeda's weapon, gave a small shrug.

"Go on," Meggie encouraged with a whisper. After all, what other choice did they have? And taking a deep breath, her fists clenched, Bethan tried to smile.

"I'm awake!" she then called, only just managing to find her voice. "I'm here!"

The words echoed dully against the white stone, and with one knowing look at each other, Nickolas and Dromeda then stepped away from the entrance, hiding themselves in a nearby corner just in time as the door swung open and sure enough, Barabus appeared, carrying what looked like a loaf of bread and a jug of water in his arms.

"Good morning-" the elder element started politely as he tried to concentrate on not dropping anything. But there was nowhere to hide, not really, not in that tiny space and the moment he looked up and noticed the other three elements, the three women who shouldn't be there, all staring at him, wide-eyed, he knew.

Instantly Barabus dropped his load, reaching automatically for a weapon, any kind of weapon, but Nickolas was too quick for him. Signalling to Dromeda, both leapt on him and in one rough movement the element was pinned against the wall, his arms spread across the stone, defenceless.

"Nickolas!" Barabus panted. He sounded surprised, and yes, angry, as he struggled to look from one man to the other. "Dromeda! What are *you* doing here?! You should not be here! Let me go!"

"Not until you listen," Nickolas grunted in return as he crushed their captive's hand against the stone with his own.

"Ow! Wha - why?! Listen to *what*?" Barabus stuttered furiously, but Nickolas just looked at Dromeda again.

"Hold him fast until he sees sense," he instructed and Dromeda grimaced.

"My pleasure," he mumbled, trying to keep Barabus still with an elbow to his throat, the knife still tight in his hand. The man was very strong, but not strong enough for the other element, almost twice his weight in muscle, and obviously seeing that he had no chance of escape, Barabus quickly ceased in his bid to be free.

"Of course I will listen to you, old friend," he tried tamely. "Now please release me."

It was obvious to everyone watching, what the man was doing; that he had already weighed up his odds at fighting and seeing they were non-existent, was now changing his tactics; but though the warning in his heart told him to know better, Nickolas also knew that they had to give the other element a chance.

"All right," he said, slowly stepping away.

Barabus gasped with pain as Dromeda's arm pressed against his gullet and Nickolas glanced at his friend. "Leave him," he added quietly. "He cannot do us any physical harm." And straight away, to everyone's surprise, Dromeda obeyed. As he dropped the man like he had some kind of repulsive disease, an inhuman growl rumbled from the depths of his throat, but he didn't say a word in protest.

Released, Barabus's eyes meanwhile flicked over the room's inhabitants again, his expression clearly controlled.

"Where did you all come from?" he then asked, his voice level, forcefully detached. For a second longer than all the others, his gaze seemed to linger on Bethan, as if noting how nervous she looked.

"We came from the outer city," Nickolas replied shortly, not giving too much away. He too, seemed on edge. Barabus could feel it in the room, could almost taste it; the tension, the anxiety. And taking another moment to calculate his chances, he bent to pick up the scattered crumbs of the bread, retrieving what was left of the water that hadn't spilled and was now seeping in one long trickle across the floor.

"Did you not receive word?" he asked carefully, all the time watching Dromeda's knife, still clasped firmly in one hand. "About the separation?"

Nickolas and Dromeda made eye contact and straight away, he could see the indecision on their faces.

Neither of them were sure which was better, to lie and claim ignorance or to tell the truth and suffer the consequences. However, whatever they were planning, neither were ever given the chance.

"Yes they 'received word' about it," the element he knew to be Meggie then spoke up bravely. He looked at her. The smallest of the four, smallest and yet somehow the most threatening. "But *they* chose not to obey it."

Chose not to obey...?

And suddenly realising what was really happening, what he had *really* walked in to, Barabus couldn't help himself; he couldn't help but turn on her, outrage bursting from every pore.

"You did not obey the Builder?" he challenged, all control, all pretence gone in a moment. He glared at the other two men as if he couldn't quite believe his eyes.

Dromeda though, had already had enough.

"No, we did not!" he barked. "And you do so needlessly, Barabus!"

But it was pointless. The elder element's words had fallen on ears already deaf to human reason and suddenly, like a coiled spring waiting all this time for release, Barabus flung himself at the wall of the white hut.

With a cry he smashed the jug of water against the stone, sending shards of pottery shivering everywhere and in one leap then lunged for Dromeda, a long dagger-like fragment clutched in his now-bleeding hand.

There was a flurry of movement as the two collided, one with stone, the other with his knife still ready and willing. Dromeda didn't look so much surprised as *pleased*, as if he had been waiting for this moment, for this chance, for centuries. Nickolas however, was there in an instant, shoving his body between them, reaching for his own knife as the four women looked on in complete horror.

"ENOUGH!" the elder element shouted. "Dromeda! Barabus!" He was almost pleading as he took hold of one, then the other and like a mother separating her squabbling young, physically wrenched the men apart.

Adrenaline pumping, Dromeda almost shoved his friend aside, but suddenly seeming to remember himself, he then stepped back, taking a moment to draw breath. Barabus meanwhile shuffled away, pressing himself against the wall as if he longed for it to swallow him up. Neither of them lowered their weapons but even so, everyone else visibly relaxed a little.

"Where is Gergo?" Barabus panted, as, once again, he glanced about the room, clearly assessing his options.

Dromeda sneered, his knife-arm twitching.

"You always did need his protection!" he taunted.

And Barabus shot Dromeda a look of clear loathing. None of the watching women had any idea what had truly happened between the pair, but all of them could see that the hatred between them wasn't just from today, from this one argument.

"At least he has the sense, I see, not to be a part of this *madness*," Barabus snarled only for the listening Bex to square her shoulders.

"You're wrong! He helped me!" she spoke up, feeling it right to defend Gergo's honour in this. "He gave me as much information as he felt he could…"

Barabus, instead of arguing though, just stared at her in disbelief.

"*So*," he muttered. "You are all in this together. You are *all* defying the Builder's orders."

Nickolas gave something of a weary sigh.

"Barabus," he said, his voice surprisingly calm. "You know in your heart that what we are doing is right. What allegiance do we owe the Builder? He brought us all here against our will." And he spread his hands pleadingly. "You know how we felt when first we came here! How *lonely* we were! We are aiding these women to keep them together. They care for one another. Surely you can understand that?"

They were strong words, daring ones and for a moment, it was almost as if Barabus *did* understand. His face softened, his eyes again roving over the earnest and anxious faces of the four women as if absorbing their pain, appreciating their worry and then, on to Nickolas, seeing the face he had trusted, he had known, open to him now, offering friendship. But then;

Dromeda.

Though his comrade was trying desperately to make peace, the other element, clearly wanted none of it and looking finally into the hate-filled eyes of his companion, Barabus couldn't help but react.

Straight away, the element's face scowled into a frown and then the shard of pottery was rising again as he stepped away from the wall, his safe haven, his makeshift weapon at the ready.

"I am sorry," he then lied, "but you have disobeyed a direct order and I must take all of you to the Builder, as my captives. You must be punished for this disobedience."

Hearing the words and knowing now that trying to reason with him wasn't going to work, Nickolas gave a groan. Dromeda however, still fuelled with his resentment, laughed.

"And just how do you propose to do that, *Barabus*?" he mocked. "There is *one* of you and *six* of us!"

Nickolas shot his friend a warning look.

"Dromeda!" he spat through his teeth.

"Have you not been listening to a word I have said?!" Barabus shouted, losing his cool again. It was strange to see him so rattled, almost frightening.

"Have you?" Dromeda retorted. "Your way is madness, Barabus! Not ours!"

But his words only made the element angrier. Gone was the cold, controlled exterior Bethan had known, and in its place, danger.

"We are the chosen!" he spat wildly, brandishing his slither of stone like a sword. "You all made the choice to come here!"

"The choice?!"

Dromeda's eyes flashed.

"It was all a *lie*!" he yelled. "We were never saving our world, and we are *still* not by remaining here!" And he gave a crazy laugh then, as if realising for the first time how stupid all of it sounded. "All this time, this long long time of *nothing* and we still do not even know *why* we are here! And yet it was *you* that drove us here in the first place! Traitor!"

"I never *forced* you through the flames!" Barabus's face was red now. He was inching closer and closer to Dromeda all the time, the pottery moving perilously in his hand, with all eyes in the room on the blade…

"Stop it!" a voice suddenly bellowed. "Just stop it now!" And as if the whole room had frozen again, everyone, including the two enraged men, fell silent with a start.

It was Bethan.

Her face was distraught and despite her fainting fit from the night before, also now red.

As all eyes fell on her, she too then held her hands wide.

"Just stop! Please!" she begged, her voice shaking, and as if knowing this was his chance, Nickolas stepped forward again, ready to try peace one more time.

"Please, Barabus," he said, knowing somehow that it was his last opportunity to make the other element see. "Remember what it was like for us. We have never been imprisoned. We were never forcibly separated as these four have been. They just want to stay together. They are friends, just as we once were…"

"*Once*. A *long* time ago," Dromeda sniffed quietly to himself.

Barabus's boiling face relaxed slightly. But though he had been right to try, to hope; just as both Dromeda and yes, Nickolas had predicted, it wasn't enough.

"I am sorry," Barabus said again and with that, he finally lowered his weapon and before anyone could say another word, before anyone could so much as try to stop him, he was sprinting for the door and crashing out into the alley; gone in a moment.

For what felt like a minute afterwards, the others all just stared after him, slightly stunned by what had just happened. But time, seemingly, was of the essence, especially now, and the first to gather his senses, Nickolas suddenly sprung into action, gathering up what was left of the fallen bread from the floor before hurrying to the washbasin to fill the empty flagon with water.

"What are you doing?!" Meggie asked, stepping to his side in a kind of daze. "Where has he gone? Will he be back?"

Nickolas glanced at her briefly.

"Collect everything that we have. We need all of that bread and if you can find another flagon, fill it," he looked at the empty bed. "Plus the blankets, get those too. We have to leave right now."

"Leave? Why?" Saz joined in, she too, moving towards him slowly as if utterly bemused by the whole thing. "He's gone now. Surely…"

Did they not understand?

And finally pausing, Nickolas turned to study the elements then, *really* study them, realising perhaps for the first time how innocent and vulnerable they all looked, huddled near each other, their eyes wide with worry, with mild confusion at what they had just witnessed. What hope did they have? What chance did they really stand without him? Without Dromeda? And though a part of him had determined not to let it, Nickolas realised that the truth of that answer *worried* him. The future, *their* future worried him.

"Barabus has gone to find help," he then explained carefully. "If we do not leave soon, this place will be swarming with Diggers ready to take us away under lock and key." And he turned back to his work, not wanting to see the realisation on their faces, the recognition that once again they were in danger.

"But where will we go?" Dromeda, finally sheathing his knife, approached the basin, keeping his voice low. "Where *can* we go where he will not find us?"

Nickolas, distracted, didn't look up. There was barely any water left now, certainly not enough for any long journeys, but it would have to do. They had no other choice.

"Anywhere. Somewhere. Away from here…" he replied. "Maybe back to the outer city or-"

"Northwards," Saz suddenly suggested and everyone looked at her in surprise.

"Well why not?" and she gave what was supposed to be a shrug. "Let's stick to the plan! Let's find this world of the dead! What other choice do we have?"

It was a fair point. No one had a better suggestion and no one *needed* more persuading right then that leaving was the best plan any of them could have.

And so it was that the group seemed finally to move into action, grabbing what sparse supplies they had to prepare themselves for the potentially long and dangerous journey ahead.

TRAVELLING TO DEATH

For the rest of the day, the crew of the Karenza were very quiet, few words spoken between the remaining five companions as the ship carried on its noiseless path up the dark river.

The deadening trees were thinning the further north Eliom's wind pushed them and yet a strange gloom seemed to hang over them all, even as the first signs of civilisation began to appear.

Elanore was the first to spot them, the squat little fishing huts and docking bays scattered with empty but clearly still-used boats.

"Merchant's Wreath," she remarked to Edmund as the Explorer leaned over the bulwark, straining to glimpse the first few houses along the shoreline. There seemed to be no one about this far south, but the place was obviously inhabited.

Instead of looking hopeful though, the human seemed only wary.

"Will there be any trouble?" he asked. All of them had been shaken by the nimphs, more perhaps than they'd want to admit.

But Elanore shrugged.

"I don't expect so. It's a human settlement, I think. They're not likely to harm us."

"All right." And just as he had for hours, the Explorer fell back into thick silence, lost in his own thoughts.

"About time."

Thom was standing only a few paces away, leaning on his axe absently. But though he grumbled as usual, there was something, just like everyone else, subdued about him. Even his spirits were poor. "We need a decent meal and if humans are good for nothing else, it is certainly food."

Edmund couldn't help but give a weak smile at his friend's clear attempt to make him argue, to rouse himself from the numb grief of the early hours.

"Indeed," he remarked and then, as if the dwarf's intentions really had done their job, he straightened up, finally turning to cast his eyes across the rest of the empty deck. "Has anyone seen Eliom?"

Not to his surprise, Thom gave a grunt.

"No. Not for a while," the dwarf remarked. "He is still in the cabins. I do not think anyone has spoken with him since... this morning."

And Edmund nodded, trying not to show his worry at what Thom *really* meant. *No one has spoken with him since Eldora was taken...*

Feeling suddenly dizzy, the Explorer clasped the side of the ship for support. Though the nimph poison seemed completely removed from his system now, he still felt weak. Weak and tired. All he wanted to do was lie down in his bunk and sleep. But sleeping right now, he knew, wasn't really an option.

"Should we dock?" Elanore asked, going back to the issue at hand and she gestured to the land where already, during the last minute of their conversation, the huts and small docks had given way to cabins and small wooden houses set in clusters along the riverbank. Up ahead was the main port, empty but for a few vessels peppered with late arrivals and fishermen bringing in their wares from the day.

Edmund stared up at the already lengthening sky. Had the afternoon almost passed already? Had it really been so many hours...?

He gave a small sigh.

"Yes," he decided aloud, not knowing until that second what his answer would be. "I think it'll be good to stop for a little while. We're making good enough progress..."

As long as no one else tries to hold us prisoner and take our crew...

Elanore nodded gladly.

"Very well then," she replied before, with a meaningful pause; "Though I'm going to need *all* hands on deck."

From the way she said it, Edmund knew this meant Eliom too. And reluctant as he suddenly felt, he also knew what *that* in turn would mean...

"Do you want me to-?" Thom started, seeing his expression, but the Explorer soon shook his head and straightening up again, pulled his cloak more tightly about him. Though the sun shone now through the diminishing trees and the air was warm, he still felt somehow cold.

The presence of the Lectur was still with them...

"I'll go," he said, before, turning back to Elanore; "Give me a minute to speak with him. Do what you can in the meantime to get underway."

And Elanore gave another nod before heading off to the other side of the ship, followed by Thom as Edmund, without further ado, then hurried for the cabins.

He had no idea what he was going to say, that much he knew straight off. He had no idea even, what he was going to find when he confronted his friend.

The wizard had changed of late; he wasn't so blind that he hadn't noticed. *How* or *why* he had changed, the Explorer didn't quite know, but he *did* know that something hadn't been right with his life-long companion for a while now and it wasn't the first time he'd recognised it even in the past few days. The differences were subtle, but they were there. And right then, he knew he was *afraid* of what he might find in that cabin, afraid of what might happen if the wizard was disturbed…

Edmund however, needn't have worried, for just as he reached the trapdoor and paused, taking a small moment to prepare himself, to try and think, it was then that he heard the movement from below and suddenly the door was thrown open of its own accord and appearing up out of the darkness beneath, a figure he recognised.

Straight away, Edmund studied his friend's face.

Despite the time to himself, the time Edmund hoped he had spent resting, the wizard looked tired, more tired than the Explorer thought he had seen him yet. His face was white, *grey* even and there were dark circles starting to gather under those perfect brown eyes. He looked almost *human* in his weariness and realising that it was because of him, because of what he had made the wizard do, Edmund instantly felt the familiar crush of his guilt, the *shame* at what had happened.

He felt ashamed by the fact that he hadn't handled the situation with the nimphs better, the fact that, by his own stupidity, he'd allowed himself to be poisoned, and then that he hadn't been able to wake, that his body had been incapable of fighting for itself and once again his friend had been forced to risk his own life to save his. He had witnessed the change in Eliom after freeing everyone from the Dark Mist, the strain taken without complaint, without comment. But to do it all *again*?

And as for Eldora…

Edmund was afraid to dwell on *that* and whatever emotions, if at all, her arrival and awful departure had stirred up.

Whatever he had been expecting of his friend, as he looked upon him though, Edmund was half surprised to see the wizard give a little smile, as if he recognised the Explorer's feelings and was trying to tell him that all was right and thrown off, Edmund opened his mouth, suddenly struggling for words.

"I was just coming to get you," he commented pointlessly. "But I see…"

Eliom bowed his head.

"I know," he said, his words somehow steeped in meaning.

Then, before they could talk anymore, Elanore, seeing Eliom emerge, had descended on them, issuing orders left, right and centre.

"Eliom! Edmund!" she cried, hardly pausing to breathe. "Ropes! Now!"

Eliom glanced at Edmund questioningly.

"What-?"

"We're stopping at Merchant's Wreath," the Explorer explained.

"Ah." And the two separated to perform their tasks, all the while Edmund trying not to dwell on the tiniest yet concerning detail - the fact that the wizard had had to ask...

—

"And 'ow long do yer plan ter be stayin' for?" asked the dockhand, looking pointedly at Elanore. "Miss…?"

"Elanore. Elanore of Lordan," the sea captain replied from the front of the group before turning to the others inquiringly.

Edmund stepped forward to address the man.

"Just one night," he said. "Then we'll be on our way."

And appeased, the dockhand gave a smile and a nod. His eyes roved over the strange assortment of travellers from the Karenza semi-curiously until he reached Eliom, at which point he seemed to freeze, his jaw slackening, before, remembering himself, he tried to smile all over again.

"Do yer need anythin' movin'?" he started politely, obviously wanting to be of some help. "Any supplies or…?" But Edmund soon shook his head.

"No, no. We can take care of ourselves…but thanks."

"Very well." The man's grin widened. He had several teeth missing and those that were left were worn almost to stumps, giving him a sort of grotesque lopsided sneer. "If yer need any 'elp, there are plenty o' men aroun' here willin', for a bit o' coin."

Edmund cleared his throat.

"Thank you," he repeated, before, throwing a look at the others, he then started off down the jetty, the rest all following behind him, not a word passing between them. Only as they reached the end of the planks did the Explorer then suddenly pause as if remembering something and turning back, he too tried to give a smile.

"Can you recommend any places to stay around here?" he called. "Give us directions perhaps? And supplies, where can we get them?"

The man, who had already made to move to the next landed boat, much smaller than the Karenza, halted and swivelled in his tracks, clearly delighted.

"Yes, I mos' certainly can!" he cried and hurrying towards them, he almost tripped in his eagerness.

Thom meanwhile leaned in closer to Fred.

"Is he really the most reliable source?" he muttered.

But the warrior only gave him a half-withering, half-amused look.

"Never judge a man by his appearance, Thom. You should know that by now."

And the dwarf let out a rare laugh.

"If we judged *all* humans by their appearance, we would never have anything to do with them," he remarked sardonically as the man then pushed past them to the head of the group and Fred hid a smile.

"I can do one thin' better! I can shows yer!" the dockhand exclaimed and then, beckoning to another man nearby, who was dressed in nothing but a dirty loincloth, his voice grew even louder; "Benn! Giv' us a hand 'ere would ye?"

The man called Benn, strolled over like he had all the time in Tungala.

"Can you show som' of these…" the toothless dockhand continued, searching for the right word, "… *peoples* 'ere, the supply yard?" and Benn nodded lazily.

The crew all glanced at each other. This was the first time they had been separated in a while and despite the dockhand's friendly manners and Elanore's assurances, the nimphs had left all of them feeling wary.

"Elanore, can you take Thom and Fred to buy any supplies that we might need?" Edmund then requested, taking charge again. "We'll meet you later…"

The sea captain just nodded. The trio would be safe together.

She, Fred and Thom then followed Benn off towards the supply yard just beyond the border of the docklands.

The helpful man with the toothless grin didn't seem particularly keen on being left with a wizard – every now and again he would throw Eliom what could only be described as a fearful glare - but he kept to his bargain and signalling for Eliom and Edmund to follow him, he gave yet another smile.

"This way gentlemen," he then said exuberantly once the others were gone. "I'll find you the nices' accommodation this side of the Eastern territories," and without anymore to-do he led them across the docks towards a group of cabins and the outskirts of the small town.

The elements and their companions hurried wordlessly into the evening light, dodging the open spaces and sticking close to the alleys as they drew ever closer to the edge of the City.

Nickolas took up the front of the group with Meggie and Saz immediately behind. Bex and Bethan followed along after whilst Dromeda brought up the rear, his knife in hand, despite his friend's earlier warnings of no more bloodshed.

All day it had been quiet - they'd heard no hint nor seen any sign of *anyone* Digger *or* human - and it was this more than anything that worried Nickolas.

"Where *is* everyone?" Meggie hissed, detecting his fear as they rounded yet another corner to find an empty, silent street. But the elder element just shook his head, keeping his eyes on the way ahead, and taking a moment to check on the others, Meggie glanced behind her.

In the faint light, her own eyes were distracted by the glint of metal and noticing the weapon in Dromeda's hand, her pace slowed a little. The way the elder element moved, the way he held the knife reminded her of something, of some*one* she had known back on Tungala and even amidst the urgency of their situation and her fear, she couldn't help but wonder for a moment what was going on there, how life was for those left behind, for Fred – *that* was who Dromeda reminded her of – Thom, Edmund, Eliom and the captain of the ship, Elanore.

Had they managed to leave the temple? Did they ever think about her and the others? Did they even know they were still alive?

Ahead, Nickolas peered carefully beyond the next alley wall, holding up a hand to stop the others.

"Wait!" he mouthed and everyone halted behind him, their hearts beating crazily in their chests, their lungs burning from the run.

After a moment or two, the elder element then nodded the all clear and beckoning for them to follow suit and duck, they did so without question, trailing after him in a doubled huddle as he rushed across to the far side of the alley, keeping, as always, to the edge of the buildings. Even though the huts cast no shadows, just as nothing did in this place, staying close to them felt like the only protection the rebels had from prying eyes.

Reaching the end of another thin street, Nickolas yet again held up a hand to stop the others as he cautiously checked ahead. They couldn't be too careful and though the last few hours had felt like nothing but run, stop, check, and run again, no one had any better ideas.

This time however, as the elder element scanned the way ahead, being careful to keep himself hidden, something was different. Meggie was the first to notice as a look of horror flashed clearly across Nickolas's face and stepping back from the corner the elder element then straightened up, but instead of so much as glancing at her and the others, he turned to look directly at Dromeda.

Clearly detecting something was wrong, Dromeda was ready.

"What is it?" he mimed, studying his friend's face. But Nickolas just beckoned for the other element to approach the front of the group and creeping past the women quickly, Dromeda obliged.

The four remaining elements looked at each other in growing confusion. *What was going on? What had he seen?*

But watching as Dromeda took his own look beyond the corner of the next street, only to snap back into hiding, his face a mask of shock; confusion soon turned to icy cold fear.

"What is it?!" Meggie hissed. "What's wrong?!" But though she looked straight up into Nickolas's face, almost waiting for him to reassure her, reassure them *all*, both he and Dromeda for the moment, seemed to ignore her.

"We can take them," they heard Dromeda mutter as his hand visibly tightened around the handle of his knife. He then made as if to move out into the open, but even before any of them had worked out what was going on, Nickolas was quick to grab him by the scruff of his tunic and drag him back.

"No!" the other element spat. "There are far too many of them! Barabus must have spread the word fast! Somehow he must have known we would try and leave this way…"

Dromeda just looked indignant.

"We cannot die remember? No matter what they try and do! What is there to lose? They cannot murder us!"

Murder. The word sent a thrill of horror shuddering through the group. Even though all four of the listening women had heard, had been told that humans didn't die in the Digger world naturally – the two men standing in front of them were the very testament to that fact – none of them had ever really considered *murder*. Humans couldn't die here. They could be injured, yes, but being *killed* seemed an entirely different thing altogether.

Could it really be? No matter what happened, would they really *never die*? And thinking about it, the sheer magnitude of such an idea, Meggie massaged her wrist. It hadn't troubled her for a while now but all of a sudden, she could feel it throbbing all over again.

They could certainly feel *pain*; that was for sure.

Nickolas, meanwhile, shook his head, still concentrating on Dromeda.

"I do not like it. Perhaps the gate is not the only way after all…"

"It *is* and you know it! Stop trying to delay!"

Dromeda looked angry and stepping in then, Meggie grabbed both of them by the arm, her gaze flitting up from one face to the other.

"What's going on?!" she repeated, her voice almost reaching normal levels. "We need to know!"

Dromeda and Nickolas seemed to give a collective start as if they'd forgotten she and the others were there.

"Shush! Keep your voice down!" Dromeda warned with a sharp hiss, looking even more annoyed.

Nickolas, on the other hand, was more tender.

"We have reached the gate," he said. "We are at the northern end of the City."

That was it? They were there?

Upon hearing this, the rest of the group seemed to stir and as if she couldn't quite believe it, it was then Saz, who, pushing past the others, headed for the end of the street.

"Well let's go then!" she whispered, remembering to keep her voice low, "what are we waiting for?!"

But before she had a chance to so much as reach the end of the wall, Dromeda had grabbed her roughly by the shoulder, pulling her back and Saz gave a gasp of surprise as she was shoved roughly against the alley wall.

"We cannot just *walk out there*," Dromeda all the while growled in her face. "Stay!"

Saz opened her mouth to reply but Bethan got there first.

"Why?" she asked fearfully. "What's out there?" She too had moved towards the end of the alleyway, but unlike Saz, she was holding back a little, looking at Nickolas and Dromeda, waiting for answers. All four women were beginning to suspect what was coming, but it took Nickolas to prove their fears right.

Obviously thinking it better to show rather than tell, the elder element gave a sigh.

"Come on," he then whispered and the elements moved up to join him at the very end of the street.

Signalling for them to stay well hidden, he then glanced at Meggie, still the closest of the four.

"Take a look," he said. "But do it slowly. And for everyone's sake, *stay low.*"

Meggie nodded seriously.

"Will do."

Little by little, the smallest element then peered out beyond the wall, just as Dromeda had, and before him, Nickolas himself, only to stifle a cry as she saw what was holding them back.

Before her was a wide open square of white stone. It was currently empty but clearly a space dedicated to a day market, with great stone supports where stalls would usually stand and pavements carved into the rock beneath. But what drew her eye the most, was what stood beyond, for at the end furthest away she could just make out two great gates. They were intricate, beautifully crafted with thick golden bars and a design of what looked like a creeping plant curling up between the spokes.

They were stunning, but they were also at least fifteen metres tall and almost just as wide.

Meggie sucked in a big breath.

They looked heavy, *very* heavy, impassibly so and to make things even more impossible, there was, she could see now, two chains twined between them, dense as a man's arm and attached to them, locking the gates together, a great padlock, rusted with age.

This though, wasn't the worst of it. Not by far, for illuminating the gates' thorny golden bars were hundreds of little lamps, flickering in the evening air and as she watched, as she saw and understood, so it was Meggie truly began to fear, for each little lamp, flickering in the suddenly stifling air, was held by a Digger.

There was a great crowd of Diggers standing silently before the elements' only exit, weapons open in their hands and glinting in the dim glow.

Weapons ready and waiting.

Waiting, Meggie realised with an even greater chill, for them.

—

Stretching out on the bed, Edmund couldn't help but give an appreciative groan as he let his head roll back onto the plush pillows, his eyes closed.

"Ah," he murmured, finally allowing his tired body to relax. "You have no idea how much I have missed this. A normal, *human* bed."

Eliom, from his position by the window, said nothing in return though, and reminded that things were clearly not well, Edmund soon got up again, propping himself up on his elbows to watch as his companion drew back the corner of the lace curtain and stared out of the frosted glass beyond. His face, its usual unreadable self, was still very pale.

Edmund glanced at the other bed across from him.

"Eliom, it's late," he remarked seriously.

He didn't dare tell the wizard to rest, much as his friend clearly needed it. He rarely ever saw the wizard sleep. He didn't usually need to, but this was different. This time...

As if he knew what his companion was thinking however, Eliom gave the smallest shake of his head, his eyes never leaving the street outside.

"Not until the others return," he replied. And though his voice gave nothing away, Edmund was immediately concerned.

Forgetting his own need to sleep, he was back at a sit in seconds, his eyes turned to his sword, propped at a reachable distance from the mattress.

"Do you suspect something?" he demanded, as, obviously seeing his full, Eliom then let the curtain fall.

"I do not know," the wizard replied truthfully. "I only... I do not trust this place. I detect..." He paused, as if unsure what to say, how to explain but though Edmund was trying not to look too urgent, he couldn't help himself.

"What is it? What do you detect?" he hurried. Was it the nimphs? Was the Lady Charlee going to go back on her word after all? Or was it something even worse?

"I do not know," the wizard repeated. He sounded almost *confused*. "I could be wrong but..."

Could be wrong?

Edmund felt truly worried then.

"You're rarely *ever* wrong about this sort of thing Eliom!" he said. Getting to his feet as if he was going to go right then and check everything was all right for himself, he then reached for his cloak. "They *are* late…" he offered. "Maybe I should-"

"I said, I could be wrong," Eliom interrupted, his voice unexpectedly sharp. But as Edmund looked taken aback, the wizard too got to his feet and slowly made his way towards the inviting bed, the unexpected moment gone. "Maybe I do just need rest after all."

"Right," Edmund responded absently, still stunned by his friend's uncharacteristic outburst. "Yes. Rest." It was clear that even now the wizard still hadn't recovered from the morning's trauma.

The morning.

Edmund could hardly believe that it had been only *that morning* that his body had still been pumped full of poison, fighting for its life. *That morning* that they had given Eldora to the nimphs, let her sacrifice herself needlessly for the good of their own lives...

Did Eliom *feel* something about that? Was that why…?

And feeling a sudden chill, the Explorer shuddered. He desperately needed sleep. They probably all did.

"On second thoughts, I think I shall stay awake for a while longer, just until the others return. However, you must rest. You are tired," Eliom then said suddenly, making Edmund wonder whether his friend had read his mind…

"You should be the one resting," the Explorer argued feebly, but all of a sudden, he couldn't seem to do anything else but yawn, his eyes incredibly heavy and seeing Eliom make his point with a wan smile, Edmund released his cloak and flopping back onto the bed, was asleep before he could so much as clamber under the blankets.

―

Eliom sat awake well into the night, replaying the past day over and over in his head.

Strangely weak and exhausted as he was, he felt no need to sleep. He so often didn't. He wasn't like the others. And yet…

The nimphs. Going into Edmund's mind and Eldora's sacrifice. They swam round and round in his head, making him feel unnaturally drowsy, unfocused.

Eldora.

He remembered the final words he had spoken to her, his final thoughts as they had connected and oddly, it bothered him.

He had *felt* something, something that he still felt now; the breath of something not quite an emotion but still enough to trouble him.

Was it sorrow? He wasn't sure.

Even though he'd been unable to love Eldora in the way she'd wanted, the wizard found himself strangely regretting that he couldn't have made her happy.

Was it guilt then?

He'd never really experienced guilt before, not before the Lectur had come back into his life. It was new and strange, like a deep aching, a deep gnawing in his core. He'd *witnessed* it, of course, seen it play out plenty of times, often in humans. But *feeling* it himself?...

He remembered Edmund's guilt in Bor's village and the anger he himself had felt. The anger at wanting the stupid human to see sense. It disgusted him now. Anger was such a weak emotion, not one fitting for a wizard.

Not that *any* emotion was fitting for a wizard...

Eliom knew that he was to keep his head at all times. He had been trained to do so; since the very beginning, the control, the shield he had built within had grown to be a part of him and yet somehow things had slipped recently.

Maybe it was the weaker-willed humans with their constant shifting emotions that were making things difficult.

It was not the first time he had reasoned this, over the last weeks especially, but for the first time since then he found himself recalling the words of Joshan - The Great, the head of the wizard Order, or so he had believed him to be before realising he was an illusion, a dream of the Dark Mist's making.

"You grow too close to these humans, Eliom. You must not let them control your actions. That is weakness," he had said.

Had he been right?

Eliom had, after all, been captured. The Dark Mist had managed to imprison him in a world of fantasy, of horror all of his own making, despite the fact he was a wizard. He was emotionless, he dealt only in reason, he *had* no fantasies and yet still he had been fooled...

We both know why you are here. Although we also both know this is not where you would truly wish *to be!*

Again Joshan's words replayed themselves in his head; the words that had secretly plagued him since the very moment they had been spoken... But quickly, just as he had every day since the Mist had taken him, the wizard shook them off, turning his mind to other things.

He didn't want to think about those words now. About what he knew they meant.

He couldn't and he *wouldn't*. And luckily, right then he didn't have to.

"You are late," he whispered, unable to keep the sudden edginess from his voice as he got to his feet, his staff in hand at the arrival of a very tired-looking Thom and Fred. He studied both faces in the dim light from the corridor before gesturing warningly at the bed across from him where Edmund still lay, sound asleep.

Fred and Thom glanced at each other.

"Ordering supplies took longer than we had expected," the warrior offered. He looked at Eliom strangely. "Plus, there was a delay at the night market-"

"A fight!" Thom broke in eagerly, his voice perhaps a little too loud, and Eliom blinked at him.

"A fight?" he echoed. He sounded calm but the same sense of foreboding that had been growing on him the entire evening only worsened.

Fred nodded absently and moved to another of the four beds in the room, unbuckling his sheath and pulling off his cloak as he went. He propped his sword next to the pillow within fingers' reach.

"Yes. No doubt you will hear all about it from the locals tomorrow," he mused, obviously none-the-wiser to the wizard's odd concern before adding as an afterthought; "Elanore is on the next floor. She will explain what we bought in the morning," and before Eliom could say anything in reply, both Fred and Thom had slumped onto their own beds and within less than a few minutes were dead to the world.

The night was almost entirely black now, the smallest hint of an almost-rising sun glimmering on the horizon, but despite his own exhaustion and the growing snores around him, Eliom still sat awake, alone with his raging thoughts.

He didn't sleep that night.

―

"What are we going to do?!" Bex hissed after she'd taken one more fleeting look. "It's our only way out!" And then, quickly; "Isn't it?"

"It is," Dromeda confirmed, his voice grim, as the others just stood in a sort of speechless silence.

Nickolas's mind all the while, was reeling with indecision.

As far as he could see, the group had only a few choices. They could either stay within the City and lay low, hoping to find somewhere safe to conceal themselves until the crowd dispersed – not that *that* looked likely to happen any time soon – or if that didn't work, give up on any plan of escape and try and find somewhere more permanent to spend their remaining long days in hiding. The elder element glanced around. Although the chances of doing that too, of finding somewhere safe away from the eyes of Diggers, away from Barabus, with a continuous food and water supply were nigh on impossible…

Their other choice then, was to continue on as planned and take their chances with the crowd at the gates. Yes, there were many Diggers in the waiting throng, all with weapons ready to be used, but the elements had to hang on to the fact that all violence against them would be useless. Nothing could harm them. Not really. Pain was an option, but death wasn't.

They couldn't die…

Not really.

And not for the first time, Nickolas glanced at Meggie.

The little element looked worried, but at the same time he could see, just as he had from the first day he'd met her, that she also carried with her a strange dogged resilience. She'd obviously weighed up the same options he had – what other choices were there? - and come to the same conclusion, the same realisation that whatever they did would now involve considerable risk. Instead of panicking though, as anyone naturally would, the element was waiting, silently, almost calmly as if for fate to take its course.

This woman, he could see, had truly known death. She had known pain, *real* pain in her past life; yet although she was still afraid of it, she didn't let it control her and despite their circumstances, despite the urgent decision they had to make, he couldn't help but admire that.

"We should carry on," Bethan was then the one to say it, half surprising them all and as the group's eyes fell on her she bit her lip. "Can we *really* do anything else? The Diggers obviously know about us, and if this is the only way out of the City…"

"But, hold on."

It was Saz's turn to speak, and as if a last-minute sluggish thought had struck her, the element held up a hand, grabbing everyone's attention.

"Why didn't we think of this *before?*" and she looked then at Dromeda, as if demanding answers. "What about the way *we* came into the City?" she asked, gesturing at Meggie and herself. "We were on the outskirts even of the outer city, way out in the desert. Surely there must be a way of…"

But straight away Nickolas shook his head.

"I ask again, do you think no one has ever tried this before you?" he said a little sceptically. "That no other human has ever tried to escape this place except for this man Belanna spoke of? We do not talk of it, but *everyone* knows that beyond the outer city leads to nowhere. There is a wall, a great impassable wall," he gave a small sigh. "I have never seen it myself but…"

"So, let's take the gates then," Bethan interjected firmly. She seemed suddenly very determined, as if she could somehow see the barrier of death right before her eyes, could feel the freedom beyond… "In any case," she was searching for any reassurance, "you said that we can't die no matter what. So what do we have to fear?"

Nickolas's face was grim.

"Precisely," Dromeda chipped in. He was positively shaking with nervous energy. Though none of them hoped for it, all could see that the elder element was ready for a fight. "So," he added, looking from one face to another eagerly. "Is it decided?"

"Wait!" And suddenly, Meggie had stepped into the middle of the group like the captain of an army, her little face firm. "Before we decide *anything*, we need some sort of plan, don't we? Or are we just going to charge at them and hope for the best?"

Dromeda pulled a face.

"She's right," Bex pointed out and Meggie glanced at the other elements before turning again to Nickolas, that same stubborn spirit wild in her eyes.

"How about; I'll distract them away from the gates and then you can all run?" she suggested bravely.

But immediately Nickolas shook his head.

"No!" he argued and then, seeing her expression change, he added more softly; "I will go. After all," and he met Meggie's wide glare with a strange acid kindness, "*You* are the ones who wish to leave…"

He sounded angry and for some reason, the little element felt her face redden at this, but unable to understand why or to fathom Nickolas's sudden coldness, she looked away.

"What about me?!" Dromeda then interrupted. "Do I not get a say in this?" but Nickolas turned to him, his face unreadable.

"Lead them onwards," the elder element replied simply. "And then, if I do not return…"

Meggie looked straight back at him.

"Stop it!" she snapped. "Don't start talking like *that*!"

But though she was expecting, willing Dromeda to join in, to maybe make a joke out of his friend's half-goodbyes, the other elder element suddenly looked very lost.

"You cannot die," he repeated. But the statement sounded more like a consolation for himself than his companion; a request, more than a fact and Nickolas replied with a wry smile.

"Well, we will definitely know for sure soon enough," he joked and he plan made, he looked no one in the eye then, instead, drawing out his own knife and taking a moment to inhale three long, calming breaths.

"Try not to kill too many of them," Dromeda remarked, filling the suddenly tense silence and then, when his friend finally looked at him, he gave his own grin. "You know how much I love Diggers."

"Yes," was all Nickolas said, and then, with that, with no more final words, no ceremony, the elder element stepped out into square and like a being crazed, began to run. Within seconds he was gone, swallowed up in the darkness before the flickering light of the lamps, and the four women and Dromeda were left alone, ready and waiting to make their move.

Almost straight away, both Meggie and Saz made as if to go after him but Dromeda soon held them back.

"Wait," he murmured. "He needs to draw them away from the gates." And sure enough, even as the words came from his mouth, they all heard a great shout well up from the crowd. The Diggers had spotted him and all four women felt a shudder as they recognised the unmistakable clash of metal on metal.

Already they had turned on him. Already he was fighting.

Nickolas was fighting. Alone and desperately outnumbered.

Taking this as a sign to move, Dromeda then craned his neck out into the square, looking for their moment of opportunity.

To the women, it felt as if time itself had slowed right down as minutes seemed to pass, minutes littered with the shrieks and cries of confusion, of pain, the collision of weapons and running feet as all four waited for the go-ahead, trying to focus on the task before them and hoping against hope no one would get hurt.

Finally, Dromeda then turned to them, something of a hungry glint in his eye. He was ready.

"Only half of them have been drawn away," he spat. "The darkness is only working partially in our favour. We will have to take our chances with the rest." Before, seeing the anxious looks on the women's faces; "Stick by me, whatever you do. None of you are armed so do not try to be heroes. Just remember, you cannot be seriously harmed, so do not fear. Just run and keep running until you are free." Turning back to what now seemed to be a growing battlefield, he then pushed himself to a ready crouch, for a moment looking like an animal ready to spring up and attack, ready to draw Digger blood.

"When I say go…" he said, his voice rising above the growing noise.

The elements prepared to jump into action themselves, each trying to picture, very differently, what lay ahead.

Then it was time.

"*Go!!*" Dromeda yelled, and just like that, he disappeared at a sprint, the four women, without another thought, running after him, rushing straight around the bend and out into the thick of confusion.

In the dark flurry of bodies and movement and sound that now filled the once quiet square, the first thing the elements saw was that, sure enough, the number of Diggers had lessened. Nickolas had obviously managed to coax half of the crowd towards the west, away from the gates and despite being one man against many, others lay injured, some even, horrifyingly, *dead*, the lamps they had once held now dribbling burning oil onto the dry white stone floor already tinged with blood. The whole place seemed to have transformed, but seemingly unaware, or rather, *unmoved* by the bloodshed all around him, Dromeda ran straight for the great gates, the women hurrying to keep pace with him, trying not to lose each other in the night.

The remaining Diggers now stood before them, some watching what little they could see of the fight clearly going on just beyond the square to their right – one human versus at least twenty Diggers - others talking amongst themselves, others on the alert, shaken by the sudden attack. Seeing the approach of Dromeda and the four women however, soon drew them all together, reminding every Digger why they had been summoned there in the first place and immediately each began to ready his or her weapon, snarls of incredulity rising on their faces.

But despite their orders, despite what they had clearly been told to expect, what the throng *hadn't* bargained for, was Dromeda's speed. The elder element was like an arrow loosed from a bow and before any of them could truly react, he was there. With a great cry of adrenaline-fuelled hatred, he was leaping into their midst, swinging his knife effortlessly and already Diggers were falling to the ground.

Bethan, who took up the front of the sprinting women, wanted nothing more than to turn away and *fast*, as she noticed the number of Diggers all focusing on her, and her alone, ready to hack her down the second she was within reach. The faint flicker of the remaining lamps made their faces seem contorted in the darkness, frowns turning to great evil scowls like dark spirits ready to do away with them all. But swallowing her fear, she too let out a cry, an inhuman wail to push herself on and without another moment's worry she dashed headlong into the throng of armed bodies, the others following her.

Dromeda was already expertly slashing a kind of pathway through the Diggers and stunned and horrified as it was to see or even contemplate – for *where* had he learnt to kill so many so very fast? – Bethan, Saz, Bex and lastly the smaller Meggie simply took it without question, ducking and diving out of the way of bodies, weaponry and blood as each and every one tried to fall between them and their exit.

"Nearly there!" they heard Dromeda shout from ahead somewhere, but despite his talents, he was getting worryingly far away, and the path was gradually starting to close in with eager Diggers, all prepared to injure or be injured trying and before they knew it, the elements found themselves completely surrounded with nowhere to go. Soon all four of them were forced to slam to a halt, chests heaving and eyes wide in fear as the circle of angry Diggers pressed in around them.

"Where are *you* going, miss?" one of them sneered. There was an odd hint of reverence in the Diggerman's voice, but all respect and fear of the humans had clearly crumbled the moment Nickolas had raised the first weapon. "You can't defeat us. You have no weapons."

Bravely, Meggie held her head high, staring the man, who was considerably larger than her, straight in the eye.

"Leave us alone!" she shouted above the chink of metal and mutters from the other Diggers pressing in to watch. "You can't defeat *us* either! We mean you no harm and we can't be killed by you! So let us pass!"

"You can't be killed?" another Digger sniggered, pushing forward through the crowd to get a good look at the women. "You may be blessed by the Builder with long life, miss, but we can soon put your *killing* theory to the test!" Meggie's point though, had obviously worked and some of the other Diggers were starting to look a little uneasy. Several of them even moved back, widening the space between human and Digger.

"And - and... what would your God say about *that*?" Meggie challenged quickly. "The Builder brought us here for a reason. If you try and hurt us, he'll want to know why!"

That was it; another mention of the Builder and half of the remaining Diggers were lost now, stepping away in fear. A good few though, still remained in the tight circle.

"We're under orders to stop you should you try to reach the gates," another Digger said indifferently. "*You* are the ones who are disobeying the Builder."

So it was true then. Just as they'd suspected, Barabus *had* had a hand in this. Somehow he had known that they might try to make a break for the desert and fast running out of ideas to talk themselves out of the situation, Meggie glanced at the other women uncertainly.

What did they do now?

And where on Tungala was Dromeda? Where, even, was Nickolas?

What could they really hope to gain without so much as a *knife* between them?

"Has anyone got anything sharp?" Saz, the most experienced fighter of them all whispered helplessly, bringing a snigger from several of the Diggermen. But even before the words had fallen from her mouth, they all heard the cry from the back of the group, followed by the sound of crashing metal and suddenly the Diggers began to turn, to move aside as something, or rather *someone* began to charge through them.

It was a dark figure, a man, slashing left and right and as he neared the centre of the circle, pushing aside the last of the now-frightened Diggers, he called out.

"Meggie! Bethan, Bex, Saz! This way!"

Splattered in blood, sweat and dust as he was, Nickolas appeared to be miraculously unscathed and knocking the last Digger standing between him and the women aside with the flat of his blade, he stood before them all, panting hard.

Sweeping the women with a cursory glance; as seemed to be usual, his gaze fell on Meggie the longest.

"Quickly!" he then commanded again as none of the elements moved, all of them unknowingly frozen in place by what had just happened. "Follow me!" And released from their shock, the other four instantly obeyed as he turned and began to lead them at a run towards the gates.

But there were still some Diggers on their feet and as the small group made their way onwards, Nickolas continued to do battle. The amount of bodies littering the ground were less than those willing to stand and fight and it was getting harder and harder for the elder element to wrestle them on his own...

The elements could barely see now, what with the darkness growing ever deeper as more and more lamps fell, and the bodies pressing around them. Each just kept pushing and pushing forward, ducking and careening away from any enemies as Nickolas fought them off, his energy waning more and more with every stroke.

And then suddenly, before they knew it, the great golden gates were looming over them and there to meet them was an exhausted but equally unhurt Dromeda.

"Nickolas!" the elder element exclaimed, unable to hide the relief in his voice as he saw that his friend was safe. "Nickolas! You are all right!"

Nickolas, however, didn't have time to celebrate.

"Get the... gates open... *now!*" he ordered breathlessly. "We have to... get them... out of... here! There are more... Diggers... heading this way! I saw them!"

More?

And his face paling as he realised that the fighting was well and truly not over, Dromeda just nodded, tucking his now bloody knife in the band of his trousers before turning to the gates.

The gates.

In their haste to flee, to get past the Diggers, no one had really thought about *them* and so it was right at that moment, as they stood before the glimmering gold, that the group then realised the impossible truth that they hadn't even paused to consider for a moment; the truth that their only way of escape was closed to them, was locked shut by a padlock the size of a human head.

And none of them had the key to open it.

"How are we going to get through?!" Bex cried shrilly, glancing behind her. The remaining Diggers seemed to be keeping their distance, for now. Something had frightened them; perhaps Nickolas and Dromeda's strange resilience, perhaps something else, but either way, it was only a matter of time before more of them came, and united, they would be strong again.

Dromeda cursed loudly and Bethan let out an exasperated groan.

"Come on!" Nickolas growled and sheathing his own knife, he made straight for the padlock and gripping it in both hands, braced his feet firmly on the ground.

The others all just stood and stared at him in shock, unsure of what to do, panic ringing in their ears.

"Do not stand there!!" the elder element grunted, as he strained against the lock. "Help me!" and again, when no one moved; "Dromeda!!"

Hesitating, Dromeda then whipped out his weapon once more and after a moment of consideration, threw it to the nearest element, Saz.

Saz caught it mid-air.

"Take this," he then hissed gruffly. "Watch out for any more Digger-scum." And Saz nodded, holding the knife firmly in both hands as Dromeda dashed to help.

The feeling of the weighty metal between her fingers, warmed by Dromeda's hand and yes, the blood of tens of Diggers, somehow felt comforting to her. She could remember the last time she had held a weapon like this, remember how Eliom, the wizard, had given it to her. She'd only known him a few days then but he'd handed her the golden blade, the perfect fit for her fight-worn hands, almost as if he'd made it for her...

Eliom.

As she thought about him, recalling his friendly yet aloof face to memory, Saz felt a sudden unlooked-for hope, eliminating some of her fear.

Eliom would come for her, she realised. If anyone was going to help them be free of this place and back in the world where they belonged, it would be him.

The wizard would not have forgotten them. He would not have left them for dead. He would *know,* and despite everything going on around her, almost as if by doing so, she could somehow connect with him, Saz felt herself give a little smile.

They could do this.

Dromeda and Nickolas, meanwhile, were both red in the face, but no matter how hard both men heaved, the rusty padlock didn't so much as groan. It wasn't giving and the more they tried, the less and less it seemed that it was ever going to.

"Come on!" Meggie urged and in a moment of decision, she too rushed forwards to grab hold of the metal, along with Bethan and Bex. "We need to break this lock!"

The shout waking her from her thoughts, Saz stayed where she was, standing guard, the knife held bravely out before her as if challenging any Digger to come near. For a long while though, still nothing seemed to be happening as the five elements pulled with everything they had, knuckles and fingers turning white.

But then, suddenly, as if it had been waiting all along for some show of teamwork, the padlock gave an odd screech as ancient metal began to grind against ancient metal and before they knew it, the whole thing started to loosen and feeling the lock shudder beneath his grip, Dromeda gave a cry of encouragement.

"Yes!" he shouted his battle-like yell. "For the elements!"

"For freedom!" Bex added as she hauled with all her might, her feet rooted solidly to the hard ground.

For Edmund. Bethan thought to herself, passion urging her to carry on even though every bone in her hands and arms were screaming at her to stop.

And then, in one tiny moment there was a satisfying click and with a thud, the group fell to the ground in a heap as the padlock gave way.

As one, the great chains began to snake with an ear-splitting clatter across the metal bars, loosening at last until their ends fell away entirely and the gates were free.

They had done it and Dromeda being the first to get to his feet, quickly brushed himself off before reaching out for his knife. Saz returned it gladly.

"Is everyone all right?" Nickolas meanwhile asked, helping Meggie, the closest element, to her feet. Incredibly, everyone still seemed unharmed and unable to help himself, Dromeda let out an exhilarated laugh.

"We really *are* invincible!" he exclaimed and for what seemed the first time that evening, Nickolas gave a proper smile, the expression lighting up his whole usually-stern face.

"We're not free yet!" Bex then said, and drawing everyone back to the matter at hand, she soon gestured back across the square.

Sure enough, just as Nickolas has predicted, they could now make out the glimmer of more lamps as Diggers in their hundreds began to flock into the square, marching in a rabble towards them. The group of elements had minutes before they would be completely surrounded and even more vastly outnumbered. They would have to move fast and forgetting their minor victory for the moment, the humans immediately leapt back into action.

"Open the gates!" Nickolas shouted and diving for the left-hand gate, he braced himself to heave. To his surprise however, despite its size, the gate felt like nothing more than a feather in his hands and in less than a breath it was open.

They only needed one and without delay, Dromeda then sprinted over the threshold of the Digger City followed by the four women, Nickolas taking up the rear to push them on into the dark nothingness ahead.

Already the first of the Diggers were at the gates now, any others that had held back before, finally gathering their nerve to join the growing mob of noisy soldiers.

"Keep going! Do *not* look back!!" Nickolas bellowed to the others and obeying, the group ran wildly into the blackness, away from the City and its glow.

Just as they had been told, before the six of them seemed to be a kind of desert prairie with no light either natural or unnatural, at all. But though very soon they knew they would be running blind, though all of them felt already exhausted, already ready to rest, the Diggers hadn't stopped their pursuit at the gates. They were following them onwards at a seemingly relentless pace and sweat already pouring into his eyes, Nickolas chanced another glance behind him.

The Diggers weren't going to give up, he could see that. Not now there were so many of them, encouraging each other on, fuelling each other's rage.

Despite his secret hopes that none of them would dare to adventure out onto the forbidden land, they weren't going to cease, even if it meant following them, running for days on end, wherever it might lead… Believing themselves to be acting on behalf of the Builder, they weren't going to stop. Not unless someone *stopped* them and turning back to the others ahead, he then suddenly began to slow.

"Dromeda!" he cried and from the head of the group, Dromeda turned.

"What?!"

Nickolas knew he had to do it.

"I am… going to… hold them back!" he then called, every few words coming in a breathless, hurried gasp. "Keep… the others… running as… fast as they… can! Do not… come back… for me!"

But instead of agreeing, Dromeda slowed his pace right down too, almost forcing the others behind him to stop.

"No!" the elder element retorted. "Definitely not! I am staying with you!"

Perhaps he knew what it was Nickolas had planned, perhaps not, but too tired to argue, Nickolas just shook his head. It was very dark now and he could barely even see Dromeda in the faint light from the City behind. He could barely see *any* of them.

"I will… catch up… with you," he promised. "Trust me."

And though Dromeda still seemed unsure, the elder element knew he had him and with one final nod, Nickolas then stopped running altogether.

Almost straight away the others seemed to disappear into the darkness as they carried on, their pace weakening but determined, clueless as to what they were leaving behind.

He had a few seconds before he would be truly alone. And then a few seconds more before he would be in company again, a very different company, and taking his time, Nickolas once again drew out his knife, pausing a moment to catch his breath as he turned back to the City.

She had heard his shouts, but too distracted by the sheer will of putting one fast foot in front of the other to really think what his words could mean, it was a good while before Meggie realised that Nickolas had gone. Glancing back, she could see Saz and Bethan just behind her and then, beyond that…

"Nickolas!" she shrieked and suddenly, she too had halted, almost causing the other two to run into her as she just made out his silhouette in the darkness, standing there, knife in hand, facing into the growing lamplight. "Nickolas! What are… you *doing*?!"

But before she could say another word, before she could do anything, she felt the rough tug of a strong hand on her arm and Dromeda was there, pulling at her, almost lifting her up in his desperation to keep her moving.

"He will be *fine*. Please! Just keep going!" he cried violently. "Leave him!" Nevertheless, however much he tried to make her move, no matter how many times she almost fell as she was dragged, Meggie couldn't seem to pull her eyes away from that one lone figure.

From his position nearer the City, Nickolas took a long, calming breath.

He'd had more time than he'd thought and the crowd of Diggers seemed to be slowing.

Just as he'd hoped they would be, they were clearly nervous of him, nervous because of who he was, because of what he had done back in the square, because he had stopped running and they didn't know why. And because of it all, they too began to stop, to swarm into one big group, half-circling him so that he stood like some barrier between them and the other elements behind.

Good, he thought to himself. He was giving the others time. Time to disappear.

His plan, so far, was working.

"Are you admitting defeat, human?" one of the older Diggermen then dared. "If so, you're choosing the right path. I expect the Builder may show you mercy. Even if *we* wouldn't!"

Some of the others made their agreement known with a cry but Nickolas merely looked at the speaker, not a hint of an expression on his face.

"I have nothing against you or your people," he replied. "I spilt Digger blood today and for that I am sorry… But you left me with little choice."

There was a murmur amongst the crowd, but no one so much as inched closer.

Seeing Nickolas surrounded, both Meggie and Dromeda has ceased running now, both of them just standing, watching with baited breath the single man, looking so small and helpless in the dim light against a great armed mass of Diggers. But though his strength was nothing in comparison to theirs, he had one advantage above them all, the advantage that still kept every Digger in their place, too afraid to touch him; Nickolas was human, therefore Nickolas couldn't die. He couldn't lose his life and none of them would dare try to take it, for he was a chosen one. He was an element.

"Bind him!" another Digger then called out from near the back of the group and the first speaker, obviously not as nervous as the rest, stepped forwards, in his hands a metre of rope clearly brought for that very purpose. But before he could so much as reach for the elder element's hands, Nickolas was swinging forward with his blade, and within seconds, the Diggerman's fingers, along with the rope itself had fallen to the floor, blood bursting silently onto the virgin ground.

Immediately there was uproar in the ranks of Diggers as many stepped back in fear, others letting out a fresh cry of outrage, and knowing that any moment of peace was now gone, Meggie turned desperately to Dromeda.

"Help him!" she pleaded. "He's on his own! *Help him!*"

Instead of running to his friend's aid though, as she had hoped, Dromeda just bit his lip.

"He will be fine… Just watch," he insisted. "Just watch!"

Meanwhile, another Digger had stepped forward from the rest to make himself heard.

"The Builder will *kill* you human!" he spat loudly at Nickolas. "Mark my words! You will *die*!" But though he was within a foot of the element, still he wouldn't touch him and fuelled by the hold he still seemed to have over them, Nickolas turned on him.

"The Builder *cannot* kill me!" he challenged, shouting loud enough for the whole crowd to hear. He sounded pleading. "He need not be your god and you have the chance to turn away from him now! Take it!"

But this only caused more outrage as the throng began to jostle with each other, cursing and shouting and raising weapons.

"The Builder *is* god!" the Digger at the front retorted. "You blasphemous scum!!!"

And Nickolas levelled the man with a pitying stare.

"He did not create me or my kind," he said calmly. "Is that not the makings of a god?"

"No, but he can destroy you!" one Digger replied and then, just like that, without warning, the chanting started.

At first it was low, no more than a small suggestion, but quickly it began to spread through the ranks of the crowd, fuelled by their anger, growing into a shout.

"Kill him! Kill him! Kill him!" they demanded. "Kill him!"

Kill Him.

Hearing the call echo across the plain, Meggie gave a groan.

"Kill him! Kill him! Kill him!"

And thinking of nothing else, she made as if to go to him, to step in, to stop this madness. But though she tried to move, Dromeda still had hold of her arm and no matter how hard she struggled, he wouldn't let go.

"Kill him! Kill him! *Kill him!*"

If Nickolas was unnerved by their shouts, he didn't show it. Instead, he lowered his knife, as if willing them to see reason and sure enough, one of the Diggers closest to him, still looked anxious.

"We *can't* kill him," the man said, his voice only just audible above the chaos. "They can't die. We know that…"

"He's right, they can't…" another added and watching to see who it was who had spoken, Nickolas couldn't help but feel a wave of relief.

There was still definite doubt there, doubt that could work to his advantage. Maybe no one else needed to get hurt. Maybe he could persuade them to leave, to return to the City and leave the elements alone…

But then;

"I still say we *try!*" another shouted and suddenly, from amidst the bustle, a giant of a Diggerman stepped forwards.

Towering above even Nickolas's considerable height, and wielding some sort of curved sword with notched edges in his beefy fists, he seemed to pause only for a moment, as if assessing the path he was about to take before, without warning, he stepped back and swinging his arms forward, chopped out at the element's head.

With barely a second to react, Nickolas threw himself aside as the blade missed his left ear by an inch, but the effect was instantaneous as immediately, the Digger crowd fell into silence, too stunned by what had happened, by what had just been attempted, to do anything else.

No one had ever raised a weapon to a human before. Not *like this*. Not with the real intention of *killing*. But as they watched Nickolas duck and roll away as the large Digger had another go, swiping and stabbing at the air where his body had been but a heartbeat before, their confidence began to grow and soon, they began to raise their voices again, to shout and laugh, to encourage the fight, enjoying the strange sport enfolding before their eyes.

Diving nimbly away from the Digger's giant blade, Nickolas rolled onto his back, his breathing coming fast.

"Stop this!" he cried. "No more bloodshed!" He didn't want to kill this man, he didn't want to slay another Digger; he had already killed so many that night. A pointless waste of life.

But the giant only sneered at him.

"No more of *our* bloodshed!" he taunted and lunged forward, his blade pivoting in mid-air.

As the sword flew towards him though, this time, Nickolas was ready, and with a clash and whine of metal, his own small knife rose up to meet it in the air. Just as he'd hoped he would, the Digger man looked surprised for a moment and stepped back, almost falling into the crowd and giving Nickolas the window of opportunity to leap back to his feet.

In the meantime, Meggie, Dromeda and now the other three women who, hearing the commotion, had also stopped, were watching the ensuing fight with growing horror. Again, Meggie tried to free herself from Dromeda's grasp, to do *something* to stop this, but still the elder element clung on, reassuring her over and over again that Nickolas was going to be fine, that they'd all see.

As he got up, Nickolas tried to use the Digger's moment of weakness to stab him. But he missed, swiping just short of the tall man's belly and the momentum sent him turning about on his heel to face out towards the prairie and his watching friends.

But though it seemed only small, a tiny mistake, a second in a much longer encounter, it was then that it happened; the moment when everything they knew was altered. The moment when, as Nickolas raised his arms, preparing to turn back and finish his enemy, the Digger then lunged forward and with a warlike cry, thrust his weapon straight into the elder element's back.

The blade slipped through Nickolas's body like water, stabbing him all the way to the front of his chest and with a sickening crack, it sliced up through the front of his tunic, where it protruded towards the sky in a curve of triumphant blood and metal.

Instantly the entire prairie fell utterly, horribly silent. All mocking smiles of sick enjoyment fell from the Diggers' faces in a moment, a few shuffling away in terror, the other elements merely watching in disbelief as Nickolas then gasped, his face contorting in confusion, in pain.

The Digger who had done the damage, all the while, fell back in alarm, releasing his hands from the weapon as if it had burned him, as Nickolas just stood, rocking on his legs for a few moments, blinking back tears of surprise as blood began to seep softly around the blade, staining his light tunic red, bubbling up from the deep wound in his chest.

There was a dreadful hush across the plain as all watched, waited, astonished.

And then, it happened. Just like that, the element buckled forward and with barely a groan, he fell to the ground with a lifeless, horrible thud.

For a moment it felt as if the entire Digger world had somehow *stopped*, as everyone, every Digger, every human just continued to stand and stare, utter astonishment echoed in every face, every being unable to really fathom what they had just witnessed.

But then, Dromeda, being the first to come to his senses, gave a start as the reality of the situation, the reality and the realisation that he had been wrong, that they had *all* been wrong, hit him.

They could die.

The elements could die.

"We have to go. Now!!" he bellowed, the unexpected shout seeming to waken both Diggers and elements alike as all began to rouse themselves, and turning on his heel, the elder element started to sprint back into the darkness, out towards the prairie and freedom, trying to drag Meggie with him.

THE ENTITY OF SOULS

It took a few moments for the other women to register what was happening, but then, just as it had for Dromeda, the sudden awareness hit them well and truly in the face.

They were no longer safe, and fuelled by the sudden horror of this fact, each of them set off, now running for their lives.

Meggie, however, still tried to stand firm. Despite Dromeda's best attempts to pull her away, the little element's eyes were wide, half-glazed in shock.

"No..." she began to mutter, refusing to tear her eyes from Nickolas's corpse, refusing to move. "No.... No. No. No! It can't be. No!"

"Meggie!" Dromeda shouted, physically shaking her. "We have to move!"

But the little element was too much in shock. It had just been so sudden, so unexpected. She hadn't even had a chance to say goodbye, *none* of them had. One moment he'd been there and then...

He was gone.

"*Meggie!*" Dromeda tried again, his voice angry now. "Leave him! Do you *want* to die?!"

But instead of snapping back to her senses, of realising the danger and making her move, suddenly, the little woman was glaring at him, a confusion of pain and anger, of numbness, of *accusation* in her fierce eyes.

"You said he'd be fine! You said! You promised he would be all right!" she screamed, and then, she was lashing out at him in her strange grief, pushing him away. "You promised...!"

Dromeda looked horrified.

"We have to go!" he almost pleaded, his voice cracking. "Please Meggie!" And then finally, as if not knowing what else to do, he seized the little element by the waist, to try and pick her up, to *carry* her to safety.

But though he tried his best, Meggie was having none of it. Quickly, she squirmed away, hitting out, almost slapping him across the face.

"We can't leave him there!" she retorted, flailing her arms, desperate to avoid Dromeda's grip. "He's your *friend!* How could you-?"

"Meggie! We *have* to!" the elder element cried. And then, finally managing to lay hold of the struggling woman's shoulders, he pulled her forcefully towards him, encasing her in his arms like a firm embrace.

"No! We have to help him! He's hurt..."

"We cannot help him now! The Diggers will *kill you!*"

"But he-!" Meggie pleaded.

"Meggie!" and Dromeda, almost yelling with frustration, with the pain of what he had to say, nearly crushed her in his arms. "*Nickolas is dead!*"

Dead. Dead. Dead.

The prairie rang harshly with the word and up ahead of them, the other three elements halted again in surprise, panting for breath.

They'd all known it. They'd seen it with their very eyes. But to hear it spoken aloud, so very soon…

Meggie too, seemed to freeze all over again and seeing that he really wasn't going to be able to move her any other way than by brute force, it was then that Dromeda took his moment. Without so much as a warning, he grabbed the element by the waist and hoisting her up, he flung her across his shoulders before setting off once more at a run. But though he held the little woman tightly to his body, ready to feel her struggle, to feel her lash out all over again, all fight seemed to have left Meggie now and she just lay there, limp, silent and numb, as if resigned to her fate.

"Come on, follow me," Dromeda then ordered the other women as he caught up to them. "If we want to get out of here alive, I suggest we keep running until morning." And unable to say so much as a word between them, the others just nodded dully, following behind their new leader as he steered them into the abysmal blackness, away from the crumpled body of their companion.

A SURPRISE GUEST

"Hello there!" Elanore said brightly as Edmund made his way onto the deck of the Karenza in the warm morning light. "Sleep well?"

As he bent to shift a wayward crate, the Explorer replied with something of a smile.

"Better than I have a while," he admitted before, thinking better of it, his grin grew sheepish. "Not that there's anything wrong with your-"

But Elanore merely laughed and stroking the wooden bulwark like it was her well-loved child, she gave a shrug.

"She's not the most comfortable place in the world, but she does the job," she said fondly and Edmund chuckled.

"She does," before, feeling the need to suddenly be serious; "And we owe her *and* you so much, Elanore." She had no idea where the praise had come from all of a sudden, but even so, feeling modest, the sea captain brushed the compliment off with a shake of her head as she took up another crate of food and heaved it towards the centre of the deck where all the other supplies waited.

"Well, that's enough of *that*," she teased. "I don't want-" but then, just like that, the whole mood of the morning seemed to change as they heard a movement behind them and, distracted, both turned to see Eliom approaching.

The wizard's face looked a little haggard, and still pale, but it was, to Edmund's silent relief, its ever-calm self. Even so, the Explorer's smile still faded as his mind returned to what had happened the very morning before to make his friend look so exhausted in the first place…

"Hello," Elanore repeated. She sounded less cheerful than before, a lot more *careful* and for a second, Edmund wondered if she too, even in the short time since she had known him, had noticed something different about Eliom.

"Good morning," the wizard returned and then, not wasting any more time with pleasantries, he stared straight at Elanore; "I hear that there was a fight last night."

If the sea captain was surprised by the sudden question, she didn't show it. Instead, depositing the crate with the others and dusting off her hands, she gave a little frown.

"Yes there was, but we didn't get too involved, thankfully."

"A fight?" Edmund asked, bracing himself, as he too picked up a heavy crate. It was the first he'd heard of it. "What fight? What happened?"

Elanore however, shrugged again, heading for another crate.

"Well, some men tried to pick a fight with us-" she said.

"But it was nothing, we held them off," Fred interjected as he appeared from the cabins, making his way across the deck with a coil of new rope. He nodded in greeting to both Edmund and Eliom as the wizard watched him, his expression giving nothing away.

"They picked a fight with *you*?" Edmund paused a moment. "What did they want?"

But instead of answering, Fred just glanced at Elanore almost warningly.

"They don't much like strangers in these parts. They'd just had a bit too much ale, that's all," the sea captain returned, implying that that was as much an explanation as they were going to get on the matter. It was a weak dismissal, but it obviously worked, for his concern waning at the mention of a drunken brawl, Edmund soon went back to his work.

"Perhaps it's good we're moving off this morning then," he replied quietly and then, completely forgetting the whole thing; "Where's Thom?"

Fred jerked his chin upwards.

"Crow's nest."

"Ah."

And straightening up as he dropped the crate, Edmund then turned to Eliom.

The wizard was still, oddly, watching Fred, something obviously bothering him, but the Explorer knew better than to ask him what the problem was outright, in front of everyone. He had a feeling that whatever it was, it was something not to be shared and he made himself a mental note to try and ask his friend about it later.

For now, he was keen to be getting on and looking back to Elanore, he gave another, slightly less cheery smile.

"Have we got everything?" he asked and Elanore, hands on her hips, surveyed the pile of supply crates like an army commander surveys her troops, before nodding.

"I will let us go, then," Fred offered.

"Yes, please do. We'll be off in no time. The wind is in our favour today," Elanore glanced sideways at Eliom, "without any help!" And the warrior made his way towards the ship's side where the landing plank led down to the dock, Edmund following to help him heave up the hefty wood.

"On three," Edmund suggested, bending down to grab the edge of the board. But as he did so, another movement then caught the corner of his eye and glancing down at the dock below, he was the first to notice a lone figure standing there, just at the jetty's edge, watching them.

It was a beautiful fair-haired young woman garbed in a grubby cloak and having gained Edmund's attention, she soon gave a companionable wave.

The Explorer had never seen her before and unsure what to do, Edmund just blinked at her for a moment. Meanwhile, realising that his companion had stopped, Fred soon followed his friend's gaze.

To Edmund's surprise, the warrior's eyes widened in amazement.

"What is *she* doing here?" he then muttered and amazed himself, Edmund couldn't help but look from him to the woman and back again.

"Do you *know* her?" he asked incredulously and Fred nodded.

"Yes, I do," the warrior said. His voice was grim. Then; "It is Soph. My life-partner."

—

Soph moved swiftly up the gangplank towards the watching group of mismatched travellers as if she owned the place. Reaching the top, and taking one small glance about the Karenza, her expression completely unmoved, she then offered each member of the group, including Fred himself, a formal nod, before her eyes then fell on Edmund and to everyone's surprise, stayed there.

"At last, Edmund of Tonasse, we meet!" she cried and taken aback, the Explorer gave a shocked smile, offering her his hand. Soph took it, her grip remarkably strong.

Like Fred; the warrioress, as they now knew her to be, appeared young, no older than a human in the early years of her twenties, and yet the Explorer knew better. She had shoulder-length dirty blond hair, shorn in a direct, straight cut – no doubt slashed with a sword to keep it out of her way – and wonderfully untidy. Her grey eyes looked soft and calm, but like her life-partner, her firm set lips spoke of something else altogether.

Like Fred too, she also wore trousers – strange to see on a human woman, not so on a warrior – only hers were cropped and thinner and instead of a tunic, underneath her travelling cloak she wore a bodice of leather, which seemed to accentuate every curve of her lithe body.

Overall, despite her scruffy, weather-worn appearance, Soph was extremely attractive and for a bizarre moment, Edmund found himself wondering how Fred had ever managed to leave her behind in Mawreath all those years ago.

"Have we met before?" the Explorer managed, knowing that they hadn't – the warrior *certainly* made an impression – but interested as to how Soph could possibly know who he was. As far as he was aware, Fred hadn't seen Soph, his wife - or 'life-partner' if proper terms were to be used – for at least fifteen years in human time**,** meaning that the last time they had set eyes on each other would have been when Edmund was only a child.

"No, we have never met!" Soph chuckled in reply. Her voice too, was soft, womanly and yet also fierce; like a dangerous creature, tamed but ready to turn at a moment's notice. "But I have heard many stories on my travels!"

Stories? At this, the whole group seemed to tense up, used as they were to being cautious, but noticing their reactions, Soph soon gave a reassuring smile.

"If you were trying to lay low, you have done a good job," she replied. "Do not worry on *that* score. No," and her eyes glistened a little, "I have met with Bor, the Chieftain of the Tribe of Water. I do believe he is a comrade of yours?"

And immediately, everyone relaxed.

"Yes," Edmund replied with obvious relief. "He and his people were a great help to us."

"Indeed," Soph mused, "so I have come to understand." And introductions clearly over, she then turned back to Fred, a new kind of smile, small, almost shy, playing at her lips.

"Greetings," she whispered and his expression giving nothing away, Fred simply bowed his head again, for a rare moment, looking stuck for words.

"You look…" He paused. *Amazing? Beautiful? Radiant?* That's what they were all thinking, himself included, but somehow the words didn't feel right, didn't seem to come naturally to him right then, so instead he settled for; "content."

Regardless of his struggle, Soph didn't look at all disappointed by his choice. Instead, her eyes glistened all over again.

"Perhaps," she said. "Although, it has been a long hard road, I can assure you." And finally seeming to draw to the point, the reason for her presence there, Fred looked oddly severe.

"Why are you here, Soph? How did you find me?" He gave something of a sigh. "I intended to return to you sooner but-"

"There were complications," the warrior-woman interrupted vaguely. "Yes, I am aware of that." She then pulled back her travelling cloak and reaching into a pocket woven in the well-worn fabric, she started searching for something. As she drew back the material, the others noticed that she was carrying a large, obviously well-loved sword sheathed at her side.

She really was a true warrior then, like her partner.

Finally, after much scrabbling around, Soph pulled out a well-folded piece of parchment and handed it to Fred briskly.

"I came to find you, because I was asked to give you this," she then said, and without a moment's pause, Fred unfolded the paper and began to read.

The note was obviously a long one, for he seemed to stand there for some time whilst the others all studied his face, waiting for some sort of explanation.

Soph meanwhile, was sweeping the Karenza with her eyes again.

"I was hoping to give this, to Crag instead," she continued nonchalantly. "But I can see that he has chosen not to venture with you this time…"

Crag.

At the mention of the warrior's brother-in-arms, the other crew members all glanced at each other uncomfortably, Fred's face growing forlorn as he finished with the parchment. Folding the paper up neatly, the warrior then tucked it away into his own pocket before turning his attention back to Soph.

"Crag fell," he said simply, cutting the sudden tension on the ship quickly and decisively. "He is no longer with us."

"He is dead?" and a look of clear distress flashed across his partner's face as she seemed to realise what he was saying. "Kell will suffer. They have a son," she muttered and then, looking up into Fred's eyes she laid her hand on his arm, the first touch the couple had shared in over a decade. "I am sorry for your loss."

Fred didn't even seem to react.

"I meant to return to Mawreath to tell her myself of the news-" he said instead. He sounded strangely aloof, stiff even.

"But you were needed here," Soph finished.

Straightening up slightly and removing her hand, the soft look in her eyes was then gone.

"And now you will be needed back in Mawreath more than ever. It is no longer just me who seeks you, but the entire colony."

Despite the urgency in her voice however, Fred shook his head as the others listened and watched on in growing confusion.

The entire colony? What was Soph talking about?

"They cannot ask it of me," the warrior began to retort as if he had forgotten anyone else was there. "It was never my intention-" but Soph soon held up a hand.

"You have no choice. You are all that they have left," she said and straight away, Fred lowered his gaze as if her words had somehow shamed him.

Unsure what was going on, the rest of the group all eyed the couple uncertainly. Though they were husband and wife, in human terms, the pair seemed almost complete strangers to one another. There was clearly no love here, no warmth, no embrace after so long being parted and though Edmund understood that warriors were connected at birth, betrothed to their life-partners and many never bonded, it was still alien to see. There was some kind of barrier between them- that much he could make out. Soph seemed glad in some small way to see Fred, but Fred appeared to be holding back.

Was his coldness something to do with the note? Something to do with Crag's death?

What did the colony, the warriors of Mawreath need from him?

And looking at the others briefly, Edmund saw that Elanore and Thom, who upon noticing the new arrival from the crow's nest had descended to find out what was going on, also seemed none the wiser. Both of their expressions were blank yet curious. Little to his surprise however, Eliom seemed to be following the warriors' conversation as if he had been a part of it all along.

"Can they not ask it of *you*?" he suddenly addressed Soph, making the warrioress turn to look at him in surprise, before, noticing his staff, she shook her head.

"I am female," she explained. "And besides," she gazed at her fellow warrior again, reading him up and down with her grey eyes; "I cannot leave Fred's side. Not now. We have been parted for too long…"

"There *have* been female Sovereigns before," Fred pointed out. But even as he spoke, his argument only sounded half-hearted.

Straight away the others looked even more baffled.

Had he said…?

"Sovereign?" Thom then piped up rudely, voicing the confusion of the other three listening innocents. "What are you talking about?"

But instead of explaining, Soph glanced at him.

"Do you not know of Fred's position in the West?" she asked in obvious confusion herself. "Do you not know who he *is*?"

Before she could say anything else however, Fred had flashed what appeared to be a threatening glare at her.

"No, they do not. I have felt no need to tell them," he said firmly and looking suddenly appalled, Soph fell into silence.

"I had my suspicions," Eliom sounded apologetic. But instead of blaming him, Fred just gave a dry smile.

"I knew I could not hide it from *you*, old conjurer," he joked. "I could not even try to."

"Hide *what*?"

And bringing the fact of the matter back to the waiting three, Thom sounded and looked impatient now, as did Edmund.

What were they talking about? What had Fred hidden? What did they not know?

It was obviously something important, that much the Explorer could tell just from the stunned yet severe look Fred's partner was levelling at him.

They had mentioned the word Sovereign.

Was Fred-?

"Why have you not informed these people?" Soph then demanded fiercely. "Why have you not told them?"

But Fred only shook his head again.

"I did not think it *necessary* to tell them," he insisted. "They never needed to know."

And though Soph was slighter than him, a little shorter too, straight away the others could see the rippling muscles in her arms, the strength in her fingers as she reached for her sword hilt, just as her partner so often did, clearly ready for a fight.

"Well, they certainly do *now*!" she argued. "Now that you must leave them!"

This got everyone's attention. Finally, they seemed to be getting somewhere, and looking even more surprised, Edmund turned directly to Fred.

"What?" the Explorer demanded. "Why do you need to leave? Why now?"

But it was no use, Fred was still giving nothing away and obviously seeing it as her duty to intervene, Soph took charge.

"The Sovereign of our people is dead," she started. "He was killed in battle with a neighbouring colony less than a human month ago and I was sent out to find Crag, to give him the official summons from the council to return to Mawreath..." She then trailed off, looking to Fred as if expecting him to interject and help her. The warrior, however, remained utterly silent and cool.

"Why would Crag need to return so urgently because of the Sovereign's death?" Edmund asked slowly. Somehow he could sense what was coming, could see all the parts of the mystery moving to fit together, but he knew he had to hear it aloud to truly believe it. And he had to hear it from *him*.

Fred rubbed the back of his neck, looking uncharacteristically awkward as Soph didn't reply. But then;

"Crag was the heir to the Sovereignty, to the throne of Mawreath," he finally answered, his voice strangely quiet. "But he has gone..." And as if the final few words brought with them every meaning, understanding then dawned, the shocking realisation clear as day on the faces of Elanore, Thom and Edmund.

"And you were - are - the next in line after Crag? You are the new Sovereign?" Edmund cried, filling in the missing link and to his amazement, Fred, shooting Soph another angry glare, gave a cheerless nod.

Elanore and Thom just gawped.

Fred, the warrior, the unassuming backbone of their party was a Sovereign. Fred was a *king?* The idea felt almost completely-

"So, you see now why he must leave you and return to his people," Soph finished, moving back into focus. "They need a ruler, more now than perhaps they ever have."

But despite everything his partner had said, despite everything that had been revealed in only a few moments, Fred still seemed adamant.

"I will not be that ruler," he spat though gritted teeth. "You cannot ask it of me! That role was never intended for me!" And though his face was controlled, every part of him seemed to reveal his distress, his anger.

"Wow! Fred! A Sovereign!" Thom exclaimed, looking impressed despite the tense atmosphere that had suddenly fallen on the deck all over again. "Who would have thought it?!"

Meanwhile, ignoring the dwarf, Soph too gritted her teeth.

"You *can* be the Sovereign, Fred," she argued. "It has always been meant for you!"

But this only seemed to make matters worse.

"How can you *say* that?!" Fred cried. And finally, as if he'd been waiting all along, he then turned away. "The position was *always* Crag's. He was born to it. He wanted it, he was raised for it. I do not *want* to be Sovereign. I cannot be and that is the end of it! They will have to find someone else!"

Soph looked about ready to strike him, her face a mask of cold outrage. Edmund could see her hand tightening, as Fred's had so many times, on the sword at her belt and knowing Fred, he had no doubt in his mind that if Soph was anything like him, the conversation could very easily turn to bloodshed.

None of this was any of his business, or even the business of the rest of the group watching, but even so, knowing he had to do *something* before things got out of hand, the Explorer then made his move.

"What's so wrong with being a sovereign?" he asked to his friend's back carefully. "I know men who would kill for the opportunity to rule. Think of all the good you could do. Of what you could achieve…"

He knew he had no right to get involved and rightly so, Fred rounded on him; luckily for Edmund though, the warrior's own anger seemed to have already fizzled out.

There was no use in arguing. The warrior had clearly given the issue thought before and knew his mind. He would not be persuaded.

"Humans are different," he replied shortly. "I will not give up my life to this cause." And again, he turned away as if to make for the cabins, to get away from the still-awestruck gazes of his companions and Soph, who looked as if someone had punched her in the stomach.

"You would have your people *leaderless*?" his partner said, sounding almost breathless. "You would not give your life to defend them?"

Fred closed his eyes in exasperation.

"Of course I would give my life to defend them," he said. "I would die a warrior's death for them, but I will not give up my life for something I do not believe in."

He wasn't backing down and Soph seemed truly at a loss for a moment. But though the others looked at her questioningly, she only had eyes for Fred now.

"But Fred, we have been through this before…"

"And you know my opinions on the Sovereignty, Soph," Fred pleaded, his voice still cold. "It has needed disbanding for years and you know it. We have a Captain. He leads us well. The Sovereign?" he threw his hands wide with a sneer. "He does nothing. He gives up his life to sit in a chair and for what?!"

"He gives hope," Soph sighed. "He brings strength."

But as if the words were a terrible curse, a new stab in his back, Fred rounded back to face her with fresh anger.

"It was never my path. It was never meant for me," he repeated. "I never wanted it. It was Crag's!"

Soph's voice was rising now.

"But Crag cannot walk the path any further, so it is yours! You are his next of kin! It is your *duty*!"

"Why not Crag's son? Or Kell?" Fred sounded desperate. "We have had a Sovereign Queen before. I am not good enough to fulfil what they ask of me…"

"Not good enough?!"

But to the watching crew's surprise, instead of fuelling her obvious rage, *this* seemed to make Soph quieten for a moment. Suddenly, the fierce, powerful face of the warrioress looked almost sad and taking a step towards him as if she was going to reach out and touch him again before thinking better of it, she drew a long, deep breath.

"You are the best of them *all*," she replied wretchedly. "Why can you not see that?"

But Fred had truly had enough. Filled with fresh emotion as he looked on that sorrowful face, the face he hadn't known for so long, the face that demanded so much from him, he hurriedly turned away and before anyone could try to stop him this time, he was striding towards the cabins, away from his friends, away from his partner and the burdens of their people.

"Fred!" Soph called after him, but it was too late, the warrior had already wrenched open the cabin door and disappeared below, his quick steps banging out across the deck.

The argument, for now, was over and the others, forced into awkward silence, could only watch as their companion disappeared.

No one knew what to say. No one really knew how to react. *None* of them, not even Eliom, had truly been expecting the spectacle they had just witnessed and as if realising the trouble she had unknowingly brought, Soph, quick to recover, soon looked to Edmund kindly.

"I am sorry that you had to witness that," she said. "But he *must* be made to realise his duty."

She seemed adamant and though Edmund opened his mouth to reply, Eliom got there first.

"Duty may not always be as it seems," the wizard mused wisely and as if remembering where they were, what has happening, the path that lay ahead, the Explorer then looked up at the sky.

Time was getting on; it was already mid-morning. They needed to leave, but the question was, did they go with or without Soph?

Staggered as he was by the news that his long-time friend was now the Sovereign, the *king* of the Mawreathan warriors, this didn't change anything. Not right now. They still had somewhere to be, as fast as they possibly could; and knowing that he had to make a quick decision, Edmund soon turned to Soph, offering her what he hoped was a smile.

"Soph," he said. "You are welcome to stay with us as long as you need, or want to, but we're leaving this town, today."

He was aware he sounded more rushed than he'd wanted to, but even so Soph gave a nod. Already she looked herself again, or rather, the 'herself' they had all welcomed on board, calm, collected and ready for anything.

"Of course, thank you," she replied politely, returning his smile as if nothing had happened. "I will gladly accept your offer. Do not let me hinder you on your important journey."

And that settled, the crewmembers that remained on deck, with the help of their new comrade, then set to work heaving up the gangplank and setting the sails, readying the Karenza once again for the river and their destination ahead.

—

The elements and their lone guardian ran into the morning without a single word between them.

All five of them were exhausted from a night spent in fear and dazed grief. Dromeda and Meggie were especially quiet. But as night had become day, their relentless pace into nowhere had gradually started to slacken as fatigue took its toll and it was Bex who was the first to stop.

"Please," she begged, her voice hoarse as she almost fell to her knees, wiping desert dust from her spectacles. "I need... to rest."

And slowing a little but not halting completely, the other three women looked to Dromeda.

The elder element's expression hadn't changed for the last few hours. His eyes were glazed and he looked more lost than any of them, but on hearing

Bex speak suddenly, he shook his head as if waking from a dream and glancing at her, halted in his tracks.

"Yes, of course," he replied, his voice absent as he downed the pack tied to his back. Unfortunately, Nickolas had been carrying the other wad of their supplies tied to his waist, so food was sparse. But they had little choice but to manage.

He fumbled around distractedly for the remaining half of the bread they had taken from Bethan's hut, tucked as it was within the folds of the only blanket left. Tearing it into eight, he then handed a small piece to each element, tucking the rest back inside the bundle.

Bex, Saz and Bethan all ate in ravished silence, Meggie meanwhile, refusing the food with a shake of her head, as she sat on the hard, dry ground, gazing off into the distance.

In the daylight, the prairie looked as if it stretched on for countless miles, a meagre desert with no food, no water and no shelter from the gathering warmth of the day, and already feeling the heat, inexplicable in a world with no sun, Dromeda pulled out the flagon of water next.

"We may as well rest here for an hour or so," he said stiffly. "Then we should move on," and finishing her bread, Bethan nodded as if her agreement spoke for everyone.

It did. No one argued.

Dromeda held the water out to Meggie after taking a swig himself and this time, the little element took it. There was no point in dehydrating.

"Thank you," she said, just as stiffly, the first words she had spoken in a long time. But though she was talking to him, she didn't dare look at him.

She couldn't. Not yet. Not while she felt like this; so angry, so full of loathing for him, for the Diggers and, most achingly, for herself.

Again and again, she couldn't help but play the moment in her head. The moment she had watched Nickolas die right in front of her. The moment when she had tried to go back to him, to help him.

And Dromeda had stopped her.

She felt like lashing out at the unfairness of it all, like hitting something; like hitting *him*. But at the same time, she just wanted to stay there, to just curl up in a ball right there, right on that very desert and do nothing.

Nothing.

Meggie wiped her dry eyes tiredly.

She had known death before, she had seen it, she had tasted it. Her whole family was gone, every single member in sudden, suspicious circumstances. She knew what it was to feel bereft. To feel the denial, the anger, the pain, the sorrow, and then finally the numb acceptance. But not like this.

This time, somehow, it was different. This time, for some reason she just couldn't seem to understand, she felt well and truly *empty*.

Nickolas, a man she had known for what felt like five minutes, was gone and she felt *empty* because of it.

She couldn't understand it.

What did it even *mean?*

"Bread?" Dromeda tried giving her the food again, but for the second time, Meggie shook her head.

"No," she replied.

Just no.

And turning away from her, Dromeda muttered a word that sounded unmistakably like sleep before unravelling the blanket again, he flung it at her.

"You will have to share," was all he said to the others as he then stepped away from them, obviously intending to keep an eye out from afar. The Diggers had dropped back many hours before, clearly too frightened to follow the elements any further into the 'forbidden' land, but it still didn't hurt to be wary.

The other three women approached Meggie wordlessly, soon curling up on the ground in a huddle beside her to stretch the thankfully-large blanket between them. Fraught as their nerves, their emotions were, they were asleep within moments and realising how tired she was herself, Meggie lay down beside them, resting her head on one arm as she tried to get comfortable on the stiff ground. As she lay, watching Dromeda restlessly begin to pace here and there, still clutching the knife at his side, she then found her eyes starting to droop and before long, the little element had fallen herself, into a dreamless sleep.

—

Edmund took another bite of the fresh red fruit, his leg resting up against the bulwark as he stared out at the trees. The peaceful, rhythmical breeze pulsing through the Karenza's sails seemed to calm his spirits and finishing his snack, he threw the fruitstone overboard and stood to his full height, taking a deep gulping breath.

Despite everything he had been through, despite everything he had seen, everything that had happened, a day like today couldn't help but soothe his very soul, couldn't help but make him relish in the rare elation of being alive.

He had been through so much and, he had a feeling, was likely to go through much more, but still he was here. Still he was breathing, fighting, willing himself on to finish what he had started; to find the elements and bring the journey he had taken all those years ago, full circle.

Bethan.

Edmund closed his eyes, trying to dredge up every tiny scrap of memory he had of her, allowing each image to form together in his mind like one long tapestry. Every day they headed further upstream was another day he was closer to finding her, to being with her again. Every day he longed to see her, to hold her once more in his arms and this time, never let go…

Soon, he thought to himself.

Soon. But not yet.

Not quite yet.

"We should reach the town of Ophelius before long. Perhaps even today if the winds remain high."

Edmund opened his eyes and turned to see Eliom standing nearby.

He too had his eyes closed as if enjoying- if that were such a thing for him - the air just as much as his friend was. The Explorer could tell though, by the very tone of the wizard's voice that all wasn't well. Something was clearly bothering him and reminded of his concerns watching Eliom and Fred earlier, Edmund couldn't help but feel anxious all over again.

Now was the time, and scanning the rest of the deck as if to check they were definitely alone, he leaned in closer to his friend.

"Are you all right?" he asked. "I didn't want to say anything before in front of the others but-"

But without even bothering to let him finish, Eliom went straight to the point.

"Edmund, last night, in the inn," he started. "I had a vision."

A vision.

The word brought with it an instant chill of dread these days and in less than a second, all of Edmund's happy thoughts had well and truly fled.

No. Not again…

"It was unclear, very unclear, for I could not rest and my mind was not… *prepared…*" Eliom continued. But this only made Edmund's fears worsen. If he didn't know better, it sounded like the wizard was trying to keep from the actual point of what he'd Seen, trying to reassure the Explorer before he'd even started. Which could only mean that he was about to reveal something terrible…

The elements.

Please no.

And straight away, Edmund's patience failed him.

"What is it?" he found himself blurting out. "What's happened? What's *going* to happen?" He had to know. He just had to know that they were safe, that *she* was safe… "What did-?"

But before he could go any further Eliom had already stopped him mid-flow.

"I felt an overpowering sense of death last night," he said, without warning, without explanation. "I cannot describe it. But I am almost certain of it."

"Death?" Edmund echoed.

This was the worst news he could have heard, the worst of all. He hadn't been ready for it.

To think that only moments ago he'd been thinking, dreaming…

And without knowing he did it, the Explorer let out a groan. Suddenly he felt lightheaded, sick even, but more urgent than ever, he almost grabbed the wizard by his robe.

"Eliom, is it *them*? Is it her?" he demanded, looking almost pleadingly into his friend's eyes. "Please! Tell me!"

But instead of confirming one way or the other, the wizard only tilted his head to one side.

"I wish I could tell you for certain," he intoned. "I have failed you in the past and I-"

"Failed me?!" Edmund was suddenly incredulous. "You've done more than I ever could have asked from *anyone…*"

Somehow, hearing the wizard talk like this, felt more horrible than anything else.

What was going on here? Where was this coming from?

"I spent the night thinking it all through," Eliom insisted, as if trying to make sense of things. "I kept trying to make the images clear in my head, trying to find the answers. But none came. None came."

And watching his friend, perhaps for the first time, Edmund found himself truly worried. Eliom's eyes were wide and almost *wild*, not like themselves at all and the Explorer couldn't help but notice how incredibly… *human* he sounded.

This wasn't right. This wasn't how things should be. He needed Eliom to be aloof and wise and powerful. Now, perhaps more than ever, he needed his friend to be normal, to be himself; but for some reason, at the very back of his mind, as the Explorer saw the wizard's gaze wander blindly to the sky, glazed in thought, in *worry*, Edmund knew that that wasn't going to happen.

Perhaps, he realised, it would never happen again…

And trying despite his fear, to stay focused, trying not to let the rising panic control him, Edmund forced himself to turn back to the matter at hand.

"Is it them?!" he repeated, his voice quavering in expectation. "Eliom, you must have *some* idea…"

"It *is* to do with them, yes. I just…." Eliom hesitated. "I do not know *who…*" and as the wizard gripped his staff tightly, Edmund suddenly wanted to cry out, to grab his friend and shake him until he told him everything he knew, shake him until he was back to his usual untouchable self.

But it was too late for that, and somehow he knew it. The damage, whatever it was, had been done.

This whole ordeal, their whole mission, had done more than Edmund could ever have realised. He had recognised a change in his friend; he had recognised it several times over the past few weeks but now it was becoming more apparent that it wasn't just a change. Something had clearly broken within Eliom and along with it, his whole tranquil exterior was slowly starting to collapse.

Edmund could see now that the shield that held the wizard's emotions in check was beginning to fall.

And if it fell completely, who knew then what would happen? Maybe the wizard would finally start to experience the emotions that the Explorer battled with every day. Happiness yes, enjoyment, but also fear, shame, guilt and most worryingly of all... *rage*. It was clear that a part of him, however distant, was, little by little, beginning to practice them now...

But what if that continued? What if it grew? What if his emotions became uncontrollable? What if *he* became uncontrollable? Edmund couldn't help but think ahead to the future, however immediate that might be.

Could his friend really become a danger?

"I know what you are thinking," Eliom then said, startling Edmund from his thoughts. His voice shook a little. "And perhaps you are right to. I know that you fear for yourself and the others."

Edmund didn't need to ask what the wizard meant. He wasn't even upset that Eliom might have read his mind. Instead, he shook his head, hard.

"No," he denied. "No. I fear for you, Eliom," and hearing the quiet sadness in his friend's voice, Eliom gave something of a dry little smile.

"Perhaps he was right," he mused. And then, before Edmund could ask who 'he' was; "Maybe I *have* spent too long in human company."

But almost as soon as the words had fallen from his mouth, his hand flew to his lips as if to stop them. "No," he muttered to himself. "No..."

Too long in human company? Was this change, this brokenness because of *him*? Edmund could only watch on in growing dismay, but before he was given the chance to reply, before he could even *think* of how to, Eliom had turned his back on him and without another word, was making his way swiftly towards the cabins.

Fred, who had just stepped up to the pair from across the deck, glanced at the wizard as he hurried past before shooting Edmund a questioning look.

"What happened?" he asked, as he approached the human's side.

But Edmund merely shook his head again, his shocked gaze never leaving Eliom's retreating back.

"I don't know," he replied truthfully. "I honestly don't know..."

—

Meggie felt the drop of cold water on her face almost before she was awake. It was cool against her warm skin and not completely uncomfortable and yet...

Suddenly, the little element opened her eyes and sat straight up, groaning as the glare of the reddish noonday light momentarily blinded her.

More drops were falling around her, falling from the sky, growing in number, the ground already turning from a sandy dry yellow to a murky brown and for a moment or two, her sluggish brain just couldn't seem to understand what was going on.

Where was the water coming from? What was happening?

And then, just like that, it dawned on her.

It was raining.

Despite the fact that there wasn't so much as a single cloud in sight - the sky was a perfect reddish blue - it was *raining* and getting to her feet, Meggie took a moment to look about her.

The others were already waking up, rousing each other as the rain began to fall thick and fast around them.

"We need to move, *now!*" Dromeda was commanding at a half-shout, already forced to raise his voice over the sound of the droplets drumming against the hard ground.

And before any of them knew it, all five of them were then soaked to the bone, water running cold down their backs, drenching their thin clothing as they struggled between them to fold their single blanket, tucking safely inside what was left of the bread and the flagon.

Meggie could see that Dromeda seemed tenser than usual and forgetting for the moment the fact that she could barely even *look* at him, let alone speak to him at the moment, she turned on him, confused.

"What is it?" she bellowed over the sound of the rushing water around them. Already it had grown into a steady thrum. "It's only rain! We get rain all the time in Tungala!" She could remember it well. Remember how the water used to roll in great big sheets from the dilapidated roof of her house, the hideaway she had chosen from the rest of the world, spluttering on the glass of her garden windows.

But Dromeda shook his head, his shaggy mane matting to his brow as water dripped down his nose.

"It *never* rains here," he said simply and suddenly, as if someone had lit a splint in her mind, comprehension struck. Meggie had no idea *where* it had come from or how she could ever have reached such a conclusion, but all of a sudden, there it was, in her head, as if someone had placed it there. And despite how crazy it sounded, it also made perfect sense.

The Builder. The Builder knew what they were doing. What they were *trying* to do. And he or she was trying to stop them. By any means necessary.

Meggie turned her face to the sky, a hand over her eyes.

The Builder, the supposed god of this place was making it rain.

But whilst that somehow seemed logical, nothing else did. Why, for instance, would the Builder choose to use *rain?* How could a bit of rain stop them? It was hardly likely they were going to *drown*...

Dromeda, however, soon answered *that* question.

"The dirt is turning to mud!" he warned as, ready to go, the group started off at a lumbering run. "We must keep moving or it will suck us down! Watch where you put your feet!"

And sure enough, even as Meggie started off, she could feel the growing sludge between her toes beginning to stick to her skin, making every step that little bit harder.

It was, then, a trap. A *death* trap.

"Where are we going?!" Saz cried, desperately trying to brush water from her eyes. It was getting hard to see already and all of them were shivering beneath the torrential downpour. The air had turned sodden and cold.

"North!" Bethan bellowed back. "We keep heading north!"

"But which way is north?!" Saz retorted, almost tripping over her own feet. "I can barely see where we're going!"

"Just keep moving!" Dromeda hollered, pushing them onwards.

Just as he had said it would, the ground beneath their feet was softening, little puddles joining larger puddles, joining rivulets of water to become fully-fledged streams of ever-growing mud. Several times the elements fell and several times they pulled each other up until each and every one of them were coated in thick muck, thin dresses plastered to their trembling bodies.

"We need to find shelter somewhere!" Bex wailed desperately. "Look for a tree or something!"

"A tree?!" Meggie spat, urgently flinging her long hair away from her mouth and eyes. She choked as water went up her nose, her short legs straining to keep up with the others. "There *are* no trees out here!"

There was nothing. Nothing but the prairie.

Just as Nickolas had said...

"We just have to keep moving!" came Bethan's reply, her eyes closed against the mud as they continued to scurry through the deluge. "And hope that the rain stops!"

But Meggie and now the others, had a feeling somehow that the rain *wouldn't* stop... not until the Builder had their way.

—

Fred and Edmund continued to stare at the cabins for quite some time after Eliom had left, both of them in deep thought before the Explorer finally broke the silence.

"Not that it's anything to do with me," he started, clearly not wanting to discuss whatever it was that had just happened, "or with *any* of us really, but have you-?"

"Yes," Fred interrupted. "I have."

And not sure whether his companion was annoyed or not, Edmund looked at him.

The warrior seemed much more his normal self now. Gone was the coldness displayed before Soph and in its place, calm sincerity.

"I remain decided that I cannot return to Mawreath."

And yet, whilst he had almost expected it, Edmund couldn't help but look a little surprised.

"At all?" he questioned before finally turning too to look on his human companion, a frown twitched on Fred's lips.

"Whilst I was willing to return before, to speak with Kell, as was my duty, *now* I am not so certain," was his honest reply. "All I know is that I cannot do what they ask of me. I cannot be the Sovereign."

"But why not?"

Edmund had no idea where the words were coming from, but suddenly they were there and then, as if it had just occurred to him; "are you afraid?"

The Explorer wasn't sure who looked more shocked, himself or the warrior. But even more surprisingly, instead of rearing up, his pride offended, Fred seemed only to hesitate a moment, before, avoiding Edmund's gaze, he turned to look up at the sky, leaning against the bulwark.

"If you would call it that then, perhaps I am, yes," he then pondered quietly, "I am afraid." And afraid himself to say another word, Edmund just waited.

He had never heard Fred talk like this before - he doubted *anyone* had - and though, yes, a small part of him had been secretly hurt that the warrior, his friend, had never thought to inform him of his position, he found himself strangely pleased that he seemed able to confide in him now.

Warriors *never* admitted fear. They lived for strength, for the fight and both of them knew it.

"I am afraid for my *people*," Fred then elaborated as if suddenly desperate to be understood. "For what I cannot bring them."

And Edmund too, looked up at the sky.

It was a beautiful clear blue, an innocent blue. How he had admired it only a matter of minutes ago, before Eliom had revealed his worrying vision, before *this*…

"If it helps, I think that you would make a great ruler," he offered, even though he knew that his opinion wasn't of the slightest importance in the matter.

Fred just smiled wanly.

"I thank you but I cannot agree with you. I have no desire to rule." He gave a sigh. "I have no desire to sit and decide who should live and who should die."

And hearing the solemnness underlying his words, Edmund's gaze was straight back on his friend in a moment.

"The Sovereign decides who... he *knows* that?"

"Oh yes," Fred said. He sounded bitter. "The old Sovereign, Omegan, Crag's father – may his soul rest –" he lowered his head a moment in a sign of respect, "he knew exactly where I was, no doubt until his final moments, even though I have not ventured to Mawreath for years."

The warrior stroked the bulwark distractedly.

"He was the one who decided that I should leave the West in the first place. The Sovereign decides who comes, who goes, who lives, who dies. He is wise, he knows *all*."

"But how could he possibly have known where you are now?" Edmund asked outright, not quite able to believe it. "You've been walking Tungala for fifteen years! You could have been anywhere!"

Fred shrugged with a grimace.

"What can I say?" he spoke dryly. "He has - had - his ways of keeping track of our men. Especially those in line to the Sovereignty."

Had his ways.

And hearing him admit it, for a moment, Edmund looked at his friend in a new light.

To all the world, it sounded as if Fred was saying that the Sovereign had magic.

The warriors of Mawreath were an ancient race and beyond doubt, if the myths were to be believed at least, there was some form of power within them. But magic such as that?

Edmund felt his head spin a little.

Was that something else Fred had kept to himself all this time?

How much had he ever really known about the warrior?

"Couldn't you abdicate? Couldn't you step aside and give your place to someone else, like you suggested? Maybe Crag's son?" he said, trying in his own small, human way to help his friend.

But Fred dismissed the idea with a shake of his head.

"No. The boy is far too young. And besides," he sighed up at the sky, "it has always been this way. I can only pass the Sovereignty on to the next heir if I die. Crag's son could never have the throne."

Edmund didn't understand.

"But why not? If it was Crag's *father* who ruled then surely…?"

"Our lineage is different to humans," Fred was patient. "Your rulers pass rights down from father to son, father to son. We, on the other hand have warrior-brothers to think of," and he paused a moment, a flicker of grief alive in his eyes as he remembered his own warrior-brother Crag, a man so close they had almost been as one flesh.

"The Sovereignty passes from father to son, yes, but only once the father has been granted a true warrior's death." And by this, Edmund knew he meant death via battle, the ultimate honour of a warrior.

"And then," Fred continued, "once the son has also been killed, the right passes to his warrior-brother. Only once the warrior-brother is killed, does it then pass to his first-born son and so the cycle continues…"

Edmund gave a shrug. It had been worth a try, and though it seemed strange to him, he knew he couldn't argue with centuries of tradition.

"You talk as if no one ever dies naturally in Mawreath," he remarked instead, only for Fred to give another shrug of his own.

"That is because none of my people ever *do* die naturally. At least," he paused for a moment, "there has not been a natural death for centuries… of our time. You know our origins. You know where all the great beings first originated."

"From the elves, yes," Edmund said.

"Exactly." Fred's face gave nothing away. "And you know that after the third century war and the disappearance of the elven men, so the elven women turned to other races. Just as Lecturs are the making of an elf and a witch or a wizard and are gifted with long life, so are we warriors, once shaped from man and elf, almost immortal. We could survive for hundreds, if not thousands of years untouched, but none of our kind have ever lived that long." His eyes shone then, for the briefest of moments. "We are warriors. We live a life of danger, of war. It is not our way to wither and grow old. It is not our way to die without honour."

Without honour.

And even though he had known this all along, known the very doctrines ingrained into his friend since the very moment he had first drawn breath, Edmund couldn't help but take a moment just to let the fact of the matter sink in, to mull over how very different Fred's life, his outlook, was.

Fred's thoughts, his worries and dreams were so radically unlike his own and seemed, right then, so much *greater* than his own that for a moment, the Explorer found himself feeling, not for the first time, small and insignificant.

He had always been aware of the warrior's vast age, just as he had Eliom's. The two of them, especially Eliom, had lived long before Edmund's own parents had been but a glint in his grandparents' eyes and would no doubt continue to live long after he himself was gone.

They were, to him, his friends, and yet suddenly he was struck, as he had been at other moments during his short lifetime, by how incredibly *lucky* he was that either of them gave him any time at all, let alone *listened* to him, making him to be some kind of leader amongst them.

To them, he was young, almost a child. A simple human child. And yet they had never made him feel that way. No matter what their thoughts were on the subject, no matter how much older, wiser and stronger they were, they had never, for one moment, pretended otherwise than that they were equals. And it was this that made him respect them and right then, that made him brave enough to try.

"If you *do* go back, couldn't you just disband the Sovereignty altogether?" the Explorer then asked after a time, trying to sound knowledgeable. "You said before that you didn't believe in it…"

But when Fred only looked amused, Edmund couldn't help but feel stupid. The warrior obviously found it funny that he was trying to help, that a *human* was trying to help, in a situation he could never hope to understand.

"Perhaps," he said fairly. "But it would cause great hostility within the colony. There are many supporters of the Sovereignty, of what it stands for. Any move to disband it could create open war between my people. A pointless war of pride."

And thinking about what that could mean, Edmund couldn't help but shudder. One warrior alone was fearsome enough, but an entire army, a battle of fighter against fighter, willing to bleed, willing to die an 'honourable' death all in the name of superiority, didn't bear imagining…

"What if-?" but even as the words started from his mouth, Edmund stopped as he noticed the droplet of water falling, as if from nowhere, onto Fred's shoulder.

The single bead landed straight onto the warrior's tunic, absorbing into the fabric in a moment, and instinctively, the Explorer and the warrior glanced up only to find, to their complete surprise, that in the short time they had been standing there, the sky had completely changed. Where there had been brilliant warm blue moments before, there was now thick blackening grey, already starting to dribble with rain.

Just like that, they were in a growing rainstorm. An incredible, *impossible* rainstorm that seemed to have come out of nowhere and instantly recalling a moment very much like this before, Edmund couldn't help but shudder all over again.

He could remember a day such as this, a day when one moment the skies had been empty and clear and the next, full of storm clouds; the day before the elements had reached the Temple of Ratacopeck.

That day, it hadn't rained for years and only hours before the elements had taken their final steps into the Temple had it happened, just as it was happening now. One moment dry, the next wet.

This then, wasn't ordinary rain; he knew that already. No, this was something else.

And whatever it was, the Explorer had a gut feeling that it wasn't good.

The elements were almost wading through the sludge now as the once parched land turned to a thick river of mud, sucking and bubbling to their shins.

Tired wasn't really enough of a word for what they were. Every step felt like an effort and every effort was thrown into every step, the mulch taking everything from them; their energy, their enthusiasm, their desire to push on. But despite their worst fears that things were only going to get worse, that nothing was going to give, the rain, at long last, seemed to be subsiding.

The torrent from above had calmed now to a dull splatter and as the companions pushed on through the drizzle, they were finally allowed the chance to slow their pace a little and turn to each other, amazed they could even recognise themselves at all through the mud caked to what felt like every inch of their bodies.

And then, just as it had suddenly started, the rain was gone altogether and straight away, all five of the companions turned their eyes to the clear sky in amazement.

It had stopped. It was over. Finally. But whilst this revelation made them all relax a little, none of the group felt even slightly relieved.

"What's going on?" Saz was the first to say it. "Why's it stopped?"

And pausing in the mud, Dromeda continued to look at the sky for some moments, as if trying to work out the answer for himself. Now that he had stopped moving, the ground beneath him seemed to feel different somehow than it had before, much softer and sure enough, before anyone could even cry out in warning, the elder element could feel himself starting to sink, the thick mud sucking him down as the land gave way.

Panicking, Dromeda quickly lifted his knees up high, stumbling forward a few steps to save himself.

"I do not know why it has stopped!" he exclaimed. "But *we* cannot! The ground will take us!" And not needing to be told twice, the four women immediately picked up their pace again, pushing their exhausted bodies onwards, each step higher than the last as the mire grew thicker and thicker.

Meggie especially was struggling. With her legs considerably shorter than the others' in the group, the little element had very soon fallen to the back, the moment the rain had begun. The mud easily covered her knees and with the long thin dress of the Diggers dragging through the slush like a dead weight and her long hair matted to her shoulders, she was straining even to hold her head up.

But despite it all, everything was not lost, for after a few more minutes of battling on, it was then that Saz gave the shout from the front of the group.

"Look!" she cried, gesturing crazily at the horizon. The others soon followed her gaze. "The ground! It's dry up ahead!" And sure enough, up ahead of them, a clear line could be seen in the dirt, on one side, the dark murk of wet mud, on the other the yellow of dry, cracked earth...

This was all any of them could have hoped for and with cries of delight, all five companions pressed on until finally, the lake of mud gave way and the elements found themselves stumbling once more onto dry, dusty ground.

Straight away, without so much as a word to each other, the group all collapsed to their knees, panting breathlessly, secretly thankful to feel the warm hardness of safety beneath them.

Whilst they could guess, none of them really knew what had happened, or why it had happened- not *really*. But whatever it was had put them all on edge and after only a few moments, Dromeda was straight back on his feet.

Dropping their single bundle of supplies to the ground, he quickly began to assess the damage. The outer layers of the blanket were soaked and encrusted in mud but peeling it back gently he saw, to his relief, that what remained of the bread and water were still clean and undamaged.

"We should rest here," he said. "But only for a while. We need to keep moving." And he handed out the water flagon to the four women, watching as they took grateful gulps of the lukewarm liquid between them. Despite the fact there was no sun in that place, the reddish light above them seemed to radiate some kind of heat and now that the rain was gone, all of them could already feel it drying the wet mud to their skin in thick uncomfortable clumps.

As her body began to dry, Meggie looked down at herself in disgust. Her long hair, stuck to her face, was knotted with dirt. Her skin was stiff and itchy and her very eyelashes were peppered with dried dust. And her dress- not that she cared for such things - was a state. No longer a pale beige, it was caked in a deep brown. Even now she had stopped, she could feel how heavy her clothing was – her shoulders seemed to hurt with the weight of it and as if suddenly realising that she could do something about *that* at least, she took the very bottom of her skirt and, in a moment of annoyance, began to tear, ripping along the seams and peeling the fabric away from her legs until the hem sat just above her knees.

"Good idea."

Meggie glanced up to see the other three women watching her, before, as one, each began to take her own dress and copy the little element's example, seeming to find some kind of fresh energy in the moment of destruction.

This was the first time they had stopped properly for hours, and however short a time the rest might be, so it was the group were finally given the chance to just sit, think, and most importantly, mourn.

Almost the moment she had finally stopped, had finally taken a chance just to draw breath, Meggie could feel the fresh grief, the pain of her strange emptiness creeping up on her all over again.

Much as she'd hoped it would, it hadn't gone. That dull ache. The numbness. The anger. And suddenly unable to keep it to herself for another second, it was then that she finally turned to Dromeda.

The elder element had his back to her, to them all, staring out on the horizon blankly, perhaps fighting his own demons, but this time, Meggie knew that she couldn't just leave him.

Before, she had been too stricken with emotion to talk to him, to so much as *look* at him. But now? Now all she wanted was nothing *but*.

"You let him die."

The words came without warning, stabbing into the weary silence like an arrow and clearly having no doubt as to who she was talking to, the other three elements lowered their gazes as Dromeda, drawn from his own thoughts, turned to face the smallest of the group slowly.

His face was vacant.

"You let him die," Meggie repeated more strongly. Her voice shook. "You could have saved him. But you *didn't*."

Whilst a part of her had hoped he would argue however, Dromeda just looked at her, his eyes still a little glazed, almost as if he didn't *want* to defend himself and seeing where the situation might lead, Bethan soon looked up, eying both of them anxiously.

"You could have done something! You could have *stopped* them!" the little element tried again and then, all of a sudden, she was on her feet again, unexpected tears springing to her tired eyes. "*Answer me!*" she almost screamed. "*Why didn't you stop them?!*"

Clearly unsure of what she was capable of, Dromeda got to his feet too, his hands held out, palms up, as if to defend himself at last.

"I could not have stopped them all," he retorted feebly, "Nickolas knew what he was doing…"

But Meggie just clenched her fists and moving towards him sharply, she looked for a moment as if she was going to hit out.

"You called yourself his *friend*! You could have pulled him away! Stopped him! Or stood by his side! *Anything*!" she cried, her words echoing across the empty space, ringing in every eardrum. "You could have let *me* go to him!"

You?

Dromeda's lips formed the word as if he would throw it back at her, demand to know what *she* could possibly have done, but his heart obviously wasn't in it. He was still just staring, his gaze not completely all there and knowing that things could only take a turn for the worse, it was then that Bethan finally held up a hand.

"Stop it!" she cried, before, leaping to her own feet; "Stop it! Both of you! Neither of you are to blame for this! So please! Stop this now!"

And yet, though both heard and understood, Meggie seemed *incapable* of stopping now. It was too late. The blame was flying from her thick and fast. It needed to.

"He could have *done* something, Bethan!" she argued hotly, turning on her companion now as if shifting the blame to her. "But instead, he just *stood* there telling us Nickolas would be all right!"

"I thought that he would!" Dromeda finally seemed to be waking from his stupor, and incensed, Meggie rounded back on him, the clogged hair on her little head flying.

"You saw how outnumbered he was! He couldn't possibly have taken them all!"

But even as she spoke, as she thought back to Nickolas's final fight, she couldn't help but recall how fast the elder element had moved, how prepared he had been and yes, *experienced*.

Dromeda too, back in the City, the way both of them had fought; it had been like watching skilled marksmen, killing Digger after Digger after Digger...

The little element blinked.

"How did he even *fight* like that?" she demanded as her thoughts just spilled out. "How did *you*-?" and Dromeda, looking a little taken aback seemed to soften a little.

"You want to know-?" he started, before; "Both of us. We were soldiers. Long ago-"

But already Meggie held up a hand.

"You know what?" she spat, her expression livid with torn emotions. She couldn't stand it anymore. Any of it. "Shut up! I don't even *care*!"

Dromeda's expression instantly shifted.

"How *dare* -!"

"*Stop it!*"

Bethan's yell then rent the air like a knife and straight away Meggie and Dromeda gave a start, turning to look at her. The element looked forcefully calm and for the first time, both realised that she had a hand pressed to each of their shoulders, physically holding them apart.

"Please." And seeing she had finally grabbed their attention, Bethan soon dropped her arms, looking from one to the other as she began again;

"If we all start arguing about how things *might* have been and start *blaming* each other," she said gently. "We might as well-"

Her words however, were soon lost, for right at that moment a great gust of wind blew across the plain, blasting grit and dust before it in one big swoop.

The drift was so strong, so fast and so unexpected that the group had no time to protect themselves before the air was rent with grime. In less than a second, dirt and muck flew into eyes, noses and mouths, stinging faces, making all of them cry out. And in just the same amount of time, all argument was dropped as the five elements realised the very worst.

"The Builder!" Dromeda just managed to choke out before yet another great blast hit them. And knowing straight away that they were in danger all over again, everyone was back on their feet, ready to run in a moment, Dromeda pulling his tunic up around his mouth and nose and Meggie and Bethan wrapping the spare material from their dresses about their own faces, ready to protect their skin from the bitter sting of dust.

But *standing*, let alone running was already hard. Each new buffet of wind held the force of a gale and several times, Saz and Bex, the last two to get up, fell in their attempts to join their companions.

With help from the others, they were soon standing upright though, and taking the only refuge they had, the four women huddled together, Meggie the lightest of them all, held tightly by all three of the other elements to stop her from falling.

Dromeda, finding it difficult to stay upright too, approached the small group, gesturing for them to follow him – words were no use now over the howl of power - and the women obeyed, hurrying as fast as they could without being knocked down by the growing storm at their backs.

Only Bethan, trying to keep her hair from whipping into her eyes, took a moment as they retreated, to glance back at the muddy land they had left behind.

The swamp had almost completely dried up now- despite the fact it had been *minutes* since the rainfall - already adding fuel to the dust swirling through the air. The gates of the City had long since disappeared.

Why was this happening? Why now? Why to them?

It felt as if the entire world of the Diggers was against them, the element thought to herself, before realising with a frightened jolt, that it probably *was*.

This place belonged to the Builder. It was his – or her – world, his creation. He had a reason, a plan for all of this, for the Diggers, for the human elements.

And he didn't want that plan to be ruined.

Bethan blinked the dust furiously from her eyes as her brain began to whir.

If this wind, like the rain, was all down to the Builder then it was certain that he had to know what they were doing, and also, more importantly he had to know that they were getting close, for why bother to try and stop them if there was no need? Why bother to prevent them escaping if escaping wasn't possible?

And realising what that in turn meant, the element almost stopped in her tracks.

They were going the right way. They *had* to be. Why else would they be in such danger?

THE ENTITY OF SOULS

They were heading in exactly the right direction, drawing closer to the barrier between life and death and with that, the answers they needed.

And frightened, battered and tired as she was, surrounded as she was by the flurrying, howling winds, Bethan couldn't help but smile.

The swift gale that had followed the rainstorm only helped to worsen Edmund's fears as he huddled with the rest of the crew below decks, away from the storm.

"At least the wind is still in our favour," Fred pointed out. "We should reach our destination earlier than expected, if it continues after the storm."

"If we reach it in one piece," Thom grumbled and as if to make a point, the Karenza gave a lurch beneath them, straining against the anchor chain keeping her in place until the worst of the weather had passed.

Soph in the meantime was pacing up and down, biting her lip. Whether she didn't enjoy being cooped up in small spaces or was oddly unnerved by the sudden change in the weather, none of them knew.

Except, so it seemed, Fred.

"Sit down," the warrior chided her coolly. "The storm will pass." And, equally as coldly, Soph glanced at him.

"I do not much care for ships," she remarked, but she soon stopped nonetheless and taking a seat beside him on his bunk, proceeded to fiddle with her fingers instead.

"Where's Eliom?" Elanore suddenly asked. She seemed to be trying to make conversation, but Fred simply nodded towards the other cabin, the room where the elements had previously slept.

Edmund looked up from his own bunk at the door between the two cabins as if half-expecting his friend to appear there. It was wishful thinking though. After his strange behaviour up on the deck, Edmund had a feeling that Eliom probably wouldn't be resurfacing for a while, and knowing that his long-time companion was out of sorts, he couldn't help but feel even more on edge.

If anyone had any idea what was happening up above them and why, it was bound to be Eliom. And yet…

Just go to him, a voice spoke in his head. *Just go and ask. Go and talk to him.* But the Explorer knew he wouldn't. What, after all, could he say? Did he just pretend that everything was alright? Pretend like nothing had happened and that he wasn't worried about what Eliom had said before, how he had *acted?*

I felt an overpowering sense of death last night… I do not know who, he had said. *I do not know who…*

And feeling suddenly uncomfortable, Edmund shifted his weight, staring down at his hands without a word. It was only after Soph had asked the question twice that he then even realised he was being spoken to.

"Why do you think this is happening?" she asked. She was addressing him as if she thought that he would know, that he could be the leader in this and for a moment, the Explorer just looked at her blankly.

"What?"

"The weather, the sudden change?" the warrioress took up the question patiently. "What do you think is causing it?"

And Edmund drew a long, deep breath, trying to push his other worries aside as he remembered his thoughts on the deck, remembered the night before the Temple of Ratacopeck…

"I don't know," he then admitted with a frown. "But I can't believe that it's natural, or even good. It's all too *sudden*… Although," and he glanced at Fred. The warrior seemed stiffer somehow, more aloof than usual and as Edmund glanced at Soph, he noticed how far apart the couple were sitting. It was almost as if his friend dared not touch even the smallest inch of his partner as she sat perched beside him. "On a more positive note, Fred's right. Hopefully we'll reach Ophelius in less time than we thought if the wind carries on."

"The wind is blowing upriver at least," Elanore encouraged. She gave a shrug. "Which *is* something. We just need it to lessen enough for us to go up…" and she glanced at the ceiling.

At the mention of their destination, something seemed to light in the listening Soph's eyes and looking from Fred to Edmund, her expression grew bold.

"So why *are* you heading to Ophelius?" she asked innocently and then, when she saw the reaction in the others' faces; "If I am going to join you for the time being…" Fred's mouth twitched. "It would perhaps be wise for me to know."

Straight away, everyone seemed to have tensed up and Edmund immediately felt that very familiar pang of anxiety that had been his burden for the past few weeks and beyond.

They had been so used to secrecy travelling to the Temple of Ratacopeck that sharing any information still felt somehow *wrong*. And yet, looking at Soph, something told the Explorer that though she had been with them for less than a day, the warrior was already a *part* of them.

Unlike Eldora, their last visitor, and despite Fred's icy behaviour towards her, Soph didn't feel like an outsider. There was something trustworthy about her, something *warm* and looking into those sincere grey eyes, Edmund knew that keeping secrets from her was going to be impossible.

What was the point now, anyway? he reasoned. Who now was going to try and stop them?

They had no more enemies. At least, right now… The nimphs were gone, pacified. No one outside of the group – bar Eldora - knew their true purpose. And as for Renard…

Edmund felt the sharp pain of remorse pang in his chest. It had been a while since he had thought of his brother… About what had happened, what they had been through…

But realising that he was still being watched, he tried to smile.

"We could be down here for a while," he then reasoned as if it had only ever been a matter of time and nothing. "So, all right. I'll tell you…"

———

Bethan felt it again, that prickling sensation on the back of her neck, the uncomfortable feeling of being watched and for the fifth time she struggled to turn and look behind them, shielding her eyes against the wind with a hand.

Thick dust clouded her senses, the air stinging with it, but even though she could see nothing but dirt, dirt and more dirt as the Builder's gusts continued to pound across the plain, she somehow knew that she was right.

The group were being followed.

She was *certain* of it.

And picking up her pace, forcing herself almost diagonally into the wind, Bethan hurried towards Dromeda as he strode just up ahead.

"Dromeda!" she shouted into the whipping gale as she approached him and grabbing him by the arm, swung him around to face her as she pulled the covering from her mouth. "Dromeda! We have company!"

But looking down at her, the elder element just scrunched up his face.

"What?!" he yelled in reply. "What did you say?!" and taking action, Bethan pulled his head closer to her own, almost choking as a clog of dust and hair flew into her mouth.

"Someone is following us!" she said more loudly and then, as Dromeda shook his head, still unable to hear her, she almost bellowed; *"We are being followed! I can feel it!"*

Understanding seemed to dawn this time and straight away, Dromeda turned back on the way they had come, searching the prairie with sheltered eyes. But his eyesight was no better than Bethan's and unable to see more than a foot or two behind them, the windstorm making it nigh on impossible to make out anything, he shook his head again. Whether he could see anything or not, the elder element was clearly not prepared to take any chances though, for he soon drew his knife, the same thought clearly crossing his mind as it had Bethan's, the moment she had realised they were no longer alone.

Digger.

It had to be.

The horde had obviously decided to follow them after all, determined to finish the work they had started with Nickolas. As the others wandered blindly through the maze of sand, it would only be a matter of time before the stranger – or *strangers* - could start picking them off one by one in the swirling darkness, and clearly determined not to let that happen, it was Dromeda's turn to pull Bethan close.

"*Get the other three!*" he yelled in her ear, as he too lifted the covering from his mouth for a moment. "*We need to stick closer together!*"

"All right!"

And Bethan made a show of nodding before making her way, still almost at a slant, to where she could just make out Saz and Bex a little further ahead. The pair were walking together in a tight huddle, leaning towards each other as if in some small protection from the ferocious weather and touching them both on the shoulders to grab their attention, Bethan pointed back to Dromeda.

"*We need to keep together!*" she cried, her voice already cracking under the strain of shouting. "*Go to Dromeda!*" She didn't bother trying to explain - explanations would be too much effort right then - but thankfully for her, neither Saz nor Bex seemed to want to talk either and signalling that both of them had heard and understood the pair slowed their pace, waiting for Dromeda to catch them up.

Bethan then paused a moment to scan the space around her, trying not to let the threatening panic grow in her chest.

Where was Meggie?

The little element was nowhere to be seen. The last Bethan had noticed her, she'd been at the back of the group, but despite her height, still managing to just about keep up.

Had she fallen? Had they somehow managed to leave her behind?

Bethan felt the familiar lurch of fear in her belly.

What if the Diggers had got to her first? What if it was too late?

For a second, the element thought about calling out, but then almost immediately decided against it. There was no way that Meggie would hear her; Bethan's voice was too weak now, the winds too loud and strong. And besides, the noise could only attract trouble. The Diggers couldn't be far behind. And if she made too much of a racket…

She had to do *something* though, and quickly making her decision, Bethan soon struck out the way they had come, being careful to keep Dromeda and the others in the corner of her eye whilst all the while scanning the mud plain for any kind of movement…

To her immense relief, it wasn't long before she then got lucky.

Meggie was hunched on the ground, doubled up over something and for a passing second, Bethan almost mistook her for a stray rock, muddy and small as she was. But then, the little element moved, her long matted hair flailing in the wind and recognising her straight away, the element wobbled to her side, almost throwing herself to her knees.

Closer to the ground, the wind seemed strangely lighter and taking her chance to pull the covering from her face, Bethan was quick to assess the situation.

The little element's mouth and nose were still shrouded in material, but Bethan could tell, almost before she saw, why it was that Meggie had stopped.

The little element's eyes were closed, her face, beneath the muck, pale, as unbidden tears of pain leaked from beneath her eyelids and worried about frightening her, but knowing that she had to get her attention somehow, Bethan gently touched her on the arm.

"*Meggie!*" she cried out. "*Are you all right? What's happened?*"

Meggie visibly flinched as she felt the unexpected contact, her eyes snapping open, but seeing Bethan, she soon looked glum.

"It's my ankle!" she shouted, only just audible over even the quieter wind. "I fell… I think I've twisted it!" And sure enough, looking down, Bethan could see that Meggie was cradling her right foot in both hands.

Her stomach did an even nastier lurch as she saw the swelling already growing at the ankle, red and raw. The element had twisted it all right. And it was bad.

"I'm sorry!"

Meggie was still talking. She seemed completely oblivious, for a moment, to their surroundings, to *anything* as she stared off into the distance, the shock, the pain, the agony of her unresolved fight with Dromeda finally seeming to be a little too much for her.

"I'm sorry!" she repeated. "I'm so sorry!" And then; "Just go on without me. Leave me here!"

Leave her?

And pushing her hair from her face, Bethan looked momentarily surprised. This wasn't something she had expected at all.

"Don't be stupid!" she tried to soothe. "Don't be sorry!" but even as she spoke, the element's gut gave yet another horrible twist as she suddenly realised, that even if she'd wanted to, she couldn't have taken Meggie anyway, for the rest of the group had gone.

In her moment of concern for the little element, she had lost sight of the others. The swirling world of dirt and dust had swallowed them up and quickly re-covering her face, Bethan immediately leapt back to her feet, spinning all around in horror.

The others had gone. They had left without them. She and Meggie had been abandoned and trying not to let her new fears show, Bethan, making yet another quick decision, dropped straight back down to Meggie's side.

"*Of course I'm not going to leave you! Come on!*" she shouted through her covering and her mind working quickly, she held out a hand to help the little element to her feet.

Meggie took it, only tentatively and soon, supported by Bethan, the pair then began to make their slow way forward, pushing into the roaring winds.

It became clear very quickly that the little element could barely walk and it took everything Bethan had to keep her moving. But whether she could move easily or not, the further they trudged, the more the real panic then began to sink in.

They were lost; Bethan knew it. They had to keep moving north, that much the element was aware. But with the dust and the wind, she had no idea which way north *was*. They were completely lost with no food, no water or blanket, with *nothing* to help them. And even worse…

There it was again. That feeling, the prickling along her neck and suddenly, Bethan stopped to turn back.

The Diggers. They had to be here somewhere. They had to be closer. And sure enough, to her unending horror, as she began to turn back, she was just in time to see the lone figure, cloaked in a muddy swathe appear through the swirling haze, its head bent, its hands at its side, reaching for something.

A weapon…

No.

"*Go! Go!*" Bethan half-screamed and not knowing what else to do, she began to run, dragging Meggie behind her as the little element, also seeing their pursuer, desperately tried to speed up.

But it was too late. The dark figure had seen them and it too was running, its arms now outstretched and pumping, something glistening between its fingers.

A knife.

The figure was taller than them both and faster, so much faster. They had only seconds to move, to get away and filled with fear, Bethan tried to sprint. But before she knew what was happening, she felt her grip on Meggie begin to slip and then the little element was down, falling to the ground with a hard smack… right at the dark stranger's feet.

Rushing to turn and help her friend any way she could, Bethan could then only watch in terror as the figure stopped, looming right over the little element, looking down on her, its face covered. She could only watch as Meggie, on her front, her eyes wide, tried to crawl away, to pull herself across the dirt as the stranger then began to reach for her, the knife still clutched in its hand…

"*Meggie!*" Bethan shrieked, her voice lost in the howling chaos. "*Meggie!*"

But though she shouted, though she moved back to aid the little element with no thought for herself, several things then happened so fast that Bethan barely had time to put one foot in front of the other before everything had changed.

Meggie, rolling onto her back and turning to look up into the face of the stranger, suddenly seemed to freeze. For a moment, just a moment, she seemed suddenly mesmerised somehow as the two just stared at each other, the tall stranger and the tiny woman.

But before either of them could move, before either could even speak, something shifted and Bethan saw the flash of metal, felt the brush of movement as another large figure then appeared as if from nowhere.

It was Dromeda, his own knife held high and without a moment of hesitation, he had barrelled right into the stranger, knocking both of them heavily to the floor.

There was a moment of confusion as both struggled to gain ground, but Dromeda soon managed to triumph and pinning the figure to the floor using his sheer bodyweight, he pulled back his weapon, angling it at the intruder's throat.

The stranger dropped their knife, raising their hands as if to plead for mercy. But it was Meggie who then surprised them all.

Suddenly it was as if she had come alive.

"*No!*" she screamed, and then, she was scrabbling in the dirt, frantically trying to clamber back to her feet as Dromeda, who couldn't even seem to hear her, or at least understand what she was doing, didn't even look up.

"No!"

Urgently, the little element, fighting against the gale and the pain in her foot, tried to move towards the pair, but right at that second, it was then that the wind chose to stop.

Just as it had been, so it wasn't and the change was so sharp, that for a good few seconds all Bethan could think about was the ringing in her ears as the air parted to reveal a sudden painful silence.

Just like that, all dust and dirt had settled back to the ground and as Bethan gazed around her, completely disorientated, she was mildly surprised to see that they hadn't been as lost as she'd first thought.

Saz and Bex stood only a little way away, both of them looking just as stunned as she probably did at the sudden change, both already reaching to remove the muddy coverings from their faces, their eyes turned to the sky.

Meggie.

But remembering what she had just seen, Bethan turned her attention quickly back to the little element, her heart racing.

Despite her best efforts, Meggie hadn't moved and Dromeda still held his weapon to the stranger's throat.

Nothing had changed, but now that she could view them properly, Bethan saw in a moment that the stranger was in fact a man, or man-shaped, with a tall build and wide shoulders.

She could also see that he too, like the rest of them, was covered in mud, his face shrouded in wrappings to keep out the dust and to her surprise, she just as clearly saw that he *wasn't* a Digger. Beneath the mud, she could see that just like Dromeda, the man too wore nothing but a simple tunic and simple trousers, once beige, now almost brown…

Meggie's bellow then came loud and clear, the only sound in the suddenly hushed world.

"No Dromeda!" she shouted. "*Stop!*" and as if the noise had awoken something in her, Bethan found herself running to her friend's side as the little element fell to the ground, stumbling over her swollen ankle.

"Meggie!" she breathed. "Meggie! Are you all right?"

But Meggie's face was urgent, her eyes wild.

"Bethan!" she cried, grabbing hold of her friend's skirt as she stood above her. "Bethan! You *have* to stop him! Please! Stop him now!"

But Bethan was confused. Quick as she was, as she had been to react, her brain was still slow, still finding it difficult to understand…

"Stop who?"

"Dromeda!"

Dromeda? Why?

And still confused, Bethan just swivelled to watch as the elder element, ignoring Meggie's pleas, lifted his knife, clearly ready to finish the stranger off in one swift thrust of his blade. His other hand was around the man's throat, strangling him and it was obvious from the flailings of the stranger, that he was doing a good job.

Bethan looked at the second man again.

What if he was a Digger after all? What if he was just waiting for Dromeda to do just that, to let him go, so that he could be free to kill them all?

But the tunic. And the trousers…

Could it be?

And suddenly, acting on a crazy whim, it was then that Bethan dashed towards them.

"Dromeda! Stop!" she commanded, unsure of why or what she was doing and reaching him, she grabbed him by the arm, trying to wrench him away.

Surprised by this sudden attack from behind, Dromeda looked up at her. But whether he had ever intended to listen or not, as he did so, his grip on the stranger's throat weakened a little and just as Bethan had feared, it was then that the man seized his chance.

Snatching Dromeda's clutching fingers away with full force, the stranger rolled to his side, in one movement dislodging the element from his chest and escaping all at once. Dromeda, startled, only just managed to shove Bethan out of harm's way as he fell to the ground. But then, like a warrior, he was leaping back to his feet, his knife raised again, ready to fight.

"Come on!" he yelled, pumped full of adrenaline. "Come on!"

THE ENTITY OF SOULS

But to the watching everyone's surprise, instead of reaching for his own weapon, the stranger, also getting to his feet a little more slowly, simply held out his hands, palms up in a sign of peace. Bethan could clearly hear the sound of rasping from under the shroud covering the man's face as he fought to catch his winded breath.

Dromeda cursed aloud.

"Why did you stop me?" he snapped at Bethan, his pride wounded more than anything. "I had him!"

But Bethan could only shake her head.

She had no idea. Not really. She had no idea why Meggie had shouted, why she had thought to stay Dromeda's hand.

And yet...

By this point, the stranger was already regaining his breath and just like the others, he too reached a shaking hand up to uncover the cloth at his mouth.

As he did so, he then spoke, causing a jolt of astonishment to shudder across the prairie.

"Stop, Dromeda. It is me," he said in a familiar deep voice and Dromeda, suddenly seeming to struggle for breath himself, dropped his weapon in horror as the stranger then peeled away his cloak to reveal his face.

Bethan could only gasp then as she found herself staring into the face of a ghost... Or what *should* have been a ghost.

For the man standing before her was no man. The man standing before her was dead. Or *should* have been dead, for they had *seen* him die.

The man standing before her, before them all was Nickolas.

EVER ONWARDS

Fred glanced up absently from his work to watch as the dark shape of the mainland glided by beneath the crow's nest. The trees were fewer and far between, the banks of the river ever closer as they headed further upriver, and from his position he could see for miles into the undergrowth, sometimes thick with vegetation, other times flattened into farmland, worked into crops, scattered with remote farm buildings. The touch of civilisation.

Turning back to his sword, Fred ran the whetting stone along the blade slowly, lovingly, his thoughts returning to times gone by. To memories of his homeland, of his past, of the choices he had made leading to this point.

The strange storm had cleared now. It had been gone for hours, but with the crew still edgy, especially Edmund, only the warrior had dared to venture on deck and once the anchor had been winched again, stay there, the first volunteer to keep watch from the nest. And gladly.

The solitude was what he needed right then, what he yearned for; the time to just sit and ponder quietly, alone with his thoughts in the growing evening starlight. Alone with his decisions…

But though none would have dared to disturb him right then; there was always one.

Always her.

Fred *felt* Soph approaching even before she'd had a chance to climb the last few rungs of the ladder and step up on to the decking. But still he didn't so much as look up as she drew closer, giving her time to come forward and take her seat a little way from him, hugging her legs up onto the crate beneath her before he spoke.

He gave his sword an extra long rub.

"So what I would like to know; is how you *really* found me, Soph," he then said with a grunt.

Still he didn't look up as the warrioress gave a little smile, a part of her clearly pleased that her partner still knew her step. Instead of replying though, Soph turned her focus to his sword.

"I see you still spend your time preparing," she mused. "Do you even now expect a fight?"

Fred raised an eyebrow.

"You can never be certain *what* will happen," was all he said. "As you well know."

Soph made a neutral sound.

"Perhaps." And as if finally resigning himself to the fact that she was there, Fred at last put down his work and turned his head to look at her. He knew his partner hadn't come to discuss his sword. He'd known that the moment she'd appeared.

Why then, was she here?

"You did not answer my question," he stated. "How did you *really* find me? You are not a tracker. You could not have known that you would intercept us at Merchant's Wreath. And Bor could not have been aware of our whereabouts. When last we saw him, we had sailed for the West. So *how?*"

But almost as soon as he'd asked it, the warrior knew the answer. The smallest blush on her cheeks said it all. And straight away his voice was as hard as rock.

"Timo," he half-growled. "Timo told you."

There was a moment of silence, almost as if Soph was considering a different answer but then she nodded. Her expression was blank but still he could see the hint of redness just at her temples and looking away, Fred went back to his sword.

"You are still his companion then, after all this time?" he asked. He wanted to sound nonchalant, uncaring, but somehow it came out icier than he'd hoped.

Soph cleared her throat.

"Not of late. But we *are* still friends, yes. His life-partner was killed and well," she rubbed the back of her slender neck. "I believe he felt ashamed that he had spent more time with me than with her. They never had any sons."

Fred grimaced a little but made no comment.

"So, he has been spying on me," he replied instead and Soph's brow furrowed.

"He was *watching out* for you. He was granted with the knowledge to See, why should he not use it? Just as you should use *your* skills." And again, just as she had before, on their first meeting, she laid her hand gently on his arm, as if trying to speak to him through her touch.

Fred however, pulled away.

"I know why it is they have sent you here," he reasoned, his eyes studying her face. "They somehow think you will be able to *persuade* me..."

Soph let out an exasperated sigh. Already they had come back to this.

"They *sent* me here to find Crag! I had no-"

But Fred glared at her so suddenly then, that she was forced to stop.

"You see!" he insisted. *"This* is where your story falters!" his eyes visibly darkened. "Firstly, if Timo had *Seen* where I was going then he would have also understood *why* and Edmund would not have had to explain it to you! And secondly," and as if suddenly overcome by the heat of his own anger, he jumped to his feet, turning away from her, "if Timo had truly *Seen* then he would have known that I was here, *alone*. He would have known about Crag. He would have..." But as if unable to continue, he trailed off and Soph's mouth fell open.

If she had been prepared for this kind of argument, she certainly didn't seem it.

"I-" she faltered. "I did not-"

But Fred was impatient.

"So tell me," he said. "I have my suspicions, but I want to hear it from you - why are you really here?"

Soph's big grey eyes were wide with what looked like shock.

"Fred!" she cried and then, she too was on her feet, her movements as agile and powerful as a wildcat. "This is not like you! All this doubt and mistrust! It is not the way of a warrior!"

But Fred simply brushed her words aside with a shake of his head.

"Stop avoiding the issue, Soph. Why are you here?" he repeated angrily. "Just *tell* me!"

Soph gave another exasperated sigh. She seemed reluctant to tell him the truth, the warrior could see it as clear as day, but *why* he'd no idea.

What was going on? What was she *hiding*?

"They needed someone to send word! Timo did not tell me of-"

"He *must* have! Why would he have kept an important piece of information, like Crag's *death*, a secret?!" Fred cried. "You are lying to me! I can see it in your eyes, Soph!"

But though Soph clenched her fists, breathing slowly and evenly, as if to calm herself, still she said nothing. She was as rigid and secretive as a locked vault and knowing that he wasn't going to get the confession from her lips by force, Fred immediately changed his attitude.

"So," he started again and moving away, as if to get his bearings, he began to pace, "why did they send *you*? Usually they send trackers to find strays..."

Soph seemed to roll her eyes.

"Everyone else was occupied!" she insisted. "I was the only one able to - !"

But not accepting the excuse, Fred continued to stride about, his sword still in hand, before, taking a moment, he then turned slowly back to her, sudden comprehension clear on his face.

"I was right! They sent you," and he pointed at her accusingly then, "because they *knew* I was to be Sovereign. Just as they also knew that I would refuse." He smiled grimly. "They sent you because they *knew* how dangerous this mission might become…!"

Soph seemed to be unsure as to where this was going but she clearly didn't like his tone of voice.

"I cannot-" she began, sounding more uncertain by the minute.

"We do not have a child. That is what they want," Fred carried on triumphantly. "They sent you so that I could give you a child, a son! And then if something were to happen to me, the Sovereignty could continue. In fact, yes," his eyes flashed fire. "They may have arranged for my death already…"

"*Fred!!*"

Soph's cry was so loud, so shocked and yes *angry* that Fred almost froze. And then, suddenly she was rushing to his side, taking him by his broad shoulders, forcing him to finally look at her, her grasp fierce and strong.

"Stop talking like this! These are your *people*! How could you suspect them of such a thing?" and looking at her, Fred could see her own eyes were filled with a kind of horrified wonder. "What has happened to you!? You sound like a – you sound so-"

"Human?" Fred offered dryly.

The word hung in the air like a foul curse and releasing her hold, Soph closed her eyes in irritation, as Fred gave his own sigh. In a moment, all heat seemed to have fled from them both as they realised that this was no longer about the Sovereignty, about Soph's reasons for being there, about Fred's duty…

"Soph, the humans I have met," Fred muttered, stepping away from her again. It was almost as if it pained him to stand too close to her. "They may be primitive, they may seem misguided and irrational, but I would trust them with my *life*. Edmund is wiser than many a warrior I have met. If all of them were like him, I would be *proud* to be one of them."

The confession was unusually heartfelt, but instead of making his partner see reason, Soph's eyes were downcast.

"I *hate* to hear you like this," she half-whispered. "It is not like you." Her voice shook a little and for a moment, Fred seemed to soften. But only slightly.

"I may not be the warrior that you once knew, or even the life-partner you desire," he paused a moment, as if the words had stuck in his throat. "And for that I am truly sorry; but I cannot help my feelings, *or* my suspicions." And the last word reminding him of their argument, he then turned his back on her again, his voice sharp.

Soph glanced up at him, slowly. But something in her finally seemed to have given way.

"Do you want to know why I am *really* here?" she then spat.

Fred said nothing.

"Do you really want to know?" she threw her arms wide and then, just like that, the vault opened; "They were going to forbid me from coming to you! They were going to forbid me and I begged them to let me find you, Fred. *Begged* them! Timo was never supposed to grant me the information, but he did so because I pleaded with him. Because I-" and she paused a moment as if the memory of whatever she had offered was too much, before; "He could only tell me a *scrap* of what I needed to know. He only told me where you could be found... But that was all! I knew nothing of Crag's death. I swear it!"

And despite his best efforts to remain aloof, Fred couldn't help but swivel to her in surprise then, as everything came spilling out.

"I was told of the Temple," Soph carried on, her voice uneven as another angry tear escaped, "I was not told why it was you ventured there. I found Bor's village myself. But you were already gone. And then, when the chieftain told me of your voyage, I knew that you would be heading east, not west – Timo had spoken as much. But beyond that? I knew *nothing else*." Her lips drew themselves into a thin, thoughtful line. "I did not even hope to find you. But when I saw the vessel in the bay, I knew-"

"But, why?" Fred asked quietly. For some reason he found himself feeling oddly numb.

He hadn't expected any of this. Not *really*...

He hadn't been prepared to be so very wrong.

Soph, her eyes a little damp, wiped them with a rough hand, growling at herself for her moment of weakness.

"The council cannot have known of Crag's death either. I genuinely came to inform him about the Sovereignty," she said. "That, and I had to – I wanted to..." but she soon trailed off.

"To what?" Fred urged. "What did you want?" He could feel himself moving back towards her, as if drawn to her by the weighted silence.

Soph hung her beautiful head.

"Do not make me say it," she said. "You *know* why."

But Fred just shook his head. He was almost upon her now.

"Please," was all he said. Suddenly he seemed desperate to hear what she had to say, as if, whether he knew what it was or not, he wanted to hear her speak it aloud. *Needed* to.

Soph didn't look up, even as Fred stood over her.

"I came because I wanted to *see you*," she then admitted. "I hoped, in vain - *that* I can see now - that you would wish to return to Mawreath with me. To live together, to have children, settle down." And then as Fred just stared at her, Soph's last few words were muttered almost beneath her breath. "I have missed you."

The warrior was less than a hair's breadth from her now, their bodies almost touching, but though he had come so far, they both had, in such a short time, still Fred stopped, his face filled with doubt.

"But what about Timo and all the others you have-?" he started, but for some reason his own voice seemed to fail him.

Soph shook her head.

"Fred, you are my life-partner," and finally, as if the word held with it every meaning, she dared to look up into his eyes. "None of them ever compared to you. I thought I could be content with another. You were away so much, and for so long, I-"

But she didn't get a chance to finish, for it was then that, moving on a whim, Fred suddenly took her head in his hands and kissing her tenderly on the forehead, finally pulled his lover into a warm embrace.

As the twin moons passed by overhead, so it was that the couple then stood there, without so much as a word, just holding each other after so many desolate years of being apart.

—

Meggie woke from her doze with a start. Pain, sharp and unexpected was searing from her ankle, and her eyes snapping open in agonised confusion, she almost cried out.

What was happening? Where was she? And why did she hurt so much?

She was struggling, for a second to remember. And not just that. She was struggling to remember *anything*...

But then, as the little element rolled to her side, curling her body into a tight ball, she knocked against something solid, something warm and alive and everything came flooding back in an instant.

Nickolas.

The elder element was asleep beside her, his face shifting, his eyes flickering as he dreamed and distracted for a brief second, Meggie just stared at him, wondering if she was really awake herself.

This man had been dead.

She had watched him die. She had watched the sword enter his body and his breath leave it. He couldn't possibly be lying here, next to her on the desert floor, *in the flesh*.

And yet somehow he was.

Somehow Nickolas had returned to them, to her. And though he was pale, paler perhaps than she had ever seen anyone, and yes, *weak*, exhausted, as if death had been nothing but a long fitful sleep; there wasn't a scratch on him.

He was whole. Whole and alive.

And just as she remembered him.

Just, Nickolas.

But for the pain, she still felt utterly numb and shifting to her other side, Meggie tried to tear her focus away to the other body beside her.

Bethan seemed to be dreaming too, her eyes flitting about under their lids, a hint of contentment on her lips, making Meggie wonder what she was thinking about.

Home, family, Edmund…

The little element gave a long sigh.

That was it. That was all the rest *she* was going to get. And knowing somehow that sleep wasn't going to be her friend any more that night, Meggie sat up in the growing dimness, still clutching at her ankle.

The swelling, remarkably, had gone down a little, but still, as she ran her hands tenderly over the wound, she couldn't help but wonder if the bone was broken.

It certainly *felt* broken – the shooting pain was enough to make her believe that – but there was no real way to tell. Where the skin had once been red only a few hours ago, already it was turning to a deep purple bruise, spreading in an ugly welt across her foot. But though it didn't *look* as bad, it still *hurt* like nothing else and suddenly touching a nerve, Meggie felt the yelp burst out before she could stop herself.

The sound split the silent evening like a crack of thunder as the little element instantly clamped a hand over her mouth. But it was too late, almost before she heard his groan, she felt the movement at her side and turning back, she just watched as Nickolas pulled himself up to a sit, rubbing at his tired eyes.

His movements were stiff, laboured, and feeling suddenly awkward, Meggie, for a second, didn't know what to say, before something seemed to make her speak anyway.

"I'm so sorry," she tried timidly. "I didn't mean to wake you."

Nickolas glanced at her. But though he looked ready to collapse all over again, still the elder element managed a bleary smile.

"It is fine," he replied kindly as Meggie just stared at him, unable, for the moment, to smile back. "I have rested enough for now anyway."

And noticing where her other hand still lay, Nickolas's face then fell into frown.

"Is it your ankle? Is it broken?" he said, sounding worried. "Are you in pain?"

Meggie continued to stare but then, as if suddenly realising he was waiting for her reply, she nodded, her own expression blank.

"Yeah, it hurts a bit," she found herself mumbling. "I don't know that it's broken though. It could just be sprained."

Nickolas's frown faded.

"Ah." It seemed as if he too was finding it a struggle to speak. And then; "you may be right."

THE ENTITY OF SOULS

Meggie gave a non-committal shrug and once again, the pair then slipped into a long, silent pause, both elements shifting their bodies uneasily on the hard ground.

The companions had much to talk about, that much was obvious. Much to ask each other, to come to terms with, but for the moment, neither of them seemed willing to be the one to speak, to question, to offer any answers. Both of them could feel the tension between them, it lay like a thick blanket in the air, and yet...

"You must be in more pain than I am."

Meggie didn't know why she'd said it. The words had just sort of come out, but the moment that they had, the little element felt something like a tiny relief. For suddenly they were *there*; with the statement disguised as a question, along with so many of the unanswered demands hanging like a weight above their heads, so many questions like; what had happened? How was Nickolas even *there*? Why was he still alive?

And - Meggie suddenly thought with a cold shudder- was he even *him*?

Was the Nickolas beside her really who he said he was? Who he seemed to be?

How could she know for sure? For all she could tell, this man could be a stranger, another trick of the Builder's. A Digger in disguise or worse -

"Meggie."

Nickolas's voice was strangely soft and realising that he was just staring at *her* now, Meggie gave a start.

"Yes?"

Her voice was almost a squeak.

"It *is* me."

And as if to prove it, Nickolas looked her straight in the eyes. Eyes, she knew, that were still wide with dazed disbelief, wide with the pain, with the shadow of her grief...

She had truly grieved for this man, Meggie thought. Or started to.

But now she didn't need to any more. Now he was here. Right here. Right in front of her, close enough to touch. And she was supposed to say what? Supposed to *do* what? What was supposed to happen when someone you knew was one moment gone and the next moment back again? She didn't know and feeling suddenly overwhelmed, the little element blinked.

It was barely a flicker, barely a flinch, but it was enough, and suddenly the moment was gone as Nickolas turned back to her ankle, all business again.

"May I take a look?" he asked, pointing towards the wound.

Meggie just nodded again blankly, before, suddenly appreciating what he meant, her face fell.

"Please don't move it," she begged. "It's still pretty... tender."

"I will keep it still, I promise," Nickolas said and leaning in close as Meggie removed the hand still absently clutched to the ankle, he then scrutinised the swelling carefully with his eyes, squinting in the diming light.

"How did you do this?" he asked, before, as if unable to help himself, he reached down to run his finger across the base of the bruising like an expert. "You must have fallen pretty hard!"

Meggie though, didn't get a chance to answer, for instead, the moment the element touched her, she let out a squeak of surprise and startled, Nickolas immediately flinched away.

"Sorry," the elder element hissed in alarm, "where does it hurt?" but to his surprise, Meggie gave a nervous laugh.

"No! It's fine!" she said. "You didn't hurt me. It's just... your *hands*! They're so *cold*!"

Cold.

The word sent an odd kind of chill through Meggie's body as she realised what it was she was saying.

Nickolas's hands were cold to the touch. *Deathly* cold.

Could it be?

And again, Meggie's thoughts couldn't help but turn to what had happened.

Was this really Nickolas, alive again? Living, breathing, just as she was or - Meggie could feel the thud of fear in her chest - *or* was he something else entirely?

She could remember Tungala vividly, remember the Temple of Ratacopeck and the four ghostly men they had spoken with there. What if that was Nickolas's fate here, now? What if now, he was some kind of *spirit* in this world too? Not quite dead, but not quite alive...

Would he even know it?

And carefully, the little element studied what she could now see of her companion's face in the early evening darkness.

If it was true, it would certainly explain his appearance – his lack of injuries, his pale skin, his frozen touch...

But be that as it may, even as the idea entered her head, Meggie somehow knew that it was a ridiculous one. Though she clearly still wasn't ready to accept it yet, a part of her *knew* that Nickolas truly was alive.

His touch had been cold, yes, but it had also been living, solid flesh. And as for the rest, yes, he was pale, unscathed but she could see him breathing, watch as his chest rose and fell, could see somewhere in the depths of his eyes that despite appearances, he was suffering, masking the pain of what he had been through with his unreadable face.

Yes. Nickolas was alive, as alive as any of them ever would be. Though she may never understand how or why, she knew it in her heart to be true and as if suddenly desperate to prove it, the little element suddenly reached out and grabbing his hand in hers, held it fast. Sure enough, his fingers *were* freezing, but even as she pressed them to her own, she could feel something oddly warm and comforting beneath the skin. There was a familiarity there... and then, realising the painful silence she'd created, Meggie soon met the other element's gaze.

"I- I tripped," she stuttered finally, as if the past half a minute or so hadn't happened. "When we were running through the dust, I couldn't see where I was going and -*ow*!"

Nickolas was touching her ankle again with his other hand.

"You must have been running very fast," he said slowly. He seemed to be contemplating something, but what that was, Meggie had no idea. "I think though," and gently extricating his fingers from hers, he then brushed his hands together, dirt crumbling away from the skin, "that this may be more than just a sprain this time. I would definitely say that your ankle is broken."

"Really?"

And forgetting for the moment everything else, Meggie gave an exasperated sigh.

Great, she thought. That was *all* they needed right then, an invalid who could barely walk.

Watching as Nickolas then sat back on his haunches though, making the smallest wince as he pulled his legs to his chest, she couldn't help but wonder whether she wasn't alone...

The elder element looked away.

"Do not worry," he comforted. "You will not be left behind."

His words were kind, but there was something in them that was oddly cold, and studying the side of her companion's face, Meggie gave a wan smile.

"Thanks," she replied before, trying to sound a little more like herself; "I'll just have to limp all the way."

The image of doing just that, seemed almost funny to her. And for a moment, an odd chuckle rose to the back of her throat.

She wasn't sure if Nickolas was smiling, his face was still turned away from her, but all of a sudden it was then that she felt... *wrong*.

The moment seemed to have crept up on her from nowhere. The pain, it was suddenly there all over again, throbbing along her leg and aware of the sensation, of her head spinning and the dark prickle of unconsciousness sparking at the corners of her eyes, the little element gasped.

"Meggie?" she heard Nickolas's voice. He sounded strangely far away all of a sudden. "Meggie!"

And then she felt his cold hands again, this time on her back, steadying her, his eyes back on her face, searching her expression for a sign. But she was barely able to focus now and unable to manage anything else, Meggie groaned as nausea welled to the back of her throat.

What was *wrong* with her? Why did she suddenly feel so *ill*?

One moment she'd been fine. The next…

And remembering the only other time this had happened before, Meggie felt suddenly very afraid.

Was it happening again?

"It is probably the shock."

The other voice spoke out of the evening darkness as if from nowhere, but seeing him approach above them, Meggie couldn't help but notice how drawn Dromeda looked.

Like Nickolas, his skin – what could be seen of it – was almost white, his eyes carrying the dark shadows of restlessness and despite her weakness, Meggie wondered briefly, spitefully even, if the element was suffering with his guilt; the guilt of leaving his friend behind, of not defending him when he needed him.

He seemed reluctant to come too close – instead he had stopped a few feet away, almost as if worried that at any moment Nickolas would recognise his shame, realise what it was for, what he had done and punish him for it. But whatever his companion's feelings, whether guilt or just the stunned numbness that came hand-in-hand with the shock of seeing your dead friend alive all over again, Nickolas just glanced up at him before turning his attention back to Meggie.

"She needs something to drink," he said shortly and obeying, Dromeda went straight for their pack of provisions, drawing out the flagon of water.

He made no comment about how little there was left.

"And do you have a *clean* blanket?" Nickolas added as an afterthought.

Dromeda looked at him a little oddly.

"We only have the one," he muttered, gesturing to the other three still-sleeping elements as they lay snuggled together beneath the cover.

Nickolas looked utterly confused for a moment, before, realising his error, he soon shook his head.

"Yes, of course." Neither Dromeda nor the half-living Meggie dared ask where the other blanket and bread that the elder element had been carrying *before* were now. "I will need something else then," and he glanced around them in the almost-blackness as if the very ground could help. "Pass me the cloak."

Again, obeying, Dromeda moved to take up the cloak Nickolas had used to cover his face during the sandstorm. And again, neither he nor Meggie knew nor asked where it had come from. Neither dared to even imagine…

All the while, taking Meggie fully in his arms, Nickolas laid her gently to the ground, before, grabbing the cloak from Dromeda, he got to his feet. In her state of half-consciousness on the ground, Meggie saw him disappear from her eye line, but had little time to wonder what was happening before she then felt it.

This time she didn't even try to stifle the cry as pain, sharp, fast and horrible fired up her leg.

"Argh!"

In her fear, her confusion, she tried to sit all over again, to stop it, to somehow defend herself, but to her surprise she found that Dromeda was there holding her down, muttering encouraging words in her ear, words she never thought she would hear the man say as Nickolas continued to bandage her wound.

"Nearly there," she heard him speak, but his voice sounded like only a whisper in her mind.

The darkness was deeper somehow, deeper and, for a lulling second, almost comforting.

She felt suddenly very much like sleeping. Her eyes were closed now, clamped shut against the agony. Really there was nothing to stop her.

Nothing at all...

Meggie.

Nothing but the faint shaking at her shoulders and the voice constantly calling in her ear.

Meggie.

She thought it sounded like a woman, like Saz, but she couldn't be sure... just as she wasn't really sure of *anything* but how tired she was and how much she wanted to just ignore it all, ignore the pain, the pressure on her shoulders, the voice's protests and just let her body drift away with it, let the blackness take her.

She could wake later, one day. If needs be.

All she wanted now was to fall into the nothing that welcomed her...

Meggie's eyes flew open as the trickle of water hit her in the face and immediately, she sat up, instinctively gasping for air.

"Wha-?" she started, but her voice a mere whine, she tried instead to recognise the faces around her, to regain something of herself.

Nickolas was there, as were Saz and Bethan – the elements were awake now – with Bex just behind them and a little way off, Dromeda. All five of them were peering into her face, all five of them looking concerned.

Who had thrown the water, Meggie had no idea, but she could see now that it was Nickolas who had hold of her shoulders, even now holding her upright, she realised, as she felt her body weaken for a second.

Saz was saying something again but Meggie could barely hear her as she squinted, trying to focus her eyes properly. It was getting almost impossible to see now. Very soon the friendly figures around her would just be silhouettes in the night.

"She will be fine."

She could almost feel the rumble of Nickolas's voice through his hands. "She just needs some more time." And looking into all the gazes still directed at her, Meggie could feel her bloodless cheeks growing warm. Nickolas was right, she was fine, really. Although she still wasn't entirely sure what had just happened, there was no need for all this fuss…

She swallowed slowly, trying to control herself, trying to build herself up to speak. But to her and everyone's surprise, it was Dromeda who got there first.

"Well, I expect you are right," he suddenly said. "She probably *will* be fine." And turning his eyes on Nickolas, his mouth was set in a grim, dangerous line. "After all, we know for a certainty now, that we cannot die."

No one else had spoken of it yet. No one had asked the burningly obvious question, no one had dared to and yet now the moment seemed to have come, just like that, as without a word, all attention fell, not with shock on Dromeda, but Nickolas, as if they too couldn't help themselves but yearn to know.

Meggie felt Nickolas's grip on her tighten, just a little. But despite it all, his expression never altered and clearly feeling braver, Dromeda took a step closer to the group, for some reason, the little element noticed, his hand moving to where the knife lay concealed at his waist.

"Tell us Nickolas," he then said, finally speaking the words they had all longed to. "Tell us what happened. What *really* happened. Tell us why you are here."

And the prairie fell once again into deathly silence as no one said a word. Everyone seemingly waiting…

For a good long second, not even Nickolas stirred. Meggie felt his fingers clench even more, enough to almost hurt her, but she didn't cry out.

"Dromeda," Saz then began, breaking the tension. "Dromeda, maybe we should just-"

But just as determined as Nickolas seemed not to explain, so Dromeda seemed, suddenly, to get the answers he wanted.

"Tell us, what happened!" he echoed, not even trying to hide the growing impatience from his voice. "Do you expect us not to ask? Do you expect us not to wonder? To just turn up? Breeze back to us without so much as an explanation? In fact," and he gestured at the elements, his eyes flitting to Bethan, "frighten *them* half out of their wits believing we were being followed, without so much as a word as to why?!"

Bethan looked ashamed, as if somehow it was her fault that any of this had happened.

"Injure *her*!" Dromeda carried on, pointing directly at Meggie, "without apology, without a reason?"

Nickolas's face twitched and seeing where things were likely to lead, the little element tried desperately to shake her head.

"No!" she just about managed. "No! This wasn't his fault!" But the effort making her feel weak for a second time as blood pounded in her head, she soon fell quiet again as Dromeda carried on.

"You expect to come back to us without anything at all?" he spat, visibly shaking with anger now.

For a moment, Meggie wasn't sure whether Nickolas was breathing anymore he was so rigid. The elder element was utterly utterly still, staring straight ahead without so much as a blink.

Dromeda's hand meanwhile flew to his head in despair.

"We watched you die!" he positively shouted. "No one could have survived a wound like that! No one! And yet you have not a speck of blood on you! No tears in your clothing!" And he stepped away in disbelief, almost disappearing into the night. "We watched you fall!" And then finally, as if it had all been leading to this point, his voice cracked. "*I* watched you fall, Nickolas! Meggie was right. I could have helped you and yet I did nothing! And now-"

And as if something in his friend's words had finally got to him, Meggie felt the grip on her shoulders loosen as Nickolas, at last, moved. Like a machine, stiff and unthinking, he laid the little element back to the ground and then turned to stand to his feet. But though he stepped towards Dromeda, the other element seemed suddenly unable to look at him, his face contorted, his whole body seeming to shudder.

It was shock; Meggie had seen it, had felt it so many times before, yet witnessing it in such a place, with such a man felt almost alien.

That was why he had seemed so quiet, so distant, so unable to defend himself against Meggie's own emotional pain, the little element realised at last; because he hadn't known how to handle his own. The shock of everything, of seeing his only certainty gone in the blink of an eye, of watching someone he obviously cared about, someone he had known for hundreds of years, die right before his eyes had caused him to almost shut down.

But now? Now his emotions were falling over themselves to be let out; the grief, the guilt, the sorrow and with them now the stunned disbelief, the *relief*, the growing joy...

And though Nickolas moved closer, his hands outstretched a little, Dromeda could only move back, move away, his body almost completely invisible in the dark evening light.

"How do we even know if you are *real*?" he hissed in repulsion, echoing Meggie's own earlier thoughts. "How do we know this is not another trick of the Builders? He can create Diggers, he can control the *weather*, he can-"

But Nickolas had heard enough.

"I am standing here!" he said and as if to illustrate his very existence, he spread his arms wide, doing a half-turn to show them all. "I am speaking!

Look, I am breathing!" and he touched his chest where the wound had been. Meggie noticed that true to Dromeda's word, he didn't have any markings on his tunic where the weapon had pierced right through him.

"But how do we know it is you?" Dromeda blurted out. "Prove it to us!" He seemed desperate to hang onto this wild thought and even as Nickolas just gawped at him, he stood tall, his hand now positively clutching the knife at his side. *"Prove it!"*

"What do you mean how do you know it is me?! Who else would I be?" Nickolas challenged, his own voice growing angry.

"Like I said, the Builder has many tricks!" Dromeda's eyes flashed. "How do we know that you-?"

But Nickolas shook his head.

"No," he said flatly, the word stopping everything in its tracks before his face saddened a little.

"You think I am your enemy," he said. The quiet words were more of a statement than a question. And his eyes now, were back on Meggie. But though the little element opened her mouth to answer, Dromeda got there first.

"Well what proof do we have otherwise?" he retorted. "You have given us nothing so far!"

And just like that, Nickolas snapped around to look at his friend. If there had been any hope of calming the matter, it seemed to be long gone.

"What *proof* do you want from me? What can I possibly say or do to *prove* to you that I am the *real* Nickolas?" and then he was reaching for his tunic, his own expression livid.

"Is *this* what it will take? Is *this* what you wanted to see?" he challenged. And before anyone could avert their eyes, Nickolas had grabbed hold of the muddy material and almost ripping the fabric in his rage, he lifted the shirt high, tearing it away to reveal naked chest beneath.

No one had been ready for what they saw, but as they did so, the whole group seemed to take one collective gasp of breath as all eyes fell on what lay above the elder element's heart. It was no longer bleeding, no longer a hole, it had healed in its own small, miraculous way, but it was there, red and bright and sore, wet with pus, a perfect slit right where the Digger's blade had sliced neatly through the back of his ribcage and out the other side.

Feeling sick and faint all over again, Meggie looked away. The others meanwhile just continued to stare until, as if suddenly realising what he had done, Nickolas, all anger subsiding, lowered his arms, pulling the tunic back to where it should be.

"I am sorry," he said quietly. "I did not- I know it must be a shock."

But though he had seen it for himself, though he had seen the very proof they surely all needed, still Dromeda, stunned and pale as he was, looked uncertain.

"It could be a trick," he demanded, sounding more and more doubtful by the minute. "It could be a-a-" But whether the others were ever with him or not, they certainly weren't now. The wound had spoken a thousand words no other explanation could, except…

"Nickolas," and glancing down, the elder element looked half-surprised to see Meggie's pleading face looking up at him once again. Her hand, he saw, was rested on his shin, though he could barely feel it through the crust of mud coating his legs. "Just tell us what happened. It's the only way *some* of us," and her eyes flashed with something like irritation, "are ever going to be *sure*."

His story was the proof they wanted, the proof they all truly needed to hear and as if finally realising this, it was then that Nickolas let out a long sigh.

"Fine," he said at last. "If that is what you need, then I will tell you." And then, when no one said a word; "I did not wish to speak of it, truth be told. I still do not. Death is not something that *should* be spoken of. Not like this…" And his brow furrowed. "Besides, I was worried you might… that you…"

"That we wouldn't believe you?" Saz finished with a wry smile as the elder element trailed off. Dromeda, meanwhile, crossed his arms, looking at the floor.

"Exactly," Nickolas caught on, glancing at his sceptical friend before taking another deep breath. Now was the moment of truth. And there was no going back.

"When you saw me fall, it felt as if…" still he seemed lost for words, "well… It felt, what I always imagined death would feel like. Like my life was leaving me piece by piece.

"I could not breathe. I could not think. I could see the blood rushing out of me, my very life-force," and he looked down at his chest as if half expecting to still see the weapon sticking out from between his ribs, "but somehow, I could not believe that it was *me*. And it was such a… *pain*." The weight of the word seemed to send a chill through the rest of the group. "I could hardly describe it to you. It was *deeper* than pain. More like a *knowing*. Just a *knowing* that it was all over. Like I knew that I would never be able to breathe, to move, to feel ever again. And then everything began to grow dark and-" but as if the very feel of it still haunted him now, the elder element stopped, closing his eyes just for a moment.

The others were hanging on his every word, questioning horror echoed on every face. But still it wasn't enough and seeing that he needed prompting, Meggie took action.

"And what happened after that?" she asked gently. Still she had hold of him. Even beneath the mud and material she could feel how cold he was.

He lost a lot of blood, a funny reality whispered in her head. *No wonder he's so cold.*

Nickolas opened his eyes again, looking up to the blackening sky above.

"After that?" he said. "After that felt like a lifetime. A lifetime of… *nothing*, I suppose. I could not hear, or see, or smell or *feel* anything. I just somehow *knew* that time was passing beneath me. That somehow, despite it all, I still existed. And then," his brow furrowed again, only this time, he looked more confused, more troubled than any of them, "I woke up."

The words felt short, almost meaningless and there was a short pause as everyone took a second just to comprehend before;

"You woke up?" Saz asked. "Just like that?"

Nickolas frowned.

"Yes. I did. I just remember waking up. And being alone. The Diggers had gone. They had left me, covered in a cloak," he glanced at the binding on Meggie's ankle. "Too afraid to move me, by all accounts." Dromeda let out a small snort. "I think they were just as frightened, just as shocked as… well…" He eyed them all. "But for all *I* knew, *years* could have passed. For all I knew, I had been lying there for a lifetime. Exactly where I had fallen."

"So why did you carry on?" It was Bex's turn to speak. Pushing her smudged spectacles up her nose, her own pensive frown mirrored his. "If you thought that so much time might have passed, why did you follow us? We could have been *long* gone…"

"My clothing was undamaged and unstained, I checked," Nickolas explained, turning to look at her. There was something uncertain in his expression. "But my blood was still fresh on the ground. Still red," some of the others paled a little, "so I *knew* I still had a chance of finding you."

For a moment he then looked thoughtful.

"Besides," and he gave something of a shrug, "what do I have left in the City? If I simply walked back through those gates, do you think the Diggers would have taken kindly towards me? Do you think they would have welcomed me with open arms?"

It was a fair point, and a fair explanation. If this manifestation of Nickolas wasn't real, he was certainly convincing and finally facing Dromeda, he then threw his arms wide all over again.

"So, do you believe me now?" he asked his long-time friend without so much as a hint of spite. "Can you finally accept that I am who I say I am?"

Dromeda's already-ashen face had gradually been growing whiter and whiter as Nickolas's story unfolded. But he'd stopped shaking now. Gone was the anger, the suspicion and in its place, was finally the remorse.

"I should have aided you," he muttered, continuing to stare at the ground, avoiding all eye contact. "Meggie begged me to help you and I- I just *stood* there. *Watching.*" He released a long sigh himself, "you would be right to blame me-"

But half to everyone's surprise Nickolas suddenly started to chuckle. The sound was deep and surprisingly warm in what had been a cold few hours.

"Blame you?" he laughed. "How could I blame you?" And then; "We all know now that I am the better fighter!" and, just like that, the whole mood on the plain seemed to lighten.

It was as if the whole group had been living under a heavy fog that had suddenly lifted as smiles, genuine and thankful began to break out amongst them and the first then to move, Dromeda was hurrying to his friend and in one swift moment, the pair were embracing tightly as the elements looked on, each with her own astonished relief, glad that everything was once again well.

But like all things, everyone knew that their happiness was certain to be short lived.

They had others things to focus on now, the task ahead to consider and as was usual, the first to sober, Nickolas was soon to turn to the horizon.

"We should get moving," he pointed out. "The Builder obviously knows we are out here. That dust storm was no accident."

Dromeda's smile barely faded.

"Why rush?" he demanded, already seeming much his old self. "Let's rest awhile." And then, realising the real truth of it, he gave his own laugh. "The Builder's fight is futile anyway; we cannot die."

But though he had made a joke of it only moments before, still Nickolas continued to look grave.

"No, we cannot die," he said. "But the argument remains the same; we *can* still be injured," and nodding towards the crippled Meggie, he appealed to the whole group. "We can still feel pain. And the Builder knows it. The more of us who are injured, the less of us will be able to make it *anywhere*. We should leave as soon as possible. Something tells me we still have a lot of ground to cover."

"But it's already nightfall," Bex spoke up. "How're we supposed to see? How do we even know which direction we're supposed to be going?"

It was a good point. Though they had run that first night away from the City regardless of anything but escape, they couldn't afford now to just keep walking blindly.

None of them knew where they were going. *North* had been Belanna's instruction. North, north, north until they found the barrier. But which way north *was*, none of them really seemed to know for certain anymore. There were no stars to guide them, no moons, no landmarks. The prairie was flat; flat, dusty and dry.

All they were really relying on was a kind of *feeling* and the hope that at some point, the landscape would change.

The great boulder shaped like a tree. That's what they needed to find. But in the dark? In the growing blackness where, before long, none of them would be able to see even so much as their own hand in front of their face, what chance did they have of *that*?

Nickolas was right though, they couldn't afford to rest any longer. The Builder knew they were there, *had* to know where they were headed. And wasn't happy about it.

No, the quicker they got to the barrier between the worlds, the quicker they all felt that they would be in any way safe and suddenly having an idea, Saz's face brightened.

"I might be able to help," she said mysteriously. "But first I'm going to need some kind of stick…"

Edmund reached the top of the crow's nest ladder, a burning candle clenched between his teeth.

Luckily for him the breeze was soft, almost non-existent now, so there was no danger of being plunged into darkness, but even so, the Explorer moved slowly, trying to keep the wick alight and any hot wax from his chin.

Down below, much as he dared to look, the Karenza deck was all-but empty except for another flickering light at the helm where he knew Elanore was at her maps, checking and rechecking the route ahead. The sea captain had dedicated herself that evening to learning the layout of Ophelius itself and he had left her to it with the assurance that it wouldn't be long now until they finally reached their destination.

The hour was a late one, but despite it all, Edmund felt oddly awake and as he looked up into the nest, he was soon surprised to see that Fred, much as he had assumed he would be, wasn't alone.

The warrior was entwined together with another, their face buried in his chest, Fred's hand rested on their head. Only as he approached did he then recognise Soph and shocked, the Explorer froze, unsure for a moment whether to go on and interrupt or quietly leave, pretending he had never been there.

The pair were talking, Fred muttering something in Soph's ear and Soph replying with a quiet laugh. They were completely oblivious to anything else but each other and as he looked on, Edmund felt something of a pang as he recalled what it was to feel like that, to care, in that moment, for nothing else but that tiny little world of companionship.

Unaware as the lovers seemed however, there was no fooling Fred.

"Edmund," he said, looking up and then, just like that, the couple pulled apart.

Their movements were slow, as if they chose to leave one another out of respect for their new company, out of politeness, not in the usual way that two secret lovers leapt away from each other, embarrassed by the moment of discovery. Not, Edmund reasoned, that Fred and Soph *were* secret lovers.

The warriors were life-partners. For all intents and purposes, they were husband and wife and although Edmund couldn't help but be surprised to find them together after Fred's clear coldness towards Soph during the day, he also knew that here was a partnership that had developed long before he had even so much as been *thought* about and would probably go on far after he was dead.

The Explorer cleared his throat.

"It's my turn to keep watch," he explained hurriedly, spitting the candle from his mouth. Though they didn't seem embarrassed, for some reason he was. To him, it didn't feel right to be intruding into what was clearly a very private moment, but to his continued wonder, neither warrior seemed at all bothered.

As Soph shot him an earnest smile, Fred took the candle from Edmund's hand and propping it in an empty candle bracket, he stifled a yawn.

"There is not much to report," he then said. "We passed a village about an hour or two ago."

Edmund glanced at Soph then back at Fred, giving a nod.

"Was probably Yawton Corner," he reasoned. "Shouldn't be too long before we reach Ophelius." And looking away from them both, the Explorer then gestured to the ladder, for some reason feeling his face flush a little. "Now go, rest."

Fred and Soph seemed to consider each other for a second, but though their expressions were warm, they were still controlled, as was the warrior way.

"Very well," Fred then said. "We will bid you a good night." And without another word, he headed for the ladder.

Soph, for a moment, followed him, but as Edmund stepped back to let them pass, she hung back instead to watch as her partner disappeared into the blackness, giving Edmund the sneaking suspicion that the pair had made some kind of decision between them.

The warrioress clearly had something to discuss with him, but not waiting to find out what it was, the Explorer soon took his seat on an empty crate and turning his eyes to the dark land below, he scanned the black trees, looking for signs of the next village; Basherby. All the while Soph remained where she was, as if waiting for something, scrutinising him until;

"Fred has great respect for you," she spoke eventually. "As do I. And I must thank you again for letting me board your vessel uninvited."

Edmund, a little taken aback, couldn't help but turn to her with a modest smile.

"It's no problem, really. Any…" and he paused for a moment, searching for the right word, "*friend* of Fred's is a friend of mine," his smile grew a little wry. "We've met a lot of interesting people on our travels…"

"So I have heard," Soph mused. Still she was on her feet, making it evident that she didn't plan on staying for long. Even in the dim light from the candle though, Edmund couldn't help but notice how much brighter she looked. Even though he'd only known her for a matter of hours, the warrioress's whole manner seemed to have changed, to have softened somehow, making her look more beautiful than ever - if that were possible - and the Explorer didn't need to guess why.

Funny how their lives could be so very different and yet somehow so fundamentally the same.

"Can I ask you something?" he then found himself saying before he could stop himself. And then, once Soph, looking first surprised, gave a nod; "Do you think… Do you think that if you hadn't been paired with Fred, you'd still have-?"

And the warrioress smiled herself, looking strangely shy.

"Found him? Still have cared for him?" she offered.

Edmund nodded too and the warrior looked thoughtful for a moment.

"I do not know," she reasoned, looking for all the world in that tiny moment like a human woman, a girl giddy with love before, sobering a little, she turned her eyes directly to his, scrutinising him all over again. "Fate though, as it were, has a tendency of getting things right."

Fate. It had been a while since he'd heard *that* word, and remembering what it meant, Edmund's brow darkened.

"I'm not sure I would always trust in fate to make the right decision," he replied. "We wouldn't be in this situation if it weren't for *fate*."

Soph's lips turned down in a curious frown. Perhaps she understood his reasons, perhaps she didn't, Edmund couldn't tell, but either way, he knew that he didn't want to underestimate her.

"Have you told Bethan of your feelings?" she then asked almost out of the blue and stunned, Edmund just stared at her for a moment.

Bethan?

How did she know? How *could* she know? Unless Fred…

But Soph, seeing his clear amazement, just laughed.

"It is obvious," she pointed out. "I may not be human but I can certainly tell a human's emotions. They are not so dissimilar to our own." And her laugh turned into another warm smile. "Your face lit up when you spoke of her earlier, when you told me of the elements. She obviously means a lot to you."

Edmund released a long breath. He'd forgotten for a moment who he was speaking to, *what* he was speaking to. How simple humanity must seem to her, to any of the others…

"Yes," he admitted. "She does mean a lot to me. And I *did* tell her before she… left."

Soph smiled again, the secret grin of someone with a shared confidence, a shared feeling and unable to help himself, Edmund felt himself smiling back as he remembered once again the few stolen moments he had shared with Bethan in the Temple. It was a memory he never wanted to forget and vowed one day to relive... when he saw her again.

If he saw her again.

And his thoughts suddenly casting back to Eliom's still unanswered vision of death; fear, thick and fast quickly clutched his heart.

If.

Was it Bethan? Was it her? Was it she he had Seen?

If she'd been able to detect his feelings before however, Soph seemed oblivious now.

"And I take it Bethan reciprocates these feelings?" she carried on cheerfully, unaware of Edmund's thoughts.

For a moment it was as if the Explorer hadn't heard her.

"I'm sorry?" he said with a blink.

"Bethan," Soph repeated. "I assume she cares for you in return?"

"Yes," the human said automatically. "She does." But almost the second the words had fallen from his mouth, he knew something wasn't right.

I assume she cares for you in return? Assume?

And forgetting about Eliom, about his fears for a moment, Edmund stopped in his tracks as the full meaning of what Soph was asking, hit him.

Of course, he had all along *assumed* that Bethan felt the same way as he did. The way she had kissed him by the roaring fire, her tears near the end... all of it had been heartfelt, passionate, *real*.

Hadn't it?

But then, he realised with sudden shock, at the same time, she had never *said* it. She had never expressed those feelings in words. Not like he had.

She had never given him hope. Not really.

Had he then, all this time, done exactly that? Had he just *assumed?*

And for the first time ever, Edmund could feel himself start to doubt the one certainty he had been sure of all along.

Did Bethan love him? Or had the tears been nothing but a cry for help? The kiss nothing but some last few moments grabbed desperately before what she thought was her death?

Did it even really matter? he tried to reason. *He* loved *her*; he knew that much. He would still try to find her no matter *what* her feelings... He would still do anything for her. For any of them; any of those he cared for. They were his responsibility, his burden. He would do anything, despite it all...

Wouldn't he?

Noticing Edmund's unexpected silence but seemingly with no idea of the destruction she had caused, Soph all the while peered out over the edge of the crow's nest to check on the passing land below.

"We are nearing a town on the starboard shore," she said suddenly. But Edmund just nodded, his expression absent and detecting that the Explorer was in a world of his own making now, it was then that the warrioress finally turned to leave.

"I too bid you a good night then," she said softly, and headed towards the ladder.

Edmund barely even noticed her leave, too wrapped up as he was now in his own thoughts.

—

Saz stood apart from the others, the knife cupped in her hands, muttering under her breath as the others watched in the last shards of dying light, waiting for something to happen.

"What is she doing?" Dromeda asked flatly. "If she breaks my knife…"

"She's lighting it with a spell," Bethan hissed, not wanting to disturb Saz's concentration. She could vaguely remember Edmund performing the same trick before they'd entered the Temple of Ratacopeck and sure enough, even as the words fell from her tongue, there was a loud click and suddenly the tip of the knife burst into bright flames, making everyone hurry to shield their eyes.

"There," Saz said, turning back to the others with a triumphant grin. "I *knew* I could do it."

Dromeda though, just stared at her, wide-eyed.

"How did you do that?" he asked.

"Eliom taught me," Saz replied, looking pensive. "He only got a chance to show me how to do it once. I wasn't sure whether I'd be able to… I hadn't tried it before- not until now- so I just sort of…. guessed."

"Good guess," Nickolas congratulated her with a pat on the shoulder as he then passed to see to Meggie.

"Come on," he said gently, bending to pull the little element up by the arms. "Up you get."

Meggie complied with a groan of pain as she stood to her feet. Not daring to use her injured ankle though, she ended up doing a half hop, almost falling as Nickolas held her steady.

Dromeda meanwhile, was still amazed by Saz's spell.

"Will it burn out eventually? Will it melt the knife?" he asked in a flurry of interest. "And who is Eliom?"

Saz laughed at his burst of questions.

"Eliom is a wizard. A great wizard," she said, surprised somehow that he didn't know. "And no," she looked at the blazing metal proudly, "I don't think it will burn out… Although," and for a moment, her face was worried,

THE ENTITY OF SOULS

"to be honest with you, I don't know for sure. It depends if the spell's strong enough, I guess."

"Either way, I think we should get moving," Nickolas added, ducking slightly to allow Meggie to reach up and wrap her arm around his shoulder as best she could for support. "We do not know who else can see us now."

As if knowing that meant danger, Nickolas then drew his own knife and handed it to Dromeda without a word.

"Better to see where we're going than to be caught in the dark," Bethan justified.

And the group then set off, Saz in the lead, holding the light aloft.

The little flame gave them just enough light to see a good few feet ahead and for a long while, the others tried to keep together within the circle of its warm glow. After a less than a good hour of walking though, it soon became clear that staying with the others wasn't going to happen for Nickolas and Meggie.

"I'm sorry," the little element said timidly for the umpteenth time as her ankle gave way again. "I really am." Despite her best efforts, she could hardly walk, but still Nickolas just gave a weak smile.

The elder element's back was growing sore from the effort of stooping so low to support her and though he would never admit it aloud, he was still exhausted, the remnants of the wound in his chest a constant aching reminder of what he had been through.

And yet still his thoughts only seemed to be for her.

"Stop apologising," he said kindly. "It is hardly *your* fault that you are hurt."

But Meggie didn't answer.

In truth, she was finding it difficult to breathe with the effort of keeping up with Nickolas's long strides, and trying to block the pain from her ankle out of her mind was requiring nearly all of her concentration. Just like Nickolas, she was trying her best to hide her discomfort, but unlike him, she couldn't and very soon the little element was panting aloud, completely out of breath.

Nickolas heard the gasping, it was difficult to miss, yet though it worried him, he somehow knew it best to say nothing. Something told him that the last thing his companion would want him to do right then was ask after her wellbeing. He could see that she was trying her hardest to move, to carry on like nothing was wrong, for everyone's sakes. But finally glancing at the others and the circle of light ahead as it gradually shifted further and further away, the elder element knew that enough was enough and halting completely, he turned to her.

"Come on," he muttered, and then, before she could refuse, he was taking Meggie by the waist with one arm and, lifting her legs out from beneath her with the other, hoisting her up to his chest like a mother cradling her baby.

Searing pain burned through his wound as Meggie's weight pressed against his heart, but he ignored it as, shocked, the little element threw her own arms up about his neck.

"What are you *doing*?" she squealed. "Put me down! Put me down *now!*"

But Nickolas just shook his head.

"I am carrying you," he replied matter-of-factly and adjusting Meggie's body until it was comfortable for him to walk, he then set off at a faster pace, hurrying to catch up with the others.

For a moment, he was surprised at how light Meggie felt in comparison to the last time he'd carried her. Back then she'd been unconscious, her body overwhelmed with a different kind of pain, a different kind of shock, the shock of moving between worlds.

How things had changed since then.

"Please, put me down!" Meggie persisted. "Honestly! I can walk!" but still Nickolas was having none of it.

"Stop arguing. That ankle will not have a chance to heal properly unless you take the weight off it. And anyway," and he tried to smile again, "you almost sound like you *want* to be left behind."

He had, of course, been joking but when Meggie didn't reply, simply shifting her body in his arms again, Nickolas couldn't help but look into the younger element's face, a few inches from his own, in astonishment.

"You *want* to be left behind?" he challenged incredulously. "You *want* to stay here?"

"Oh. No."

This time, it was Meggie's turn to shake her head.

"No, I don't!" she said, but despite her words, there was definite hesitation in her voice and as Nickolas continued to stare at her in the almost-pitch-blackness, the little element then finally seemed to give way and breaking eye contact, she looked at the ground. She could feel the thrum of Nickolas's heart beating beneath her, deep and fast...

"Well," she stumbled, feeling suddenly like she needed to justify herself. "That's not to say I don't- I'm just not sure if I *should* go on..." her eyelids flickered. "I'm - Because- well, back in my world... I'm sort of-," but before she could give any further explanation, the pair were interrupted then by a shout from Saz and both turned their attention to the way ahead.

The element was in the lead still with Dromeda and the makeshift torch.

"Cliffs!" she was crying in triumph. "Up ahead!" and on hearing the news, Bethan and Bex, who were only a pace or two behind them, both surged forward, squinting into the blackness. Nickolas too, taking one last look at Meggie, his expression unreadable, then hurried on until they were level with the rest of the group.

Saz meanwhile held the light as high as she could and sure enough, in the distance the group were just able to make out the silhouette of something very large, dark and flat...

"We're nearly there!" Bex said. "We're nearly at the barrier! We *must* be!"

And straight away Saz and Bethan both let out long sighs, as if both of them had been holding their breath. But whilst the others were all smiles now, Dromeda looked uncertain.

"How can you possibly be sure?" he asked. "We are looking for a *rock*, not a cliff!"

Saz though, interrupted by throwing him a sceptical look.

"Boulders don't just appear from nowhere, Dromeda," she said. "This is the first rockface we've come across since we've been here. There are *bound* to be boulders around here somewhere, old parts of the cliff that have broken away. Belanna's boulder *has* to be here!"

It made perfect sense and Bethan and Bex both stifled laughs then as Dromeda's expression turned sheepish, before, taking his opportunity, Nickolas leaned in close to his old friend.

"Bet you wish you had never said anything now," he mocked.

Spirits were too high though for anything but play and instead of taking offence, Dromeda simply grinned naughtily.

"If you were not *hiding* behind someone else," he replied, gesturing at Meggie, "you know I would kill you where you stand." And the four female elements laughed as Nickolas smiled quietly.

The group then continued on their journey with double speed, all of them excited at the prospect of reaching the boundary into the land of the dead at any moment.

—

Soph entered the first cabin with quiet steps.

The room was dimly lit with a few candles, and in the faint light she could see, as well as hear, that Thom was fast asleep in his bed; Eliom hadn't emerged from the second cabin, where the elements apparently used to sleep; and that Elanore was nowhere to be seen. The sea captain, the warrior assumed, was either resting somewhere else or perhaps, still on deck, looking through her maps. But either way, it was none of these faces that she truly sought and her eyes scanning the cabin again, she soon found who she was looking for.

Fred, she noticed gratefully, was still awake and sitting on his bunk, waiting, she assumed, for her. But though he looked pleased to see her, his face, for a moment, revealing all the emotions he had expressed in the crow's nest, seeing her own expression, he soon frowned.

"What is it?" he murmured as she moved towards him, and sighing, Soph pulled off her cloak and weaponry sheath before sliding onto the bunk next to him, settling herself amongst the blankets. "What has happened? Are you well?" Her partner kept his voice low, being careful not to disturb the general peace in the cabin as he pulled her into a knowing embrace, slowly kissing the crown of her head.

Soph closed her eyes in contentment before giving a nod.

"Yes, I am well," she confessed. "But I fear that I may have done something… wrong," and just as she had expected he would, when he heard her tone of voice, Fred suddenly pulled away, holding her out at arm's length as he studied her face.

"What have you done?" the warrior asked sharply. Soph couldn't help but notice how suspicious he sounded but though she knew that she should be hurt by his mistrust, the warrioress also knew that she looked ashamed.

She *felt* ashamed.

"I am not entirely certain," she answered truthfully. "I was talking with Edmund and I fear that I may have spoken out of turn. I may have said something to injure him…"

"Injure him?"

Fred seemed to calm then, knowing as he did how sensitive Edmund had been over the past few weeks. He *was* human after all. It was only natural.

"I am sure it is nothing," he then said, obviously trying to comfort her. "Edmund has been under a lot of pressure recently. He has been through a lot. More perhaps than any human ever should."

But when Soph just made a neutral sound in the back of her throat, Fred couldn't help but chuckle softly, and reaching up, he stroked her hair.

"You do not believe me," he challenged. His warm touch, so long forgotten and yet so familiar, like no other, sent little shivers of pleasure down Soph's spine.

Her grey eyes widened.

"I believe you!" she retorted, before, remembering to lower her voice; "I just think that... You should have seen him, Fred," she whispered. "That is all."

But detecting that that *wasn't* all, Fred shifted into a more comfortable position on the bunk.

"Tell me," he mumbled simply. "What did you say to him? What troubles you so much?" and looking up into her partner's face, Soph knew that she would have to bear all.

"We were speaking of Bethan… I asked him about her and I think that maybe he begins to doubt whether she returns his regard."

Having spent less than a full day with her life-partner's companions, Soph was aware she had much to learn, but to her fear, when Fred grimaced but said nothing, she couldn't help but wonder if this was a bad sign.

"I always used to believe that we were so different from humans, that we had *grown* to be different, more superior," she mused, glancing down at her lap. For some reason she was twisting her hands together there. "But now I am not so certain…"

It was the most admittance he was likely to get out of her, but even so, she *felt* more than saw Fred's surprise as he gawped in mock shock. He had changed much since they'd last met, but his ability to make fun of her, to put her in her place had stayed the same.

"Is that doubt I hear?" he teased. "A *human* emotion? You, of all people, thinking that humans might not be too bad after all?"

Soph smiled at this. He always did know how to make her laugh and feeling a sudden rush of longing, she pulled him to her roughly, forcing him to encase his arms around her in a shell of possessiveness.

She'd missed conversations like these. They would tease each other for a little while, perhaps even argue half-heartedly but things would always go back to the way they were; peaceful.

She'd built relationships with many warrior men during the years that Fred had been gone. Not just to the human eye was she beautiful - Soph was considered one of the most stunning Mawreathan women in their colony and she knew it. Yet somehow, none of the warriors she'd been with, much as she'd cared for each of them in their own way, had ever quite been the same as her intended partner and sitting with him now, feeling his embrace, his soft heartbeat against hers, after so many years of being apart, gave her a secret thrill.

He made her feel safe, secure like no other, and for a warrioress with the strength of ten human men, and a fierce, ferocious independence, that was a big ask. She revelled in his power, much as she did her own. She was proud of it.

"We do not *feel* so differently from them," she carried on casually, almost forgetting her regret at upsetting Edmund. "And I must admit, seeing you now, like this," she looked up into Fred's face, "I am beginning to like it."

"You *like* me being more human? Showing my softer emotions?" Fred muttered into her hair and Soph nodded, resting her head against his chest with a small sigh.

"Our people are so consumed with strength, with the fight," he whispered, "they seem to forget all else."

"But you have always relished it," Soph replied conversationally, listening to the rhythm of her partner's breathing as it mingled with her own. "The fight is what we live for. And you are never a few feet away from that sword of yours."

"Neither are you," Fred pointed out. His voice was growing softer by the second as he relaxed. "Neither are *any* of our kind. I fight because I have to. It is my duty. I do not particularly care for it…"

Soph gave a little yawn. Fred's heart was beating slowly and loudly in her ear, like a single calming drum, making her feel drowsy.

"If you do not care for war," she carried on in a doze, "then I cannot understand why you do not care for the Sovereignty."

But unknowingly, she had gone too far and like a spark of lightning, Fred's entire body suddenly seemed to stiffen. She felt it, the moment he turned back to ice, to strength and anger, instantly warning her that she'd stepped over the line and detecting that she had ruined the moment, Soph immediately tried to go back.

"I am sorry," she said hurriedly. "This is not the right time…"

But it was too late.

"There is *never* a right time," Fred hissed, his manner still rigid and then, before she knew it, he was pushing her away from him again more firmly, making the whole bunk swing with the force as Soph almost lost her balance.

The warrioress spread her hands wide, her own anger rising. She couldn't help herself. They were back to the point, to the plague that would always fester between them. And she would fight her corner as fiercely as anyone.

"Why do you hate the Sovereignty so much, Fred? You just said so yourself, you only fight because it is your *duty* to do so. Well, the Sovereignty is your duty now!" she demanded.

But at this, Fred sprung to his feet, turning away from her, the bunk jolting crazily as he left, almost causing Soph to topple out of it again.

"I would rather be a warrior out in the world, fighting for my life and others' than a *statue*, Soph," he murmured dangerously, clearly still aware of where they were. "Because that is all the Sovereignty is reduced to now. A statue. A pointless *monument*."

There. He had said it and for a long moment, Soph just stared, her jaw slackening as the partner that she cherished finally seemed to spill out his feelings, throwing malice at all that she knew.

"The Sovereign has no power!" Fred spat, his voice still low. "And never will! He is just required to *sit there* upon a throne of pride for the rest of his days, giving pointless, meaningless orders…"

"That is not true!" Soph gasped. "And you know it! Omegan fought in battle. He *died* in battle! He made the choice to fight. So could you if you were the Sovereign!"

But Fred was starting to pace now, his footfall silent.

"I do not have the wisdom to lead our people, Soph!" he retorted. "And that is the end of it!"

"But you do!" and leaping to her own feet then, in a desperate appeal for him to see reason, Soph glared at him right in the face, her pride wounded. It always seemed to come down to this argument and she was sick of it.

"There is no one wiser than you!" she cried, her voice almost loud now. "You have been out in the world for years, far away from our colony. You have seen more than many of us ever have! You know more than any of us ever could! Do not pretend! You knew that this day would come! That you would be required to take up your place…"

Fred turned on her.

"Yes, I *did* know that this day would come," he growled, his own voice rising, "but I hoped I would be long dead by then. Slain by an enemy, as Crag was. Given a warrior's death!" And much as she had hoped, Soph could see from his face that she wasn't going to win him over with this argument.

She'd never seen Fred so passionate about anything before. He was almost shaking with defiance, his anger like a thick scent in the air. And not knowing what else she could do, she changed tactics.

"If you would only return to Mawreath, you would have the power to change things," she tried more quietly. "You could ensure that the Sovereignty is demolished, if that is what you see fit…"

But though, straight away, Fred seemed to soften all over again, clearly as fed up as she was of arguing, she saw the sadness in his eyes, felt it in her heart like a physical wound.

"Why are you saying these things Soph?" he asked then, all fight gone. "You told me that you came because you wanted to be with me. So why-?"

But seeing where this comment was leading, it was then that Soph dashed forwards and regardless of everything, threw herself into his arms.

"I did, I *do*," she whispered into his chest. "I… I only want you to make the right decision…"

Yet though she thought it was over, for now, Fred soon pushed her away again.

"And that is the very point," he said sharply. "It is *my* decision and mine alone. You *cannot* make it for me, no matter how much you might want to!"

"*Your* decision?"

That had done it, and suddenly, Soph scowled, her face, in that instant, ugly and terrifying to any foe.

"If I was *male*, if I was Crag, you would listen to me!" she exclaimed. "If I was *male*, I could take your place!"

"Nonsense," Fred argued, before, pausing for a second as if realising something, he started again; "I can see why they let you come. They wanted you to *persuade* me-"

Soph let out a groan.

"Not this again!" she hissed in despair, closing her eyes as if to block out her frustration. "Stop saying that! I came because I *wanted* to-"

"I know why you *say* you came," Fred insisted hotly. "But how do I know this is not all a charade to make me weak? How do I know they did not send you to *confuse* me? A few smiles, a few kisses, then I will do what the council want? Is that it?"

Soph gawped at him afresh then, hurt evident in her face and even Fred found himself wondering if he'd gone too far. But then;

"I came-!" Soph cried, her voice shaking with badly-controlled emotion. "I came because… I love you." And having spoken the words aloud, she soon looked away. "Even though, right now, I really do not understand *why*…"

Her voice seemed to trail off into the thick silence that followed and as if suddenly tired of it all, Fred covered his face with his hands. The fight seemed to have gone from them both now and there was a tense hush, followed by a particularly noisy snore from Thom – their loud voices were obviously not enough to wake him – before either of the pair then spoke again.

"Perhaps being more human is not as good as we imagined," Fred muttered eventually and as an admission of his guilt, he removed his hands from his face, turning to look at his partner properly. "Doubt, for one, is not something I wish to feel…"

Soph smiled for a moment, but though the expression was dry, Fred seemed to take hope from it.

"I am sorry Soph. I did not mean to distrust you," and in a moment of decision, he moved back towards her and taking her by the waist, pulled her close as if nothing had happened.

Soph's frustration seemed to melt with his warmth.

"I know," she only just managed to speak.

Like so many of their arguments, she knew that all of this would soon be forgotten, and already she felt relieved.

Everything resolved for now, the couple then stood for a few moments, in the calm after the storm, just breathing deeply, relishing in each other, listening each to the other's heartbeat and Thom's snores, before, as if having a sudden thought, Soph then pulled back and staring up into Fred's worn-out eyes, she looked almost afraid.

"But tell me something, foolish and *human* as it sounds…" she started.

And Fred, clearly deciding that there had been enough conflict for one day, gave his own smile.

"Anything."

"Do you care for me?"

The question came out all in a hurry, as if she wasn't quite sure how to say it.

"Because after my talk with Edmund… I hoped… I thought perhaps…"

But Soph paused as she saw the smile gradually starting to spread its way across Fred's face, now joined by the sparkle in his eye.

"Of course I do," he muttered, his voice oddly throaty, and as if to prove it, he then pulled her towards him and without further ado, kissed her full on the lips.

The warrior's touch was strong yet also soft and familiar and realising that it was this feeling they'd both been waiting for all along, the lovers quickly seemed to mould together, lost once again in their moment of just being as one, as they always should have been and always now would be…

After a while - how long a while, neither could have said - it was Soph who then broke away, grinning.

Fred hadn't professed his undying love or declared that he would die for her, but, to her, *this* was more than enough. She knew that she would never hear those three words of affection spoken aloud - that wasn't the usual warrior's way - but somehow it didn't bother her. Although he was more human than before, he wasn't *that* human.

And neither was she.

The warrioress gave a laugh, but just as she opened her mouth to speak again, it was then that they were interrupted as the cabin door flew open and Elanore swept down the steps, her coat loose about her shoulders.

She seemed to be in a hurry, but spotting Fred and Soph awake, the sea captain soon paused, her face brightening.

"Ah, good. Someone's up," she remarked. "Both of you, I need your help," and glancing at each other, a secret meaning passing between them, Fred and Soph moved apart, just as they had before.

"What sort of help do you need?" Fred asked, standing to attention as Soph moved to grab her cloak and sheath. "We are more than willing to give it."

"Edmund just reported," Elanore hurried, "we're nearly there! We've nearly reached the town of Ophelius!" And looking briefly at the snoring Thom, she then turned back to the couple. "But I need your help. Very soon, we're going to be docking for the night…"

THIN BOUNDARY

"And how long are you planning to stay?" the dockhand asked, his eyes squinting slightly in the bright sunrise. "A day? A week? Longer?"

"Um…"

Elanore looked to Fred for support but the warrior could only glance at Soph and Thom beside him before turning back to the empty gangplank for the third time.

"Indefinitely," he answered for her and pulling out a very blunt slate pencil and a roll of parchment, the dockhand soon turned from Elanore to Fred and back again, his face mildly questioning.

"Name?" he said blandly.

Elanore glanced at the gangplank herself.

No one had seen any sight of either Edmund or Eliom that morning and it worried her.

"Elanore of Lordan," she replied decisively.

The man wrote this down and then looked up, boredom etched into his aging face. He obviously asked the same questions day-in, day-out and to him, this day was no different to any of the others piled high behind him.

"And how many of you are there?"

The question was clearly a routine one, but Fred automatically touched the sword at his side and noticing his movement, the dockhand couldn't help but give a nervous flinch.

Perhaps this day *would* be different after all.

There was something strange about these people, no mistake, something suspicious, and although he tried to pretend he thought otherwise, the man replaced the paper and pencil with a shaky hand.

"Why do you need to know?" the warrior meanwhile asked, his voice calm.

The dockhand opened his mouth to respond, timidly searching the eyes of the four beings standing before him, but as he reached the shortest, Thom, it was then that he heard footsteps, and glancing up, could only watch in wonderment as a tall, cloaked figure in white paced towards them down the wooden plank.

The figure's face was set and expressionless, almost as if carved out of stone and glimpsing the staff of wood at his side, the simple man instantly recognised that here, before him, was a wizard of the highest order, a being of great power.

The dockhand visibly gulped.

This day was *definitely* going to be different and as the white stranger marched towards them, the man couldn't help but stare, his eyes wide with awe.

He'd never seen a wizard before - people of the town rarely had - but he'd heard the stories, the myths and the legends, just like everyone else…

The others meanwhile, hearing movement, turned to greet Eliom as he approached, all welcomes a little more subdued than usual. None of them had seen the wizard since the previous day and none could mistake the fact that he looked worse-for-wear for it. His face was even more drawn than it had been before, almost white enough to match his robes and his eyes were blood-shot and watery.

It was obvious that he needed rest but hadn't been granted any. Something, whatever it was, was haunting him and each and every one of them dreaded to think what it might be…

"Have you seen Edmund?" Elanore asked the wizard softly, trying but failing not to sound concerned. Their leader too, had disappeared for the night after they'd docked, hardly speaking to anyone.

"He is coming," Eliom stated. To everyone's silent relief, his voice sounded much the same as its usual tranquil self. And sure enough, even as the words reached their ears, it was then that the Explorer appeared at the top of the gangplank.

As if drawn, all eyes seemed to fall on Edmund as he marched down towards the group, his dirtying cloak flapping in the breeze. Yet, despite the attention, his face, like his friend's, was set and as if he couldn't see those looks, some of concern, some of blank greeting rising to meet him, the Explorer simply brushed through his friends towards the still-gawping dockhand, his own expression unmoving.

"Here, this should be enough," he muttered, thrusting his hand at the man.

In his clenched fist were five gold coins and no one could mistake the way the dockhand's eyes lit up as he saw the flash of tinkling metal.

"Um, excuse me sir…" he positively stammered, "the cost is-I mean to say it's only-" but Edmund was already halfway down the jetty and turning to Fred, the next in line, as the others, exchanging uncertain glances, followed on after, he held his hand out to return the load.

"Keep it," the warrior murmured as he moved passed the surprised dockhand. "Just make sure you take extra care of our ship until we return."

For a moment it was all the man could do to stare in astonishment at the golden coins before, turning to look on the warrior's retreating back, he gave an odd smile.

"I will, sir!" he stuttered with a wave, as the group hurried away from him. "I will!!"

In the early morning light, the cliffs seemed to loom even higher than before, giving the elements hope with each passing step.

In the light of day, they were white, bright chalky white, standing brilliant against the scrubby brown terrain of the prairie and the reddish-blue sky. But whilst they stood out like a shining beacon against the dullness, leaving none of them without the question of how and why the rock faces came to be there in the first place, all attention lay on the path ahead where none could mistake the promising shape of many giant stones, a forest of them clustered at the base of the cliffs.

The group hurried on without a word, all of them keen to reach the boulders as soon as possible, to find what they had come so far to reach.

"I can't see any that look like a tree," Bex commented as they came to the first of the rocks and scrutinised the way ahead like an expert studying a piece of artwork. "What would a rock shaped like a tree even *look* like anyway?"

Dromeda shrugged.

"It depends on what you *think* a rock shaped like a tree would look like," he replied dryly, and Bex glared at him, making both Saz and Bethan laugh.

"Hold on though! I've just had a thought!" Saz then quickly sobered, making the others look at her. "How would Belanna even know what a tree *is*? There *are* no trees in this place!"

It was a good point, a very worrying one in fact, but before it could go any further, Bethan held up a hand.

"There is a tree," and she gestured at herself and Bex. "We saw it on the way to our meeting place in the City. I'm pretty sure it was dead, or at least *dying*, but it *was* a tree…"

"I'm sure once we see the rock, it'll be obvious," Bex soon added with growing conviction. "We'll find it in no time." And turning to the nearest elder element, who just happened to be Nickolas, she gave a small smile, as if waiting for his assurance.

Nickolas nodded but he said nothing, too concerned about waking Meggie to have his say.

The little element had been asleep for over an hour now. The pain of her ankle coupled with the trauma of the last day or two having finally got the better of her, she now lay in the elder element's arms like one dead, but for her breathing and the occasional quiet mumble as she spoke in her dreams.

Even though she was very light, Nickolas's arms were beginning to ache with the strain of carrying extra weight; yet although he wanted nothing more than to stop and rest, maybe even suggest that Dromeda carry her for a while, he would glance down at that quiet, calm face and know that he couldn't. Or, more accurately, that he *wouldn't*.

There was something about her, something so fragile under that stubborn exterior that somehow fascinated him. The way her little chest slowly rose and fell as she breathed; the way her eyelids fluttered a little every now and again, her lips gently parted; the way that little tuft of hair hung out of place just below her hairline, moving in the breeze... Somehow he found himself simply captivated.

As Nickolas watched her this time, however, it was then that the little woman shifted and suddenly, just like that, her eyes snapped open.

"Oh!" she yelped, seeing her companion's gaze on hers and shocked, the elder element almost dropped her as he glanced away, his whole face suddenly burning.

"Sorry!" he cried, clearly embarrassed. "I did not mean to startle you. Are you all right?"

But Meggie, seeming a little disorientated for a moment or two, simply rubbed her forehead with a thumb and index finger before tucking the stray hairs Nickolas had noticed, back into place.

"Yes," she said sluggishly. "I'm fine."

Her little brow crinkled.

"Though I just had the *weirdest* dream about a man in a black cloak... He kept calling my name, but every time I tried to see who he was, he kept turning away and I-" but she stopped, and feeling it safe to look at her again, Nickolas did so. The little element's eyebrows were furrowed, obviously troubled by what she had seen, still caught up in her confusion. But then as she blinked and her head cleared, slow recognition began to dawn on her face and all of a sudden, she was sitting up, wide awake, causing Nickolas to almost drop her all over again.

"How long have you been carrying me like this?!" she cried, squirming in his arms to meet his eye.

Nickolas fixed his face into unreadableness. Already he could see where this was leading.

"Only a little while," he replied. "Just an hour or so. You needed some sleep, so I let you rest."

But just as he knew she would, Meggie was having none of it.

"An hour?!" she echoed, looking horrified and then, as if she had finally come to her full senses, her face was suddenly stern and her voice dropped to an angry, determined whisper.

"Stop," she commanded. "Stop now."

Nickolas glanced up at the others. They were a good few feet ahead now, eager to get on, and not wanting to make a scene, he found himself dropping back even further.

"I think *I* should be the one who decides when we stop," he retorted, trying to make light of the situation. "I am the one carrying you, after all." But teasing wasn't going to stop her and somehow, he knew it.

"I mean it Nickolas!" she said more forcefully. "Stop! Stop now!" and without warning, the little element began to wriggle in his arms all over again and then, before he could stop her, she was kicking her legs and positively writhing about, struggling to be free.

She was determined, that much was clear, but so, suddenly, was Nickolas too and for a moment, the elder element, instead of letting her go, just clung on all the harder, making her shout even more.

"Nickolas! Put me down! Put me down now!"

"Stop struggling!"

"Put me down!"

"No!"

"Put. Me. Down. This. Second!"

"Will you stop-?!"

A different voice then cut across them both.

"What's going on?!"

Disturbed by the sudden shouts, the others had clearly abandoned the boulders ahead and turning back to the pair, both Bethan and Saz were now hurrying back towards them, looking concerned.

"What's happening?!" Bethan demanded again, looking from one element to the other. "Is it your ankle?" But instead of replying, Meggie just gave another kick with her good leg.

"Put me down!" she hissed firmly. "Now!" and not wanting to cause any more fuss, Nickolas finally complied. Stiffly, he lowered Meggie to the floor, wincing as the still-healing wound in his chest gave a twinge.

"What is going on here?" Dromeda echoed as he also came back to investigate, Bex right behind him. He too glanced from Nickolas to Meggie before repeating the question.

"How should *I* know?" Nickolas said between gritted teeth, looking to Meggie for some sort of answer. Even though she was standing – one foot on the ground, the other, troubled foot, not quite - he still kept a steady hand on her shoulder as if afraid she might fall.

"Nothing," the little element replied hotly and then, obviously regretting the fuss she'd made, she softened. "Nothing, really. I just… I think that Nickolas shouldn't have to carry me anymore. He's barely slept and he's-"

But before she could even finish her sentence, the other five had all started talking at once.

"But your ankle, Meggie-!"
"You have to let him carry you! You can barely walk-!"
"Maybe let Dromeda take you for a while…"
Dromeda looked put-out.
"No! It will slow me down!"

It was Nickolas, however, who spoke the loudest. Raising a hand, he closed his eyes in irritation.

"Just let me rest for a while," he said forcefully, "and I will be fine to carry on just as we were."

"But we may not *have* a while," Dromeda replied and knowing that he was right, the group fell into silence. "You said it yourself. We need to get moving. Who knows what else could happen the longer we stay out here? I doubt the Builder is done with us yet."

But Nickolas just looked at his friend as if he'd only just noticed him.

"Why are *you* worried?" he retorted. "As far as *you* are concerned, this place can throw anything at us and we will survive."

The others were surprised to hear him talk like this when only a matter of hours before he had been the one encouraging them on as Dromeda had argued exactly that. The other element however, had clearly seen sense.

"I am worried about the rest of us ending up like *her*," Dromeda argued, gesturing at Meggie's bandaged ankle. "I hate to remind you, but we *can* be injured. You said that yourself too!" and Saz, seeing that a pointless argument was about to brew all over again, stepped forward.

"Look, Dromeda," she said firmly. "Surely you can carry her for a little while or so?"

But when Dromeda looked at Meggie, his expression was uncomfortable.
"I told you," he mumbled. "She will slow me down."

It had to be the oddest excuse – but something in the way he spoke made the others think that whatever his real reasons for not wanting to help, he wasn't going to change his mind any time soon.

"I couldn't possibly slow you down any more than I already am," Meggie snorted and hearing the defeat in her voice, Nickolas shook his head.

"You are *not* slowing us down," he muttered angrily. Again, he was reminded of their conversation from before, Meggie's almost insistence on being left behind, and again it baffled him.

Why was she talking like this? He knew it wasn't just because she was feeling guilty for being what she considered to be a burden. It was something else, something deeper and though she'd started to try and explain the little element had never got the chance to finish…

What was she hiding?

"So, what are we going to do then?" Bex asked. "We can't just stand here and argue all day."

It was another good point and as silence fell amongst the group, Nickolas glanced at Meggie again before answering.

"My suggestion is that you all carry on ahead. I will rest for a little while and then, when I am ready, I will bring Meggie along with me," he said.

Dromeda sighed.

"That is the worst idea I have ever heard," he retorted. "It could take you *ages* to catch up." The elder element looked to the cliffs. "And anyway, how will you know where to find us? There are *hundreds* of boulders up ahead. You will be lost in minutes."

"Dromeda could carry Meggie a little way, just until Nickolas is ready," Bethan offered, trying the idea again.

"If it's a big problem, *we* could even carry her," Saz added, gesturing at both herself and Bethan, and Bethan gave an eager nod.

"Maybe we could make some sort of stretcher…" Bex suggested.

"There's the blanket…"

"No, I think we should do what *I* said…"

Meanwhile, as the others began to talk over each other again, quarrelling as if she wasn't there, Meggie just stood there, Nickolas's hand still on her shoulder, staring at the ground, growing more and more frustrated by the minute.

The point was, though she didn't dare make it aloud; she didn't want to be carried by anyone. She didn't want to be anyone's burden, anyone's problem. But whilst she felt a stubborn resistance to the help being offered, she also knew that it was more than that.

You almost sound like you want to be left behind.

Nickolas's words from hours before sprang suddenly to her mind.

She knew he had been teasing her, all be it a little coldly, but still the sentence had stuck.

Did she want to be left behind?

She didn't think so, and yet something, whatever it may be, *was* making her feel reluctant to go on and not just because of the pain it cost her to walk or the embarrassment it cost her to be carried like a broken thing.

Was it *fear*? Fear of what lay ahead? Of what they would find beyond the boulder shaped like a tree, beyond the barrier between this world and the next?

Partly, perhaps. But still that wasn't completely it.

Something was holding her back. Something she didn't fully yet understand and all of a sudden, as if expecting him to tell her the answer, to explain, Meggie couldn't help but glance up at Nickolas.

The elder element wasn't looking at her. He was still arguing, still trying to make the others see sense and with a sigh, Meggie shifted to stand to her full height, both feet on the ground, ready to give her best shout, ready to make them stop.

THE ENTITY OF SOULS

As she did so though, it was only then that she let out a gasp of realisation.

The sound was quiet, barely a sound at all, but it was noticeable enough to make all conversation cease and suddenly everyone was looking at her all over again.

"My ankle!" the element whispered, biting her lip and straight away misunderstanding, Nickolas, took her by both hands.

"Careful!" he started. "Lean on me..." but feeling suddenly impatient, Meggie, shook her head.

"No!" she cried. "No! It's fine! My ankle, it's fine! It doesn't hurt!" and as if to prove the fact, she shrugged Nickolas's hands from her shoulders and reaching down, began, with shaking hands of her own, to unravel the bandage from her foot.

The binding was tight and it took her a good minute or so, but as her ankle finally fell free, it was then the turn of the others to gawp, for true to her word, the swelling and bruising on the little element's ankle, which had changed to the shade of a ripe plum fruit only hours before, had almost completely disappeared. Less than a day ago the bone had been broken, she'd been unable to put *any* pressure on it but now, the limb looked as good as new.

Meggie walked a few ginger steps forward under the wide, disbelieving eyes of the rest of the group.

There was no pain. No pain at all. It was like nothing had ever happened and remembering something else, Meggie looked down at her wrist, the wrist she had injured when the Digger had attacked her those few days ago, the wrist that had been red and sore and twisted and until that moment, almost completely forgotten. Now there wasn't so much as a bruise or a mark on her skin. It had all completely healed and suddenly overwhelmed, she gave a burst of surprised laughter, breaking the silence that had fallen across the plain.

Looking up into the faces of the rest of the group as they just stared, her mouth then slid into a smile.

"Well *that* solves a few problems," she remarked. "I can carry *myself*."

—

The town of Ophelius was buzzing with life as the morning started to draw on.

It was the day of the weekly market, and traders and buyers hurried from here to there, tending to their stock, exporting and selling, haggling and chattering, no one paying the slightest attention as a group of travellers containing two Mawreathan warriors, a wizard, a dwarf and a ship's captain, all led by a stern-looking man in a rugged cloak, pushed through the side streets on their way to the town centre.

Thom, who lagged at the back of the group, gawping at the wide variety of buildings ranging from very short to towering wooden halls, paused not for the first time to stare at a passing stranger. The woman had a certain feline elegance about her, a certain elvishness, and realising that she was indeed, an elf, the dwarf couldn't help but be reminded of the great elf queen, Emmine and the short time he had spent amongst her people with the element, Bex. Perhaps this elf came from Emmine's domain and was here on her travels, perhaps trading, perhaps still in search for the lost elven men. Either way, thinking about Bex, Thom couldn't help but feel a little saddened. It all felt so long ago now, almost another lifetime since he had broken into the element's home and the pair had set out together on the road to Stanzleton, little knowing what really lay ahead of them...

"Come on," Thom heard Fred's voice in his ear as the warrior, falling back to match the little dwarf's stride, soon took him by the shoulder to chivvy him along. "Keep moving."

Thom tore his gaze away from the crowds.

"Humans are not the only beings here," he mused in return. "I do not know why, but it surprises me."

Fred though, just frowned.

"Ophelius is a popular port," he offered briskly, "come on," and he pushed the dwarf in front of him. "We are not here to sightsee."

Thom gave what sounded like a disgruntled cough but soon quickened his pace, making Soph, who was by Fred's side, hide a little smile of amusement.

"Like to buy a fish, miss?" a gap-toothed youth asked, suddenly obstructing the warrioress's path with a devilish gleam in his eye. "You can have even have this one for free if you like, a pretty thing like you..." he said with a wink.

Fred's eyebrows rose.

"No, thank you." Soph turned the young man down kindly before glancing at Fred, laughter twitching at the corners of her mouth. Both warriors knew that Soph was very attractive, especially to younger humans who most often mistook her for a woman in her early twenties. The joke though, was on them, for if any had known her *real* age and what she really was, many would almost certainly be less keen...

"Well, feel free to come back!" the man called after her hopefully as the group continued and very soon disappeared into the crowds.

"This is definitely one of the largest towns I've seen!" Elanore commented to Eliom as they walked a few paces behind the striding Edmund. The wizard seemed almost back to his usual self. Quiet and calm, with a placid look on his face, he walked purposefully after their leader.

"It is almost considered a city now, I believe," he replied conversationally and hearing the odd note in his voice, Elanore glanced at him, feeling curious.

"Have you been here before then?" she asked and his eyes never leaving Edmund's back, Eliom gave a tiny frown.

"Many, many years ago, yes. Long before it was renamed."

"Oh?" Before the sea captain could ask any more though, a seller had barred her way and she was sucked back into the crowd. It didn't take her long to re-emerge as Elanore dodged expertly aside, but half-running to catch up with Eliom's long gait, she couldn't help but notice how no one ever seemed to get in *his* way. Already she'd had to work hard to cut and duck through the busy streets; whereas a path appeared to simply melt through the throng before the wizard, as people merely *stepped away*.

That's magic for you, she reasoned. *And fear.*

"This place used to be known as Mithwaya, before the prophet Ophelius came," Eliom then continued, as if they had never been parted and unable to help herself, Elanore looked confused.

"Mithwaya? That's no human name," she pondered aloud.

Eliom gave a little smile this time.

"No, indeed," he replied, clearly impressed with the captain's knowledge. "It was once an elvish settlement, but the humans took over and the town gradually spread inland."

Elves. The word sent a thrill through the captain as she glanced around her in fresh amazement.

"Elves lived here?"

And still, Eliom continued to stride onwards, seemingly unmoved.

"Yes, indeed. Although it was a smaller colony back then. Much smaller." He too looked about him, as if reminiscing. "And much quieter too."

"Wait," and as if realising for the first time what he was saying, Elanore then almost stopped in her tracks, the crowd swallowing her up again for less than a moment before she resurfaced again, incredulous. "Do you mean to tell me that last time you were here, was when the *elves* were here?!"

"They were growing fewer in number then, even in those days," the wizard confirmed, before glancing up as they passed a block of wooden houses, three storeys high, set out in a central square. "The buildings were much different, much more *natural* back then. The elves used to live more at one with their surroundings. It is often only humans who feel the need to build. Although," his eyes flickered a little, "of course, this was all before the elven men…" and he paused a moment, as if in thought, before continuing. "A small minority of elves still reside here. If you are lucky, you might see some."

The sea captain seemed to be in her element.

"So, you've met elvish men?" she hurried, seemingly stunned by this more than anything else. The elven men had disappeared centuries upon centuries ago…

Instead of replying as she'd hoped however, Eliom soon surprised her.

"Yes, I have," he said with a grimace, before, seeing Elanore's shocked expression, he continued with uncharacteristic sharpness; "and may it be said that they were not *all* the noble beings that legend speaks of. It was pride that led to their extinction. Pride and nothing more. They had no reason to go to war."

Elanore didn't dare think that the wizard could possibly be referring to *the* war; the war of the third century, the war started by man and finished by man, but more importantly in this case, the war that had come about over a *thousand* years ago, almost as far back as when records began.

Could the wizard have *possibly* been there? Could she even *fathom* that?

If what he said was true though, if he had truly met with elvish men then…

Elanore tried not stutter, but somehow, she couldn't help it.

"The gr-great war, from long ago?" she breathed, her head spinning a little as she realised just how incredibly young, how incredibly *small* she was. "I grew up with the tales, the stories but-"

"And all of them may not have been truthful," was all Eliom had to say. He didn't seem to want to push the point any further than that though, and as he fell back into aloof calmness all over again, it was only then that Elanore realised that the rest of the group had stopped.

Ahead of them now was a vast market square crammed full of yet more stalls. Hordes of people swarmed around them like flies to a feast as they came and went - the smell of fish and spices strong on the air - and for a shuddering moment, Elanore couldn't help but be reminded of Stanzleton, the port Edmund's brother had razed to the ground in his frantic attempts to kidnap the elements.

It too had been a bustling, sparkling place, filled to the brim with life.

But not any more…

Quickly, forcefully, Elanore pushed those thoughts aside as her eyes were then drawn to the centre of the chaos where a great wooden statue stood tall above the crowds. The carved figure was that of an old man staring wistfully into the skies above. In one of his hands lay an open book, in the other, an orb decorated with sea pearls…

The sea captain stared long and hard.

Ophelius.

Despite his death at least a hundred years ago, *this* was the man who had brought them here. This was the town's namesake, the so-called prophet who had brought them all to this point.

The man who was going to save the elements.

Taking a moment to look themselves, Thom, Fred, Soph and Eliom then surrounded Edmund, waiting for his next instructions. The noise of activity all around them was almost deafening.

"We need to find a guide!" the Explorer had to shout, the first words he'd spoken to them for a while. "And quickly!"

"A guide?" Thom repeated in confusion, chewing on a small titbit of fish he'd 'borrowed' along the way. "I thought you had been here before!"

But though it was true, Edmund, for some reason chose to ignore this comment, and turned to scan the crowd, the others following suit despite the fact that none of them really knew what or *who* they were looking for.

As the rest of the group were distracted, it was then that Eliom approached Edmund's side and leaning in close, his staff pointed away from him as the crowds bustled by, he whispered so that only the Explorer could hear.

"Where is the tomb?"

It was the first time the long-time friends had faced each other since Eliom's vision of death. But even though he stood so close, Edmund didn't seem to want to look at his companion. As far as he was concerned, he was too busy studying the throng around him; or at least, *looking* like he was, to worry about meeting the wizard's eye...

"It's on the outskirts of the town, but we'll need transport," the Explorer replied, equally as quietly. "It's a fair way and it'll be difficult manoeuvring through these crowds."

Unshaken, Eliom too stared into the square before them, watching as the multitude of life flooded past.

There was then only a short pause before he spoke again.

"I would ask how you are," he started. "However-" but straight away, Edmund cut him off.

"I'm fine," he said, before, sensing the heavy silence he had caused between them, he finally chanced a glance at his friend. "Really. I'm fine. Don't worry about me." Even as the pair met eye contact at last though, both of them knew that he was lying. It didn't take a wizard to see it.

"Do not doubt."

Eliom's voice was nothing more than a mumble, making Edmund marvel for a moment how it was that he could hear it above everything else in the great mass of noise.

What he *didn't* marvel at, however, was how the wizard, as usual, seemed to have got straight to the point, straight to the crux of what he was thinking, what he was feeling, neither of which he wanted to deal with right then and drawing himself up, the Explorer gave a sigh.

"We need some sort of carriage-handler," he said firmly, turning his attention back to the job at hand. "And not an expensive one either-"

But just then, as if by some strange fate, an almighty cry rang out, cutting him off and Edmund gave a start as he heard his own name bellowed from across the square, making several people in the crowd turn their heads.

"Edmund of Tonasse! *Is that you?!*"

And recognising the voice, a voice he hadn't heard for a long time, a slow smile began to spread across Edmund's face as he turned to watch a giant of a man push his way towards them through the mass of people.

The man was certainly extremely large – he towered well above the rest of the horde - and extremely scruffy with hair tumbling to his shoulders, a wild look in his eye and a chin hidden by a rough beard. His face was kindly, open, but the smile that spread across it as he saw Edmund only helped to emphasise the presence of a huge scar that stretched from his nose all the way to the lobe of his left ear, red-raw and ugly.

Nearing the Explorer, the man then broke into a run, positively shoving the crowds aside until, leaping forward, he grabbed Edmund and pulling him into his arms, delivered him a gigantic bear-hug, the Explorer almost disappearing from view for a moment in the fat folds of the man's multiple cloaks.

"Martynio!" Edmund cried once he'd managed to extract himself from the giant man's arms. "Just the man I need!"

Martynio's grin only widened. But realising that Edmund wasn't alone, he soon turned to survey the rest of the group, his expression waning a little as he saw the two warriors and the dwarf, all armed, all looking serious.

His gaze lingered on Eliom that little bit longer as he noticed the wizard's staff.

"What are you doing back here?" he then asked, patting Edmund on the back. His hands were three times the size of a normal man's. "And with such a…" he shot a look back at Eliom, "interesting crew?"

Remembering why they were there, Edmund's own smile faded.

"It's a long story," he said hurriedly. "For another time. But I need your help." And he stared up into his new companion's face hopefully. "All I need to know is; can you take us to the tomb?"

Whatever the Explorer may or may not have expected however, as soon as the question had been asked, Martynio's face fell

"At *this* time of day?" He sucked air sharply between his teeth. "It could take an age! Plus, there are laws about that sort of thing nowadays…" Surprisingly though, Edmund seemed ready for this kind of answer, and biting his lip, he soon began to rummage in the inside of his cloak.

"I'll pay you everything I have left, if that's what it'll take," he started. "We *need* a carriage-handler and there are none better than you…" He seemed to be making a show of searching for the money, taking a particularly long time about it, and before long, the others realised why as, flushing with pride, Martynio soon waved a hand.

"I don't want your money," he said with a sigh and then, taking a glance back the way he had come as if trying to make his decision, he turned back. "If that's what you really need, then this one's on me. For old times' sake. But I'm telling you, there'll still be problems…"

"Look, can you help us or not?"

It was Thom who had spoken up so impatiently and Martynio, looking down at the dwarf so many feet below him, couldn't help but smile again, albeit a little uneasily.

These people really were strange and so *solemn*...

"I can certainly try," he said with a twinkle in his eye. "Edmund was right. I'm just the man you need." And the deal struck, he reached out a hand and Edmund took it, before, looking once more with obvious uncertainty at Eliom, the giant man then turned, beckoning for the group to follow him.

"This way," he said and the companions soon found themselves being led not through but *around* the outskirts of the square, each of them struggling to keep up with Martynio's gaping strides as he powered through the crowds before making a sudden turn down a side alley, to lead them along a narrow lane back towards the docks.

Running to keep up with the others, Thom looked up at Fred.

"What is a *carriage-handler*?" he spat gruffly. But even as he asked the question, so he soon found out the answer, as already, Martynio began to slow, turning yet another corner only to emerge into a wide street flanked by warehouses. The buildings were tall and unkempt with vast metal doors and at the furthest end from them stood what appeared to be some kind of enormous animal pen, the gate, taller even than Martynio, locked with a padlock and hefty chain.

"I don't usually wake them on market days," Martynio remarked, as he pulled a jangling set of keys from his belt, and Thom glanced at Fred again. The dwarf looked more than a little uneasy.

"What are *'them'*...?" Soph muttered under her breath. Unlike Thom however, the warrioress looked only intrigued as the group then watched Martynio unlock the padlock, wrestle the gate open and disappear inside the pen, pulling the gate tightly closed behind him.

Elanore suddenly let out a little groan.

"I hope these aren't what I think they are," she said, sounding wary.

The others glanced at her.

"What do you think they are?" Thom echoed, automatically reaching for his axe.

The sea captain grimaced.

"I've dealt with these creatures before, in a few other human colonies. They're great strong brutes, but mighty hard to tame."

"Should we be worried?" Fred asked. He too, was reaching for his weapon, his automatic reaction to uncertainty. But Elanore just gave a wan smile.

"Probably not.... I just had a bad experience once," she said. The sea captain didn't get any time to elaborate though before Martynio then reappeared at the gate. He looked a little flushed and out of breath but still pretty jovial.

"We ready?" Edmund asked and the great man nodded.

"They're up and awake at least," he remarked, then, smiling at Edmund; "Alora remembers you well."

Edmund looked slightly amused.

"Well, they do say Ramundas always remember a face," he commented.

"Ra-*what*?!" Thom spurted hesitantly from the back of the group. But to his growing horror, Elanore frowned.

"Ramunda," she repeated. "Just what I thought," and then; "Elvish creatures originally, I think. Quickest way to travel long distances between towns."

The dwarf looked startled.

"But I thought that the tomb would be *here*!" he retorted grumpily. "I do not like the sound of these… Ramunda." When no one made to answer him though, Fred just smiled and patted his friend on the shoulder, more relaxed now that he understood what was before them.

"They are just like mules," he reassured him. "Nothing more."

Elanore snorted quietly.

Martynio meanwhile, leaned on the gate.

"I'd ask you not to aggravate them if you can possibly help it. They seem a bit… *irritable* this morning. Always know when a market day's here…" he said placidly.

Edmund nodded.

"Of course." Turning to the others he then stepped forward. "Let's go," and as Martynio threw the gate open, the Explorer walked into the pen followed first by Eliom then the uneasy Elanore, the confident warrior couple and finally, a still-very-anxious Thom. Martynio brought up the rear, shutting the gate behind him as always.

The pen was just as gigantic inside as it had looked from the outside. It was dim - the sunlight from above, beaming down through cracks in the wood to play on the mud and straw strewn across the floor - and up ahead of them were six individual stalls, wide enough and high enough to fit a small house in each. The whole place stank of animal manure and sweat and soon everyone, bar Martynio and Eliom, had their noses scrunched up or covered.

The smell was the least of their worries though as, after a moment's silence, the whole pen seemed to rumble and all clearly heard the groaning and thudding of large restless animals, straining to be let loose…

Thom gripped his axe even more tightly as his eyes strained to see what lay ahead.

Martynio just gave an amused smile.

"You won't be needing that, little man," he said kindly, gesturing at the dwarf's blade. "I'll make sure they don't harm you."

Thom visibly bristled at being called 'little' but continued to wring his hands along the carved handle of his weapon before Fred leaned in close to his ear.

"Ramunda hide is a thick as a fortress. You would not even cause a scratch," he whispered, and though Thom responded with a snort of disbelief, he finally seemed to give in and the axe was put away.

Standing by the warrior's side, Soph just chuckled.

Making his way to the front of the group, Martynio beckoned for the rest to join him before the entrance to the first of the great stalls. Turning his back on them he then shouted so suddenly and so loudly that even the sturdy Fred flinched.

"*Alora*! *Nolwe*! *Raumo*! *Ratullo!* Come!" he cried and immediately the whole place seemed to come alive, the first stall ringing with the drum of many feet and the ground beginning to quake as four giant creatures then rushed into view.

Each beast was roughly the width and breadth of five fully-grown men, with coarse scale-like skin, which amazingly, seemed to reflect whatever colour was around them in an act of wonderful camouflage.

Despite their size, with small eyes, long trunk-like noses and large flapping ears, the creatures looked almost comical. No one in the group, was laughing though, for each animal also had a single gigantic horn protruding from its forehead, on the largest of the animals, reaching to several metres long and as thick as a tree trunk, spinning to a sharp point.

As the companions stared at their rides, Martynio then made a step towards the closest creature, which was slightly smaller than the others.

"Nolwe," he muttered, stroking the beast's trunk before he turned back to the group, surveying each of them in turn as if deciding which of them to pick. Finally, he settled on Thom.

"You," he said with a smile, gesturing for the dwarf to come forward and Thom did so reluctantly, his gaze ever wary of the sharp horn on the animal's head.

Martynio reached up behind the creature Nolwe's left ear and pulled down some reins which were connected to a cushioned saddle near the skull.

"You may ride Nolwe," he said, handing the reins to the dwarf and as Thom took them uncertainly, Martynio laughed again. "Nolwe is one of the wisest and oldest that I have here," he comforted, patting the great creature's nose fondly. "She'll look after you, don't worry…"

Pausing, he then looked at the group again, before pointing to Elanore.

"You can join him. She's an easy ride."

The sea captain looked utterly unconvinced by this, but came forward anyway as Martynio then moved onto the next creature.

"Two…" he said, once more glancing at Eliom, "*people* to each carriage should do it."

The second animal was larger than the first and looked as if it had taken some great lengths to tame. It had only one big ear and half a horn, proving, more than anything, to make it look all the more dangerous.

"Raumo," he said. But though he sounded just as proud, if not more so, than he had at the side of Nolwe, this time, Martynio made no move to pat the animal. Instead, he just surveyed the group of awaiting customers again.

"Raumo is... well, he's a bit more *vigorous*," the great man said carefully. "Do I have any takers?"

It wasn't a great selling point, but to everyone's surprise, Fred wasted no time in stepping forward.

"We will take him," he said, gesturing at Soph with an excited glint in his eye. Soph just smiled and followed her partner as he approached the beast and Martynio handed him the reins before moving straight onto the next Ramunda.

The third creature needed no introduction to Edmund, for she had been his daily carriage during the time he'd spent in the town years before, but still Martynio spoke her name with a kind of loving reverence.

"Alora," he said, and, without another word, held the reins out towards him. Edmund took them gladly, and approaching the Ramunda, began to rub her heartily on the flank, just where she liked it.

"Hello, girl!" he muttered as Alora made a strangled hooting noise, showing her satisfaction. "I've missed you!"

Martynio said nothing to the waiting Eliom, but nodded only briefly as the wizard also moved towards the female Ramunda. The large man then strode over to the last and biggest Ramunda of the lot and grabbing the reins, he scaled the side of the animal almost effortlessly, using the ropes to hoist his body into the little saddle just behind its head.

The others just watched him in amazement, and in the case of Thom, disbelief, as they realised that they would have to do the same themselves.

Only once Edmund, almost as smoothly himself, had mounted Alora did anyone else then even try, and after much pushing and straining, everyone was eventually astride his or her designated beast; Thom needing more help than the others from a rather flustered Elanore to get his little legs up and Eliom simply seeming to *appear* behind Edmund in the saddle. Once the group were ready, Martynio steered his steed towards the gate, blowing an odd whistling noise through his teeth. The Ramunda all responded with a loud hoot.

"Come on everyone!" the carriage-handler then cried. "Keep with me, mind the crowds and we should reach the tomb in no time!"

—

"How about this one?" Bex asked, pointing to a looming rock on her right and the others paused to peer at it for a while, Dromeda even tilting his head to one side as if considering a sculpture. But it was no use. The boulder simply looked like a boulder and not for the first time in those last few minutes alone, Bethan let out an exasperated sigh.

"This is *hopeless*!" she snapped, clearly voicing how they were all now feeling. "How are we supposed to know what we're looking for?! Does it *actually* look like a tree, with leaves and everything or is it supposed to be *artistic*?"

"I'm sure it'll be really obvious," Saz echoed Bex for what felt like the hundredth time, "when we find it…" But though she'd been repeating this like her own personal chant for the past hour, everybody was starting to lose faith in it.

"I agree with Bethan!" Dromeda cried as Meggie stared up at yet another rock, her eyes squinting in the strange reddish light of the day. "None of these boulders look anything like a tree!"

"Stop being so negative!" the little element said, never tearing her gaze from the way ahead. "Saz is right. It *must* be obvious. Why would Belanna have told us it looks like a tree, if it doesn't?" The element of fire smiled at her gratefully. "We just have to keep looking."

The elder element frowned, but, half to everyone's surprise, didn't argue back. Instead, he simply turned to Nickolas, as if waiting for him to suggest a solution and then, when his friend said nothing…

"Perhaps if we split up," he started, "we could cover more ground…" but almost straight away, his companion shot the idea down.

"No," Nickolas said firmly. "You were right not to split us up before. It could take even longer. There are hundreds of boulders here, one of us could easily get lost…"

And Dromeda gave a tired growl.

"That is my point," he moaned. "There are hundreds! It could be days before we find it," and he gestured to the bundled blanket slung across his shoulder, their only provisions. "By that point we could all have perished of hunger, or even dehydration if that gets us first…"

It was the first time anyone had spoken aloud of how little supplies they had left and as his words trailed off feebly at the realisation of what he was suggesting, the others couldn't help but find themselves imagining what it would be like to be so hungry, so thirsty yet unable to do anything about it. Unable to just lie down and die…

Bethan shuddered and rousing herself, started off towards the next boulder with new determination.

"Come on!" she commanded. "We're not going to find this thing any faster if we just stand around complaining about it!" and without another word, the other elements trailed along behind her, not daring to admit to themselves the gradual dwindling of their hopes…

—

The Ramunda moved surprisingly fast and before long, despite Martynio's previous assertions, the group were nearing the edge of the town. After mumbling some kind of explanation about new laws preventing carriages too near the square, so far, under the carriage-handler's instructions they had kept to the side streets, never merging with the rest of the throng pushing into the centre of the market.

Now the noise of the bustle was behind them as they were met with the suburbs. Here, there were many little huts, interspersed with roads and fields, where workers were picking vegetables, children were running here and there and cattle were being herded.

Martynio pulled at the reins of his beast, Ratullo, and the Ramunda slowed to a gradual halt.

"We're reaching the edge of town, which means we'll have to take things a bit more slowly from now on. The roads are narrower here," he remarked to Edmund, who was riding directly beside him at the front of Alora's neck. The Explorer also pulled on his reins, causing Alora to hoot and slow as Martynio turned almost fully about in his saddle to check on the others.

"All still here then?" he said cheerfully. "We haven't lost any?"

Thom and Elanore, who were right at the back of the group, were clinging onto their Ramunda for what looked like their lives. Thom had his head down and eyes shut; he didn't say a word. Fred and Soph meanwhile, having suffered a little trouble keeping the energetic Raumo under control to start with, had soon managed to strike a bargain with the animal. It involved a sharp prod to the ear - the softer part of the Ramunda's thick hide - with Fred's sword, every time Raumo misbehaved and soon learning his lesson, the creature had been nothing but docile from then on.

Having checked the safety of his customers, Martynio then turned back to the front, making a sharp clicking sound with his tongue. The Ramunda all strolled forward willingly, keeping to the rough-hewn path of dirt up ahead with surprising grace.

Once they were back on the move, Martynio then glanced at Edmund again.

"The tomb's changed a bit since we were last up there," he said conversationally, before turning back to keep his eyes fixed on the way ahead.

"Oh?" Edmund replied, pulling at Alora's reins gently to keep her straight on the road. "What have they done to it?" He seemed to have spent much of the journey lost in his own thoughts but had revived a little now that they were somewhere quieter.

"Well, I guess you didn't hear, but there was a robbery after you'd gone." Martynio gave another sideways glance. "Or rather, an *attempted* one, sin0ce there wasn't much left to steal…"

Edmund looked suddenly alarmed.

"A robbery? Really? What happened?"

Alora hooted as he squeezed his thighs a little too tightly together, and he gave her a reassuring pat on the head.

"Well, they were arrested of course," Martynio said, pausing briefly as he directed Ratullo onto a path leading off to the right. It led down a narrow passage between huts, forcing the animals to walk in single file and the great man to speak over his shoulder. "No one knows what they were after. But I must warn you, after that, the security increased two-fold. It's nearly *impossible* to get anywhere *near* the place these days."

"Why would someone try to rob the place? I thought Edmund had excavated everything?" Fred commented. His Ramunda had suddenly charged forwards, putting him just behind Martynio and Edmund. The warrior gave the animal a quick poke with his blade.

"I did," Edmund murmured absently. "The place was virtually *empty*…"

Martynio meanwhile just shrugged.

"Who knows? But you best think of a good reason to get back in there, or the guards won't let you pass," he warned.

"They will let us pass," said Eliom, who until then had been entirely silent, and as if to make the point, Fred raised his sword a little.

"If we have to, we can use force," the warrior said.

"Not that that will hopefully, be necessary." Edmund was cautious and Martynio, turning the herd of Ramunda into yet another narrow passageway, gave another click of his tongue, causing the animals to slow a little more. The space really was minimal.

"You haven't said; why it is you want to go back there anyway?" he then mused aloud. "Anything worth looking at is logged at the library, you saw to that yourself…"

It was inevitable that it would come to this and, Fred, from his position behind, glanced at the back of Edmund's head, followed by Eliom's as if trying to judge their response.

Sure enough, the Explorer seemed to hesitate before giving a reply.

"There's just something…" he started, but almost just as quickly he seemed to stop himself, as if wondering for a moment how much to tell Martynio.

He would trust this man with his life – that much he knew. The pair's friendship went back a long way, even before his excavation of Ophelius's tomb. He had known Martynio back in the west before his friend had headed east in search of better fortune, but whilst that may be true, and whilst his heart may be in the right place, at the same time, Edmund also knew that if Martynio were notorious for *anything*, it was his failure to keep a secret.

He had never told Martynio about his discovery of the map, of the information he had found, of the Temple of Ratacopeck back when he had been there last time, even *before* he had known of his brother's treachery and feared it. And back then it had been with very good reason; the less shared with his friend was definitely the better.

But then again, he found himself reasoning; that had been back then. This was now and now things were a little different. After all, did it even really matter what the man knew? He had willing told Soph of their purpose, so why not Martynio? Regardless of what his friend may or may not tell anyone, why would anyone even try to stop them now? Renard – that name again - his brother, was dead, his army destroyed and no one else knew of their whereabouts, or even *cared*.

But… and almost as soon as he'd thought it, Edmund remembered the words of the Lady of the nimphs and Ophelius's written warnings, Eldora's visions…

The Builder.

There was still this mysterious he, or *she* – who knew? - to think about. This unknown foe they had yet to understand or face.

Considering what they had been through so far then, maybe it *was* still better to be safe than sorry…

"We are assisting some friends."

It was Fred who had spoken and surprised, Edmund threw him an almost grateful look over his shoulder as Martynio moved on with a sudden smile. Though keeping a secret wasn't his strong point, reading people, and in this case, the group's reluctance to explain, certainly seemed to be.

"Fair enough," he remarked, seeming to brush the whole thing off, before, thinking for a moment, he then gave a bit of a chuckle. "Not brought that brother of yours this time then, eh Edmund? What's Renard up to these days? Always said that lad needed a bit more adventure in his life… he's a bit of an odd one, if you don't mind my saying so."

Of course, the giant man couldn't possibly have known, but right then, everyone within earshot thought that perhaps it would have been better for him to try and force the subject of why they were there as, hearing his brother's name spoken aloud, Edmund's face immediately darkened.

Renard.

Every time he heard it, he could do nothing but remember. Like some crazy nightmare, it still haunted the edge of his thoughts; the way his brother had tripped, had fallen into the flames of the Keeper of the World, screaming for help; the way he had simply *crumbled* before his eyes, boiling and melting. And all the while with Edmund just standing there, watching on, helpless...

"Renard." The word almost caught in the Explorer's throat. His voice was quiet. "Yes. He's not here this time. He's... He's not-" but seeing his friend's downtrodden face, Martynio's eyes soon widened in realisation.

"Oh Edmund! I'm so sorry!" he cried, his whole face twitching awkwardly. "I didn't... He was such a... What a waste...I-" But he soon broke off as Edmund straightened up with a sigh, flicking Alora's reins.

A waste. Edmund found for a moment, he wasn't sure whether to agree with Martynio or not. Either way though, Fred was the one who spoke first.

"He brought it upon himself," the warrior said. His voice was short and firm. "Renard received nothing he did not deserve." And hearing those words spoken, so very harshly yet truthfully, Edmund felt a new wave of regret.

Renard had been a lot of things. He had been hateful, malicious, jealous, ready to stop at nothing, so it seemed, for what he wanted. He had been, at the worst, a killer; a *murderer*. But despite all of that, he had still been his brother.

To the rest of the world, he was a nothing, a man who had been given his just desserts, but to Edmund he had been flesh and blood... and filled with the sudden need to argue, the sudden need to inexplicably defend him, the Explorer opened his mouth to do just that.

Right at that moment though, Martynio pulled firmly at his own reins, calling out for the group to stop and as the Ramunda immediately obeyed, Edmund soon lost his chance as the great man then began to dismount, turning to the rest of the group as he did so.

"We need to tie them up," Martynio said, gesturing at their rides. "The tomb's just over there, but we'll need to walk from here."

"How are you feeling?" Meggie asked as her eyes turned to a particularly tall boulder in front of them. It wasn't the boulder they were looking for; there was nothing special about it and it certainly didn't look like a tree, but even so, she couldn't help but pause to wonder how it or any of its kind had even come to be there in the first place. Each and every rock seemed to be an entirely different shape, some ragged and sharp, some smooth and rounded, others with gaping cracks or holes, yet from what she had been told, there was never any rain or wind here to weather or break them - or at least, there hadn't been until now - so, why or how they had all fallen from the cliffs in the first place, felt like a mystery.

Nickolas blinked as if he had forgotten for a moment what the little element was talking about. As usual, both of them were lagging at the back of the group, Meggie's little legs struggling to keep up, whilst the elder element just looked tired.

Without realising he was doing it, Nickolas then moved a hand to his chest.

"I will be fine," he said. "I am just taking a little longer than you." And reminded of her now-healed ankle, Meggie glanced down as if she still couldn't quite believe it.

Even now, now she had witnessed such a thing several times, she realised that in truth, she *couldn't*. With every passing minute, this whole place, this whole world, was stranger, more different, to her own than she had ever imagined. And yet…

Meggie frowned.

"I don't get it. You were-" she faltered. The word. She couldn't say *dead*, "*hurt* before I was. But you're still not all right."

She didn't really know what kind of answer she wanted but instead of giving any, Nickolas just gave a little smile, peering up at yet another towering boulder as they passed. Even though there were no shadows in this place, the boulders rose high above them in a long corridor of rock, casting an odd dimness on the group below.

"This is all new to me too, you know," he commented. "I have never died before."

Never died before. The words, used so flippantly, sent an odd shiver through Meggie. Even so, she still managed to look sceptical.

"Yes," she said, "but are you telling me that you've never hurt yourself the whole time you've been here? That you've never noticed how quickly our bodies seem to heal?"

"No." Nickolas paused. "I am not claiming that I have never injured myself. I have… But never quite like this."

He was teasing her but as he turned to meet her eye, he noticed that she was already staring at him and seeing the odd look on her face, his smile instantly disappeared.

"What?" he demanded, unable to hide his sudden concern. "What is it? What is wrong?" But as soon as he caught her gaze, Meggie had already looked away.

"Nothing," she muttered, before staring up at yet another rock and forcing Nickolas, unconvinced as he was, to drop the matter.

In the ensuing silence, the elder element soon slowed his pace a little, putting more distance between them and the others.

"I think perhaps I understand," he then said mysteriously, making Meggie look up at him again, confused.

"You understand what?"

"Why I have not healed as quickly as you," he mused, his often reserved face, thoughtful, and then, before Meggie could open her mouth to reply; "it is nothing but a theory, but perhaps it is because of the time I have spent here; because of my age," he seemed to falter a moment. "My *real* age, I mean.

We already know that on your world, you are still alive, whereas I am not." And then, with what looked to anyone else like a shrug; "maybe that has an effect here. Maybe because you are younger, more alive than I am…"

As soon as he had spoken the words 'your world' though, the same expression he had seen only moments ago, fell on Meggie's face and as she turned away all over again, something gave way inside him.

"Meggie, what is it?" Nickolas snapped impatiently. "What are you hiding?"

Meggie's cheeks reddened a little, but still she didn't seem to want to give in.

"I'm not hiding anything!" she insisted a bit more loudly this time. But though she seemed adamant, suddenly the little element began to pick up her pace, obviously intent on creating a distance between them and more seriously worried, Nickolas reached out to grab her.

He had only meant to make her stay, to stop and explain, but the little element almost fell as his hand clamped around her wrist and he pulled her back, spinning her around to face him.

"You are lying! Tell me!" he cried, trying to find her eyes with his own. For some reason, he felt angry. "What are you hiding?! What is upsetting you?" But the little woman seemed determined to look at everything else *but* him.

"Get off me!" she spat, surprisingly sharply. "It's none of your business! Leave me alone!" and whether it was her words or the way she suddenly snatched her arm away, Nickolas immediately released her, only to watch as she then turned her back on him and almost running, hurried off to join the rest of the elements without so much as another word.

Nickolas felt stunned, and for a second, not knowing what else to do, he stopped.

What was going on? The elder element had never seen this side of Meggie before, at least, not like this. The woman was stubborn, that much he had worked out; she was passionate. But *this*, what he had just witnessed, had been so much more than that.

Something was wrong, very wrong. Something had upset her, badly and he had a feeling that judging by her fierce reaction, whatever it was had been going on for a while, whether she had realised it or not.

It's none of your business. The words she had spoken in anger, stung; he couldn't deny it.

It was true, it really *was* none of his business what Meggie thought or felt or even really, what she decided to do from hereon in. He was nothing but a bystander, a companion to help her and the others on their way to freedom. Yet even knowing that, he also knew right from that very moment that whatever it was that was upsetting her, he very much intended to find it out.

Whether it was his business or not, no matter how hard she denied it, or how hard she fought it, he knew suddenly, that he wasn't going to back down on this. Not yet.

He would find out what was wrong. And if it were possible, he knew that he was going to try to fix it…

Nickolas squared his shoulders, ready to carry on after the others.

He owed that much to her after all.

All the while, Meggie had almost caught up with the rest of the group ahead.

Her thoughts were in a whirl, her emotions, she could feel, all over the place. Something had happened to her - she realised that now - something she didn't understand and yes, hadn't anticipated and now, as she marched away from Nickolas, not daring to look back, all she could do was feel *guilty* about it.

She hadn't meant to snap at him like that. She didn't even know *why* she'd suddenly got so *angry*. And yet for some reason she just had.

The way he had teased her, just brushing his own death off so lightly when she had been so grief-stricken. The way he had mentioned Tungala, *her* world, again making out as if he had never been a part of it and never would… All of it had somehow upset her and in the heat of the moment, she'd just reacted.

She knew she was in the wrong. She'd had no real reason to act like that. And as she got closer and closer to the others, the more she was convinced that the right thing to do was turn right back around and apologise. Try and explain things, if she even *could*…

But though that may have been her intention, and perhaps, in another life, it would have been exactly what she would have done, just then, there was a shout from up ahead.

"I can see it! *I can see it! We've found it!*"

It was Saz, once more at the head of the group.

"It's there!" and hearing the excitement in her companion's voice, Meggie instantly started to run, kicking up an air-full of dry dust as she rushed to level with the others.

The other three women and Dromeda had all stopped in their tracks and as she reached them, slamming to a stop herself, the little element felt a brush of air as Nickolas also dashed up to join them.

He stood close, very close; she could almost feel his breath panting through the hair on the top of her head, and distracted for a second, Meggie thought about turning to him, trying to say sorry for what had happened. But the sight ahead soon drew every bit of attention she had as the six elements all just stood and stared in wonderment at what lay before them.

Stretching out ahead there was a great open plain, shadowed - if that were possible in this place - beneath the great cliff faces of white. Gone was the valley of boulders, gone, in fact, was everything bar one object, for standing alone against the brilliant white stood one last pillar of rock. Taller and thinner than all the rest, the boulder reached up like a drawn-out stalk towards the bright sky, from its base, three bough-like segments breaking away from it, twisting up like writhing snakes in the noonday light.

Saz had been right all along. There was no mistaking it.

Before their very eyes, within their reach, was the great boundary separating the world of living, breathing and feeling, from that of the unknown. That of lifelessness.

Before them, stood the boulder shaped like a tree and beyond that, the boundary between life and death.

—

The elements seemed incapable of even moving in the awe-filled silence. No one spoke, no one seemed to so much as blink for several moments, as if none of them could quite believe what they were looking at. But then, as one, it finally seemed to hit them and the first to speak, Dromeda opened his mouth.

Somehow his voice was croaky.

"We made it," he said as if he'd never really thought that they would. "We are here."

The others didn't reply. There was no need to. The smell of fear seemed already all too thick in the air; for suddenly, faced as they were with the reality of what lay before them, women and men alike were frozen with dread.

"Look!" Bex cried, pointing at something ahead, her eyes wide.

None of them needed to question what she was looking at. They could all see it and it was this more than anything that made them fear, for drifting before the menacing tree-like rock, was a thin kind of mist, a haze of... well, all any of them could describe it as was, colour.

It was a wall of shifting colours of every kind, only just visible in the bright daylight; blues, whites, reds, oranges, purples, yellows all twisting in and out of each other, thrashing together like fish in a dying river, knowing that any moment could be their last. And beyond that, the boulder itself, a greyish-white; the patch of sky overhead, darker and more sinister, the air beyond the colours all the more oppressive.

The land of the dead.

It was there. It was real and looking on, Bethan suddenly found herself wishing that she was anywhere else but before the sight that none would see, *should* see until the end.

The element felt her entire body grow cold.

Could the group really just *step through* the strange barrier, into death? Or had they just been kidding themselves all along, holding on to something impossible?

Bethan took a few deep breaths and trying hopelessly to calm her nerves, her thoughts couldn't help but turn then to home, to the world she had left behind, to the world she had, all this time, hoped to reclaim; the very reason she was even *contemplating* doing this in the first place.

She had to leave this place, this world – she was sure of that. She had to return to life as she had known it, to find Edmund again… And it was possible. They all knew that, deep down. Ophelius had done it, after all. He had managed to free himself. He had managed to return to Tungala and that was now why they were here. To speak to the man himself, to find out what he knew…

However long it takes, Bethan thought.

For it was true, she'd never really considered it before now, but just *finding* the prophet in the first place was bound to be hard. Millions, *billions* of people, of races died all the time; every minute, every second of every day, mind-numbing numbers, incalculable figures of them – perhaps even more than she'd ever dreamed of, for who knew now how many worlds actually existed out there?

Did all the dead come here, to the same place? And if they did, what would it be like? How would they be able to recognise who they were looking for? Did they just simply walk through the layer of colours and he would be there? Or would they spend the rest of their days just searching, endlessly, for that one lone figure they'd never even met?...

Turning to her fellow elements then, Bethan wondered if they too, were having similar doubts, similar fears, but no one met her gaze. They all just seemed to be staring, as if mesmerised by the floating, winding colours, every face set into one of glazed fright.

It was Saz who then finally blinked and as if waking from a trance, she also looked to the others.

"We should get going," she said in a voice that suggested that she too wanted to do nothing of the sort. "We're wasting time standing here."

The other women just nodded.

Only Meggie flinched as she felt something touch her arm.

It was Nickolas, his hand warmer than it had been in days, his fingers firm. For a moment, she'd almost forgotten he was there, standing right next to her, but remembering the way she'd spoken to him last, she found her face reddening again and turning, she opened her mouth to apologise.

Nickolas however, surprised her by speaking first.

"Must we go?" he said. "There *must* be some other way." And shocked, Meggie just stared at him for a moment.

He had a look in his eye she didn't recognise. But then again it was so difficult to know *what* he was thinking under that usually set expression, that the little element found it hard to be sure if she was imagining it.

"We'll be fine," she brushed him off. "Don't worry."

She had to be strong. She *had* to be, otherwise she knew she wouldn't be able to go through with it. She wouldn't be able to walk through to… that *place* stretching out before her.

It was less than a mile away. A few hundred steps and she would be…

Would she be *dead*?

Meggie had no idea, and it was this that frightened her above all else.

What if they walked in there and couldn't ever come out again? What if they could never return to the land of the living, be it Tungala or-?

She glanced up at Nickolas.

"We don't all have to go."

It was Saz who had pointed it out, and turning, Meggie was surprised to see that her fellow element was looking at her. Was her fear so obvious? But much as she wanted to agree, much as she was afraid, the little woman immediately gave a tiny shake of her head.

"No," she argued, her voice suddenly weak. "No. We should all go together…"

Even she wasn't entirely sure what she'd meant by that. Somehow it had felt right to say it, but on the word 'together', Dromeda suddenly looked horrified and taking a few steps away from them all, he lifted his hands as if hoping to push the barrier further away.

"H-hold on! *I* am not going!" he stuttered. "I mean-" and he seemed to backtrack a little. "Of course, I want to help but we," he gestured at himself and Nickolas, "*we* cannot go in there! Who knows what might happen? For us it might mean permanent *death*!"

Saz looked at him open-mouthed.

"Well, you don't have to come if you don't want to," she said. "After all, this is *our*…" and she glanced at the other three women, unable to finish her sentence.

"Precisely," Dromeda took yet another step backwards, looking worried. "I think it only wise…"

But having listened silently to the unfolding situation, it was then that Nickolas suddenly seemed to snap.

"Well! The truth finally comes out Dromeda!" he spat in disgust and to everyone's shock; he swivelled to glower at his companion, his expression livid. "How often has it been now that when faced with danger you turn and run like a coward?"

Dromeda had never looked so surprised. Suddenly his friend seemed to be positively *shaking* with rage, his usually calm face a sneering mask.

"I am *not* a coward!" he retorted and then, as his own anger began to rise, he clenched his fists. "How dare you!"

Everyone turned to look at him, but watching Nickolas still, Meggie laid a quick hand on his chest as the elder element made to move.

"Stop it! Both of you!" she threatened. "Don't!" But though she tried to hold him back, Nickolas was almost twice her size and with everything he had now channelled at his long-term companion, the elder element just pushed past her like she was nothing.

"He has had this coming the entire journey!" Nickolas growled. He too, clenched his fists, although in his current mood, he looked more likely to use them. "He turns tail and runs at the slightest hitch, the slightest threat to his wellbeing! He always has!"

"What is wrong with you?!" Dromeda roared. "This is not our foolish mission!" and all of a sudden, he reached for the knife in his tunic as Nickolas stepped closer.

The move seemed to enrage Nickolas even more and he too, reached for the place where his own knife would be, only to his horror, to find the space empty. It took everyone only a second to realise that Dromeda had both of the blades. After using Dromeda's knife as a torch, Nickolas had handed over the only weapon he had to his friend, never thinking to reclaim it... Until now.

Being almost defenceless wasn't enough to stop him though and seeing that things were about to get very bad, the four women turned to each other in panic, none of them quite sure what to do.

"Stop it!" Saz tried, "Nickolas! Dromeda! Come on!"

But both men ignored her.

"You never once think about others, do you?!" Nickolas hissed, his voice threateningly low, his eyes set on Dromeda like a hunter's on his prey. "Not unless it is in your best interests!"

Dromeda laughed bitterly as he eyed Nickolas's weaponless fists.

"What are you going to do?!" he taunted. "Hit me? Throttle me? Kill me? Is that what you want?!"

"Stop!" Saz persisted, meaning to step between them herself. "Please! Think about what you're doing!" But suddenly there was no need. Nickolas seemed to have frozen and startled, Dromeda eyed him warily.

Even though he knew his friend couldn't harm him, he also knew there was a small chance Nickolas would win if they fought. Weak as he was after his ordeal, he had always considered his companion the better fighter, the better soldier, the better man...

However, even as Dromeda watched on, expectant, the elder element's expression changed all over again. Suddenly, he looked no longer angry; suddenly his face was no longer hard. Instead, he seemed to soften and for a moment, he looked something even worse than mad, something Dromeda found even more unbearable.

Disappointed.

Nickolas looked disappointed; in him. And for a moment, as he stared into his friend's face, Dromeda almost wished they'd fought, wished Nickolas had tried to throttle him. For anything would surely feel better than this.

Anything at all.

Nickolas then lowered his fists and opening his mouth to speak, his voice trembled.

"Kill you?" was all he said. "Like you left me to be killed?"

The words seemed to cut deeper than any knife could have, as a deathly silence followed and the four on-looking women glanced at each other knowingly. Bex bit her lip.

Dromeda just stared.

"I-" he started, but almost straight away, he knew there was nothing he could say. Much as Nickolas had seemed to forgive him, or seemed to think nothing of it, he *knew* that his friend was right. The very fact of it was; Dromeda *had* left him. Instead of going back, of stepping in to help him with the Diggers, as Meggie had begged him to do, as his own conscience had begged him to do, he had simply stood there and done *nothing*. And for that perhaps, the element would never forgive himself; for that, he knew, he deserved worse than a hit.

Seeing that things had gone on long enough, it was then that Meggie stepped back between the two men.

"Both of you! Stop!" she cried, as if instead of just standing there, the two had been shouting at each other, fists in faces. But it was already clear that all fight had left Nickolas now just as it had Dromeda and as one, Dromeda lowered his knife and Nickolas his hands.

The little element then glared up at them both before delivering her own blow.

"This whole argument is pointless because neither of you are coming!" she finished in defiance. "You can both stay here and wait for us." And snapping straight back to his senses, Nickolas was the first to gawp at her.

"What? No!-" he started to protest "I am-!", but Meggie just shook her head, the matter already decided.

"Dromeda's right. Who knows what will happen if you both go in there?" she said, glancing at Dromeda, who remained silent. "It's too risky."

"But *I* am prepared to take that risk!" Nickolas argued. "I will follow-"

"No!" Meggie snapped. "You could *die,* Nickolas! For real!" And as her voice rose to desperation, she suddenly realised that for some reason her hand was back on his chest. She could almost feel his heart thudding beneath her fingertips. It was running fast and hard.

"Meggie's right," Bethan added as she too understood what the elder element could not. "You're too old. We've only been away from our world a matter of days. But to Tungala, you're already dead... and if you went in there," she waved in the general direction of the field of shifting colours, which, as if sensing the imminent arrival of the elements, had started to squirm all the more. "If you went in there, you might never come back."

Meggie stepped away then, pulling her hand from Nickolas, but though she meant it only as a sign that the matter was over, the elder element, overwhelmed with the reality of the situation, felt suddenly disgusted.

Bethan was right. He was so old, older than existence, than life... and Meggie, the other elements, they were so young, like blooming spring flowers compared to his shadowy carcass.

Perhaps that is why Meggie moves away, he thought sourly to himself. *She is disgusted too. She does not wish to touch a corpse.*

But whilst he felt nothing but bitterness and self-loathing right then, his face gave nothing away.

"I understand," he replied aloud instead, his voice almost sad. "I may *actually* die this time."

He thought about adding, *would that be so bad?* But decided against it, for never would he reveal aloud the crumbling of his hopes, the true understanding that had been a long time in coming; the acceptance that he was never going to leave this place.

He had, of course, known it for years, but perhaps he had never really realised until now how much he had secretly yearned, secretly wished otherwise. Somewhere deep inside, he'd always held on to the impossible hope of freedom, of one day being returned to his own home, the way it was, the way *he* was. But now he was finally beginning to understand, to know that *this* world was his home now. His eternal home.

Whilst Meggie and the others were one day going to leave, to return to what they had known, to live their lives, to grow old and die as was the natural way of things, still he would remain there, in that place, until the very existence of the world he had once known had fallen to dust, his senses a distant memory along with the grass and the blue skies without the tinge of red he was so used to now. There was no turning back. No escape for him.

Nickolas glanced around him, taking in the dry crumbling boulders behind, the paling sky without a sun up above.

For him, there was no hope.

Mortality was just a dream, and this dusty, sun-less place was his only reality.

But could he really bear it? Could he really *stand* to stay there?

Or was death really within his grasp now? Was it what he wanted, what he *needed*...?

Only Saz's words seemed able to bring the group back to some kind of focus as once again, she broke the silence.

"We should go, before we never will," she pointed out and giving a sigh, Bex turned to Meggie who turned to Bethan who then glanced back at Bex.

They were as ready as they ever could be.

OPHELIUS AND THE TOMB

Somehow, up close, the field of colours seemed to change, the reds and greens giving way to a semi-transparent shimmering. It was like looking through the surface of a vertical lake into an underwater world; a world of darkness. The elements could even see shadowy reflections of themselves against the sky, their faces pale, expressions drawn and set in frightened determination.

There was a disturbing smell of dust here. The very air around them seemed to waft with it, the heavy feeling of death seeping from the barrier into their very cores, willing their souls forwards. Willing their spirits to leave them…

The women looked at each other again.

Meggie could see in each of the others' faces, the same dread that threatened to overwhelm her. She felt as if only a tiny thread were holding her emotions in check, stopping her from running away from this place, far *far* away.

She was fighting, as they all were, not to give in, for with every step closer to the world ahead, they had all felt it. Like a niggling at the back of their minds, a twinge in their hearts growing stronger by the second; the silent call of mortality beckoned to them all, willing them to leave behind the world of the living and embrace that of death beyond.

The feeling was strong and terrifying; Meggie could sense it like a physical weight on her chest.

Just a few more steps, it seemed to say. *Just a few more steps and it will all be over. All your worries, all your cares, your hopes and dreams… Everything.*

Just embrace it and come.

—

From a safe distance, Nickolas and Dromeda watched in silence.

Nickolas had his knife back now and it was clutched in his hands, his knuckles almost white against the metal as he forced himself to remain. It felt as if everything he had was working to stop him from running forward to block the elements' path. Everything he had was working to make him just stand and watch as Dromeda all the while also looked on, unspeaking, unmoving, his expression glum as the four women paused to stare at their waiting fate.

There was nothing either man could do now. Both of them knew it, and yet a single bead of sweat trickled from Nickolas's brow as his eyes bored into the back of Meggie's head. For some reason he couldn't seem to tear his gaze from her as he struggled with himself inwardly, willing her on, willing her to be brave and save herself and yet at the same time...

He just couldn't stop thinking about what the little element had said, or rather *not* said. The strange way she had looked at him right before she'd brushed him off, running from him to join the others. The way she had acted this entire journey; *reluctant.*

He cared about what happened to her - he had worked *that* out long ago. She had been put under his charge from day one and from that very first moment he had done everything he could to keep her safe.

But now? Now, all Nickolas could do was watch her leave, secretly willing her to turn around and come back, to turn and run from the clear danger ahead. And yet all the time knowing that what she did was the right thing.

For what, after all, was left for her here?

If she did turn away from the land of the dead, what did she really have to turn away for?

Nothing. She had nothing. And the truth ringing loud and clear, Nickolas felt another pang of self-hatred. There was nothing for Meggie here but a twisted half-world that she would never be able to leave; a world with nothing to offer but sand and dirt and living death.

No. This was her chance, her *only* chance for freedom, to live a full and happy life.

And no matter how strangely reluctant she may have seemed, both of them knew she had to take it. It was the only choice she really had.

The elements were moving again now. Slowly but surely, they were walking as they had all that time ago into the orb flames, as one, their bodies so close to the roiling wall of colour that they almost seemed to be a part of it.

Less than a few more steps and they would be there.

They would be gone.

And it would be too late.

Nickolas's eyes flickered.

Too late.

And then suddenly, just like that, he couldn't hold it back anymore. Without another thought, a word, or a warning, Nickolas housed his knife and in one burst, sprang forward, hurling himself towards the barrier at a run.

Dromeda barely had a moment to work out what was going on. Catching a glimpse of his friend as he shot past though, he too lunged forward with a cry, flinging out a hand to grab him. But whilst he was quick, he wasn't quick *enough* and the element's fingers found nothing but air.

"Nickolas!" he yelled in horror. "No! Nickolas! What are you doing? *Stop!* *Stop!*

The shout echoed across the space, loud enough for all to hear, but despite it all, Nickolas didn't slow down. He was sprinting now, running full pelt at the barrier and hearing the sound, Meggie turned back, only to freeze in helpless alarm as she saw him shooting towards her like an arrow from a bow.

It took her only a second to realise what was happening, to realise what he was doing.

"No!!" she screamed, rooted to the spot by both the terrible pull of death, the terrible tug that every second felt more and more impossible to resist, and her own fear. Her voice sounded strangely dull, almost as if the semi-transparent wall at her back had absorbed it. Still though, Nickolas kept running, still he kept on toward the barrier, and frozen in place, for a moment, Meggie didn't know what to do.

He had to be stopped. Someone *had* to stop him. For if Nickolas came too close she knew that that would be it.

Just a few steps more… death called to her. *You are so close. Just a little more…*

And Meggie shook her head, trying desperately to clear her thoughts.

If this was what it felt like for *her*, someone so young, so far from her natural end, what chance would the elder element have against the quiet coaxing, the silent deadly pull?

But whilst she stood there, frantically looking on, as if by simply watching, by willing Nickolas to stop, he would, she realised that what she hadn't bargained for, was Dromeda.

"Stop!" she heard his shout again, loud and clear. He sounded just as desperate as she was, just as terrified. And then, to her utter surprise, she saw that he too, was running, tearing towards them like a man possessed.

Suddenly he was throwing himself towards Nickolas, low and frantic. But though he was taller, his stride longer and faster, though he lunged for his companion's waist in a mad attempt to tackle him to the ground, yet again, Nickolas was too quick for him and Dromeda crashed to the hard dirt in a useless heap of dust, choking and spluttering.

"Nickolas!" he bellowed, his harsh cry added to Meggie's. "*Nickolas!*" Yet still Nickolas seemed bent on ignoring them both.

By now, the other elements had all turned to see what was going on, and realising the situation rolling out in front of them, all three also froze, horrified, adding their own shouts to the mix, pleading with the elder element to stay back.

He was barely fifty yards away now. In only a moment he would be there and, at the rate he was going, he wasn't going to stop...

Meggie's breath caught in her chest.

He was going to collide with her. He was going to collide and they would fall, fall into the world of the dead. And he would *die*.

She couldn't explain *how* she knew it, but she just did.

Nickolas was going to die unless someone did something. *Unless someone stopped him.*

And feeling nothing but utter panic right then, the little element looked around her.

For a fear-stricken second, she considered running to meet him herself, wrestling him to the floor. Chances were, it wouldn't work, and not only because moving *away* from the field felt impossible now; but because she was so much smaller, so much lighter than him. She was hardly likely to make any impact at all. And yet... the more the thought lodged itself in her head, the more she realised - what other choice did she have?

Just a few steps more and you won't have to worry... the barrier spoke. *Just a few steps more and nothing will frighten you any more...*

Meggie braced herself.

I have to.

She wasn't sure if she'd spoken the words aloud but whether she had or not, they were definitely there and suddenly turning on the others, who were still shouting, she then yelled to get their attention.

"Go on!" she cried to the three baffled women. "Go on without me! I'll catch you up!"

And with a small cry, the little element broke free of her immobility and with a strength she'd never realised she had, charged towards the speeding Nickolas as if her very life depended on it.

His life certainly did. The element knew it and as he drew closer and closer to the field of darkness, so Nickolas began to realise it too.

At first it was just in his chest, a pain where the wound still healed, a slight annoying throb. But then it was *deeper* than that, and suddenly, with every passing step, it was spreading, as if something just below the level of his skin was aching, groaning to be set free.

And the pull...

He could feel a tugging at his heart, an overpowering wrench like nothing he had ever felt before. And a voice seemed to be speaking to him, telling him first to run to Meggie, but then past her, past the others, past the barrier, on into the world before his eyes, the world that called to him, inviting him to enter...

The barrier was sucking him into the darkness beyond, it was saying his name, whispering it on the air, drawing him with every breath to his rightful home. And only now did he understand that he was too weak to resist, his body, his mind too weak to fight it. He was too old, too fragile...

"Nickolas!"

Her shout made him blink and as he looked away from his fate, it was then that he saw her again.

Meggie.

She was in front of him, *right* in front him and coming at him, *fast*. And before he could understand what was happening, Nickolas felt the force hit him like a smack in the face as the two then collided.

The element charged squarely into his chest, the momentum bowling him backwards, and before he could so much as catch a breath, he was falling to the ground, Meggie on top of him, her whole weight thrusting itself against his aching ribs.

The onlookers watched in horror as the pair skidded across the hard dirt, the sheer force of Meggie's leap propelling them through the air until they crash-landed in a confused heap of breathless limbs.

Meanwhile, having witnessed the whole thing from the ground himself, Dromeda leapt back to his feet and began to lope towards the now motionless pair, only to be stopped by another shout.

"Dromeda! No!" one of the other elements warned, and realising the danger of what he was about to do, the elder element froze halfway, waiting anxiously, as they all now were, for signs of movement, for signs of life...

Meggie was up first. Pulling herself together, the little element clambered to a sit, her knees astride Nickolas's chest. The skin on one of her arms was rubbed raw from her journey across the ground, but ignoring it, she threw a glance back at the barrier where the other three elements, having completely ignored her final instructions, were still waiting for her, before turning back to her winded prisoner.

"What were you *thinking*?!" she hissed in his face. Her words came at an angry pant and she winced as her damaged skin began to bleed a little.

Nickolas looked up at her in blinking confusion. But though his eyes were on her face, they didn't *see*. The pull of death was too strong, even here; he couldn't get away from it, he couldn't seem to concentrate on anything else, even his own injuries, as the impact of the fall began to throb through his battered body, and seeing his vacant expression, Meggie's anger instantly evaporated.

"Nickolas?" she pleaded uneasily. "What is it? What's wrong?"

Nickolas dared not move, dared not get up for fear of seeing the barrier once more. For fear of what he might do.

He could hear a strange voice murmuring in his head, a voice he didn't recognise and didn't like.

What did it matter if he died? He had wanted to die before, always, secretly. He had yearned for so long to be free, to welcome death. Now was his chance…

Just a few more steps and he would be free…

Just a few more steps…

"What is it?!" Meggie sounded more urgent. "Speak to me!"

But Nickolas could scarcely even open his mouth to reply, his mind so consumed by the dark world beyond the boulder.

He hadn't known it would be like this. All he'd wanted to do was save Meggie, to keep her from harm. And yet now…

"It… calls…" he eventually managed through gritted teeth. The pain was almost unbearable now, the physical dragging ache of his body, willing him to get up and go onwards.

Meggie didn't need to ask what he meant.

Just a few more steps…

The little element looked once again at the barrier behind her.

"Come on," she then said and climbing slowly to her feet, she reached for his arm to try and drag him back, back and away from danger. But no matter how hard she pulled, even throwing all her weight into it, Nickolas wouldn't budge. He was too heavy for her, alone, to handle. She simply wasn't strong enough and cursing aloud, Meggie straightened up as she noticed Dromeda only a little way off.

"Dromeda!" she implored. "Help me!"

But though the elder element had thrown himself after Nickolas before, he too could feel it. He too could feel death like a painful burn in his soul and he shied away from it now in terror. He had done all that he could and cursing again, Meggie knelt back over Nickolas.

"Come on, get up!" she begged. "You have to get away from here! You have to move!"

The elder element closed his eyes, trying to block out his thoughts, but they were still there, even in darkness. They wouldn't leave. Not until he gave in.

Come on. What are you waiting for? Just a few steps more…

"Meggie…" he managed her name weakly and then; "I am… sorry."

Meggie was getting desperate now. The more time he spent there the more difficult it was going to be to draw him away. He was almost lost; she could see it in his face. He was almost giving up and she wasn't ready for that. Not yet.

"Don't be," she replied and then, throwing herself back to her feet, she tried dragging him back again, holding him under the armpits. She could barely even lift him. "Just, please, *please* get up!"

"I cannot," Nickolas mumbled. And then; "What is the point, Meggie?... I should give in… I *should* die... I want to…"

"No!" Meggie hushed him quickly. She suddenly felt like crying. "Stop it. This isn't *you!*" Her voice cracked, before, the idea suddenly coming to her, she leaned in close; "You have to wait here for me, for when I get back. You have to! *Promise* me!"

Nickolas opened his eyes then and Meggie could see a great washed-out sadness there. Like water seeping away, he was losing the will to live rapidly, if he hadn't lost it already. Yet despite this, something was clearly holding him back.

"What if you never return, Meggie?" He seemed to enjoy speaking her name, almost like he *needed* to. But his voice was emotionless now, drained of all hope, all life and Meggie, swallowing her own feelings, attempted to smile.

"Don't be stupid. Of course I will," she said. "If I know you're here waiting for me, I will. I promise."

She could see that Nickolas was trying to smile back, but his mouth refused to work properly.

At least though, he was *trying*, which was something and Meggie looked back into the dark distance where the other women still stood, waiting for her.

"I have to go," she muttered. If she didn't leave now, she never would. "But you need to get up. You need to leave…" and this time, half to her surprise, Nickolas nodded. Something in what she had said had clearly reenergised him, had made him want to fight, and though she didn't know, or maybe just didn't want to admit she knew what it was, she was silently thankful.

"Go," he replied quietly. He was *looking* at her now, properly looking. "Go. I will wait here for you," and Meggie met his eye uncertainly, never more reluctant to turn and walk away as she was at that moment.

How could she just leave him there, this close to his death? What if he changed his mind? What if he wasn't strong enough?

And what if he was right? What if she never came back?

How long would he wait for her?

"Do you promise?" she whispered to him, barely able to talk herself for the threat of sudden tears she couldn't quite explain. "Do you promise to wait?"

Nickolas tried to smile again, and this time was more successful.

"I promise."

Then, as if to prove it, before Meggie's very eyes, the elder element began to crawl to his feet.

It was a slow and painful process, almost as if his whole body were fighting against him every inch of the way, but before long, it was done and, resisting the pull of eternal rest with all of his might, he faced Meggie one last time.

"Go," he repeated and with that, he then leant forwards and taking her shoulders in both hands, he pulled her towards him and reaching down, planted his lips on her dust-covered forehead.

The kiss seemed to linger, warm and soft for a moment before Meggie pulled away and staring up at him, alarmed, surprised, but with an equally tiny smile, she turned on her heel and ran back towards her fellow elements, her steps suddenly light.

Not daring to watch, Nickolas then turned himself away from the world of darkness, away from his last glimpses of Meggie and her friends, away from death, as, behind him, the four elements, reunited once more, reached for each other's hands and stepped forward into the barrier.

"Where is this tomb then? We seem to have walked for miles!" Thom grumbled as usual.

"Miles?" Fred snorted and then turning back to the dwarf, he tried not to smile. "Would you rather we rode on the Ramunda again?"

Thom's face was a look of horror, making Soph, who was walking with the pair, give a laugh.

"He is teasing you," she assured him and Fred smiled.

Up at the front of the group, Martynio, Eliom, Edmund and Elanore were striding onwards, the latter almost running to keep up. Hearing Thom's complaints though, Martynio turned briefly, barely slowing his pace.

"We're nearly there. Just round this corner," he said. But gone in the last few minutes were the friendly smiles and loud cheerful voice. The carriage-handler looked positively worried and hearing his solemn words, all smiles fell from both Soph and Fred's lips. Silently, the warriors drew their swords.

"Eliom, we may need you if the guards refuse to let us in," Edmund meanwhile muttered to his cloaked friend.

The wizard said nothing.

And then, sure enough, just as Martynio had promised, the tomb was there, right before their very eyes.

As if appearing from a dream, a great statue, the twin brother to the wooden carving of Ophelius in the square, loomed above them from the trees and behind it an enormous clearing with stone pillars mounted about a great crack in the earth. The crack was large and dark, but as the group moved closer, all could see that it was in fact the entrance to a marble stairwell leading down into a chasm beyond; Ophelius's resting place.

It all looked very opulent and giving a suspicious sniff, Fred was then the first to properly study their surroundings.

"Where *is* everyone?" he asked suddenly, voicing all of their suspicions. For it was true; the crowds of pilgrims, the hordes of guards they'd all been expecting were nowhere to be seen. The clearing was entirely empty, everything silent and still, with barely even a breeze to flutter the treetops.

Edmund all the while, having scrutinised the stillness with his eyes, soon looked to Martynio. But whilst the Explorer's gaze was questioning, the carriage-handler said nothing. To all intents and purposes, he appeared just as clueless as the rest of them.

"Something is afoot here," Thom then muttered and soon his axe was in his hands once again.

Edmund glanced at Eliom.

"Can you sense anything?" he asked.

But the same worrying expression of doubt that he'd witnessed on his friend's face not so long ago, was already starting to appear at the corners of the wizard's mouth. He felt nothing, and knowing that fact, fear began to rise in Edmund's chest.

They had to keep moving. They had to keep Eliom from troubling too deeply. He had to remain controlled. They would just have to enter the tomb blind, and quickly stepping into the clearing, the Explorer gestured for the others to follow him.

"Come on," he ordered. "Let's go before someone comes."

But even though he had made to move, Fred held out a wary hand.

"Edmund, what if this is some kind of trap?" the warrior hissed. His piercing eyes were scanning the space again. "It seems odd that no one is here." And listening in, Martynio's brow furrowed as he nodded in agreement at what Fred was suggesting.

"There are *always* people here, Edmund," he whispered in caution, not daring to break the silence too much. "Always."

There was something strange in his voice, something *beyond* concern but the Explorer was too busy thinking to notice it. Instead, stepping away from Fred's hand, he reached inside his cloak to draw his own sword.

"Well we'll just have to be extra careful," he replied, pointing to Elanore, Eliom and Martynio with his blade. "You three, come with me. The rest of you can keep watch."

Turning back to the tomb, he then made to set out across the clearing again, Elanore and Eliom moving, without question, to follow him, with only Martynio, to everyone's surprise, holding back.

"I'll stay out here if it's all the same to you," their guide muttered edgily, backing away and looking back at him, Edmund couldn't help but frown.

"But Martynio, you've been here before," he said. "You know this place like the back of your hand!" Still though, the big man shook his head.

"As do you, my friend. You know the tomb better than anyone. I'll just... I'll stay and help keep watch." Before, seeing Edmund's obvious confusion,

Martynio then looked at the sky, inhaling deeply. "I don't like it here. I think I'll be better as a look out."

There was definitely something troubling him. Again, the odd tone to his voice, the look in his eyes... it was all very *strange* and worried, Edmund studied his friend's face for a moment, wondering what was going on. Before;

"Let him stay," Fred said, and settling the matter, he moved between Martynio and Edmund. "We will keep watch. You go on ahead."

The matter was decided and glancing once more at Martynio, Edmund sighed.

"Fine," he then said. "We'll see you soon," and moving off again, he beckoned Eliom and Elanore on behind him.

As the small group headed off towards the tomb, the others, Martynio included, then spread out, weapons at the ready, alert for any sign of other life. The carriage-handler had not come empty-handed. As he stepped back through the trees onto the path leading back to town, he pulled from between the folds of his many cloaks what looked like a hand-held mace, giving a nervous smile as Thom eyed it, clearly impressed.

Meanwhile, being the first to reach the marble steps, his sword in hand, Edmund scurried down into the darkness without a moment's hesitation. It was true, he knew the place well, for within seconds he had disappeared from view and pausing for a moment at the very edge of the chasm below, Elanore bit her lip.

Eliom, who was just beside her, also stopped. His expression was still troubled, but something of his usual self was still there.

"Are you all right?" he asked calmly and surprised, the sea captain gave a start.

"Oh, me? Yes, fine," she nodded.

Glancing at the pale wizard, she then looked doubtful. "I just - why did Edmund ask *me* to come with him?" she asked aloud. "Why not take Fred or Thom?"

But instead of replying, Eliom just frowned a little, his eyes somewhat vacant.

"The same reason he asked me, I expect," he said bluntly and moving on before her, he headed off down the steps, vanishing into the blackness without another word.

—

Like plunging into the depths of an icy pool, Bethan gasped as all feeling fled from her body in a frozen crash. The very air in her lungs seemed to catch in her chest as her eyes closed against the slamming force that pushed against her skull, smashing the world around her into a dull silence.

It was like nothing she had ever heard before, that soundlessness, for *silence* didn't seem to really cut it. It was *beyond* silent, almost as if there was no sound at all, and never had been or never would be again. It was an utter muteness, and feeling it pulse at her ears, everything within Bethan wanted nothing more than to turn back, to return to the world of living and feeling and hearing and sensing, the world that, even in what must have been only a few seconds, already felt like a memory of the distant past.

For a moment, the element wondered if all of this was one big mistake, one step too far, and she was actually dead. Had they been wrong to think that they could just step through the barrier into the world of the dead without so much as a scratch?

Were she and the others now standing in their own frozen grave?

The others...

And with a sudden surge of panic, Bethan realised that she couldn't feel Saz's hand any more. She remembered grabbing it before the four women had stepped into the gloom, she remembered its warmth, but now... she was barely aware of having a hand of her own, a *body* of her own, let alone anything else.

Had her body, her senses, been left behind in the living world? And where were the others? Was she now alone?

Trying desperately to turn her head and dredge up the strength to open her eyes, Bethan shrieked in agony as the field around shoved her back, keeping her in place.

Still there was no sound. *Did she even have a mouth to shriek with anymore?*

There was only really one way to find out, only one way she could move: *forwards,* and trying to rally up every bit of strength she had, Bethan pushed herself on, driving herself, *willing* herself through the rest of the barrier into the space beyond.

Just one more step.

One more step.

Less than a breath later, she was then through and feeling the wave of air hit her like a slap, she was sprawling forwards, throwing her hands out just in time before she hit the dirt face-first.

Her hands. She still had hands after all.

"Ow!"

Without even realising it, Bethan let out a cry, startling herself with her sudden ability to hear again. She could feel pain jarring up through her knees, where she'd landed, spreading up towards her thighs. She could feel the rough sandy dirt beneath her bare legs. She could hear her own breathing as she took a deep sigh, relishing in the fact that she was still alive. But even as she delighted in the simple pleasure of existing, she just as suddenly became aware of exactly where she was.

The air she was inhaling was sour; as if she were trapped in a room no one had drawn breath in for years, and her heart skipped a beat as the truth of the matter hit her.

The reason the air felt so stale, so unused was because it *was* dead and unused. She had crossed the line no living soul should ever cross, maybe, *would* never cross again.

She was in the world of the dead.

"Oh!"

Even as these thoughts filtered through her mind, Bethan then heard another thud and yelp beside her and finally opening her eyes, the element swivelled to see, with immense relief, the other three women, kneeling just as she was, in a small line in the dirt, each as bewildered and scared stiff as the next.

They all looked the same as when last she had seen them – what felt like *years* ago – and yet somehow, they all seemed different. Something, in those few moments between the other world and this, had changed them, something that Bethan couldn't place straight away, but realised later, when she thought back on her time in that place rarely spoken of.

They all had a shadow. Each woman, including herself, had a shadow beneath her, as if there were a bright light high above, shining down on them, casting their silhouettes in the dust. After the shadowless world of the Diggers, it felt somehow eerie; especially as there *was* no light there, only greyness... But at the time, Bethan felt only the hairs rise on the back of her neck, felt only the twinge that something was out of place.

Saz, the closest element to her, then turned her head.

"You all right?" she asked, seeing Bethan's bewildered expression. If she had noticed something too, she said nothing about it. Her voice sounded strangely muffled and far away, despite the fact she was within touching distance. The air was too dead, too old and thick to help the noise along and not knowing what else she could really do, Bethan just nodded dumbly.

Saz then looked to the other two and Bethan heard the question repeated. Already her focus had moved elsewhere though and taking her own chance to turn, the element took a proper look at their surroundings.

Before them was a land much like that they had left behind. It was a barren wilderness of dust, with nothing but the great tree-like boulder to be seen for miles. And yet, though it was almost the same, like the shadows, it seemed different.

The cliffs beyond had gone and in their place appeared to be nothing, nothing but a deep lifeless grey stretching on as far as the eye could see. Like a thin film hanging in the oppressive air, the whole place felt utterly... endless. And utterly dead.

"What do we do now?"

Bethan heard one of the other elements speak, but she couldn't tell which one. Their voices were like whispers. Yet there was only really one answer to that question and they all knew it.

They had to go on. There was no turning back now they had come this far and the first to move, Saz got to her feet with a grunt.

As she did so, the element's whole body then gave a terrible shudder and it was only as Bethan leapt up too, panicked, that she realised why. At standing level, the temperature was *cold*. More than cold, it was *freezing* and within seconds, Bethan felt goosebumps begin to spring up on her arms, spreading along her shoulders to the back of her neck as she too, gave a shiver.

Reluctant, the other two women also clambered to their feet, trembling in the sudden cold, arms hurrying to wrap themselves across their chests in some attempt to keep their warmth. The silky dresses of the Digger world though, as well as the dried mud still caked to their arms and legs, did nothing to help whatsoever.

"Wha-whatever we do," Meggie remarked. Her teeth were already starting to chatter. "We h-have to get m-moving." And the others nodded.

Saz looked up towards the gloomy horizon.

Only a little way ahead now stood the boulder. It too had changed from a brilliant white to an eerie dead grey and seeming to consider it for a moment, her eyes blinking furiously in the cold, her face fell into a frown.

"I guess we head for the rock," she started, not wanting to point out the obvious question; *what other choice did they have?* But even before she or any of the others could take a single step forward, a gloomy voice then drifted out of the blue.

"Good eternity, ladies," it said, and all four women gave a start of horror as they noticed that the way ahead hadn't been empty after all.

Before them stood a man - for want of a better term, for although he stood barely a few feet from the ground, his face was not that of a child's. A long bedraggled beard hung limply from his chin, wisping up around his ears, and beneath those ears were deep wrinkles, furrows upon furrows of them, running all the way down his cheeks to his thin-set mouth, making his face seem like nothing *but* folds of skin. The eyes too, were small and thin, like a wrinkle themselves and strikingly uneven, one planted almost at the top of his wide forehead, the other down by his bulbous nose, making it look as if he were scrutinising them all with his head constantly to one side. His clothes - a tunic and trousers with a grubby cloak much too long for him - were grey, much like their surroundings, and worn down to rags, his sleeves covering any hands he may have.

He was so odd-looking that for a moment or two, the women could do nothing but stare. Stare in surprise, in awe, in *disgust* until;

"May I take your baggage?" the man spoke again. His voice too, was muffled by the cold air, but unlike the elements, he didn't seem to be shivering.

He also didn't seem to be *breathing*, and Saz, the first to swallow her nerves, tried to give a polite smile.

"Baggage?" she echoed. "We're not carrying any baggage..."

"No baggage?"

And turning his tiny eyes on her, the man barely seemed to raise an eyebrow – if he had had any.

"Everyone carries baggage, Miss," he replied dully. "All I ask is that I take it for you." And shuffling towards them on tiny little legs that seemed to drag rather than lift themselves, he then began to walk down the line, studying each woman in turn, scanning them up and down, almost as if he were perusing a tapestry on the wall that mildly interested him.

"Were you all in a fight together?" he asked before any of the elements could say another word. "Or is this some sort of odd coincidence?"

Still utterly baffled, Saz looked confused.

"Fight?" she retorted, taken off-guard.

"Yes, Miss." The man seemed almost to be shouting now, his voice deliberately slower, like he thought they were all stupid. "Were you involved in a war of some sort? A battle? Maybe just a little scrap? Who started it?" He glared at Saz long and hard. "I bet it was *you*..."

Saz just gawped at him and seeing their collectively blank expressions, the little man then gave a grin. The movement was ghastly, his mouth sneering upwards to flash a gaping toothless hole. Bethan looked like she was going to be sick.

Composing himself, the man then ended his tour of the elements with a little sniff. His large nose quivered.

"Mean no disrespect," he said. "Jus' seems strange to me that four women, who all seem to know each other, would suddenly appear here, together. Figured you must have all come as a group. And you're young too, so, being killed in a fight seemed only natural... Unless it was a plague?" he looked suddenly horribly eager. "Was it a plague?"

"Oh, we're not dead!" Meggie interrupted, finally understanding, and she glanced at the other three as if for reassurance. "We weren't killed in a fight or by plague. We're still alive!"

But though the little man looked quickly disappointed, he also looked just as quickly very *bored*.

"No baggage and not dead, eh?" he mused. "Ah, I see. You're going to be some of *those*."

The women looked even more confused.

"Some of *what*?" challenged Meggie and the little man, seeming startled for a moment that anyone had heard him, forced another repulsive smile.

"Mean no disrespect," he repeated, as seemed to be his way. "All I meant is, I can see you're going to be some of those that take a bit more *convincing*... It's quite common you know..."

"No, really!" And this time it was Bex who spoke up as she realised what was going on. The little man obviously thought they were in denial. Every smug little wrinkle on his face reeked with it. "We're not dead. We just passed through this barrier here," and she gestured behind her absently, "We just walked into this... place. You've got it all wrong. We didn't die."

The man just seemed to look at her for a long time, before giving a blink.

"Oh, you did, did you?" he replied, still sounding utterly bored and utterly unconvinced. "Well, if that's the truth of it, then tell me; if you simply 'walked' here, through a 'barrier', where is it?"

Bex frowned.

"It's right-" But it was then that all four elements turned and saw, with cries of dismay, that sure enough the wall of colour, the barrier they had pushed through, the barrier that had separated the living world from this world of death, the barrier that would prove to be their only way home, had gone. It had vanished and with it the Digger world behind it.

They were stranded.

Bethan gave an extra shudder as she realised for the first time just how very very cold it was.

The air was close and stale and icy, making it difficult to breathe and the understanding that they were stuck suddenly dawning, panic began to rise thick and fast.

It was only a matter of time before they really *would* start to die...

"W-who *are* y-you?" the final element then challenged aloud, barely able to get the words out through the sudden shuddering of her jaw. It was the first time she'd properly spoken in this place, and she was shocked to hear how far away her own voice sounded.

The man turned his lopsided eyes on her and Bethan found herself wondering how many times he'd been asked this question.

"I am the one who collects the baggage," he said in a tired voice. "Like I told you."

There was something sinister about him now, more so than before. It wasn't likely to be long before he started to get impatient... "So, may I please take yours, Miss?"

"And like we've already told you," Saz stepped in bravely. Her cheeks had grown red in the bitter coldness. "We *have* no baggage!"

"No baggage?" the little man threw back and then suddenly, true enough, he lost his rag and with one little lunge, he was right there, staring up into Saz's eyes threateningly, his little mouth a hole of anger.

"I've had enough of your games!" he hissed as all four of the elements flinched, taking a step back. Saz almost fell over. Despite the man's size, there

THE ENTITY OF SOULS

was something about him, a hidden power that none of them wanted to awaken.

"Only the dead enter this way." His voice was growing louder with every syllable. "No living thing has ever passed into this world. And I should know!" He prodded himself in the chest in indignation. "I've been here from the beginning! The very existence of this world is down to me and me alone! Don't you think that I know this world as I know myself?! I tell you again, it is impossible to enter here without being dead!"

And, as if to prove his point, the little man suddenly leapt towards Bex and before any of the elements could react, a rusty dagger had appeared, as if from nowhere, in his sudden claw-like grasp and without so much as a warning, the little thing was grabbing Bex by the scruff of her dress and with an irritated growl as he yanked her towards him, had sunk the blade straight into her arm.

Bex screamed in agony and fell again to the floor, gulping for breath with shock as the other three, utterly stunned, just watched.

For a second, the whole world seemed to fall into silence, as the little man with the blade stood over the full-grown woman, his dagger clutched in his hand, his tiny little eyes on hers. But then, all leapt into action and Saz and Meggie, hurrying to Bex's side, surrounded her, trying to help her up, trying to protect her, trying to stop the tears, the howls of pain, as Bethan turned on the little man, grabbing for his hand in a moment of heroic outrage. But though the element reached for the dagger, not knowing what she could possibly do if he didn't drop it, she just as quickly realised that there was no need, for almost straight away, the little man had fallen back, recoiling from Bex as if he had been stabbed himself. Where they had been nothing but slits before, now his eyes were wide, wide and eerily blue, his mouth a gawping black hole, his whole wrinkled face a mask of total shock as he let out a moan.

Taking a shaky step backwards, he then held the little dagger away from him as if it were poisoned, turning his gaze on it as if it were a monster ready to strike out at him. But though he stared at it, it was still nothing but a rusty old blade. A rusty old blade that was now blood red and dripping…

"It can't be!" he cried as the other women tried desperately to staunch the bleed of Bex's wound. "She - she bleeds! It's… *impossible!*" And then finally, as if the words had released his grip, he dropped the dagger, *threw* it from him into the dirt, his eyes crawling back to the scene unfolding before him.

Saz had managed to tear more material from the bottom of her dress, and was now binding it tightly around Bex's arm as her skin turned a slippery, deep red.

She wheeled back on the man, no longer afraid.

"Do you believe us now?!" she challenged him with a growl, fear replaced with fury. "Do you believe us? Does this prove it?!"

And the little man who collected the baggage just nodded.

Hearing the mutter of a few words followed by the flicker of the torch bursting into life, the first thing Elanore saw by the new light of Edmund's spell was that they stood in a thin corridor. Like the stairs, it too seemed to be carved from marble and up ahead of them she could just make out a cave-like room constructed in the same way.

Edmund and Eliom were moving ahead of her through the small dim space and hesitating for only a moment, she soon followed, stepping out into the marble room the size of a hall with a little gasp.

The walls, although more roughly cut than they had looked, were intricately decorated with design upon design of gold and silver etchings, shining as they caught the dancing light. Some were faint and hard to make out, others she could distinguish in great detail and as she entered, casting an awe-filled eye about her, she soon spotted what appeared to be pictures dotted amongst the scribbling of symbols and a language she could not understand. Over to her right, near the doorway, was a drawing depicting a man in full body-armour fighting with a giant four-legged beast she didn't recognise, whilst right above it, she could just make out the glimmer of a golden baby lying beside a silver river that wound all along the wall…

Taking another look around, Elanore was then surprised to note that the room was entirely empty. There was nothing there, nothing but the carvings and the four steadfast pillars that stopped the curved ceiling from caving in on itself and beneath her feet, a carpet of soft red sand, making her footsteps almost soundless. The whole place smelt oddly damp.

She sucked in a deep breath.

"Is this it? Is this the tomb?" she then asked aloud to no one in particular and when no one in particular answered, she glanced up to see that Edmund was standing now some way off, hunched over the map once again, Eliom having already disappeared across the other side of the room out of her line of vision.

"*Inside my crypt there is a secret compartment,*" Edmund read to himself, loud enough for the others to hear. "*A secret compartment guarded by all the magic I know and have ever known.*"

But although they were finally there, and although they had the instructions of Ophelius himself, none of them seemed to have any answers. Even Eliom, who began moving closer to the other two, simply stared around him expressionlessly and as Edmund followed his friend's gaze, his brow crumpled.

"I spent so long searching this place," he said in exasperation. "If there was anything here, surely I would have found it by now?"

Feeling suddenly wary, Elanore came forward.

"Not necessarily," she pointed out, gesturing at Ophelius's scrawled handwriting in Edmund's hands. "Not if it was guarded by some kind of magic... and look here," she leant in closer over the old parchment, "it says it will only open for the worthy."

Edmund glanced at her a little sharply.

"What are you suggesting?" he asked and though Elanore wasn't sure if he sounded angry or not, before she had a chance to think about defending herself, Eliom had stepped in.

"She is perhaps suggesting that before now, you were not worthy of opening such a compartment," the wizard said. "When last you were here, you had not yet been burdened with the knowledge of the Keeper of the World, therefore you would not have had the need to understand Ophelius's secret," and although the words were wise ones, the wizard's voice still wavered, reminding both Edmund and the observant Elanore that he wasn't quite himself...

All of a sudden, the sea captain then understood why it was that the Explorer had asked *her* to come with him into the tomb, instead of any of the others. It was obvious really, now that she thought about it; Elanore was the most emotionally stable in the whole group. In terms of magical understanding and power, Edmund needed Eliom to help him find the hidden compartment - if there was one - but for serious, rational thought, she was currently the most reliable of all their companions. Edmund, with each passing day seemed to be growing increasingly edgy and withdrawn again and Eliom... there was something about him that felt a little unpredictable. As for the others; Fred and Soph were distracted by each other, Thom was prone to grumpiness and Martynio had refused to even follow Edmund down the steps.

Yes, she was the most level-headed of the whole group at the moment. And that, clearly, was what Edmund was hoping to use.

The Explorer rolled the map up and returned it safely to his cloak.

"Any idea where to start?" he then asked the room in general and both Eliom and Elanore looked about them again, their eyes scanning the empty space, the decorated walls, this corner, that design, this crack in the marble...

"If fate intended us to find it, it will be found," was all the cryptic wizard had to offer.

Edmund just cursed under his breath.

"Let's hope so," he huffed, before heading for the nearest wall. Watching him as he began to feel his way along the marble with his hands, the other two then followed suit, each heading for a separate wall to search for any kind of clue to the hidden knowledge beyond...

—

Bex's wound had finally stopped bleeding, but her breathing was laboured and heavy, the cold biting at her lungs making every breath a painful stab.

The other three women too, were really starting to struggle. Fingers and toes had grown numb and every pair of lips was blue. They were running out of time. And realising just how quickly, Bethan got straight to the point.

"Listen," she said, turning once again to the little man. He was still just standing there, staring, his eyes on the once-oozing blood. His face was aghast with fright and seeing that he no longer seemed a threat, the element realised that any possible fear she had felt of him was now gone. "We're looking for someone. Can you help us?"

The little man didn't even blink, didn't even move and when he didn't respond, Bethan tried again.

"Hey!" she snapped. "Listen to me! We're looking for someone. Can you help?"

She took a step towards him and just as she'd hoped, the man suddenly seemed to come to life again, flinching away, as if at any moment she was going to hurt him.

"Why should I help you?" he then said. He sounded troubled. "Tell me that!" and Meggie, who had been easing Bex back to her shaking feet, gave a growl of frustration.

"You hurt our friend!" she cried. "I think you owe us!"

"*Owe you?*" The man turned his lopsided gaze on the little element as if sizing her up, but obviously deciding that Meggie was too much of a threat to him, he soon turned back to Bethan instead, an ugly scowl on his face.

"I suppose may be able to help you…" he said slowly. "But only on one condition…"

Condition?

The other three looked suddenly alarmed and Bethan's heart skipped a beat all over again.

She'd been dreading this since the moment he'd appeared, dreading making some kind of deal with this man. She'd had a feeling that the guardian of the dead would want some kind of payment for the information they wanted, whatever they had to do to get it. And more than likely, it was going to be something she knew none of them could possibly give…

"What condition?" she replied uneasily. "What do you want?"

The man gave a wicked smile.

Did he know what she was thinking? Bethan hoped not.

"Mean no disrespect," he then said, dragging out the sudden hold he seemed to have over all of them, "but I don't help *anyone* for free. Why should you be any different?"

He sounded smug and although Meggie looked about ready to murder him – if that were possible – Saz soon held her back.

"Well?" she asked, clearly struggling to keep her own calm. "Spit it out then. What do you want?"

The little man gave a little shuffle. He was clearly enjoying this more than he should. He had shown his weakness when Bex had been stabbed, but now he was back in power.

"Only a small thing, a trifling thing," he replied, his grin widening to leave a great gap where a mouth should have been. All four women visibly shuddered. "It's nothing really. Not when there're four of you…" he was babbling now. "But it has to be done." And as he cleared his throat, the elements could almost feel themselves leaning in to listen. "In return for helping you, I ask only this… the price of one soul."

No.

This was *exactly* where she hadn't wanted this conversation to go and Bethan, knowing what he meant, bit her lip furiously. It was so numb with the cold, she barely felt the pain.

"One s-soul?" Saz questioned, her voice wavering.

The little man nodded again, his grin fixed in place now.

"One of you must give me your soul, *willingly*," he said and then, as if speaking to a group of children; "in return for my help, one of you must die."

Bex let out a choke of pain as the other three elements lapsed straight into silence.

One of you must die.

He'd said it. He'd said what they had all secretly feared to hear and for a second, no one, *no one* knew how to respond, bar, it seemed, Meggie.

"No! No way! No deal!" the little element spluttered and then, as the other women just looked at her, her face hardened. "Please don't tell me you're even considering this! It's too much to ask, of any of us! It's not worth our lives!"

But though she had said exactly what most of them were thinking, still the others said nothing, each of them already deep in thought and turning back to the little *thing* before them in appeal, Meggie almost begged.

"Surely there must be something else we can do, something else that you want? Nothing is worth death," she pleaded.

The man though, just shrugged, his smile never budging.

"Mean no disrespect, but you'll all be here one day anyway. What more could I have to ask of you than a death? I am the baggage collector. It's my *job* to collect from the dead. One more death means one more job for me…"

"But surely one more death can't even matter to you?!" Meggie wasn't giving up. "It's just another job! A job you can do at any time! Thousands- no! Millions! – must die every day!" She gestured at her friends. "To us, life is all we have!"

But already the little element could see that her argument was useless. The baggage collector collected baggage day in day out and had been doing so from the beginning of time. Death was him, he *was* death and no matter how much one small insignificant person tried to argue with him, that was that. He had never budged and never would. And as if to make the point even more, his own face hardened, every wrinkle in his face as solid as a rock.

"My job is all I have," he said simply. "Would you ask that I sacrifice that for the sake of you?"

It was, in its own way, a fair point and overwhelmed with what it all meant, the elements just turned to each other, indecision in every eye.

There was no question in their minds that someone's *life* was too much to sacrifice for the lives of the others. And yet in each and every one of them was a great aching desire to be free; for Saz to see her family, her little sister Charlie again; for Bex to feel the rain on her skin once more; for Bethan to hold in her arms the man she loved…

Meggie meanwhile, infuriated beyond words that it had come to this, was thinking, searching deeper than she thought she ever had for a solution. The iciness was becoming almost unbearable now. Her whole body was shivering beyond control, as were, she noticed, those of the other elements. But she had to concentrate.

There had to be something else; something she could bargain with. There had to be some way to get what they needed and get out of there, out of the cold, out of the deadness pressing in all about them. And she knew that useless as it *felt*, she wouldn't stop until she had found it.

"There must be other things to live for than just your *job*."

She wasn't sure where the words had come from, but suddenly they were there and sticking with it, she then levelled the baggage collector with pleading eyes.

"Is there nothing else you desire? Anything at all?" she asked.

For a moment, the man stared back at her, his expression just as stony, just as hard as it had been before. It was like looking into the face of an ugly statue, rigid and fierce.

But though she had thought their cause to be hopeless, though she had thought him unmoving; Meggie had been wrong.

"Anything?" the man echoed and then, suddenly, without warning, his face seemed to cave in on itself. Furrows, deep and quivering seemed to join into long tremulous lines as his eyes closed, disappearing against the grey skin. And then he was shaking, his whole body crumpling into a little ball and with complete astonishment, the elements just looked on as the baggage collector, the lord of the dead, then began to cry.

The sight was a pitiful yet disgusting one as fat wet tears started to roll down his face, sticking in his damp beard, getting caught in the crevices of his cheeks and he let out a loud wail, his mouth wet with saliva. Staring at him all the while, Saz, Bethan, Bex and Meggie just gawped, none of them sure how to respond until, feeling oddly guilty, Meggie then stepped towards him, reaching out a hand to take him by the shoulder. Moving though, only seemed to make it *worse,* as, seeing her outstretched fingers, the weeping stump of a man soon let out another cry and backed away, clearly frightened.

"Don't touch me!" he snapped. His voice cracked. "Keep away!"

Meggie paused.

"I won't hurt you…" she tried, but the man, shuffling further away, held his deformed hands out as if to push her back.

"The living cannot touch the dead!" he barked. "Keep away from me!"

Already though, he seemed to be regaining his composure and as he wiped away the water on his cheeks, eying the element uncertainly, it was then that Meggie finally realised just what was going on.

Despite appearances, this man wasn't human. Chances were, he wasn't even alive and probably never would be.

All he had ever known, all he had ever seen was death; until now; until those four *living* women had stepped through a barrier between worlds; a barrier that had then disappeared, leaving them stranded there; a barrier that was no doubt some kind of anomaly, some kind of *mistake* that even the baggage handler, the eternal friend of death, had never seen before…

That was why it was only after stabbing Bex, after seeing her pain and the living blood oozing from her wound, that he'd finally believed and understood that what they spoke was the truth.

And that was why he was crying now; because he knew nothing else but death, and by being not quite alive himself, he really did have nothing else but his job, the job he'd performed forever and would continue to perform long after all that the women had ever known was gone.

He was crying because he had never known life. Though he desired it, he could never have it and it was then that Meggie finally understood, *really* understood that there was nothing else she could do, nothing else any of them could do.

There was no other bargain they could make except a life. The little man could want nothing else because he *knew* nothing else. Money, beauty, love, anything that could have been offered was entirely useless and unwanted.

"Listen," Bethan then said again. Perhaps she had reached the same conclusion as Meggie. Perhaps she too knew that it was useless, but either way, she looked unhappy.

"We have to think of a way to-" But before she could finish, Saz had interrupted, her voice so quiet, even in that muffled, airless place, that the others took a second to register what she had said.

"I'll do it," she muttered and when Bethan, Bex and Meggie all turned as one to look at her, she gave an odd sort of grimace.

Bethan looked confused.

"You'll do what?" she asked.

And as if it were nothing, Saz nodded towards the man, her head low, not meeting anyone's eye.

"What he wants," she replied simply. And then; "I will give him my soul if he helps us find Ophelius."

—

Sweaty and breathless in the warm tomb air, Edmund's sore fingers traced the curve of what he thought was a globe etched into the wall just above his head. It curved round in a great golden arc but as he neared the end and saw the snake's head, he let out a sigh. It was the fifteenth coiled reptile he'd outlined in the last few minutes alone. They seemed to be everywhere, and just as useless as each other. So far, he'd come across snakes, some writing and a picture of a tree, none of which seemed to have revealed themselves to be hiding a secret compartment.

Eliom meanwhile, was sweeping the wall across the other side of the room with his staff, muttering quiet incantations under his breath. The words flowed over his lips in rich deep flurries of power and pausing in his work, Edmund listened for a little while before getting to his feet with a groan.

He still couldn't quite believe what was happening, what they were doing. Days he had spent down in that tomb years ago and yet he'd barely paid any attention to what was on the walls. Back then he'd only been interested in what the walls *housed* and in all that time he'd completely missed the compartment.

The compartment which, if they ever found it, would lead him to the elements.

Lead him to Bethan…

I assume she cares for you in return?

Edmund shook his head fiercely but before the doubts of her feelings started to take grip again, like they had back on the Karenza, he heard Elanore gasp from a small distance away and straightening up, he held the burning splint he still carried, that little bit higher.

"Everything all right?" he asked, trying to keep the excitement from his voice as it echoed through the space. The sea captain was seated in front of what looked to be a sizeable carving of a key. "Have you found something?"

Elanore looked up. But instead of smiling, it was the captain's turn to shake her head and Edmund's heart returned to its normal rhythm as she touched her hand to her lips to suck on a freshly-bleeding finger.

"Cut myself," she said sheepishly, pointing to the bottom of the jagged key with her uninjured hand. On the wall there was now a patch of blood where her fingers had been.

Edmund frowned.

"All right."

He felt like saying something sarcastic, snapping at her in his frustration but instead he simply looked away. Why was he feeling so touchy? Was it just because of what Soph had said, the hesitation it had unearthed within him? Or was it something else?

It wasn't Elanore's fault that they couldn't find the compartment. None of this was anyone's fault…

Was it?

He wasn't given time to analyse his troubled thoughts any further though, before Eliom suddenly stopped in his work and in one swift, inhumanly fast moment, he was at Edmund's side.

"Of course!" the wizard exclaimed as if he'd finally solved a puzzle that had been irritating him for months. "Blood!" and before either Elanore or Edmund could say anything, he had delved inside his robes and pulled out a knife sheathed all in white.

"Here," he then said and drawing the blade, he reached for Edmund's arm.

Elanore, watching the two companions from afar, opened her mouth to cry out, only to close it again as, without a word, the Explorer lifted his hand, willingly offering it to the wizard. No matter what had happened to his friend, no matter what strange turmoil he was going through, Edmund still trusted Eliom with his life and taking that trust, Eliom soon lifted the knife and without ceremony, dragged it right across the middle of Edmund's outstretched palm.

Edmund winced in pain as blood welled up from the wound and Elanore gawped in disgust. But the wizard wasn't finished. Waiting for a few seconds as the blood began to pour freely, seeping over Edmund's fingers, Eliom then grabbed Edmund by the wrist and marching him across the tomb, finally thrust his friend's hand, cut and all, up to the wall where Elanore's own blood still stained the marble.

Nothing happened for several tense seconds.

"What are you-?" Edmund started but Eliom got there before he had a chance.

"Using blood as a key is one of the oldest and most common forms of magic," he explained as if they all, especially him, should have realised this fact a long time ago. He grimaced a little. "I spent too long looking for complicated spells or cracks in the wall, when all the time the answer was staring straight at us!"

Edmund's hand, still pushed up against the rough old marble, was beginning to ache as more blood throbbed to the surface, but he didn't complain.

"Where you cut yourself, Elanore," Eliom continued, gesturing to where he'd placed Edmund's palm, right at the edge of the carving of the key. "It was supposed to be there. It was supposed to be sharp enough to draw blood… but," and he gave a small smile, "just not yours."

Edmund's hand was really starting to sting now and he gritted his teeth.

"If not Elanore's though, why mine?" he questioned. "Why am I so special?"

"Because," and Eliom appeared to give yet another smile, "this spell, a simple spell - although to a human like Ophelius it would have seemed a magic of great power. It would have taken him years to master it - this spell, only reveals its magic for-"

"-those who are *worthy*," Edmund finished, the words of the map echoing in his mind. He was starting to feel excitement building within him all over again now. What the wizard was saying made sense… Sort of.

"And those who are worthy in this instance," Eliom continued as if he'd never been interrupted, "are those with a connection to the one who has cast the spell."

"A connection?" Elanore looked confused, and as she looked from wizard to Explorer, her brow furrowed. "What connection could Edmund possibly have with-?"

But her words were lost by the sound of a groaning crack from deep within the wall as suddenly, before their very eyes, the bottom of the key where Edmund's bloody hand was pressed, then started to glow.

The light was faint at first, faint and red but then it started to grow stronger and as the trio watched in amazement, it began to spread out, creeping along the outline of the key, spreading up towards the ceiling. The wall gave another noisy moan as the light traced the top of the key, down the straight, along the round bulb and back down until…

As if he knew what was coming, Eliom then grabbed both Elanore and the bleeding Edmund by the shoulders, pulling them back and out of harm's way as, with an almighty boom, the marble within the shape of the key then crumbled outwards, piling debris at their feet.

—

Once Saz had spoken, it took only half a second for the other three women to then burst into life, all at once filling the silent world of the dead with their worried cries.

"Saz, No! None of us will do this! Don't be stupid!"

"Why would you say such a thing?! We can't let you die!"

Surprisingly to everyone though, Bex proved to be the loudest of the three.

"You can't do what he asks!" she cried, straightening herself up from cradling her injured arm. "You have a family, a home to live for!" and then, suddenly looking even more determined, she turned to the others. "If it needs to be done, then I will do it!"

Meggie immediately looked outraged.

So, it had started...

"No, if anyone is going to go through with this then it's me," she said. "My family are all dead. I've got no real reason to go back to Tungala. I might as well be the one!"

But though the others began to argue, Saz had clearly spoken her piece.

"No!" She was almost shouting. "I've said I'll do it and I will. I mean it." And there was something in the way she spoke, something so firm, so decisive and final that both Meggie and Bex found themselves falling into silence.

Bethan however, had yet to have her say.

"Hold on a second!" she cried, and stepping forward, she looked at each element in turn, challenging them all with her glare. "This is not a competition to see who has the least to live for!" She glowered at Bex and Meggie sceptically. "You both have just as much a reason to live as any of us. There's some other way around this. There must be!" Clenching her fists, her voice cracked with emotion as the cold pressed against her chest. "None of us will die. There must be some other way. Saz, you are not doing this!"

But though she had secretly hoped for more arguing, for more indecision, for more answers, the silence that met her words spoke volumes. Somehow, with barely a discussion, they all seemed to have decided, to have resigned themselves to the situation; all of them, except her and she couldn't help but pale, her whole body juddering with the cold, numb shock of it.

"You're not actually going to let Saz do this are you?!" she asked in amazement to anyone who would listen. But when no one gave her a reply still, she smiled bitterly. "No one's going to try and stop her?"

"We just did..." Bex began. She looked like she was about to cry, but before she could finish, Saz was shaking her head, suddenly finding her feet very interesting.

"We'll never reach Ophelius unless one of us gives in," she muttered, gesturing at the little man, who'd done nothing but look immensely stunned since her offer. "He wants nothing else. There is nothing else we can possibly give him. We all know that and need to stop kidding ourselves that we don't."

But though Bethan, still totally amazed that no one seemed to want a way out of this except her, struggled to stutter some kind of excuse, words seemed to fail her. She had never seen Saz look so determined, so *sure,* and as if the floor had somehow given her strength, she looked up at the baggage collector, her expression fierce.

"So, what do I have to do?" she asked. "How is this going to work?"

Still looking amazed himself, the ugly little man-thing stared at her intently for a good minute.

"Well, if that is your decision. I will make a pact with you," he then said, solemnity hanging on his every word.

And Saz nodded.

"Very well," she replied. But the way she spoke, so finally, so resigned to her fate, only seemed to stir Bethan up all over again.

She couldn't believe this was happening. She couldn't believe that as a group they were letting Saz do this and suddenly turning, she grabbed the element of fire by the shoulders as if to shake the entire ludicrous decision right out of her.

"No!" she cried. "I won't let you do this! Are you insane?!" and then, in a moment of desperation; "I will go, if anything!"

It was the first time she had said it. And yes, the first time, she realised, with a pang of guilt, that she had even considered it, *really* considered dying in this place for the sake of her friends' freedom.

She wasn't the only one to be wholly unconvinced by her efforts though and Saz, tearing herself away, looked suddenly *angry*.

"Just stop it!" the element then yelled in Bethan's face, finally seeming to reach the end of her tether. "Why are you so desperate to prevent this?!" And then it came; "I'm making this choice for *your* sake. For *you*, Bethan. So stop fighting it!"

Bethan's eyes widened, as did the eyes of all of the others and Meggie, seeing that things were about to go too far, started to speak, but it was too late.

"What?" Bethan demanded. "What do you mean for my sake?! You're doing this for everyone!"

But Saz's own eyes shone with a cold intensity now.

"You're the one who wants so desperately to escape," she spat, her voice as icy as her stare. "To return to *Edmund* again! So don't pretend to care about my welfare. You would gladly see me die to be with him again - and you know it. So don't you dare try and stop me because *it makes you feel better!*"

It makes you feel better. Despite the close air, the words seemed to hang there for a moment, just echoing into the nothing as a deadly hush fell amongst the group.

The whole place seemed suddenly to feel that little bit colder as Saz finished her tirade and Meggie and Bex, astonished by her harsh words, could do nothing but stare.

Bethan meanwhile, remained silent. She *had* nothing to say, no response to give as she watched Saz give her life away. The fight was gone from her now and later she had often wondered why she'd spoken nothing in her own defence, why she hadn't begged Saz to reconsider again, why she hadn't denied her friend's charges. But then, it was only then, only later that she really understood…

THE ENTITY OF SOULS

Deep down Saz was right, and it filled Bethan with a shame like no other that ached in her chest slowly every time she thought about it. It was a shame that would always be in the back of her mind whenever she remembered her fellow element in the times to come; a shame that would follow her to the grave, when she joined this place of the dead as a true citizen.

But right then, right at that moment, she did and said nothing. And neither did anyone else, except the collector, who, acting as if nothing had happened, then turned to Saz himself.

"I propose..." he started in a business-like manner and Saz shifted her attention back to the little man. Her expression was strangely blank.

"I'm listening."

The man smiled again horribly, almost as if he were enjoying himself, enjoying the chaos he was creating.

"I propose," he then repeated with a dramatic wobble of his head, "that I take all of you to find this person that you seek, in exchange for your soul," he pointed at Saz, "But," and he waggled a gnarled finger, "I *am* prepared to make one small concession."

Concession?

This immediately got everyone's attention. After all that, was there some kind of hope for them after all?

Saz's face didn't change.

"What concession?"

The little man looked pleased with himself.

"I *will* take your soul," he said. "But only when your purpose is done." And he paused then, as if expecting someone to argue with him.

Everyone just continued to look at him, slow confusion passing across each face.

Meggie's brow wrinkled.

"Her *purpose*?" she asked uncertainly. "Are you saying-?"

"Yes." The man barely glanced up to see who had spoken. It seemed that he only had eyes for Saz now; yes, for the one more soul he would be adding to his collection. "I'll only take her soul *once* her job is done, for she yet has a very important purpose to fulfil..."

None of the women knew how to respond for a moment. None of them had really prepared for this.

"Hold on. Do you mean to say, that you're not going to kill me now?" Saz tried to clarify. Suddenly, there was an odd light alive in her eyes. "That I don't have to stay here *now*?"

The wrinkles on the little man's face seemed to furrow even deeper.

"Oh gods, no!" he cried, almost sounding disgusted at the idea. "Like I said; it is not your time quite yet." But he was still smiling that awful smile, keeping every nerve on edge and not even Saz could feel too excited just yet.

"How long do I have then?" the element hurried. She couldn't help herself, she looked relieved. They all were in some way. The man wasn't going to kill her. Not right then at least. Which meant she had time... "Weeks? Years? My sister, Charlie, will I see her again? And my Mother? And Eliom-?"

"It's not my place to say," the baggage collector replied simply. Apart from the disgusting grin, *his* expression gave nothing away, making all of them wonder if he even knew the answer to Saz's questions or not.

Discussions clearly over though, Saz then sobered.

"All right then," she said seriously and holding out a hand towards the little man, she gave a nod, as if waiting for him to shake it, to finalise their agreement.

The baggage collector stared at her outstretched fingers as if each long bone were a poisonous barb.

"No," he said and remembering that he couldn't touch living flesh, Saz soon dropped it awkwardly. Instead, the little man then bent down and in one quick move, had hold of the dagger, still dripping with Bex's blood, from where it had lain in the dust.

All four women immediately stiffened, but seeing their obvious fear the man only looked amused.

"*This* is how we will make the pact," he explained, before carefully, so as not to make any contact, handing the dagger hilt-first to Saz and demonstrating the movement with his own imaginary knife; "draw it across the centre of your palm."

Hesitating, Saz stared down at the rusty-looking blade, the colour draining from her face.

This was it; this was the end, and as the dagger met her skin and blood began to ooze onto the already gory knife, none of the other elements found themselves able to watch, to watch and know that their friend was giving her life away, however long or short that may be, for their own freedom.

Her palm stinging, Saz winced a little, but she kept her eyes on the baggage collector.

"What now?" she muttered, her tongue seeming to stick in her mouth. *His* eyes were greedily watching the blood as if every morsel were his.

"Now, repeat after me, quickly!" he ordered as Saz finished the job, "*I...*" he paused. "What's your name?"

"Saz," Saz broke in weakly. "Saz of Bretherton." Her whole hand was throbbing now, the blood flowing thick and fast. The cut was deeper than she'd thought...

"*I, Saz of Bretherton,*" the baggage collector continued, *"agree to honour the contract made between myself and the other world."*

"I, Saz of Bretherton," Saz started tonelessly. This time no one argued with her. There was no point. It was too late… "agree to honour the contract made between myself and the other world."

"Good," the little man crowed, "and say- *'that in exchange for the information I seek, I will give my soul and my life to the collector without question and whenever it is seen fit for him to take it'*."

Saz gave a small sigh before continuing herself.

"That in exchange for the information I seek, I will give my soul and my life to the collector without question and whenever it is seen fit for him to take it," she said.

And then, at the exact same moment of her last word, as if to seal the very agreement itself, the fresh trickle of blood from her hand seemed to cease and before Saz's very eyes, the cut began to heal. Quickly it closed up, leaving nothing behind but a long brown scar, serving as a record of her pact; a sign to remind her that at any moment she would be taken back to this cold, desolate place, *forever*.

"Well," the little man then said. And reaching forward gingerly, he carefully extracted the dagger from Saz's hands. In his eyes, the deal was done and he wasn't going to waste any more time. He had baggage to be seeing to elsewhere. "Shall we get moving then?"

The others, including Saz, all seemed to give a start, as if suddenly being lifted from a daze, each of them too stunned by what they had just witnessed to remember why it was they'd come in the first place.

"M-m-moving?" Bex stuttered, her voice quivering.

"Yes," the man's grin widened, making the whole lower part of his face seem like one gaping hole. He was obviously greatly satisfied with himself now that he had another soul to add to his lot, at his own bidding. "If you want to find someone, then we must reach the opening." And he pointed towards the great tree-like rock far before them, the rock that had shown them the way.

The women could do nothing but hate him, him and his grotesque smiles. But there was nothing they could do now. They had travelled there for a purpose and it would be a waste if they did nothing; a waste of time and effort; a waste of Saz's life.

They had no other option now but to follow and meet the dead.

"Lead the way," so Bethan then muttered, finally finding her voice again and without another word, the small group started off, the ageless hunched little man leading the four living, breathing elements.

—

As the dust settled and the trio waited to see inside the long-looked-for compartment, it was Eliom who heard the noise first.

Straight away, the wizard stiffened, his grip tightening on his staff, but too transfixed on the gaping hole in the wall, blinking in the dirt-filled air, Edmund and Elanore noticed only too late the sound of rushing feet.

Within seconds, a horde of men were then upon them and without a sound, Eliom had reacted, twisting round sharply as he delivered a deadly blow to the first. It was a stout man waving a scythe and as he fell to the floor with a grunt, making the others suddenly aware that they were no longer alone, Edmund and Elanore snatched for their own weapons, Edmund quickly shifting his sword to his uninjured hand. Both of them barely had a moment to register what was going on though, before more men were pressing themselves forwards, every single one of them armed and dangerous.

And then, just like that, they were fighting for their lives; Edmund slashing out at the knees of a grubby-looking fisherman as he tumbled towards him, waving a knife, Elanore rolling with surprising skill under the slash of another figure's longsword.

Diving to the floor as he thrust his sword into the belly of another fighter, Edmund quickly tried to get some kind of grasp on the situation.

What was going on? Who were these people? And where were they all coming from?

Although he had no way of knowing, from his new position, he seemed to see everything more clearly. To his left, Elanore was confronting what looked like a dwarf, or otherwise a very short man, hacking at the only thing she could reach; his head. Eliom meanwhile, had somehow managed to make his way to the other side of the room and was almost effortlessly ploughing back the crowds of fighters trying to push themselves into the tomb.

There seemed to be an endless stream of them, cascading, roiling, sprinting down the steps, crashing into the marble walls. Where it had once been utterly empty, the whole room was simply thronging with people, including now, he realised with a hint of relief, Fred, Thom and Soph.

Soph was just as impressive a fighter as her partner. Already she had managed to kill three men, leaving a bloody pile at her feet, her movements fast, agile and calculating; whilst Thom's axe was in full swing, chopping at the legs of those taller, ducking under metal, meeting each fighter with a growl. Close by, Fred was a blur of smooth movement as he battled his way through the throng with seeming ease.

Seeing another figure approach him, Edmund swivelled to meet his unknown foe. But as he turned to fight the stranger head on, he then saw something that made his blood run cold and the sword in his hands almost fall loose, for before him in the dim light of the tomb stood a slim figure. It was young, with a child-like face, brown ringleted hair and bright eyes... a girl, a beautiful cherub-like girl and as the two met eye contact, she opened her mouth slowly to smile, to reveal beneath rosy lips, a set of pearly-white fangs…

An audible groan fell from Edmund's lips.

"No!" he hissed in horror, backing away from the girl, from the clone. Renard's clone. "You - you were destroyed! All of you! You were killed!"

But the girl's disgusting grin only widened. Death didn't frighten her. *Nothing* frightened her.

"You have taken our master, human!" she roared instead, in her high squeaky voice. "And for that *you* must die!" And so it was, she then lunged at him, all teeth and shining metal as she wielded a heavy sword.

Thankfully, stunned, horrified as he was, Edmund reacted straight away, his reflexes jumping into action as he watched the girl charge towards him. Without any thought or hesitation, he fended her off with a leap to the side and then, spinning, drove his sword straight into her face.

The smile disappeared with barely a cry as the girl sank straight to the floor, dead. But whilst she posed no more threat to anyone, for some strange reason, the Explorer found himself feeling suddenly breathless as he stared down at her body, pulling his blade from her forehead with a nasty pop as his mind whirred.

Who were all these people? Why were they here? The same questions were back, but now with new ones, most importantly; where had *she* come from? Why was *she* here? And how had she come to challenge him without Renard's orders? Renard was *dead*…

All answers, however, came sooner than he'd thought as a loud voice then rang out above the confusion.

"*Edmund of Tonasse!*"

It was as if his name had some sort of magical effect, for all of a sudden, the fighting then ceased. Everyone stood still and silent, panting and sweating in the crowded space, Fred, Soph, Thom, Elanore and Eliom staring about them, their weapons still raised, confusion evident on their faces.

Searching the room for the origin of the voice, Edmund then noticed a robed figure pushing its way towards him through the throng and apprehension forming like a lump in his chest, he simply watched as the stranger then wasted no time in pulling its hood back to reveal a face he immediately recognised.

And immediately hated.

"Jen," the Explorer spat bitterly. The name was like some kind of curse on the air and straight away the rest of his companions all tensed. "I thought you were dead."

The woman, almost completely identical except in clothing, and yes, age, to the girl Edmund had just killed, smiled joylessly.

"Thought or *hoped?*" she replied and Thom, who was surrounded by men almost twice his height, gave a low snarl, which everyone ignored.

"Bor told me you were found after the battle at the village." Edmund sounded almost pleading. "Your sash and cloak…"

But the captain of Renard's army, just gave a small laugh. She was never one for flamboyance. She'd never had a chance next to Edmund's brother.

"Yes, it's quite helpful having a whole army that look exactly like me, sometimes…" she mused, a grin still plastered across her face. Although she didn't have fangs like the rest of her look-alikes, she was still monstrous.

"You coward!" Thom exclaimed, brandishing his axe as if to charge at the woman and slay her once and for all. "You dressed one of your fighters to look like you! Instead of staying to fight like a man!"

Jen though, just shot him something of a withering look.

"If you haven't noticed; I'm *not* a man," she replied before smiling again as Thom scowled.

Edmund all the while, was trying desperately to calm his wildly beating heart.

Jen had never frightened him before. Not really. Not the way the clones had. But now…

"What do you want?" he asked, suddenly aware of the time they were wasting. He hoped that no one had noticed the hole in the wall, or, more importantly, whatever lay beyond it…

And hearing the impatient tone in his voice, Jen's face grew serious then, serious and yes, *angry*.

"You know *exactly* what I want," she replied, with barely a blink. "I am here to reclaim my master, of course."

Reclaim her master?

He wasn't sure what he had expected but even so, for a moment, Edmund just looked at her blankly.

Reclaim Renard?

And slowly, before he even really realised he was doing it, the Explorer found himself starting to wipe his bloody sword on the corpse at his feet, as if preparing to use it all over again.

Something told him that whatever Jen meant, whatever she had come for; things were unlikely to end well…

"What makes you think I can help you?" he asked, stalling for time as it then suddenly dawned on him.

Of course. The chances were; Renard's followers had no idea what had befallen their leader.

The last time any of them had set eyes on him, he'd been fighting his way through the trees of Bor's forest towards the Temple of Ratacopeck, alone, ready to ambush the elements and their companions.

For all Jen knew, Renard wasn't dead. For all Jen knew, Edmund and the others could have captured him and had him imprisoned somewhere…

And Edmund's eyes looked to the ground as if suddenly afraid Jen would be able to read his mind, for if this was what she thought, then it also dawned on him that as soon as he admitted the truth, his life, and the lives of his friends, would be in serious jeopardy.

"You were the last to see him," Jen pointed out, much to Edmund's growing fear. "He came to find you."

He was right then. She *didn't* know...

"And what, you assume that I know where he is now?" Edmund replied, trying urgently to think of a way out, of a way of keeping her from what he really knew.

Looking about him cautiously though, as he considered a plan, he could see straight away that any chance of fighting their way out of the situation were pretty slim. Each of his friends was completely surrounded by men and yes, he could see them now, identical young girls. Somehow Jen had managed to find herself a significant army and the group were well and truly outnumbered.

"Don't play games with me, Tonasse," the captain sneered, raising her weapon irritably. "Only two things could have happened to my master, and either way, both lead to *you*." And she thrust her sword at Edmund, as if meaning to kill him, only for the blade to fall just short of his chest.

The Explorer didn't move as she held it there, the metal quivering a little beside his tunic.

"You've either captured him and are holding him prisoner!" Jen continued. "Or," and right then, she looked oddly smug, "he entered the flames with the elements and is still alive."

Still alive?

And much as he'd thought he was prepared for anything, Edmund couldn't help but looked shocked at this.

How did Jen know about the flames? How could she possibly know what had happened in the Temple of Ratacopeck? Even Renard hadn't foreseen the real fate that awaited the four elements once they stepped into the fire...

Had he?

"Oh yes," Jen muttered, much calmer now that she clearly had the upper hand. "I know," and as she pushed the sword just that little bit closer, Edmund winced as the cool metal nicked through the fabric of his tunic, scratching his skin. "So, once you find whatever it is that you're looking for to 'save' your friends, you can take me to my master."

Having clearly had her say, the captain then cast her eyes lazily about the room and watching her, Edmund felt an odd twinge of hope. Her gaze wasn't a *searching* one, she wasn't studying the space, trying to find an answer. Clearly then, she didn't know about the compartment. She knew - somehow - that Edmund and his companions were there to bring the elements back from wherever it was they were, but she obviously had no idea why or how.

Not, the Explorer reasoned, that the great gaping hole in the wall wasn't obvious… but then again, maybe that was just it. It *would* be obvious - *if* the room had still been empty. If Jen had wandered in alone, the hole, the debris on the floor from where the wall had fallen, all of it was as clear as day. But bringing along what seemed to be her entire force was in fact an unknown disadvantage to their enemy. With so many bodies packed in so tightly, an open compartment was easy to hide.

Perhaps, Edmund realised silently, *there might be a way out of this after all.*

But first…

"Before this goes any further," he then addressed Jen, making her fix her roving eyes on him. "Tell me how you know. How do you know about the true nature of the Keeper of the World? How do you know what the elements had to do?"

If Jen seemed a little surprised by Edmund's questions after such a long silence, she didn't show it.

"I've done my research," she replied shortly, before adding, almost despite herself; "and I've asked around. Quite a few have been extremely… *helpful*."

Edmund raised an eyebrow, trying to look unconcerned, but inside, his thoughts were already turning to one thing now and one thing alone.

How was he going to kill Jen?

This woman had offered Renard, his brother, her own blood to clone a mob of soulless fighters who lived for nothing but their master's bidding. This woman had then taken those fighters, that army and commanded it, controlled it to the cost of a blameless town, to the cost of Stanzleton, to the cost of hundreds of lives, and then on to the Tribe of Water, to the slaughter of innocents.

He had no idea what her intentions really were now, or even whether he was going to come out of this situation alive. But either way, he knew that he wasn't, he *wouldn't* die alone…

"Who have you tortured?" he demanded bitterly. "Who did you hurt to make them help you?"

And Jen gave another small chuckle, nothing like the sound of the high callous laugh of her clones yet still just as chilling.

"What makes you think I tortured anybody?" she snorted, before, seeing Edmund's face darken, she then laughed again. "Maybe I just *persuaded* them!" and she rubbed her finger and thumb together with a sneer.

From amongst the crowd, Thom gave another snarl and moved as if to spit at her. Unfortunately for him though, he was too far away.

"Which coward was it who betrayed us?!" he roared instead. "I will kill him with my bare hands!"

Jen actually seemed to be enjoying herself now. For the first time, the captain was coming into her own and she *liked it*.

"I might as well tell you all the full story and get it over with!" she cried, raising her voice to the rest of the tomb. But her eyes remained firmly anchored to Edmund's, each of them sizing up the other, building up a secret animosity that was sure to get the better of them both at any moment...

"After the battle on the shore with those tribespeople," she then started, "I donned a clone with my uniform and hid away under cover of the trees, waiting for my master." Thom's lip curled. "I knew he would be heading north, following the trail you had left and once I found him, I tracked him for a time, hoping to catch up." Jen looked almost embarrassed for a moment. "As you might guess though, the forest was too thick for me to carry on for long. I lost my bearings and for a while was utterly lost..."

Thom snorted.

"What a shame!" he mocked.

Jen ignored him. She only had eyes for Edmund now.

"I was in the forest when the earthquake struck, when the sky burst with light and the trees bent almost double. And I –" she almost faltered. "I admit. I was afraid. But then, when I found it, the building - the Temple - and I saw *you*," Jen jabbed her sword at Edmund again. "I knew what had happened. I knew that my master had failed. That he'd reached his goal only to have it *stolen* from him! But I couldn't see him with you..." Her eyes narrowed a little. "I knew that you must have him hidden somewhere out of reach, somewhere I couldn't get to, so when you left again for the village, I followed you..."

"How?"

The voice was sudden and unexpected and distracted for a moment, Jen couldn't help but turn to scan the crowd as it then continued; "How could you have tracked us undetected? We would have known of your presence."

Eliom was standing only a few feet away, surrounded, like the others, by a circle of foes. Unlike the rest of his friends however, no one seemed to want to get too close to him, every man or child standing at least a full arms-length away, and giving him a look that spoke of her own silent fear, Jen sneered.

"Don't you already know the answer to that, sorcerer?" she replied, sounding perhaps braver than she felt. Though the woman's confidence had clearly grown since her master's disappearance, she was not foolish enough to challenge a wizard.

Eliom eyed her coolly.

"You did not get as far as the village," he stated and Edmund found himself relieved to hear his friend sounding calm and confident. He also couldn't help but notice that Eliom seemed to be muttering something under his breath. His mouth was twitching, almost as if his lips were forming words, but from where the Explorer was standing, he couldn't hear a sound...

"C-correct," Jen said to the wizard. Was that nerves that made her voice quiver? Or just loathing? "I didn't reach the village, because on the way I found the rest of my master's army. Those who had escaped…"

"Escaped?" Once again, Thom took his moment to interject. "I thought your army were supposed to be fearless! Run away did you?" and he threw a rude gesture at a nearby clone, making the girl rear up in rage, the only emotion she knew how to respond to.

"We feel no fear!" she snarled, looking as if she wanted to kill Thom right then and there. "We feel no pain!"

"Well maybe you can feel-"

But Fred stepped in.

"Thom!" the warrior hissed aloud and immediately Thom fell silent.

They had to be more careful. Causing another fight was the last thing any of them really wanted to do right then.

At least, not yet anyway…

"Yes, listen to your little warrior friend…" Jen snapped at the dwarf, finally acknowledging his existence. But though she had meant it as nothing but a flyaway comment, drunk as she was on her own sudden power, on hearing the insult, it was Soph's turn to flare up, and shoving against one of the men holding her in place, she looked about ready to start killing all over again.

"Silence your tongue!" she hissed angrily. "Do you not know who it is you are talking to human…?!"

"Hush Soph!" Fred cried suddenly. "You forget yourself!" and although Edmund couldn't see his friend amongst the crowd, he guessed that the warrior was also being held. The throng of fighters had clearly decided that leaving both warriors free to move wasn't a good idea…

"Anyway," Jen continued, turning her attentions to the Explorer once again, now that there was finally silence. "Shall I carry on?"

Edmund just looked at her.

Did any of them really have a choice?

"The girls and I, we headed east, avoiding the village as best we could, striking out for the nearest town to find supplies and followers…" she glanced at the swarm of bodies, alive and dead around her. "And of course, a boat big enough to take us. It was only a day or two after that that we spotted the sails of your ship and set off after you. I knew that if we followed you, we would soon find our master."

None of the Karenza's crew dared question aloud how it was that another ship, clearly large enough to hold the entire tomb-full of fighters, had managed to follow them completely undetected… but just then, Eliom spoke out again.

"But how could you be certain that Renard was still alive?" he asked and hearing the almost bitter tone of his friend's voice, Edmund grimaced.

He still wasn't ready for Jen to find out the truth. They needed for Renard to be alive right then; just for a while longer. He still needed time to make a plan and turning his head slightly, he tried to catch the wizard's eye.

Eliom, he thought to himself. *If ever there was a time to read my mind, it's now...*

Jen too, seemed a little shaken by the sudden question, but despite the shock on her face, she recovered quickly.

"I knew that Edmund wouldn't hurt his own brother," she replied with a slight scoff. "My master spoke of nothing else but how *weak* he is."

Thom's fingers curled. He couldn't seem to help himself.

"Weak?" he blurted out. "You are the weak one here! Only brave enough to face us with an army at your back!"

Jen looked at the dwarf as if he'd spat in her face.

The move gave Edmund more time to think, but though he felt like retorting, adding his own fight, he said nothing. Already he could feel the deep shame he had pushed aside, beginning to resurface as he remembered what had *really* happened at the temple...

How wrong Jen is, was the only thought crossing his mind now. *How very wrong.*

He *had* been prepared to kill his brother and he knew it. For a few moments in that temple, Edmund had really wanted to hurt Renard, to punish him for what he had done, the destruction, the suffering and deaths he had caused.

Who knew what would have happened if the flames hadn't consumed him? If Renard's life hadn't been taken out of his hands? Who really knew if his brother would have walked away from it all unscathed?

He certainly didn't.

The flames...

And just then, as he remembered the fiery orb, as he remembered his brother's final moments, something flared up inside Edmund; the inkling of a thought he'd ignored all this time, or maybe hadn't even realised was there...

What if...?

What if Jen was right? What if Renard *hadn't* died? The elements had entered the flames and still lived. What if the same had happened to his brother?

But just as Edmund began to think it through, to feed this small hope, he realised that Jen was talking again.

"Of course," she was saying, "nothing could be achieved without a spy."

A spy? *This* caught the Explorer's attention. And not just his either...

"Coward!" Thom roared again. "Threatening some poor wretch to scout us out!"

The anger in his voice hid the surprise the crew all felt, but this time, no one tried to shush him. Jen even smiled.

"How many times do I have to tell you? I didn't *threaten* anybody!" she replied evenly. "Actually, funnily enough, the spy I used was *her*," and to the friends' complete disbelief, Jen was gesturing with her sword to the dead clone at Edmund's feet.

The Explorer just looked at the girl he had killed like he'd never even realised she was there.

"And very good she was at that! She boarded your ship and *none* of you," Jen continued with a quiet laugh, "not even *you*," and with this she glared at Eliom, "noticed her! She lay hidden in the belly of your ship, listening to your every word for days and days on end! And *none of you knew*!"

Her words rang harshly in the crowded space, and for a moment, there wasn't a sound to be heard in reply. None of the group could quite believe it, could quite yet accept how far the conspiracy had gone, how *blind* they had all been to what had been right under their noses all that time…

"Bu-but how did she even make it on board without a boat?!" Elanore's voice suddenly rose indignantly above the throng. "From what I've heard, your army can't swim…!"

"Does the name Merchant's Wreath mean anything to you?"

Jen's own voice was triumphant.

Merchant's Wreath.

And hearing that name, Fred let out an annoyed groan as Eliom closed his eyes in understanding.

The fight. The fight on the dockside at Merchant's Wreath. Fred had stopped Elanore from telling Eliom what the men had said, the men who had surrounded them when they'd been gathering supplies, who had started on them without any warning…

The warrior had thought that he was protecting the wizard. One of them had started insulting their 'white robed friend' and before long, both he and Thom had fallen into a fight for the Eliom's honour, two against five.

At the time, the warrior had thought nothing of the scrap… but now, he realised; it had been a decoy all along. Those men had almost certainly been paid by Jen to distract the group from loading the Karenza with supplies, giving the spy clone enough time to smuggle herself aboard and hide, completely undetected. And none of them had told Eliom about it. The one being who could have worked it out, the one being who had detected something was amiss at the time, but had no idea what it was. None of them had told him the truth and now they were paying the consequences…

Edmund was almost roasting with anger now; anger at himself for not knowing there was a clone on board all along, for not thinking to check after they'd left the dock, for making port in the town in the first place. But more importantly right then, he felt an almost overwhelming anger towards Jen, an anger he knew at any minute he would not be able to control any more…

Jen though, hadn't finished. Unknown to the group, she had more ammunition yet.

"Well," she said. She seemed to be speaking more quickly now, almost as if she was dying to get her whole story out, to prove to the world at large, the power she herself owned. "The girl made the perfect spy. My master's creation share a collective mind, you see. So it wasn't difficult to get the information I needed. I heard *everything* you told your new companion," and she glanced towards Soph then, who looked suddenly as if the whole thing were somehow her fault. "I heard all about the flames of the temple, what you found written on the back of the map, where you were headed… *everything…*"

"Everything except exactly why we were headed here of course," Edmund heard Thom mutter. "Or you would have taken whatever it is for yourself…"

"Ah, but you see," Jen threw the dwarf another look of deep disgust, "*that* doesn't matter. I didn't need to know *why* you were heading here. All *I* needed to do was follow you and observe. Wait to see what it was you wanted from Ophelius's tomb so badly." And she looked once again at Edmund. The Explorer could tell that she wasn't going to stop until she'd explained everything. "We docked not long after you, so had time to make some arrangements. To clear the way…" she didn't elaborate, but the group could all tell that she had been the one responsible for just how empty they had found this place. "And after speaking to a local… shall we say *guide?* - someone I think you know quite well - persuading him to help you, we pushed on ahead and lay in wait…"

"When you say persuade, I suppose this time you mean threaten," Fred pointed out coolly.

Despite her tale, Jen was starting to get impatient now, Edmund could tell by the way she shifted on the spot, her sword, back in its place at his chest, quivering against his skin. His tunic was flecked with blood.

"No, as I said before," the captain snapped, losing her calm for a moment. "I didn't threaten anybody! It was just a case of finding some leverage. Something easy where your friend Martynio was concerned…"

Martynio?!

Of everything that had happened, it was this that truly sent the room into a stunned silence as all six of the captured friends gawped.

Martynio had betrayed them? The friendly giant with his numerous cloaks, had been working with Jen all along?

Only Eliom made any sound as he continued to mutter under his breath. To Edmund though, this was finally it. Finally the Explorer had reached the end of his tether, and before Jen could even blink, suddenly, he gave a yell of rage and flicking his wrist around, he swept his almost-forgotten sword up towards her neck stopping it barely a stroke away from the skin.

"You *lie!*" he roared, his blade-hand shaking with fury. "Martynio would never betray me freely! What did you threaten him with?!"

Jen released a slow breath. Was that fear in her eyes?

"Haven't you noticed how he's not here?" she remarked, gesturing about her with her spare arm, the other still holding her own sword to Edmund's chest. "Didn't you notice how he wouldn't come into the tomb, even when you practically *begged* him to?"

Edmund growled like an enraged animal.

"Answer my question!" he shouted, his spit flying in Jen's face.

Jen flinched and just like that, Edmund suddenly saw and understood.

For the first time, in that one tiny second of reaction, he realised her weakness and from that, the Explorer realised his point of attack.

The captain was afraid of him.

With a whole horde of people to do her bidding, Jen had been confident in telling her story, in taunting him, but when she was this close to death? This close to Edmund and his blade, with no one to help her? She was actually afraid...

"I just made a bargain," she tried tentatively.

"What kind of bargain?" the Explorer demanded, his voice shaking almost as much as his sword. At the back of his mind, he was suddenly starting to be aware of just how much pain he was in. The hand Eliom had cut to open the compartment was still bleeding freely, more than he'd realised and he was starting to feel a little lightheaded with it.

Luckily for him, Jen didn't seem to notice.

"He agreed to take you to the tomb in exchange for me not killing you," she replied finally. "That's all." And almost relieved, Edmund gritted his teeth.

He'd known not to doubt Martynio's intentions. And he'd been right not to. Though he had seemed out of sorts outside the tomb, the Explorer knew that his friend would have been incapable of hiding anything bigger, anything more underhand than this. He may be the worst secret-keeper Edmund knew, but he was certainly one of the most loyal. Chances are, he'd had no idea of the fate waiting for his charges, only that by obeying, he thought he was saving their lives.

But Jen hadn't finished yet.

"He came deliberately slowly on those creatures of his, giving me time to... *clear*... the tomb of others so that we could wait for you."

Edmund dared not dwell on Jen's idea of 'clearing'. Instead, his thoughts had turned to what was now left; the future.

Jen had reached the end of her story, which meant that he now had a decision to make.

He had a clear shot of the captain's neck. With his blade pressed to her gullet, he could finish her off in a second, sending the crowds into a panic without their leader. But at the same time – the Explorer glanced down - Jen had an equally clear shot of his chest, a blow, he knew, that would probably prove to be just as fatal.

Edmund secretly studied Jen's face. If Renard's captain had any idea of the real danger she was in, she didn't show it. Instead, she seemed to have only one thing on her mind too, the one thing she had come all this way for, and clearly wasn't going to leave until she had.

"So where is my master?" she asked stubbornly. "Tell me where he is or I'll give the sign and your friends will die."

Edmund didn't say a word.

Perhaps there was a chance after all, a chance that Renard was still alive, and if he was, that he, Edmund, could undo it all. He could save him from death, from himself. He could bring his brother back…

"Tell me!" Jen repeated more forcefully.

Renard could turn over a new leaf, become the brother he had hoped for. He was capable of change, Edmund was sure of it. If only he could be given a second chance…

"Where is he?!" Jen was almost screaming with frustration now but still Edmund ignored her as his thoughts just as quickly changed, darkening.

Who was he trying to fool? Renard would never change.

He'd always been a disappointment. Though Edmund had tried to deny it in the Temple, he had known it. He had known how hard his brother had fought to impress, to feel wanted, to feel like he *mattered*…

"*Where is Renard*?"

And Edmund had seen Renard *die*.

He'd seen him burn in the flames.

He'd heard him scream in pain…

Surely no one could have lived through that?

Surely it really was too late?

"Tell me! *Where is your brother*?!"

Brother. The word, spoken so shrilly seemed to have an effect then and blinking, Edmund looked into Jen's face, *really* looked as she stood there before him, her pupils searching his, her mouth a thin angry line, his sword pressed to her quivering throat. In that moment, it felt to him as if everything was waiting on his next move, his next few words, the truth that he knew, the moment he spoke, would cause yet more suffering, yet more pain. Yet more death.

But he had to say it now, there was nothing left.

He couldn't hide the fact any longer.

"My brother," the Explorer said, levelling the captain with his gaze, "is dead."

And, it was in the split second that followed these words that Edmund of Tonasse then finally took action. As Jen's expression changed, as the words sifted themselves through to her brain and understanding began - the shocking realisation that her master was gone - he lunged forward those last few centimetres and in one swift, bloody movement, slashed the captain's throat.

As if her death was a sign of its own, the Karenza's crew instantly reacted and leapt at their enemies, blades flying in a whirl of fury as the throng responded with equal ferocity, slamming themselves, swords, fists and teeth into the five friends.

But no one witnessed what happened next. No one saw. Everyone was too busy fighting for their lives to notice Jen as she took her final fall. Because with only moments left to live, as the life drained from her throat, Renard's captain careened towards Edmund, all of her weight behind the thrust of her sword; the sword that was still pressed to Edmund's chest.

The Explorer gave a breathless moan as the blade entered him, slicing through his ribs in one smooth move. And then, for a moment, he was just standing there, bloody weapon in one hand, the other cradling the sword now a part of him.

This was it.
It was over.
Edmund blinked again.

And then he was falling, the noise of battle so loud that no one heard as he crashed to his knees on the dusty ground, Jen's body crushed beneath him.

This was it.
He was gone.

And with nothing left but a soundless cry, Edmund of Tonasse fell forwards into the bloody puddle he'd already made, his last few moments swallowed in blackness.

———

After what felt like an endless time of silent, frozen trudging, the little man finally signalled for the elements to stop.

They'd reached their destination, they'd reached the dead and even without knowing that fact for certain, somehow all four women could feel it.

The rock loomed far above them, casting a dark shadow countless miles across, and it was on the edge of this shadow that they stood, a cold wind from nowhere suddenly whipping their faces, making everyone shudder all over again. Everyone, except the baggage handler that is, who barely seemed to notice the sudden change in the once breathless air.

"We're here," he said simply, sounding almost bored. "Do as you must." And the elements, who had barely made eye contact since they'd set off, for fear of seeing their own dread reflected in their companions' faces, turned to look at each other.

"What do we do?" Meggie was the first to ask. The others seemed just as uncertain, but whilst it was a fair question, the little man looked at her like the answer was obvious.

"Mean no disrespect," he replied, like he was tired of this whole affair already, "but speak the name of the person you seek and they will come, of course."

At the way he said "of course," Meggie frowned but Bex soon squeezed her arm in warning. Now was not a good time to anger the guardian of the dead. They could still need his help yet...

"Although, just to warn you," the baggage handler continued, "whoever you want to speak to, may not want to speak to you in return. Therefore, your trip *might* have been in vain."

"What?!" Bethan erupted as the others looked completely aghast. None of them had even considered *that*. Was the baggage collector just teasing them or was there really a possibility that they'd come all that way, given so much for *nothing*?

The little man gave his horrid smile, brightening up.

"Sorry, did I not mention that before?"

"No, you *didn't*!" hissed Meggie hotly and suddenly, she made as if to lunge towards him.

The baggage collector, without so much as a flinch quickly took a step back, moving into the shadow of the rock.

"Oh!" he hurried. "And I should mention or rather suggest that you don't step into the shadows."

Straight away, Bex was quick to grab Meggie's arm again before she could go any further.

"Why not?" Saz spoke up, not sure if she even wanted to know the answer.

As it turned out, she didn't.

"The shadow of the rock is where the dead live," the man replied smugly. "And as we are all well aware, you are not dead. *Yet*." His beady eyes flashed as he looked at her and Saz blanched a little. The other three shifted uncomfortably, all trying hard to forget the pact the element had made on their behalf...

"Come on!" the little man then snapped. He obviously wanted the women to leave. No doubt fascinating as this whole ordeal had been for him, he was still wary of the living creatures and the blood that ran through their veins, the life that had no business being there in his world.

The elements looked at each other again, the same question on all of their minds.

Who was going to do it? Who was going to call on the dead Ophelius?

But before anyone could ask out loud, Meggie had stepped forwards bravely, her feet just on the very boundary of the dark shadow.

"Ophelius!" she shouted, her voice almost lost on the cold windy air. The other women trembled in expectant fear, his name like the call of doom to their beating, living hearts. "Ophelius! Please come and speak with us! We need your help!"

And then, just like that... nothing happened.

For what felt like minutes, and then even longer than minutes, nothing happened, as they stood there, just watching the great shadowy darkness expanding on and on into eternity.

The cold seemed to lie in their bones now. It felt like a part of them, yet further on, into that gloom, each woman somehow knew that it was even colder. Though breathing felt hard, though every blink seemed to stick, beyond the shadow, into the place of death, they knew that none of that existed.

And then, with every passing moment, as each of them stared, wondering now what they were even hoping for, the darkness seemed to shift.

At first it started as an odd sort of flicker in the very centre of the horizon, as a tiny patch of darkness lightened to pale grey. It was so quick even, that for a moment the elements all thought they'd imagined it. But then, there it was again, the flicker, before the colour started to harden, growing and lightening from grey to cream then on to white as it grew and grew.

And as it grew it began to change from a formless bright blob. It began to grow legs, a waist, a chest, arms, neck, head, all featureless but unmistakeable, brilliant, almost blindingly so, against the deathly darkness...

"Ah, I guess you're lucky," the baggage handler mused as the white figure then began to move, as if it were walking out across the space, striding towards them with purpose. "Your friend has come to see you."

"Meggie," Bethan warned with only a word, as she noticed just how close her friend was to the shadow, to the spirit as it moved closer and closer. Luckily though, the little element didn't need telling twice and she almost fell as she stumbled back a few paces, her eyes never leaving the shifting figure of light.

No one's eyes could leave the *thing* in front of them now, even if they'd wanted to. There was something fixating about it, something beautiful yet horrifying and as it reached the very edge of the rock's shadow, there was a frightening moment where all four women expected it to step out of the darkness, to break that invisible line they had somehow all forged in their minds; the line between life and absolute death.

Thankfully though, the figure of light stopped just short of the divide and for the first time, the elements saw that it had grown features.

It had hands now, fingers, long and thin, clothes, muscles, and the face of an old man; an old *human* man, worn and wrinkled with age yet open, smooth and understanding, the face of wisdom. He had a long white beard that ran from the bottom of his nose all the way down to the centre of his chest, thick and well-cared for. And as for his clothes; he wore a long simple cloak tied with humble roping, the shade of which seemed to match his bright eyes.

Ophelius.

None of them, for the moment, could quite believe it and for a good long while all the elements could do was just stare and stare at the figure all in white, white hair, white skin, white cloak, not daring to believe what they were seeing; not daring to believe that right in front of them stood a man who had been dead for hundreds of years; the man who had started all of this, for them; the creator of the map that had dragged them from their ordinary lives to the Temple of Ratacopeck, to experience things they had never even dreamt of. The man who had brought them to this place. And now, the man, the *only* man who could help them.

"Ophelius, sir," Bethan was the first to start. Her voice squeaked. "We-" but before she could go any further, the ghostly man interrupted.

"I know why you are here, my children. Do not fear me," he said, his own voice surprisingly deep and strong for someone who was no longer alive. "I will help you." And a smile then cracked across his age-worn face, a smile that was so warm despite the chilly dead air, so bright in the darkness, that all four of the anxious elements felt their fears abate a little. A few of them even stepped forward as if drawn to the pleasant glow of Ophelius's light.

"Will you tell us then?" Bex continued shyly. "Will you tell us how to escape from the world of the Diggers? How to return to Tungala?" Now that they were there, finally there, the elements found they'd never felt so eager. There were no pleasantries to be said, no introductions, suddenly they just *needed* to know answers...

Ophelius eyed Bex kindly.

"I will tell you," he replied, making her give a visible sigh of relief. "But," and he frowned a little then, his old wizened brow crinkling, "first I must speak of a few things. Things you must know. You must be warned."

"Warned?" and unable to help herself, Bethan looked worried all over again. "Warned about what?"

Slowly, Ophelius turned to her, almost as if he had been waiting for a long time to do just that and taken aback, the element found herself meeting his eye only to look away again.

The sorrow, the heart-wrenching pain of death seemed to seep from the very depth of the man's pupils. The blackness there was like the blackness of nothing, and giving a shudder, Bethan physically turned herself away, knowing that that look, the abyss of time without end, would haunt her in the times to come.

She said nothing more for a long time.

Ophelius however, soon carried on.

"The Builder is powerful," he said, turning back to the others. His dead eyes seemed to look at Saz the longest. "He is everywhere. And he is not a force to be underestimated."

"The Builder?" Meggie piped up. None of them had noticed Bethan's reaction or now, Saz's, as she too seemed to turn away, biting a pale lip. "Is he definitely a he? Who is he?"

Ophelius's gaze was patient.

"The question is not who he is, but *what* he is," was his cryptic reply and then, seeing the confused expressions on the listening Bex and Meggie's faces, he cleared his old throat. "But that is not why we are here, that is information for another time… For now, you must understand that the Builder is the reason you are caught in the world of the Diggers. He is the reason you are here right now. And most importantly, he is the reason I could not tell you about the fate of the elements using my map."

"I did wonder about that," Bex pointed out, "why it was you directed us here, or rather to the Temple, under false pretences… telling us we would save the world, only to end up…." She spread her arms in exasperation.

Ophelius looked pained.

"My child, I did not lie about your role in the Temple. You did prevent what I said would occur in my writings. There is a balance between the Digger world and yours…" He paused as if reconsidering something. "But again, that is not important now. What you must know is that I could never write about the true reasons, the true consequences. I could never warn about the flames. The Builder has spies in every world. Not just that of the Diggers. If I had said anything, he would have caused great harm…"

Caused great harm. His admittance, surprised them all somehow, but none more than Saz, who seemed to snap back to herself then, her expression suddenly fierce.

"So that's your reason?" she cut in. "You couldn't tell us what was really going to happen because you were afraid the Builder would kill you?"

Was it true, that all this time, they could have avoided their fate but for the fear of an old man?

"No," Ophelius sounded oddly calm. "The Builder would not have killed me. He would have damned me to a life of eternity. No, my child," and he looked so sad, that even Saz, despite her fury, seemed to soften. "He would have kept me, tortured me for all of time. I would never have died. I would have gone on and on. Alone. Forever in pain. You are young. You have not known what forever truly means. Until you have seen it for yourself, you cannot understand. At least here there is…" and he glanced behind him at the blackness as if he could see a whole other world there, "Well… it is not right for me to tell you." Slowly, his eyes turned back to Saz. "But do not judge me too harshly, please. It was only by the Builder's permission that I was able to live at all once I had been freed…"

Bex looked horrified.

"So are you saying that if we *do* manage to escape, the Builder will just kill us anyway?" she cried.

It certainly *seemed* to be what he was saying, but even so, Ophelius appeared to take a long moment to consider before answering.

"Is it a chance you are willing to take?" he asked gravely. "I cannot predict your future, only you can decide it."

Saz's eyes were on the ground.

"It's a chance I'm willing to take," she spoke up seriously and the other three women, including Bethan, looked at her. "I want to see my family again and… the others, before I…" and she trailed off, her gaze shifting to her scarred hand.

"You are not alone," Ophelius encouraged then. "Help will come your way. I may not have told you and your friends directly about this other world but I have left my mark."

And at this, fresh hope suddenly seemed to leap to every chest.

Mark? Did Edmund, Eliom and the others know where they were? Was this the escape plan? Help from the outside?

"Oh yes," Ophelius said, all smiles again. "I have used several spells - simple magic- to conceal messages for your friends, so that they might know where to find you, for at the time I knew that everything would happen just as it had before and before even that. I hoped that I could make escape easier for the next elements to follow in my path."

"What kind of spells?" Bex was excited all over again.

"All kinds," Ophelius explained, his eyes twinkling to see the element's enthusiasm. "A hidden message on the back of my map; a secret compartment concealed in the walls of my resting place… a dream…" and he stopped and to everyone's surprise, turned once again to the silent Bethan. "I have spoken to Edmund," he added and hearing that name, the name always at the back of her mind, Bethan gave a start, her heart giving an extra surge.

"You've spoken to him?" she echoed, breaking her strange quietness before the surge of questions came. "How? Is he all right? Is he coming for us? What did he say? How did you know about him?"

"I did not speak *with* him," Ophelius admitted seriously. "I sent him only a brief vision. I showed him what has been, what is at this moment and what may come to pass. Most importantly I gave him the seed of hope that you may still be alive, so that he would know to continue searching for you… Whether he has or not, however, time will tell." He gave another thoughtful frown. "As to how I knew of him? I have my ways, even in death, of seeing and hearing things in the world of the living. Edmund has spent a lot of time with my map… I knew it was him I must communicate with."

Before he could offer any further information however, it was then that the baggage collector stepped forward and the elements all gave a start, having completely forgotten for the moment that the tiny man was even there.

"Mean no disrespect," he started, "but I thought I should let you know; someone else wishes to speak with you," and his lopsided gaze levelled on the four women in turn until no one was in any doubt as to who he was talking to.

Ophelius's frown increased, dragging great lines across his kindly old face.

"What do you mean, 'someone else wishes to speak with you'?" Meggie ventured uncertainly, the only one to notice the dead man's reaction.

The baggage collector looked smug.

"One of the dead calls to me," he said. "He wants to know if he can approach you. Do you want me to agree or not?"

And realising what this meant, all four elements couldn't have looked more shocked if they'd tried.

Someone dead wanted to speak with them? Someone else, out in the blackness of nothing, in the hidden world of the dead, had asked for them?

But who?

And the first to realise the possibilities, Bex's face suddenly lit up.

"Is it my father?" she gasped. "He was killed... an accident when I was young..."

No one had really thought about *that*. About the fact that past relatives, past friends who had gone, could be reached again in an instant; that they were all accessible, right there in front of them.

"It could be mine," Meggie pointed out. She looked a little less enthusiastic. "Or my brother."

Saz however, was the practical one.

"Who is it?" she asked suspiciously. "If we know who it is then surely we'll know whether to agree to see them or not."

The little man nodded, cocking his head to one side as he did so and it was only after a while of watching him behave so oddly that the elements then realised; he was listening for something.

Sure enough, the baggage collector then straightened up to turn to his live guests. But instead of looking to Saz to answer her question, his eyes swivelled straight to Bethan, with what could only be described as confusion on his ugly face.

"He wants to talk to you in particular," was all he said, and astonished, the other three women turned to join him in staring at their friend.

"Me?"

Bethan surprised as she was too, urgently tried to quieten her throbbing heart.

Part of her was afraid, terrified even, that she had been singled out to be faced with the unknown; to be faced with the dead. But then again... The dead spirit obviously knew her, or knew *of* her, which surely meant that it had be a friend, or a relative...

Right?

What then, was there to be scared of?

"Bethan?" Bex asked quietly, and Bethan, realising that everyone was waiting for some kind of response from her, took a deep cold breath. She couldn't even feel her lips anymore.

"Sure," she replied, trying to sound nonchalant; to sound like this sort of thing happened to her every day. "If they want to speak to me then... fine. Let them come."

And without further ado, the little baggage collector then stepped back up to the line of darkness and with one hand to his mouth he called out unceremoniously;

"You may come!"

As the elements watched, another rift of shifting colour appeared in exactly the same way as the first. Only this time, somehow, it was different; for already the light was changing into a figure, white and featureless at first but growing, so quickly and so much brighter, more brilliant than Ophelius. It was moving towards them in no time at all, with all speed and purpose and staring at it wonderingly, Bethan found herself questioning at the very back of her mind whether this spirit was younger somehow, whether maybe it had died recently, was still clinging on to life and that was why it shone.

"Who is it?" Saz whispered as the figure drew closer and closer to them at such rate, it looked, just as Ophelius had, as if it were going to overshoot the line of death.

Bethan squinted into the darkness as if screwing up her eyes could help. All she could make out so far was a cloak, a billowing cloak, and a strong, tall build with broad shoulders...

"I have no-" she started, but then, just then, just as she saw it all, her words caught in her throat and suddenly, she couldn't breathe. As she looked on, staring ahead at the figure now approaching, in sheer horror, it was as if her lungs, her heart itself had stopped.

The cloak hood, a vivid otherworldly white, was pulled up over the figure's head, but even as the ghostly stranger joined Ophelius at the line between life and death, she could see the ever-so-slight stubble of weeks spent sleeping rough, the thin tentative lips.

The square jaw.

No.

No.

Just no.

And recognising the man just in the same moment, no one made a sound, neither Bex, Meggie nor Saz daring to speak, daring to believe what they were seeing.

None of them could say it. None but Bethan.

And Bethan just wanted to scream. To just open her mouth and scream and scream until everything she had was spent.

Instead though, she could do nothing; nothing but put a name to the figure before their eyes.

The name they all knew.

"Edmund?"

AN ESCAPE ROUTE

Fred finished the last of his opponents with relish as two fell under the swipe of his blood-caked sword. Neither of them made a sound as they slumped to the ground and for a moment the warrior paused, breathless, waiting for the next charge, before, hearing none come, he straightened up to take a look around.

The room was virtually empty of life now, nothing but a mass of strewn bodies, the scrap of a fight still raging here and there.

Over in the far corner he could see Thom and Elanore fending off the last of Renard's clones as the girl tried to push them both to the wall. The little dwarf aimed low as the sea captain aimed high and the fighter, like so many others, fell, biting and kicking to the end. Eliom, meanwhile, was stepping smoothly over the remains of those who had tried to take him, all his efforts concentrated on a single man, the only man left, as he tried like so many others had before him, to scramble towards the marble steps and escape. Unfortunately for him though, too much death stood between him and freedom and tripping, he sprawled his last amongst the mess.

Suddenly, Fred felt a hand on his shoulder and whipping around, he raised his sword, ready to fight, ready to die all over again… only to find a rather dishevelled Soph smiling at him. The warrioress's hair was matted with gore, her tight tunic and trousers a blood-stained mess, a small sheen of sweat shimmering on her forehead, but her eyes, like his own, were wild, aflame with the call of the warrior and for a second Fred couldn't help but stare, struck dumb by her absolute beauty…

"I think we did it," she remarked, looking leisurely to a cut on her upper arm and Fred just nodded, too breathless to say anything before;

"Come here," he muttered as he saw Soph wince. She was trying to tend to the wound but it was deeper than she'd realised, blood thick and red oozing from between her fingers.

"Nicked by a clone's blade," the warrioress groaned but obeying, she moved closer, allowing her partner to tear a piece of cloth from his own travelling cloak and bind it like a tourniquet about her arm.

As he did so, Soph too, gazed around her at the massacre they'd caused. Amazingly, despite the hordes of men and children demanding their deaths, they'd somehow managed to survive. Thom and Elanore, unscathed, were wiping themselves down now and seeing to their weapons, the dwarf taking to cleaning his axe as Elanore slumped against the once-white wall, trying to catch her breath. At the same time, Eliom was standing in the centre of the mess, his last foe defeated, doing just as Soph was, scanning the room with his eyes.

Watching the wizard look about him though, Soph soon frowned. Unlike the warrioress, the wizard's gaze was urgent, searching, and as Soph followed his line of sight to the mass of bodies strewn all over the dusty tomb floor, it was only then that she suddenly realised why.

Where was Edmund?

—

Bethan couldn't move.

She was frozen, unblinking, unbreathing in place, unable to do anything, so it felt, but look in dull disbelief at the man standing in front of her. The man she loved. The man who was dead.

Edmund was dead.

The three words seemed to buzz round and round in her head like a swarm of insects, stinging her with every letter.

Edmund is dead.

Edmund is dead.

And yet, for some reason it all felt meaningless. As if the words were just strings of loose sounds all tied together that meant nothing, that were just noise.

Edmund is dead.

Edmund? Dead?

Edmund is dead.

No. It isn't possible. And though she knew she was in denial, knew that her brain was trying to assure her that what she was seeing was a trick, a hoax, some big joke, just to save herself from the pain she could already feel beginning to build up in her chest, deep and thick, she held on to it for a little while longer. She grasped it as if it were her very sanity, as if the lie would somehow hold her together, keep her hope from shattering just that little bit longer.

But then she knew.

It *was* happening. It was there right in front of her.

Edmund was dead.

How could she deny it when the truth was standing there for everyone to see? *He* was standing there for everyone to see…

Edmund is dead.

And just like that, she felt herself starting to give.

Bethan wasn't sure if the groan came from her or somewhere else entirely but suddenly something seemed to snap within her and then, it was as if her whole body were suddenly deflating, crumbling in on itself and without a word, the element keeled over, heading straight for the ground like a dead weight.

"Bethan!"

Only just in time to grab her before she hit the floor, Saz looked into her friend's face.

"It's all right. It'll be all right," she soothed pointlessly, the same horror reflected in her eyes as she tried to help Bethan back to her feet. But Bethan's legs didn't seem to be interested in straightening out, in ever working again and she simply flopped back into Saz's arms, as her fellow element, not knowing what else to do, laid her to the ground, cradling her as if somehow just by holding her, she could help. Bethan though, barely seemed to know that the other woman was there. All she could think about now, was how much she wanted those arms to be *his*, how much she wanted to feel *his* warmth.

But never would again.

Edmund...

Bethan closed her eyes as she realised the cold hard reality.

The thought of seeing him again, *alive*, had been the driving force of her return to Tungala.

Yes, her need to return home, to be back in the world she had known and loved was strong but she knew that it was really her desire to see the Explorer again that had kept her going through thick and thin, through everything…

And yet now?

Now he was gone.

Now she was without him. And only now was she realising just how much her yearning to be with the man she cared for, had spurred her on, had given her hope.

You barely knew him. Already the voice of reason was trying to cut in, to do some damage control. *It's stupid to think you were doing all of this just for him.*

But straight away, the element was firm.

Yes, she had, in reality, barely known the man. She had spent only a few weeks in his company. But she'd thought she'd have the time to get to know him, for them to get to know each other. She'd bargained on returning to Tungala to find him. To give them that chance.

But now…

Now it was over.

While all of this had been happening, the hooded figure of Edmund, shrouded in his dead cloak, had looked on, motionless, wordless, watching as Bethan had fallen, her face whitest white; watching as the others had crowded around her, trying desperately to offer some kind of comfort.

But then finally, as if he had waited long enough, he opened his mouth.

And laughed.

The sound rattled out across the nothingness, sharp and mirthless, and stunned, none of the elements could help but turn to look as the man they had all known then spoke, his voice harsh.

"Classic," he sneered. "Our parents used to fall for that one too. Sometimes."

Without waiting another moment, the man then lifted his shadowy head to stare straight into the Bethan's now-opened eyes and, meeting his gaze the element let out a gasp.

At the same moment it was as if her heart had suddenly started working again and her chest heaved, beating with renewed strength as she studied the pitiless face staring back at her.

This man wasn't Edmund.

The new information was already filtering into her head, replacing the old, forming into words; much better words. Words of relief.

It isn't him. It isn't Edmund.

Yes, the man standing before her in the world of the dead *looked* like Edmund – he had the same-shaped face, the same eyes – but it *wasn't* him. It was someone much younger, much wilder, much *harder*...

His brother.

Renard.

Bethan gawped.

The man standing in front of them was Renard. The man who had tried to hunt them down; the man who had wanted them killed; the man who had razed Stanzleton to the ground in his thirst for power. The man they had watched die in the flames of Ratacopeck, who even now was glaring at them like he wanted to finish the job he had set out to do...

And somehow, in that moment, Bethan could feel her own power returning.

She had been mistaken. In her moment of fear, she had lost all hope, but now, seeing the Explorer's brother standing before them, ghostly white, a sneer on his face, meant to her only one thing.

Edmund was still alive.

The man she yearned for, still lived; for if the spirits could choose to come forward as his brother had, she knew that he would have too. Edmund would have asked to see her, if only to say goodbye. And filled with the sudden energy of fresh faith, the element found herself clambering back to her feet, the colour returning to some of her face as horror was replaced by anger.

"What do you want, Renard?" she spat, her first words in a long time. Already she was beginning to marvel at how she had managed to mistake the younger, more rugged features as those belonging to Edmund. None could doubt that the pair were related, but the same person? No.

Renard glanced at the other elements and then at Ophelius. The older ghost had been standing patiently, waiting for the drama unfolding around him to end. But now that it had, all could clearly see the look of repulsion on his worn-out face.

"You are not welcome here," the old element said, barely looking at the younger ghost, and for a moment, Renard just gazed at him, his head cocked to one side, considering the wiser man, before, turning away with equal dislike, his beady white eyes were then on Bethan.

"I thought I should issue you a warning of my own," he said in answer to the element's question, his face screwed in a bitter smile. "From what I saw, you and my brother seem a bit fond of each other."

The other elements, who'd obviously been just as shocked to find out the true identity of the new spirit, were staring at Renard, wide-eyed. It was an uncomfortable sensation, watching someone who they'd seen die, standing right before them, clear as day, and each of them couldn't help but remember the image of Renard's burning body, his melting face, his screams of pain as he'd fallen into the raging flames...

When there came no retort to his comment, Renard's confident sneer widened.

"You do know that he's a murderer, don't you?" he said wryly, obviously trying to cause trouble.

But though she could tell already what he was trying to do, Bethan still shook her head, too angry for a moment, to care.

"Shut up!" she couldn't help but snap. "He's never *murdered* anyone!"

Renard laughed all over again.

"Of course, of course," he taunted. "No one but his own brother!"

It was so obvious he was trying to goad her, but even so, the element clenched and unclenched her fists. Suddenly she wanted nothing more than to run at him, to wipe that smile from his smug face. But just as quickly she became aware that Saz was holding her all over again.

"Don't," she heard the element hiss in her ear. "Leave him be. He wants you to go for him."

At which point, Renard's amusement only seemed to increase.

"You'd better listen to her, my dear!" he cried, making both women give a start as they wondered how he could possibly have heard. "Or else you might end up dead. Just like I did when Edmund-"

"Edmund had nothing to do with your death!" Bethan spat. She could still just about feel Saz's firm grip on her shoulder through the numbing cold. "He tried to *save* you!"

But no matter how hard she sounded, Renard's eyebrows rose in mock surprise.

"Is that what you call it? *Saving?*" he demanded angrily, making the element realise, with shock, that this time, he wasn't just teasing. He really believed it. Renard really believed that his own brother had been the death of him and whilst it made her feel somehow afraid, it also saddened her.

"If he hadn't tried to kill me in the first place, I would still be alive now!"

"If your *greed* hadn't led you to the temple, you would still be alive now!" Bex join in loudly, saving the suddenly-quiet Bethan from the lonely fight.

Renard sent her a withering look and now that his eyes had moved from hers, Bethan felt herself relaxing a little. Slowly she shrugged herself away from Saz's hands. There was no need for them now.

"I notice how you're all still alive," Renard said. "And yet my brother was so determined to make you walk through those flames, like I did... Although," and he paused a moment, pondering them all. "You *are* here..."

"You were not one of the chosen," Ophelius piped up. He was actually watching Renard now, his disgust verging on obvious loathing, making the others wonder if he somehow knew who this man was, what he had done. "You did not survive because you were not destined to do so. It was foolish of you to think that you could harness the orb's power."

Renard swivelled on him, equally as hate-filled.

It was a frightening thing to see, two spirits facing one another in mutual hatred. For a second, their glowing white skins seemed to shift to a deeper grey as they glared at each other, daring the other to look away, their gazes so powerful that for a good moment the elements felt as if they were somehow intruders watching a private argument.

"Because I wasn't a precious element, I deserved to die? And they to live?!" Renard spat, not tearing his eyes away from Ophelius's wrinkled face.

Ophelius looked completely unmoved, his once kindly eyes, suddenly fierce.

"What did you expect but to be burnt alive?" he replied matter-of-factly. "It *was* a fire." And Renard scowled.

"I knew that-"

But it was right then, as the true argument started, that the pair were interrupted as the baggage handler, who up until that point had been watching the scene before him unfold with a degree of bored fascination on his ugly face, cleared his throat noisily.

"Mean no disrespect," he started, making all four women whip their heads round to stare at him in surprise. "But I have things to do, baggage to collect.

THE ENTITY OF SOULS

I gather quite a large group have just come in… And your time is running out."

"Time?" Meggie was the one to echo it sceptically, as the others all look suddenly shocked. "You never said anything about a time limit!"

But the little man simply smirked.

"Mean no disrespect," he replied, causing the still-frustrated Bethan to give an annoyed growl. "But you never asked! *However*," and raising a hand to stop any obvious protest, he carried on, "if you *had* in fact asked me, I would have told you that a spirit may only resurface for a short time. Fifteen Tungalan minutes, I believe, to be precise. Of which you have now had…. Ten…. No sorry," he cleared his throat again pompously, "eleven minutes."

Four minutes? That was all they had left?

"But there's so much we need to know yet!" Bex cried. "We don't know how to return to Tungala!"

"Fifteen minutes?" Saz challenged at the same time. "That's ridiculous! You're just making that up!"

But the baggage handler rolled his lopsided eyes.

"All I'm saying is you had better hurry up…" he said, ignoring the second remark completely and turning to the spirits he seemed to bow a little, not looking into either face. "I'd tell them what they want to know if I were you," he said and then stepping back, he seemed to merge into the shadow.

Renard, who was still glaring at Ophelius, looked away then, as if realising something for the first time, something else far more fulfilling, far more entertaining than a fight with the prophet.

"What's this?" he asked, appealing to Bethan once again. She seemed to be the weakest link of them all when it came to him and they both knew it. "You're trying to escape?"

But choosing to ignore him this time, even though the way he spoke implied that he *knew,* maybe had known all along about the world of the Diggers, about the true sacrifice of the Keeper of the World, Bethan appealed directly to Ophelius.

"Please, tell us how you escaped," she begged. "How did you return to Tungala?" and hearing her desperation, the wise old man blinked slowly, an action which somehow had a calming effect on all four of the anxiously awaiting elements.

"Yes, please do!" Renard mocked, even though no one was listening to him anymore. They had far more important things to focus on now.

Without further ado, Ophelius then started.

"Listen and remember," he said. "In the centre of the City of the Diggers is an opening to your world. At a certain time, this opening will appear and," he pressed his hands together for emphasis, "it is during this time that you must then be pulled through from one world to the other."

An opening? Another barrier or door? Could it really be that simple? And reeling with what seemed like the sheer straightforwardness of it, for a moment, no one knew what to say until;

"Where exactly is this opening and when does it open?" the fast-thinking Bex asked, greedy for more information before it was too late and as if trying to remember the end of a tale he had heard repeated long ago, Ophelius looked pensive.

"The gateway is at the top of the statue," he replied after much thought. "Yes... the top of the statue, where the flames are..."

The women glanced at each other.

"Statue?" Saz asked. "Which statue?" None of them could seem to remember any statue right then, and certainly not one with *fire*...

However, instead of Ophelius, it was Bethan who answered. As if the mention of flames had alighted something in her mind, the element of earth suddenly found herself recalling the great white monument she had seen from the window of that first building in the City, the statue she had noticed only a day or so after their arrival...

"The statue!" she exclaimed, her excitement rising. "I saw it when I was with Barabus! A huge great thing!" and she gestured wildly with her hands. "I remember now! Though I didn't really recognise it at the time... it looks *just* like the Keeper of the World – the platform and everything! - but instead of the orb of fire, it's got four big glass balls, in different colours, like the necklaces-"

"Of course!" Saz added with a gasp. "I saw that too. You're right, it looks just like the platform in the Temple of Ratacopeck..." and Ophelius nodded encouragingly.

"Yes," he agreed. "That is the one..." and then; "that is the door to your world. As you stepped through the flames into the Digger world, so you must step through the fire of the Diggers to return to your own."

Fire? Though all of them could now recall the monument in the centre of the City, still none of them remembered seeing a fire... but running out of time, Bex was the first to press the issue.

"When?" she repeated quickly. "When will this 'door' open?"

"When the fire upon the statue is lit," the old man then said. "It is a ritual performed by the Diggers once a day at sunset – sunset that is, in both that world as well as your own."

"Sunset..." Meggie muttered as she mulled everything over. But already Bethan had given a start as she saw the vital flaw in an otherwise simple-sounding plan.

"Sunset?" she questioned. "But there *is* no sunset. The Digger world has no sun..." She could remember now, her very first day in that new place, looking up at the sky... the beautiful *sunless* sky.

"Very true," Ophelius said and he gave the element a heartening little smile, straight away soothing Bethan's anxious heart. "The Digger world indeed has no sun... But it still has a sunset. You will know when it is time. When the light fades and the darkness begins, as the day transitions to night; *that* is when the gateway will open... But," and then, suddenly, he was raising a finger in warning, his smile gone, "be aware. The opening will only exist for a few minutes at the most and in that time, you must be pulled through to your world by those ready to meet you on the other side... Or you will fail."

His last word echoed through the cold air like a death knell.

Fail.

And then there was a pause as the four women began to realise the potential problem of this plan, the problem that was growing larger and more worrying the more they all thought about it.

Pulled through.

They couldn't just do what they had before and step blindly into the flames. They had to be *pulled*. Which meant...

"Will Edmund and the others know what to do?" Bex asked, voicing their collective concern. "Will they know where to go, to 'pull us through'? You said before that you've spoken to Edmund, you've told him that we're alive. But does he know how to help us?"

"As I said before," Ophelius replied calmly. The old man didn't seem to be at all put out by the idea that the two groups could miss each other entirely. "I have left my mark in places. On the back of the map, I left them hidden instructions. Instructions that we can only hope they will have taken."

"I know Edmund would have followed them," Bethan insisted straight away. "He'd want to save us."

"And Eliom," Saz added. "He'd never leave us, knowing we're still alive."

"Noble," Renard smirked quietly from the side-lines and Bethan glared at him, having, for the moment, almost forgotten he was there.

"But where do they go to reach us?" Bex continued her questions hurriedly, aware of how little time they had left with their guide. "How will they know when to reach in and 'pull' us out of the Digger world? You say the opening only lasts a few minutes, what if they miss it? What if they pick the wrong sunset or-?"

Ophelius, however, shushed her with a shake of his head.

"Listen again to me now, and listen carefully, I can already feel myself fading," he said hastily. And it was true, for even as he spoke, all four of them saw the figure of Ophelius begin to ebb a little, waning to a light grey as his inner light diminished. The baggage collector hadn't been making anything up after all. "They will know what to do, but only once you have instructed them."

"Instructed them?!" Saz exclaimed looking at the old man as if he were mad. "Are you joking? Instruct them how?"

"Think, my child," the prophet replied patiently. "Think. By using the only way of communicating through different worlds. By speaking to them through their inner most thoughts…"

By using dreams.

All four women were looking at him like he was insane now. Each of them had witnessed how Eliom, Edmund, Fred and Thom had all used visions to communicate, but the thought of one of *them,* one of four human women who up until a month ago had never even believed in such magic, being able to perform such a feat, seemed almost laughable.

"That is how I returned to Tungala long ago," Ophelius explained, ignoring their doubtful glances. "Fortunately, I had learned the art of communication using the mind before I entered the flames, so I could use such a skill to communicate with my brother from the Digger world. Together we worked out what to do…"

"Just like that, eh?" Renard butted in. He clearly knew Ophelius's time was fading and in some desperate attempt at whatever revenge he was exacting, he seemed determined to waste it.

Ophelius, however, still ignored him.

"I had had my suspicions about the statue, having observed it during the fire-lighting ceremony…" he mused. "But that is unimportant," he gave a shake of his old head and then, looking at each in turn; "You must communicate with Edmund or one of your other companions and instruct them in what they must do. This will ensure that the timing is correct and ultimately your transition is successful."

"How do we go about doing that?" Bethan asked.

But just as the words came from her mouth, Ophelius turned back towards the darkness, the shadow of the rock behind him, almost as if it had spoken his name, as if it were calling him back from the edge of life.

"My time is up," he said quietly. "I can feel myself being pulled back… But I shall fight it for a little while longer." And his face crumpled suddenly as if he really was fighting to hold on to that brief spark of life, fighting with his whole greying body.

Bethan wanted to rush forward and shake the old man so that he would tell them what to do. They were so close to escape! They were so close to their goal! Yet she knew she couldn't act on her impulses. She knew he was trying his hardest and she also knew that the dead weren't meant to mix with the living… Who knew what would happen to either of them if she touched him?

"This place," Ophelius eventually stuttered. "This world of death… it has a connection to every world ever created. Everything, everyone has the potential to arrive here eventually…" He faltered as his face collapsed again, some kind of other-worldly pain spasming through his body. His white eyes flickered. "You must concentrate on who it is you wish to speak to and it shall happen... This world offers an easy link to the inner mind in *any* world... for *everyone* dreams of death... Death is constant and comes for us all."

The words were chilling but true and though he knew it as well as they, Renard sneered.

"How lucky that you're here where it's easy for you to send a dream without any training," he said, staring out at the elements, challenging them.

But though his words were harsh, Ophelius just looked at him as if the younger spirit were nothing but a child, a pitiful child playing at a game he would never understand.

"It is not luck," he answered solemnly. "It is never luck. It is fate." And something in the way he spoke seemed finally to have an effect as the ghost of Renard fell silent.

Turning to the worried elements for what would be his last time, Ophelius then gave them a smile.

"Do not fear, I have left your friends a helpful gift in my tomb. A gift that will aid them in receiving your message," he said. "However, I suggest you choose wisely. You may only have one chance to speak. Choose someone you have a real connection with, be it blood or otherwise. If you do not, the vision may not be strong enough..."

"But what if the others don't find the gift in time?" Bethan ventured anxiously. Suddenly she couldn't help but conjure up horrible images of creating a dream, their only chance of escape, only for it to never be noticed, overlooked by Edmund and the others...

The entire plan seemed to rely on a lot of "what if's".

But the form of Ophelius was fading fast now. He was nearly transparent, almost as if the darkness beyond were draining all colour from him, dragging him back into nothing...

He opened his mouth and for a moment, nothing came out. But then; "If fate intends you to return, then you will," he replied. His voice was quiet, drifting away on the air like everything else about him as he battled on to the very last.

"Thank you for waking me."

And with that, he gave one last smile, a grin so bright, so full of joy that it was almost blinding and then he was gone, leaving the elements to stare heavy-hearted at the space where the great prophet had once stood, searching the shadows with their eyes for any last trace.

It was over. They had done what they had set out to do. They had their answer now, but still it was a good long moment before anyone said a word, or even so much as moved.

Bex was then the first to react, and cradling her injured arm, she turned away from the shadow line, back to life.

"Bethan," she said and Bethan looked at her, her eyes quizzical. "It's got to be you. You must send the message." And straight away all of them knew what she meant.

Choose someone you have a real connection with…

As they had before, so now they knew their lives would rest in the hands of Edmund of Tonasse and as if someone had spoken his brother's name aloud, Renard then shifted again, his cold white eyes glaring at them all like frozen fire.

"Who told you you can leave?" he spat nastily. "I'm not done yet!"

But though before, his words had been venom, though before, Bethan had risen to his taunts, she knew that she never would again. Though once he had been an enemy, a man to fear, the dead Observer was unimportant now. They had other things to be afraid of and no one so much as questioned the silent decision; no one needed to, for though each worked through their options for a second, considering each of Edmund's group in turn, Eliom the wizard – the obvious choice, Fred the warrior, Thom… all four women had the odd sense that the element of water was right.

Bethan had to be the one. She was *meant* to be the one. For Ophelius had also been right. Their plan of escape didn't rely on luck. It relied on what felt a lot like *fate*.

"*Over here!*" Elanore yelled and throwing herself to the ground she tried to heave aside the bulk of a dead man twice her size, only to curse as the body wouldn't budge. "*Help me!*"

The others scrambled over from the four corners of the crowded room, Fred, the first to reach the sea captain, searching the throng of corpses with his sharp eyes.

"There!" Elanore wiped sweat from her face as she pointed to something amongst the mess of drying blood and limbs, and true enough, Fred saw the cut and bloodied hand that he almost certainly recognised…

"Eliom!" and he swivelled as quick as lightning to find the wizard. "He is being crushed! Help him!"

And in less than a moment, he was there.

"Move!" was all the wizard said, the very command making every person in the group step back and then suddenly he was raising his staff, the close air of the tomb alive with a flurry of light and incantations as bodies, warped and messy began to shift, sliding apart from each other, limb after head after torso moving aside to reveal others below. Sure enough, as the corpses moved apart, it was then that the others could gradually begin to make out the motionless body, the white face of someone they all knew…

Elanore almost cried out, as did, surprisingly, Thom, as Edmund was finally unveiled and for the first time the group saw what they had all secretly dreaded.

The Explorer was sprawled on his front, his face and skin ashen-pale beneath a clot of thick blood, his legs buckled under him where he had fallen, one hand still holding the sword that had slain Jen, the other outstretched, palm upwards, Eliom's tell-tale cut still red beneath his fingers.

His tunic and cloak were soaked in blood, but regardless of whether it was his own or not, all of them could see straight away that their friend was dead.

No one could mistake the sword-hilt sticking at a horrible angle from under his chest, the fatal weapon that had killed him. No one could mistake the expression on his face, his eyes open and glassy, gazing off, unseeing into the world beyond...

The tomb was utterly still. Barely even a wisp of breath seemed to move as the group fell silent, stunned to their very cores by what they were seeing.

Edmund of Tonasse was dead.

After everything they had been through, everything they had fought for, their friend was gone.

Their leader was dead.

"No."

Someone uttered the word as they all stood there, uselessly staring, uselessly fighting their denial.

The evidence was unmistakable. It was final, so final and yet after only a moment of looking upon the body of the fallen Explorer, Eliom made his move. Suddenly, the wizard was lowering his staff and in one quick swipe, he leaned towards his friend, pushed him over onto his back with surprising strength and began to reach for the sword in Edmund's chest.

Immediately, both Fred and Thom looked horrified.

"What are you *doing*?!" the warrior cried, reaching out as if to take the wizard by the arm. "Do not touch him!"

At the same time, Elanore, whose face was almost as white as Edmund's, gave a groan.

"Leave him!" she moaned. "Leave him be!"

Even later, no one was quite sure who the captain was talking to, but Eliom, heeding neither of them anyway, continued to reach for the sword and taking the hilt firmly in both hands, to the group's collective disgust, he began to pull the metal back through Edmund's ribs.

The weapon slid surprisingly easily through the Explorer's body but it seemed too much for Fred and all of a sudden, as if overcome by some strange rage, the warrior drew his own sword and with a flick of his wrist, he pointed it straight at Eliom's unprotected throat.

Elanore, Thom and the watching Soph gave a collective gasp.

"Stop!" Fred challenged aloud, his voice shaking. "Leave him alone! Do not defile his body!"

But instead of so much as pausing, instead of even turning to explain his actions, Eliom said nothing. Glancing up for a second, the wizard simply continued in his task and as if the word 'defile' had released a rage in him as well, Thom too made a move for his weapon, swinging the axe round to face the wizard.

Elanore's gaze flitted between all three, her expression fearful.

"No…" she warned weakly, but no one seemed interested in listening as Fred stepped nearer, his blade almost touching Eliom's skin.

"Face me, sorcerer!" the warrior snarled in a tone none of them had ever heard him use before. He sounded *beyond* angry and straight away the sea captain could see that things were going to get out of hand. Fast.

"No!" she repeated at a shout, finding her strength. "Don't! All of you! Edmund wouldn't want *any* of this!"

Again, no one was quite sure who she was talking to, but either way, it was already too late. Both Fred and Thom were starting to close in on the wizard now, as if hunters ready to take their prey, each of them incensed, in the ways of their people, that Eliom could dare touch their dead friend.

The wizard continued in his work carefully. Though it had started off as easy, the last of Jen's sword seemed to be stuck in Edmund's chest, making the going slow now.

"Wait," was all he said, his voice oddly strained with exertion. But though the word was a command, it held no magic, and not convinced for a moment, neither warrior nor dwarf lowered their weapon. For dwarves and warriors alike, dying by the sword was seen as a great honour, a true fighter's death. To them, removing the weapon that had killed their friend, only moments after his death, was the greatest insult imaginable...

"Wait for what?" Thom sneered. His blood-covered beard quivered, reminding everyone just how dangerous dwarves could be. "He is barely even cold and already-!"

"Stop!" Elanore warned yet again, still helpless. "Come on!"

But Fred's eyes blazed.

"I swear by the blood of my kin," he suddenly spat, "I *will* kill you if you do not stop *this instant*!"

The look on his face told them all, shocking as this statement was, that he meant it and as if realising for the first time that his own life might be in danger, Eliom finally halted. For a moment, it seemed, as if the wizard was even stuck there, his pale hands gripped on the sticky sword-hilt, looking as if he were, for that tiny second, actually contemplating his companion's words, considering what he was doing, what it looked like... But then, without so much as another word, that moment was gone and he began again, heaving with a firm grip, murmuring soundless words under his breath.

He had no account for his actions; no, it appeared, empathy for the others' pain and it seemed this more than anything that made Fred then snap.

Like a wild beast finally released, the warrior lost control and springing forward, he thrust at the wizard's exposed neck. But whilst the move was quick, and accurate, ready to find its mark, before Eliom could so much as drop Jen's sword and raise his staff in defence, Fred felt the sudden slam of something metallic and *hard* smash into the side of his head and careening off course, he fell aside, stunned.

Stars erupted in his head, blinding him for a moment as both Thom and Elanore, witnessing the unexpected attack, whirled around to meet their new foe. At the same time, as all other attention was pulled away from him, with a final tug, Eliom heaved the last of the blade from Edmund with a nasty crack...

As the warrior regained his sight, he made to swivel back on his assailant, his sword raised again for the attack. But it was too late. He felt the blade pressed cold and tight to his own throat, holding him in place and before he could open his mouth to cry out, a firm voice was hissing in his ear.

"If you do not drop that sword right now. I will kill *you*."

And for a second, as he recognised the sound, Fred paused, shocked by the realisation of what was happening before he let out a wild growl.

"Unhand me, Soph!" he snarled, still filled with pent-up rage. "Do not make me take arms against you!"

Soph though, was just as much a warrior as her lover and unafraid, she simply jabbed her blade closer to Fred's neck.

"And what would that achieve?" she demanded, shooting Thom an equal look of contempt from the corner of her eye. The dwarf, utterly surprised to be in this situation in the first place, was quick to lower his axe.

"Whose side are you on?!" Fred panted. He was positively shaking with unspent aggression, with yes, *grief* he clearly didn't know what to do with, but despite it all, Soph suddenly grabbed him by the jaw and forcing his head around to face her, her expression was hard.

"I am on Eliom's side," she said bitterly. "Your *friend's* side."

She too, sounded angry, but even so, Fred gave another growl, seemingly too lost right then to care who was friend or foe.

"He is no friend if he dares to taint Edmund's honour!" he snapped, struggling to release himself from Soph's grasp on his face. No matter how he tried to move away, her fingers wouldn't let go. "You know the ways of our people, Soph! You know he must not be touched! His body must be burned! He must-!"

"Edmund is - *was* human, *not*-" Soph started but then, as if thinking better of it, her hardened face fell into a fierce frown. "Eliom does not defile him!"

By now, Thom had completely stepped away from Eliom, stunned once more into silence at what was happening in front of him. None of them had seen Fred like this - not since Crag - so filled with an unquenchable, grief-stricken rage - a rage that made him turn against even those he loved - and it frightened them all.

Twice, Renard or those in league with him, had taken someone he had cared for from him and twice he had been unable to reap his revenge. For someone such as Fred, such as his people, the idea was almost unbearable…

And none of the others really knew what to do. Only Elanore, who seemed more than anything, worried for Soph as Fred fought against her, his sword dangerously close to *her* body now, turned to Eliom as if in appeal. To her surprise though, as her eyes darted to where the wizard had been only moments before, she saw that he was now crouched beside Edmund's motionless body, feeling the Explorer's brow and rubbing his hands together. Still he was mumbling to himself as if in a trance and not knowing what else she could do, the sea captain called out to him.

"Can't you do something?!" she tried. "Say something? Make him stop before he kills someone?"

From the strange way the wizard was behaving, she hadn't known whether to expect anything but half to the sea captain's disbelief, distracted by her voice, Eliom glanced up at her as if suddenly realising that he wasn't alone. Concern creased his usually calm face and for a stupid second, Elanore wondered whether the wizard hadn't even noticed what was going on.

He paused in his mumblings just long enough to speak.

"Soph knows what to do," came his short reply. "He will not kill any more this day." And just like that, he was turning back to his deceased friend to mutter more words, his hands busy at Edmund's chest now as if the matter didn't bother him in the slightest.

Soph's grip meanwhile, had moved to Fred's sword hand, clamping her strong fingers about his wrist as she struggled to keep hold of him.

"Eliom does not defile him!" she repeated, desperately trying to make eye-contact with her partner. "Leave him be."

But Fred's own eyes were roving wildly, his whole focus on nothing else but trying to break free and avenge Edmund. It was like Crag all over again; like the hatred he had felt for Renard, the hatred he could never get rid of, could never quench, was directed now at the wizard. And it was so sudden, so intense that deep inside he wasn't sure he could stop it even if he wanted to.

"I must stop him!" he snarled. "I must! It is our way, Soph."

He was weakening though, just a little, his life-partner could see it and straight away she seemed to feed on it, as her face softened and reaching up again, she began to stroke her lover's cheek with the back of her own sword hand, her grey eyes wide with her own concerns.

"I know you must punish the wrong done to Edmund," she soothed. "I know that it must be done, as you are a warrior, as you wield that sword, as you draw breath, I know. But this," she glanced at Eliom. "This is not the way… Eliom is not your enemy."

THE ENTITY OF SOULS

But though Fred was looking at her now, meeting that large softening gaze, it was as if the words couldn't reach him. He was struggling so hard against Soph's grip that without knowing it, both Thom and Elanore had already taken a whole extra step back.

Once he broke loose, who knew what he would do? And Soph, seeing her efforts were more fruitless than she'd hoped, seemed to harden all over again.

Suddenly her expression was terrifying, and with a strength none of them had expected, she dropped her hand from Fred's face and twisting her other hand on his, she yanked his arm up to his chest, pressing the flat of his blade to his tunic.

"If you cannot listen to reason, then listen to this!" she then snapped. "If anyone has insulted Edmund's honour this day, it is *you* Fred!"

The words, clearly long in the coming, seemed to render the air like a magic spell as suddenly, Fred stopped in his struggle, stopped trying to force his strength against hers and just stared, his own eyes wide in what could only be disbelief.

"Yes!" Soph cried triumphantly, glaring straight back at him, as she finally managed to gain his full attention. "You!"

"Me!?" Fred started, his anger seeming to abate completely for a second. "I would never... could never-!"

"Well, you have," Soph was firm. "The moment we find him, you set yourself upon your friend, Edmund's friend in some desperate attempt to seek revenge! Turning on him just because he tries to clean Edmund's body!"

Fred just gawped at her. So did everyone else.

"Do you think Edmund would have wanted that?" the brave warrioress continued. "Do you think he would want you *slaughtering* each other?!" And with this, she also glared at the now ashamed-looking Thom. "I know the rituals! I know the rites! I know we do not move the bodies of our dead! We do not hide the honour in how they died!" she gestured vaguely towards the Explorer. "He died bravely. We can all see that. He died by the sword, a *warrior's* death. But there is no *revenge* you can seek here," her voice gave a little. "You do not know who it was who killed him. You cannot name them. They are either slain or are far from here by now."

Almost stunned into silence, Fred said nothing, but just like that, his sword hand seemed to relax and gently, Soph released her grip, allowing him to lower the weapon as she, in a sign of peace, dropped her own to the floor. The couple moved closer, their bodies touching in the quietness.

"There are other ways to deal with this," she said as she searched his down-trodden face. "He is not to blame. Eliom is not to die this day."

But mentioning the wizard's name aloud again seemed to release something in the warrior one more time and quick as a flash, he was moving away from Soph, his sword once more taut in his hand as he stepped forward, ready for the kill. This time though, things had changed and shocking them all, instead of turning back on Eliom, still crouched by Edmund's side, Fred swivelled and his weapon cutting through the air with fast, ferocious precision, the edge of the blade landed, not at the wizard's throat but a hair's-breadth from the defenceless Soph.

Immediately, the onlookers responded, Elanore crying out and turning away, unable to watch, as Thom once again raised his axe in some desperate show to try and protect the now powerless warrioress.

But not even giving a flinch, Soph just stared up at the warrior she loved, her face as cool, as collected as a still lake.

"Fine," she murmured. "If death is what you seek, then take me instead."

Her words were soft, but even so, Fred frowned, almost as if considering it. He was breathing heavily again, struggling to control himself, the angry warrior blood surging through him, the grief he didn't fully understand.

"Kill me," Soph repeated. "Go on. Do it."

Fred's sword hand shook.

Elanore gave another moan.

"Please!" she begged. "No more bloodshed! Hasn't there been enough?!"

But Soph and Fred continued to stare at each other for some time, a tension filling the room as everyone waited with dread, waited for that second or the next when Fred would react, would finally take his revenge and spill blood for blood.

"Do it," Soph whispered, hot tears of frustration rising now to her eyelashes as she waited fiercely for her partner's judgement. "Do it."

Inside, Fred battled with his anger, trying desperately to quench his desire for revenge. Trying desperately to quench the despair that threatened to overwhelm him, to make him weak…

He wasn't usually like this. In fact, he was sure he had *never* been like this before. But somehow the pain of Crag's death, the pain of that loss, that great big hole in his life he knew would never be filled, followed by *this,* had all tangled into one great ball of fury at the world, at anything and *anyone* standing in his way…

But staring into Soph's bright grey eyes, damp now with heartbreak, he could already feel himself beginning to calm, and something else to seep through, starting to abate his rage, replacing it with the shameful truth of what he had done, what he was doing…

If anyone deserved to die, it was him.

The thought was brief and yes, foolish, but it was there.

Soph had been right. *He* was the problem.

He had threatened Eliom, Edmund's life-long friend, been prepared to *kill* him just for the almost meaningless fact of moving the Explorer's body and now here he was with his sword pressed to the chest of someone else entirely innocent, of the one being, the one person he had left to care for in all the world.

How could he knowingly kill such a beautiful, fierce creature as the warrioress who stood before him?

And looking into those eyes, he could see that she was thinking the same. How could he even consider killing the warrioress he *loved*?

Yes, he had never said it aloud, he had never thought it, but he knew that it was true.

The word was a human one, but he understood it well enough.

He loved Soph. He always had. And he always would.

No. *He* was the one who had acted dishonourably, not Eliom, not Soph… He was the one who had let his rage control him, his *emotions* control him, bringing shame upon himself.

If anyone deserved to be punished that day, it was him.

Perhaps in those moments of quiet, Soph somehow knew what was going on in the other warrior's mind, perhaps she didn't, but either way, as Fred then finally lowered his sword, Soph lunged that last tiny gap and taking her lover in her arms, she embraced him fiercely for all to see, and reaching up, kissed him again and again.

Fred looked surprised - scenes of public desire weren't the warrior way - but he didn't pull away. Instead, he tugged her closer, running his hands through her matted hair, holding her as if she were a part of himself, his one saving grace. And in that long moment of passionate apology, the warrior's weapon fell to the floor to join his lover's, no longer a threat to himself or anyone else.

Averting their eyes, Elanore and Thom both breathed an inward sigh of relief.

The danger was finally over.

Now they could turn to dealing with what had happened. Turn to face their mourning…

But even as the collective thought crossed their minds they were interrupted by a sudden groan and everyone's attention, including Fred and Soph's fell straight back on Eliom, until then, almost forgotten.

The wizard was standing again now, his once white cloak stained red, his hands blackened by the blood from Edmund's chest. But though the sight was disturbing, most importantly and most mind-blowing of all, was that he didn't stand alone.

For a second the whole tomb was utterly, deadly still as the two warriors, the dwarf and the sea captain looked on in amazed, *horrified* silence at the figure before them. The man that only moments ago they had all thought gone forever…

Edmund of Tonasse then gave another groan and his face, already whitest white, blanching all the more, he clutched at his chest and staggered a little, only just managing to stay upright as Eliom steadied him with a hand.

"What…?" his voice started weakly. "Wh-what happened?"

Everyone just stared at him.

Thom even opened his lips to speak, to ask the question the others were all thinking – *how?* For some reason though, his voice simply wouldn't work and not knowing how else to respond, the dwarf soon found himself taking a step towards their leader instead, Elanore and Soph following suit as if none of them could quite believe what they were seeing.

None of them really could. None of them had seen a dead man come back to life before, and frozen in place, so it seemed, by his shock, only Fred stayed back as Eliom, calmly studying Edmund's face all the while, gave a little nod. If any of the others had looked at the wizard during that moment, they would have seen the hint of tell-tale relief flash across his face. But as it was…

"You will be fine now," was all he said and Edmund in turn just looked at him, his own eyes searching those he knew so well, questioningly.

Thom then finally seemed to get a grip.

"Ed-Edmund!" he spluttered, letting out a loud laugh. The sound felt odd somehow after everything they had just been through, but with a grin, the dwarf hurried up to the shaken Explorer, offering him a hand in human friendship. Edmund took it and as if suddenly awoken, Soph and Elanore too broke into smiles and came forward to greet him, to embrace him, touch him as if to prove to themselves that he was real, that despite everything they had believed, Edmund of Tonasse wasn't dead.

"How…?" Elanore tried, turning to Eliom for some sort of explanation as she shook Edmund's newly-working hand warmly. "He was dead! We *saw…!*"

But instead of the wizard, it was Edmund who answered her question as he too turned back to Eliom.

"The muttering," he said. His voice sounded raspy, tired, but strengthening at every moment. "You cast a spell on me." And to everyone's surprise, Eliom nodded once again.

"A simple shield spell," was all he said. "Although, for a while, I too was uncertain whether I had been successful…"

A spell. Of course. It explained everything that had happened. The way Eliom had seemed so distracted, the way he had headed straight for Edmund's body, to removing the sword, no doubt to force the magic to work… But whilst it made sense now, getting their heads around it wasn't going to be easy for any of the group and Edmund frowned, his eyes glazed for a moment.

"Did I –?" he asked tentatively. "Did I… *die?*"

Eliom though, gave the smallest of grim smiles.

"Only you can answer that question," he offered. And deep down, it was only Edmund who ever knew.

The others, still surprised, still overjoyed that Edmund was, despite it all, still with them, just smiled all the more. Yet even now, Fred hung back, his face utterly expressionless as he watched the others' clear relief.

"Go to him. It is over now."

Soph had returned silently to her partner's side. But though she had tried her best to banish it, she could still see it in his eyes; the shame at what he had done or tried to do, made all the worse now by the fact that his friend was still alive.

The warrior had fought for nothing, he had tried to kill Eliom, to kill his lover for nothing, because here Edmund stood, shaky but very much still breathing…

Hearing the silent plea in her voice though, Fred stood tall with a stiff nod and obeying, finally stepped forward to greet the Explorer. Just as the others had, he too held out a hand, but oblivious to what had gone on before, Edmund soon pulled him into an embrace.

"I am sorry, Edmund," Fred said awkwardly. "I believed you to be dead…"

"Sorry?" Edmund asked lightly before, realising what his friend was saying, pulling away from him in confusion. "Why do *you* need to be sorry?"

But Fred, stepping away too, looked at Eliom, making it clear that the apology was really meant for him.

"I did not explain my actions," the wizard said before the warrior could speak again. "I understand why you acted as you did. It was, in its own way, honourable."

Fred lowered his gaze, but pacified for now, everyone else couldn't help but think what would have happened had it not been for Soph.

Honourable? Still confused, Edmund all the while looked from one companion to the other, searching for some kind of explanation. Before the Explorer could speak though, everyone heard a loud grunt and turning, the group were then surprised to see that Thom had moved off and was standing now at the hole in the wall, the almost-entirely-forgotten secret compartment, his hands full of debris.

"We should get a move on," he said as he shifted the rock away, clearing the space. "Jen may be dead, but that does not mean her fighters are. I assume this hole is what we were looking for?"

It was a good point and as if finally remembering their mission, the very reason they were there in the first place, the others hurried to help him, grabbing handfuls of stone between them to clear the entrance to what, every moment, looked like a dark cavern beyond.

With six of them working hard, the hole was widened in no time at all and as they finished, all stopped for a moment to gaze into the blackness.

The compartment was bigger than any of them had expected, for instead of a room, the space seemed to fall into a long wide tunnel leading deeper into the ground. Here there was no white stone, and as Eliom muttered the lighting spell and held his staff aloft, everyone could see that the tunnel was in fact constructed of dried dirt, as if the passageway hadn't been planned with the rest of the tomb at all but added as a hasty afterthought.

"Where do you think it goes?" Elanore whispered. For some reason she felt suddenly afraid to speak too loudly.

"I don't know," Edmund admitted. He swayed a little again, but grabbing hold of the edge of the wall for support, he quickly turned to Eliom. "Maybe only a few of us should go. The rest can keep a look out again."

The wizard inclined his head calmly. Despite everything that had happened, he seemed to be back to his usual placid self.

"You are our leader," he said.

"Right." Edmund blinked. Yes."

The Explorer meanwhile, looked and felt truly worn down.

"In which case," and he glanced vaguely at the others, "Eliom and I will go. The rest of you can stay here. Just in case…"

None of them needed him to explain what he meant by 'just in case' and half to the Explorer's surprise, no one argued either. Thom was right. Who knew if the crowd of fighters had been the last of Jen's onslaught? Who was to know whether their lives could be in danger yet again, at any moment?

Gesturing for Eliom to go first, Edmund then took one more quick look at the blood-strewn tomb around them before the pair disappeared off into the unknown.

Edmund.
Edmund.
She repeated his name over and over in her mind like a chant.
Edmund.
Edmund.
Edmund of Tonasse.

But no matter how many times she seemed to say it, still nothing happened. Still she was there, in the world of the dead, in her own body. Still she could feel the rattle of cold breath in her chest, feel the freezing air on her cheeks, feel the presence of the elements standing around her, their eyes on her face.

She had to concentrate. She knew had to go deeper. Deeper into herself. But *how* she could only guess.

Edmund.
Edmund.
Edmund of Tonasse.
Harder.
She had to think harder and desperately she tried to conjure up an image

in her mind, an image of where he could be now, what he could be doing, what he could be saying, the people he might be with.

She could see his face, the square jaw, the deep blue eyes, the lips she had kissed so briefly, so clumsily in those last few moments. But these things she knew already, could sense even *without* knowing anything else.

Edmund, come to me, she begged the air.

Please listen to me.

Edmund of Tonasse.

Bethan took a deep long breath, forcing herself to concentrate.

Edmund. Please.

Where are you?

And then, just like that, it came. Suddenly, without any warning, she could see him. She could see his body. She could see him moving, *living* – her stomach did a little flip. He was walking away from her, walking in a place she had never been before, the details so clear that she could make out the muscles straining in his legs, his arms swinging from side to side, his chest rising and falling, hear his heart thrumming very fast, his sword in hand...

Edmund.

Edmund, come to me.

Edmund.

She called out to him in her mind, longing for him to know her, realise that she was there, but though she could see him, still he continued regardless.

He was somewhere dark; she was able to notice that now, to focus on something other than him for a second. He was somewhere gloomy, spacious, with nothing but torchlight...

Was that blood?

And Bethan couldn't help but recoil then as the vision shifted, as he turned suddenly and she was finally faced with *everything,* from the bloodstains on his tunic and cloak, to his pallid face and the cut across one hand.

The element shuddered in horror.

What was happening? Was he in pain? Was he dying?

Suddenly she felt desperate to know.

Edmund.

Edmund.

Edmund, listen to me! Please listen to me!

It crept up on her long before she even realised it. She knew she was almost there. She could hear his breathing now – no, *feel* it as if it were her own, *feel* the pull on his legs as he moved, *feel* the ache in his chest, the ache from a wound so deep...

And then, the world of the dead was gone. The elements were gone. She was *in* the gloom and yet still she was alone. Still he could not see her. Still she was waiting for him.

Edmund.

Edmund.
Edmund, come to me.

—

Edmund suddenly stopped in his tracks.

"Bethan…" he breathed, his eyes roving the dark tunnel in blind confusion.

The word had slipped out unbidden, but upon hearing him speak, Eliom suddenly swung around, the light from his staff illuminating their faces.

"What is it?" he asked, searching his friend's face. "What can you see?"

He sounded surprisingly urgent but even so, Edmund just frowned.

"Nothing," he mumbled. "I can't *see* anything. I thought I heard something. A voice…"

It sounded mad, even to him, but although he tried to shrug the issue away, Eliom's expression soon flashed with concern.

"A voice? That is not nothing," he offered wisely. "Voices are *rarely* nothing." And he gestured further into the tunnel. "Let us continue. It may grow stronger."

Edmund nodded, but almost the second they started off, he had stopped all over again.

Edmund, come to me.

"That!" he challenged the air. "Did you hear that?"

And Eliom studied the tunnel around them, his expression calm again.

"Someone's whispering! Calling my name! Can't you hear it?" Edmund demanded, spinning around, covering all angles with his gaze as if expecting the culprit to emerge from the muddy wall at any second. "Listen!"

"I hear nothing…" But then, right as the wizard spoke, as if it had been waiting for that very moment to reveal itself, they both saw it.

The bag.

It lay on the tunnel floor, in the dirt at their feet as if it had always been there, even though Edmund was almost entirely certain that it *hadn't* a second before… and for a long while both of them just stared at it.

It was a simple pouch made of rough sackcloth tied together with string, just small enough to fit in the palm of a hand and as Eliom reached down cautiously to pick it up, turning the fabric about in his fingers to examine it in the dim light from his staff, Edmund couldn't help but feel his heart drop.

"Is this *it?*" he realised aloud, trying to fight his rising disappointment. "Is *this* what we've come all this way for? A bag of…"

But the wizard didn't answer as he continued to run the little pouch across his hands, weighing it warily. The way he inspected it, made it clear he was looking for something in particular; but whilst Edmund had no idea what that something was, watching his friend's careful expression made him

THE ENTITY OF SOULS

wonder if it was a little too early to be giving up hope just yet...

"This may be more than meets the eye," the wizard then confirmed.

As he glanced up, his face suddenly then flashed with realisation and without a second's warning, he was tossing the little sack to Edmund.

"Open it!" he commanded urgently. "Quickly!"

And almost dropping the mysterious bag, Edmund immediately began to fumble at the knot in the string. The pouch felt strangely heavy in his hands, its shape shifting easily as he turned it about.

"It feels like... *sand*," he muttered, cursing as his fingers shook. The knot was surprisingly fiddly.

"It is. Of a sort. If I am not mistaken," Eliom replied, taking another scan of the chamber around them as if it was him now who expected someone to appear at any moment. "If it *is* what I believe it to be though, then we must hurry. The timing is crucial."

Edmund had no idea what the wizard was talking about, but just as he felt like crying out in frustration – the knot was not only fiddly, but *tight* – the string suddenly loosened and just like that, the little bag fell open.

Both man and wizard leaned in close to look at the contents.

From what Edmund could make out in the dim light, the bag appeared to be filled, just as he had suspected, with sand. It was fine and pink and as Eliom moved his staff closer, it glistened slightly, glimmering like millions of tiny particles of glass. It shifted like fluid in the Explorer's hands as he cupped them together, trying not to spill anything, but even as he stared at it wonderingly, recognition began to dawn.

"Is this *sleeping powder*?" he asked, looking up at his friend as he forced himself not to be disappointed again too soon. It looked exactly the same as the powder Eldora the Lectur had given to him that night on the ship, the night that had changed everything, and yet as Edmund glanced between the pink sand and Eliom, he saw that the wizard's eyes were wide in wonderment.

"Amazing," he mumbled as if he hadn't even heard the Explorer speak. "Amazing. I had no idea that it still existed..." And confused, Edmund looked down at the powder again.

Now that he thought about it, it did seem finer than the stuff he remembered, finer and much more... *shiny*.

"What...?" he asked, feeling suddenly nervous. "What is it?"

Eliom however, still didn't answer, for just then a tiny slip of folded parchment seemed to *appear* amongst the powder almost as if, like a little living thing, it had slithered its way to the top of the bag, desperate for air. It met Edmund's fingers and wasting no more time, the Explorer gently prised it out and, handing the bag of pink sand to Eliom, hurriedly unfolded it.

The parchment was old, crumbling and saturated in dust and as Edmund's hands continued to tremble, he pulled it apart to reveal a single line of scrawl.

The writing was in black ink, faded and smudged with time, but still readable.

Only one who is destined will find a way.

That was all it said, and turning the parchment over several times, just to make sure he hadn't missed anything, Edmund read the sentence another two times before he spoke.

Only one who is destined will find a way.

"Only one who is destined will find a way… why do I recognise that?" he mused. His mind felt oddly fuggy in this place. He certainly wasn't feeling himself since Eliom's spell, but down here, down in the tunnel, it felt worse, almost as if someone had pulled a sack, much like the one in Eliom's hands, over his head, blocking everything out. His memories and thoughts were jumbled.

Only one who is destined will find a way.
Only. One. Who. Is. Destined. Will. Find. A. Way.

Was it some kind of code? And suddenly the Explorer couldn't help but felt irritated as he realised that yet again, he was faced with another frustratingly cryptic message he didn't understand.

He was certain that the words meant something to him. He'd definitely come across them somewhere before. Or at least something *similar* anyway. But *where…?*

Only one who is destined will find a way.
Destined will find a way…

"Ratacopeck." And finally, just like that, Eliom had the answer. "The Temple of Ratacopeck. *Only those who are destined will find a way*. It was engraved over the entrances."

"Of course!" Edmund exclaimed, almost crumpling the telling parchment in his excitement. Although he hadn't been with Eliom at the time he had translated it from the old wizard tongue outside one of the four entrances to the temple, the wizard had spoken of it afterwards.

The old man had said it too. He could remember it now as clear as day, the words from his dream… Only *those* who are destined will find a way…

But then that well-known bitter feeling washed over him and without knowing he did it, Edmund's lip curled.

Destiny. Yet again destiny was there. Was in control. It was destiny that had led them to the Temple of Ratacopeck. It was destiny that had made him lose the elements, lose Bethan, in the first place. And now…?

Edmund. Edmund, come to me.

Suddenly, the voice was there again, hissing in his ear as if she, Bethan, were standing right beside him, and shocked, Edmund snapped back to his senses.

"Only one can fulfil this task," Eliom said. If he'd been able to read the Explorer's face or mind in the last few moments, he didn't show it. "Only *one* is destined."

"Destined to do what? What *is* this stuff?" Edmund asked, exasperated. Hearing the voice on the air again had given him a new sense of urgency. Though it had felt so much closer, it had also sounded weaker, fainter than before.

Whatever it was, wherever the voice was coming from, it was fading. They were running out of time...

Eliom turned to look at his friend then, for what seemed one long, hard moment. Edmund was still pale, his face ragged and worn-out, his body coated with the now-dried remnants of his own blood, but still his eyes were alive, energetic, determined and looking into his companion's face, the wizard knew, as he had all along, that there had only ever been one person to save the elements, just as there had only ever been one to lead them all. Yes, the Explorer had been helped along the way by his friends - they'd been through much together – yet still Eliom could see in that moment, staring into that resolute gaze, that Edmund alone was the one to bring them back, to bring the elements home. Much as the Explorer fought it, whatever he thought he knew otherwise, it *was* his destiny...

"Hold some of the dust in your hands," the wizard then instructed quietly. "There is little time. We may already be too late." And obeying without question, Edmund immediately took the bag from Eliom and poured a small mound of the fine pink powder into his cupped fingers.

"Now," Eliom continued, "you must inhale it, in one sharp breath and think of them. Think of the elements."

Edmund nodded. It was just as he had done with Eldora's powder. Simple yet effective...

"But be aware," and suddenly, the wizard sounded almost worried. "The magic will only last for a few minutes. Dream dust is very powerful, but only temporary."

"Dream dust?!" Edmund cried, glancing down at the sandy substance in his hands with a new feeling of nervous excitement.

"It was once a common form of communication," Eliom explained, "even for *my* kind. But it was used too often, too much. I thought the practice had died out centuries ago. It is grown you see, not *made* and we had to find new ways of communicating over vast distances, new spells..."

"What does it do?" Edmund asked, moving the sand across his palm with a finger. The powder was soft to the touch.

"You were correct in one sense. It is like a sleeping powder, but it is much more potent," the wizard replied. "It opens the mind, allowing you to see beyond what is possible and, in many ways, *probable*. Like a dream." Eliom seemed thoughtful. "In a dream you can see things, hear things, experience things that are not real. They can seem to last forever, to stretch on for days, years, when in reality they only take a few seconds for us to comprehend. Dream dust allows control over the part of our minds that govern our dreams, our deeper thoughts. It sends the user into a dream-like state, where anything is possible. When two or more *beings* use it at the same time and think of each other, they can speak, experience things together over large distances."

"Like a vision?" Edmund started, thinking about the ways in which Eliom had communicated with him over the years.

The wizard frowned a little.

"In a way, yes. But the dreams the dust creates are much more powerful, much stronger."

"But if I think of the elements," the Explorer began again. Already he was starting to see the potential flaw in the entire plan, "if I think of… Bethan, surely she'd have to be using the powder too, at the same time, in order to speak to me?" Wherever Bethan was, whatever she was doing, the chances of her being able to communicate with him at *exactly the same time* were infinitesimally small. But though he was half-expecting Eliom to look horrified as he realised the truth in what the Explorer was saying, the wizard was calm.

"That is the greatest magic of all," he replied instead. "We must trust that Bethan is already prepared to communicate with you." He glanced around the tunnel again. "That voice you keep hearing, it is undoubtedly her, already trying to reach you. We must trust this time in-"

"Fate." Edmund gave a very wry smile. "Yes, I know." He sighed. "Why does everything always seem to come down to *that*?"

"A great mystery for another time perhaps," Eliom said. "But quickly now. The timing is vital."

And realising how much time he really was wasting, Edmund nodded and looked down once more at the sand in his hands.

He could hear his heart pounding in his temples.

Could these special little grains of dust really take him to see Bethan again, after all this time? Could they really help him to save her and the others?

There was only one way to find out.

And without so much as another thought, the Explorer then lowered his head and with a great gasping breath, snorted the dream dust up into his nose.

SEPARATED REUNION

*T*angy *pain seared into Edmund's lungs and he choked, his vision suddenly blurred by a stream of tears. The dim light and Eliom began to swim before his eyes, but instead of darkness, both began to grow lighter and lighter and lighter until all was white. So white, it almost hurt.*

And with that whiteness came a faint ringing at his eardrums, getting louder by the second, pounding his every sense.

His head felt heavy. No, not heavy; as if it were being pulled, as if the back of his neck were being tugged by some unseen force, straining his head back and back and back...

Until with a snap, he was released and Edmund found himself propelled forward, almost to his knees.

"Argh!"

Stumbling to stay upright, the Explorer cried out. His voice sounded oddly disjointed, not quite a part of him. It made him jump.

He felt suddenly sick and taking a moment just to breathe, to calm himself, it was only then that he paused as he realised for the first time where he was.

He was standing in the white room he knew only too well.

The ground was shimmering, brilliant white, as white as the bright air around him, and the walls, well - there were *no walls - only white blankness. No shadows, no edges.*

The world of visions.

He had been there many a time before, summoned there by Eliom. It no longer frightened him, no longer took him unawares. But for the first time, it felt different.

The wizard; he wasn't there, standing in front of him. He wasn't in control, and yet Edmund wasn't alone.

The Explorer felt himself blink. Hard.

There was a figure standing only a little distance away who seemed suddenly to have appeared and yet to have always been there. Just as he felt he had always been there...

A woman.

She was tall, slender, with a rugged dress of pale silk, dirtied with mud, the hem torn. Her bare legs and arms were dirty, caked in mud, spattered with grit, her long dark hair tangled over her shoulders.

From where he stood, he couldn't yet see her face. Somehow it was blurred. But he didn't need to be told who it was.

Edmund.

The air whispered again, stronger this time, wafting all around him.

Edmund. Come to me.

"Edmund!"

And then, the voice became clear and Edmund knew that it was the woman who had spoken and his stomach gave a churn as he saw her, truly saw her. The eyes, the nose, the lips that had haunted his dreams, his every thought.

She was there. Finally. She was there. And the very sight of her seemed to make him freeze.

"Edmund!" *Bethan repeated. She sounded shocked, breathless. As breathless as he felt right then just looking at her, still not quite believing it...*

And for a good long moment, he couldn't seem to focus on anything else but how overwhelmed he was, not just by this place, by what was happening, what he was seeing, but by the realisation as he looked into that face how much - no matter what his doubts had been the past few days - he wanted her, how much he longed to hold her in his arms, to tell her she would soon be safe, that he wouldn't stop trying until she was by his side again...

Bethan.

But somehow, his feet wouldn't budge. Much as he tried to rush to her, to comfort her, his body wasn't listening to his commands. It was numb, motionless. He couldn't move...

His own voice echoed strangely in the weird expanse.

"Bethan... I-!" *But Bethan was quick to cut in.*

"I don't know how long we have! You have to listen to me!"

She looked tired, he realised, tired and afraid, and the reality of the situation hitting him hard, the Explorer found that he felt afraid too.

Where was she? Was she hurt? Was she in danger? Why did she look so bedraggled?

"Just tell me you're all right," *he replied.* "I just need to know you're all right..."

But whilst Bethan nodded, she didn't smile.

"I'm fine. The others are here too. We're all fine. But we need your help! You have to listen now!" *And Edmund, worried as he still was, immediately clamped his mouth shut, ready to hear her.*

The element looked urgent.

"You have to return to the Temple of Ratacopeck," *she said, getting quickly to the point.* "And climb the platform by sunset tonight."

Edmund stared at her, uncomprehending.

The Temple of Ratacopeck?

"Tonight?!" *he echoed out loud. He could feel his hope starting to waver a little.*

"Yes. By sunset," *the element repeated.* "At sunset, the gateway between the two worlds will open and you* must *pull us all through. That's the only way we can get out of here!" Her words were fast, she was barely leaving herself time to breathe.*

But still confused, Edmund just shook his head.

"How do you know all this?" he asked. "How do you know it will work?"

"Ophelius told us," Bethan said simply. "He was just here..."

Here?

Ophelius had been there, with the elements?

Edmund felt suddenly very sick all over again. This time for an entirely different reason...

"Where are you?" he insisted, fearing for the answer. The prophet was surely dead; he knew he was dead... Yet she'd told him all was fine...

"Don't be worried," Bethan replied, and then, for the first time, she looked a little sheepish. "And I don't want you to... well... But..." she gave a little sigh. "I'm in the world of the dead."

Edmund gave a start, but before he could say another word, Bethan's face was pained.

"Oh, Edmund!" she cried, and she reached a hand out through the expanse towards him. "I thought- I thought..."

"It's all right," the Explorer tried to soothe.

The short message, however confusing, however bizarre, was delivered and now all Edmund wanted was her.

Again, he desperately tried to move to her, but still his body was frozen. He couldn't even reach out his own hand to touch her.

She was so close and yet so far away...

"What's happened to you?" Bethan cried. Her voice was shaking. "Is that your blood? Where are you? Are you safe?"

"Hush, I'm fine," Edmund tried. She too had obviously noticed his dirty clothes, the dried blood, his pale skin. "We're all fine here too. Eliom is with me. Fred, Thom and Elanore as well. We're coming to get you. No matter what."

"I was so afraid..." Bethan continued. He could see the tears rising to her eyes, see how much she was trying to control herself. Something had happened to her, something to truly shock her, but what that was, Edmund couldn't be sure.

"Hush now. It'll be all right. Everything will be all right," he said. But still Bethan looked ready to cry.

"I thought the worst had happened. When I saw- I saw-." And the element hesitated then, before, wiping a hand furiously across her eyes, she seemed suddenly to sober. "Edmund, your brother. I've seen him. Renard. He's here."

Renard.

The name seemed to send a shockwave through the white expanse and there was a stunned silence as Edmund paused.

Renard. The brother he had been prepared to kill... the brother that he was trying even now to forget...

And his thoughts couldn't help but return to what had happened in the tomb, to Jen and her desperate search for her master, his vague hopes that Renard could still be alive, right before she had stabbed him...

His brother truly was dead after all then.

"How-? Does he-? Did he-?" somehow the words struggled to come out as a lump formed at the back of Edmund's throat. Suddenly, for some reason, he just had to know that Renard wasn't angry with him, that he didn't blame him for what had happened and it shocked him. Selfish as it was, his first thoughts were of redemption, were of saving himself from his own guilt, his own shame at doing nothing as his own flesh and blood had died before his very eyes…

"He *is*, was…" Bethan was clearly searching for the words but little did the Explorer know that the element was understanding right then and there that she could never truly tell him of Renard's hatred, of his blame, his bitterness. What, after all, would it achieve, but hurt? More hurt, more torture at the hands of a young man who had caused so much pain already…

"I'm not-" she tried again, but before she could finish, Edmund suddenly let out a gasp as he felt the pulling at his neck again.

It was faint but growing stronger by the second. And he knew.

The dream was ending. Already, their time was up. The power of the dust was running out.

And already, Bethan's voice was far away again, a voice on the air.

Edmund. I… I love you.

It was too quick. He had no time. No time to look on her face one last second, to store it there to fuel him on.

He didn't even have the chance to say goodbye.

"I love you too," he whispered. And then, just like that, Bethan and the space of white were gone.

SUNSET

"Careful. Take it easy."

Meggie's voice sounded very far away, but still Bethan opened her eyes, only to find herself sitting on the hard cold ground, staring up into the faces of her fellow elements.

All three of them looked cold, pale and worried.

"Are you all right?"

It was Bex who spoke next and still a little disorientated, Bethan reached up to touch her own face only to find it damp with fresh tears.

Her heart panged.

Edmund. He'd been there, right before her very eyes, right within touching distance. She'd spoken to him and he'd-

"Bethan, are you all right?"

"Yes, yes," she managed to stammer a reply. Everyone was staring at her, watching, waiting, probably wondering why she'd been crying.

And to her horror, as she thought about it, casting her mind back to what she'd just seen, she realised that she was beginning to wonder *that* herself…

"What happened? Did you find Edmund?" Meggie asked. She looked urgent for some reason and Bethan's brow furrowed.

Edmund? Had she seen him?

Everything felt suddenly very fuggy.

"Yes… I saw him. I think…" But for some awful reason, she was finding it difficult to focus and though it scared her, she couldn't remember *why* she was even feeling so upset in the first place. Had something happened? Why did they all look so concerned? "Yes. I'm pretty sure I saw him. And I told him what needed to be done…"

The other elements glanced at each other. She was only *pretty sure* she'd seen him?

"Are you certain?" Saz asked, to which Bethan nodded, paused and then, after a moment of consideration, shook her head. Her vision of Edmund was somehow fading, drifting away like a leaf on the breeze. She'd only seen him a moment ago and yet already it felt like an age...

"And how was my murderer?"

The cold voice reminded them all of the lurking presence of the baggage collector, and the even more unwelcome Renard, but even so, none of them so much as glanced their way.

"Shut up," Saz snarled. "Leave her alone." And though Renard gave an uncaring laugh, he surprised them all by saying nothing more as Bethan then turned to stare up at him, long and hard.

He looked so like his brother, it almost frightened her. Again. But no doubt against his wishes, his words had reminded her.

Edmund, your brother. I've seen him. Renard. He's here. Those were *her* words. She could remember that much. And feeling a clearer sense of conviction, the element grimaced.

"Yes. I told him," she said with more confidence. They'd spoken of Renard right before everything had faded and he'd said...

Nothing.

Edmund. I- I love you. She could recall screaming it; the first time she had truly spoken her feelings out loud, her voice cracking as all had dissolved. They were the last words she'd heard. The last words spoken.

And for some reason this bothered her.

Right there and then, despite the urgency of their situation. Right there and then, sitting on the floor of the world of the dead, a place no living creature had ever before dared to tread, it bothered her that Edmund hadn't replied. It bothered her that he hadn't said the same, affirmed what she was fighting for... And an irritated flush rising to her cold face, Bethan reached out a hand to Bex, who helped haul her to her feet with her good hand.

The tourniquet was doing its job well, Bex's arm no longer seemed to be bleeding.

"So, what happens now?"

Saz was the one to say it, but all of them knew they were each thinking it. They had come, they had spoken with Ophelius and they had their answer.

So what did *happen now?*

"We get to the statue by sunset, and return to Tungala," Bex said. It really sounded that simple, but somehow, the others doubted it would be in practice. The statue was miles away, back in the City, back through the barrier that had disappeared, back across the prairie and through the Builder's wrath, back beyond the crowd of angry Diggers waiting to hurt them...

"I told Edmund that it had to be *this* sunset," Bethan recalled aloud. "I know that doesn't give us a lot of time but... it's probably for the best."

None of them looked surprised though. After all, all four of them knew that to wait any longer would only give the Builder and the Diggers more time to potentially find them... and stop them.

Impossible as it might seem to get back in time, they had to strike as soon as they could. The sooner the better.

"But how long do we have until sunset?" Meggie asked. "Will we have time?" and realising the potential problem ahead, Saz frowned.

"Who knows?" she cried. "For all *we* know, we could have been here for *days* in Digger time. Time could be… different here. How do we even know that the sunset we'll see is at the same time as the one Eliom and the others will see? We could be *years* too late or-" and struck by their lack of answers, she turned then on the baggage collector. "We need Ophelius," she demanded. "We need more time with him."

It was the first time any of them had addressed him in a while, and the baggage collector, who, up until then had been observing the elements with a sort of morbid interest, gave a start, his ugly face squirming in surprise at the sudden attention thrust upon him.

"He had his time," he said unhelpfully. "I told you, a spirit may only surface for fifteen minutes. Especially one as old as him."

"What, fifteen minutes, ever?!" Meggie challenged incredulously. "That's *stupid!*"

"Ever." The little man smirked a little. "Mean no disrespect, but that man wasted his last few moments with *you*."

That silenced them all then as the four women felt an equal sweep of horror at knowing that Ophelius had resurfaced just for them, wasted his last few precious minutes of what appeared to be consciousness, to save their tiny little lives…

"Just like he's wasting his now you mean?" Saz suddenly piped up, glaring towards Renard. But to everyone's astonishment, the ghost of Edmund's brother had vanished.

"Where'd he go?" Bethan demanded, forgetting Ophelius for a moment. Had his time been spent too? Had Renard really wasted his last remaining minutes on them? A small, angry part of herself hoped so.

"He left," the baggage man replied with something like amusement. "Mean no disrespect, but I should think he didn't want to share the same fate as your friend. He is saving his last few minutes for someone else no doubt…" and for some reason, Bethan found the knowledge that Renard wasn't done with the living yet, unnerving. Fury for what he had done, the pain he had cause, still burned like a flame in the pit of her being. If anything, he *deserved* to have his time wasted…

But then again, despite it all, he *was* Edmund's brother. Edmund's flesh and blood…

Edmund, I-I love you.

Her mind returning momentarily to the dream, Bethan realised that her troubling thoughts were still there, ready to resurface at the smallest hint and straight away, the element took a deep breath, trying to remain calm.

She needed to focus. They all did. As Saz had said, who knew how much time they had?

"We have to get moving and hope for the best," she offered aloud then, turning back to the problem at hand. "If it worked for Ophelius, it can work for us. We just need to reach the statue by the first sunset once we're out of here. It *must* be at the same time."

It had to be.

"How long have we got?" This question was directed at the only one present who could possibly know. But the baggage man only shook his head.

"What does it matter?" he retorted. "After all, what makes you think you can even *leave* this place?"

It was difficult to tell if he was taunting them or not. His face was still a twisted, grimacing smile, enough to make every hair on their skin stand on end, but even so, the women stared at him, stunned.

"Don't you think you've done *enough*?!" Meggie positively growled, gesturing at Bex's bandaged arm. The baggage collector gave a small shudder as he remembered the thick, warm, *alive* blood. "Can't you just help us now?"

"And anyway, we made a pact," Saz added, stepping forward to hold out her hand. Where the baggage man's knife had crossed her palm only a while before, the scar had already changed from brown to black, the skin around it shrivelled like an old wound. Bethan avoided her fellow element's eyes.

You're the one who wants so desperately to escape, she told herself, echoing Saz's words form earlier. *To be with Edmund again. You would gladly see Saz or anyone die so that you can escape...*

Whether he feels the same way or not...

The baggage handler uttered a low snarl of irritation. But despite it all, he soon seemed to give in. He had, after all, exactly what he wanted now. A soul.

"Very well then," he said. "You may leave. If you can..." he gave an odd sneer. "But you should know one thing..."

Despite his obvious attempts to antagonise them, no one rose to it at first and all four women remained silent. But seeing that nothing would be dealt with otherwise, it was Meggie who then rolled her eyes.

"What," she said flatly.

"Sunset," the baggage collector then pointed out. He definitely seemed to be enjoying himself. "In the world you have come from..."

"Yes?" Saz groaned impatiently.

"Well, mean no disrespect, but I thought you ought to know... it's in less than a few hours."

—

"We have until sunset," Edmund told Eliom the second he was awake. The wizard was crouched over him, the light from his staff held high to reveal the presence now of Fred, Thom, Soph and Elanore.

THE ENTITY OF SOULS

All were staring down at him, looking nervous and for the first time, Edmund realised that he was lying on his back on the tunnel floor. The ground was hard, and giving a groan as he tried to move, he gave a start as he noticed once again the dried blood on his chest and blackened clothing.

No wonder they look so worried, he found himself thinking. Only minutes ago, he'd been almost dead... Or was it longer than that? The dream had seemed so short and yet at the same time it felt like it had lasted a lifetime, just as Eliom had said it would. For all he knew, he could have been out for hours.

Remembering the dream, his heart then wrenched as he pictured Bethan's saddened face. Now that he had seen her again, face-to-face, he felt more determined than ever before to find her, to save her, and that meant that he had to move, *they* had to move - *fast*.

"What happened, Edmund?" Fred asked. "We heard a cry, and rushed through to find you like this. What did Ophelius leave us?"

"Time for explanation is later, my friend," Eliom offered quickly. "But first, let him speak. There is little time before the dream fades. Edmund." And knowing the next few moments were vital, Edmund found the wizard's face and tried to focus on it. For some reason he felt completely exhausted, his eyes still fuzzy, his nostrils still sore from inhaling the dream dust. "Edmund," the wizard repeated. "Tell us what was said, what you saw. What is happening at sunset?"

What *is* happening at sunset? Edmund, with a jolt of horror, realised that he'd already started to forget Bethan's message. All he could see was her face, a picture of beautiful sorrow. He could remember his own emotions, the warmth flowing through him at seeing her again. His determination to help her... But her words?

"She said... something... something about a temple..." he faltered, unsure, to which Thom gave a big huffing sigh.

"*Another* temple?!" the dwarf snapped unhelpfully and Fred shot him a warning look.

"You *can* remember, my friend. Tell us." Eliom was calm, trusting, as were the others. They were all looking to him, once more, for guidance. Guidance that yet again, he wasn't sure he could give...

"Why can he not remember? Can you not delve into his mind?" Fred suggested to the wizard.

Eliom turned to the Explorer.

"It is certainly possible..."

But Edmund immediately shook his head. Whilst at certain moments, the wizard seemed entirely himself, the Explorer could see how drained Eliom still was, the healing spell having exhausted him even more. Unbeknownst to the others, Edmund knew that whatever Eliom had done to protect his life back in the tomb had to have been very advanced magic, no matter how little the wizard had made of it.

He would have to recall the dream without help. Without magic.

... by sunset tonight.

What?

He could remember some of her words now, but they were somehow jumbled in his memory. Scraps of phrases thrust together, like a giant puzzle of letters and sounds.

Why couldn't he remember?

Edmund found himself angry all over again.

He could recall *other* dreams, Ophelius's words, his own nightmares, but this? *This* felt somehow impossible. Almost as if his memories were falling through a sieve, lost in the abyss with every passing moment...

And then suddenly...

Ratacopeck.

The name hit Edmund like a slap.

The Temple of Ratacopeck. The place that had taken the elements away from them, that had taken Bethan away from him. The place where his brother-

Edmund, your brother. I've seen him. Renard. He's here.

The sudden memory stung him with surprising force, pulling his focus away for a moment.

His brother. His brother was dead. And unable to forgive him.

Renard was dead and had to *hate* him for it.

She hadn't said as much, but he'd seen the expression on Bethan's face when he'd asked her, or tried to ask her. She may have tried to hide it, but she hadn't been fooling anybody...

"Time is of the essence. What have you remembered?" Eliom's sober voice cut into Edmund's consciousness and coming to his senses, the Explorer tried to concentrate all over again. He had to focus on finding Bethan and the others now. Renard was already gone. The dead were for later...

"The Temple of Ratacopeck," he said, finally getting to his feet, his joints stiff. "We must return to the temple by sunset." His brow furrowed as he tried to focus on repeating Bethan's words exactly as she'd said them. They seemed to flow easily now. "At sunset, the gateway between the two worlds will open and we must pull them through. It's the only way we can get them back."

"Ratacopeck?!" Thom spoke up and this time no one tried to stop him. They were all thinking it. "But that's *days* from here!" The distance was clearly impossible...

"How long until sunset?" Elanore asked of anyone who could answer. "The Karenza might-"

"Less than three hours," was Fred's flat reply. "We cannot reach it by ship."

The sea captain's face fell.

"No," she replied pointlessly. "Even she can't perform miracles."

There was no way they could reach the temple in that time by *any* means and there was a long and hopeless silence as all pondered the question of what was to be done.

Less than three hours…

"Is that it?" Thom was the one to finally declare. "We have come all this way only to find we can do *nothing*?!"

"Hush Thom," Fred chided, but even then, his effort was only half-hearted. "Ophelius will have an answer, surely." And with this, the others began to stare about them in the dim light, as if somehow expecting one to appear from the plain mud-covered walls. But there was nothing; nothing but emptiness and a bag of used dream dust which Edmund soon retrieved from the floor.

"There may be no answer this time," Eliom said. "Perhaps Ophelius meant only to lead us here. No further…" It sounded like defeat in his tone, but still, the others weren't quite ready to give up yet.

"What about the map?" Soph offered suddenly. "Does the map say anything else?"

Eliom gave a thin smile.

"The map has been studied already. Ophelius gave us nothing more."

"It may have more hidden magic." Fred wasn't completely out of hope. "After all, we would not have discovered his directions in the first place if the water-"

"There is nothing," Eliom repeated, surprisingly firmly. "I have checked."

To everyone's surprise, he truly sounded as if he had given up and suddenly frustrated all the more, Thom gave a growl.

"*How* have you checked?" he demanded. "You did not know of its hidden powers before and yet now you-"

"*Stop!*" And all of a sudden, Edmund snapped, the word reverberating around the now-crowded compartment before shooting out into the silent tomb behind them. "Just stop it!" He sounded angry, and surprised all over again, everyone turned to him.

If they expected their leader to have a solution this time though, he was soon to disappoint.

"Turning on each other isn't going to solve *anything!*" he said instead, making Fred and Thom glance at each other as both of them recalled what had happened back in the tomb when Eliom had tried to save Edmund…

"I agree," Soph piped up. "There must be an answer to all of this; we are just not aware of it yet."

"We've been in worse situations before," Elanore agreed. "We'll find a way."

Find a way…

And for a moment, as the others carried on trying to work things out, the sea captain's final words clicked in Edmund's mind and stayed there.

Somehow they reminded him of something; something, he was certain, of great importance, but putting his finger on why, after the fogginess of the dream, was hard.

"Whatever we do, we have little time to do it in!" Thom remarked.

"Yes, we are all well aware of that, Thom…" Fred was starting to sound impatient now.

Find a way…

And turning away from his companions a moment, Edmund tried to concentrate on his thoughts, his recollections, anything that could tell him why those three words were important right now. He fumbled with the empty sack that had once contained the dream dust, scrunching it in his hands, thinking…

"What is the quickest way to travel long distances?" Fred meanwhile asked the tunnel at large. "Short of riding or sailing…?"

Find a way…

"I don't know," Elanore mused. "*Is* there anything quicker?"

Edmund continued to run the sack between his hands.

The quickest way to travel…

Find a way…

Then, as if by magic, something fell from the bag into Edmund's fingers.

The scrap of parchment was still open, rolled at the corners, but readable and for a moment, despite knowing what it said, the Explorer just stared at it.

Only one who is destined will find a way, he read again.

Will find a way.

As the answer then hit him, Edmund felt a surge of hope.

That was it!

Only one who is destined…

But could it really be the answer?

And before he even knew he was speaking, the word was out of his mouth.

"Transportation!" Suddenly Edmund couldn't help but smile at the simplicity of it all. How could they not have seen it before? "That's it!" And then, when no one said anything, he laughed, making the rest of the group, all except Eliom, give a start. Hearing his friend's obvious excitement, the wizard simply blinked slowly, almost as if he'd been expecting to hear Edmund's outburst all along…

"Transportation! That's the answer! Ophelius *can* help us!" the Explorer insisted and dropping the now useless bag of powder, he waved the little note up high as the others just looked at him in blank confusion. "Only one who is destined will find a way. Only *those* who are destined will find a way," he declared. "This phrase. It's followed us everywhere. It was at the temple, it was in my dream, it's here now. But what does it *mean*?!" And as the others continued to look completely stumped, Edmund almost laughed again. "It means exactly what it says! *Destiny!*" before, glancing at Eliom; "Though I hate it, the very *idea* of it after everything that's happened… what if it's the answer now?"

Fred's was the first brow to wrinkle.

"Edmund, what are you talking about?" he said carefully. "How is destiny the answer?" But though the warrior was staring at their leader with the kind of concern shown for the insane, nothing could destroy the Explorer's moment; not now that everything was so clear for the first time in so long.

"Perhaps Ophelius knew who would be here today!" he cried. "I don't know how, but maybe he knew who would find this compartment, knew who would try and save the elements. And that's why he's given us no obvious answer," he swung his arms wide like a performer coming to the end of his show. "Because the answer's already here, staring us in the face." And then, when no one seemed to have anything to offer; "Maybe *all of us* were destined to be here. Maybe I was destined to be here to use the dream dust, to find out where the elements are and how to save them." And finally, as if he had been waiting for this moment all along, he turned back to Eliom, who, already ahead of the others, was nodding. Everyone else looked at him too. "And maybe it's our destiny, *your* destiny, that right here, right now, we have *you*, a wizard. And not just *any* wizard. A wizard of the highest order. A wizard with the power, the right to-"

"Transport…" Fred finished, and slowly, a smile spread across his own face as he finally got it, as he finally understood.

Soph nodded too, obviously reaching the same conclusion as her partner, but still, despite the obvious confidence of their companions, Elanore and Thom continued to look confused.

"I don't mean to be stupid," the sea captain pointed out. "But what *is* transportation? I've never heard of it…"

"You wouldn't have." Edmund was gabbling now. "Only wizards truly understand it."

"It is the ability to travel a great distance in a matter of seconds. In fact, in almost an instant," Fred meanwhile explained.

"Yes. And only few can achieve it. It requires a great amount of power," Soph added.

It sounded remarkable, impossible but even as Elanore looked from warrior to warrioress before her eyes then fell on Eliom, she was smiling a little too now, in on the secret.

Thom however, still seemed to be behind.

"What is all this? What has destiny got to do with anything?" the dwarf grumbled. But more explanations truly were for later. They had to move.

"You have grown wise, my friend," Eliom spoke quietly to Edmund. "I began to wonder when you would finally understand."

"I'm not sure I do, completely, yet," Edmund replied, clearly humbled to hear such words spoken by someone so great, but before he could go any further, Thom was cutting in again.

"Hold on!" he snapped, more than a little perturbed that no one was paying any attention to his questions. "Finally understand? If you knew," he glared at Eliom, "and understood all along how we could get out of this, why did you not say something straight away?!"

Even though the dwarf made a valid point, Eliom still looked at him, the smallest hint of amusement in his eyes.

"It was not my place," he said. "It was not my destiny." And Edmund, energized by this new solution, this new hope of saving the elements, gave another laugh.

Everything would be all right now. He *knew* it somehow... Everything felt like it was fitting into place and he was elated by it, excited that they were finally doing something.

But whilst he had been lost in the moment of his realisation, in the thrill of finding the answer to their seemingly impossible problem, he had missed the most important thing of all, and turning back to his long-time friend, watching the wizard's face, the Explorer soon felt his happiness start to dwindle as he remembered again what had happened; as he remembered how Eliom had saved his life, not once, but *twice* in the last days alone, first from the nimph's poison, and then from Jen's sword; remembered how the wizard had been before, how he had changed since; remembered how, despite all appearances, *frail* he was.

Even now, as he studied Eliom's expression, he could see the haggard bags under the wizard's eyes, too small perhaps for the others to notice, his face, pale and wane, his eyes dimmed with fatigue. Eliom appeared to be exhausted and for the first time, Edmund wondered whether he'd done the right thing...

The crux of it was; would his friend *be able* to transport them all those miles to the temple?

He knew that Eliom *would*. Now that the others understood that it was an option, Edmund had no doubt in his mind that the wizard would go ahead with it. It wasn't in his nature to back down, no matter what the risk; he had already proved that time and time again. But then the question really wasn't *would* he, but *should* he?

In all their years of friendship, Edmund had only heard Eliom speak of transportation once. He had been young, not much older than a boy when the wizard had told him the tale and at the time, he hadn't understood it, *really* understood it. To him it had been fantasy, just another story. But since then, he had really seen magic, really seen the impact it could have, and not just on those around the wizard…

Hundreds of years it had been, perhaps even longer, since Eliom had transported. Transportation, so the Explorer had been led to understand, was a great power, a desperate power, reserved usually for only the greatest need. *"The further the distance, the greater the price,"* the wizard had told him.

It had not always been as it was now. Edmund was hazy on the specifics, having only ever snatched small details of his friend's previous life here and there, but long ago, Eliom had been tasked by the great wizard council to dispose of another; a wizard, disbanded from the Order.

Eliom had never explained what it was the wizard had done wrong, why it was the Order of Wizards wanted him banished, or even what it *meant* to be banished, but even in his travels as an Explorer in the early days, Edmund had heard tales, myths almost forgotten, of the great fight, of towns, cities destroyed, humans and other races alike driven from their homes, many of them killed. The battle had raged on for many months, *years*, so the stories said; wizard against wizard, until, in a moment of weakness, his staff - the epitome of his power - almost shattered, the renegade wizard had taken hold of Eliom, turning in his final moments to petty strangling in an effort to kill his foe, rather than be taken himself.

And then they had disappeared.

An elderly lady Edmund had once known, from a village not far from his own, had told him most of the details as she knew them, the history passed on from generation to generation of her family. She had told him how the two great beings had simply vanished into thin air, one moment there, the next moment inexplicably gone. And though Edmund had questioned his friend, though Eliom had given him only sparse information himself, from what the Explorer had learned, in one last attempt to destroy his enemy, Eliom had transported them both hundreds of miles out of reach of civilisation.

The wizard had never told him what had happened next, and the Explorer had never pushed him far enough, even as an adult, to find out any more, but growing up, the rumours surrounding him spoke of how, drained by the endless fighting, by the great strain of power he had used in that one moment, Eliom had drowned his adversary in a nearby river, turning like a human to the only thing he had left – his own bare hands…

Edmund had no idea how much of the story was true. It had been years since he had even thought of it, even spoken of it, even contemplated that his friend, so calm, so collected, so placid, could have even done such a thing in the first place. But whatever the relevance of it now, of one thing, he was certain; transportation was a dangerous task, a very dangerous task, and one that could very much mean the end for Eliom. Not *death* – at least, he hoped not - but certainly the end of *something*. Something that Edmund dreaded to think of…

Could they really ask this of him?

This time was different from the stories. This time it wasn't one on one. This time there was six of them. And this time, Edmund thought, searching, it seemed, for every possible negative angle; the wizard was older. If that kind of thing made any difference...

Just as he knew he would though, the Explorer became aware all too quickly that the wizard was reading his friend's face just as much as Edmund was his.

"You doubt me too much," he murmured, sounding, if anything, *hurt*, and embarrassed to be caught in his own thoughts, Edmund immediately frowned.

"I don't doubt you," he replied hurriedly. "I'm... I'm afraid for you."

But his fears couldn't matter right now, and he knew it. It was clear that Eliom was going to transport them whether *he* wanted him to or not.

"All right then, let's get moving!" Thom cried eagerly, grimacing as he turned to Eliom. Like the others, he had no idea what it was he was asking, of the risk they were all taking. "How does this... *thing*... work?"

And straight away, the wizard held his free hand out, palm up.

"Take my hand. All of you. *Quickly*," he chided as Thom hesitated before gingerly taking the wizard by the fingers. Fred was quick to follow suit, encircling Eliom's wrist with his hand.

Edmund all the while returned Eliom's gaze that little bit longer, as if waiting to be sure, waiting for that moment of hesitation in the wizard's eyes. No matter how pointedly he looked though, Eliom's face was calm, unreadable, and realising he had little choice now but to obey, the Explorer soon took his friend by the arm.

Surely the wizard wouldn't really go through with it if he didn't think he could do it. Would he?

"Soph, come. We have to go," Fred then said as he turned to see that his life-partner hadn't moved. But to everyone's surprise, despite his words, Soph remained where she was, as did Elanore, both of them seeming to avoid his eyes.

Fred shifted impatiently.

"Hurry! We have little time!" he insisted, holding his spare hand out to her. But regardless of his urgency, still Soph didn't take it. Instead, she glanced at Elanore, and as if agreeing to some secret pact, the sea captain nodded, her hand moving slowly to the sword sheathed at her side.

"We will stay here," Soph then replied quietly, her gaze still avoiding the warrior's. "And wait for your return." And for a moment, dumbfounded, Fred just looked at her, his expression entirely blank. Though his partner appeared adamant however, the warrior still seemed intent on taking her hand.

"No," he said, almost as if he was speaking a fact. "You are coming. Come and take hold."

But Soph just shook her head, and her eyes instead turning to Eliom, Edmund felt a wrench in his chest as he realised that she too had understood the potential cost of what they were about to do.

"Five is too many," she then confirmed. "Eliom cannot take *all* of us. It could kill him."

It was the first time anyone had ventured to speak of the possible dangers aloud and whilst no one could be sure that it would, then again, no one could be sure that it *wouldn't* and realising too what this meant, Fred also glanced at Eliom before turning back to his partner in a moment of indecision.

"Then I will stay here too," he decided and before anyone could stop him, the warrior had let go of Eliom's wrist and stepped away.

The group were down to three now. Three and counting, for already Edmund could see Thom's look of unwillingness as he too started to think through their options. Fred had his eyes on Edmund as if waiting for his blessing, as if waiting for him to tell him it would be all right, but despite the silent plea on the warrior's face, despite even, his own misgivings about the whole thing, Edmund felt suddenly resolute.

The elements needed Fred. He had no idea *why* or *how* he knew this, but something about destiny, if he were to trust in it now, told him that Fred's role in this was yet to be over. Much as he could sense his friend's reluctance to be separated from the one he loved, a reluctance he himself had known, he was also certain about this.

As, so it seemed, was Soph.

"The elements need you, Fred," she said firmly. "You must go. We will see each other again soon. I promise. I will find you."

"We'll set off as soon as possible," Elanore added, trying to be helpful. "As soon as the Karenza is up and running we'll set sail for the temple. We can be there in-"

But Fred looked suddenly angry.

"No!" he cried and just as she had in the tomb, regardless of the others around him, he took Soph in his arms roughly, pulling her body close to his. "I am not leaving you again!"

Nestling her head against Fred's shoulder, Soph gave a small growl of defiance. Every fibre of her being secretly wanted him to stay as she breathed in her partner's scent, felt the muscles of his chest pressed beneath her own. But at the same time, she knew what had to be done.

"Go. Honour me with this," she commanded, her voice muffled by her lover's cloak. "You have to go. Now!" and as she saw that he too was torn between his sense of duty and his feelings for the warrioress enclosed in his arms, she reached up then, and taking his head in her hands, delivered him what would perhaps be their last lingering kiss.

"*Go*," she whispered and her arms moving back to his chest, she gave her life-partner a shove towards his waiting friends, her grey eyes suddenly fierce. "Go Fred, or so help me…"

Fred still seemed unsure, but there was something changed in him now.

"All right," he said numbly and taking hold of Eliom's wrist once again, he gave a small sigh. "We should go."

Slowly, Eliom then looked at each member of the group in turn.

"Are we ready?" he asked and as each of them nodded, including, finally, the glum-looking Fred, it was then that he lowered his staff to the ground. The wood made an odd clunking noise as it hit the hard mud. "First I must perform a spell to build my strength. But then the transportation will be almost instant." He let out a long calming breath. "I warn you that the experience may feel a little strange. But whatever happens, no matter what you see, hear or feel, *do not let go of me.*" And again, the others all nodded.

"Elanore, Soph," Edmund started as he looked to the two they were leaving behind. "I can't begin to" But Elanore soon stopped him with a wave of her hand and a tight smile.

"Again, it's been a pleasure. But," and she glanced at Soph again, "no goodbyes, just yet. We'll find you."

"Good luck," was all Soph said, her voice still merely a whisper. All the strength seemed to have gone from her now.

"You too," Edmund replied, seeing that Fred was unable to reply. None could mistake the sorrow in his eyes, but like a true warrior, he was trying to hide it. He had other things to focus on now.

Edmund then looked to Eliom.

"Let's go," he said and Eliom nodded. Now was the time. They were all ready.

It didn't take long. Almost instantly the light from Eliom's staff began to shift from white to a deep red as the wizard began to chant, to speak the words under his breath, preparing himself for the spell. But as the whole tunnel began to glow with it, the light growing brighter and brighter, as they all stood, waiting for the moment to come, the moment when they would be somewhere else, there was a sudden crash.

The sound came from the tomb beyond and as everyone turned to look, they all heard it; the voices, the shouts, the scramble of many feet.

The first to realise, Soph immediately drew her sword, turning her body fully to face the tunnel entrance. Elanore too began to draw hers, swivelling towards the commotion.

"What is that?" Thom exclaimed, raising his own weapon in his spare hand.

But it was too late. As the red light grew to an almost blinding level, Eliom's staff began to *hum,* deep and loud and as Eliom, his eyes closed, continued to chant, his words were soon drowned out by the clashing of metal and the bustle of bodies as suddenly, a horde of jostling figures appeared through the darkness of the tunnel entrance, all of them brandishing swords, bows, axes, all of them young, with brown ringleted hair, childlike faces and fangs...

"*Soph!*" Fred yelled, drawing his own sword as he realised what was happening. But still it was too late. As the warrior, dwarf and man watched, the group of figures then leapt at the two women, instantly burying them in a pile of thrashing teeth and metal and before any of them could react, there was a sudden dazzling flash and everything had gone.

—

"Less than a few hours?!" Saz echoed in shock. "But that's impossible! How are we supposed to get to the statue on time?! It took us days to get here! And it was daylight when we... how can it be almost-?"

"Time moves quickly," the baggage collector remarked, gesturing at the cold expanse around them. "There *is* no time here as such – not in the same way there is in other places - but I like to keep track of what's going on in the outside worlds... call it a *hobby*. You've been gone for hours... possibly even days, I'm not sure..."

Days?!

"Nickolas and Dromeda!" Meggie suddenly cried. They'd nearly forgotten all about their companions out in the Digger world and the elements suddenly found themselves full of concern. What if the men had been waiting for days? They had next to no food left, no water, no shelter.

What if the Diggers had found them?

What if Nickolas tried to follow us after all? Meggie thought to herself. She remembered their last few moments together, his struggle to turn away from the call of fate, his promise to wait for her, the kiss... and for a moment, despite the freezing cold, Meggie felt her cheeks warm as she hoped against hope that Nickolas had gone back on his word, that he and Dromeda had left, returning to the potential safety of the City.

"How do we get out of here?" Bex asked the baggage handler. If they really had less than a few hours until sunset, the group would have to move. Quickly.

"The same way you came in, I assume," was the little man's unhelpful reply. "Mean no disrespect but-"

"You *assume?*" Saz's words were bitter. At that moment she wanted nothing more than to grab the wretched little thing and hit him, hard. But knowing that would be utterly pointless, instead, she simply clenched her fists, taking a deep breath.

The baggage collector shrugged. Just like everything he did, the movement was grotesque.

"You may not have noticed, but this sort of thing doesn't exactly happen to me every day!" he snapped. "I don't fully understand how you came to be here in the first place, let alone how you can get back!"

Bex glanced around them.

"How *did* we get here in the first place? Which way did we come from?" she asked, panic starting to creep into her voice. None of them could see anything even remotely distinctive in any direction; nothing but the black shadow of souls. The line between death and life…

"I have no idea," the baggage collector replied, making Saz's fists tightened.

"Well, there must be some way," Bethan suggested and then, the idea only just striking her, she looked suddenly hopeful; "How do the *dead* usually get out of here?"

"Dead? Get out of here?!"

This seemed to make the little man stop a moment. His eyebrows rose, or rather his face shifted upwards a little, causing his ugly sneer to slacken into a look of disbelief.

"This is the world of the dead!" he cried indignantly. "*None* can leave this place!"

Catching on to Bethan's point though, Meggie gave a frustrated sigh.

"Of course they can!" she joined in. "How else do you explain *ghosts*? Spirits? that kind of thing? You can't tell me that's always a *story!*"

But the baggage handler just frowned, his wrinkles deepening into furrows.

"Ghosts? Spirits? They're nothing but anomalies," he retorted, making it clear that this was the only explanation they were likely to get. Straightening up to his full tiny height, he then cleared his throat. The sound was horrible. "Mean no disrespect but, this world is connected to every living world that ever existed. Each gateway is a one-way system only. Sometimes the dead can't find their way here. Or they slip back through somehow…"

"Just like *we* slipped through somehow," Bethan finished. "The barrier…" And losing herself for a moment, she paused to think, pondering on something the man had said.

The land of the dead serviced every world. Whilst the existence of more than one world had once seemed impossible to her, their very surroundings, their very journey through the flames and then through the barrier, spoke otherwise.

If there were ghosts in every world - although Bethan had no idea if that were true or not- then surely there had to be barriers, much like the one they had walked through, *in every world*.

And if there were barriers in every world…

The thought process, the idea that was forming in Bethan's mind, seemed to be slow in coming. But like a spark it suddenly sprung up and unable to help herself, Bethan nearly yelped.

"Tungala!" she cried. And then, when the other three women just looked at her in confusion, she let it all out, the flurry of excited words; "He just said this world is connected to *all others* right? Well if that's true, then what's to stop us from going straight back into *our* world?! What's to stop us walking straight back into Tungala?"

In that moment, it all seemed to make sense. There would be no need to go back to the Diggers, no need to worry about timing, about the sunset. They would be home again in an instant, with no more plans to go wrong, no more waiting. She could find Edmund and all would be as it should be...

But even as the thoughts of hope, of home, overwhelmed her, Bethan looked down on the little man to see that his expression hadn't changed and the smile that had risen to her lips, immediately fell.

"Surely you must know how we can get out of here," she begged. "You must. You've been here forever! You said so yourself! You said you know every part of this place!"

The baggage handler seemed to ponder her words for some time and watching his smug little face contort as he considered his options, considered his own pride, the elements were left in no doubt that he'd been lying to them all along. He clearly *did* know how to leave this place, but though they could sense it now, still that mischievous ugly grin soon reappeared.

"What if I do know how to leave?" he then asked. "What reason do I have to let you go? And," he added as, almost shaking with rage, Saz made to show him her hand again, "mean no disrespect, but before you start accusing me of going back on my word," he snarled. "May I remind you that I said I would let you leave, not that I would help you to, see?"

To maybe everyone's surprise though, Saz didn't seem at all thrown by this. In fact, it was almost as if she'd been expecting him to say it all along.

"And may I remind you," she retorted, "that if you don't help us leave, if we don't reach the free, living world; and more importantly, if we don't reach Tungala, the real world that we're from; *I can't die.*"

Her voice was loud, but shocked to hear her sounding so calm, so decisive about her own fate, the others looked at her.

"Saz..." Bex started, worried that the element was about to make another bargain, but Saz soon talked her down.

"*No,*" she insisted, glaring at the baggage collector, who was also looking slightly stunned. "Hear me out. You say that time has no real place here, that it's not quite the same. Which means that, if I stay here, if *we* stay here, time will just keep going and going and going in the outside world, and we'll just stay alive here, with you, *forever*. Right?" She included the other three elements in a sweeping gesture. "Even if you let us go back to the world of Diggers, we, or most importantly for you, *I* can't die there! But, if you let us go, help us even to get back to Tungala, then one day I will die. One day I'll belong to you, just like this pact here," and she gestured at her hand, "says I will. Just as you said I will, at the right time. One day my soul will be yours."

Pausing for effect, just to let her well-played argument wash over the baggage handler's little head, she soon saw him turn away with a grimace. He knew now what was coming, she could tell, but for the benefit of all, she wasn't done just yet.

"That is, after all, what you want isn't it?" she continued, challenging him, daring him to argue. "Souls? You deal in nothing else. So surely it's in your *best* interests to help us back to the world of the living, until my time, until all of our times are up and we're ready to return here... properly."

It was a good point. A very good point and they all knew it as Saz then looked to her fellow elements, her eyes flashing with triumph. She was right, the little man really had no choice but to help. If he didn't, he would be going against the pact made in blood himself.

And so it was, after a considerable pause, that the baggage collector then turned back to them, his face reluctant.

"As I said. This world is connected to all others," he began. He spoke more quietly now, all sneers and arrogance gone for the moment. "And the gateways between these worlds *are* flexible."

This brought about a collective sigh from the women as they all turned to each other with big smiles. They were going home. *Finally.*

"*But,*" and the little man held up a deformed hand, making them all hesitate again. "Though I can show you a way out of here, it is only back to the world you came from. *Not* to Tungala."

And once again, the elements' hearts fell. They were so close and yet every time hope dared to grow...

"Why?" Bex protested. "Why not? If this world is connected to all others, why can't we go back to our world?"

"I also said," the baggage collector explained, his voice bitter, "that the gateways to other worlds operate with a strict one-way policy. The world you came from, is a world like no other. And because of it, its gateway is weak. It must be since you managed to walk through it so easily!" His mouth pursed with obvious annoyance. "So I'd say that it's your best and probably *only* chance of getting out of here."

Walking from the line of shadow then as if ready to leave right that second, he levelled each one of them with a lopsided eye.

"I can show you how to reach the gateway..." he started again and all four of the elements couldn't help but turn vicious glares on him, outraged once again that the man had done nothing but *pretend* all along, wasting what precious time they had. But he hadn't finished. It was almost as if he had to force the words from his mouth, but eventually they came. "And even better. I can take you to where you want to go. To this... *statue.*" And when the women all looked completely bewildered, he sniffed proudly. "I did not mention it before, but I alone have the power to change, to move the barriers between life and death. As long as they remain on their own worlds, they can be shifted to anywhere…" He straightened up. "I might be willing to do this for you…"

Despite their first disappointment, it was more than any of them had hoped for and once again, the elements felt their faith daring to rise. Finally something was happening. Finally their escape seemed real, seemed possible. If the baggage handler could take them to the statue, they would have plenty of time before sunset, plenty of time to be ready, ready to go back…

Go back.

"Wait," and the hopeful smile that had played at the corner of her lips vanished as Meggie then realised. She had never truly forgotten, only pushed the thought aside until now. "What about Nickolas and Dromeda? We can't just *leave* them at the rock, while we skip straight past them! They could be waiting for us forever!"

In any other situation, 'forever' might have seemed like a foolish word, but right then all four of the women knew what it really meant just as they knew that Meggie too, was right. Who knew how long Nickolas and Dromeda would stay there, waiting for them? Nickolas had made a promise, Meggie had seen to that and with everything they had been through together, all of them had a feeling that he would stick to it.

Even as she thought about it, Meggie couldn't help but already imagine the worst, imagine as he and Dromeda starved to death, or died of dehydration. Only… in her mind they didn't die. They just kept coming back to life, just as Nickolas had before, resigned to a perpetual existence of suffering, wasting away again and again as they just sat, waiting…

No, someone had to go back for them. She knew it. Just as much as she also knew, deep down, who that person needed to be…

"Who are Nickolas and Dromeda?" the baggage handler asked the women at large, sounding more curious than anything. "If they're so important, why didn't they come with you in the first place?"

Bethan was eying Meggie's face carefully. Perhaps she knew what was coming.

"They can never come here," she tried to explain half-heartedly. "They're sort of already… dead."

"*Dead?*"

The baggage collector, surprised, looked as if he were about to argue, but before he could reply;

"I'll go back for them," Meggie said, the moment finally come as she looked to the others. "You go on ahead. I'll go back and we'll just have to try and reach the statue as fast as we can on foot."

Both Saz and Bex looked horrified.

"But Meggie, the statue is too far!" Saz objected. "You'll never make it in time! It's *impossible!*"

But though Meggie bit her lip, realising it was probably true – the likelihood of her and the elder elements getting from one place to another in three hours after what had taken them several days was pretty non-existent - she'd already made up her mind.

"It's not impossible… and it's a risk I'm willing to take," she replied. "I can't just leave them. They've been good to us…"

"She's right," Bethan added. They *had* and every element knew it. Nickolas and Dromeda, despite the latter's protests, had looked after them from their very first arrival to the Digger world. They had cared for them when they had been confused and sick, brought them together against the odds, turning against an easy life of obedience just to keep them that way and all for what? So that they could be *left* there? Abandoned at the door to death, forever doomed to wait…

Somehow it seemed wrong. Very wrong.

Bex's voice was slow.

"Maybe," she suggested tentatively. "Maybe we should *all* take our chances. If we hurry, perhaps we can make it in time from where we left them…" But almost immediately Meggie shook her head.

"No," she demanded. "No way. There's no need for *all* of us to start from where we left off. The more of us there are, the slower we're bound to be. It makes no sense for no one to get out at the risk of one," she gave the smallest shrug of her shoulders. "You three go ahead and wait for me and if I'm not there by sunset, go without me."

It was as if Meggie had uttered some revolting curse word, and even Bethan looked surprised now as all three women opened their mouths to protest.

Go without her? Could she really mean it?

The little element raised a hand.

"Go!" she insisted. "I take this upon myself."

"Well, whatever you decide, hurry up," the baggage collector took his moment to interject. He sounded fed up now. He really did have other things to be getting on with and what had started as an unusual diversion, seemed to him, to be turning into something a lot less exciting. "Mean no disrespect, but you've already wasted minutes in the Digger world just talking about it."

"It *is* decided," Meggie said, and before anyone else could object, she hurried forward to embrace the other three women, each of them returning her hug numbly. Everything was moving so fast…

"Be safe," the little element whispered to each in turn and as they finally realised what was happening, each replied with their own personal goodbyes, hoping against hope that it wouldn't be their last.

That done, Meggie then turned back to the ugly keeper of the dead. She wasn't going to waste any more time. She had a lot of ground to cover.

"So how do I get back the way we came in?" she asked matter-of-factly.

This time there was no smirk, no avoiding the question, no demanded payment. Something about Meggie's decision had obviously touched the little thing in some way he'd never thought possible and so it was the baggage collector then turned and pointing off over Meggie's right shoulder;

"Just head that way. And keep walking. Don't look back, or you'll be lost."

Lost.

All of them had a sense of dread in the pit of their stomach, the sense that the little element was more than likely lost already, but ignoring it, Meggie straightened up as if drawing every bit of her strength in one deep breath. With nothing else left to say, the smallest of the elements then took one last look at her friends and with a nod, started off into the cold dimness, never so much as glancing back again.

The others just stood and watched for a minute or two as Meggie drew further and further away, until she was nothing more than a dot on the horizon. And then finally, it was time.

"Follow me," the baggage collector commanded once he was sure that the fourth and final element was gone. "And I will lead you to your freedom."

The second they landed, Fred leapt away from the group, wielding his sword.

"Take me back!" he shouted. "Take me back *now*!!"

But before he could stop himself, he was falling, his head spinning, dizzy stars erupting before his eyes as he collapsed to his knees.

The others too, all fell, Elanore flat on her face, Edmund stumbling forward onto his calves and Thom... there was a retching sound as the dwarf hastily threw up.

In the few tiny seconds since the tomb, all of them had been through the most disturbing experience of their lives. After the flash of blinding light, they had felt the great push. It was like a force shoving them forward yet pulling them back, grinding them down and heaving them up all at the same time. And then before they knew it, the world was upside-down, spinning in circles, shaking from side-to-side, a deafening humming rocking at their ears; their only central point, their only anchor, Eliom's body, the one object they all clung to with every bit of strength they had. Breathless and unable to cry out, all three had closed their eyes, a wind from nowhere whipping at their faces, the droning, the screaming hum seeming to fill their every sense.

And then, just like that, they'd been released and with a great *crack* the ground had opened up before them and they were there, on the grass, alive and unscathed, miles and miles from where they had been only moments before...

Fred's own face was a horrible shade of green.

"I have to go back," he mumbled weakly, disorientated as he tried to make sense of his own body all over again. For some reason his legs wouldn't work. "Take me back! Please!"

"There *is* no way back," Edmund retorted, his own voice just as weak as he closed his eyes again, willing the dizzy spinning in his head to go away. Gulping in big breaths he then heard a soft groan and turning to his right, he realised that it was coming from Eliom.

Like the others, the wizard too was sprawled on the grass. But his face was so white, so terribly white that his cloak, inexplicably clean again after the tomb, appeared almost *dirty* against it. His eyes were closed and unmoving and straight away Edmund was roiling back to his feet, scurrying the tiny gap across the grass like someone possessed.

"Eliom!" he cried. "Eliom, can you hear me?"

There was another gagging noise as Fred too, threw up, but Eliom made no sound, no sign that he even knew the others were there.

No. Dazed as he was, Edmund felt the panic begin to rise inside, the fear. *No. This couldn't happen...*

"Edmund, I have to go back!" Fred repeated, his voice louder now, more demanding. "Eliom needs to take me back! You saw what happened. Soph... she..."

"*There is no way back, Fred!*" Edmund almost shouted as, feeling stupid but not knowing what else he could do, he studied Eliom's body for any signs of injury.

Of course he knew he wouldn't see any - the wizard was beyond his help - but he had to try, and taking Eliom by the shoulder, he gave him a shake.

"Eliom," he tried again. "Eliom."

No. Please no.

The wizard gave another groan, but he didn't open his eyes.

"Soph." Fred tried to get to his feet, but suddenly something like a powerful sob erupted from his chest and he fell all over again. *The tomb.* They'd all seen it. The clones, the horde of fighters and their swords, a volley of hate and malice, and the warrioress and sea captain standing alone to face it...

"She's strong," Edmund tried pointlessly as he gave Eliom another shake, willing him to wake up. Nausea welled up in his throat but he swallowed it down. "Maybe even stronger than you... She can fight them."

Though how long she could possibly last that *outnumbered...*

He didn't dare say, or even *think* it, but the Explorer heard another sob then and to his surprise, as he looked up, he was astonished to see Fred's face screwed up. The warrior, for a moment, looked almost as if he were *crying...*

"I know," was all he said and the pair just looked at each other for a good long second, pain in both of their eyes; pain, uncertainty yet resolve, determination to carry on and worry later.

"Help me," Edmund said, turning back to the unconscious Eliom. Still the wizard's eyes were closed, his eyeballs barely even moving in their sockets. But though Edmund knew, *hoped* that his friend just needed rest, he was also very aware that they had to keep moving. They had to enter the temple, to reach the platform on time, or everything, all of this, would have been for nothing.

The temple.

Struggling back to his feet, Edmund then chanced to take a proper look at his surroundings.

He was standing on the edge of a clearing. No, not a clearing, a vast plain, miles wide, bordered by a blossoming forest of white and green. The sun, as was to be expected, hung low in the sky, the blink of the first twin moon just hanging on the horizon as a gentle breeze drifted lazily by, but apart from that; there was nothing else. No movement, no other living soul and, Edmund realised with growing horror, no Temple of Ratacopeck.

"Where is it?"

Thom was the one to say it aloud as he too realised, just as the Explorer had, that the temple was nowhere to be seen. Had Eliom somehow brought them to the wrong place? And looking up at the fading sky, cold hard fear replaced the nausea in Edmund's stomach.

Where were they?

He'd never seen this place before – he swore it. The Temple of Ratacopeck had been ginormous, unmissable, and shrouded not in the lush foliage they could now see sweeping at the edge of the green, but in the black, thick forest.

What was going on?

"Where's the temple, Edmund?" Fred took up the call now. *"Where is it?!"* He too was just starting to understand, to realise that he'd left Soph to fight Renard's remaining clones outnumbered and all but alone... for an empty clearing.

"I don't know! I don't know!" Edmund cried, raking his hands through his hair as he began to think the worst.

What if they'd landed *even further* from where they needed to be? What if they were lost? What if it was too late? They needed to know, *and quickly*...

Hating himself for doing it, but knowing he had little choice, the Explorer then fell back to Eliom's side and taking the wizard firmly by the shoulders, he began to shake him violently.

"Eliom!" he practically shouted in his friend's face. "Eliom, you *have* to wake up! Come on!"

The wizard let out another moan as his head lolled uselessly again and again, but still he didn't open his eyes.

What had they done?

"Let me try," a voice then hissed in his ear and before he could stop him,

Edmund felt Fred shoving him aside, his strong hands ready to do their worst as his frustrations took over.

"Fred!" Edmund warned, as the warrior reached for the unconscious wizard's head. "Careful!"

But just then, as if someone had lit a fire under Eliom's body, his eyes suddenly snapped open and quick as anything, he was sitting up, his face a mask of alarm, making both human and warrior alike give a start.

"Where is it?" he said. "*Where is it?*" and Edmund's heart sped into even more of a panic as he saw that the wizard was staring out into the grassy space beyond in a way that made him realise the awful truth: *the wizard was just as clueless as they were.*

"Obviously it is not here!" Fred spat angrily. For a moment he looked as if he was going to go for the wizard again. "Are we lost?"

Eliom though, just blinked, his white face still screwed in concern.

"No," he then started and slowly, like an old, frail man, he reached for his staff and began to lever himself to his feet. "No. I-" Edmund quickly grabbed him by the arm as the wizard stumbled. He'd never noticed how *thin* his friend was...

"I-We are not lost," Eliom insisted, his gaze still spanning the empty clearing. "We are in the right place. I am certain of it. I could not have mistaken the distance..."

"Well then, where *is* it?" Thom joined in. He looked positively green in the face but fairly steady on his feet. "A building as large as that temple, cannot have simply *disappeared.*"

Edmund was struggling to try and remain calm.

"Could it have been destroyed in the blast?" he asked quickly. "After the elements walked through the flames..."

"No." Eliom's voice was weak but he sounded firm, certain. "You saw it with your own eyes after the blast. It was completely unharmed."

"But like Thom said, a building can't just *disappear*... can it?" The Explorer was finding it difficult to concentrate, to just stop and think and work things out. They hadn't anticipated anything like this...

"Perhaps that is exactly what happened."

And to everyone's surprise, it was Fred who had spoken. Suddenly, it was as if he had accepted their fate, accepted Eliom's answers and just like that, his anger, his upset was gone, pushed aside and in its place, hard focus.

"Perhaps once the elements walked into the orb and the temple had completed its purpose, it disappeared," he continued seriously, once he had everyone's attention. "You said it yourself, Eliom. The building has magic beyond anything you have seen."

For a moment, Eliom looked thoughtful.

"You may be right..." he said. But already Edmund didn't look convinced.

THE ENTITY OF SOULS

"No!" the Explorer cut in, remembering his dream like the shadow of a memory. "Why would Ophelius tell the elements that we had to come back if he knew the temple wouldn't be here?"

Thom frowned, swaying a little as he clutched his axe for balance.

"Maybe he had no idea," he offered unhelpfully. "Maybe he thought it *would* be here?"

"Well, either way, what do we do?"

And Edmund wrung his hands together, his fingers trembling. The effort of just trying to control himself, of just trying to stay calm as time trickled away, his hope threatening to trickle with it, was almost too much right then.

He knew there had to be an answer; there always *was*. A large part of him refused to believe that the prophet, the great man Ophelius could have led them all this way for nothing and much as he hated it, much as he fought against it, Edmund knew he would never rely more on the idea of fate than he wanted to right then...

Eliom's face was gradually regaining some of its colour now, but still his cheeks were haggard, the darkness under his eyes a disturbing grey. And yet, though every second Edmund half-expected him to fall, for each moment to be his last, still his friend stood, calm now and as always, so it seemed, with the answer they needed.

Looking at Edmund, the wizard gave a careful frown.

"I suggest that we do the only thing that we *can*," he then said, as the others stood by him, just staring at the empty grass; "We wait until sunset."

Meggie wasn't sure how long it had taken her to reach the barrier, but whether it was minutes or even hours, all of a sudden, she was there.

The heat was the thing that hit her first, the heat and the reddish light, like some wave almost knocking her flat and as she stepped into the Digger world, she couldn't help but take a gasp of air, her lungs revelling in the sudden burst of freshness, her pupils shrinking crazily in the glare of a sunless sky on the bright plain. Almost straight away, like the touch of magic, she began to feel her skin warming itself, happily gathering energy, releasing stiff muscles cramped in the frozen world of death, her heart throbbing that little bit harder in her chest as if to remind her what could have been.

She had returned from the world of the dead. She was back and she was still alive.

Thank Tungala...

"Meggie!"

The shout met her ears almost right away, and before she even knew what she was doing, Meggie then found that she was running, faster perhaps than she ever had in her life, her feet slipping and sliding on the hot dusty ground, her mud-encrusted dress sticking to her knees.

"Meggie!" and before she could stop herself, the little element had thrown herself into his arms.

His chest was hard but warm, so warm and comforting as she buried her face there, overwhelmed for a moment, just as he was, by the strange joy of it all as he murmured her name over and over again into her matted hair.

But there was no time. They had to move. They had to go and pulling herself away, Meggie eyed the plain.

"Where's Dromeda?" she panted hurriedly and then, looking up to finally meet his eye; "We have to head for the City, *now*."

Instead of moving though, Nickolas, letting go of the little element slowly, just stared into her face as if studying every part of it, committing it to memory, his eyes wide with concern. He looked so tired, she realised, so tired and - was she imagining it? - *thinner* somehow, that her stomach roiled.

How long had he been waiting? How long had he been suffering because of her?

"Nickolas, where's-" she tried to start again, but Nickolas got in there first.

"What happened to you?" he asked. "Where are the others? I thought-"

"Listen. There's no time to explain, we have to go!" Meggie exclaimed, and knowing that they had such an impossibly short time, she grabbed his hand and, turning her back on the giant tree-like boulder that marked the land of death, started to run again.

"Where's Dromeda?" she repeated, as Nickolas, finding himself suddenly dragged along, began to jog to keep up.

"I sent him back to the City hours ago. I did not see the point in both of us…" but he didn't finish his sentence. He didn't need to.

He didn't see the point in both of them staying only to die. If the barrier hadn't finally called them on, hunger or thirst would have got them eventually, again and again and again…

Good, Meggie thought, for the first time pleased that Dromeda had chosen to save himself. *One less person to worry about.*

"We have… to keep… moving," she then gasped breathlessly. In such a short time they already seemed to have reached the odd valley of rocks that had guided them to the barrier. Perhaps the distance wasn't as incredible as they'd thought… "We've got… just under… three hours."

Nickolas's legs were longer than hers but he didn't pull ahead, instead he seemed to slow a second, looking confused.

"Three hours?... Until what?" he panted.

But Meggie couldn't answer, she was already running too hard.

—

THE ENTITY OF SOULS

"Here we are," and all of a sudden, the baggage collector just stopped, making all three women almost walk into each other, as they too, paused to look.

Behind them lay the boulder shaped like a tree, this much they knew, though none had dared to look back, and ahead...

Ahead was nothing.

Nothing but more endless miles of flat dark land, black and shapeless.

"Here?!" Saz rounded on the little man in disbelief. Was he trying to trick them again?

But even as the word fell from her mouth, the air changed. At first it was like a tiny spark, a glistening of light in the space just in front of them. And then, just like that it began to grow, to fizzle into a volley of blues and greens, shifting to and fro, multiplying into hundreds of bright colours wriggling in and out of each other like little creatures of light...

Recognising what could only be another barrier, Bex and Bethan instantly hurried forward, suddenly desperate to escape the cold world of death. None of them wanted to linger more than they had to, but even so, Saz seemed to hang back for a moment, and turning again to the collector, all anger gone, she gave a little smile.

"Thank you," was all she said. "Thank you for helping us."

The little man looked shocked for a moment before giving a nod.

"Of course," he replied quietly, no hint of smugness anywhere. Little did the element know that 'thank you' had never been a phrase the baggage collector of the dead had heard, that never in all of his life, if his existence could ever be called a 'life' had anyone shown him an inch of such kindness. Anger, bitterness, sorrow, regret, *this* he met with every day; this was his food, his drink, his breath. None were ever truly ready for death and though he had learnt to grow hardened to the bartering, turn a cold shoulder to the begging, to laugh at their tears, it had, one being by one, drained him, leaving him nothing but a dried up, ugly husk. Until now; until this moment, and as if she somehow knew what she had done, as Saz watched the little man then turn and leave, loping back off into the darkness, she made an unspoken promise deep within herself. When she returned, she vowed, she wouldn't cry, she wouldn't spit and shout and scream her hatred, she wouldn't beg or blame. She would face death like an old friend. She would face *him* like an old friend. For in that moment, as the little man had moved his face away, turned his ugly head one last time, Saz knew she had seen tears once more in his lopsided eyes.

"Saz!"

Bethan's voice brought Saz back to the task at hand and turning back to the barrier of colours she noticed that both Bethan and Bex were standing at the very edge, the very gap between life and death, waiting for her.

Obediently she rushed forward to join them and as all three then stared at the way ahead for a moment, stared into that other world, all of them felt afraid.

None of them knew what they would find on the other side. None of them knew if they were truly going to make it. But it was all they had and Bethan taking Saz's hand tightly and she in turn grasping Bex's good arm, without another word, the three elements stepped forward.

The barrier was as cold and hard as ice, but none of them seemed to feel it as it slammed against them, willing them back, pulling at their hair, their clothes, their faces, forcing them into a world of painful silence before it was all over and in less than a second, they were out and falling to their knees on the hot dusty floor of the Digger world.

Instantly all three of them took a gasp of fresh warm air, shielding their eyes against the waning brightness as the world around them erupted with light. And the *sound* - it was almost deafening; the shout of voices, the hustle and bustle of movement, the cries of young Diggers mingled with the noise of their own beautiful breathing. It was life again; pure and simple, and as Bex, the first to react, clambered back to her feet, she couldn't help but let out a laugh of delight.

They were back. They were back in the Digger world. But not only that, just as the baggage collector had promised, they were back in the City, the very heart of it all, surrounded by the busy market and the streets of squat stone huts and a little way ahead, the gigantic stone structure towering above everything, its four giant gemstones gleaming in the light of the dying day…

The statue.

"We made it," Bethan breathed as she got to her feet as well. "We actually made it!"

And reaching out a hand, she helped Saz up too. But as the final element stood to her full height, looking at the marketplace around them, she alone, didn't smile.

Yes, they were back, yes, they were where they needed to be but… there were Diggers *everywhere*. They were surrounded by them, all talking, eating, buying, selling, sharpening weapons and packing away their stalls before the evening drew in. Or at least, they *had* been. Until now.

And it was only as Bethan and Bex saw it, that they too then froze.

For every eye was now on them; every Digger, no matter what he or she had been doing, was now staring at them, staring with mixtures of surprise, of confusion and, in most cases, *anger*…

And just like a slap to the face, the elements remembered what had happened.

Kill him! Kill the human! they'd demanded in their hordes before one of them had stabbed Nickolas, before one of them had dared to lay a hand on one of the Builder's chosen and left him for dead. And now here the three of them stood, the humans who had defied the Builder, the humans who had dared to leave the City…

A whole minute seemed to go by as the women just stared at the Diggers and the Diggers stared back, as if all waiting for the other to react, to draw weapons, or in the case of the women, the three *defenceless* women, without a weapon between them, do the only thing they could; *run*.

Before anyone could so much as move a muscle though, a voice they all recognised then rang out across the square.

"Where is the fourth? Where is the fourth woman?"

And striding purposefully through the crowd, Barabus appeared, a look of absolute triumph beaming across his face, all the more so as the three elements soon turned to him in complete surprise.

Barabus. They'd all forgotten about him…

"Well?" and sauntering along the line of them like a general inspecting his troops for battle, he looked each element in the face, pausing for a particularly long time at Bex to eye her bandaged arm with a look of blank curiosity. "Where is she?"

"What do you want, Barabus?" Bethan almost spat. "This has nothing to do with you."

"Oh?" Barabus stopped right in front of her then, meeting her eye with such coldness that Bethan couldn't help but look away. "This has everything to do with me. You disobeyed the Builder. You must be punished."

The Builder. For the moment, they'd almost forgotten about *him* too. Their only thoughts had been of nothing but escape. Nothing but going home…

"And how do you intend to punish us?" Saz spoke up bravely. "We can't die and you know it."

At the mention of death, the Diggers in the crowd shifted nervously, but Barabus didn't even blink.

"That is not what I have heard…" he said and his gaze moved to the crowd where the women could just make out another face that they recognised. It was the large Digger, the one who had fought with Nickolas outside the city gates, but this time his sword was sheathed, his expression worried and it was clear that he was hanging back, keeping away from them. Never would he lift his blade to a human again.

Of course, none of them knew what had happened…

"Nickolas is alive. We've seen him with our own eyes," Saz announced and then, looking at Barabus, her own expression triumphant; "so like I said, there's nothing you can do."

Barabus couldn't hide his surprise, and neither could the crowd of watching Diggers. Murmurs and gasps of shock soon broke out amongst the throng, but raising a hand, the elder element made all fall silent again.

"How do I know you are telling the truth?" he challenged, sounding unsure.

"You don't," Bethan stepped in. "So move out of our way." And her movements braver than she felt, she made as if to leave. Just like that though, Barabus was on her, his body a barrier between her and escape and where he had looked shocked, now his face was suddenly set, something like a glimmer of victory in his eyes all over again.

"Oh no," he said. "I cannot let you go. I have something prepared for you... something you might think is much worse than death."

"Oh?" Bethan threw his own phrase back at him, trying not to meet his eye as he stood so close. Despite her feigned coolness, she could already feel her heart starting to thud in fear.

"Indeed," Barabus replied and then, giving an odd smile; "I know where you have been. And I know why you have returned here... You wish to leave this place."

This got the elements' attention and instantly all pretence at bravery was gone as the three women stared at him in horror.

How did he know? But more importantly; How *much* did he know?

Was he bluffing or did he somehow know about the statue? About the sunset? About how little time they had left...?

But suddenly, whether the elder element was aware of all of these things or not, wasn't important, for with a nod of Barabus's head, several Diggers then emerged from the crowd, carrying what appeared to be rope. Before any of the women could move, they were then surrounded and grabbed, two Diggers to each, their arms wrenched behind their backs and in moments, bound tightly.

"I am sorry," Barabus then said unapologetically, as he watched them struggle. "But I cannot let that happen." And to the elements great dismay, he turned to the Diggers now holding them captive, his face serious.

"Take them away," he commanded.

—

Meggie was slowing down. She could feel it, but despite her best efforts she couldn't stop it. With every gulp of air, her lungs felt like they were about to explode, her legs and arms raw and aching as she pumped them onwards, her feet slapping on the hard mud. She could see Nickolas, just ahead of her, his legs pushing with their longer stride, but though he was covering twice the ground she could, with half the effort, he too was starting to slacken his pace. Every now and again he would glance back, as if to check she was still there. And every now and again, he would slow all the more, waiting for her to catch up.

This time he almost stopped.

"Are you... alright?" he asked, each word coming out in a short breathy gasp.

Meggie just nodded, too breathless herself to talk. Every ounce of energy she had was devoted to her legs, devoted to just moving...

She had known it would be hard - yes, like the others had said, almost impossible - but not quite *this* hard. And all the time she just couldn't help but question over and over again why she'd done it, why she'd offered to stay behind, why she hadn't gone on ahead with the others...

Nickolas was still watching her, but she couldn't give him anything. She hadn't even told him where they were going, what they were doing. And though she kept trying to convince herself it was because they didn't have time, she knew that that wasn't entirely true...

"*Argh!*"

Before she knew what was happening, one of her ankles, the very one that had given up only days before, suddenly twisted and Meggie fell heavily, face-first into the dirt, the momentum sending her skidding across the mud like a stone across water.

Crying out in pain, the little element cursed as she felt the skin beneath her hands split, her shins grazing across the floor. Though she could tell straight away that the injuries were only small, they already stung, bringing tears to her eyes and a lump to the back of her throat and, not wanting to waste any precious time, she swore again as she pulled herself up onto her knees.

Why hadn't she been more careful? They didn't have *time* for this. She had to keep going...

Her ankle was throbbing like anything, all over again. Had she broken it?

But before she could try to brush herself down and clamber up onto her worn-out feet, Nickolas was there. Without a word, he was crouching by the element's side and then, as if the movement were effortless, he took her by the waist, and pulling her back onto her feet like she was made of nothing, he turned and grabbing her by the thighs, hoisted her up onto his back.

In less than a moment, he was starting to walk and then, slowly, to run...

"You... all... right?" he repeated, shifting Meggie's body weight to make her more comfortable. But still unable to speak, for very different reasons now, Meggie just buried her face in the back of his neck. The smell of his skin felt somehow comforting to her, kind of muddy and warm, the brush of his hair surprisingly soothing on her face. Beneath her she could feel the strength of his back muscles, his legs pounding to and fro and not for the first time, no matter what else she might be feeling right then, she realised that she felt safe. Nickolas made her feel *safe*.

They'd been running non-stop for almost an hour now and unprotected from the heat of the ensuing evening, with no water and no food, and with nothing but hot air to breathe in, movement was almost unbearable. Meggie had no idea how far they'd run, or how much further they had to go, or even whether they could possibly ever reach the City in time. But she knew that they had to try.

And right at that moment, as she encircled Nickolas's neck with her little arms, though tears still glistened in her eyes, the element felt an odd buzz of contentment, a sense of certainty.

She'd done the right thing. Though she had doubted, she knew that she'd had to come back. She knew she could never have left Nickolas there, waiting for her and for a few seconds, she even found herself wondering whether she would really mind if they didn't reach the City in time after all…

She had thought about it before; endlessly - it felt - thought about why she was even slightly reluctant to return to Tungala, why it was she so dreaded leaving this place. And though she had tried to speak of it before, though Nickolas had asked her she had never-

"Did you… feel… that?"

Nickolas's question came from nowhere and startled, Meggie looked up, drying her unshed tears on the back of her arm.

"Feel what?" she muttered, finally able to speak. But right as she said the words and then opened her mouth again to ask what he meant, she *did* feel it; a drop of water, from the sky, and her guts churned.

It was starting to rain.

Again.

Which could only mean one thing…

"We have to move!" she cried, and then, squirming in her seat, she tried to get down from Nickolas's back. "Let me down. You can't run as fast, carrying me…"

But Nickolas wouldn't let go. His arms were clamped around her thighs, keeping her pressed to him like a vice. And suddenly, as if all this time he had somehow been holding back, he began to speed up, his run turning into a full sprint.

"No," he panted. "You… cannot run… at all!"

And knowing, much as she hated it, that he was right, Meggie just turned her eyes to the sky. Already one drop of rain was fast following another and another and another…. Before they knew it, they would be drowning in a rainstorm and remembering what had happened before, Meggie felt panic beginning to rise thick and fast.

The Builder. Just as they had suspected before, he - or she - had to know what they were planning and trying to force her already damp hair from her eyes as the wind began to pick up, she gave a howl of frustration. If trying to reach the City had seemed impossible before it was nothing compared to *this*. Before long the ground would be thick and slippery with mud, the way ahead nothing but a wet blizzard, making running impossible; making her *escape* impossible…

As if he knew her fears, Nickolas tilted his head back towards the falling sky, taking the nourishing droplets on his tongue, his legs continuing to pump despite the growing slush beneath his feet.

"We can... make it!" he shouted as the noise of drumming water began to grow to deafening heights. "Just... hold... on!"

"I know!" Meggie yelled in his ear. And even as she said it, she did. Though Nickolas knew nothing of their plan, he had obviously guessed, at least in part, that getting back to the City in the few hours they had left, was all that mattered, and to her that felt like enough. She had faith in him, she realised. She trusted him and if Nickolas said they could make it, then chances were...

Nickolas shook his head, flinging cold droplets from his eyes. Water was streaming down his face, his arms, his torso, his legs, sliding down his neck, washing through his clothes. Meggie too was drenched through, her dress clinging tightly to her back and thighs, mud running in rivulets from her legs and arms, dousing her face. Despite the warmth of before, both were soon beginning to shiver and as she desperately clung on, squinting into the growing darkness ahead, the little element was the first to see the flash of something bright streaming across the sky.

"What was that?!" she cried in fear.

Nickolas didn't look up, his eyes focused on the slushy ground. Still he continued to run. And then the rumble of thunder came and Meggie felt the hairs on the back of her soaking neck stand on end.

It was a storm. This time it was a proper storm and already it was torrential. Little rivers of mud were flowing past them now, and with every step, she could feel Nickolas working harder. With the added weight of wet clothes and sucking sludge, the elder element was beginning to tire and ultimately slow...

It was no use. Meggie had made her decision.

"Let me down!" and this time, without knowing she did it, the little element redoubled her efforts, taking Nickolas by surprise. For a moment he almost dropped her. "Please! You're tired!"

"You... are... hurt!" Nickolas argued back, bellowing over another loud grumble of thunder. His legs were pushing even harder than before, propelling him forward with added determination, and not for the first time, Meggie found that she suddenly didn't care about reaching the City before sunset, before time ran out. She cared about *him*.

He had to stop. If he carried on much longer, he was going to collapse, she was sure of it. And realising that she was the only one who could do something about it, she just as suddenly let go of Nickolas's neck and pushing herself up with her good leg, she launched herself backwards.

Nickolas had no time to react, no time to grab hold of her as she fell out of his arms, but the moment she was gone and lying in the wet mud, winded, he shuddered to a halt and rounded on her.

"What are... you doing?!" he roared, leaning on his shins in some desperate attempt to get his breath back.

Meggie heaved herself to her knees, attempting to stand. She could feel a shiver of pain stabbing from her ankle but she tried her best to ignore it.

"I told you to put me down!" she yelled, spitting water from her mouth. She could barely see Nickolas through the field of rain, but from what she could make out, she was surprised to see that instead of understanding, or apology or even concern for her leg, like the last time he'd carried her, the last time she'd made him stop, he looked suddenly livid.

"You are... so... stubborn!" he then yelled, the words falling from his mouth as if he'd been keeping them in all this time. "Why... do you... never... listen to me? Why... do you... never let... anyone... help you? I said... I would... carry you! And that... is what... I am going... to do!"

For a second, Meggie just looked shocked at his outburst but then, seeing him come towards her as if to pick her up all over again, she struggled away.

"No!" she cried, a little taken aback by his reaction as she scrambled to her feet. "If you keep carrying me, you'll-!"

"Stop being... so stupid... for five... seconds!" Nickolas interrupted. His expression was beyond angry now, it was furious and as he spoke, rain exploded from his mouth. "You can... hardly... *stand*... let alone... run! You... cannot... make it... without... me!"

Stunned, Meggie felt her own anger growing. How *dare* he, she thought. How could he speak to her like-?

"I could've made it perfectly fine without you!" she then spat aloud. "I could be at the statue right now if it wasn't for you! I only came back here in the first place because of you!"

She regretted the words the second they had shot from her mouth, but it was too late; she had said them and though Nickolas knew nothing about the statue, though he knew nothing of her plan, he still understood and instantly, he fell silent, just looking at her as if she had punched him in the chest, *hard*.

The rain continued to hammer down around them, saturating their already soaked bodies, but for the moment, neither of them cared. A flash of lightning ripped overhead.

"I never... asked you... to come... back for me," Nickolas then said eventually, his breathless voice almost lost on the wind. But the anger had dissolved away now, and in its place, Meggie could see hurt. Hurt that she had caused. Hurt that she found she hated herself for and unable to bear it, she found herself stepping towards him.

"Nickolas..." she started, wanting to explain, to make him understand what she'd *really* meant, to try and make it better. "I-"

THE ENTITY OF SOULS

But before she could go any further, the pair were interrupted.

"Nickolas! Meggie! What are you doing here?!"

And from out of the stormy gloom a man then appeared.

He was as drenched as they were, from head to foot, if not more so, but he was still very much Dromeda and recognising his friend as he approached, Nickolas almost laughed.

"Dromeda!"

He sounded relieved and for a moment, Meggie couldn't help but wonder why. Eyeing first Nickolas and then Meggie however, Dromeda soon frowned.

"Where are the others?" he asked, his voice raised to cut across the storm. "What have you done with them?"

Nickolas didn't look at Meggie, making her chest pang, but she knew she was the only one who could answer.

"They've gone a different way," she said loudly. "It's just us."

Dromeda nodded, looking confused, but didn't say anything more about it.

"I thought that maybe you had returned!" he shouted instead. "As soon as it started raining, I guessed you might be back! The Builder must know what you are doing!"

"Yes-" Meggie started, but to her surprise, Nickolas then spoke up.

"You have come... at the perfect time. We have to... reach the City *now*!" he shouted through the rain. He appeared to have finally caught his breath a little now, but still he seemed determined not to meet Meggie's eye.

"*Now?!*" Dromeda exclaimed as another crash of thunder exploded overhead. "But the City is nearly a day from here, maybe two if we walk!" He didn't seem interested in asking *why*, for which Meggie felt suddenly grateful. She didn't think she could try and explain it. Not now.

"We are not walking! We are running!" Nickolas bellowed and without so much as a glance at Meggie, he then took a step toward his friend, as if to lean in close. "Can you carry her?" his voice was quieter but still Meggie heard it. "She is injured. And I do not think I can..." he trailed off.

The little element, remembering very well what had just happened, felt her cheeks reddening. But this time she didn't argue. And neither, to everyone's relief, did Dromeda. Instead, with yet another nod, he offered his hand to Meggie, blinking water from his eyelashes.

"May I?" he asked. And then, without waiting for an answer, much as Nickolas had, he took hold of her waist and swinging round, he pulled her up onto his back. Quickly Meggie flung her arms around his neck, tucking her legs to his sides and trying not to dwell on the fact that it felt different somehow than before.

Nickolas meanwhile looked at the sky again.

Still the rain wasn't abating. If anything, it was getting worse. But noticing that the others were ready, he yelled, "Come on!" and set off at a sprint.

Just as his friend had before him, Dromeda paused only to adjust Meggie's weight before following suit. The mud was thick beneath their feet now, thick and slow. The journey would be hard. But perhaps not completely hopeless just yet…

"I'm sorry, Bethan."

The apology came out of nowhere and having been lost in her own thoughts, Bethan blinked.

"What?" she asked and then straining against her bonds, she turned to look at Saz.

The element's eyes were on the dusty ground. She looked solemn.

"I'm sorry," she repeated, never raising her gaze and still surprised, Bethan just stared at her.

"You're sorry?" she asked again, not understanding. "For what?" Saz was tied to a chair just a few feet away from her, but even if she'd wanted to, she couldn't have offered her any comfort, her own hands tied to the bed, her ankles loosely bound. Bex was secured to a table leg in the corner opposite, nursing her bandaged arm.

Saz hung her head.

"I just…" and she paused, as if struggling for the words. "I said some things I wasn't proud of before, in the world of the dead. And I'm really sorry."

For a moment Bethan had no idea what her friend was talking about, but what she *did* know was that she was determined to stop it. Saz was apologising as if she'd never get the chance to again and right then, Bethan wasn't ready to face the idea that her fellow element might be right. Somewhere deep inside she was still clinging onto the hope of freedom. Despite being tightly bound in the well-guarded Digger house, with little less than two hours until sunset, she wasn't yet ready to accept that everything might not work out fine.

"You have nothing to be sorry for," she offered quickly, trying to dismiss the issue. "Don't worry about it." But despite her tone, Saz wasn't having it.

"No," she almost mumbled, her eyes, though staring at the ground, glazed over. "I shouldn't have accused you of being selfish," she insisted. "It was wrong of me. I don't want you to think that I believe you capable of that. Because," she paused again, "I don't."

And it was then that Bethan understood, that she remembered Saz's harsh words in the world of the dead, her allegations that Bethan's feelings for Edmund were swaying her judgement, that it was preventing her from making the sacrifice needed. And once again, as she had at the time, Bethan felt, not anger, as Saz obviously expected, but the wash of shame; shame at the knowledge that despite her apology, the other element had been for some of the part, right.

You're the one who wants so desperately to escape! To return to Edmund again! So don't pretend to care about my welfare. You would gladly see me die to be with him again - and you know it.

Saz's words replayed in her head like sharp daggers, every bitter stab a kind of truth. She'd known it at the time and she knew it now; Bethan *had* let Saz bargain her own life away for her - for the man she loved. For the man who she still believed she was miraculously going to see again.

Despite the fact he hadn't told her he loved her back.

Part of her knew it was irrational, that it was stupid, childish, and yet still it was there, that little niggling doubt, just as it had been for the past hour as she'd sat there, thinking, wondering. Much as she had tried to convince herself otherwise, it really bothered her that Edmund hadn't spoken out in the vision, that though she had called to him, told him for the first time of her feelings in words, he had said nothing in response. She had *tried* to think nothing of it, but despite her best attempts, her thoughts just seemed to have grabbed the idea and run with it...

What if Edmund didn't love her after all? He'd told her he loved her before the flames at the Temple of Ratacopeck, when he had taken her in his arms and kissed her – the memory still made her a little giddy – but then that had been when she thought, when they'd both thought she was going to die, that those moments were likely to be her last...

Had he really meant it?

Bethan shifted uncomfortably, trying to fight the wave of odd emotions threatening to overpower her.

What then, if it had all been nothing? And what if, now, just as she did, he felt ashamed, *guilty* for where he had taken her, taken them all? Without him, none of them would have known about the Keeper of the World. Without him, none of them would have stepped through those flames in the first place. What then, if he was just trying to help the elements out of duty? To help *her* out of duty?

What even - and this was the worst thought of all, the thought she most tried to suppress and yet seemed ever at the forefront of her mind – *what if he wasn't even trying to help them at all?* For all she knew, Edmund could have been anywhere, at any time, somewhere far away from where he needed to be, far away in a place where he had long forgotten them all. How did they even know he and the others would come? He'd seemed as if he would, but what if he'd changed his mind?

What if sunset came and there was no one there?

"You have nothing to be sorry for," Bethan found herself repeating the words aloud then, her voice suddenly dull as she realised that this time, she really meant it. No, if *anyone* should be sorry, it was her, for letting Saz offer up her life, all for the sake of nothing, or so it was all starting to seem…

The three women remained silent for some time after that, each of them lost in their own thoughts, questioning as time wore on, whether they would ever see home again. With perhaps accidental cruelty, the Diggers had locked them in a little hut facing out onto the main City market square and, from their positions, Bethan, Saz and Bex could all see the great statue in the centre, a stark contrast of white against the darkening sky as the light dimmed on the horizon.

It wouldn't be long now.

—

"Two hours to go, by my calculations," Eliom told the pacing Edmund and on hearing his words, the human, dwarf and warrior all looked to the sky, the scraping of metal ceasing as Fred paused in sharpening his sword. But as he had watched the fading sun countless times before in the past hour, without much of a change, Edmund gave yet another impatient sigh, continuing on his march as Fred went back to his blade, the sharp noise ringing out across the quiet space.

Thom all the while gave a groan of annoyance.

"I cannot bear this waiting," he growled from his position on the ground. Being slower to recover than the others after transporting, the dwarf had taken to lying in the grass, his axe held loosely at his side in readiness for something, *anything* to happen.

"Well, there is little other choice," Fred returned, each word almost chanted to the rhythm of his work. He'd remained fairly quiet throughout their wait, his thoughts no doubt still on Soph, Elanore, and his last memory of the clones overpowering them. No one had dared attempt to comfort him or insist that leaving the pair behind had been necessary, partly out of fear, but also partly because, at that moment in time, all of them were starting to doubt the reasons themselves.

Slowly, with each passing minute that the Temple of Ratacopeck didn't appear, all four of the friends had started to feel their hope slipping. None of them could help but wonder if they were somehow too late, or if the temple really had just *vanished* with no intention of return, but with no other plan but to wait it out and see what happened, that was exactly what they were doing.

Edmund, finding it best to think about anything else but his frustrations, took some time to subtly study Eliom. His friend was seated on the grass, his exterior its usual calm self; but though he looked almost normal – or as normal as a wizard could be - his eyes were half-shut as if he were fighting to stay awake, his face still a ghostly pale, and though his staff was lying by his side now, he made no move to touch it.

The fact of the matter was; Eliom was suffering. Just as Edmund had worried it would, the transportation had damaged him. It hadn't hurt him, as the Explorer may have feared, but it *had* weakened him substantially, and not for the first time during that long hour of wait, Edmund found himself hoping that if something *were* going to happen at sunset, it wouldn't involve anything…. *bad*.

Eliom was almost completely powerless now, even Thom, often the most unobservant of them all, could see it. There would be no helping him if a fight broke out. The wizard would be almost defenceless, just as they would be down a fighter, if it came to it…

Not, Edmund realised stupidly, that he was necessarily expecting a fight. There was no one, nothing to fight with. But for the previous elements and Renard, the Temple of Ratacopeck had been all but empty last time. Except for-

"The keepers of the necklaces!" he suddenly exclaimed and slightly startled, the others looked at him. Eliom even opened his eyes.

They'd forgotten about the trials, about the four great creatures that had guarded the fire, that had tortured warrior, dwarf, wizard and human until the four women had given up the gemstone necklaces, the keys to the inner temple. The creatures, gigantic and hideous and powerful had stood in their way before, demanding the jewels, demanding the four elements in exchange for access to the Keeper of the World. And now Edmund and his companions had neither necklace *nor* element to bargain with…

"We can fight them," Fred said steadily. "They will not stand in our way." But, to the group's surprise, it wasn't Edmund who disagreed.

"Do you not recall their power, my friend?" Eliom's voice was quiet, controlled. "They were bred from deep magic, too great for any of us." He gave something of a sigh. "Even me…"

Edmund rubbed his forehead in aggravation. It was still spattered with dried blood from the tomb.

"*Especially* you," he chipped in with concern as his eyes turned once again to the sky. It really was getting noticeably darker now, shadows of the trees from the side of the clearing looming across the green as if to swallow it whole.

"No," he then said absently. "If there's to be any fighting, you will stay here."

It was strange, but though he wasn't looking at his friend, he somehow *felt* the wizard's annoyance, like a change in the wind, and sure enough, as he turned, he wasn't too late to see Eliom's expression change. One moment it had been calm, the next, *annoyed*.

"I will *not*," the wizard then replied, shocking them all with the sudden sharp tone in his voice. "I will see this through. I owe it to Saz and the others, no matter what you believe. I can fight as well as the next man."

"But you're not a man." And alarmed, worried for his companion as he was, Edmund too felt his frustration starting to get the better of him. "You're a wizard. And you're not... You're unwell. Don't try to deny it."

Thom and Fred glanced at each other.

"They might not be there, anyway," the dwarf reasoned out of nowhere, obviously attempting to cut the sudden tension. "After all, the creatures already have what they wanted; the gemstones. We have nothing more to offer them."

"Except our lives," Fred mumbled. "Which I, for one, will not give up willingly."

"Me neither," Eliom said, before, closing his eyes as if he had tired of them all, his face then relaxed back to blank. "It will not be too long now," he whispered.

Edmund kicked at a tuft of grass in aggravation. Still they were waiting, and still nothing was happening. What if Bethan was waiting for him, in that other place? What if she'd lost hope that he would ever come for her? What if the elements had given up and resigned themselves to their fate – whatever that may be - and they never saw them again?

What if he never saw *her* again?

"She said sunset."

The exhausted wizard's voice was very quiet, but thankfully calm, and surprised but relieved to hear it, Edmund turned to look at his friend in amazement.

"Did you just-?" he started, feeling suddenly hopeful, but Eliom just gave a wan smile. His eyes were still closed.

"You were right," he replied. "I am a wizard. But even..." he paused before continuing, "even as I am... I can still read you like a book. You have done nothing but doubt since we got here."

Edmund grimaced half-heartedly but he couldn't help but feel a sudden warm regard for the wizard. Eliom had never doubted their journey. Even now, even as they waited for seemingly nothing, he still believed that the temple was there, that they could rescue the elements yet. And despite all his own misgivings, just then, Edmund couldn't help but find his friend's faith contagious...

The Explorer had to believe that in less than two hours the temple would reappear and they would enter, little knowing what obstacles would stand in their way, but knowing that no matter what, eight of them were going to return; a man, a wizard, a warrior, a dwarf and four elements.

—

The rain had stopped long ago, but the damage it had left behind was almost impassable. The mud, now up to their knees, was gradually beginning to dry, forcing Dromeda and Nickolas's steps to slow all the more as each footfall met a half-sloppy-half-caked trap.

Neither men could speak, all energy driven into plodding ever on through the thick slush. Long ago they'd stopped arguing with Meggie's fresh pleas to be put down, and over time she too had stopped making them, resigning herself to the fact that she couldn't walk. Already her arms were beginning to ache with the weight of holding her own body against Dromeda's neck and her twisted ankle, now swollen to twice its original size, jostled painfully against the elder element's knee every time he moved forward. But though it hurt, so it seemed, every second, Meggie was past caring, knowing that her suffering was *nothing* compared to the other two as they slaved onwards.

They were dehydrated beyond description, exhausted beyond understanding and yet all three of them knew, no matter how painful, how hard their bodies cried out to fall down and die, they couldn't. The Builder wouldn't let them. And this, they had realised with heavy hearts, was his punishment now.

The rainstorm had fulfilled its purpose. Though mercifully short, it had left behind this perpetual torment and much as they felt like they might want to, the elements of past and present couldn't stop it.

Meggie raised her head slowly to the horizon, a line of more sucking sludge, devoid of all life in the small light of the dying day. There was nothing but a faint glow, dry heat and miles and countless miles of dead ground and as she watched the daylight sinking ever lower, Meggie's hopes couldn't help but sink with it

They weren't going to make it, she was beginning to realise this now. The other elements had been right; it really had been an impossible task, one they should never have attempted, one she should never have forced these poor weary men to undertake with her, and all over again, part of her began to wish that she'd never come back for them, that she'd left Nickolas and Dromeda to their own fate. Yes, she reasoned, maybe they would have waited for a while, but eventually? They would have realised that the women were gone. They could have made their own way back to the City, with no pain, no exhaustion and no regrets. They could have led better lives, instead of being *stuck* in this living abyss with her...

No. It was over. Regardless of whether she was reluctant or not, she was willing to admit it, and feeling overwhelmed with a mixture of emotions, the little element suddenly released her hold on Dromeda.

"We should just stop," she mumbled aloud, her first words in at least half an hour. Her voice was strangely hoarse and quiet despite the expanse around them, and yet both men heard.

Unable to see everything the way she did, Nickolas, unsurprisingly, was the first to shake his head. It took a while before the words then made their way out.

"No... We... will... get... there." he said, his own voice barely a whisper. "We... will... make... it."

After their argument an hour or so before, the elder element still hadn't really met her eye and though Meggie, in her stubborn way, tried to pretend that it didn't bother her, it only seemed to make her feel worse.

"It's pointless," she returned instead, her heart only half in it as she almost ticked the reasons off on her fingers. "We have no idea where we are. We could be going completely the wrong way," for it was true – with nothing to guide them, the flat expanse felt utterly directionless. "And it's almost sunset. We're not going to make it in time."

But despite all the evidence in Meggie's corner, the elder element still didn't seem prepared to give up.

"We... have... about an hour... or so," Nickolas insisted. "There is still... time. And... anyway..." and he paused for breath, his eyes turned to the ground to watch each arduous step. "You could... be at the... statue right now... if it... were not... for me. I... owe you this."

Hearing her rash words repeated back at her so bitterly, whether Nickolas had understood them or not, Meggie almost wanted to cry, but though a lump rose again in her throat, no tears would come.

She knew she couldn't possibly escape back to her world now, despite Nickolas's assertions, and she'd said some unforgivable things. She'd blamed him for her fate, which was now looking bleak. And sorry as she was that she had said it, they both knew deep down that technically she was right; it was his fault that she'd come back, that she hadn't gone with the others and there was no getting away from it, from this place...

Or so she thought... for just then, Dromeda, who had been eyeing the horizon every now and again too, suddenly began to quicken his pace, making Meggie grab hold of him again.

"There!" he cried, startling the others. "I... see... it!" And amazed, both Meggie and Nickolas looked to where he was now pointing to see that sure enough, through the smoky haze of drying mud, something was glinting at them in the dimness. Something shiny and bright against the darkening sky...

Meggie's heart leapt, the lump in her throat almost reaching bursting point as she let out a cry of unexpected joy.

The City gates.

Somehow, inexplicably, *impossibly*, they were nearly there! They were nearly at the City! They were nearly at the statue!

After all that, she really would be free at last!

And forgetting all else for a moment, Meggie looked for the one person she suddenly wanted to share in this moment with above all others, grinning from ear to ear as Nickolas gave a little smile in return. Witnessing his relief as well, only added to her lightened mood – it felt good to see him happy again…

"We have to hurry!" she then cried, and reenergised by her optimism, both Dromeda and Nickolas broke into a run.

—

"You know something I'm going to miss?" Bex said as she gazed absently out of the darkened window. "Flowers."

She paused a moment to contemplate before counting with nods of her head.

"And animals. And trees. The dawn chorus. Rainclouds on a spring day. Snow. The little things I always took for granted, you know?"

Both Saz and Bethan shifted uncomfortably in their bonds. No had said it aloud yet, no one had wanted to, but they were all beginning to think it now; to know that it was too late. Half an hour and sunset would have been and gone. Half an hour and their freedom would be lost.

Saz suddenly let out a growl.

"Don't!" she snapped, as Bex opened her mouth to list some more things. "Please *don't!* I don't want to hear it!"

Her companion said nothing in reply, but the other two women were pretty sure they heard her swallow a small sigh. Bethan meanwhile sighed herself, trying to control her emotions. Her eyes stung with threatening tears, her throat dry, but she didn't give in.

"Well, at least we won't have to visit the baggage collector anytime soon," Saz tried again more calmly as if in some desperate attempt to lighten the mood. "At least we can live forever here. Some people in Tungala would kill for that…" But despite her best efforts to make the others feel better, no one smiled.

"I can't bear it," Bethan muttered instead. Her voice shook a little. "I can't bear the idea of living always knowing what we had and what we…" and she took a deep breath, her sentence remaining forever unfinished.

Lost.

They all knew it; Saz would never meet her family again; Bex would never smell the flowers and Bethan would never again see the face of the man she loved.

And right then, it was all too much.

"What do you think the others will do when we don't turn up?" Bex offered the air in general, her eyes closed now against her own hidden tears.

It was a pointless question, but as soon as she spoke again it was as if all three women instinctively realised that talking was all they had. If they stopped now, if they fell once again into silence, all of them knew that they would have nothing left, nothing but their own thoughts and the heavy despair hanging over every one of them.

Saz shrugged, trying to look noncommittal.

"They'll wait a week or so, I suppose," she replied, her voice beginning to sound flat, hopeless. "Meggie will realise what's happened. She'll tell them."

Meggie.

And at the mention of the fourth element, all three of them took a moment to wonder how she was doing, how far she had come, whether they had been mistaken to leave her behind…

"Maybe they could somehow get here through the flames themselves and help us," Bex continued, determined to keep the impending silence at bay for as long as possible. Bethan sat up a little.

"You saw what happened to Renard," she chipped in, catching on to the idea of a discussion, however depressing. "Only the elements can walk through those flames unharmed."

"But *why?*"

And for the first time in over an hour, Saz also seemed to physically perk up a bit. There were still so many unanswered questions, questions that until then had been pushed aside, ignored or forgotten…

Bethan frowned a little.

"Why what?" she asked tiredly.

"Why is it only the four elements who could walk into the flames? That's what I can't understand?" And she looked around her, as if expecting the almost-bare room to hold some kind of answer. "I mean, what *is* this place? Why are we even here? What's the *point* of it all? And *why*," her eyes flashed and she almost seemed to interrupt herself as an idea came to her, "*why* is it only today that we have a chance at freedom? Why not tomorrow or the day after or the day after that?!"

It was a good point and both Bethan and Bex's couldn't help but feel their spirits lift a little. Why *did* they have to leave during that day's sunset? Why *not* tomorrow or the day after or the day after that? Did they really believe that once Edmund and the others had tried one time and failed, they wouldn't try again every night until they succeeded?

"Yes, every day has a sunset!" Bethan cried, pulling against her bonds in her growing excitement. "You're right! We just have to work out how to get out of here and try another night… And by then Meggie will have –"

"But maybe we're not *supposed* to leave another night."

Bex sounded suddenly glum, and immediately, the mood seemed to dampen all over again as the others strained to look at her. The element of water looked sheepish.

"I mean, it might be," she carried on, once both sets of eyes were on her. "…it might be that we're meant to leave during this sunset," her gaze fell on Bethan. "You told Edmund this sunset…"

"Yes, but I'm sure he won't give up," Bethan argued a little hotly. "Ever." But even as she said it, she could feel herself starting to hesitate. They were thinking about *days* here, days for them to escape from their prison and somehow make it to the statue, days to try the sunset; but what if it was longer than that? What if it went on for weeks, for months, maybe even more? Would Edmund and the others really keep trying for that long? Could *any* of them really hope for that long?

"Even so," Bex mumbled. "We said this sunset and Ophelius said that if it's our fate to escape, then we will. I'm just saying that maybe it *has* to be this sunset."

"Maybe what has to be this sunset?"

The chilling voice spoke out across the tiny room so suddenly that all three friends jumped and much as they were allowed, spun towards the door, to find, to their dismay, that they had company.

Three figures now stood just within the door of the hut, two, their captors, fierce-looking Diggers armed with hefty swords and the third, the one who had spoken, a smug-looking man with tufted hair and beady eyes.

"Maybe *what* has to be this sunset?" Barabus repeated and then, when no one answered, he took a menacing step further into the room, glaring at each element in turn. "*What* has to be at sunset?!"

But though his voice was already a shout, still the three women bitterly held their tongues, determined not to give their enemy anything. For that was what he was now, there was no doubt in anyone's mind; Barabus was their *enemy*. He had tried to prevent them from coming together, then from leaving the City and now, he was trying to keep them from the thing they all wanted the most – their freedom. He deserved nothing.

Obviously impatient, Barabus then gave an annoyed groan and leaping towards Saz, the closest woman within his reach, he grabbed her by the chin and before anyone could so much as protest, he was whipping out a knife from his waistband and pressing it up to her cheek, the blade just touching her skin.

With a look of victory, he lowered his face right to hers, his eyes glaring. But though he hoped to frighten her into submission, though he hoped to frighten all of them, to make them give what he knew they wouldn't willingly, Barabus couldn't help but be surprised as no one moved. None of the women so much as let out a gasp and Saz didn't even flinch. Instead, meeting his gaze with a hard one of her own, the element simply gave a smirk.

"And what are you going to do with *that*?" she mocked. "Kill me?"

Taken aback, Barabus just blinked. As he did so, his hand slipped a little and the blade nicked Saz's flesh. A few drops of blood welled to the surface but still Saz didn't move. There was something about her now, something powerful, something *invincible*. Nothing could touch her here and somehow, they both knew it.

"You know what?" she asked instead, her voice low and deadly. "When we get out of this hut. *Which*," she emphasised as she saw Barabus's smugness threatening to return, "we will one day. I think none of us will have anything *better* to do than tie *you* up and make *you* bleed."

A little stunned, Barabus gave what was supposed to be another self-satisfied smile.

"And how do you propose to do that?" he asked. No one was quite sure if he was teasing or genuinely worried. "You cannot escape from here. You are surrounded. And making me bleed?... As you just pointed out, we cannot die."

So, he believed them. Despite what the Diggers had told him of Nickolas's death, he believed that the elements spoke the truth of his return to life.

Interesting, Saz thought.

"No, we can't die..." Bex then joined in suddenly and distracted by the sound, Barabus turned to stare at her, the knife pulling away from Saz's face to leave the small cut behind. He appeared almost to want to say something in return, to think of some answer, but before he got a chance, it was Bethan's turn.

"But we *can* hurt you," she said loudly. "We *can* make you suffer."

Barabus snapped his head round quickly to look at her and in that moment, as he stared into his fellow earth element's face, Bethan was sure she could see a glint of fear there.

He was afraid of them, she realised. He was afraid they were desperate enough to actually go through with it, if given the chance... but even so, even as she thought it, the moment was then gone and in its place his expression was triumphant all over again. Threaten him they might, but to his mind, the women had no way of escape. To him, they were bound, guarded, with no friends to help them, no one to aid them to safety.

Yes, it was true that he didn't know where the fourth element was, but right then, he didn't care. What could one woman, a small one at that, achieve against him and his men? What could one woman achieve against the *Builder*?

And suddenly he seemed to find his voice again.

"Just as I can make you suffer now, you mean?" he hissed aloud, squaring up to the women's defiance. "If I wanted to, I could separate you. And then keep you tied up for decades... or *millennia*. With no company, no food, no water, no escape and no death. Oh yes," and he began to pace between the three of them, clearly revelling in the power he held right at that moment. "You will starve, you will thirst, you will *suffer*," he spat. "And there will be no alleviation. There will be no death, no matter how hard you cry out for it." It was his turn to smirk, his turn to be defiant. "So you see? It will be *I* who triumphs. *The Builder* who triumphs, not you."

Stopping his tirade, he then stared into each face, waiting for that fear, waiting to see that they had been beaten. But helpless, hopeless, as the elements now felt, not a single one of them gave him the satisfaction of looking back. Every eye turned away the second they were met and his frustration flaring all over again, Barabus scowled.

"You may as well tell me," he demanded, bringing them back to the matter at hand. "What is happening at sunset?" and then, with more of a sneer; "how were you planning to escape?"

Bethan couldn't help but pale a little, but the only one to respond, she also dared to look up.

"How do you know that's what we were planning?" she challenged, trying to hide the quiver of dread from her voice. Yes, they may have nearly missed *that* day's sunset – outside, the sky was almost dark now - but no matter what Bex had said, a little part of her still held out hope for another sometime in the near future. One day, they would escape this world, she was sure of it... *almost*. But if Barabus knew about their plans, what hope would they have then?

"Just an educated guess," Barabus replied. He was eying her now, as if, despite his confidence, he could be wrong. "Why else would you have been discussing it when I entered?"

"If you knew what we were talking about when you came in, why did you bother asking us about it?" Saz mocked coldly from her chair and distracted, Barabus's eyelids flickered in irritation as he turned on her.

"Knives can still hurt, even if they do nothing," he threatened. But seeing Saz's unafraid expression, he suddenly gave a thoughtful smile, changing tack. "You know," and slowly, he moved towards her, still fingering his knife. "You do remind me a lot of my friend Dromeda."

"*Friend?*" Saz snorted. The others could tell that the element was determined to fight with everything she had right then, even if it was only words. They all were. Regardless though, even Barabus couldn't miss her look of surprise.

"Oh yes, you remind me a lot of him," he continued. "Very determined both of you. Very *fiery* tempers." He gave a small chuckle, waving his weapon towards Saz's cheek again.

"Hilarious," the element of fire said flatly. But clearly Barabus wasn't finished, the punch line for him was still to come and turning on Bethan, his eyes narrowed a little.

"The Builder did well to pair each of us off," he carried on. "Each element the same as the one before. So you see Bethan, you and I are not so very different..."

Bethan looked like she was going to be sick, but though she wanted nothing more than to be strong, to fight like Saz, to keep her head and look away, she couldn't help herself.

"I told you before!" she cried angrily. "I'm nothing like you!" And for the first time since it had happened, she found herself remembering the last time Barabus had spoken like this.

The situation hadn't been much different. She'd still been held captive against her will, kept away from her friends, from those she loved... just as she was now. But back then, the other earth element had almost seemed sympathetic, willing to be kind, unlike *now;* now when she could see nothing but coldness in his eyes, nothing but triumph over her. They'd long missed their chance of ever becoming friends, and as she saw, ever being alike, and the idea that she was somehow 'the same' as him made her feel physically ill.

"I think you are," Barabus teased. He was on to something good here. He had finally got to them and though Saz soon shifted in her bonds as if to reach out and hit him, the elder element just ignored her.

"Leave her alone!" the fiery element threatened with a hiss, but Barabus just stepped away.

"I'm not," Bethan retorted all the while, more tears springing to her eyes in fury. "I would-"

"Never do what I have done?" Barabus interrupted. "Yes, you already told me that once before. But you see," he gave another strange smile. "I believe you already *have.*"

All three women looked utterly stunned now, Bethan's face almost green in expectation of what the elder element could possibly mean. Not that they had long to wait and find out.

"Let me explain," and Barabus began to pace once more between the helpless friends. "What have I done but sacrifice a few things for what I truly believe in?"

"Sacrifice a few things?!" Saz blurted out. "Is *that* what you see this as?!"

"Hush!" Barabus gave a snarl, instantly silencing her. He glanced at the two Diggers who still stood at the door, until then completely forgotten, and one of them drew his sword as if ready to drive it through Saz's throat at a single word.

"That is where you and I are the same, Bethan," Barabus then continued, once more pausing at his fellow element. He leant in close, searching her pallid face. "We are both passionate about what we believe in. And once we have found that special something to believe in and treasure above all else, we will sacrifice anything to obtain it. No. Matter. What." He patted the flat of his knife on Bethan's shoulder with every last word as the element just stared up at him, her eyes wide in disbelief.

"Determination and dedication is the key," he carried on, gently sliding the weapon from Bethan's shoulder up to her neck, where it rested there for the duration of his torment. "That is the key to who we are. We do not give up, you and I. And that," his voice dropped to a whisper, "*makes us the same.*"

"Don't listen to him, Bethan!" Bex joined in now, struggling against her bonds. "You're nothing like him! He's just trying to hurt you!" and Saz merely watched in amazed horror as tears finally began to fall from Bethan eyes, dribbling down her chin and onto the blade held now at her throat.

"I don't know what you're talking about," she mumbled. But slowly, like a deathly poison, Barabus's words had crept into her mind and begun to take root there.

He was right. She hadn't given up, not really, not ever. She *had* been prepared to do anything to get back to Tungala, anything to get back to Edmund. Even letting Saz, her friend, give up her life… and what kind of person did that make her? It made her just like him. It made her heartless, cruel, selfish…

Just like him. Just like Barabus…

And suddenly knowing that she couldn't bear to think about it anymore, that she couldn't bear for him to say another unfeeling word, Bethan let out a cry and yanked forward, trying to tear herself from her ties. Even Barabus didn't seem to have expected this, but just quick enough to pull the knife from her neck before he did some real damage, the elder element sprang away.

"See?" he cried to the room at large, as he realised what he had done. "See? She knows I am right!" and he turned his back on Bethan to pay his full attention to the rest of his audience. "Do you want to know why I have done all of this?" he gestured at the room around them. "Why I have you here? Why it was I who tried to stop you all meeting in the first place? And why it is I have not allowed you to escape?"

Saz and Bex looked blank. Bethan's chin was resting on her chest, her eyes closed.

"Because," he said slowly, "I have found my treasure. I have found what I desire right here." He jabbed a finger in the air with zeal. "Right here. In this world. In the world of the Builder. And because it is he who can give me what I desire, what I treasure above all else, I must serve him." His eyes were aglow with some strange light now. "Even if it means making a few sacrifices here and there…"

Bethan didn't lift her head, but still she spoke up.

"What could you possibly treasure here?" her voice trembled as she tried to stop her tears.

What could this world possibly give Barabus? There was no greenery here, no animals, no shadows, no proper food and drink, no rain, no sea, no sunlight, no elves, no dwarves, no wizards, barely any *humanity*…

But instead of a fallen expression, the realisation that his idea was flawed, Barabus's face only brightened, the light in his eyes glinting with something of a madness.

"I treasure life," he replied shortly. "Everlasting life. That is what I believe in, what I cherish and will do anything for. Even if it means, like you, trampling over others to get it!"

"Bethan would never trample over anyone!" Saz interjected for her friend. "So whatever you're suggesting, it's rubbish!"

"But that is where you are mistaken," Barabus insisted, not even bothering to turn and face the element of fire. Once again, he only had eyes for the trembling Bethan. "Bethan here *also* has something she believes in and treasures above all else. And she has already made sacrifices in order to try and get it."

"All *three* of us want to leave-" Bex started in an attempt to outsmart their foe. But Barabus was too quick.

"Yes indeed!" he cut in. "But there is a *reason* above all others why Bethan wants to return to Tungala." And he smirked. "Because of a man. The thing she treasures above all else is her love for a man. And she is willing to do anything to keep hold of it. Even if it means sacrificing her friend..."

Sacrificing her friend...

All three women paled in horror then. *How could he possibly know?* - the question was at the forefront of every mind. How did he know about Edmund? How did he know about Bethan's feelings for him? Bethan didn't recall ever telling the elder element but then again, the kiss in the Temple of Ratacopeck hadn't exactly been private...

Most importantly though, what had he meant by 'sacrificing her friend'? Did he somehow *know* about Saz's pact? Did he somehow know about what they had done in the world of the dead? And if so, *how?*

"Th-that wasn't her fault," Saz soon stammered after the initial shock. Questions as to how the older element knew about their journey beyond the great gates were for later. Right now, Bethan needed her. "One of us had to choose," she insisted. "It had nothing to do with Bethan. I was upset, I didn't mean anything I said about her... but one of us had to make the pact and *I* decided that it would be me, no one else. It was *nothing* to do with her!"

To Saz and the rest of the elements' surprise though, instead of looking smug, Barabus's expression, for a moment, looked only confused.

"I do not know what *you are* talking about," he said, making everyone's heart immediately give a thud of relief. But then; "*I* was referring to your friend. Your Digger friend, Belanna."

Belanna?

And with none of them expecting *this*, all three women gave a start.

Belanna! They'd almost completely forgotten about their helper; the Diggerwoman who had risked all to tell them of the barrier between this world and death, who had risked all to help them escape, and at what cost?

"Yes, remember her?" Barabus mocked, once again leaning into Bethan's face. "Well, when I discovered her, she told me everything. All about the man with the blue eyes... And all about your plans for escape..."

"What did you do to her?!" Saz cried, horrified, for it was true, there was something deeply unsettling about the way he spoke of her, something that told them Belanna had not given him what he wanted to know willingly...

"I did nothing," Barabus sniffed. "But then, Diggers can die here; so hurting her was a bit more of a threat," he smiled just a little, looking at Bethan. "So there you are. Sacrificing for what you want. And your friend's life too. Which is worse than what I am doing. Did you even give her a second thought or were you too busy thinking about..." he paused, pretending to have difficultly remembering. "What *is* his name? Did you ever find out?"

But once again no one gave him the satisfaction of answering, all now too wracked with the guilt of what Barabus was telling them. Despite what the elder element said, none of them were left in any doubt that Belanna had been tortured in some way to gain the information he'd gleaned from her...

Although, all of them reasoned, as guilt was replaced quickly by anger, at least now she had a chance of rescue. No doubt the Digger was locked away somewhere, just like them and would have remained so if Barabus hadn't told them. Now though... Now they had even more of a reason to get out of there.

Whether he knew the effect his words had had on them or not, Barabus still appeared to want to talk, to draw every last shred of information from them, and moving back down the room, he seemed to start all over again for the third time.

"So," he said, almost conversationally. "What are... or rather *were* your plans for sunset? You might as well tell me," He was untouchable now. He had the women where he wanted them. And for that he *would* know the answers to his questions. Or so he thought...

"Tell me or I will-" but just as he started, he was cut short as the door to the hut flew open with a loud crash and the evening air spilled in.

The Digger guards were the first react, but even they were too slow, as two figures then leapt into the room, lashing out with fists and feet. The intruders moved quickly and within seconds, the guards had fallen noisily to the floor, unconscious. Meanwhile, Barabus, realising who it was who had entered, who it was who had come to defy him, tried to turn and run. But it was too late, for spotting him, one of the two new strangers soon sprang at the elder element, barrelling him to the ground with a growl. There was a horrible crunch and Barabus let out a cry, but the wind knocked clean from his chest, he barely made a move to struggle as the man – for so it was – didn't hesitate to straddle his body, his hands at his throat.

The second figure, all the while, still standing over the bodies of the Diggers, straightened up and twisting round, began to unload something or rather some*one* from his back...

"Meggie!" the three women seemed to shout the name in unison and breaking into a wide grin, the little figure of Meggie soon limped forward, brandishing a knife of her own.

"Oh good," she said. "You're all here!" and without another word, she set straight to work cutting at the ropes tying her friends' hands and feet.

"Meggie!" Bethan breathed as the little element hacked at the rope binding her wrists. Somehow the element of earth couldn't quite believe what was happening. "Meggie! You're here! We thought- How did you-? But," and she took a gasp of air, realising she'd been too amazed to even breathe. "But what happened to your leg?" and for the first time, all three seemed to take in Meggie's bedraggled appearance. Her ankle was swollen and although caked in mud before, the element looked even dirtier. But though there were so many questions, Meggie soon silenced any more with a shake of her head.

"Later," she said. "We have to hurry! Sunset's in about fifteen minutes!"

Bethan, Bex and Saz all gave an eager start.

"Fifteen minutes?!" Saz exclaimed, so overjoyed then she could barely stay still as Meggie, freeing Bethan and then Bex, began to start on her. None of them questioned how she knew the time so accurately...

"You have to go, now!" Nickolas cried from his position on the ground. He was the one who'd lunged at Barabus, and was now pinning him to the floor with obvious ease. Whatever strength he had left from their gruelling run, it was still clearly enough to hold his weaker foe down, for the elder element, after the initial winding shock had worn off, now seemed to be struggling with everything he had. He was biting, scratching, flailing, but all to no avail.

"Help! Help me!" he began to scream as a last resort. "Please! Help!" But quick to take action, Dromeda staggered forward, still panting from their exertions, and taking a piece of the now-cut rope, shoved it roughly into Barabus's open mouth, silencing him in a second.

Finishing with Saz's bindings, Meggie then turned to her own fellow elements. They were standing there now, energized by their freedom, yet confused, shocked, unsure what to do, of how to say thank you to Nickolas and Dromeda, of how to express the sudden leap of joy in their hearts, of how to say goodbye...

They had no time to contemplate though. They had to go, and Nickolas knew it before they even could themselves.

"*Go!*" he repeated more firmly. "You need to get to the statue *now!*"

And spurred into action, the four elements, carefully dodging the still-comatose bodies of the Digger guards, immediately ran for the door. In less than fifteen minutes they could be free, in their own world! And they were all looking to that now. There was no turning back.

As the women then spilled out of the Digger house into the impending darkness, only Meggie hesitated for a moment.

Pausing on the threshold, she looked behind her, back into the room where Nickolas and Dromeda still stood, looming over their victim.

Neither of them were looking in her direction; neither of them could say goodbye and she realised, with a painful sting, that she couldn't either. She'd barely spoken to Nickolas since their argument on the plain, a fact which was beginning to pain her more than anything... How could she possibly say goodbye to him now? And taking a deep breath to stop the lump that was strangely threatening to rise in her throat, Meggie turned back towards the alleyway beyond the hut, determined to force herself onwards.

Just overhead, towering above the other Digger houses she could make out the statue, a faint white glow in the dimness.

It was what she wanted, she told herself. It was what they all wanted. Escape was in her reach now and no matter what her doubts had been in the past days, she knew she had to take it.

Tungala waited for her. Normal life waited for her, away from the red light, away from eternity.

She had to go.

And so it was that Meggie took a step forward, ready to dash after her friends. As she did so though, her ankle began to throb and she almost cried out. The pain somehow felt worse now, almost as if the Builder were still trying to hold her back, to remind her of what he could do, what he *would* do, and gritting her teeth, she tried her hardest to remain calm.

"Would you like some help?"

The soft voice in her ear was so warm, so kind, that Meggie, for a second, felt as if all her pain were evaporating. And then, before she could move another muscle, there was a presence at her elbow, a strong arm around her waist and, a wave of relief sweeping over her, Meggie couldn't help but smile. Just hearing Nickolas's voice again, no longer angry at her, no longer hurt, gave her more joy than anything else, even the thought of reaching the statue in the few remaining minutes they had left...

Unable to look him in the face for fear of the lump in her throat overcoming her, Meggie bowed her head.

"I would love some," she muttered, her voice choked.

And without another word, Nickolas tenderly but firmly reached for Meggie's arms and twisting round, as was his way, he hoisted the little element into position on his back.

Though he had run countless miles those last few hours, though he was exhausted, famished, at breaking point, he was still ready for that one last dash and straightening up, the elder element then set off, hurrying after the three disappearing women ahead, Meggie just clinging to him, once more burying her face in his back.

—

Minutes had passed and still nothing had happened; the sun now so low in the sky that it had long since disappeared behind the trees, casting the clearing into an almost-darkness. And yet still, in the ever-growing light of the twin moons, the four friends remained where they were - silent, expectant, waiting.

"Not long now," Eliom spoke up again. "It is only a matter of minutes." This time though, the others made no sign that they'd heard him, each of them too busy squinting anxiously into the blackening space.

"I think it may be time to accept that nothing is going to happen," Thom broke the stillness for at least the third time. Again, as they had every other time, the rest of them appeared to ignore him. Even so though, the dwarf didn't seem to care. "After all, even if it did," he pointed out to the clearing at large. "It will be far too dark for us to see it anyway!"

At his implication, and barely realising they were doing it, everyone snuck a glance at Eliom then, but as if detecting their silent questions, the wizard only frowned.

"The light from the moons will help," Edmund hurried vaguely, realising a split second before the others, the full impact of what they were thinking. The spell to generate light wasn't too hard; it was something the wizard had taught Edmund himself and any of them could probably do it, but to keep it going for who-knew how long, to be that bright? That needed a wizard.

A wizard at his greatest power...

"We could *build* a fire," Fred offered, as he too remembered their friend's powerlessness. "I, for one, would welcome the distraction." And as if he'd been longing for something like this to happen all along, Thom immediately jumped to his feet.

"Good idea!" he cried. Anything was better than standing there, staring into nothingness, trying desperately to keep hope alive. "Edmund!" and he turned to the human with an eager glint in his eye. "Come!" But whether the Explorer had heard the dwarf or not, he was still looking off into the distance, hardly seeming to notice what was going on around him. "Take your mind off this wait and collect some wood with me! It will not take a minute."

Fred, however, was the one to step forward, laying a hand on Thom's shoulder.

"Leave him. I will help," he muttered. Then, a little louder to Eliom; "Let us know when something happens." He did not use the word "if" and the wizard, his expression unreadable once more, gave a nod, as, without another word, the dwarf and warrior then hurried off towards the trees at the edge of the clearing, disappearing quickly into the looming night.

"By the light remaining I would say we have twenty minutes left," Eliom commented, his voice breaking the suddenly weighty silence. To Edmund's surprise, the wizard then took hold of his staff and stabbing it firmly into the ground, began to slowly lever himself to his feet again. The movement was painfully frail and daring to tear his eyes away from the clearing for just a moment, Edmund couldn't help but feel a pang of something in his chest as he watched his friend, the young-looking wizard, turn to an elderly man in his eyes, stiff and crumbling with age. The sight had lasted only a few seconds, but it was long enough to make the Explorer turn away again, feeling suddenly uncomfortable, as if he'd witnessed something he had no right to, an embarrassing weakness…

"Do you still doubt?"

The words came out of nowhere, and for an odd second, Edmund had no idea either what they meant or even who had spoken them.

He cast his eyes to the sky.

"Doubt?" he echoed uncertainly. Hadn't they already spoken about this an hour or two before?

"Yes," and as if he had planted the very question in his mind, Edmund then found that Eliom didn't need to elaborate. He knew *exactly* what it was his friend was asking and a tiny smile, a hopeful smile played across his face.

"No," he replied, studying the growing brightness of the stars. "Not anymore. She told me that she loves me. In Ophelius's tomb. The dream – Bethan told me that she loves me." He lowered his gaze for a moment, considering his own thoughts. "I was stupid to worry about it. But it was something Soph said. It made me question myself, my motives for doing this…"

"And what about now?" the wizard said. "Do you still worry that nothing will happen? Do you still worry that the temple will not reappear?"

Moving his eyes to the clearing ahead of them, Edmund surprised himself by shaking his head.

"No," he repeated. "I've realised that you were right. What you said before. Bethan told us to be here, at sunset. And I trust her."

"Hmm," Eliom mused, "Whilst that may be true, it may not be a question of trust. Why, after all, did you not go with the others to collect wood? Why do you still so anxiously watch nothing?" This was followed by the muffled swish of grass as the wizard stepped forward to stand alongside his companion. From the corner of his eye, the Explorer saw that his gaze too was drawn to the darkness around them and for a second he wondered what it was the wizard truly saw there.

Edmund's smile faded. Eliom had a point. He always did. But this time he wouldn't freely admit it.

"Why don't *you* doubt?" he retorted gently and finally he looked straight at his friend. "How do you know that the temple will be there? Why do you have so much faith?"

Eliom's face was cast in shadow, nothing but a wisp of paleness in the growing moonlight but even as he spoke aloud, Edmund already knew what it was the wizard was going to say. And he was right.

"Destiny," Eliom's voice was firm. "You know as well as I that throughout our travels, destiny has played a great part. And I trust that it has a hand in this."

"Ah right. Destiny," Edmund scoffed, glancing back toward the spot where the Temple of Ratacopeck had once stood. So it always seemed to come down to *that*.

"You still do not believe in fate, after everything we have been through," the wizard said.

Edmund wasn't quite sure if it was a question or a statement, but either way, it made him feel uncomfortable all over again.

"You were so certain back in the tomb when you realised about the transportation. You seemed certain only an hour ago. What has changed?"

"I know. I have my moments. And I *do* believe... I think... but... at the same time, fate hasn't been amazingly kind to us so far. I mean," and Edmund gestured to where the temple was due to arrive at any moment, "it was supposedly down to *fate* that the elements had to walk through those flames in the first place. They were sacrificed because of *fate*. They had a choice, but what kind of a choice was it?"

"True," Eliom replied. "But fate also made it possible for Bethan's dream to reach you at the exact right moment back in the tomb. Fate counted on your feelings for her."

Edmund made a face then and Eliom turned his body fully towards him, as if ready for an argument.

"Do you not remember what I told you, so long ago?" the wizard continued. "Do you not remember the inn?" and for a moment, the Explorer paused. He had known Eliom for most, if not all of his life. Yes, they had not always been together, each going their separate ways, as was their want, but again, despite the fact that the memories he shared with his friend were almost countless, so it was that he somehow understood exactly what the wizard was asking.

He remembered very well what Eliom had told him. Memories of that one particular day had never *really* left his mind; that day in the bar, alone together, years ago, when Eliom had spoken of another vision, a vision concerning his future, his brother, Bethan...

Funny to think how he had dreamed of those moments almost on that very spot not so long ago...

"I remember," he replied aloud. "How could I ever forget? You told me that I would fall in love with Bethan. And because of it, because of *fate*, I fought it, Eliom. I tried so hard to feel nothing. I tried so hard to distance myself. You know that. You know that's why Fred came with me to collect her. He was supposed to be a kind of buffer, something to keep me under control. But then once we heard of Crag and he had to leave…"

"Fate had other ideas," Eliom commented quietly.

"Exactly." It was as if something had given inside Edmund now and suddenly it was all he could do to hold back his frustration. "And though now I wouldn't change it for anything; the way I feel about her, it feels like it's something outside of my control… something *fixed*," he insisted. "Or so I was too scared to believe back then… because if I accepted it, if I gave in to my feelings for her, accepted that my future was set in stone, that meant… if there was nothing I could do to stop it, then there was nothing I could do to stop any of the rest of it either."

Though Eliom's face was hard to decipher, Edmund knew that the wizard was looking at him questioningly then and his own expression turned sour.

"Oh yes," he said. "I remember it all. Not just Bethan. I remember too, what you told me about my brother. How he would betray me…"

"That was not your fate to control," Eliom replied, his voice ever patient. "Renard knew what he was doing."

Edmund gave a sigh.

"Yes. I know, but-"

"But do you also know, do you also remember what I said *after* the vision?" and Eliom's eyes were back on the sky as if the very words were written there for all to see, making Edmund follow suit. "I said that every action that you take, affects what your life holds. Fate is not one fixed path, Edmund," he said. "You are given choices. When you found the map in Ophelius's tomb, you could have chosen to see it all as folly, to believe his writings those of a madman and do nothing about them. You could have chosen never to act upon your growing feelings for Bethan, you could have chosen another to collect her-"

"I tried-!" Edmund cried.

"You could have chosen so many other paths, and though many may have led to the same conclusion, not everything is 'fixed', as you say." He looked thoughtful again. "But *I* would say it is a comforting thought to know that through fate, certain events are more likely to occur," and he leaned heavily on his staff then as if he was straining to stare more closely at one of the shimmering moons just above them. "For instance, I strongly believe that fate brought you and Bethan together to save the elements' lives and perhaps the lives of countless others not yet known."

For the first time since they'd been there, *this* seemed to gain Edmund's full attention and ignoring his watch on the clearing for a few precious moments, the Explorer immediately swivelled fully to face Eliom.

"What?!" he cried. "You think-?"

"Fifteen minutes," the wizard mumbled, still keeping time despite everything.

"You think - Do you mean to tell me that fate *made* Bethan and I – us -" Edmund spluttered, "for some kind of *reason*?!"

"I think you are misunderstanding the point," Eliom said calmly. He too had turned away from the sky now, his tired eyes almost glowing in the dimness. "What I mean to suggest is; without your feelings for Bethan, the elements could not be saved from this situation."

"That's stupid! The elements could still be brought back without my help." Edmund wasn't sure what to make of the whole idea, whether to see it as good or bad, but either way, he felt utterly overwhelmed. Eliom's vision had never said anything about *this*. "*You* care for them too. Not in the same way but... You would still have come back for them without me."

"Perhaps so, yes," Eliom replied. He spoke slowly, as if he had given the matter much thought but was hiding his conclusions. "However, it was your humanity, your passion and I suppose, in some way, your inability to accept Bethan's death that has driven us on to this point. You forget, Edmund, how much has happened in order for you to be here," and when Edmund remained silent, the wizard continued. "Think of how many trials you have been through in the last few months. Think of how many times we have been attacked, how many times you have been injured, but never killed. Think of Eldora. She sacrificed herself, gave herself willingly to Hoclee and her kind, because she realised that her destiny, her *reason*, was to aid *you*, in order that you might be here, at this exact time. She realised that you are important. And you *are*, for many reasons we may not even understand as of yet. But certainly, without you, Bethan would not have been able to contact us, to tell us what we needed to know in order to return her and the others to Tungala. Therefore, without you, we could not save the elements. And *that* is why," Eliom finished, "I believe that in only a matter of minutes, the Temple of Ratacopeck is going to appear and we are going to walk inside and finish our task."

For a few seconds, Edmund just gawped at his friend, too stunned to speak as he mulled over everything that had been said, amazed at how the wizard could know so much. Could Eliom be right, as he so often was? Could all of it, everything that had happened, been leading up to this? And if this were so, had he ever, despite the wizard's earlier assertions, had a choice?

Was he, Edmund of Tonasse, the Explorer, somehow *important*?

Suddenly he felt lightheaded.

THE ENTITY OF SOULS

"I-" he began, struggling for some kind of answer, for some way to respond, maybe even to argue all over again, but before he could get the chance to do anything, he was interrupted by the noisy return of Fred and Thom carrying firewood.

"Where do you want it?" Thom grunted, and the moment broken, Eliom was the first to look up and respond.

"Pile it here," the wizard said, and pointing to a spot not far off, he turned away from his astonished friend. Discussions were for later. Now, as it so often had been throughout their time together, was the time to act, and doing as commanded, with no idea of what had just passed, the warrior and the dwarf threw what little kindling they'd managed to find in that short a time, just where the wizard had instructed.

"Almost ten minutes," Eliom said and then, glancing back at Edmund. "You remember how to light it?"

Edmund blinked like someone waking from a deep dream and realising then what was about to happen, he gave a nod.

"Of course."

Without another moment's hesitation the Explorer then crouched over the wood and began to mumble the words of old the wizard had taught him, trying to concentrate on the pile in front of him and not the memory of the last time he had been there, the last time he had use this spell and watched Bethan's amazed face as the splint had come alive with light...

Bethan, I'm coming, he vowed silently and even as the others watched, the kindling gave a fizzling spit and flames flickered into life, casting a warm glow across every face.

Their hearts in their mouths, the company then swivelled towards the plain.

It was almost time. Although none of them knew how Eliom could be so accurate in his counting, how *any* of them could really, all of them could somehow feel it...

"Ten minutes," Eliom counted down. Then, as they waited; "Nine minutes... Eight."

Still there was nothing, all eyes searching desperately in what little light the fire gave them. For some reason, as he dared glance to the side, Edmund noticed that both Fred and Thom had their weapons unsheathed in their hands and not knowing why, he too reached for his sword.

"Seven minutes..."

And then, just like that, it started to rain. The dark sky above, one moment clear and speckled with stars, glimmering with the light of the twin moons, was suddenly clouded over and down the water poured in one great rush.

In less than a moment, the grass of the clearing was sopping wet, the trees at the edges bending and groaning under the growing deluge. But though the world around them had changed; though all four could feel the cold wetness on their skin, drenching through their cloaks; though the little fire they had built guttered, almost going out, none of the group so much as stirred.

"Five and a half," Eliom continued, his voice rising above the thrumming of the water. "Five minutes..."

And at that very moment, without so much as a sound, a movement of wind, a smell of stonework, it arrived, as if it had always been there. Suddenly, before the four travellers, a great wall of white had appeared, looming high above them, stretching far beyond the naked eye, blocking out even the sky with its vastness. And there, cut into that wall, barely a few metres away from where they were standing, already spattered with the gathering raindrops, were hundreds of carvings and symbols rising up over a large gaping entrance; the entrance to the Temple of Ratacopeck.

It was there. They'd finally made it.

"Only those who are destined will find a way," Eliom muttered, once again reading the inscription above the door, the words of an old wizard tongue almost lost and forgotten. In the dying light of their drenching fire, he then turned to Edmund, who in turn looked at Fred and Thom.

None of them could quite believe it. Not really. But whatever magic, whatever power this place clearly held, there was no time to appreciate it, for once again, now was the time to move, the time for action and filled with a new energy, the dwarf, wizard, warrior and human, all set off at once, bounding up the steps of the gaping doorway and straight into the dark abyss beyond.

THE FIRE

No one tried to stop them. In fact, no one even seemed to notice as Bethan, Saz, Bex, and Nickolas – still carrying Meggie - all hurried towards the centre of the City as fast as their feet could possibly carry them.

Pushing through the quietened evening streets, the five humans flew past the few straggling Diggers, dodging the last market stalls and cutting their way around the little Digger houses, the giant gemstone statue the only thing in their sights. Every time a woman fell, another would help her up without a word, such was the scene as the four elements sprinted their way towards their only freedom from the Digger world.

"We are… nearly there!" Nickolas panted, full of adrenaline as he forced his exhausted legs to keep moving. Seeing Bex almost trip a little ahead of him, he reached an arm out to help her in case of a fall, only for the element to soon regain her balance, and glancing back to check that Nickolas and Meggie were still on the move, continue on her run.

The elder element leapt aside only just in time as an evening merchant stepped in his path, laden with his wares from the day. The Digger cried out, a few items tumbling from his hands, but did nothing else but stare as the human ran past.

"That… was… close!" Nickolas laughed but feeling Meggie's face still buried in the back of his neck, he soon turned his head a little to the side, trying to study her from the corner of his eye.

"Are you… all… right?" he asked, his expression changing completely, but though Meggie nodded her little head against his skin, still she said nothing.

For some reason the lump that seemed to have developed at the back of her throat felt like it was growing larger and larger by the second. She dared not try and speak for fear of crying, but then again, *why* she felt like crying in the first place, Meggie had no idea.

Surely she should be smiling, laughing, joyful that at any moment now she would be back home, back in her own world with all those things Bex had said they were missing. The flowers, the dawn chorus, trees, snow… And yet all Meggie could seem to think about, all she could seem to picture in her mind, was Nickolas' face the second they'd seen the City, the second that the impossible had become the possible; that smile of relief, and yet, what she had chosen to ignore at the time - the all-too-telling sadness in his eyes. And not for the first time the little element knew that saying goodbye to him was going to be hard. Really hard.

"Meggie," Nickolas said. His voice sounded more strained than usual and Meggie wondered if he knew too, if he could somehow sense what she was feeling and understood what it meant.

She managed to open her mouth.

"I'm fine," she lied. "Just keep going."

And he did.

Up ahead of them, Bethan was at the front of the running group, her lungs fit to burst, her hair flying in the dry evening air as she pushed her way through the streets of the Digger city. Her every muscle was calling out for her to stop, but she knew that she wouldn't. She *couldn't*.

The excitement, the hope, the anticipation of once again being in Edmund's arms, or even just *seeing* him again was almost too much for her to take in. All she could do was stare at the statue, focusing all her energy on reaching it before the time ran out.

Somewhere nearby she thought she could hear Saz breathing heavily, and a little way off, the slapping of Bex's feet as they all ran that race of freedom, pressing themselves to get there. But these noises were faint, quietened by the beating of her own heart as it forced her along, everything else dimmed by the image of the statue burned in her sights.

And then, suddenly, before she really knew what had happened, houses and alleyways and Diggers had given way to a great clearing and she was there, at the foot of the great sculpture, and slamming to a halt, Bethan, for a moment just stood, panting, gawking up at the large platform right before her, waiting for the others to catch up.

Crafted from white flawless stone, much like everything else in that place, the statue was taller and more menacing than Bethan had ever imagined. It towered above her, forty, fifty feet, maybe even more, high like a giant arm reaching up to the sky, its four stone trellises - ornate replicas of the ladders leading to the platform at the Temple of Ratacopeck - like thick organic webs crawling up its base, each one, Bethan noticed as she looked closer, covered with hundreds of symbols carved delicately into the perfect white, swirling in and out of each other in a flurry of surprising beauty.

Up above, as she craned her neck, was then the podium where the four gigantic globes stood, each the width and height of a man, each perfectly formed and each exactly matching the colour of the original gemstone necklaces - blue for water, orange for fire, green for earth and clear glass for

THE ENTITY OF SOULS

air. And amongst them, nestled at the very centre of the platform she could see a slight glow, the flickering of something small but bright that she hadn't noticed until now. A fire...

"The Diggers... light a fire there... every night... around sunset... It is a kind... of shrine... to the Builder."

It was Nickolas who had spoken, and turning, Bethan realised that she was no longer alone. The other three women's faces expressed awe equal only to her own.

"What do we do?" Bex was the one to ask aloud to no one in particular. "Do we just climb it, like we did in the temple?"

Bethan licked her lips. She felt suddenly very thirsty. Thirsty and tired. And admittedly, afraid.

"Yes, I think so," she said. "Ophelius said something about being pulled through... up at the top of the platform, where the flames are. Maybe we just have to walk into the fire again."

Just, the word was almost laughable, as all of them remembered what had happened before and up to this point, and yet no one was laughing. Nickolas, who only now seemed to have realised why it was they had come there, looked suddenly pale.

"But that," Saz pointed, never taking her eyes away from the statue, "looks like a *normal* fire. If we walk into *that*..."

Bethan glanced at her in surprise.

"The other fire looked like a *normal* fire. Didn't it...?" she argued anxiously. "And we managed to walk through *that* alright."

Instead of agreement however, Bex soon turned to Bethan herself.

"I think I know what Saz is saying," she said. "This fire is small. It's manmade... or rather Digger made. That other fire in the temple? Well..." she bit her lip. "I don't know who made it, but it was definitely not normal..." No one could ever have called the Keeper of the World, the great fiery orb of power normal. "What if we walk into these flames and just..." She trailed off, not wanting to say it.

It was a fair point, and a point that couldn't help but frustrate all of them. Had they really got this far only to find yet another obstacle?

"We have to try it. What else can we do?"

This time it was Meggie who spoke up and as the others turned to look at her, Nickolas gently lowered the smallest element to the ground, offering her his arm as she stood to her feet, only for her to brush his help aside as she hobbled to the level of the others.

"What's the worst that can happen?" she pointed out, as all eyes were on her. "If we're not supposed to go through the flames, the worst we can do is suffer a burn or two!" and she glanced at her injured ankle numbly. Her eyes were dry, but though she wasn't crying, there was something in her face wholly unreadable.

"She's right!" Bethan added, taking up the case quickly. They were so close, and with so little time left – the element had no idea just *how* little - they had to *try*. "Why are we just *standing* here? We need to move!"

But just as the element of earth then made as if to lead the way to the trellis and start climbing, everything changed. Suddenly, as if from nowhere, a great wind whipped across the square, throwing dust and debris from the day's market, spiralling into the air. The wind was loud, howling and *angry* and hair and dirt swirling into faces and stinging eyes, the four women and their companion cried out, too late to shield themselves as the force slammed its way past them. But it didn't stop there. In an instant, the gust had passed across the square, over their heads and reaching the base of the statue, in a flurry of moving dust, it then began to wind its way *upwards* from the very bottom, towards the platform.

As the almost-blinded elements watched, the airstream then seemed to circle the four gigantic gemstones once, twice, three times before it hit the flames.

The reaction was instantaneous. For at the exact moment the strange wind touched the burning sticks of the little Digger-made fire, the flames erupted in a boom of crackling ash and smoke, soaring into a towering inferno, at first screaming high into the sky before fanning out in a great whoosh of power to envelope almost the entire podium, glass orbs and all.

All five of the watching companions drew back in alarm and for what felt like a long minute, no one said anything. It was all Saz, Bex, Bethan and Meggie could do to just stare. Stare and marvel and *fear*.

But the first to come to her senses, Saz couldn't help then but let out a laugh.

"I guess we know exactly what to do now!" she shouted above the sudden loud roar of fire. Just as they also knew exactly what time it was.

It was almost sunset. And finally, this was their exit.

But though smiles broke out amongst them all, including Meggie, all four women knew that they weren't quite free yet. Above them loomed the four trellises, wider and deeper than any ladder; their only chance to reach the statue platform in whatever time they might have left. None of them wanted to guess how long the flames would stay, and unwilling to find out, it was Bethan who, with a quick nod of goodbye and a thank you to Nickolas, then made her move and sprinting for the nearest trellis, reached for her first handhold. The stone came at waist height, meaning she would have to climb, not step, but nothing was going to stop her now and turning back briefly, she beckoned to the others.

"Come on!" she bellowed above the noisy flames. "Let's go home!"

—

Bounding up the steps leading to the entrance, the four companions thought little of what they would find on the other side. The archway was dark, darker even than the suddenly wet night around them, and yet without hesitation or even a light to guide his way, Edmund, the first to reach the top, leapt inside with the others following wordlessly, all of them expecting the murky tunnels and dank passageways that had led them before to the small square rooms, the monsters' lairs and then the main hall, the house of the Keeper of the World.

What none of them had expected however, was the light.

It was sudden and blindingly bright and reaching straight away to shield their eyes with arm and sword, the four friends stepped into it gingerly, huddled together in fighting formation. But though they were ready for combat, ready to shed any blood necessary, it was a fight that would never come, for as they inched their way further into the temple, each of them trying desperately to see beyond the brilliance, it was Eliom who realised it first as he turned his gaze to the white ground beneath their feet...

"Remarkable," he then commented aloud. "We are here." And believing himself adjusted to the glare, he removed the hand covering his eyes to take a proper look around. Sure enough, they were all standing in the colossal hall of white stone, exactly as he'd remembered it; the roof, still supported by the many great pillars, each one intricately hand-crafted with symbols and words, and the skylight, now dark, still wide, each stone surrounding it impossibly big.

And the fire.

There before them, in the centre of the magnificent room, burned the brilliant orb, the source of the blinding light. The flames licked and roared with fierce, hot intensity as if it had always been there, unquenched and unchanging and far above their heads, the platform reached by the four stone ladders, was brilliant in marvellous white as if it too had never been touched, as if it too were still ready and waiting for the four who were destined to climb...

The Keeper of the World.

It was there, right before them and the second to let his eyes adjust, it was Thom who then let out a cry of amazement.

"Impossible!" he gaped, his head tipping so far back as he looked up towards the grand ceiling, that he almost toppled over.

"Impossible," Fred echoed in awe.

"What happened to the tunnels? The creatures?!" said Edmund, as he too stared about him, completely overcome once again by the sheer scale of the place.

"Thom was right," Eliom offered. He appeared to be the only one unaffected by their surroundings. "The creatures already have what they desired; the necklaces. We have nothing more to offer them. Perhaps we do not pose a threat."

"Despite the fact we are here to help the elements escape from whatever place *they* sent them to," Fred replied somewhat wryly. Despite the fact the gigantic beasts of the temple were clearly not there, the warrior still hadn't lowered his sword.

"That does not account for us being *here*," Thom added in his usual rough manner. "I do not know about the rest of you, but I specifically remember having to *walk* a fair way before getting anywhere near this place…"

Eliom *had* said that the building was magic. Was it possible, then, that it could not only disappear, but somehow change its very structure too? And looking completely blank for a second, it was then that Edmund remembered something, a moment brushed aside that had meant nothing at the time…

What do you mean how did I get in here? I just walked in. There was a door, I stepped through it and here I am.

Renard. Edmund could remember his brother's very words on his appearance at the temple.

I just walked in…

Had he too then, just stepped through the archway and found himself in the inner sanctum? And if so, how and *why?*

Eliom meanwhile was giving the dwarf a long-suffering glance.

"As *I* said," he replied coolly. "The creatures are born of a deep magic, too powerful for any of us to understand." Looking once more at the spotlessly white floor, he gave it a little tap with his staff, before; "It is evident from what has happened here, that the structure itself may share in some of this magic. Perhaps it already knows why we are here and hopes to aid us…"

"Why would it do that?" Fred asked. He sounded more suspicious than anything as his own eyes roved the hall. "Why would it *help* us?"

But Edmund soon cut in.

"Look, we don't have time for this," he pointed out. If what Eliom said was true, how long would the temple stay like this for? Would it disappear again if they didn't save the elements in time? He certainly didn't want to find out and clearly able to sense his desperation, Fred then straightened up.

"All right. We need to get moving," he encouraged. But giving one more glance about the place, he then turned straight back to Edmund. "What do we need to do?"

It was a simple enough question and yet…

Suddenly, Edmund realised with a growing panic that he didn't know.

He didn't know *what* they had to do. What had Bethan told him in the dream? She'd told him to return to the Temple of Ratacopeck, but after that?… He couldn't remember. Somehow it had all faded to nothing. All of it. Every word of what she had spoken in the dream… Gone.

"You spoke of a gateway between worlds," Fred tried as all three saw the Explorer's face slowly fill with horror. "You said that we must 'pull' the elements through. But how?"

Eliom meanwhile, touched Edmund on the shoulder lightly.

"Just take your time," he encouraged. "It will come."

Would it? Would it really? *What if it didn't?*

Wiping a hand across his brow – it was so hot in the temple, the air felt sticky with fiery heat – Edmund was all too aware of how ridiculous he felt and it angered him. Why was everything so *hard*? How could he have forgotten something as simple as a few small instructions?

"Just take your time," Eliom repeated. His voice was low, so low that Edmund wondered if the others could hear it and he closed his eyes, trying to make his frustration subside.

"We don't *have* time!" he snapped, but as if Eliom had spoken a spell over him, Edmund could already feel his mind slipping into blankness, nothingness as everything closed in around him. As he tried to concentrate, he could feel the heat fading, the hardness of the stone beneath his feet leaving him, the awareness of the others drifting away as he began to search within himself, to remember. It was like falling asleep, or falling into a chasm, he wasn't quite sure which. And then, it was working.

He could see her, conjure her up in his mind, the image of Bethan, and she was standing in a white space, *the* white space, her hair matted, her dress muddy and torn.

It was cloudy, this image he had of her, fuzzy round the edges, but it was her and as he looked on her hopeful face, he felt the familiar ache in his chest, the sudden breathlessness as he looked upon the woman he cared for. She was right there, within his reach. And yet not quite yet... Not until he could remember.

Listen to me. She was speaking, the memory of her words returning as if they had been dragged through thick mud to be there. *Listen to me,* she said. And he was, desperately.

You have to return to the Temple of Ratacopeck. Ophelius told us. He was just here.

Here?

The familiar fear filled him, just as it had in the dream. Where was she? Why was Ophelius with her? The prophet was *dead*. Edmund had seen his tomb...

Before he knew it, the Explorer was then playing the whole thing out all over again.

Is that your blood? Where are you? Are you safe? The words were coming fast now, but they were a jumble of statements, too quick to understand, to grasp onto. *I was so afraid...* Bethan said. *Your brother. I've seen him. Renard. He's here.*

Edmund. I... I love you.

This threw him off and Edmund's heart thumped harder in his chest as he longed to tell her, the image of Bethan, that he felt the same. *Had she heard him?* he found himself wondering. As they'd left the dream world, had she heard him? Had she heard his whispers?

Whether she had or not though, he wasn't allowed to dwell for long, for Bethan's next words soon caught his attention. *At sunset,* she said. *The gateway between the two worlds will open and you must pull us all through. That's the only way we can get out of here.*

Fred.

That was what Fred had said. Edmund could remember that too.

But what gateway? And where?

The gateway between the two worlds...

And then, just like that, he *knew* and it was so obvious, so completely, absurdly obvious that in seconds he was back in the temple and his eyes were opening with a victorious laugh.

Of course...

"The platform!" he then cried aloud, taking the rest of his companions by surprise.

Climb the platform by sunset tonight. Those had been her words. Her exact words – he could hear them ringing in his ears now.

And climb the platform was what they were going to do.

Without another word, Edmund then turned back towards the orb and began to sprint full-pelt for the platform surrounding the curling, living flames.

And without question, without so much as a comment, the dwarf, warrior and wizard followed.

Though only a short distance away, as the four friends neared the diamond-shaped podium and its four steep ladders, each could feel the blasting heat of the burning orb growing more and more intense as the roar of the flames rose to deafening heights. As sweat began to bead on every forehead, dribble down every back in the unbearable hotness, none of them could help but recall the last time they had felt like this, the last time they had been so close to the temple's heart to watch the four women climb to the top of the white stone and disappear into the hungry flames...

As they reached the closest ladder, the stonework seemed to reach high above their heads further than any of them had remembered and for a second, all four just paused to stare and wonder.

For some reason, Eliom found himself recalling Edmund's fight with Renard and the Explorer's collapse not so far away, his brother's knife through his chest. In his mind, he watched, almost like a spectator, as he had knelt over his friend, instructing the stunned Saz to find some water. How pale she had looked, yet determined...

Thom's mind all the while turned to the four ghostly men, the elements of the past; Barabus, their leader of sorts, or so it had seemed, offering Bex and the others a choice, *the* choice.

Would the world ever have been truly destroyed if they had refused and never walked through those flames? he found himself questioning.

Would they ever know for certain?

Fred's thoughts had turned to his argument with Edmund at the foot of the platform, his accusations of his friend's guilt getting in the way of the elements' sacrifice. How little he had known then, how little he had understood of Edmund's motives, of the feelings he had felt for Bethan, the very same emotions now alive in him, woken by his life-partner after such a long, long time.

Soph…

For Edmund, standing once again at the foot of the platform could only make him think of one thing. As he had so many times before in the passing weeks, the memory of his last moments with Bethan seeped into his waking mind. *Please, Bethan. Don't go,* he'd pleaded with her as she'd stood, right on the very spot he was now, all that time ago, ready to leave him. *I love you.* And then he had kissed her, he had pulled her into his arms and like it was only yesterday, he remembered it all; the desperate feel of her lips against his, the sweet smell of her skin, the brush of her soft eyelashes against his cheek, the warmth of her body pressed to his so tightly… the heart-wrenching pang, the physical pain as she had then turned around and left him, as she had made her decision, climbed the ladder, the very one before him, and disappeared.

Bethan.

And not really knowing why he did it, Edmund found himself reaching out to take the first rung. The stone was surprisingly cool, hard, but even so, he hesitated, just holding it for a second as if it were something important.

Bethan.

He could save her now. They could save *all* of the elements now and filled with some new determination, the moment was then gone and turning to the others, his eyes bright, he gave a sort of smile.

"Thom!" he cried. The dwarf blinked. "Take the north ladder! Eliom!" the wizard met his gaze calmly, "the west! Fred!" the warrior was ready, "south! And get climbing!"

No one needed telling twice and each nodding his consent, the three companions instantly took flight, each taking to his own designated ladder like a spark to a splint of wood.

With only moments to go before sunset, Edmund paused for a second to watch his friends' progress, but then it was time, and taking the first rung in his hands more firmly, he heaved himself onto the ladder of stone, beginning the long climb to the platform as fast as his limbs could carry him.

Following Bethan's example, Bex and Saz hardly hesitated to make their speedy goodbyes to Nickolas before running for the statue trellises. Time was of the essence, and there was little of it left to stop and think.

Only Meggie paused longer than the others as she made her move to leave.

Knowing she had to say something, or at least try, she soon turned back towards the elder element, but as she did so, words failed her and unable to look into his face, she just stood there, her eyes on the ground.

What was wrong with her? Why couldn't she just say goodbye and get it over with?

Nickolas's own gaze, all the while, still seemed to be on the statue, almost as if he couldn't quite believe that it was there.

"Do you need help?" he asked, the moment he realised she hadn't gone. His voice sounded surprisingly cool, but though he had offered it and though she knew she probably needed it, Meggie just shook her head, still avoiding his gaze.

He thinks it's because of my ankle I'm still here, she realised. *He doesn't know... he doesn't understand.* And neither really did she. She had no idea why the idea of saying goodbye to a man she barely knew, her companion of no more than a few weeks, a man she would never see again, felt so incredibly, incredibly difficult...

"No," she mumbled, feeling foolish. Why was it so hard just to speak? And why did her throat have a lump in it again? She was nearly free - she should be happy. All she had to do was say a few words, turn around and climb; it was all it had to take. And yet in those few seconds, for some reason Meggie couldn't seem to move.

"What are you doing then?" Nickolas asked.

She noticed he sounded softer, but not much so. He seemed distracted somehow, distant, yet, for the first time, she also noticed how close he was standing. His voice came from just above her head; she could feel his warm breath on her scalp, tingling at the hairs on her neck. His feet were just within her eye line as she stared at the floor, her heart pumping suddenly faster. Was that his hand on her shoulder? Comforting and warm... *Did he know after all?*

But then all of a sudden, the warmth had left and his feet disappeared as he stepped away.

"What are you waiting for?" she heard him snap. "You have your chance to leave. Take it and go!"

The words were true enough, but it wasn't so much *them* themselves that somehow stung Meggie; it was the way he had spoken them. Nickolas sounded impatient now. No, not impatient; *annoyed.*

He wants rid of me, she realised. He *wanted* her to go. He *wanted* her to leave. And all of a sudden, Meggie felt incredibly stupid.

Here she was, imagining somehow that saying goodbye was going to be one of the most difficult things she would ever have to do and yet here Nickolas was making it clear that to him it wasn't a problem at all, that to him it didn't even matter – that *she* didn't matter.

Before she knew it, Meggie could feel her face flush as her own anger then took hold.

"Fine!" she retorted and gone in an instant was the lump in her throat, the threat of any tears as her body positively shook with indignation. "I *will* go!"

In her heart of hearts, she hadn't meant for it to sound so final, for those words to be her last to him, but it was too late, they had been said. There was no going back now and still without throwing Nickolas so much as a glance, it was then that Meggie turned on her heel and doing her best not to cry out with the pain of it, the frustration of it all, she made her way towards the statue.

The going was slow as she hobbled, the stab of her swollen ankle sending spasms of pain along her leg with every step, but determined to doing nothing else but move, she carried on, until, reaching the closest trellis, the very one Bethan was climbing, she stopped.

Even though every *ladder* – for want of a better word - was only really wide enough for one person to climb at a time, the other element had already made a pretty good head start and looking at the distance between trellises, Meggie knew this would have to be the one, regardless of whether it was already occupied or not. She didn't dare consider trying to walk any further for fear the pain would be too much and she'd fall, or what felt like *worse* right then; have to give up entirely. But it wasn't any of these things that had made her pause, for as she reached for the first rung, her hands still quivering with rage, it was only then that she realised how much she was going to struggle, whether her ankle was hurting her or not. Where each stage of the trellis had come up to the other women's waists, to the smaller Meggie, it reached almost to her chest...

The little element stared up along the length of the stone lattice. There had to be at least thirty rungs-worth. And every single one of them was going to require every last bit of arm strength she had...

Meggie felt herself give a sharp sigh.

There has to be a better way, she reasoned. After all, the Diggers managed to get to the platform every night to light what was even now, despite her hesitation, still a towering blaze. Was she supposed to believe they did exactly what she was about to do, *every single night*?

But though she knew that she could quite easily turn back and ask just exactly how it was the Diggers made it, a stubborn voice inside her head wouldn't let her.

I never want to talk to him again.

And just like that, Meggie found herself starting to climb.

During the tiny scene on the ground, the other three elements had made surprisingly good progress. Already almost halfway to the top, a strong breeze had begun to whistle in their ears the higher they climbed, sweeping across the evening Digger world.

As the giant gemstones grew larger and larger in her sights, Bex thought that her pounding heart would never still. Her arm was aching, the injury from the baggage collector a sore reminder of what they had been through to get this far, but despite it all; the excitement beyond words, the feeling of imminent freedom, seemed to propel her on, climb after arduous climb as she threw one hand up to the next ledge, then another, before pushing herself up on her knees and starting all over again.

Sweat clung to her brow, to the back of her neck as she just concentrated on breathing, her lungs struggling with the exertion. Meanwhile, her mind turned to home, to her own world, Tungala, and for a moment she felt like laughing as she thought of all the things she was going to see, to hear, to smell, to feel, the very things she had lamented never experiencing again, tied up in Barabus's little hut. The smell of fresh flowers, the blue sky, the dawn chorus, a spot of rain on a spring morning, a warm bath, the sea, her own house… A whole world of possibilities.

At the same time, on the opposite side of the statue, Saz's thoughts were also on all of the things she'd missed and would soon know again. With every new rung, a new reason to be free, a new reason to return to Tungala seemed to pop into her head. How she longed suddenly, to see her family, her mother; to laugh with her little sister Charlie; to teach Allan, the fighting instructor, who'd been replaced all that time ago by Eliom, a thing or two! And as for Eliom himself, it seemed like a lifetime since they'd first met and ventured out together. And yet, though she may never have realised it until then, despite his cool, calm ways, she knew she had grown fond of the wizard. He felt like a true friend to her, a friend she knew would never let her down, who she knew would be waiting on the other side of that fire for her, ready as ever with his words of wisdom…. and thinking it through, the element of fire couldn't help but glance down at her hand and its blackened scar, the seal of her fate.

Perhaps he'll be able to change things, she thought to herself. If anyone could change what had happened, could somehow reverse her pact with death, she knew it would be him. The very idea made her smile a little and tugging herself onwards and upwards, she tried to imagine the happy reception that awaited them all on the other side…

Ahead of the others, Bethan meanwhile took a moment to pause and rest. She too felt breathless and hot, her heart thrumming like a drum as she thought of what was to come, as she thought of her freedom, and more importantly, what could be waiting for her on the other side of the flames above her head. As her eyes dared to look out across the space above the City, marvelling a little at the almost beautiful picture it painted of little huts and glowing lamps, dotted with dark squares, she was very much aware of how suddenly *nervous* she felt. All she wanted, was hear that gentle voice, see the smiling face with those deep blue eyes, but as she contemplated her reunion with Edmund, she knew that she was afraid.

The memory of her dream, of what she'd said and, more importantly, what he *hadn't*, still haunted her. The reality of it was; she and the Explorer barely knew each other. They had been acquaintances for only a matter of weeks before the Temple of Ratacopeck and then separated for only a few more. Was it enough? Or could her absence have made them both virtual strangers all over again?

As she thought about the last time they had been together, *physically* been together, the lingering kiss of the temple that never really left her mind, she felt the colour rising to her already hot cheeks.

Was one kiss enough to make him hold on? she found herself wondering again. Did he still mean what he had said then, that he loved her?

And did it really *matter* as long as he was there?

Whatever the answer, whether good or bad, Bethan knew that she was eager to find out and glancing back to check that the others were still following, the element soon continued on the drudging climb to the platform edge, ever aware that they were running out of time.

All the while, her anger forcing her to forget the throbbing of her still-swollen ankle, Meggie continued to haul herself up the great ladder. Already her arms and chest were starting to burn as she pulled her whole weight up onto each stone slat, using her chest to rest before she crawled to her knees. Despite her size though, her determination had got her almost a quarter of the way and as her body groaned, her mind raged with unwanted questions.

Why did you ever think you meant something to him? she scolded herself. *Why were you so* stupid *to think he wouldn't be sorry to see you go?* After all, she'd been nothing but a burden to Nickolas since day one, having to be looked after, cared for, carried when she fell, fed and watered. And her constant questions, her demands for answers…

Yes, after years, real *years* of quiet for him, she'd come along and made a lot of noise. And fuss. She and the others had tried to alter the way of things, and judging by the way Barabus had reacted, none of it had been good. Nickolas had almost *died* because of them, died because they wanted to change, they wanted what no other human had tried, bar one; they wanted freedom and for that... how could she possibly *blame* him for wanting to see the back of them?

Why did I even go back for him? Meggie's thoughts turned bitter as she reached out for yet another stone rung. Why hadn't she left him at the world of the dead? Because she'd thought he would have waited for them, for her? Because she'd thought that he cared? Or had none of that mattered?

Meggie bit her lip, trying to stop her arms from shaking even more with the physical strain.

It doesn't matter now, she told herself. She would be free of this world, of *him* soon enough and she had to focus on that now. She had to focus on the positives, on her freedom, on the glorious things she would have when she returned to the world she'd unwillingly left behind...

Tungala waits for me.

But as her eyes turned to the way ahead, to the platform above, to the raging fire, even as she tried to think of the world she had known before, of what she had lost, Meggie's mind fell completely blank and suddenly, try as she might, it hit her.

There was nothing; not a *single thing* that she actually missed. There was *nothing* that she wanted to return to Tungala for. Just as she had realised before, even tried to express to Nickolas on their way to the world of the dead, just as she had felt all along really; Tungala truly held nothing for her.

Yes, she missed the rain, the flowers, the grass, all the kinds of things that Bex had spoken about, but, she realised with a shock that made her hesitate for a second, none of that really mattered, none of that really felt that *important*. Not as important as what she *would* miss right here, in the Digger world, if she left...

And it was thinking about this that made Meggie then completely stop and turning slowly, so as not to fall, the little element dared to look back down at the way she had come, confused, unsure and alone.

Back in the square, the actions of the four human women had caused quite a stir. Despite the fact that the early evening streets had seemed almost empty, quite a crowd of Diggers had now gathered in one great mass below the statue, some waving weapons and fists angrily, others just looking on in sheer wonder as the four women climbed the trellises of their sacred monument. But amongst all of their faces, there was only one that Meggie was searching for and within moments she found it.

"Meggie!" she heard his bellow before she saw him, but then there he was, forcing his way through to the front of the throng as he saw her perilously turn. "Meggie! What are you doing? Please, be careful!"

The elder element's voice carried well across the square and his shout soon alerting the others, Bethan, Bex and Saz all paused to turn themselves.

"Meggie!" Bex, the closest of the three now, echoed. "Meggie! Are you all right?! Don't stop! Keep going!"

But Meggie wasn't listening to anything but her own convictions now, her own truths. And she continued not to listen, as, with a lump forming once again at the back of her throat, she turned back to face the trellis.

It was only when she dropped to her knees, her leg reaching down over the side of the rung that the others then realised what was happening.

"Meggie! Stop!" Nickolas continued to shout, the first to understand, and in less than a heartbeat, he was at the bottom of the trellis, his hands on the first rung, almost as if he were going to climb up and force her to carry on to the platform himself. "Stop it now!"

"Meggie, please!" It was Saz's turn to cry helplessly. "We have to hurry! What are you doing!?"

But although her fellow elements continued to yell, to plea, to worry for her, Meggie remained utterly silent and determined. Several times she almost slipped, several times she almost didn't feel the touch of stone against her toes as she reached out with a tentative foot, but every time she hardly seemed to notice. And it was because she knew now, she *knew* and it spurred her on with a strange kind of energy she had never experienced before.

He cared. Though he may have tried to pretend before - perhaps for his own sake as well as hers, she didn't know - he hadn't been able to hide it this time. She'd heard it in his voice the second she'd turned back, seen it in his far-away face; *concern*. And that was enough.

"Meggie! Come on! You're going to miss your chance! Please!" Bex bellowed, her voice growing fainter and fainter as Meggie scrambled closer and closer to the ground.

I don't care, Meggie found herself thinking. *It was never my chance. It was never meant for me.*

"Meggie!"

Nickolas's voice was growing louder, making Meggie realise that she was nearly there. In nearly half the time she'd somehow managed to make it almost to the bottom of the trellis. Very soon she'd be back on the ground and then she would have to face it. Face him.

"Why will you not listen to us?" the elder element growled up at her. He sounded angry again, but she didn't care about that either. There was only one thing on her mind now and as she reached the last rung, Nickolas, throwing his arms up in a show of anguish, stepped away to give her room. "You are so *infuriating!*" he cried as Meggie's feet touched dusty floor. "Do you *know that*?!"

Yes, she did. But it didn't matter right then, for finally, without another moment's hesitation, she swivelled and did what she hadn't dared to before; she looked directly into Nickolas's face.

The elder element's eyes, often so controlled, were alive with frustration, were searching her own face in wild confusion, wanting to know why she wouldn't listen, why she wouldn't say anything, why she'd come back… But still that was enough for her.

"Nickolas," was all she said, was all she managed. And then, before the great crowd who had gathered to stare, before her waiting friends and before Nickolas could react, Meggie, the little element of air, stepped forward and without so much as a warning, reached up and pulling Nickolas's head towards hers, planted a rough kiss squarely on his lips.

For the smallest second, it felt as if the whole Digger world had paused to watch as the little long-haired woman on her tiptoes and the tall muscular man with a rather stunned expression on his face, stood there, their faces pressed together, their skin flushed; her hands reaching for his neck, his reaching slowly for her back.

But then, just as roughly as she'd started, Meggie pulled away.

Her heart was pounding and for some reason she felt suddenly very giddy, but noticing Nickolas's shock, her cheeks soon reddened all the more.

"Look, I don't care if you're angry. Or even if you don't like me," she began, staring up into the elder element's face once again as he stood over her, his eyes wide in astonishment, his lips slightly parted, just how she'd left them. "I had to come back because if I didn't, I'd-" but she never got to finish her sentence, for in those few seconds Nickolas's whole demeanour had changed. His face softened as it never had before and gently, cautiously, he was reaching up and taking Meggie's cheek in the palm of his hand, he leaned forward, bringing his face once again to hers, and kissed her.

Meggie, almost too overjoyed to breathe, could feel something inside her melting as his warm skin met hers, and then something else, something more forceful, something not warm but *hot*, like a blazing fire rising in the pit of her stomach as he pulled her body towards him, his scorching breath mingling with her own, his arms strong and controlling, and unable to bear it any longer, she pressed herself to him, her hands pulling him down, as if she never intended to let go, oblivious to the statue behind her, oblivious to the watching crowd now staring, oblivious, so it seemed, to the world and everything in it.

Observing from above, Saz and Bex couldn't help but smile to themselves as they watched the pair below clinging to one another as if every second could be their last. Somehow, they'd always seen this moment coming, though neither of them could ever have said how.

Only Bethan, too far up the trellis now to tell what was really happening, had no idea, and balancing herself on the edge of the lattice, she soon called down to the others.

"What is it?!" she shouted. "What's happening?! Is Meggie all right?"

Saz glanced up.

"She's fine!" she called, unable to hide the grin from her face. *Or rather, she certainly would be.*

But though Meggie's fate seemed somehow certain now, though the couple continued to hold one another, after what seemed an age, Nickolas suddenly pulled away.

"You have to go," he muttered, his eyes closed from the kiss, his voice gruff. Gently he smoothed Meggie's tousled hair down her back before moving to touch her forehead, stroking her cheeks, her lips, as if desperate not to let her go, before he cleared his throat. "You have to go," he repeated. "Now."

"No," Meggie retorted, "I don't." Her own voice was quiet but firm, her lips tingling under his touch, her heart still hammering in her ears. But though she moved forward to touch him again, to bury her head in his warm chest, Nickolas seemed to step away a little, leaving a sudden gap.

"Please," he continued. "You cannot stay here. You have a chance to be free. I want you to take it."

And knowing somehow that this would happen, Meggie took a step back then to stare him in the face.

Please don't do this, she willed him silently. *Just don't.* But aloud, she was still determined.

"What if I don't want that chance?" she said. "What if I don't want to take it?"

Nickolas though, seemed just as determined to avoid *her* eyes this time and Meggie, watching him, felt a horrible pang as she saw his expression change, shift into that well-known unreadableness, as he began to bury himself and his feelings along with it.

"You will regret it if you stay here," he said. His voice seemed to barely rise above a whisper. "You must see that…"

"Must I?" Meggie almost choked on the tears she had never realised until then were still threatening to appear and reaching up once more, it was her turn to take his cheek in hand as she move forward, closing the space between them, forcing him to look her in the eye. Though he tried to hide it, there was sadness there, that same rejection, the same look that she'd noticed but ignored out on the plain when they'd first seen the City, when he'd smiled *for* her, she realised, not *with* her; the sadness that had haunted her since then, and, she realised, had made it so hard for her to think about saying goodbye.

"How can I leave?" she asked him, searching his gaze again with her own. And then, she smiled, realising something not for the first time. "How can I go when my life, my *world* is here?"

She'd known it for a long time, but had never done anything about it. She'd ignored it, tried to bargain with it, laughed at herself for being so stupid. But there it was, the truth.

Tungala held nothing for her, because Tungala didn't have Nickolas.

The elder element just seemed to look stunned as he studied Meggie's face, his gaze moving back and forth, back and forth as if he couldn't quite believe what he was seeing or hearing. But despite what she had said and what it *meant,* still he seemed to remain resolute, and giving a jagged sigh, he soon pulled his head away from her grip.

"It is not enough," he replied seriously. "Meggie, I cannot let you stay."

The little element scoffed.

"You're not *letting* me do anything. I'm my own person-"

But Nickolas wasn't finished.

"For the very reason *you* want to stay, *I* want you to go!" he snapped, making her stop in alarm. "Meggie you have no idea how hard it has been… I have *tried* to keep my distance, to force myself not to care about you… But I will *never* forgive myself if you do not take your chance and leave, if you miss out on your one opportunity to be free of this -this," he gestured at the world around him in general, "living *abyss,* where there is *nothing* to look forward to but a blank, long eternity." He turned away then with a burst of wry laughter. "I am hundreds of years old, for Tungala's sake!! I am far*, far* too old for you! And I have no choice but to stay here! If I go into that other world, I am nothing but a ghost and here? I am cursed to stay like this forever! Even when I want to die I cannot!"

Taking a moment to calm himself, the elder element then gave another sigh.

"I cannot hold you here," he started again, "I cannot and I *will not.* You have to go. Live your life. A *full* life. This place cannot make you happy."

Whilst she had expected something like this, for, it seemed, a long while, Meggie just stared at him, lost for words, struggling to take everything in. All around them, the square was deathly quiet, the crowd of Diggers at Nickolas's back, silent; all of them secretly straining to watch and hear the spectacle before them. All interest was on her now, on Meggie, and as if the attention had given her some kind of clarity, the element suddenly found herself understanding.

"You deliberately pretended you didn't care, to make me leave, didn't you?" she challenged. She waved her hand half-heartedly at the statue behind her where the other three women, despite everything, were still waiting and Nickolas, his own gaze wandering to the trellis, gave a new dry smile.

"I thought that if I could convince you there was nothing for you here, that I wanted no part of your life, you would go without remorse," he explained. "I thought it would make you free-"

"But I could have left angry with you!" Meggie shot at him. "And I *was!* I was going to leave without even saying *goodbye!*"

"It was the risk I was willing to take," Nickolas replied, the smile never leaving his face. But suddenly, his expression fell, as if he too had understood something. "And I still am," he said. And then, just like that, as if he had finally made a decision known only to himself, he turned from her and began to walk away. Still silent, the Diggers moved aside to clear a path as he strode

THE ENTITY OF SOULS

across the square, never turning to look back, but though she could not move to follow, the pain in her ankle too great to hobble more than a few steps herself, that didn't stop Meggie.

"Why can't you see that I have to stay?!" she shouted at his back. Her hands were balled into fists now, fists of rage, frustration that he just couldn't seem to *see*. "Don't you *want* me to stay?! Is that it?"

Nickolas hesitated for only a second, but it was enough.

Cursing under his breath, he swivelled back.

"I told you!" he exclaimed, his own anger still rising. "I cannot *let* you stay!"

But still Meggie stood firm.

"And I told *you*!" she growled. "I'm not leaving!"

And as if to prove her point, she then began to walk, step after step after step towards him, biting her tongue as gasps of pain sprang to her lips. She squashed them down furiously.

"What's the point in me going back?" she entreated. "What's the point in me returning to a world that has *nothing* for me? I'm not like the others." And she wildly gestured again to the other elements. "I don't have a family. They're all *dead*. My brother, my father. There's nothing I want to *do* with my life! Before I came here, I lived on my own in a run-down shack! I don't care about the grass, or the birds or not having a shadow, or not being able to die! There's only one thing I care about and that *I* see as being worthwhile and that's-" but before she could finish, her voice cracked and a yelp escaped as her ankle gave an extra hard throb.

The idea of leaving, of going back to that other world, *that* wasn't freedom to her, in fact it hadn't been for a long time now, she realised. Ever since she'd been in this world, ever since she'd thought about going back, she'd always had her doubts.

Somehow, somewhere in the back of her mind, she'd always known that she'd never leave. Like the time she'd first injured herself and Nickolas had joked about leaving her behind; the time she'd snapped at him for no reason only because he hadn't understood her turmoil, the strain of trying to decide whether to stay with him or return to what she knew.

No, that world, her *old* world, had nothing left for her now. Until weeks ago, all she had known there was pain, fear and loneliness. It would be like a prison; a prison that Nickolas seemed intent upon sending her to…

And as Meggie almost fell to her knees, lowering her head to gasp with the aggravation of it all, it was then that she felt suddenly warm as two strong arms were engulfing her, pulling her back to her feet and forwards, towards safety and a fast-beating heart.

"You are so stubborn," Nickolas spoke into her hair. But this time his voice was soft again, teasing, *happy* and Meggie, her face buried in his tunic, shifted to stare up at him. To her utter joy, he was smiling properly now, his eyes shining with a new light. "I just want you to be happy," he added. His deep voice seemed to rumble through her whole body, making her own heart give a kind of shiver and she too gave a smile.

"I am," she whispered. Then, as if to prove just that, encircling his chest with her own little arms, Meggie slowly reached up all over again to deliver another kiss.

Up on the trellises, Bex and Saz were still watching the scene with growing delight for their friend. But though it felt as if everything had stopped to let the scene unfold below, the fearsome flames of their escape were still burning bright at the back of their minds and once again, Bethan called down to her companions.

"What's going on down there? What's the hold up?" she demanded anxiously and suddenly remembering what little time they must have left, if any at all, Saz and Bex both gave a start.

"We have to go!" Saz pointed out, staring back up to the platform above. "We can't have more than a minute or so left!"

But though Bex's eyes travelled to the fires above too, the element hesitated.

"We haven't even said goodbye!" she cried feebly. All four of them had come so far together and somehow, just leaving their fellow element, their companion and friend without another word, felt somehow seriously wrong.

"Meggie isn't coming?!" Bethan shouted down in confusion.

"No!" Bex yelled back up to her. "I think she's found something worth staying here for! But," and she paused again before, giving a nod almost to herself, she then dropped to her knees. "I'm going to say goodbye to her!"

Saz almost slipped from her rung.

"Bex! No! We don't have time! We have to move!" she cried. "We don't know how long the gateway will stay open!"

Bex, however, was already starting to descend.

"Bex!" Saz tried again, but seeing that it was hopeless to stop her, it was as if something in her also broke and all of a sudden, she too was dropping to her knees to start back the way she had come. It was stupid to turn back now, turn back when they had minutes, perhaps even seconds before sunset, and yet the element of water was right; they were never going to see Meggie again...

Noticing the other two women moving *the wrong way,* Bethan too, almost lost her grip as she tried to spin fully around.

"What are you doing?!" she shouted, her voice almost hoarse with frustration. "Why are you going *back down*?! *Stop!*"

The last word was almost a scream of desperation, and as it split the air, ringing across the entire clearing, so it was Meggie broke away from Nickolas's embrace and turning back to the statue, realised all too quickly what was happening.

THE ENTITY OF SOULS

"No!" she bellowed, cupping her hands around her mouth as she watched her fellow elements on their descent. "Don't come back! You don't have time! Just go! Go now!"

Saz and Bex both paused.

"Go!" Meggie insisted. "Go! Don't worry about me! Just go!"

"But Meggie..." Bex started sadly.

"No buts! Go!" Meggie replied. "Please! I don't want you to miss this chance! Consider your goodbyes said!... And thank you!" she suddenly burst out as it finally really sank in that these words would be the very last she would ever get to say to any of them. "Thank you for... well *everything*. You've been true friends. I mean it. I'll never forget you for it." And she gave a laugh then, glancing at Nickolas, who still stood by her side, "and when I say never, I mean *never*!"

Her words made tears spring to all three pairs of eyes as Bex, Saz and Bethan all understood, truly understood that this goodbye would be their last. But though heartbroken to leave the little element behind, each knew deep down, just as Meggie had said, that it was for the best, and knowing in the same way that anything they said now would only make it worse, Bex and Saz both turned back to the white stone trellises and began to climb again....

Only Bethan, still way ahead of the others, took another moment to call down.

"Take care of yourself, Meggie!" she shouted and then, seeing Nickolas move to put his hand on Meggie's shoulder, she gave a little smile. "Take care of each other!"

"We will!" Meggie yelled. "You take care of yourself too. And give Edmund and the others my thanks as well!"

Edmund. Bethan felt her own heart racing all over again. Soon she would see him again.

But only if she hurried...

With Meggie's words still ringing in their ears, so it was then that the element of earth, the element of fire and the element of water all clambered their desperate way up to the platform towering high above the City, as the final element stood below, just watching, her throat thick with emotion, the man she had stayed for, silent and protective by her side.

—

The first to reach the top of the ladder, Edmund only just had time to shield his eyes as a fantastic blast of hot air rose to meet him. As he stepped out onto the platform, the flames licked at his face, the intense light and heat of the orb searing across the space, and without thinking, the Explorer immediately went to remove his travelling cloak, the thick cloth stiflingly warm against his sweaty back. He took a long breath.

Climb the platform by sunset tonight. The gateway between the two worlds will open and you must pull us all through. Bethan's words rang in his head, over and over and over as if they'd always been there. It was almost funny to think how he'd struggled to find them before when now they seemed to be all he could think about...

He'd climbed the platform and it had to be almost sunset, if it wasn't already – who knew how many minutes had gone by since they'd entered the temple? Now all they needed was the gateway... and uncovering his face, Edmund dared to look straight into the fire, the great Keeper of the World, before turning swiftly away again.

The fire. It had to be the answer; the 'gateway'. He knew it made sense – after all, that was how the elements had left Tungala in the first place, stepping through those white-hot flames - and yet a part of him was seriously starting to worry. All of his natural instincts were telling him to turn right back around and get himself and the others as far away as possible from the inferno tumbling, roiling and burning only a few steps away. Fire was deadly, and *this* fire... none could fail to forget the scene of only a few weeks past as Renard had fallen and burned, melting into a screaming pile of ash. And yet...

And yet somehow Bethan and the others were relying on him, on them, to *pull them through*.

What then, were they to do? Watch and wait all over again for a sign, for something to happen? Or did they just risk it and step into those flames, just as the women had before them, and hope for the best?

Sensing movement, Edmund then saw that Fred had also reached the top of his ladder and stepping out onto the platform, just as he had, the warrior flung a hand to his face as surging heat blasted at him, crackling and spitting like a raging animal. Eliom too then appeared from the other side, his white cloak billowing, followed closely by Thom, who barely seemed able to stand against the giant blast of hot air streaming from the fire, his hand out on the hilt of his axe as he pushed it before him like a walking stick.

Together, all three of them headed for Edmund and the companions once again reunited, the Explorer soon gathered them close together. The roar of the fire was almost deafening. Even standing so close, they would have to shout to be heard.

"What do you suppose happens now?!" Fred was the one to say it. He was positively yelling. "Do we just walk into the fire?!"

Edmund grimaced.

"Exactly what I was just asking myself!" he admitted loudly. The smell of sulphuric fumes was already beginning to burn his nostrils. But though the heat and the noise and the light should have made him feel drained, he could feel a strange kind energy coursing through him. They were so close now, *so close*. He could almost feel the blaze licking at his skin, just as he could almost feel Bethan's hand in his and though he knew it would do nothing but blind

THE ENTITY OF SOULS

him, he found himself squinting all over again into the burning light, imagining that somehow he would be able to see her, that she could give him some kind of a clue even now…

"Well, we have two choices!" Thom shouted. "We can either stay here and wait for the elements to appear, or we step through the flames ourselves!"

Fred straightened up.

"I will try the flames!" he offered bravely. "If they burn me then-!"

But Edmund had flung out a hand before the warrior could so much as move.

"No!" he cried, fear all too evident on his face. "You saw what happened to my brother! Only the elements were allowed to walk into the fires safely! We don't know if anything's changed!"

"But what if it has? What if it is safe now?!" Thom was the one to reply. "You told us that the elements need to be 'pulled' through! How else are we supposed to *pull* them if we cannot touch the flames?!"

What he said made sense but…

"There is only one way to find out!" Fred insisted and before anyone could stop him again, the warrior had spun on his heel and without even the smallest flinch, he was marching across the platform, straight towards the flames…

"Fred! *No!*" Edmund bellowed, his stomach lurching horribly as the image of his brother's death jumped up to haunt him. *Not again!* he screamed inside. *Not again!* He couldn't bear it again…

But just as the Explorer, in a crazy moment of heroism was about to throw himself after the warrior, Fred, instead of flinging himself into the flames as they'd all expected, then paused, right before the centre of the platform, inches from the fire and dropping to one knee, loosened one of his boots, tugged it from his foot, straightened up and without a moment's hesitation, threw it straight into the bright abyss.

The fire hardly seemed to flicker as the tiny object flew right into its core and for a split second, seemed to hang there, making the onlookers hold their collective breath. Within seconds though, the shoe then vanished as the mud and leather exploded in a ball of boiling ashes and as all four companions simply stared, wide-eyed after it, each of them couldn't help but imagine what would have happened if they'd simply thrown all caution aside and stepped straight in…

"I suggest that we wait!" Eliom shouted, breaking the stunned hush that followed, and the others nodded in silent agreement. There was no doubt in any mind now that waiting was *definitely* the best plan at this point. But for what?

"We must have to *do* something!" Fred bellowed as he moved back to join the still-huddled group. "Surely just climbing the platform is not enough? Thom is right, how can we 'pull' them through without touching the flames?"

"We will know what to do at the right time," Eliom replied calmly. "Fate will have a hand in this, I am certain of it."

"*Fate?*" Thom retorted. "If we rely on *that* nothing will *ever* happen." And Edmund couldn't help but smile to hear someone else fight it just as much as he did. Or rather… *had*. Because now, maybe, a part of him could feel itself starting to truly believe, as he revisited Eliom's words from outside the temple.

You could have chosen so many other paths… he'd said. *Fate brought you and Bethan together to save the elements' lives and perhaps the lives of countless others not yet known… You forget, Edmund, how much has happened in order for you to be here… you are important… For many reasons we may not even understand as of yet. But certainly, without you… we could not save the elements. And that is why… at sunset, the Temple of Ratacopeck is going to appear and we are going to walk inside and finish our task.*

The words echoed in his mind like they had been spoken seconds, not minutes before, but right then, no matter which way he looked at it, all of them seemed to ring true.

He couldn't help but remember the last time he had been standing at the bottom of the same ladder he had just climbed, despairing at how fate had taken away the woman he loved. And yet, despite his assertions to the contrary, since then, so many things had fallen into place to bring them to this point. He had felt so certain back in the tomb when he'd realised they had a wizard, the only being who get them from here to there in less than a blink in the eye. Why not now? After all that Eliom had said about everything he and his friends had been through, could he really believe that it had all been for nothing?

And so it was that the Explorer then opened his mouth and the words he never thought he'd hear himself say, tumbled out;

"Fate's helped us a lot through our travels, Thom!" he shouted, daring to glance at Eliom as he did so. The wizard gave a quiet little smile. "Don't give up on it just yet!" before; "Eliom's right! Maybe we just have to wait until we know what to do!"

And so, with no better suggestion from anyone else, they did.

—

Bethan reached the top of her trellis breathless and exhausted, and falling straight to her knees on the white stone, she took a good long moment just to collect herself before allowing her attention to wander to her surroundings.

Much like the platform in the Temple of Ratacopeck, the podium beneath her feet was set in a diamond shape, each corner protruding out over the four trellises, with, instead of a gaping hole, a simple dip in the centre for the Digger fire to burn. Unlike the temple though, although the flames now towered higher than was possible, they were still only small in comparison to the orb they had once known, the Keeper of the World. Instead of searing white, these flames were red, but even so, as Bethan made to clamber to her feet, she could still feel their powerful heat raw against her skin, still smell the scorching tang of burned air, still hear the roar of their hunger, the redness still bright enough to make her shield her eyes from the glare.

To her right and left stood the four giant stones of glass. Just as they had looked from below, the green, blue, orange and cloudy-transparent gems were as large as a person and rounded into a perfectly-formed sphere. All four shimmered beautifully in the moving light of the fire and before she could stop herself, the element was reaching out to touch the nearest – the emerald – with trembling fingers, only to find it smooth and surprisingly cool despite the heat.

Flattening her hand, she soon ran her whole palm across it, enjoying the sensation.

"Bethan!" she heard her name and turning, she found herself half-surprised to then see Saz approaching her across the platform, followed by Bex. Both women looked just as she probably did, red in the face, sweaty, tired and overwhelmed, but as they met each other's gaze, none of them could help but smile.

Finally they were here and finally it was time to go home.

"So what… do we do… now?" Bex said, raising her breathless voice just enough to be heard over the crackling flames. "Do we just… do what we did… before and… walk into the fire?"

Bethan turned her eyes back to the Digger blaze uncertainly. It definitely made sense. After all, that was how they'd got there in the first place, by stepping into the flames of the Keeper of the World. But some kind of doubt was holding her back. Ophelius had said that they were to be *pulled* into their world by their companions…

"Wow! Look at these!" Saz exclaimed as she too, distracted by the beauty of the glistening glass, laid a hand on the emerald stone nearest to them. "How did the Diggers get them up here?!"

"Where did they even get them from?" Bex added, also reaching out to stroke the earthen stone. "There's nothing else I've seen here but stone and dust."

"The Builder, I'm guessing," Bethan said seriously. "Didn't Nickolas say this is a kind of shrine to him?"

A shrine.

The word seemed to stick in her head for a moment as if it meant something; as if it was important.

A shrine. A shrine to the Builder. A shrine to the Digger god, or rather a shrine to who the Diggers *believed* to be their god, if nothing else.

And what did gods need?

Bethan frowned.

What did gods demand?
Faith.
Of course. And as if it was all suddenly slotting into place, she bit her lip.

"I think we have to wait," the element then said aloud, making the other two look at her oddly. "We have to wait and see."

"Wait?" Saz questioned. "Wait for what? What if the fire…" and she too glanced at it, screwing up her eyes in the brightness, "what if it… - I don't know – changes back to normal again?"

Bethan bit her lip harder.

"I don't know," she replied honestly. "I don't know what we're waiting for. But something just tells me… something in my gut, that we should. That there's going to be some sort of sign, then we'll be pulled through…"

The other two continued to look at her strangely but didn't argue. Neither of them had any better ideas, both of them secretly too afraid at that moment to brave touching the flames alone.

"It must be something to do with Edmund and the others," Bex was the one to reason aloud. "Why else would we need them here? Or rather, *there*," and she gestured to the imaginary platform she could see in her mind's eye beyond the fire. "They must have to do something to show that we can leave, before they can pull us through…"

"It makes sense," Saz replied but then, giving a small huff of irritation, her fists curled. "Why didn't we ask about all of this in the world of the dead?! Ophelius could have given us so much more!"

"He did the best he could with the time he was given!" Bex retorted and put in her place Saz grimaced, immediately sorry for her outburst.

"I know he did," she muttered. "It's just…" she gave a nervous sigh, "one minute it seems like we're going to be free and the next…"

"I know," Bethan re-joined, giving her friend an encouraging squeeze on the shoulder. They *all* knew. For once more it suddenly felt as if their hopes might be dashed all over again, dashed by the uncertainty, by the hurdle of what happened next. Waiting seemed like a very difficult option, but it also seemed to be the only one they had…

That or braving the flames.

Trying to take her mind off her excited nerves, Bethan then edged towards the rim of the platform to stare out across the City. The platform was very high up, the Digger people almost like tiny insects below, and the element's head spun momentarily with the sheer magnitude of it all. She could see for miles. More than miles. Miles upon miles, right out across the large Digger city and into the blackness beyond, the blackness where, somewhere, she knew, across the plains, was a gigantic tree-shaped rock surrounded by a wall of shifting colours…

Turning her gaze closer to home, Bethan then found her eyes returning to the crowd still standing at the base of the statue. Hundreds seemed to have appeared as if from nowhere, to watch their odd progress, but even in the dim evening light, in the flicker of tiny torches, she could just make out the shape of a couple standing a little apart from the rest, their arms clasped round each other, and she couldn't help but smile.

"I wonder what it'll be like for her, staying here *forever*."

Bex's voice was quiet, but despite it, Bethan flinched as she noticed that her fellow elements had followed her to the platform edge to stare, just as she was, down at the distant companions they had left behind.

Bethan's smile warmed.

"Staying with the man she has feelings for?" she replied absently. "I don't think she'll even notice." She could sense her heart starting to beat even faster, if that were possible, as she thought of seeing the very man she had feelings for, very soon...

"It's sad to leave her behind though," Saz added. "I mean, who knows what this place really is?" and remembering her thoughts during their short time as Barabus's hostages, she soon turned to the others, "We never did find out why people are being collected here or who the Builder is or why-"

But the element of fire never got a chance to finish, for right at that moment, the very thing they had been unknowingly waiting for, happened.

Suddenly the fire let out a gigantic boom and the elements, startled, snapped around just in time to watch as the flames began to billow out, puffing and growling with unknown strength. It was as if some invisible wind were buffeting the fire, as it moved, back and forth, roaring like some great beast, and even as they stared, grew larger and larger, the red burning brighter and brighter until it was almost white...

And then, just like that, with a great crackle of energy, the fire died back and from the very centre of its force, the very centre where the kindling still burned, something appeared.

It was an object, something small, dark and dirty that seemed to hang there for a moment before falling straight onto the white stone platform with a dull thud, as the elements looked on in complete disbelief.

"Was that-?" Bex began. "Is that a-?"

"Shoe?!" Bethan finished for her. And then, before she knew what she was doing, she was rushing forward to retrieve the thing. But though she reached for it and the boot just lay there on the hard white stone seemingly waiting for her, as Bethan neared it, it suddenly began to smoke and then bubble and then, right before their eyes, it turned to nothing, disintegrating into ash that swirled up into the evening air and was gone in a second.

The elements all looked at each other in utter confusion.

"Was *that* our sign?" Bex cried in disbelief. "*A muddy boot?!*"

"I don't know," Bethan started again. "Maybe, I-" but her eyes falling on Saz, she stopped.

"Saz? Wh-what's wrong?" she spluttered instead, for all of a sudden, the element of fire was staring about them as if she'd lost something important and was very *very* desperate to find it.

"We have to throw something back!" was all the element said, as Bex too turned to look at her like she was crazy. "That shoe might have belonged to one of the others! Maybe it *is* our sign! Maybe they're trying to contact us! We have to throw something back!"

It was a good idea, a brilliant idea, the best yet, and catching on fast, Bethan and Bex too began to look about them, searching for something to throw into the flames. But though they searched, instantly all knew it was pointless. The platform was completely empty but for the giant stones of glass, far too heavy to move, the fire and the very clothes they stood up in. They had nothing to throw in but themselves... nothing but...

Realising at exactly the same moment, all three women then turned to their already-torn dresses, the dresses that had seen them through thick and thin in their past few weeks in the Digger world, the dresses still crusted with mud from the plain, torn at the seams from the dust storm, the dresses that wouldn't miss a little more material... and as one they began to tear, bite, yank and shred at the silk-like fabric, trying to break away a large enough chunk to make some sort of impact on the flames.

"Here!" Bex cried, finishing first. She'd managed to tear off the entire shoulder of her dress, leaving the rest to flap down, revealing the thin underdress beneath; but without even reaching to cover herself, she flung it straight to Bethan, the closest to the fire. "Throw it in!" and with baited breath, the other two then watched as, bundling the dress into a tight ball, Bethan stepped forward and throwing the fabric into the flames, leapt back as it disappeared in a flash of burning ash.

It was Fred who noticed it first.

"Look!" he yelled in Edmund's ear, anxious to be heard over the great roaring commotion. "I just saw something move! Over there!" and sure enough, as Edmund and the others all turned to where Fred was pointing, all caught a glimpse of something shifting in the flames.

At first it appeared to be a small ball of some kind, just the size of a man's palm, but as it held there before them, almost floating in the light, it then began to uncurl into a long thin strip before disappearing, much as the boot had done, in a fine puff of dust.

"What in Tungala was *that*?!" Thom shouted but none the wiser, the others just stared in confusion, their eyes almost shut against the blinding light of the inferno.

"It looked like a strip of fabric!" Eliom replied. "The sleeve of a garment, I would say!"

"A sleeve?!" Thom echoed. "That makes no sense!"

Edmund, however, still just staring silently at the space where the object had appeared, could feel his hope beginning to rise all over again despite itself. Was this the sign? Was this what they had been waiting for? Were Bethan and the others trying to contact them?

Somehow he knew that they didn't have much time to find out...

"It makes *perfect* sense!" he bellowed and then, without warning, without even taking another moment to think or worry about it, he was suddenly leaping forward, his teeth gritted in preparation, ready to rely on his feelings and the knowledge that *this was it*. "Come on!" and before anyone could so much as protest, Edmund of Tonasse had shoved his entire arm directly into the searing hot flames.

The others let out cries of utter horror as they realised what was happening, as they watched powerlessly, trying to ready themselves for their leader to wail in pain, for his skin to turn red and disintegrate before their very eyes. But even as Edmund screwed his own eyes shut, ready for the onslaught, ready for the sharp, intense burning, the sense that it was all over... nothing happened.

His hand and arm just lay there, the flames rising up around them, not hot and searing but strangely cool and inviting and *safe*... and as he opened his eyes, just watching as he flexed his fingers, running them through the trickling smoothness, it was then that he knew what he had to do - what they *all* had to do.

"Help me!" he bellowed, turning back to his astonished friends with a burst of laughter as everything came together. "Put your hands in the flames!"

That was why they were here. By throwing his boot in the fire, Fred had shown the elements that it was safe to cross, and the bundle of fabric? That had been their response, the women's sign to let them know that they were waiting for him and the others on the other side of the fire to pull them across the divide. Something he couldn't do alone...

"We need to help them through! All of them!" he cried as the others rushed towards him. "All of you have to put your hands through the flames, *now!*"

And without another second's pause, the dwarf, warrior and wizard, side-by-side, obeyed and reaching out, each pushed a hand into the blaze. The heat around them was intense, the force of the fire blowing burning hot in their faces, and yet within the flames, within the power of the orb, fingers and palms felt cool and unharmed.

It was sunset and the gateway to the other world had opened, just as Bethan had said it would.

"Bethan!!" Edmund suddenly began to shout, his voice almost drowned out by the deafening snarl of the fire. "Bethan!!" He was so close to her now. So close to them *all* and catching on, the other three joined in, calling out to their friends.

"Bex!! Bethan!! Saz!! Meggie!!" The names disappeared in the close burning air about them as fast as they were called, and yet the four companions didn't give up, hoping against hope that the elements, wherever they were, could hear them.

—

Bethan. Bethan.

"Did you hear that?!" Saz cried excitedly. It was only moments since Bethan had thrown Bex's sleeve into the fire, and all three of the elements were staring into the bright flames, their eyes peeled, ears strained for any sign. And then, like a ghost, like a whisper on the air, it had come.

Bethan.

"Yes!" Bex yelled. "Bethan! Someone's calling your name!"

Bethan.

Bex.

"And yours!" Bethan added with a gasp. She felt almost too happy to speak, even to breathe because as soon as she'd heard it, she knew it; she knew that voice, the voice murmuring in the flames, the voice she had longed for…

He was here. He had come.

Saz. Meggie. Other voices began to drift through too, other speakers. Eliom. Fred. Thom. All of them were there, ready and waiting, just as they had planned, just as they had hoped for…

"What do we do?" Bex squealed, moving ever closer to the fire. The reflection of the flames danced eagerly on her spectacles making her eyes seem larger, more wild. "What do we do?"

Bethan however, already had the answer.

"Edmund! Edmund!" she began to yell and then, stepping so close to the fire she was almost touching it; "We're here! Edmund! We're here!"

"Eliom!" Saz joined in. "Eliom!"

"Thom!" Bex cried. "Can you hear us?"

Their shouts reverberated across the platform, entwining with each other, bouncing off the gemstones with an excited echo. They were here! Their friends had come for them!

As the women then paused to listen, hardly daring to breathe, nerves on edge in expectation, so it was a soft voice spoke out with the most beautiful words they ever thought they'd heard.

Take our hands and you will be free.

And then, before any of them could wonder, from out of the flames, the three women noticed the appearance of four hands, each of them outstretched, palms up, fingers ready, beckoning to them.

And without so much as another glance at each other, the three elements in the Digger world then reached forward to take one each and finding the grips strong, and themselves no longer afraid, so it was that Bethan the element of earth, Saz the element of fire and Bex the element of water stepped forward into the gateway that lay open before them.

———

Still standing at the base of the statue, Meggie the element of air, gently took Nickolas's hand in hers as they watched the tiny figures of her three friends disappear into the flames far above them.

They'd made it. They'd finally made it. The women were back where they belonged, and Meggie gave a sad smile as she silently wished them all well, at the same time knowing that she would never see any of them again.

She sensed Nickolas turn to say something to her, perhaps to give her comfort, but she gave his fingers a squeeze, letting him know that it was all right. She knew she had made her decision and though it hurt a little now, she also knew it wouldn't always.

Always. She had always…

But as her thoughts turned to the future, to *her* future and what it meant, it was then, as all eyes were still on the space, the fiery brightness where the three companions had vanished, that the statue gave an almighty groan and suddenly the fire atop of the podium, at one time so small, blasted with iridescent light and in a massive whoomph of energy, engulfed the entire platform in a ball of flame.

Meggie heard the gasps of surprise and fear all around her and she too flinched, reaching up to protect her eyes as she watched the flames then begin to build, to grow all over again. Automatically, her grip tightened on her partner's hand as the blaze began to swirl and writhe, building itself into a massive cloud of energy stretching up into and across the sky. A giant blot of light in the blackness, as the fire seemed to reach its full height and breadth, it paused, as if halting to take a breath.

Gasps then turned to screams as the swarm of Diggers below began to scurry for shelter in a mass of chaos as, in one beautiful, horrific spectacle, the inferno then began to fall, like liquid pouring in a waterfall of molten heat over the edges of the platform. In a rain of fire, it was rushing down the four trellises, hurrying in a wash of destruction towards the square below where the two humans, alone amidst the sea of panic, their hands still clasped firmly together, stood and watched.

Realising all too soon what was about to happen, Meggie just had time to turn to the man by her side, a new smile on her face.

"Are you glad I stayed now?" she asked, her eyes suddenly damp with happiness.

And Nickolas, smiling too, responded by pulling her into his arms, burying her face in the warmth of his chest as the blaze rushed towards them.

"Yes," he breathed in her ear as they held each other tight. He closed his eyes, pressing his face into her hair. "I am."

And so it was the liquid flames hit the ground in an eruption of light and heat, tearing, burning at flesh and bone and stone alike, sweeping out across the square towards the Digger huts as they lay, already deserted.

There were screams, there were cries, there were feet pounding in fear, but even as the terrified men and women of the Digger world fled before the deluge, it was as if the Builder himself had reined in the forces of nature and just as quickly as it had started, so the fire dwindled and in a puff of hot ash and sulphur, it was gone.

And then all was silent and deathly still.

The elements had been saved…

ACKNOWLEDGEMENTS

My thanks go out again to the usual suspects: Mum, Dad, the besties - those who helped me mainly just by existing and being awesome.

Also, this time I have to thank my big sister, Becca, for inspiring me in multiple different ways. Although we haven't always seen eye-to-eye, there is video footage to prove I totally hero-worshipped you growing up, a fact I completely deny all knowledge of now, of course…

And to my nephew and nieces, W, E and C; none of you existed when I was writing these books, but I love you all dearly and hope one day (when you're old enough!) you can maybe enjoy them too.

This time around I also have to make mention of Mrs Potter and Mr Wella, two school teachers in particular who inspired and encouraged me to write. Mr Wella, you asked me nearly every time I saw you when you could read my first published novel – and whilst this isn't the first, here you are all the same!

And finally, again, I have to say thanks to you, the person reading this, for taking a punt with the first book and enjoying it enough to take a stab at the second. I hope you continue on to the third, but if not, it was great to see you!

The adventure continues with the final instalment:

The Treacherous Balance

With three of the elements now returned to Tungala, the travelling companions are ready to head home, whatever that means. But when Eliom, the wizard, is stripped of his staff by the Order and with Elanore and Soph still held captive by Renard's remaining clones, it soon becomes clear their journey together is far from over.

And what about the Entity of Souls? Can they really just walk away from what they know?

Troubled by questions about what they have seen, it is only as the company voyage on to save their friends that the disturbing truth about the world of the Diggers begins to unravel, leading them down a path of discovery to learn the true identity of The Builder and the means of destroying him once and for all.

No matter how much they may each wish to turn back: *only those who are destined will find a way.*

Printed in Great Britain
by Amazon